Praise for Richard Stern's Short Fiction

"If the task of reading Stern requires a greater concentration than we are accustomed to apply to mere jewels of literary art, the reward of reading him is proportionately greater as well." —Mark Harris, *New Republic*

"Stern has the temperament, the technical ability and the confidence in his audience to be by turn sharp, sentimental, erudite, whimsical, astonishing, even amusing." —Norman Shrapnel, *The Guardian*

"A depth of sensitivity and clarity rare even in novels."
—Robert Boyd, *St. Louis Post-Dispatch*

"Richard Stern has always had a wonderful way with short stories, and in his new collection is more wonderful than ever." —Saul Bellow

"The quality . . . that really disturbs and astonishes is the truth of the characters. How does Stern know how an American teenage girl in Rome perceives the world around her? How does he know how a bus driver feels on his 50th birthday when his whole family has forgotten it, a character whose stoicism and gratitude for the barest shreds of emotional response bring tears to the eyes. . . . His comprehension of people's lives is truly remarkable." —Alice Shukalo, *Daily Texan*

"Stern is a writer who uses language and situations in a way all his own. He is imaginative, with a rare eye for detail, and a bitter sense of humour that is altogether to my taste. Read him please." —Mordecai Richler, *The Spectator*

" 'Teeth,' 'Wanderers,' and 'Dying' would be the envy of any contemporary writer." —Frederick C. Crews, *New York Review of Books*

"As tightly packed and potentially explosive as the heart of an atom. In 'Mail,' for example . . . there are germs for at least five promising novels squeezed into fourteen pages. . . . Richard Stern's [stories] are simultaneously rich gifts and murderous booby traps. You open them at your own risk and for your own reward. Please do open them." —James Frakes, *Cleveland Plain Dealer*

"Every once in a while some genius of a satirist gets the exact pungency of aconite emanating from professors: Mr. Stern can do it to perfection."
—Guy Davenport, *National Review*

"Read him and laugh, read him and weep, read him."
—Thomas Rogers, *Chicago Sun-Times*

"What a feast of other people's troubles! . . . The stories are a kind of game, a sensual vicarious gambol in a room full of naked people, intense as gossip, exhilarating as a suddenly opened window on a sparkling eye-blue sea. In a nutshell (make that a coconut), Stern is fun to read."
—John Seelye, *Chicago* magazine

"Stern has done as much to pry open the possibilities of the short story and the long story as any of his more illustrious contemporaries." —Philip Roth

"I tried hard, I really did, to find just one sentence that, in or out of context, didn't provide pleasure. Of course I failed." —Albert Goldbarth

"Often compared to his fellow Chicagoan Saul Bellow, Richard Stern is an almost equally masterly creator of brainy, complex characters hell-bent on self-exploration, imprisoned by the lures and delusions of sex, and riddled with primal familial guilts."　　　　　　　—Bruce Allen, *Philadelphia Inquirer*

"Stern's best stories are written with such compactness that they seem to become tiny novels often using chapter breaks to jump across great periods of time."　　　　　　　—Will Nixon, *Boston Phoenix*

"Dry, witty and economical, [Stern] . . . never lets sentiment succumb to sentimentality."　　　　　　　—*Newsweek*

"Stern is often considered Bellow's disciple, but in the short story at least, he has proven himself the master."　　　—Arnold Klein, *SoHo Weekly News*

"There is nothing deadeningly schoolish about Stern's writing: like Auden's Houseman he 'attacks the life he leads' . . . he is incisive, economical, reserved and aware of the further irony of wishing to achieve clarity by reduction."　　　　　　　—*New Statesman*

"Stern has a poet's knack for compressing novels into inches, for breaking your heart by the perfect word without ever specifying exactly what's the matter. And yet he is never sentimental. . . . An iron fist in a velvet glove cradled around a secret."　　　　　—Mary Shelton, *Nashville Banner*

"Few writers anywhere can touch Stern."　　　—John Blades, *Chicago Tribune*

"The sheer force of imagination in Stern's work carries the reader forward: because Stern really gets inside his characters, nothing surprises us by its being included, since the characters' tiniest perceptions take on relevance."　　　　　　　—*Austin American-Statesman*

"Stern is a writer who perceives everything. He is a writer in whom intelligent people can take comfort."　　　—*Louisville Courier-Journal*

"A verbal prestidigitator."　　　　　　　—*New York Post*

"Stern is a dramatic, terse, witty writer . . . assured but not slick, wise but not self-satisfied."　　　　　—Elizabeth Jennings, *The Listener*

"Marvellously funny short stories. . . . Stern (to use the kind of image which abounds in 'Teeth') goes to work on life like a sound-wave drill, his abrasive talent ripping away at it until all that is left is some bone-dust and a fragment or two of nerve tissue . . . hard-won results of a superb technique."　　　　　　　—Francis King, *Sunday Telegraph*

"A burnished style, a burning imagination."　　　—*New York Times*

"Richard Stern is a literary treasure . . . a true man of letters."　　　—Scott Turow

"Entertainment of the highest order, entertainment as literature."　　　　　　　—James Atlas

"Stern proves conclusively . . . that he can do just about anything with narrative forms."　　　　　　　—J. Coates, *Chicago Tribune*

ALMONDS *to* ZHOOF

Books by Richard Stern

Golk

Europe, or Up and Down with Schreiber and Baggish

In Any Case (reissued as *The Chaleur Network*)

Teeth, Dying, and Other Matters

Stitch

Honey and Wax

1968: A Short Novel, an Urban Idyll, Five Stories, and Two Trade Notes

The Books in Fred Hampton's Apartment

Other Men's Daughters

Natural Shocks

Packages

The Invention of the Real

The Position of the Body

A Father's Words

Noble Rot: Stories 1949–1988

Shares, a Novel in Ten Pieces and Other Fictions

One Person and Another: On Writers and Writing

A Sistermony

Pacific Tremors

What Is What Was

Almonds to Zhoof: Collected Stories

ALMONDS*to*ZHOOF

collected stories

RICHARD STERN

TriQuarterly Books
Northwestern University Press
Evanston, Illinois

TriQuarterly Books
Northwestern University Press
Evanston, Illinois 60208-4170

Printed in the United States of America

10 9 8 7 6 5 4 3 2 1

ISBN 0-8101-5149-9

Library of Congress Cataloging-in-Publication Data

Stern, Richard G., 1928–
    Almonds to zhoof : collected stories / Richard Stern.
        p. cm.
    ISBN 0-8101-5149-9 (cloth : alk. paper)
    I. Title.
    PS3569.T39A6 2005
    813'.54—dc22

                                                2004030002

For Eli Reyes Stern and Jacob Reed Stern,
my beloved twenty-first-century grandsons,
in hopes that they and some of their contemporaries
will one day enjoy these twentieth-century stories.

And, as always, for Alane.

CONTENTS

AUTHOR'S NOTE

Forty-nine stories, and just about forty-nine years writing them.

I'd begun earlier, at Stuyvesant High School, the audience a laugh-starved class and its instructor, the kind, dour booster Mr. Lowenthal. Bless him and bless my father, another booster. The first published stories—none saved—appeared in *Carolina Magazine* when I was at Chapel Hill, from 1944 to 1947.

"Good Morrow, Swine" and "A Short History of Love," the earliest stories reprinted here, were written in 1950, when I was teaching English at the Collège Jules Ferry in Versailles. The first story published in a national magazine, "Cooley's Version," was written in Heidelberg in 1951. Its acceptance by John Crowe Ransom, editor of the *Kenyon Review,* made one of the unforgettable days of a quiet life.

The first collection of stories, *Teeth, Dying, and Other Matters* (1964), appeared after the publication of three novels.

I continued writing stories of subnovel length, although one reprinted here, "Veni, Vidi . . . Wendt," might pass for a short novel. Story forms are congenial to many narrative urges, some matters of character, situation, and theme, some formal, technical, even musical.

A few are by-blows of novels: "Losing Color" uses the characters in *Stitch* (1965); "Oscar and Hypatia," "Sylvan and Agnes," and "Wool" dropped off *Pacific Tremors* (2001); "Almonds," "Chicago, in the Depths of Feeling," and "My Ex, the Moral Philosopher" deal with the same characters but were conceived as independent stories (and will be further altered for a novel under way); finally, "The Sorrows of Captain Schreiber" was written as an independent story in 1952, then turned into a chapter of *Europe, or Up and Down with Schreiber and Baggish* (1961).

In the collection *Noble Rot* (1989), I eschewed the sort of information just supplied:

> These stories . . . aren't arranged in chronological order. (The
> collection isn't meant to display literary development or decline.)
> The arranger thinks of the reader as a story lover looking forward

to his nightly story fix. Such a reader is comparatively disinterested in the towns and times of composition, the recollected fusion of experience and invention. Fascinating stuff that, but uncooked fiction, more or less cooked fact.

I stand by most of this statement, but fifteen years older, I am less dismissive of lesser wants. Indeed, the acknowledgments at this collection's end supply more in the way of publication dates.

ALMONDS *to* **ZHOOF**

THE ILLEGIBILITY OF THIS WORLD

Tugged by sunlight and the phone from a dream about populating the universe with sperm; a spaceship stocked with fertile cells unloading on empty planets with the blueprints of civilization; the humanization of the universe. "Yes?"

"Mista Biel. Deejay."

"Jeesus. What time is it?"

"Comin on nine, cep you put the clock back. Joo member to do that?"

Did I? "Yes." On the table, the knowing pine face of the clock, gold fingers at VII and X. "It's ten of seven."

"Rilly eight."

"How many times, Deejay?"

"Was finkin you wanted those leaves up."

"The leaves, yes, me, no."

"You doan want me to come over?"

"I should say no."

"No?"

"No, come on over."

"I be over haf'n hour." This could mean three hours or the next day, depending on whom he ran into or what; what bottle, that is.

"You don't need to ring. You've got the garage key."

"I need maw bags."

Ellen wanted me to get rid of him. "Never darken our door again." I can't. We're the last people on the block for whom he can work. He botches most tool jobs. Still he can fetch, lift, carry, mow the lawn, pick up leaves, he's not stupid, he's honest, he's not always drunk; I like him. "I'll put some on the porch."

This weekend, between the World Series and Halloween, I'm alone. Ellen's in Buffalo for our daughter Annie's thirty-sixth birthday. Friday, I drove her to Midway, then went downtown to my one-room office on Adams, checked the markets, bought a Kansas City municipal, faxed a letter to our insurance agent, sent copies of our living wills to our grand-daughter—old enough now to be in on it, who knows, she might be the one to unplug the tubes—and walked five blocks to the Pub Club for the best hour of the day, lunch at the Round Table on the eleventh floor, looking over the silver river and the blue bulge of the State of Illinois Building.

I've been a club member thirty-five years. It's more important than ever now that I've retired. I used to ridicule my uncle Bert's life, a shuttle between the City Athletic Club and his rooms at the Hotel Warwick across the street. I thought that twenty-five-yard shuttle the icon of his narrowness and ignorance. Now my life resembles his. I arrive early enough—11:45—to ensure a seat at the Round Table. (It's gauche to turn up earlier, but if you come as late as 11:50, the table's full and you take your chances with less congenial company.) The table doesn't have the best view, but I've had enough scenic views in my life. I hunger for the day's stories, for jokes, for the latest aches, grandkids, market tips, slants on the news.

We usually start with stories in the *Wall Street Journal,* the *Trib,* and the *New York Times.* Royko's column gets big play from us. International, national, local news, the latest this or that. We've got fellows who follow science, books, the arts, we're all readers and TV watchers. Mondays we go over the Bears game. We cover restaurants, travel, we're a worldly bunch. We know each other's form sheet, we have roles: I'm the left-winger; three or four of us are political Neanderthals basically unhappy that Gorbachev has changed the old game. Two regulars have been assistant secretaries (one of state, one of commerce) and one of us was on Reagan's economic council; we feel we're privy to inside dope. Anecdotes about politics in Washington and Chicago are one of our stocks-in-trade.

The talk I prefer is personal. Friday, we talked about fathers; time has cleared mine of wrong, translating his naïveté into honesty, his timidity into modesty. I told how he read the morning *Times,* so lost in it he flicked cigarette ash into his coffee and drank without blinking. No one laughed. I described his going down the elevator in his pajamas, forgetting his address in a taxi. I drew another blank: the Round Tablers know what's around our own corners. We've all had operations. Bill Trask's back curls with osteoporosis, Harlan Schneirman's lip from last year's stroke. Death bulletins are a regular, if unstressed, feature of our talk.

Of his father, Harry Binswanger says, "I shcarcely knew him." Though he's been in America more than forty years, German phonemes pass in and out of his speech. Till he retired, he was my dentist, a good one, though Dr. Werner, my dentist since, says my mouth was in poor shape when I came to him. Harry — it used to be Heinz — is large, clumsy, thick fingered. I felt secure with the heft of his fingers around my jaw, though they may have handicapped the delicacy of his bridge and canal work. I've heard something of his history for twenty-five years, but there's always more to know. Nor do I mind listening to what's familiar. (I'd have to leave the Round Table if I did.) Harry's parents divorced when he was eight. He visited his father in Mainz every Christmas. "Muzzer sent him my presentss. He unwrappd zem, showed me vat they vur, zen mailed zem back." Harry shook his head, a semaphore of passed anger. "He vass eggcentric, eggcitable, unshtable, couldn't make a liffing. Muzzer's fazzer said she deserfed vat she got, marrying a *hergelaufenen Juden,* 'a Jew from God knows vere.' Fazzer had a farm near zuh Neckar Riffer. He bought turkeyss, zey drowned; he bought marigoldss — he luffed flowerss — zuh riffer flooded zem; he bought pigss, zey broke out of zuh penss. Grandpa said, 'Not even pigss vill stay viz him.' He became a portrait photographers but vass no good viz children. He vanted a picture uff me on zuh riffer, crying. I vouldn't sit on zuh raft. He tied me zere, slapped my face: 'Now cry.' He put his photographss in — vat do you say? — a cabinet viz a glass front. *Vitrine.* Tough kidss — Nazi toughss — broke it. He said, 'It's time to get out.' He vanted to go to Brassil. He'd been born in Bukovina, zuh Rumanianss lost his paperss. At zuh emigration office zey said, '*Für uns, bestehen sie gar nicht.*' 'For us, you don't exist.' He vuss schtuck. Somehow he made it srough zuh var. I saw him after, vonce. He lived in a basement room, zuh rest of zuh block vuss wrecked. Outside his vindow vur a few inches of dirt viz sree zinnias."

Driving back home along the lake by the Museum of Natural History, it struck me that Harry's in-and-out German accent was his mind's way of preserving that *hergelaufener* father of his, even as his stories turned him into comic relief.

Ellen called at eight o'clock. "How're you doing?"

"Fine. I warmed up the chicken. Delicious. How's Annie?"

She was fine, so were Chuck and little Anne, the Buffalo weather was being its notorious self; the plane was an hour late. "Take care, dear," she said. "I'll see you Monday."

"You'd better."

Though it was nice to be alone, a hue of freedom I hadn't noticed that I hadn't noticed. At the same time, the house felt loose around me, slightly spooky.

In my leather armchair, I read a new book about an escaped prisoner and stopped at a German phrase I didn't understand. (The second time today.) *Die Unlesbarkeit dieser Welt*—"the illegibility of this world." The German pleased me, and I repeated the words till they felt at home on my tongue. Their author, a poet named Celan, was born— another coincidence—in Romania. His mother was killed in a death camp—the phrase suddenly made sense—and, decades later, he drowned himself in the Seine.

There's a quiver in my pleasant self-sufficiency; but I am comfortable, snug, taken care of. (Because I've taken care?) Who knows, maybe Harry's father, in his basement, looking out at his zinnias, felt the same; having survived what so few had might have been his comfort. Harry himself had been sent to Amsterdam and, like Anne Frank, hidden. After the war, unlike Anne, he'd gone to a Dutch school. Had I forgotten, or never known, how he'd gotten to America, this man with whom I'd spent five or six hours a week for twenty-five years, whose hands had been in my mouth, to whom I'd paid thousands of dollars?

Saturday morning, I drove up to see my son, Peter. He'd moved again, the third time in five years. He gets bored with a neighborhood, seeks what he calls "action." A large, rangy boy—I shouldn't say boy, he's thirty-two—with lots of energy, he's chosen to be a salesman because he can't sit still. He sells polyvinyl traffic cones and is on the road three weeks a month. He doesn't much like the job, or any other he's had. The routines of moneymaking, the hierarchy of business authority, the cheerleading and critiques of salesmanship, the ups and downs of sales, go against his grain. And grain he has. As a boy, he was exceptionally gentle; in adolescence, he assumed a roughness which I felt contradicted his nature. He's still rough, argumentative, sarcastic, but now he mocks the roughness and regards it as a comic scurf he can remove at will. Deep down—whatever this means—is the gentle boy he was at five and six; very lovable.

A year after he graduated from the University of Illinois in Champaign he married a girl he met in a singles bar; a year later they divorced. He asked his mother and me why we hadn't stopped him from marrying. "Couldn't you see it was a mistake?"

His mother said she'd suspected it, but what could she do? I said, "I liked Louise."

Ten years and many girls later he's still unsettled. I ask him, "How long can you go on being Casanova?"

"Envious?"

"A little. Mostly worried. Not just about disease. This is a critical decade of your life. Squander it courting, you'll end up like the queen in *Alice in Wonderland,* just where you are."

"What's wrong with that?"

"I don't mind, but I think you do."

His new apartment is on the first floor of a redbrick six-flat on one of the thousand tree-lined, quiet streets which root Chicago in a domestic independence which gets it through bad times better than the other industrial cities around the lakes: Cleveland, Detroit, Erie.

The front door is open, he's been watching for me. I follow him into a bright room with an old couch, an armchair, a stack of pictures leaning against the wall, boxes of books and dishes. There's a stereo, no TV. "I don't want to get addicted." His addiction is bars, music, girls, cigarettes. There are four rooms, all in more or less the same tumbled shape, though the kitchen has a built-in orderliness. "Nice," I say. "It's light, the rooms are a good size, it's a pretty street. How much're you paying, may I ask?"

"Five hundred."

"I should move down here myself."

"Too much action for you."

"Not that I can see. Except for the hurricane that hit your place."

"Come back in two weeks, it'll be immaculate. Ready to play?"

Now and then he consents to play tennis with me. I've been playing over half a century and still get around pretty well. I know where the ball's coming and get it back. Peter has speed and power and, when he's playing well, doesn't give me any points, but I can frustrate him with tenacity and junk shots. Then he starts slamming balls out or laughs so hard he misses them altogether. Now and then he gets angry — "*Hit* the goddamn ball" — but rarely, and I enjoy playing with him. Since I had a hernia operation a couple of years ago, the old sweetness of his boyhood comes through, and he's been easy on me. There's also some — I suppose classic — resentment. As we drive a few blocks to public courts on Montrose, he tells me what a lucky life I've led. "You retired early, you've had a good marriage, you've got a granddaughter, and except for that hernia, you haven't been sick; you still play tennis, you liked your job, you've got some dough, you haven't been hassled —"

"The demographics were in my favor. No baby boom."

"Right. I'm one of too many."

"Two's more than enough."

There's some sibling resentment, though he and Annie are good friends.

It's a bit chilly. I keep my Windbreaker on but play well, serve hard, and hit good backhands. I run Peter around the court, which he needs. He sets up the game so he has to chase around. Life cramps him. He spends too much time in cars, writing reports, closed up in his apartment, in bars. On vacations he goes to national parks, where he climbs or paddles white water. A few times he's gone to the Alps and the Pyrenees. But it's not enough for him.

Sometimes I feel that I stand in his way, a wordless — usually wordless — rebuke to his life. Then too I was off a lot on sales trips — neckwear, accessories—when he grew up; he missed me and I think he thinks I sacrificed him. The travel seemed more romantic to him than the chore it was. He thinks I've seen much more than I have, know much more than I do. I feel that he hardly knows me at all, which I don't mind. Should fathers and sons know each other? Or love each other? Well, I love him, though there are gaps of cold in all affection. Yet if the love isn't constant, it is recurrent. That should be enough for security, shouldn't it?

I win the set, 6–3. A rarity. We play another, and I don't win a game. I'm delighted. I always either try hard or appear to try hard, but it's been years since I've wanted to do better than Peter at anything. I want him to have what I've had and more. Above all, I want him to have—to want to have, and have—a child.

Back at his place, I clean up in the bathroom, he washes himself at the kitchen sink. He comes into the living room, the towel working over his wet body. I haven't seen him naked for years, and I'm a little shocked. He's very hairy, has a bit of a belly. This man, who as a boy looked like an angel, is into middle age. I look away. I don't want to see him this way. There's a book open on the beaten couch, I move it and sit down. "What's this?" I ask. He's got on his Jockey shorts. His legs are enormous, they should be running up and down basketball courts or hills.

"Kafka," he says.

"Never really read him. Good stuff?"

"Not exactly." He's buttoning a blue shirt. "You ought to read that one."

"Ought to?"

"You'd understand me better."

"Maybe that's not a good idea. What's it about?"

"Read it. Take it home. But return it. I need it for my sessions."

"Your doctor's paid to understand you. All I have to do is love you."

He's put on blue jeans. "What's to love?"

"I'd better read it."

He's putting on white socks and sneakers. "How do you know it's me you love if you don't understand me?"

"That's too complicated. Do you have to understand *me* to love *me*?" As soon as I say this, I feel the discomfort of presumption. Maybe he doesn't love me. Love's too big a word anyway. It's used much too often. Morons in front of microphones hold out their arms to millions they never met and cry, "I love you." All they mean is, "How wonderful to be shining up here." I never talked about love with my wife or children, my parents didn't with me, and I'm grateful. Love was assumed. A million feelings were bunched up in it.

I'm against all domestic analysis, I'm against understanding. That word also means too much. You understand a request, a situation, but how do you understand a person? You reduce him, that's how. Do I understand myself? Does Harry Binswanger understand his father? In a way, yes, because he hardly knew him. That is, he turned his father into a little vaudeville act, a comic handle that lets him carry the hot pan around. Why did he remember "For us, you don't exist"? Because of his own fright that his father didn't exist for him, except as some snapshots of intimidation and pathos. Not enough, he knows it's not enough. Peter and I have had thousands and thousands of moments with each other, many of them, maybe most of them, charged with something you can call love. But the word itself is just a convenience, a pigeonhole that can't really hold the complexity of it all.

His blue-shirted arms lie on the seamed brown arms of the chair; he looks as big as Lincoln in the Memorial. He says, "I'm paying through the nose to find out if I'm capable of loving anyone."

That night, back in my armchair, I read the book. Had to force myself through it, though it's short, sixty or seventy pages, a story about a salesman, the support of his parents and sister, who wakes up one morning transformed into a huge bug. He can't go to work, they pound on his door, the chief clerk of the office comes to fetch him. (It's rather ridiculous.) Naturally he astounds, terrifies, and disgusts his parents and the young sister who for a while takes care of him, bringing him the rancid leftovers he prefers to fresh food. In time he annoys them so much they want him to die; when he does, they're released and happy.

Now what in God's name makes Peter think that this *Metamorphosis* story has anything to do with him? In the kitchen, I open a bottle of red wine, pour a third of it into a water glass, clip and light a cigar, and go back to my chair to think it out.

In the first place, Peter's never supported us. Au contrairc, though in the last three years he's made a point of not taking money from me at Christmas and his birthday. Still, he knows I'm there, ready to help him. "I helped your sister when she and Chuck bought the house, and I want to help you when you're ready to buy." I wouldn't dream of his sharing, let alone taking, a check in a restaurant. All right, then, what's the similarity? Does he feel like a bug? Have his mother and I made him feel like a bug? Does he disgust us? Do we want him dead? Absurd. I sit puffing, sipping. Beyond this lamplit circle, it's dark. Here, it's warm, comfortable, charged with the warm pleasure of the wine, the special, bittersweet fullness of the smoke; yet my heart's hammering away. Clearly, Peter feels that he's inadequate, repulsive. What's askew in this boy of mine?

Or is he putting it on, dramatizing himself, using the author's own self-dramatics as his crutch? (But the author invented these things and, I think, thought they were funny. There is something funny about it.)

I went to the desk and wrote a note.

Dear Peter,

You're no bug, and I hope I'm not a bit like that pompous, cringing, bullying, self-righteous father. I don't see this story as a key to you. Maybe you can explain it to me. You can do it over the best lunch in Chicago or in one of your bars. You choose.

Love — if that's still a permissible word,
Dad

I'm on my way upstairs to draw a bath when I wonder what the word actually means. *Metamorphosis.* I go down again, lift out the heavy — eight pounds, I once weighed it on the bathroom scale — first volume of the compact edition of the *OED,* for which we joined the Book-of-the-Month Club about twenty years ago. I polish the big magnifying glass on my pants and read "Change of form, from the Greek."

Upstairs, as I unbutton my shirt, I feel restless. I need a walk. I button up, put on a sweater, exchange my moccasins for the springy walking shoes Annie gave me last Christmas, and, downstairs, put on the black leather jacket young people on the street or in stores look at in surprised approval. (Sometimes they say something like "Niice.") I pat my pocket to make sure the key's there—I don't want to be stuck outside with Ellen in Buffalo. I hope she doesn't call when I'm out, getting the answering machine, worrying that I'm looped around a lamppost on the Outer Drive.

The relief of the air, the dark. There's moonlight after the early evening shower, the oak tree on the lawn has shed its last leaves, they're thick on the lawn, a sea of shapes. The branches are transformed by bareness, a predeath bareness. Lucky, in a great city, to live on a street that registers the seasons so clearly.

The cold air feels wonderful. The small lights of the small houses, the interrogative iron curl of the lampposts, the pools of moonlight on the metal skin of the cars; beautiful. I don't want to leave this. After my operation, I was so fatigued I didn't care about living or dying. Only the idea of leaving Ellen kept me going. Now I understand what I'd laughed at in the obit column this week, the eighty-nine-year-old mogul, William Paley, asking people why he had to die. I know life usually wears you down and you're ready to go. Not with him. Not with me.

A *Trib* piece said Paley was a rat, sold out everyone who loved or helped him, took credit for everything; in short, a perfect dead horse for newspaper whips. Is egomania what keeps you alive? Maybe for tycoons. I don't need an empire. Leaves are enough, the moon, the air.

I walk through the bank parking lot, turn left on Dorchester. The maples are half full of pumpkin-colored leaves. (Are the ones still there the Paleys?) Pumpkins are lit on porches. The confidence in these houses. Chairs, lamps, bookshelves, the purple flair of TVs.

I'm the only one on the street. No, up ahead, someone coming. Should I turn? No. Courage. A black man in a raincoat, eyeglassed; a fellow burgher. We should say "Good evening," the way they do in small towns, but we don't. We just pass each other, relieved. I round the brick six-flat on the corner. Back on my block a couple I know stands on their porch, white man, black woman. I don't know their names. I wave, she waves.

My block.

In the bath, my body looks heavy, fattish, knees big, dingus floating in soapy foam. God, man's ugly. No wonder people write about metamorphosis. My body. Peter's. My body forming his, my mind—whatever that is—his. Chromosomes, genes, strings of sugar and protein generating versions of themselves which somehow become others. There's some of Uncle Bert in me. Is it why I live as he did? Transmission. This floating dingus rose to Ellen's innards and generated Annie and, later, Peter. Annie's Anne has my stuff in her, and when she signals doctors to turn off my life, she turns her own spigot. Thought. Ghosts. Spooks. The world, so clear and snug, isn't. Metamorphosis. A rational man turns verminous. A rational country declares some citizens verminous and kills them.

I soap arms, armpits, the side where my scar begins, the left leg, the right, the crack, the ankles, the toes. Lovely. The mind lolls. What is a thought? Form without bulk. "For us, you don't exist." How could he not exist? He was there. But existence meant a paper, a name, a class. Citizen, father, uncle, niece, son, president. Tuesday's election day. Men and women run *to be,* to be entitled. I'll push a stylus through numbers on a card to make a governor, a senator. (Later, they could make or unmake me.) The father in *Metamorphosis* becomes a bank messenger, has a uniform with brass buttons, and, like the doorman in that old film *The Last Laugh,* swells with pride. Fired, uniform taken away, the doorman shriveled.

If I died here in the tub, Ellen would be a widow. She wouldn't know it till she came home. Knowing changed things. That's why you had to remember, especially those who did nothing memorable, had no children, planted no trees, wrote no books, carved no stones, left nothing but lines in old telephone directories, on stones in suburban cemeteries. Where is Bert buried?

What's the sense of remembering the unmemorable? Can't be helped, it's involuntary. Why hasn't evolution weeded it out? What does it have to do with survival? On our bedroom calendar, the November quotation (in blue letters beside the ironic, ethereal face of Albert Einstein) is "What I value in life is quality rather than quantity, just as in nature the overall principles represent a higher reality than does the single object." But isn't quality in the single object? What's worth more, the singular jerk or the genetic dictionary which formed him?

"Don't foul your own nest." Uncle Bert.

That was what he told me forty-odd years ago. My parents and sister had taken off for a month, to Banff, Lake Louise, the Rockies, California. I was left in our apartment alone, very happy. I worked in the Paramount Films Sales Trainee Program on Forty-third and Broadway. Weekends I went up with my cousin Andy — who had a car — to Quakerridge, my sister's club. I played tennis, swam, ate hamburgers, and signed her name to the chits. One Saturday I saw Lynette Cloudaway lying by the pool. Two months before there'd been a feature spread about her in *Life,* an Arkansas girl who'd come to New York to be an actress. A photographer followed her around snapping pictures, at work, shopping, taking a bath, kissing her boyfriend good night. I'd fallen for her in *Life,* and here she was, in the flesh, by the pool. I could hardly speak. "May I sit here?"

"Sure." The smile I recognized, the throaty voice was new, devastating.

"I recognize you."

"It's me."

"What are you doing here?"

"I'm with Willy." The guy she kissed good night. "Not exactly 'with,' he's playing golf."

"Good. You can marry me."

"What name will I have?"

"Mrs. Larry Biel."

"Set the date."

We talked schools, jobs, where we lived, siblings, boy- and girlfriends, movies, books, songs, the works. How confident Willy must be to leave this perfection by herself; he didn't deserve her. "Leave him."

"I haven't had my swim yet."

From the diving board, she jumped into the water. I paddled after her, dodging kids and dowagers. Beyond the flagstones, cigar smokers played bridge. On umbrellaed lounges, bodies toasted. Lawns, blue sky, the rich, Lynette; a Jewish Fitzgerald scene (the madness and cruelty evaporated).

Andy showed up. "Time to go."

To Lynette: "I better not miss my ride."

"You coming to the dance?"

"I will now. If I have to walk."

But I talked Andy into driving up again, white jacket and all.

Bare shouldered, breasts under lace, Lynette was in another gear of beauty. On the dance floor, I kissed her ear, her cheek, her mouth.

"We shouldn't do that."

"Why not?"

"I like it. And Willy would see."

"Let him," I mouthed. Tough guy who'd melt at a leer.

"Let's not dance for a half hour or so."

"If you think so." Snootily. But before she went back to Willy I got her phone numbers.

Monday I called her office from mine. "Lunch?"

"Tomorrow."

We met at Toffenetti's, the glittery restaurant a block from the Paramount. I brought her the Viking *Portable Fitzgerald,* told her to read *Tender Is the Night,* and asked her to go out with me Saturday.

"I spend weekends with Willy."

Thursday night she called me at home, where I was working off my passion for her by myself. "Willy's going fishing in the Adirondacks. I've got to get my shoes fixed on Eighty-second and Amsterdam. I could come by your place after if you like."

Would I like. I bought the first bottle of wine in my life, got whitefish and rye bread from Barney Greengrass, stacked records on the phonograph, and by noon was lathered out of my mind. When the bell rang, I nearly fainted. Again, she looked different, playful, subtle. How many selves was she? I trembled too much to kiss her, could hardly talk. I managed to unscrew the bottle and trot out the sandwiches. We listened to Bing Crosby sing, "Moonlight becomes you, it goes with your hair, you certainly know the right thing to wear." I had to go to the bathroom. The phone rang.

"Shall I get it?"

"Yes." Proud to show whoever called what I had going here.

"It's your uncle Bert. He wants you to call him back. He sounded funny."

"A laugh a minute. What's he want?"

"He didn't say. Better call'm."

I did.

"Larry," he said, "don't foul your own nest."

Old sap. *Foul.* Even then I felt its comic pathos. Yet also sensed the stupid debris of something brought down in stone. "She's my friend Al's wife," I said. "We're just going out."

"All right, but you don't foul your own nest."

The condom I'd gotten from the bathroom was ready, and I was getting there when the phone rang again. I didn't answer but thought, The bastard'll probably come up here. It was nervousness talking. Despite my reading, despite six months' fornicating with my first girl between rows of boxwood near the stadium at Chapel Hill, I knew nothing. (Six years after Lynette, a week before Annie's birth, I still believed children were born through the—enlarged—navel.)

Don't foul your own nest. You fouled it for me, you old jerk.

Wednesday, Lynette called my office. "I have something to show you." At lunch, she held out her hand with the diamond ring.

I never saw her again. In person.

Two years ago, *Life* published an anniversary issue, and there was Lynette as she'd been, mouth open, gawking at a Broadway street scene on her way to work. Ravishing, perfect, the girl of my life. Under the forty-year-old photograph was one of a crinkled granny: Lynette today. I tried to see the young Lynette in the old face; couldn't, not a molecule. A caption said that she and Will lived in Seattle near their grandchildren. I thought of writing her. But why? I didn't want this grandmother. I wanted, *still,* the girl who'd come to the apartment.

Remembering acts on you, not you on it.

Why remember Bert? That sterile neatness, that concupiscent propriety. Immaculate in his blue suit, white silk handkerchief in the lapel pocket, gold tie and collar pins tucking him into himself, black silk socks taut in black garters, black shoes and hair gleaming with different fluids. So clean. My mother, another acolyte of cleanliness, was, in womanliness, beyond that. You wouldn't say she was immaculate. There was flow to her, dress over breasts and rear.

Arms hooked, she and Bert strolled Fifth Avenue, mirrored paragons, proud to be with each other, going into Saks and Sulka's, Bert commandeering the service that was the chief source of his self-satisfaction. That and his Packard, his annuities, his neckties, his opinions, the blonds whose signed portraits — "To Bert with love, Jocelyn" — stood on his chifforobe.

I'm unfair. I'm repaying the resentment he felt for me as Mother's baby. There was decency and generosity in him. I needed five thousand dollars to put down on a house — it would be fifty thousand today — and he gave it to me. Every winter, he sent Ellen and me a crate of grapefruit and oranges from Boca Raton. Isn't he in that generous gold fruit as much as in the Sulka ties and antique injunctions? (The last crate of it arrived a week after he keeled over in a Florida pool.)

After Deejay's call, I try and fail to crawl back into the dream, then put cold water on my face, pee, brush my teeth, and go down the L of carpeted staircase to the kitchen for my bran flakes and muesli mix. I get out a pack of two-ply, thirty-gallon refuse bags, put them against a post on the porch, and bring in the Sunday *Tribune*.

Taking in the news with these flakes of dried grain is as close as I get to a sacrament. Today, election predictions and polls; Edgar and Hartigan in dead heat, Simon ahead of Lynn Martin. Then Hussein, Bush, and Desert Shield, features on the wives, mothers, and children of reservists yanked from their cereal and *Tribune*s. Then the usual montage of misery, the shot, the burned, the flooded, the starved, the planet's daily moil served up as digestif. Even the prick of conscience about this serves my well-being.

I wash my blue breakfast bowl — always the same — go upstairs with the entertainment and book sections and, sitting on the john, shave with my Norelco's trinity of rotor blades. Then another sacrament: a television show I've watched for years, stories about small towns in crisis, the courage of the handicapped, musicians, photographers, all introduced fluently, overfluently, by a benign, wise roly-poly.

The program's critics are literate and scornful, their taste is mine (or becomes mine). Is this the equivalent of a Victorian gentleman's hundred lines of Tennyson?

The doorbell. Deejay, holding the bags, leans against the porch post. He wears stiff black pants, a porkpie hat, a stained brown Windbreaker. His small mahogany face is, as usual, intense. There's always something pressing him. "Mawnin." A lace of booze on his breath, a flash of gold molar.

"Morning, Deejay. What can I do for you?"

"That downspout near the back porch's rotted out. You gotta get you a new one, for winter. You member that ice piled up there last year."

"Is that the reason?"

"Sure it is. What you think it was?"

I go around with him to the back porch, he taps the spout, breaks off a rusted section. "Take a look a that."

"Doesn't look good."

"I can go git one, put it on tomorrow."

Ellen doesn't want him doing any more jobs that require tools—he puts hinges on upside down, he broke our mailbox, he screwed up a toilet, he painted windows shut—but she won't be home till late afternoon. "Fine. How much do you need?"

"Ten bucks, maybe twelve. I git you the receipt."

"I know." If there's a gene for honesty, he has it. "I'm gonna do some raking with you."

"You calls it." He's of two minds about this: it cuts down his work time, but he likes company. He lives alone, somewhere in the neighborhood, has a schoolteacher brother who looks down on him. I don't think he's ever been out of Chicago. Occasionally he takes the El looking for jobs. They've never worked out. A couple of months ago, he took a quality control course which "guaranteed a full-time job." He came by dressed in a grim tie, his Windbreaker, and porkpie to borrow bus fare to the North Side. Two days later, he came by again asking if he could mow the lawn.

"What happened to the job?"

"I took that bus a hour, walked bout two miles, and this man at the plant says they doan have nothin' for me."

"I thought he told the school to send someone up."

"He said I should be bilinguial for the job."

"But you're not."

"I got a brother knows Russian, I can learn Spanish."

"It's not easy to learn a language. I've been trying to learn German since high school. Almost fifty years."

"My God, man, you old."

"And I still don't know it."

"I know some Nippon. Least I can unnerstan it, I can't talk it."

Sure, Greek and Hittite, too. Still, I was angry for him. "He should've given you the job. You went through the school."

"Maybe it's this secession."

That took me a second, but one language I've learned is Deejay. "A job's a job. He told the school he had one for a graduate."

Deejay made the old shrugging motions of human acceptance, but I was upset. That job was his, bilingual or not. Unless of course he'd started popping off about how he'd rearrange the plant or what he'd told Mayor Daley or Brother Farrakhan about running Chicago. Anything could come out of him when he got going.

"I'll do the flower beds," I said. Ellen doesn't like him working there, claims he pulls out what she plants.

We rake away within yards of each other. I pick up a refuse bag to fill it. He says, "Lemme do that." I hold, he fills.

We rake in a sort of harmony. I like it but wonder if he feels awkward. After all, I'm doing what he's paid to do, cutting into his space, his authority. Even his habits; if I hadn't been there, he'd've smoked a cigarette.

He calls over, "What you fink bout this Ayrab war?"

"Not a war yet."

"Boosh gonna get us in?"

"What do you think?"

"Somepin mean bout his mouf."

"I guess that means war." He doesn't answer that. "You been in the army, Deejay?"

"They wouldn't let me."

"Who wouldn't?"

"The army, who you fink?"

"Why not?"

"What they gonna do wiv me? Rakin' bullets? How bout you, you a vet?"

"Too young for World War II, married by Korea, too old for Vietnam."

"We bof lucky. Doan haveta shoot nobody. What you fink bout dis Hussein?"

"A tough guy. He's shot people."

"He sure has nice suits. A nice moostache too."

"You like that?"

"I like a good moostache."

"Hitler had a hell of a mustache."

Deejay breaks up at this. "You a card, Mista Biel. You oughta grow *you* a moostache. A nice white one. Look like a million dollars on you."

"I'm not old enough."

He breaks up again.

Enough. I go in the front door, then think of something. "All these years you've been coming by here, and it just struck me, I don't know your full name. Is Deejay a nickname?"

He leans on the rake and laughs, showing the gold molar and eight or nine discolored teeth. "Deejay's mah nishes. Daron James. That's the name."

"Your whole name, first and last?"

"First and last. Like Lawrence Biel. At's your name, ain't it?"

"That's it." For some reason, I come down the stairs and shake hands, as if, after all these years, we've finally been introduced.

Driving downtown Tuesday, I recover from the small dislocation of Ellen's return. Spend so many years with a person, seeing her again after even a brief absence is like seeing her in close-up. Many unnoticed things are noticed, lines in the face, white in the hair, a rawness in the voice, dents and discoloration in the body. The least strange person in the world is, for an hour or two, a stranger. Perplexing, a little frightening.

Then the indispensability of the familiar returns, feelings of reliance, confidence, the identity and accepted disparity of views. There are habits of self-restraint as well as self-expression. It's one package.

I enjoy the grace and ease with which Ellen unpacks; her reports on the trip. At supper it's mostly about Annie, Chuck, and Anne. New problems, the resolution of old ones; the death of the big oak across the street; Chuck's worry about the recession—though a pharmacist should be almost recession-proof—the new Medicare regulations. "Are things better with Bostorf?" This is Chuck's assistant, who Annie thinks is swindling him.

"He's still trouble. At least Annie's worry about him is troublesome."

We've been worried about Chuck and Annie. They express their difficulties with each other obliquely; Bostorf is one of the targets of this indirection. "And Anne?" We worry a lot about the dangers to which so decent, open, and, we believe, innocent a girl can fall into in an American high school. For someone as much concerned as I am about the future of my seed, my fear about Anne's fall into womanhood—the antique phrase that comes to me—is puzzling.

I tell her about Peter, omitting *Metamorphosis*.

While we're stacking the plates in the dishwasher, the phone rings. "Mista Biel?"

"Deejay. Didn't you get the money?"

"I got it, but I need another twenny."

It's the second time this month that he's called up to ask for more than we'd agreed. Ellen doesn't like this at all. "It's a bad month for me. Lots of bills."

"How bout ten?"

"You really need it?"

"Would I be askin?"

"Sorry."

"Spose I come roun now."

"How about tomorrow?"

"Tomorrow I doan need it."

He must be buying all the liquor tonight. "I'll leave it under the mat."

"Twenny?"

"Ten."

"You a hard man."

"That's right."

"Least you stick wimme."

And you wimme, you poor bastard.

Some afternoons are hard. After the Round Table, I play cards, or billiards, or read the magazines, then walk back to the office and check
the market close. I get going at 3:30, before the rush hour, and am
home by 4:15. We eat at 6:00 in front of *The MacNeil/Lehrer Report,*
then watch one of the scandal programs, people abusing, deceiving,
molesting, kidnapping, killing; the human works. Then we read,
watch programs, occasionally go out, or have friends in for bridge;
then bath and bed. Beside Ellen's familiar warmth and fragrance, I go
to sleep. Sometimes feelings bunch and we're active; afterward, we express gratitude to each other.

I don't sleep as I used to and often go to the guest room to read till
my eyes tire. I'm conscious of aches in the balls of my hands, my feet,
my chest. Sometimes I fear these aches. After all, how much longer is
there?

I've been a bystander, done nothing memorable. I've had no real
trouble, have lasted six and a half decades, raised—whatever that
means—what will live after me, and live in my paid-up house with
someone I love. I'm lucky. Still, now and then, it comes to me that I
don't understand anything. As if the world's speaking a language I
can't follow. Fear gets so loud, I can't sleep. Once in a while, I go back
to our room and hold on to Ellen. Sometimes this helps—like finding
a dictionary—but sometimes it doesn't.

GOOD MORROW, SWINE

The doors swung open, and a small, gray-haired man strode to the platform, jumped the two steps, and slammed his briefcase on the desk. The class rose and called, "A good morrow to thee, Mistair Perkins."

"Good morrow, swine," said Mr. Perkins.

The class sat down. Mr. Perkins unhooked a yardstick from the blackboard, raised it as high as he could, and slammed it on the desk.

"Vun," called the class and, to the yardstick's slash, "two, tree, four, five, seeks, seven, hate, hate prime, ten."

When the counting finished, Le Quillec raised his hand. "Alleviations of ze bowel, sair."

"Pity," said Mr. Perkins and waved Le Quillec from the room.

Mr. Perkins scratched his nose, and the class divided into two groups which spaced themselves single file at opposite sides of the room. Mr. Perkins took a child's coloring book from his briefcase and held it before the first boy in group 1. The boy examined the picture of a massive turtle.

"Igle," he said.

"Precisely," said Mr. Perkins, and he called for the translation of "igle" from the first boy in group 2.

"*La tortue*" was the response.

"Acceptable fiction," said Mr. Perkins, turning the page. The picture was of a boy feeding sugar to a horse.

"I forgets," said the second boy in group 1, and he held out his palm, which Mr. Perkins slapped with the yardstick.

"Ze lovair," called the third boy, and the translation from across the room was, "*Le cheval.*"

Group 2 triumphed, eleven to eight.

"Conquerors up," called Mr. Perkins. "Massachusetts."

Group 1 went down on its hands and knees, and group 2 leaped over the desks, first to straddle the Conquered and then to reassemble in a circle around Mr. Perkins's platform.

"Pang," went the yardstick.

"Vun," called the prostrate Conquered.

Boots stamping, heads jerking, the Conquerors raced around shrieking, "Oodirtydad, oodirtydad, oodirtydad, oodirtydad."

"Vun-two-tree, vun-two-tree, vun-two-tree, vun-two-tree," pounded the prostrate Conquered.

"Pang," went the yardstick, and the Conquerors froze, arms extended, sweat tickling their stillness.

"Massachusetts," said Mr. Perkins, "a bloody state." The class resumed their seats.

"Ahgony of ze bladduh," called Rigobert, the smallest boy.

"Your sentence, Rigobert," said Mr. Perkins.

Clutching his right side, Rigobert recited, "Shane ze catupilluh, sad my oncle, so hees weengs cahnt grau . . ."

"Mangle the coral and its blood will show," finished Mr. Perkins, and he waited for the translation.

"*Quand on lit trop vite, on n'entend rien.* Shokespierre."

Rigobert left the room, passing Le Quillec on guard at the door.

"Sentence, Pinot," said Mr. Perkins to a pale, fattish boy in the first row.

"Ze barbair scrimed and waved ze bloody shears," and before Mr. Perkins could add the coupling line, Pinot went proudly on with "Tinking ze infant's blood its mudder's tears. *Le mal est aisé, le bien presque unique.* Calvin Coolitch."

He drew back quickly, just dodging Mr. Perkins's spittle.

"Arrogant whoremaster," said Mr. Perkins, and he walked slowly to the windows and looked out. "The minor villainies are weighed with the major, my dears. Look at the sky, *la terre,*" and, with the yardstick, he indicated the rows of bare trees along the banks of the hidden river while the class followed the motion, wide eyed and silent. "It's made up of a trillion tentacles which, each minute, draw up our villainies to the heavens, *l'enfer,* and drop them into the destined receptacles of our blood. And, one day, our lives, *nos erreurs,* are gathered up, the vats overflow, and the sky runs with our blood." The yardstick arched slowly down to the dusty planks, and Mr. Perkins walked back to the desk.

"Strethman," he called.

A rickety form arose, trembling, in the back row.

"Strethman, you look ravishable today. Hast thee on a new frock?" Mr. Perkins was quivering.

"Sair?" asked Strethman softly. He fingered his old brown sweater and shrank back toward the seat.

Mr. Perkins waved him down with a gesture of blessing. Strethman sat and put his head on top of his crossed arms.

"*Il pleure, monsieur,*" called the class.

"There are times for weeping as for mirth, times for fronting, times for birth," chanted Mr. Perkins, and he walked back to Strethman and pulled his hair till the weeping stopped. "A new elegance today, my dears," he said, walking to the blackboard.

He printed, "A child's tears are the devil's pearls. *Le coeur pleure quand les vices triomphent.* Waldo Emerson."

"We will violate the vision drop by drop. *Nous répéterons la phrase mot à mot.*"

Mr. Perkins led the class through the sentence. They repeated it individually and in small groups. He assigned the English to the Conquerors and the translation to the Conquered. The class chanted in round fashion, Mr. Perkins guiding the repeats and phrasings with the yardstick.

"Ze bahbee's tairs are ze davil's pairls. *Le coeur pleure quand les vices triomphent.* Valdo Emairso."

When the bell rang, there was instant silence on the words "tairs-vices." Mr. Perkins erased the blackboard, took up his briefcase, and said, "Pleasant dreams, swine."

"Pleasant dreams, sair," called the class, on their feet.

They continued to call "Pleasant dreams" until Mr. Perkins disappeared down the hall on the way to his next class.

MAIL

At least it doesn't count as much as it used to: the day saved because of what's in the little steel cave. Age? Resignation? Or is it I care more for what *I* mail?

Still, it's still nice to get nice letters. Out of the unblue blue where people we're not thinking about are thinking about us. Yet not transmuting themselves (and us) into electric pulses in a vast system of immediacy. Just hes and shes, people with individual calligraphy, personal styles.

Even the salutations are special: "Dear Marcus"; "Dear Tuck"; or (one fairly recent style) "Dear Marcus Firetuck." Which is how the letter from Quito started.

The one from Sandra Lukisch began

> How I wish I could begin with "Dear Marcus." But I can't. You
> will always be the one who guided my first scale lines, reshaded my
> first choropleth map. So, "Dear Mr. Firetuck."

Sandra is director of the Lukisch Cartographic Service in Melbourne. I haven't seen her for twenty years but remember her better than people who worked in this office last year. In the midfifties, girls wore soft sweaters, cashmere, alpaca, lamb's wool. (So much memory has to do with clothes, what's inside and what issues from them. Legs, eyes, sweet—unmappable—hills, ridges, thickets; rough trapezoids, astonishing spheres; eye brightness; smiles: Sandra's was—is?—a dolphin's deep serene; earlobes; nostrils; waists.) I remember Sandra's beautiful maps. They fuse in memory with her delicate roughness. (No standard beauty.)

In my head there are thousands of maps. My dear gone father said he remembered every mouth he ever worked on. To which hyperbole Fred, my middle son, responded, "Lucky you aren't a proctologist, Grandpa." On the other hand—as it were—who is to gainsay those cavy regions? To any true investigator, every variation of the studied genotype fascinates. Nothing there can be beneath study, if not devotion.

Sandra writes she is getting married. "At forty, Mr. Firetuck. Imagine." Not difficult, Sandra. Hundreds must have thought of spending years beside—and inside—you. (I myself.) "I had to tell you, dear old master. Who first showed me what an isopleth was." (A line which represents a constant value.)

Those who have stayed in our heads live there as isopleths; though often unrepresentative of anything but themselves. They are their own color, flag, fruit, and meat, the country of Their Self. Sandra stands for Sandra. And for the feelings rising as she reenters the lit part of my head with her two sheets of typescript. Bless you, Sandra. I will send something or other to Melbourne for you and your fortunate air force colonel. (Did he use your maps?)

The letter from Ecuador was something else. Last March, a fellow called me at my hotel there. I'd flown in from the Cartography Congress in Buenos Aires to give my little spiel on Andean mapping in relation to the new high-resolution photographs we'd been getting from a hundred thousand feet. Joachim ("but called Jock") Fopper had seen the notice of my talk in *El Comercio*. (The good newspapers of that splendid little town may not have sufficient news to fill their local pages.) He wondered if the speaker could be

> the same man who'd written *Reliefs*. I did not think "Marcus
> Firetuck" could be so common a name in your country.

It is the only time in my life that this has happened. In a foreign country—and not one of the world's most populous or worldly—someone who is not a cartographer, textbook publisher, or military man has not only heard of me but also knows me in that tiny—if intense—part of my life of which *Reliefs* is the only—can I say?—monument.

A forty-four-page chapbook printed by a West Virginia press which "split the cost of printing" with me, *Reliefs* received two reviews (that I've seen, for there's no clipping service which hunts down the places in which reviews of such books appear). Yet Joachim—Jock—Fopper of Quito, Ecuador, not only owned a copy of *Reliefs,* had not only read and apparently found it—I can hardly credit and won't repeat his compliments—but he'd located— "through friends in New York whom I commission to send me little magazines from the Gotham Book Mart"—eleven of the fewer than twenty other poems I've published in publications, only one of which, *Poetry,* in my own hometown, prints more than two thousand copies an issue. Most of these journals bear the names of small animals—*Raccoon, Marmoset, Gnat*—and print fewer than five hundred copies. Yet out of this black hole of literature, Joachim Fopper had fetched a couple of hundred lines of Marcus Firetuck. "Your work meant something to me from the first three lines I read," he'd told me on the phone last March. And, no dispenser of vapor, he cited—I assume from memory—three lines from "Scratches on the Record": "They do not mean to hurt the music / They were not made by a mind / And no one will ever try to reproduce them."

These lines had "spoken to" Mr. Fopper. Mr., Herr, or Señor Fopper. There were tiny Germanic tilts in his close-to-perfect English. Yet, as his letter informed me, he'd lived "twenty-odd years" on "this godforsaken continent." I had asked him on the phone if he was a poet. "No. Unfortunately." He did not say then, nor does he say in his letter, what he was (or is). He had just seen the notice in the newspaper; he was astonished, then thrilled at the notion that it might be "the very man" who had given him "such immeasurable pleasure." (Do I detect a stylistic influence of Firetuck in Fopper? The love of internal rhyme, verbal repetition, the mix of stiffness and idiom?) He did not dare to ask me to have a drink, he had hesitated a long time before telephoning, he did not want to be one of those importunate "voice tremblers" who "intrude" into the lives of those who had "already done so much" for them.

I was travel and lecture weary and also low: Ethel had flown back to Chicago from Buenos Aires and the cartographers here assumed that I was being taken care of by "someone else." (Sweet Quiteño modesty.) So, after our seminar, I was deposited at the Colon Internacional in a heap of weary loneliness. I suppose I should have asked Fopper to have dinner with me—the hotel food was terrific—but, who knew, intelligent as he seemed, and surely as sympathetic, wasn't it better to let well enough be enough?

I did tell him how much his call meant. "This isn't an everyday occurrence, Mr. Fopper. I am not exactly Lord Tennyson or T. S. Eliot. You've cheered me up considerably."

I don't think he was set on meeting me. I believe Fopper is one of those true readers whose truest passion is literary. To encounter the actual flesh of authors (or their characters) would be a gross intrusion on their perfectly adjusted mental life. His phone call was, then, very daring. His letter is only slightly less so. Perhaps if I were a more prolific poet, Fopper would not try to drill for epistolary firetuckery.

The letter—about two thousand words long—is almost entirely literary. It begins by quoting

> one of the three French poets born in Montevideo, Jules Laforgue.
> The others, as I do not have to tell you, are Jules Supervielle and
> the astonishing Isidore Ducasse, the self-styled Comte de
> Lautréamont.

(He did not have to tell me, but I would have gone to my grave— not necessarily less happily—not knowing.)

> I know a small master's career is, as Laforgue writes, "decked
> out with rags and praise" ("*un train pavoisé d'estime et de chiffons*"),
> but I could not resist trying to sew in my rag. I hope it did not
> disturb you.

From this variation of his oral apology for "intruding," he goes on to the most intricate and subtle criticism I have ever had (and I include reviews of my professional—cartographic—publications). There are comparisons of my poems to ones in four languages, including poems by Americans of whom I've never heard.

An amazing performance by a true amateur of poetry. An amateur of Firetuck. An extraordinary letter. An extraordinary pick-me-up. (How I wish it could be sold in the drugstores with Valium and Prozac. Fopper's Uppers.)

But who is or what was Joachim—Jock—Fopper? I wonder now, and in Quito, a bit nauseous and dizzy from the height disease they call *soroche,* I wondered then. (Sucking the nausea-fighting barley sugar candy given me by an English salesman, my seatmate from Buenos Aires.) Once I even wondered if Fopper's calls were not a distortion of my dizziness. And later, over pickled *camarones* (the local shrimpy shrimp) and some *sopa quiteño* (egg and white cheese in a rich soup), served in the white and silvery dark elegance of a Colon Internacional dining room, I pursued the hints of vertigo to conjure up careers for Herr Señor Fopper. One was shaped by decades of reading mystery and spy novels. So Joachim Fopper, the only one of the two hundred million people living on the enormous continent who knew Marcus Firetuck as a poet, one of the, say, fifteen (ten?) human beings who had been enriched, expanded, *pleased* by my poems—the strangest and most beautiful of mental handshakes—this fan of mine was some Nazi dribble who'd crawled out of Europe via the Odessa Network to South America, where his brutal talents went underground to emerge only in such perverse passions as admiration for the obscure poems of a North American—and *for repentance*—Jew. Didn't such careful study of the obscure bespeak training, say, on Admiral Canaris's counterintelligence staff? Indeed, might Fopper's "intrusion" be a subtle way of establishing an American contact?

"Tell me about yourself," I will write back to Fopper.

Or should I? Here in Chicago, with the day's rich mail, his four single-spaced typewritten sheets create an island of international lucidity on my desk. Between matte-finished cellulose plastic, calipers, T squares, nomographic charts, and cartographic journals, Fopper's letter is a grail of communion. Why should I test it for fool's gold?

For five or six years now, my steadiest correspondent has been another man with whom I've had next to no physical contact. In the spring of 1973, I got away from a tumultuous house party my older children were throwing in our house in Door County and lunched myself in a restaurant in Sister's Bay. At the next table was an enormous young fellow whose head, I remember thinking then, could have been put up almost intact alongside the four presidents carved out of the South Dakota mountain. As I was marveling at this stony, eyeglassed immensity, it turned my way and asked if it could have the sweetener in my sugar bowl. That began a monologue which ended with an exchange of addresses, and this, in turn, became an epic correspondence, the most intense and one-sided correspondence of my life (excluding a shorter one with my first fiancée, Mary Joe Weil—pronounced "wheel"—of Durham, North Carolina, back in the early months of 1952). It is certainly the most peculiar.

Vernon Bowersock.

Is he out of his mind?

I think not. Vernon is just out of your mind, at least out of mine. Or was then. By now I'm used to him. Vernon is one of the very few people who very early on is hooked by a life project. His project is self-reflexive. That is, Vernon is concerned with Vernon. Or, at least, with a kind of Vernonization of the world. Vernon wishes to make sense of everything he has seen, heard, or can think about. His tools are numerology and epic poetry. Vernon is always thinking, Where will this or that fit into the *Vernoniad*?

There is a lot of this and that. Vernon runs up and down the United States getting a degree in one thing here, a degree in something else there. He marries, he separates, he divorces. He reads, he carries on his Napoleonic correspondence, and he supports himself wherever he goes as a computer programmer. (Knowing such work was useful in any city, Vernon took it up in high school.) Vernon is not a careless man. Indeed, a theme of the future *Vernoniad* is that there is nothing accidental; everything belongs in the great scheme called Vernon.

Vernon was born in the only Mississippi county which seceded from the Confederacy (or does one say stayed loyal to the Union?). His grandfathers have been the county sheriffs. "As close to being dictator as humans can get in this country," says Vernon. So it is out of this singular world of authority and pride that the future epic poet comes.

Future poet. There's the rub. Vernon has only prepared to write his epic. What's written now is introductory matter. Perhaps Vernon, dazzled so by the possibility of the *Vernoniad,* will write nothing but introductions. But if one includes the letters to his four chief correspondents — "my four compass points" — Vernon's prose already constitutes an epic, a kind of Epic of Introduction.

I answer one in ten or twelve of Vernon's letters. (He doesn't require answers from his Easts and Wests: the three others are a preacher in Binghamton, Alabama, an undertaker in Lompoc, California — "picked because it's the setting for W. C. Field's *Bank Dick*" — and a "beautiful seventy-year-old librarian in Lima, Ohio, so I can begin her letter 'Ohi-o'—'hello' in Japanese, I'm told—'Lovely Lima Lady Libe.'") Why do I answer them at all? Because through Vernon I see much of the country and encounter a mentality my small, skeptical intelligence habitually rejects. I suppose too that Vernon's numerology is a wild form of that impulse which made me both cartographer and "lisper in numbers," a desire to achieve clarity by reduction.

Vernon, always in "financial holes bigger than canyons," "thrown out by three wives, all of whom I love and will always love," always working, reading, moving on, and writing about it all, is, I suppose, my own Odysseus, the moving part of my essential inertness. I have been in fifty or sixty countries, but almost always in ways which eliminate their strangeness; Vernon has never left this county, but every inch of it is different for him.

163 Farrell Ave.
#19
St. Paul, Minn.

Dear Mr. Firetuck,

It is 6:18, and I have consumed the day's second thousand calorie. I took a four-mile walk, jogged two, did ninety push-ups, forty knee bends. Tomorrow, I go for my weekend at the Sunfare Camp. I go twice a week. Erections are forbidden. Joke: "When do the Japanese have elections?" "Before bleakfast." I am twenty-nine years, three months, four days, six hours, and thirty-one minutes old. I was conceived when George Marshall was making his Marshall Plan speech at Harvard University. Or close to it. You were

conceived when Babe Ruth was hitting the twenty-seventh or -eighth
of his record-breaking sixty home runs. Lindbergh was en route to
Paris when your—excited?—parents conceived you. *"Le hasard infini
des conjunctions."* (Mallarmé, *Igitur*—I know only this quote which is
scrawled on the back flap of Irma Rombauer's *Joy of Cooking* which
work I slobber over as I eat my broiled turbot—120 calories, 200 with
Tartar Sauce and catsup. How about the infinite romance of con-
solation to balance the infinite chance of conjunction?)

I owe twenty-one thousand nine hundred and seventy dollars,
eight thousand of them to Rosaleen who will let me pay back the
others first. (She is in Spokane, earning good money in a carob and
soybeanery.)

Your friend,
Vernon Bowersock

Imagine. I was spawned in a heroic time. My loving progenitors were
excited by Lindbergh's flight. (Had they come out of a newsreel theater? Did they exist then? Or had they news on the radio? Did they
own one in 1927? No. Too new.) Still, the excitement was in them, the
market was good. What a grand time to be conceived. Does it account
for the essential peace of my unheroism?

My own son, Frederick Gumbel Firetuck, was, I'm almost certain,
conceived the night Ethel and I went out to Midway Airport with
other lost causers of 1957 to greet Adlai Stevenson's plane. Carl Nach-
man was there, and he was paying lots of genteel attention to Ethel;
much as I liked him, my old jealousy was roused, and, that night, her
body roused me like a new one. Fred sprang from that passion. Which
explains—why not?—his blue eyes, his exceptional strength and
height, his sweet reserve. Why not?

3126 Walnut Street
Evansville, Indiana

Dear Mr. Firetuck,

You'll note I've moved again. A bit of trouble in Sunfare. A forty-
year-old blond-headed, brunette-pubed lady from Milwaukee.

Someone with such prodigious endowment should not be allowed the good clean health-fare fun of the colony. It was not before breakfast, *mais* I was elected. Bad show. The saintly Mr. Carmichael was taking his matutinal walk in the sun and nearly tripped over the barrier. He is like Voltaire's Jesus, "an enthusiast of good faith with a weakness for publicity." I was summoned, marked—though within terrible half seconds my guilty member had resigned its office—and asked to remove it and its base. Life here in the besummered north is not for such as I anyway. I am part Floridian—"oh, Florida, venereal soil"—and I don't have the manners of you northerners.

I weigh 179, though I have not eaten today and on the road was down to fifteen hundred greasy calories.

I'm on page 134 of three books, pocket jobs. I will now advance to page 184 of each. The books: *Back Swing,* a novel; *The Arnheiter Affair; My Days with the Mafia.*

Do you realize what half a century of life means? It eases my terrible approach to the *mezzo del cammin.*

Your friend,
Vernon Bowersock

There is only one other real letter in this day's mail. (I don't discount the documentary value of dental bills, charity appeals, advertising flyers, and treasure packages, expected—subscriptions, say—or unexpected—perhaps forgotten; but they are not the essence of mail.) The letter is from my old pal Lester Doyle, whose father was my teacher in Ann Arbor. (Working for the State Department in 1942 to 1944, Professor Doyle mapped the boundaries which became the three—later four—zones of postwar Germany.) Lester, a polyprogenitor, has not otherwise been as productive as his father. Nor has his life been as serene. Almost every Lester letter contains at least one piece of bad news. Yet so considerate a person is pale, tiny Lester that he manages to find some countervailing sweetness to enclose with the month's misfortune. He has so large a family—five boys, three girls—that there is always a supply of each on which to draw.

Lester teaches musicology at a remote branch of the University of Arkansas. As the only faculty member who has published an article, he has become a figure of both awe and exoticism. "I am their Paris and their Greece," he wrote me once. "But they are so remote. And so, it appears, am I." I've wondered if Lester's incessant progeniture is an attempt—like his letters—to people solitude. Today he writes that William, his second son, has had a leg amputated. "Soft-tissue sarcoma, I'm afraid, and the prognosis is not good." I hardly know William Doyle, remember only a frail, shy, small-chinned young man, a young edition of the professorial grandfather for whom he was named. William, like all Doyles, is very intelligent. He got scholarships to Milton and Williams, where he was a brilliant student of something like Provençal. A pro football freak, he knows the lifetime won-and-lost records of every professional team. He must be about twenty-two and works for the Atlanta Braves baseball team (doing something with season subscriptions). "Eileen has gone to stay with him." Eileen is his oldest sister.

> I was there for several days after the operation. William was very brave. I cannot bear the thought that we might lose him. Yet just that, we have been told, is what will soon happen.

There is other Doyle news, busy news, grandchildren conceived and jobs changed; then there is a paragraph about his research.

> I am trying to complete an article on Delphine Potocka, the randy countess who had an affair with Chopin. Chopinologists are most exercised about the subject. A lady in Warsaw discovered a cache of letters in 1945. Or did she? You can imagine what life in Warsaw was like then. Is it unreasonable to see a starving lady scholar filling her belly with the invention of her head? I don't think poor Mme. Czernicka capable of forging them. For instance, there's a line from "Chopin" about wanting to set "something precious in D-flat."
> That is a pun on the most intimate part of a woman's anatomy. Human beings surprise, but I would be very surprised to see Mme. Czernicka making this up.

Little William Doyle prepares to leave the world, and his loving father, Lester, works to fill the gap with a perhaps affair of the melancholy genius. Giving Chopin this bit of postmortuary life, does Lester somehow provide for his son?

The word "mail"—I've looked it up—derives from the Old High German *Malha,* a wallet. Its homonym, the woven metal rings used for armor, derives from Old French *maille,* link, and the Latin *macula,* stain.

I like to think of the lexic twins in Siamese unification: so in these small sacks, these envelopes, we inscribe our little *maculae,* the spots and stains of our individuality. Some we show to one correspondent, some to another. And the result is a mesh of strands from all parts of the world and of our lives. Against the day's brute fact, the fatigues and routinage of *now,* this mesh armors us.

Sandra Lukisch, Joachim (Jock) Fopper, Vernon Bowersock, and Lester Doyle, and even you, Frédéric Chopin (or your letter writer, Mme. Czernicka), though none of you has met or will meet except in my head, on my desk, you are citizens of the country of correspondence, the soul of commerce across time and space; you are society itself.

Beloved correspondents, blessed institution, may the terrible convenience of speedier linkage never triumph completely over your clumsy, difficult frailty. "Very sincerely yours, Marcus Firetuck."

TEETH

*In the multiplied objects of the external world I had
no thoughts but for the teeth. For these I longed with
a phrenzied desire.*

Poe, "Berenice"

1

Ah, Miss Wilmott, how did you come to think what you did? Is all
your interpreting so askew, so deformed by self-interest? And is your
self-interest so unbroken a pup that any street whistle seems its master's voice? To think that you were misled as wisdom itself was being
certified in your aching jaws? Those third molars, so long held back,
and then so painfully emergent, fangs and cusps clinging savagely to
the gum flesh. "Impacted," said Dr. Hobbie, and despite the kind, soft-
beaked, confident face behind the metal glasses, you shuddered. You
remembered the last one, also impacted, eight months before, also in
the Bank Building, though two flights up on the ninth floor in a large
office afloat in the strawberry light off the lake. Dr. Grant, the extrac-
tionist, Miss Blade's recommendation, a strong fellow with white mustache and a post on the executive council of the American Dental
Association, just back from a downtown committee meeting to have a
go at your trouble. A lovely May day, the creamy air swimming over
the IC tracks, enough to make you forget the pain, until Dr. Grant,

eyes asweat under his speckled horn-rims, leaned over your open mouth and blocked out the view. And then, the tugging, the hammering, the cracking, chiseling, wrestling, blood squirting into the cotton gagging your mouth, blood dripping past it down your throat, your heart pumping, your great brow streaming, your wet palm grabbed tight by the fierce little nurse, Miss Romeyne. Afterward, on the couch, another blow, Dr. Grant sitting beside you, your long legs dripping feet over the edge, hand to your swelling jaw. "How does a hundred dollars sound, Miss Wilmott? Pretty fair? Including postoperant care, anesthesia, the works. I know you're a teacher."

The pain lasted twelve days, unabated by Miss Blade's late revelation that she had been charged a hundred and twenty-five dollars. For this omission, Miss Blade would not get to know about Dr. Hobbie. Not that she'd appreciate him anyway. Miss Blade favored all the weak sisters in the department, the students with the loudest line of gab and the worst minds who took so long with their dissertations that they completed them and their scholarly life simultaneously.

Miss Wilmott learned of Dr. Hobbie through her once-a-week cleaning woman, Mrs. Spiders, whom she passed in the lobby of the bank as she was on her way to request it to honor Dr. Grant's hundred dollars, although her balance was zero until the first of June. Mrs. Spiders was on her way to Dr. Hobbie. "Yeah, Miss Wilma, mah Hobbie's a grand tooth man." Mrs. Spider's syntax obscured identification, but she spoke of him now and then throughout the year, so that when Miss Wilmott's second tooth began cracking her head open the night after Epiphany, the vision of the great dental surgeon soothed it till morning, when she phoned him up and got a noon appointment. Dr. Hobbie was seldom too busy to squeeze in a sufferer. Half his business was "street business" anyway, delivery boys feeling pain between the first and fifth floors, taxi drivers from the Yellow Cab stand, salespeople from the local stores, even receptionists from other dentists' offices in the building. A good sign. Not that Miss Wilmott needed confirmatory signs.

Except for that first day. An initial visit to Dr. Hobbie was disconcerting, especially if your appointment came on Wednesdays. Every Tuesday, he danced at the Tall Girls' Club till 3:00 A.M., and Wednesday was one long yawn for him. An unrepressed yawn, for Dr. Hobbie repressed no habit that any normal dentist would. No dentist with a smart practice walked around with his smocks so loosely tied that a skinny, peppermint-colored back exposed itself to his patients' gaping faces. No normal dentist worked in a shelfless closet which barely enabled his movements and certainly no nurse's. As for answering the phone, tucking it between shoulder and jaw while continuing to drill, or taking long looks at Educational Channel Spanish lessons while working in a silver filling, these were procedures which — Miss Wilmott imagined — might lead to dismissal from the ADA. Yes, there was almost no limit to the external defects of Dr. Hobbie's practice.

But Hobbie was a dental genius. In thirty years of agonized dental visits, Miss Wilmott had never known such not only painless but even pleasurable sensation. Dr. Hobbie's office did not face the strawberry-colored lake air but the west wall of the Bank Building; there were no couches, no magazines, in fact nothing at all in the scarcely redeemed cave of a waiting room but a kitchen chair and a coatrack. But you almost never had to wait, and when you were in the chair, there was almost no pain. The fees were ludicrously small, even for her, a low-grade instructor in the history department. Ten dollars for her impacted wisdom tooth, and for that there were sound-wave drills, the best Swedish steel, a lecture on her lower jaw, Mantovani playing Cole Porter on the hi-fi, and the sweetest of all analgesics, Dr. Hobbie's account of his personal troubles.

These came out of him as naturally as his pale, thin back out of the white smock. They were not unlike Miss Wilmott's own troubles, at least his implicit ones. They had to do with Suzanne, his tall, expert dancer of a wife, who'd left him last June to live with the Bank Building florist, Mr. Consolo, but who still somehow or other extracted money from him, though they had no child to support. Which led to another trouble: here he was, forty-two years old, the only fellow he knew who had no children, as well as the only one who had to spend half his time looking for girls with whom to dance the samba and the twist, though he had a perfectly good dancing wife of his own. The implicit troubles were, she knew, those for which she had female equivalents.

It was her early insight into their equivalence that made her think that Dr. Hobbie could help her with more than teeth. He wasn't the world's most attractive man, God knew, not even the most attractive she'd known, which said a great deal; for her timid six feet, popped eyes, and no-nose face—she'd overheard someone say she looked as if she'd been blotted—were no powerful magnet for men.

In her entire life, there were very few times she'd gone out with half-decent men. She'd come to think that perhaps it didn't matter, that she could make it without a man. If only people would stop pressuring her. Thousands of small pressures: salesgirls calling her Mrs. when she bought her father's birthday shirts; people being introduced to her at parties; being the extra girl and getting tied up with the miserable extra man, more miserable when he saw her; the hundreds and hundreds of self-pitying hours in her two rooms, Jack Paar jabbering maniacally on the twelve-inch screen while she shared him with *Middlemarch,* its pages stained with the peanut butter she sometimes thought was more faithful to her than any person on earth.

She had yens, God knows, though not as many as two-bit Freudians would think. She'd even had a little experience, a summer at Truro, where her six feet and impressive learning had substituted for a movie star's chest and model's face. There'd even been a marriage proposal, from a Wyoming historian at the American Historical meetings in '58. It turned out that he wanted introductions to the scholarly big chiefs at Chicago. At least, though, it was on the books, her chance at middle-class nirvana.

As Hobbie's big-beaked, sandy face, a good-hearted parrot's, leaned over her open mouth, even that first day, Miss Wilmott felt a kind of root tremble in her heart. A sweet man, a poor troubled fellow. Not a cretin either, though naive and uncultured. In dentistry, he was actually a scholar, full of the history of instruments, surgical procedures, technical advances. He spent weekends reading the journals, and while Dr. Grant was in ADA executive sessions, he listened to papers. He was so enamored of his profession that she began to pick up toothy tidbits for him, things she'd come upon in her ubiquitous browsing in the stacks.

"Ever read ahhh Poe's 'Ber-ahhh-niece'?"

"Nope. Spit out, Miss Wilmott."

Then, after rinsing with the sweet, violet water, "It's about a man so insanely fond of teeth that he breaks open his former fiancée's grave ahhh, pulls out all her teeth ahhh, and keeps them in a box."

"Oh, my Lord," eyes furry with astonishment. "And I thought I liked teeth. Little wider there, Miss Double-U."

Miss Wilmott read the *Britannica* on teeth and dentistry, soaked up tooth lore, began to think in tooth metaphors, and felt the root tremble in her heart whenever Dr. Hobbie leaned over to pass a steel shaft beneath her strong, white crowns. "There's a tribe called the Ndembu in Rhodesia which has a tooth ceremony called the Ihamba, ahhh. They pull out the premolar incisor, and their troubles are supposed to come out with it. Then they have a tooth dance."

"That's really something. Not much longer. Good girl. Where do you find such things out?"

She puffed her cheeks with the violet water and spat as daintily as possible into the bowl's soft whirlpool. "Periodicals."

"Periodicals?"

"Magazines. That was in the ahhh *Rhodes-Livingstone Journal* last month." Into her mouth and out, a silvery tool. "Dahhhhh."

"Just a little bit more now. There we are, almost out. I envy you book people. Myself, I can't . . . Here we are," holding up an enamel needle bloodied with nerved dentine. "That's the old troublemaker. I think you're going to be all right for a while now."

"I might as well get everything cleaned up, Dr. Hobbie. As long as I'm making real progress. I'd miss my visit anyway."

With the hand that held the silver forceps in which her troublemaker lay, he brushed the soft tip of his beak back and forth, as if to sniff out a proper response. "Might work a little on that back bite then if you really want to go ahead and spend the money. It'll run you thirteen, fourteen dollars." He opened the child's notebook in which he entered all appointments and payments. "That'll be three-fifty today, and we'll set you down for next Thursday. Four-fifteen, OK, right after Mr. Givens. He's my other book patient."

Thursday, she came a few minutes early and sat on the kitchen chair listening to Dr. Hobbie tell Mr. Givens that he had this fine teacher from the university coming right in, he wanted Mr. Givens to meet her.

At 4:14 the door opened, you never had to wait, and a short, good-looking Negro of forty, dressed in house painter's stained overalls, was introduced to her by Dr. Hobbie and said he was very glad to meet her, was she a Marxist like the other teachers up there at the university, and to her "I'm afraid not" said he was disappointed, he having been a Marxist for twenty years, *The Manifester* and *The Working Day* being his favorite books of all time.

Dr. Hobbie's other book patient. After this, most of her appointments coincided with Mr. Givens's. She wondered if Dr. Hobbie also brought his salespeople together. At any rate, she exchanged a few words each time with him while a beaming Hobbie stood by. Once she recommended Herzen's *Memoirs* to him, and another time she told him that she'd just reread the *Manifesto* and not only "The Working Day," but the whole first book of *Capital.* At this, Mr. Givens struck a great hand to his fine brow. "You mean to say there's a whole book of that, and I don't know it? Give me the name there, Miss Wilmer. I'm ashamed of myself. I'll go git it today if I got to go to every bookstore in Chicago." Miss Wilmott gave him the name, told him it was readily available, and recommended the Everyman Library Edition, one sixty-five for each of the volumes. "God," said Mr. Givens, "they could charge three or four dollars for them, and I'd git them as quick as I'm going to now." He held out his hand, and she put her own great one into it. Dr. Hobbie said, "What'd I tell you, George?"

Today Miss Wilmott's tidbit was that biologists regarded fish teeth as migrated scales. "I suppose our ancestors may have masticated on the skin," she said as he placed her head back into the rest.

Dr. Hobbie said that that sure would make dentistry easy. Then, a large shape darkened the office door, a gray fedora pulled nose level on the head. " 'Night, son," it said.

" 'Night, Dad," said Dr. Hobbie.

Though she'd not seen Hobbie's father, a doctor from the floor above, she knew that the glass cabinet of unfinished bridges and tooth sets over by the television aerial was due to him, or rather to the dying patients he felt would be comforted by his son's diverting skill. They often died in the midst of their absorption in refurbished mouths, and Miss Wilmott's Dr. Hobbie kept their work, as if, in some odd turn of the world, a mouth would appear just right for one of the unfinished bridges.

"That your father?"

"Yep. That's the old man. Been in this building since they put it up. He's a real good doctor if you need one." He was washing his hands, and she studied his reflection in the dark window. He took off his smock, and she saw his skinny, harmless back, white and pink, a rabbit scooting into a green shirt. "He helped me out with Suzanne last week. She hit a car. Two hundred bucks. I've got to pay her lawyer. That doesn't seem fair, does it? I mean Consolo is no poor man. They do well, even in winter. Three-fifty a dozen for irises." She put on her coat. "What do I owe you today?"

"I put my book away. I guess I can't charge you, or they'll be getting me up for not reporting income."

"I won't think of that," she said, and laid out a five-dollar bill on top of his sterilizer.

He took out his wallet and gave her two dollars. "I'll drive you home. It's another cold one."

"Lovely," said Miss Wilmott. She drove a '52 Pontiac which hadn't started for most of January and February.

Out on Fifty-third Street, the wind was knifed for murder. People passed like thugs, scarves pulled over mouths, hats down like old Dr. Hobbie's to the nose. Ridges of steel ice humped the streets, and every third corner had its famished crocodile of open car hood, whining for life.

I'll offer him supper, thought Miss Wilmott, though there was nothing in the kitchen but two cans of roast beef hash, eggs, and a loaf of Pepperidge Farm bread. Nor could she take the chance of asking him to let her shop. He'd not let himself be invited then. "I'd like to give you a little supper, Dr. Hobbie. If you're free, I mean."

"Gee."

"I don't get too many chances to cook for other people."

"That would be something, Miss Wilmott," but he was turning round, looking for something. "Darn," he said. "Guess what? I don't have the car today. It's in the garage. I am sorry, Miss Double-U. I'll put you in a cab. Let me take a rain check on that supper, OK? It's real nice of you." And he opened a taxi door, put her in, spoke to the driver, and said, "So long." Turned out he'd paid the fare.

But Miss Wilmott had a bad night. The heat was low, her bed was cold. She got up, put on a sweater and the furry bathrobe her father'd sent her for her birthday. February 2. Thirty-one. She turned on WFMT. Buzz. It was three o'clock. Dr. Hobbie'd be coming home from the Tall Girls. She sat back in the terrible green armchair she'd gotten at Carmen the Movers for eight dollars. A troglodyte. The only arms that ever held her. How long was it going to go on like this? She couldn't even get a man over for supper. For talk. For an exchange of troubles. The enamel crown was off, the pulp cavity cut away, and the tiny, mean, piranha nerves of the dentine sang out in the iron cold of February. Today's *Sun-Times* remarked that a marine had pole-vaulted sixteen feet, twenty years to the day after another man had pole-vaulted fifteen. A photographer, rapacious for a shot, had knocked down the bar and the record might not be official. Dr. Hobbie had said he'd come for supper, but the garage had his car. The grain of the world was wrong. What could she do? She was a Ph.D. in English history, a low-grade instructor at a high-grade university. If she wrote a few more articles and a good book, they'd give her six years as an assistant professor and then maybe tenure. She could get a tenure job right now at lots of women's colleges. Down south, where the streets didn't look like an illustration of the *Inferno,* where women were loved. But she wouldn't live down south again. She'd gone a year to W.C. in Greensboro, and she wouldn't live in a place where Mr. Givens would have to sit in the back of a bus and drink from a different water fountain. Maybe she'd go back east, nearer relatives, nearer the marrying girls of her class at Wheaton. But she'd left such dependence and such competition behind. She was a scholar. She knew her stuff. She loved to work, to find out what happened, to read two-hundred-year-old periodicals, to trace in detail the rise of sentimentality, the alteration in attitudes toward children, toward women, toward pain, toward dirt. But now, now. Tonight. She could not read, not listen to the radio, not steam a kettle. She stared at the arrested chaffinches in her stained rug border, the bricks and boards which held the books she'd dragged around for years with her, east, west, south, her swelling paunch. It was a terrible night. Only self-consciousness kept her going. She brooded on until the room turned fuzzy with fatigue, and then she went off to sleep in the troglodyte's arms.

2

Miss Wilmott did not see Dr. Hobbie again until spring. She was writing an article on the use of opium in England during the first two decades of the nineteenth century, and it took up every minute of the time that she did not give her classes, committee meetings, papers, meals, and pillow. Weekends, nights, vacation days found her in Harper Library or downtown at the Newberry reading account books, newspapers, doctors' diaries, the works of Coleridge, De Quincey, Bramwell Brontë, and other well-known users of the drug. Her fingers bore dots of yellow where the dust of the old accounts bit into the curious, living flesh: her addiction marks. When she got to the use of opium by dental surgeons, she was brought up short.

It was May, a year from her terrible encounter with Dr. Grant. Walking home from the bus stop one evening, facing the strawberry light off the lake, she felt the root tremble in her heart. "Your liking and your lust is fresh whyle May doth last, / When May is gone, of all the yeare the plesaunt time is past." Carpe diem, Miss Wilmott. Old time is swiftly flying. "Oh dear," she said, taking her long, slow strides into the fading light. "It isn't simple."

But the next morning, she telephoned Dr. Hobbie and asked if she could come in to have her teeth examined. No, there was nothing special wrong except that her jaw ached when she ate ice cream, and her bite was a little unsteady. Dr. Hobbie told her to come in on Tuesday.

Monday night, he telephoned and said he was awfully sorry, he couldn't see her tomorrow. "The old man kicked the bucket today. This afternoon. I'll be real busy tomorrow. How about Friday?"

"Of course," she said, "and I'm awfully sorry about him."

"Three-thirty, right in his office." For a moment, she thought it was her appointment time and that he was moving into his father's office. "Had his stethoscope on a patient and kicked the bucket right there, listening. Seventy-eight years old."

Miss Wilmott could not think of opium that May night. There was a burr stuck in the evening: Dr. Hobbie's mortal phrase, "Kicked the bucket." It was not worthy. Offhandedness had limits. Distaste helped blunt her disappointment at the postponement. By Thursday, however, she could hardly wait to see him.

It was ten-thirty. She must have been his first patient, for she had to wait outside the locked door. When he arrived, he said, "Don't have to work so hard now. The old man left me eighty-four thousand bucks. Never thought he was within fifty of it. Suzanne would hit the deck if she knew how much she lost out on. I'm going to New York, take in some shows and restaurants before she gets the word and tries to get her hands on it. I don't think she's given up on me. Every so often, she gets soused up and calls me on the phone, gives me a chewing out. You don't do that if you've given up on somebody. Maybe you can give me a list, Miss Wilmott." A list of what—girls? "I don't know the restaurant situation too well there."

Ah. She said she knew very little about New York.

Dr. Hobbie's hands at her mouth were sure as ever, but Miss Wilmott did not feel comfortable. He talked a blue streak. "People been calling me day and night asking about the old man. They can't figure out why his phone doesn't answer. Think they'd read the papers. That's a nasty one you have back there." He touched her with a silver prong.

"I'm on the run every minute. Have to shut off his phone, sublet his office, the apartment. Papers, you have no idea, writing relatives, the funeral. Dying is harder on the relatives than the dead man. I'll bet getting born is easier. Not that I know much about that. You ever had a child, Miss Wilmott?" He'd run on too fast and blushed. Miss Wilmott's file turned up a sentence, "A blush is a primitive erection." Her own face chugged with capillary action. "Of course not," he was saying. "Excuse me. I was just shooting off. The old man's kind of thrown me. Never had a bad word for me since I was a little tyke. Helped me through school, helped me furnish the office, helped with Suzanne." Had his old man given him the kitchen chair, the TV set, the glass case?

Miss Wilmott nearly invited him to dinner on the spot. But held back. This time she'd prepare. There'd be another appointment in a week. She'd invite him then.

Two days before the appointment she went down to Halsted Street and bought a fine roast, a Greek cheese and olives, baklava, and a beautiful eggplant which she would transform into a marvelous Greek dish she'd read about in an eighteenth-century cookbook. It took two days

to make, and Miss Wilmott turned to it from her opium with the energetic passion she knew great cooks must have.

So there she was, the day of her appointment, ready to show her
stuff. But oh how foolish was Miss Wilmott. The most untutored person would not prepare so elegantly for an empty chair. If she'd telephoned even one day early, Dr. Hobbie might have canceled his plane
tickets to New York; for that's where he was going, one hour and ten
minutes after finishing up her mouth.

Her disappointment was immeasurable. Back she walked along
Fifty-third Street, hardly looking at the colors which the sun stirred up
in the chubby western clouds, hardly aware of the birds singing good
night to her from the cottonwood as she pushed her legs past each
other down Harper, Blackstone, Dorchester, Kenwood, and then up
Kimbark toward her apartment.

Nor did she see Mr. Givens, the house painter, till he was practically at her feet. "Hey there, Miss Wilmer. How ya doing this evening?"
He'd taken off his cap, was in coveralls, and he carried a paper bag.
Miss Wilmott's heart, which had jumped with fear, calmed in recognition. And then in a brilliant flash, she remembered the beautiful dinner waiting twenty feet up from where they stood. The rest was
simple. "Mr. Givens, I couldn't be more happy to see anyone. Guess
what just happened to me," and she told him about someone being
called away from the dinner she'd cooked, an emergency. Could he
help her out and share it?

"Why, Miss Wilmer, that's really something. I'm just going on up to
Blackstone Library with a couple of hamburgers and a jelly doughnut.
I'm reading that memoir book you told me about. Best thing I ever
looked at. I'd like to come up, it's real nice of you. I'll read at it tomorrow night."

So Mr. Givens came and sat down at the table she'd set the night before, between her green troglodyte and the TV set, with her complete
supply of Wedgwood picked up in the corners of State Street pawnshops and Maxwell Street stands. It was a wonderful dinner, praised by
Mr. Givens at the last word in a lifetime of good eating.

He was not bad company, either. He had strong opinions about
everything. There were the rich, who always argued about bills, never
paid you what they'd agreed to, always trying to cut your throat; there

were the sports-crazy people of Chicago, blowing off the air-raid sirens when the ball team won the darn pennant; there were the "jawbreakers" (whom she didn't identify with John Birchers till he lumped them with the Ku Kluxers), out to loot everybody by scaring them out of their brains, not that there were too many around to be scared out of; there were these Careoaches and Milers, beat writers who were full of more hot air about colored people than Talmadge and Bilbo; there was De Goal sitting up in a French cloud while everyone in Paris killed themselves with these plastic bombs; there was the Rooshans, more *boojwa* than the capitalists, never thinking beyond their own bellies, not that he should be thinking about anything else after such a wonderful meal, for which, Miss Wilmott, I never will git to thank you enough.

With which he was up, a handsome man with a fine mustache, gray at the temples, a high forehead, a very distinguished looking and intelligent self-educated man, probably unmarried, though she didn't know and wouldn't dream of asking, and if the world wasn't the way it was, and if he could possibly get interested in her, who knows if despite everything that separated them, she would not enjoy cooking for him and taking his praise and affection every single remaining evening of her life. If she could take anyone that much, there being, after all, much to be said for freedom, one's own time, doing one's work at one's own speed, so good night, Mr. Givens, it's been a real pleasure, mutual, yes, sometime again, and I certainly would like to go out with you, no absolutely, I'm not in the least offended by the offer, I'm proud you asked me.

The next week Miss Wilmott began writing her article. It flew. Never had she written so fast, so well. In one week, she laid out a thirty-nine-page first draft, and she knew that there wouldn't be more than a handful of changes. Still, she distrusted compositional euphoria, remembered Horatian maxims, and laid the article aside for a few days before turning to the final draft.

Fatal delay.

The evening Dr. Hobbie was due back from New York, she sat in the troglodyte's arms, fingering her reference cards, thinking about plunging ahead. On the very first card, the terrible equation, "Picul = $133\frac{1}{3}$ lb." swooped toward her eyes. "Oh no," she said out loud. "No, no, no." But there it was. Her calculations about imports had been pegged at a hundred and sixty-six and a third pounds to the picul. She'd misread her skewered threes. An absurd error, yet an easily corrigible one. But, no, those thirty-three false pounds lodged in Miss Wilmott like splinters she was too fearful to dig out of her tender article. Infection set in. Her beautiful account of opium consumption, rich in psychological insight, economic analysis, social theory, and literary allusion, rose rankly to her nostrils, a festered lily.

That night her jaw throbbed in sympathetic misery. Her knowledge, her research, her opium, what were they now in the dark, stranded by her needs, errors, miscalculations, her muddled self-interest? In agony, Miss Wilmott reached for the phone and called Dr. Hobbie's home number. Four, five, six rings. The receiver was on its way down when she heard his "Hallo."

"Oh, Dr. Hobbie. Thank goodness. Forgive me for calling you. I wasn't even sure you were back. It's Miss Wilmott. I'm in awful pain."

It was right to call him, said Dr. Hobbie, he'd just gotten in, he was barely asleep. He'd meet her in twenty minutes at the office, no, better, he'd pick her up in fifteen minutes. Yawn. That too quick?

"I don't want you to have to do that. I'm just being nervous. It probably was knowing that you'd come back that made me tooth conscious. If you were in New York, I probably wouldn't have noticed."

"We'll take a look anyway, Ethel. See you in a few minutes. Bye now." Click.

He'd called her Ethel. Bye now. Bye now. By now he was taking pajamas off his long, pale body, slipping into underwear, pants, shirt.

She dressed in a flash, a blue cotton with her initials figured in the lapel, EAW, an unfinished word. Downstairs, she waited at the door, her nose blob flattened further against the glass, waiting. The first car brought her out to the stoop, but though it paused in midcareer, it was not Hobbie and went on. Few neutral cars would stop for Miss Wilmott.

There was a bite to the air. Miss Wilmott was starting up the stairs for a sweater when Dr. Hobbie's Dodge pulled up in front of the house. She ran down and climbed in beside him. "It's wonderful of you to do this."

Behind his glasses beaked the soft face. "I'm kind of proud to get a night call. Doesn't happen more than twice a year. Makes me feel like the old man."

Suddenly, Miss Wilmott was in a stew: there was not a splinter of pain left in her body. Nothing. Yet it had been genuine. Her whole head had gone out on strike with pain. There was no question of that. There may have been a psychic trigger, but the somatic twinges were genuine. Now there was absolutely nothing. Could it be that sitting beside this gentle fool, this *beau sabreur de la bouche,* was enough to soothe her gums?

At the Bank Building, all was dark. Dr. Hobbie's keys got them into the elevator and his office. He lit up his little workshop of analgesia, put a smock over his short-sleeved shirt, flipped a few switches, and before she'd summoned the strength to tell him how fine she felt, he'd sat her in the chair and stared into her mouth. "Whew. Good thing you called me. This must have been killing you. Can't remember a worse-looking abscess. We'll lance it and see what we can do."

Sir Percival. He was over her, touching, spearing, dabbing, in and out of her mouth, his beaky head swimming in a kind blue light. There was music—the hi-fi—"Is It True What They Say about Dixie?" Time flew. It was bitter dark, bitter cold, the iron February cold; she was lying down, faceup, staring at the wicked ice smothering the earth. Above her head, the whacking, cracking blade opened up the ice. Hobbie's terrible lit face, a starving bird's, gleamed in the white air. His talons, fierce Swedish tools, reached for her mouth. "Berenice," he screamed, "Berenice." And out, out they came, one by one, her thirty glorious crowns, roots, rapt from her yielding jaws. Oh it was over. She lay back, vacant, depleted, fulfilled.

Dr. Hobbie leaned over, a bloody three-pronged crown caught in his silver forceps. "There's your troublemaker. He won't bother you again. How do you feel, Ethel?"

She nodded. Her face felt shot away by Novocain. The nod was like lifting a boulder.

"We'll pick up a little painkiller and Chloraseptic for you, and I'll take you home."

She raised his good dentist's hand and patted it for thanks. For more than thanks.

In the car, she asked him if he'd seen some good shows.

"Not a one. Went dancing most of the time. Those places that sell you tickets. They're not bad. You get some fine dancers. And then last Saturday who showed up at the hotel but old Suzanne. I knew she'd smell out the old man's dough."

It was wickedly dark out. They were on Cottage Grove. The May night blew cold on Miss Wilmott's brow. Struggling through the rocky, cotton-lined resistance in her mouth, she said, "Well, well. And what did you do?"

What a question, Miss Wilmott! Where do you come off to ask such a question?

"She's not so bad, Ethel. You get used to a certain person, and then you take her faults with her better parts. Flags." Indeed there were, on stores. "Decoration Day."

"When May is gone, of all the year the pleasant time is past," said Miss Wilmott.

"I like June," said Dr. Hobbie. "I was born in June. I graduated in June. I got married in June. Of course, Suzanne ran off to Consolo last June. Every month has its good and bad times."

They were outside the drugstore. He ran in, and she waited alone in the car, her head back on the seat, aching.

"I don't have my purse," she said when he came back.

"Forget it," he said, and put the package in her lap. "They give it to me cut rate. I'll stick you next time."

Oh stick me now. Her great head leaned against his shoulder, and without warning, large tears bloomed and fell in her face. "Oh dear," she said.

Dr. Hobbie took his hands off the steering wheel and put them around her. "That's all right, Ethel. Just what you're supposed to do after an operation. You're going to be OK."

She was not going to be OK. The Ndembu's troubles left them when their teeth were pulled; not hers. The Ndembu danced to celebrate; Dr. Hobbie had not taught her the twist.

THE ANAXIMANDER FRAGMENT

1

Nibbenour arrived the day after Thanksgiving. Five of us, sitting in the shade of the tent, hear this rough purr and see a six-wheel Wombat coming out of the Great Nothing, pulling up to our twelve puffs of grass. Out come four helmets; one's removed, and there's a mess of brown curls. "Nibbenour," she says. "You guys wanna see the CIC's autograph?"

Dubbda: "General Blackhead's?"

"*The* CIC, dummy." Dubbda has a pharmacist's degree from Georgia State. "Your president. We ate Thanksgiving with'm."

Dubbda: "Old Bird in the Hand himself?"

She hands over Polaroids, one of her and President B. stuffing their faces, the other him autographing the Wombat's rear end.

We went over — not Vlach, he's reading — and there it was, a purple scrawl.

Pelz: "What's he like?"

Nibbenour: "Big. And built, for an old guy. Laughs. A lot."

Dubbda: "You thank him for sending us to this fucking resort?"

"Right place, right time, and the right butt kickers is what I told'm."

Dubbda: "A news bite."

Nibbenour: "Wanna see the Fox?"

Nothing was playing at the opera, we took the tour: amphibious, six tires, back two silicon, suck up what they ride on, analyzes for nerve agents, radiation, mustard gas, then craps weighted warning markers. "Nice?" Nibbenour's got gray eyes, rimless librarian specs, is built low like the Fox.

Pelz: "I prefer the M-9." The M-9 knocks holes in the sand berms.

Dubbda: "The M-60 for me." The M-60 rolls out a sixty-foot bridge for ditches, wadis.

Vlach's reading. Nibbenour calls over, "What's with you, soldier? Got something against the CIC?" Vlach has black eyes and a rug of black hair slapped down like an afterthought. "Excuse me?"

"The president. Chief Medicine Man. You American?"

"North American."

"Christ. Pawnee? Cheyenne? Navaho?" Vlach's dark complected, has a big, straight nose, could be Indian.

"Excuse me?"

"Forget it." Sticks out a little mitt. "Nibbenour."

Vlach went over and shook it. "Vlach."

"Where you from, Flak?"

I could see him taking that question in, *thinking* about it. I'm next to him in the tent, know his ways. She was about to throw in the conversational towel. "*To apeiron,*" he said.

"Wherezat? Carolina?"

I stepped in for him. "Georgia. He's a professor in Savannah."

"Well, well, you and I are going to have lots to talk about. Whaddya profess?"

Vlach tossed that around about twenty seconds. "Skepticism."

Nibbenour: "That's a course?"

I: "He teaches Humanities. At Armstrong."

Nibbenour: "You his translator?"

Vlach looks at us as if we're in an aquarium.

I: "He bunks next to me."

Nibbenour: "I'll bet. On, over, and between."

2

We're activated reserves out of Fort Stewart, Georgia. Nibbenour's RA, stationed in Bad Nauheim. No dummy, a soil technician. Mail call, she gets subscriptions, *Newsweek, Army Times, Scientific American,* three or four others I don't know.

Waiting for the war, she took on everyone. It'd be late afternoon, the sun sliding off the desert, full of color instead of bricks of glare, and here comes Nibbenour with her MRE (our plastic food), boots, camo pants, gas mask at the belt, a red T-shirt with SO ARE YOU over what's there. "What you Einsteins think of—?" It could be anything, Bush, Baker, Baghdad Charlie, Arabs, Madonna, newspapers, Picasso, alternative fuels, satellite grids, the superiority—her favorite—of women to men in or out of combat. Somebody would answer, she'd top him, he'd agree or he'd top her and get challenged: "Dummy." "Paper face." "Pig balls." The mitts would fist, she'd spread her legs, toss up her chin. "You looking for a guided tour of your asshole?"

Most of us got out of her way. Which left Vlach, who had no evasion skills. Somehow they talked, they walked—usually in the old lava bed, the *harra,* or behind the pile of rocks Nibbenour said was a Crusader castle.

She told Pelz, "Vlach and me're on another plane of discussion."

3

Vlach did what we all did. Up at ten, gear, rifle, mask, then crawling, sand in our mouths, noses, boots. We lay down smoke, fire beehives—pellets—flares, follow the Fox, the earth movers, cross ditches on fascines—plastic tubes dropped from tanks—back at four or five, the blue tent like Buckingham Palace, sleep the best thing on earth.

Vlach wasn't strong, but he made it, night after night after night.

Bunk four feet from a guy, he becomes part of you: his noises, smells, habits are like the hard ground and the cold, part of your life.

Wake to drink or piss, he's reading with a pencil light. He had four books. When I finished my three, I asked did he want to exchange. He hands one over: *Heidegger and the Anaximander Fragment.*

"A mystery?" Surprised, I'd figured him for *Crime and Punishment* or *Rabbit Something*.

"Unfortunately."

"Thought you'd be going for better-class stuff. Hemingway. Elmore Leonard."

"Don't know them."

He handed over the book. I turned pages, read words; a blind man at the silent movie. "I don't get it. Not a sentence."

"People study it for years they don't get it."

"So what's going on?"

He shook his head.

"You don't know?"

"I don't know if I know."

"I like to know things. Tell me what you know."

So he went on about Greek philosophers before Plato—who we read in Hum II—how there were only fragments of them quoted in other fragments. "I'm studying two sentences by Anaximander. Five hundred B.C.

"What are they? In plain English."

"It's not plain."

"Maybe you should switch sentences."

"Too late."

"Gimme a general idea, just the subject matter."

"Where things come from, what happens to them when they're here."

"Physics."

"Metaphysics was physics."

"And the words. The real words. I don't mean the Greek."

"I don't know Greek."

What does he know? Spending years figuring out a few words, he doesn't even know the right words.

He turned pages, pointed. There were two sentences in italics. I got out the tablet I write home on and copied them down.

The first wasn't bad. "*The beginning and origin of existing things is the unlimited (to apeiron).*"

"That's not bad," I said. "It's like Genesis."

"Yes."

"*To apeiron.* Greek?"

"Greek."

"Why throw it in?"

"It can mean different things. That's one of the problems."

The second sentence was something else: " 'Out of which, however, becoming relates to existing things, even though it also exists in what lies beyond; passing into obligation, for they pay just penalty and retribution to each other for their injustice, according to the disposition of time.' Something sounds wrong here."

"That's what happens. Things get passed on, mouth to mouth, parchment to parchment, and something drops off. The idea's to recover what the man thought."

"They can't even do that with this thief in Baghdad."

Out of the back of the tent, Dubbda or Oxenhandler, came a "Break it off."

"Outside," I said.

It's cold. A big moon lights the desert, looks like a huge lion. Forty billion stars. If it wasn't for what was going to happen, it wouldn't be bad. It was a place to talk about big things. Our brain cells might be doing some of the last work of their life.

Vlach's a little guy, the head fools you. It's good to have a guy like this, thinking of something else than what Mom cooks for dinner. "So whatta you think, Vlach? What did the old Greek mean?"

The big nose tilts out to the *harra*. "It almost makes sense out here." He nods awhile. I'm patient, I have no appointments. "Erosion," he says. "Things losing shape, meaning. Just by coming into existence. Existence disturbs the order of things so it has to be punished. Like this desert's the punishment for the green that used to be here. Or death. Our punishment."

"Not for a while, though, right?"

"War's speeded up punishment."

"That sounds like Jimmy Swaggart."

That he doesn't get either.

4

I'm mixed about fleshy women. I appreciate a lot of flesh, if it isn't jouncing around. (Joke: He: "Is this it?" She: "No, that's a fold.") Fleshiness can mean a woman believes in herself, isn't tuning in to what other people want. Or it can mean she's out of touch, selfish, greedy, you're another mouthful to her. Nibbenour? I'm not sure. If you like the person, you like the looks. I got used to her. She came on strong, no apology. (Why should there be?)

We didn't see that much of her. The Fox takes off an hour before we do. At base, the crew work it over, study the readouts, check its parts, treat it like you treat a new car. Still, every two or three late afternoons she was over, sometimes with Shirlee, who started walking around with Pelz, while Nibbenour ate and walked off with Vlach. You could see them talking, arguing, getting into things. Vlach watched her, hard, like he read his fragment. Nibbenour changed too: this down-to-earth, charged-up, tough-mouthed person with the strong arms out of her T-shirt, her good bottom and good top, became sort of airy, made little flutter gestures, didn't bark so much. If you were looking at her when Vlach talked, her eyes goggled; she'd taken off her specs.

Fear shows in the gut, jealousy in the stomach. Maybe jealousy's not the right word. I had no right to be jealous, not of Vlach. Maybe it was that out there, everybody else ten thousand miles away from those he cared about, these two had found each other.

5

"What do you two talk about?"

Vlach wouldn't say, "It's none of your business." He just buttoned up.

"Sorry," I said. "None of my business."

"Philosophy," he said. "She has an aptitude."

"You like her!"

"I like talking to her."

"You like looking at her?"

We're outside the tent, in the dark. "When I see her, it's pleasing."

What a person, I thought. Here we are in the middle of nothing, and this odd ghoul is making it. "You like to touch her?"

Nothing.

"So something's cooking?" Silence. "You and Nibbenour." I felt him thinking. "You and she take your little walks behind the tower." Nothing. "You been together? You made it?" Zero. "You made love? You know, fucked?"

"Twice."

6

Christmas we had something like a meal—turkey, cranberry slabs, stuffing that didn't taste like pillow filling. There was a plastic tree, toilet-paper ribbons, pop-can rings, and, underneath, packages from the States, half from strangers, candy, books, games, cards ("How we love you!"). Some liked all that.

Vlach opened neither letters nor packages. He never got personal mail.

"Your folks don't write?"

"Dead. No wife."

Naturally. I take this cactus as my lawful wedded husband. "Free as a bird, eh?"

"Freer." Then, not to explain, just thinking aloud. "It's not easy to be."

"Free?"

"Yes. And alone."

"That's what you like?"

"It's what I use." The beak tilted—to the *harra,* the dunes, the sky. "Thought comes from this."

"There's nothing else to think about. But no Platos, right?"

"Maybe they kept what they found to themselves."

He walked off. And ran into Nibbenour, decked out: bead necklace, silvery earrings, red T-shirt with the SO ARE YOU. Carrying a Christmas box with a yellow ribbon. "Merry Christmas, Walter." She handed it to him.

He didn't take it. She untied the ribbon, took out a jack-in-the-box (some kid from Kansas sacrificing his present?), wound it up to "Hickory Dickory Doc," and, whammo, out pops a red-nosed clown.

Vlach: "What's this mean?"

Nibbenour: "It's all I have for you."

Vlach: "It's more than all you have. And less than nothing. Save it for your children."

I watched Nibbenour's lights dim. Not pretty. Seeing me see it, she handed the box to me. "Merry X, Potts."

7

Pelz, out with Shirlee, saw them. "Thought it was a mirage. 'They dancing?' Shirlee asks. 'Or doing a Chinese exercise?' Then we realize. Crazy. They're hitting each other, slugging, kicking. Vlach and Nibbenour. Claws. You seen him yet? She did him good."

He's in the tent, doubled over, bloody, right eye closed, big lipped, cheek swollen, rubbing his side, groaning. I could just make out "Kidneys. Get a medic. She kicked me."

8

The next day, they helicopter him to Dhahran. Nobody said anything about Nibbenour. He'd asked for what he got. I saw him just before, in the medic's tent, blanketed to the chin, face purple, eye swollen shut. (The other looked at peace.) "You lucky bastard," I say. "You're gettin' out of here." (Though of all the Americans in Arabia, Vlach was probably most at home.) "How are you?" He had an arm outside the blanket. He points it to his face, meaning "See for yourself." But there's a little smile on it, another little message: "I'm fine."

"What in hell was it all about?"

He made some sounds. I wouldn't have understood if he hadn't given me the Anaximander poop. "Punishment . . . penalty . . . retribution."

"She was angry at you for ignoring her, refusing her?"

"I provoked her."

"I saw you. Wasn't like you. Why?"

He went on awhile. What I made out was something like this: "Something came into existence between us. We disturbed the order of things; we had to pay the penalty."

The crazy coot's fragment had gone to his head; like nerve gas. He's taken that Greek fog literally. He fought over it, fought on principle. Or so he thought.

Anyway, he does something then that surprises me, stretches out his hand and looks at mine until it shakes his, then, "Hope you make it out OK, Hugo." I didn't know he cared enough for anything human to say that.

9

The third week of February, we took off, like a line of steel bats, in a big loop west. Twenty-five hours over sand, the only breaks planes cracking the glare and a few guys driving shaggy goats. They hardly looked at what must have been quite a sight. Maybe they'd seen the desert swallow up everything, why not us?

Looping east, we run into berms, ditches, wire, antennas coming out of the sand. We tank through, bridge ditches, blow explosives. We take no fire, just prisoners, starved-looking guys materializing out of lids in the sand, waving undershirts, yelling, sometimes English— "Peace, us want, hello, thank you"—raising their arms, falling on their knees. We give them water, feed them.

Then the news, it's over. We haven't lost a man. We haven't taken fire. It's done, the air did it. It was crazy, wonderful, we'd be home before spring.

We drive south on what Dubbda calls "death row." A river of busted steel: tanks, every kind of armor, broken, smashed, charred, or just turned over, just left. Men in some of them, parts of men, and stuff: carpets, TVs, dressers, piles of new shirts in cellophane, hair dryers, calculators, neckties, a carton of lipsticks, digital watches, gold necklaces, electric fryers, tires, boxes of pills.

Sights: a pair of arms hugging an air conditioner, no body; a uniformed arm on a windowsill, no body; a shoulder, nothing else; a head of hair on half a face in the sand, nothing else; bodies swelled triple size; two guys in the front seat of a jeep, carbonized like marshmallows; a mustached guy, an officer, his hands on a wheel, and in back of his face and chest, nothing, gunk.

Some motors were running, radios playing.

The smell: take a vinegar factory, a thousand rotten eggs, a million gallons of wolf piss, age in hatred and inject it through your nostrils into your brain.

Near the border, hundred-foot spools of black smoke, the sky like a thunderstorm.

Dubbda and I walked off the road and heard "The Blue Danube." It's coming from a dead kid, seventeen, maybe less, in uniform. In his hand's a music box. "Take it for a souvenir," said Dubbda.

I didn't; neither did he.

All this built in me, I don't know what. The night before we took off from Dhahran, I let some of it out writing the longest letter I ever wrote. Odd thing is I sent it not to my folks—my mom doesn't take to bad things, won't listen, shuts her eyes—but to Vlach, care of the Philosophy Department, Armstrong College, Savannah.

10

We got back March 16. The folks drove down to Fort Stewart, so there was a big show. Turns you into what you're not, which once in a while is all right. Ten days later, things are back where they'd been, I'm doing accounts at Jordan's. Fine with me, numbers are my thing.

I take up where I'd left off looking for my own place and someone to live there with. I tell my war stories. They don't go over right; not enough blood, maybe.

I meant to call Vlach when I was in Savannah, thought of it a few times when I was home, figured I'd drive down some weekend; but there'd been no answer to my letter, I figured he wasn't interested. He had his own numbers. Then, too, he might not've wanted to be reminded of his little Desert Storm.

I watch the evening news. The minute we left, the Iraqis started banging each other around. After the first week or two, Mustache looked firm in the saddle. End of April, the news showed him on his birthday, walking through a room in a white suit, little girls kissing his cheeks, and what the reporter said was the Iraq Symphony Orchestra—nine geezers in white blouses—playing "I Did It My Way." That broke it for me.

Mama said, "*What* is humorous, Hugo? Ah didn't see anything humorous."

"I wish I'd thought to send him a present." I should have kept Nibbenour's jack-in-the-box. It would have been worth twenty bucks to send it to him, the mother of all jack-in-the-boxes.

11

May 1, a Wednesday, a letter from Vlach. It had gone through APO to Dhahran and followed me back. Green ink on an Armstrong College memo pad sheet. No "Dear Potts," let alone "Dear Hugo." Just

> Glad you and the others came through.
>
> I hope you won't have to pay for not having paid enough. Looks like the unit's only casualty was yours truly. Your account of those human fragments wiped mine out. I'm thinking of another one. By Heraclitus. Immortal mortals (*athánatoi thanetoi*), mortal immortals, living their death, dying their life.
>
> If you have any ideas about it, write me, same address. [He did sign off—it made me feel good.] Your friend, W. Vlach.

WANDERERS

"Those Jews sure did travel." Miss Swindleman reflecting as the bell-hops carried away her glowing collection, the four hundred and fifty postcards which memorialized the wanderings of Hotel Winthrop guests for a quarter of a century. A wild shuffle through the world Miss Swindleman herself knew not otherwise. Unless one counted the scenic provision of a quadriannual locomotive between New York City, her place of permanent exile, and Synod, Missouri, her detested point of origin. Some provision. The green pudding of southern Ohio, the hoarse red gullet of southern Indiana, and that scab of ambitious hummocks called the Ozarks. One week there with the surviving Swindlemans and she was ready for another four years of New York.

Though less and less ready, thanks to the Jews. When she'd first come, the Winthrop and the Depression were as new as she; they broke into the New York world together. The clientele was quiet: widows, widowers, bachelors, spinsters, a few small families, the ex-rich learning to adjust their wants to their constricted means as she learned to adjust hers to the constrictions of New York loneliness. A quiet, respectable, learning time.

Then as the Depression slid away, and the quiet goyim died, the Jews began moving in. They too were bachelors, spinsters, widows, widowers, and small families, but they had not been broken by hard times. Decades of finagling, deception, complaints, and theft had hardened and renewed them. Behind the three bronze staves of her cashier's den, she regarded their great noses twitch with the strain of hoping that she would overlook the delinquent quarters in their monthly settlements. She never did, but the strain of guardianship showed in her face.

The Winthrop too showed strain: the rotting plaster showed it, the bursting water pipes, the splintering toilet seats, the ripping carpets. And the management! No more the quiet little Jew, Oppenheim, who'd moseyed noiselessly in the corridors her first twelve years and then, fifty if he was a day, and weak as the cocktails the surviving goyim drank in the Peacock Room at five o'clock — shoring their ghetto within the ghetto — he was drafted away in '45 to be replaced by a perfect 4-F, the hunchback and supreme yeller, Nagel, a dark Jew, oily, welching, eavesdropping, and mean eyed as the skua bird Dr. Mochus had mailed her ten years ago from the Faroe Islands. Board 6.

With the onset of the Jews, though, Miss Swindleman had conceived her life's mission: their assimilation. Assimilation to the ways and manners of the older stock which she represented and which gave names to the invaded hotels of Eighty-sixth Street, the Peter Stuyvesant, the Governor Brewster, the Dorchester Arms, the Winthrop. Every check she eyed, every sum she readded, contributed to their education, to the enforcement of the rules of Western life, rules to which no amount of traveling could educate them.

They were great travelers. Great postcard senders. She'd started her collection one day after Roosevelt beat Landon, when they'd sent her three postcards from three different continents. Board 1 had gone up, and the Jews traveled to fill it. Over the years, war or no war, the boards filled with twisted, six-word cards from Sfax and Borneo, Tarsus, Rhodes, Rio, and Auckland. The fjords ran a blue storm down board 3; the statuary of board 5 made up a great museum; and board 2 carried enough exotic, mean-eyed animals — they loved killers — to stock a Bronx Zoo. If she'd used "repeats," the Taj Mahals alone could have replaced the slums of New York, but the eye which spotted the delinquent fifteen cents in Milton L. Bungalow's monthly was ruthless about filtering repetition from the world's views and could spot a repeat bend of the Trondheim fjord more quickly than a native. There were few places on the traveled earth to which Miss Swindleman lacked some sort of key. Even the Arab countries were well represented. Not only had the Jews traveled there before the war, but the

Winthrop's few voyaging goyim liked to visit there, if only to flaunt the experience before the excluded *yehudim*.

Miss Swindleman understood the desire to flaunt experience before these wanderers. Experience was a fact, like family, like money, which had to be respected. Not that it marked superiority. Miss Swindleman didn't believe in superiority. There were only greater or lesser collections of fact. She was concerned with the arrangement of the few facts under her control, because that was the human task, to fend off the disorderly, the ugly, the crooked. It was why she never turned her back on a Jew when she was in her den. "Get thee before me, Israel, I'll keep thee orderly." And she surveyed their avaricious disorder through the peeling bronze staves which never vouchsafed them more than partial views of her.

It was why she classified her own partial views, those nickel four-by-sixes, classified them by area, type, color—the blue fjords, the checkerboards of Scotland, highland, lowland. They were not an altar, but a demonstration that the world would be put into shape and, too, that there were things beyond unsteady checks, paid-up phone bills, change for a clanked quarter thrown like an insult under her staves. Stability and place were there amid the wild shuffling, amid the packed suitcases, the scarred trunks, the taxis to Pier 40.

Miss Swindleman could spot traveler types as they signed the register. They signed both easily and wearily. Half the few couples who stayed in the Winthrop traveled; about a third of the widows, three-eighths of the widowers. Under forty didn't count. She'd probably not received more than ten cards from guests under forty, usually children who had lived with widowed parents (not more than twenty regulars in her more than thirty years). She once got a Blenheim Palace from a pockmarked Mettenleiter and had discarded a repeat of Sugarloaf Mountain from a Baer twin, but that was all of the memorable.

Nothing of course from the two boys of Harvey Mendel, though they had lived in the Winthrop for fifteen years. She was the only person in the hotel—probably including Mendel—who remembered their mother. Ina Mendel, a name like a sigh, a nice Jewish woman who talked to her in a fluty little voice. No traveler, but nonetheless had once bought her a postcard of the Roman Forum before being told that only mailed postcards were pasted up. Ina took plenty from

Mendel and the two nut sons. The worst was Sonny, who, at fourteen, was nearly arrested for lowering an armchair out of the eleventh story to an accomplice on the ground in full view of Eighty-sixth Street. He'd been hauled in to Nagel by Lester, the cabbie, who looked up from examining one of the pigeons he liked to grab by the throat and pick at with his penknife. Last year, Sonny, now known as Harvey, had proved his early promise by being jailed for three months in Phoenix, Arizona, on a charge of taking pornographic pictures. The lesser nut was Burton, the railroad buff, who spent hours in the lobby memorizing the timetables but couldn't figure out change for a quarter. Ina lasted six years, then went on the operating table to be knifed to death by some Lester of a surgeon. With her passing, and Oppenheim's, the reign of half-decent Jews ended, and the Mendel type took over.

They were too mean spirited to travel, too cheap to live. Once she'd called him the monk of Eighty-sixth Street. "Are you related to Gregor Mendel, the monk?" she asked him.

He never smiled. Baby lips in a cranium the size of a great soup bowl. Between it and abnormality—water on the brain—was scarcely a hair's breadth of dispute. "What monk?"

"Invented genes," said Miss Swindleman.

"A monk in skirts invents jeans. Crazy," said Mendel.

He was a designer of men's suits and knew nothing else. An odd man; an odd looker. Under the perisphere of a head was a fat little body, maybe five feet five, and midget's feet. He wasn't a black-looking Jew. In fact, with eyes so blue they were sometimes hard to see and a nose like a soap bubble, he looked as Irish as the policemen who patrolled the streets and held their annual brawl in the Peacock Room. Mendel had once been involved in their brawl and fitted right in. Involved because he was, as usual, staring at people, from the lobby armchair where he spent half his life. Staring with those snow-blue eyes, this time at one of the Irish cops who'd staggered out of the brawl, highball in hand, and, seeing Mendel, in overcoat and fedora, staring up at him, had removed the fedora and poured the highball over the great dome. Mendel had risen, sixty-six years old, five feet five inches tall, wrenched the standing lamp out of its socket, raised it over his streaming head, and started after the cop. The cop ran, Mendel followed, the old ladies screeched, Gelb, the cigar man, ducked under his counter, and she, safe in her den, waited for Irish brains to go flying out to Eighty-sixth Street. Only half a squad of uniformed micks leaping out of the Peacock Room preserved the cop. And they made Mendel a hero, took him into the Peacock Room, shot him full of whiskey, then elevated him upstairs in triumph.

There weren't many triumphs riding armchairs in the Winthrop lobby, not many triumphs anywhere for Mendel. And the only other thing she could think of in this line was his escaping indictment after pushing Lepidus out of the window; you might as well count not catching flu a triumph.

What did she object to in Mendel?

It wasn't idleness. He worked, went downtown three or four times a week till Lepidus's death. He'd once been a success according to Ina, had managed a whole men's department in Buffalo till he'd punched a customer who'd tried to return a suit from another store. Not idleness.

Nor was he particularly crooked; only particularly cheap. The number one Jew for cheapness. The Winthrop never collected a penny more from him than his rent. To telephone, he came down to the lobby, day or night, using the pay phone and saving a nickel; he never went into the Peacock Room except to use the toilet; he never bought a cup of coffee in the Nook; and he avoided Gelb's cigar stand so conspicuously that despite twenty-five years of sharing the same lobby, the two never exchanged good-mornings. When sick, he sent for borscht with a hard-boiled egg from Sheffrin's, the delicatessen on Columbus Avenue where he ate every day of his life but Yom Kippur and Rosh Hashanah, when he took his trade to Chock Full O' Nuts. This according to the young thief Sonny, who also told Lester—his confidant after the armchair heist—that except for these two restaurants, the Yorktown movie theater—forty cents before one o'clock—and the annual Thanksgiving dinner downtown with Ina's brother, his father hadn't been inside another place of entertainment since—big leer— his mother had died.

Miss Swindleman was aware of the Thanksgiving outing. Next to Macy's parade, it was the surest sign of the holiday. Mendel and the two nut sons washed their faces, put on clean ties, and paraded out of the hotel as if they were on the number one float. Two hours later they'd be back, soiled with blots of stuffing and cranberry sauce, their faces bloated with self-satisfaction at having a Family Dinner at a Downtown Hotel.

"Mr. Mendel," she said to him after one of the expeditions. "You should try our Thanksgiving dinner here someday. Forty-six birds they cooked this year." (Jewish syntax had crept up on her twenty years ago, and she relaxed into it. She wasn't interested in self-preservation.)

Mendel had sent one of his blue-blank stares through her staves. "Family obligations, Miss Schwindleman. Nothing to do about it," and he floated upstairs, followed by the nuts.

Miss Swindleman objected to more than Mendel's cheapness and third-rate vanity. She objected to his fixity. There he'd sit in the lobby, three sofas, six armchairs, stand-up lamps, Gelb's cigar counter, bent Jews going up and down in the two elevators night and day, the blue-and-gold elevator men, her bright postcards, a little tropical island in the Eighty-sixth Street cold, plunked down there for no reason but to allow amphibious transients to crawl across it before they dived back down into the ocean. Shelter? Home? Reservoir? A sour little hotel whose only real distinction was her flash of the world and her disciplined hand on the financial wheel. In the midst of this discipline sat that unsmiling, waiting, staring Mendel, isolated like a monk in a burlesque show. It wasn't until the day Lepidus went out of the window that she understood all this about him.

Lepidus was one of Mendel's two visitors. The other was Mrs. Minnie Schlag, a hirsute, muscular woman who for years was thought to be the unlikely means of satisfying whatever passion resided in him. It turned out, however, that Mrs. Schlag and Mendel did nothing more passionate together than play pinochle. A bellhop looked in through a hole in the plaster and saw them humped over the coffee table, Mendel in suspenders and Mrs. Schlag in a blouse which showed an arm like the ones on the statues in the Oslo gardens. Board 5. Every other Saturday, Mrs. Schlag turned up for pinochle at the Brewster, and once a month on Thursdays, as Sonny told Lester, Mendel went to the Schlags for poker with Dr. Schlag, the bone man, Simon Gabrilowitsch, a bassoonist and reputed cousin of the pianist, Mrs. Schlag, and two other refugees from Vienna, one of whom sold perfume atomizers door-to-door. Lester further reported—what she was certain was a lie, until Schlag's obituary confirmed it—that as a young bone man in Vienna,

Schlag had rented rooms and lent money to an unpromising young man named—"you guessed it," Miss Swindleman would say wickedly to whatever Jew she passed it on to—"Adolf Hitler. Ha-ha-ha. Old Schlag could have saved you an ocean voyage, eh, Mr. Rappaport? A little arsenic in the chicken soup, doctors aren't suspected, and Schlag would have had a place in history."

"Wouldn't have been no history then," the paling Rappaport or Goldhammer or Mochus would say.

Though not Mendel. His response when she offered him the homicidal suggestion was a simple, "I wouldn't have much of a poker game then, Miss Schwindleman." A hard man, a bit of a Hitler in his own right. She could see him in the seat of power, bombs instead of stand-up lamps in his angry little arms.

Lepidus, Mendel's partner, was a more frequent visitor. As small as Mendel, but wiry, blue in the face, a scowler, a rapid man, cigar crunching. A stormer, of elevators, candy counters, her den. Like the last day. "Gimme change fifty," he'd said.

"You a guest of the hotel?" As icy as the roughneck deserved.

"Change of fifty. I'm a guest a guest." Meaning, "a visitor to a hotel resident."

"Who, may I ask?"

"Mendel. Harvey. Eleven C. You seen me a hundred times. I'm here five times a month. You got fifty bucks in this cage?"

"You'll have to get the manager's signature. And he's out. I can't be expected to remember every visitor to the hotel. It's hard enough keeping track of the guests."

An oath, a sneer from the penny-colored eyes, he slung himself into the elevator.

Five minutes later, a call from 11C. "I'm coming down to change fifty dollars, Miss Schwindleman."

"Swindleman."

"Next time Mr. Lepidus requests a service, I'd greatly appreciate it, Miss Schwindleman."

But Lepidus would never again request a service, and apparently her exchange with him had something to do with it. Her proper invocation of a proper regulation. What was the world without rules, she asked the detective, not adding what was appropriate in this instance, that the trouble with the Jews was that they fled rules, claiming that rules had rigged the world against them? That's why they'd had to wander since Christ's time, evading the rules, and then trying to make up for evasion by sending nickel postcards back to those they fled, the enforcers, hoping for a more than even break the next time. Could she cash checks for everyone who walked in off the gutters? The Puerto Ricans stood six deep between Columbus and Amsterdam. Give them an opportunity like that, and they'd make the Jews, who were clever or mean enough to be pikers, look honest. She'd worked nearly thirty years around other people's money, and nobody had ever suspected that her purse held one cent that didn't belong there. She personally had nothing to lose or gain by enforcement of the rules. Rules were what she went and lived by. Did Lepidus think she was a country girl waiting for wool to be pulled over her eyes? So his temper was riled. What did what happened have to do with anything but the breaking of rules?

According to Mendel, he and Lepidus worked as usual. When he, Mendel, was indisposed, they worked at the hotel. It was just as convenient as the closet they worked in on Fourth Avenue. Gotham Fabrics and Designs. A big name for a small enterprise. Two men, two desks, cardboard patterns, sample materials, drawing paper, colored pencils. Not enough for a child's Christmas. That's all they needed to carry off twelve to fifteen thousand a year. "I've been with lots of outfits, big and small," said Mendel up in his room, where she'd never been before. "There was nothing more efficient in the world than Charley Lepidus and myself. I designed. He marketed. That's all there was to it. I had pencils, he had a mouth. Three or four days a week was all the time we needed to put in. Didn't matter where, down on the avenue or here in the hotel."

That was the Lepidus-Mendel history. But every history has a history, and who more than the wandering Jews—barnacling themselves onto the histories of every nation on the civilized earth—would know that? A squad of Irish cops, Annalee Swindleman, and assorted old ladies, half of them under the earth now, had witnessed Mendel going berserk with a metal stand-up lamp. Other incidents made longer history. The punched customer in Buffalo and a doorman in Minnie Schlag's building who, according to her, had the habit of stepping on Mendel's small foot until the latter, after years of the abuse, had one day grabbed the fellow by the voice box, toppled him, and tried to throttle him there in the snow of Lexington Avenue. Yes, the huge woman went on, in some ways, he reminded her of a man she'd known in Vienna, also a docile young man till seized with rages. Luckily she mentioned the young man's name, and the detective wrote her off as a nut. Miss Swindleman, who had listened to her along with Mendel, shook with anger. There was more history to come, this time from Sonny, the ex–furniture mover and photographer, recently returned from his stay in the American Southwest. Yes, moaned Sonny, his father had raised him and his brother on a diet that would have done in a robot; by the time he was twelve, he'd eaten enough cabbage soup and kreplach to have felled a horse. Also, his father entered into frequent altercations with a waiter named Bungmeier in Sheffrin's Delicatessen, capped one day when his father stuffed Bungmeier's gray head into a plateful of borscht after being rightfully accused of dawdling over his meals.

After all this, Mendel's own story of the day did not look strong. The story was that Lepidus had been riled by the behavior of the good Miss Schwindleman. Never was Lepidus a cup of tea, but fired up, he was a terror. They worked hard, in shirtsleeves, though it was drafty, a Christmas cold driving through the peeled window frames, never strong since the no-goodnik, Sonny, had pushed the armchair through them. Lepidus talked, he, Mendel, was all concentration. When he designed, he was lost in his materials. Lepidus had started on Miss Schwindleman: piss-cold anti-*Semitischer* virgin-whore were the easiest things he said. (Blushing, head averted from her stricken head.) Then he was on to the Winthrop, the fleabag where he, Mendel, too cheap to waste piss in a pot, had holed himself up for thirty years, killing his wife with the cold and inflicting two loonies, the junior Mendels, on the world. "A Hitler with his mouth, he was," said Mendel to Detective Milligan. "A marketer, he had talent for the mouth." But he, Mendel, could take it. He was small, he was old, but he could take it. He kept on cutting his patterns. Not from cowardice, he was afraid of nobody. He took where it did no good to do something about it. Years he had taken guff from Miss Schwindleman. Why not? What could she do, poor old girl (head averted, lost in his materials), poor old cold bag, full of hate, collecting her postcards from a world she understood nothing of. Years he had taken insults from family, wife, bosses, sons, doormen, policemen, waiters, inhumane cabbies, but now and then, once in a great while, he had to strike out. The Jews had a history of taking it. Nevertheless, sometimes, they turned. The Maccabees. Suez. Jews were not Hindus, not cheek turners. For humanity, for peace, for an end to persecution, they rose up. Lepidus wouldn't stop; he got hotter and hotter. He, Mendel, caught fire and gave him a push. One push. The window frames were weak, Lepidus was small and solid. Out he went into the middle of Eighty-sixth Street under the nose of Lester knifing a tail feather from a pigeon. Out he went, like garbage from a Puerto Rican window. Unpremeditated, unintended, the victim victimizing and being victimized thereby.

Miss Swindleman, looking up at the detective without the protection of her staves, minus the glowing backdrop of her collection, smaller, chaired, sworn—though without Bible—to honesty, a gray girl from the Ozarks, up in the be-Jewed city, thought back thirty years. Every morning she walked through Central Park to the hotel. Every year it seemed bigger to her. This morning, all the familiar trees were there, branched in snow, imploring the New York sky to spare them. Bushes and shrubs were turned into crystal chandeliers, the buds alive somewhere in them, unseen but living in the icy beads, waiting. Walking in her furred galoshes around the reservoir, she'd looked through the crackling trees toward the General Motors sign flashing "8:23" and thought that she had not one single postcard in her collection from New York. It would have been perfectly all right to send herself one, for, after all, she'd traveled from her home and was still a visitor in this place, as much a wanderer as the poor black Jews she served and governed. Mosaics from Ravenna, bark-colored farmers from Sierra Leone, twisted statues from Rotterdam, skyscrapers from Brazil, mountains, rivers, pyramids, but nothing of this city where she and almost everyone else she knew was a wanderer. Her stopover, Mendel's stopover, this old-line hotel was rotting, facade intact, but pipes going—a geyser had burst from a flushed toilet only last week—and the wanderers were the only thing that sustained it, deprived people, harboring their small-time leisure, their miserable quarters. Mendel was one of the best. Polite, quiet, he hurt no one that didn't hurt him much more. The wife had seemed a good one, but who knew? Behind the flutter she could have given plenty. After all, she let her boys grow up in this hotel, went gladly to restaurants, avoided kitchen work.

Maybe Mendel had not had much from her. He hadn't much period. A monk in the barrage of Eighty-sixth Street. Cheapskate, but no quibbler. As for Lepidus, he was the blackest of the black, yes, nasty, cigar-chewing scoffer, crook, a hurrier and worrier of others. If she had riled him, well and good. If Mendel had pushed him, he deserved it. She spoke the truth, always had, had no reason not to.

So it was over, and Milligan wrote it up. *Accidental.* Miss Swindleman went back to her den.

Things were not the same. No. An opening had been made. What does one do about an opening? Send a postcard of the Empire State Building to oneself? Go to Mendel's room and say, "Mendel. I saved you. Now save me. I'm yours. Be mine"?

Or even, think more gently, speak more kindly ("Piss-cold, anti-*Semitischer* virgin-whore." "No, Lepidus."), cash checks more readily, make up delinquent quarters from one's own purse?

Possibly.

The opening was a wound in Miss Swindleman. Days passed, and embarrassment at defending Mendel was all she could stuff in to stop the raw ache. She was altered, but alteration had nowhere to go.

The incident had altered Mendel much more. He grew thinner, whiter. He no longer sat in the lobby. More and more frequent were the calls to Sheffrin's for borscht and pastrami. Two or three times he came down for coffee and English muffins in the Nook. He bought a TV set, and the bellhops reported that it was on from Garroway to the anthem. There was no more work, and no visitors except a monthly call from Burton, the timetable son, who, like his father, never frowned nor smiled and whose only nonambulatory motion was the Adam's apple popping up and down in his neck as he swallowed un-uttered words. So Mendel passed on in his own den — pneumonia, TB, heart. Everything hit him at once.

The day after he died, she took the first notice of her collection that she had taken since the "hearing" six months before. It was in wretched shape. The pasteboards were rotting: gnarled scabs of string dripped from the edges, odd swellings humped the boards where drafts and radiator heat had gnawed the fiber. She called the bellboys and told them to take it out to the garbage heap. Her wandering was over.

DR. CAHN'S VISIT

"How far is it now, George?"

The old man is riding next to his son, Will. George was his brother, dead the day after Franklin Roosevelt. "Almost there, Dad."

"What does 'almost' mean?"

"It's Eighty-sixth and Park. The hospital's at Ninety-ninth and Fifth. Mother's in the Klingenstein Pavilion."

"Mother's not well?"

"No, she's not well. Liss and I took her to the hospital a couple of weeks ago."

"It must have slipped my mind." The green eyes darkened with sympathy. "I'm sure you did the right thing. Is it a good hospital?"

"Very good. You were on staff there half a century."

"Of course I was. For many years, I believe."

"Fifty."

"Many as that."

"A little slower, pal. These jolts are hard on the old man."

The cabbie was no chicken himself. "It's your ride."

"Are we nearly there, George?"

"Two minutes more."

"The day isn't friendly," said Dr. Cahn. "I don't remember such — such —"

"Heat."

"Heat in New York." He took off his gray fedora and scratched at the hairless, liver-spotted skin. Circulatory difficulty left it dry, itchy. Scratching had shredded and inflamed its soft center.

"It's damn hot. In the nineties. Like you."

"What's that?"

"It's as hot as you are old. Ninety-one."

"Ninety-one. That's not good."

"It's a grand age."

"That's your view."

"And Mother's eighty. You've lived good, long lives."

"Mother's not well, son?"

"Not too well. That's why Liss and I thought you ought to see her. Mother's looking forward to seeing you."

"Of course. I should be with her. Is this the first time I've come to visit?"

"Yes."

"I should be with her."

The last weeks at home had been difficult. Dr. Cahn had been the center of the household. Suddenly, his wife was. The nurses looked after her. And when he talked, she didn't answer. He grew angry, sullen. When her ulcerous mouth improved, her voice was rough and her thought harsh. "I wish you'd stop smoking for five minutes. Look at the ashes on your coat. Please stop smoking."

"Of course, dear. I didn't know I was annoying you." The ash tumbled like a suicide from thirty stories; the butt was crushed into its dead brothers. "I'll smoke inside." And he was off but, in two minutes, back. Lighting up. Sometimes he lit two cigarettes at once. Or lit the filtered end. The odor was foul, and sometimes his wife was too weak to register her disgust.

They sat and lay within silent yards of each other. Dr. Cahn was in his favorite armchair, the *Times* bridge column inches from his cigarette. He read it all day long. The vocabulary of the game deformed his speech. "I need some clubs" might mean "I'm hungry." "My spades are tired" meant he was. Or his eyes were. Praise of someone might come out, "He laid his hand out clearly." In the bedridden weeks, such mistakes intensified his wife's exasperation. "He's become such a penny-pincher," she said to Liss when Dr. Cahn refused to pay her for the carton of cigarettes she brought, saying, "They can't charge so much. You've been cheated."

"Liss has paid. Give her the money."

"Are you telling me what's trump? I've played this game all my life."

"You certainly have. And I can't bear it."

In sixty marital years, there had never been such anger. When Will came from Chicago to persuade his mother into the hospital, the bitterness dismayed him.

It was, therefore, not so clear that Dr. Cahn should visit his wife. Why disturb her last days? Besides, Dr. Cahn seldom went out anywhere. He wouldn't walk with the black nurses (women whom he loved, teased, and was teased by). It wasn't done. "I'll go out later. My feet aren't friendly today." Or, lowering the paper, "My legs can't trump."

Liss opposed his visit. "Mother's afraid he'll make a scene."

"It doesn't matter," said Will. "He has to have some sense of what's happening. They've been the center of each other's lives. It wouldn't be right."

The hope had been that Dr. Cahn would die first. He was ten years older, his mind had slipped its moorings years ago. Mrs. Cahn was clearheaded and, except near the end, energetic. She loved to travel, wanted especially to visit Will in Chicago—she'd not seen his new apartment—but she wouldn't leave her husband even for a day. "Suppose something happened."

"Bring him along."

"He can't travel. He'd make an awful scene."

Only old friends tolerated him, played bridge with him, forgiving his lapses and muddled critiques of their play. "If you don't understand a two bid now, you never will." The most gentlemanly of men, Dr. Cahn's tongue roughened with his memory. It was as if a lifetime of restraint were only the rind of a wicked impatience.

"He's so spoiled," said Mrs. Cahn, the spoiler.

"Here we are, Dad."

They parked under the blue awning. Dr. Cahn got out his wallet— he always paid for taxis, meals, shows—looked at the few bills, then handed it to his son. Will took a dollar, added two of his own, and thanked his father.

"This is a weak elevator," he said of one of the monsters made to drift the ill from floor to floor. A nurse wheeled in a stretcher, and Dr. Cahn removed his fedora.

"Mother's on eight."

"Minnie is here?"

"Yes. She's ill. Step out now."

"I don't need your hand."

Each day, his mother filled less of the bed. Her face, unsupported by dentures, seemed shot away. Asleep, it looked to Will as if the universe leaned on the crumpled cheeks. When he kissed them, he feared they'd turn to dust, so astonishingly delicate was the flesh. The only vanity left was love of attention, and that was part of the only thing that counted, the thought of those who cared for her. How she appreciated the good nurses and her children. They—who'd never before seen their mother's naked body—would change her nightgown if the nurse was gone. They brought her the bedpan and, though she usually suggested they leave the room, sat beside her while, under the sheets, her weak body emptied its small waste.

For the first time in his adult life, Will found her beautiful. Her flesh was mottled like a Pollock canvas, the facial skin trenched with the awful last ditches of self-defense; but her look melted him. It was human beauty.

Day by day, manners that seemed as much a part of her as her eyes—fussiness, bossiness, nagging inquisitiveness—dropped away. She was down to what she was.

Not since childhood had she held him so closely, kissed his cheek with such force. "This is mine. This is what lasts," said the force.

What was she to him? Sometimes little more than the old organic scenery of his life. Sometimes she was the meaning of it. "Hello, darling," she'd say. "I'm so glad to see you." The voice, never melodious, was rusty, avian. Beautiful. No actress could match it. "How are you? What's happening?"

"Very little. How are you today?"

She told her news. "Dr. Vacarian was in, he wanted to give me another treatment. I told him, 'No more.' And no more medicine." Each day she'd renounced more therapy. An unspoken decision had been made after a five-hour barium treatment which usurped the last of her strength. (Will thought that might have been its point.) It had launched her last moments of eloquence, a frightening jeremiad about life dark beyond belief, nothing left, nothing right. It was the last complaint of an old champion of complaint, and after it, she'd made up her mind to go. There was no more talk of going home.

"Hello, darling. How are you today?"

Will bent over, was kissed, and held against her cheek. "Mother, Dad's here."

To his delight, she showed hers. "Where is he?" Dr. Cahn had waited at the door. Now he came in, looked at the bed, realized where he was and who was there.

"Dolph, dear. How are you, my darling? I'm so happy you came to see me."

The old man stooped over and took her face in his hands. For seconds, there was silence. "My dearest," he said; then, "I didn't know. I had no idea. I've been so worried about you. But don't worry now. You look wonderful. A little thin, perhaps. We'll fix that. We'll have you out in no time."

The old man's pounding heart must have driven blood through the clogged vessels. There was no talk of trumps.

"You can kiss me, dear." Dr. Cahn put his lips on hers.

He sat next to the bed and held his wife's hand through the low rail. Over and over he told her she'd be fine. She asked about home and the nurses. He answered well for a while. Then they both saw him grow vague and tired. To Will he said, "I don't like the way she's looking. Are you sure she has a good doctor?"

Of course Mrs. Cahn heard. Her happiness watered a bit, not at the facts but at his inattention. Still, she held on. She knew he could not sit so long in a strange room. "I'm so glad you came, darling."

Dr. Cahn heard his cue and rose. "We mustn't tire you, Minnie dear. We'll come back soon."

She held out her small arms, he managed to lean over, and they kissed again.

In the taxi, he was very tired. "Are we home?"

"Almost, Dad. You're happy you saw Mother, aren't you?"

"Of course I'm happy. But it's not a good day. It's a very poor day. Not a good bid at all."

TROUBLES

1

Trouble, Hanna knew, seldom came labeled. And her trouble was not simple sexual confusion. Everyone she knew slid up and down the sexual shaft, getting off first at this floor, then at that one. She herself was one of the straightest of straight arrows. (If there were sexual continents to explore, she was no sexual Captain Cook.)

The confusion was deeper. Certainly deeper than what diverted her or with whom she slept. Troubles were deep structures. Or structural defects. Deep, confusing, hard to assign. Cagey. Uncageably cagey.

She thought keeping a diary would help. It had helped Kafka (a pillar of her marooned dissertation, "The Dissolving Self in Braque and Broch, Kafka and Kandinsky"). Instead of burrowing into it, she bought a Woolworth notebook and began burrowing into herself, her life with Jay. It went slowly.

Kafka observed himself dissolve, described the dissolution, and put another version of himself together. That was caginess. Her first entry in the speckled, Rorschach-y book dealt with him: *Kafka's lodestone was his father. Is mine Jay? Or myself with Jay? I only know I'm bottled up. But is he the bottle or the bottler?*

Or was it the rodent life they led on the periphery of lofty mentality?

They lived like anchorites on the last fifteen hundred dollars of their Peace Corps savings and half-time jobs (Hanna in the law library,

Jay tutoring Javanese and Arabic). They ate like health-freaked Saint Anthonys: raw carrots, cottage cheese, cabbage, Bran Buds, fruit, dried milk, beans, soy substitute "meatoids" (a Jayism) frozen into "tomatoid gunk." " 'Poor, forked creatures,' yes," said Jay, "but not poor, forked, *constipated* ones."

They had spent two years among people who owned next to nothing; yet here, in their little white apartment over the Midway, Hanna felt barrenness. If only she had a few plants, something alive to care for.

Hanna was mad for flowers. Nights she got to sleep walking her memory through the forest near Sadjapaht: mangrove, sesamum, cinnamon, palm, banana trees with their edible hives, the casuarinas with whip branches, their sides bunged with vermilion fungi ("jungle whores," Jay called them).

He was no plant lover. "Not in Chicago. Not here." (Their dumbbell-shaped slot tipped over the asphalt-split greens of the Midway.) "A goldfish would crack our ecosystem. We can't import the jungle." Waving at their walls — puffed and wattled as old Caucasian skin: "We fight the dust for breath."

"Plants would freshen the place."

"Nights?" (When he worked at home, moated by monographs on social stratification, village bureaucracy, shamanism, and apple cores, note cards, dictionaries, the green vase from which he drank decaffeinated coffee. The sacred circle of his absorption.)

He's not cruel. He just hates what he has to do so much, he armors himself against anything that would tempt him from it. As far as he can love anyone, he loves me. He needs insulation. I'm insulation. He's so fragile inside he doesn't want to know about it. He doesn't want to think about himself. This turns out to be more selfish than selfishness. The egocentricity of damaged egos.

For her birthday — the funereal twenty-fifth — he brought home an African violet. He'd scooped and sieved dirt from the Midway — "In Chicago, dirt has to be cleaned" — and planted it in a washed-out jar of Skippy.

"When we get the doctorates, we'll settle in a garden. You can start a vegetable state. Every plant in creation can have its own municipality. You'll be Mother Shrub."

"Oh, sweetheart." Looking at the little purple blossoms.

Which soon curled off. But, eyes to the leaves' small fur, Hanna conjured up Java, the silver *alang* grass outside the kampong, the ferns, pitcher plants, orchids. Pods, spikes, and glumes burst, and fragrance poured over the valley. Transfixed by fatigue, loneliness, heat squatting on every bone, she took in the aromatic ecstasy like some great work of mentality.

Twenty miles away lived the polite, handsome boy she'd met during orientation period in Jakarta. One afternoon, she hitched a *samlor* ride to the paddies, where he was pointed out to her (he was shaded by the nipple-tipped straw hat which, from the road, made him look like an ambulatory mushroom). "Hey, there. Jay. It's Hanna. From Sadjapaht."

How could I tell? I'd have fallen for Dracula if he'd spoken English. Life was so nutty. All that Java courtesy that made you feel transparent. They looked through you. Not even Pua or Madame Charwa talked to me those first weeks.

She and Jay met once a week, hitching *samlor* or bullock-cart rides until they bought bicycles. The meetings were the week's beacon. On their first three-day leave, they bicycled to Borobudur and, in a hotel near that old monument to release from world and flesh, they worked out their own release.

Oddly, it was Madame Charwa who first sensed their division. Jay had bicycled over to Sadjapaht the day Pua, the old coffee-stall man — her first Javanese friend — died. Everyone in the kampong went to Pua's house. Jay told her to make a bowl of rice and go too, it was their chance to see a funeral *slametan*. She sat with Madame Charwa, Jay with the men. Priests recited Arabic prayers, Pua's black body was undressed, washed, and stuffed with cotton pads. Hanna cried. The Javanese tried to ignore this impropriety. Jay looked icebergs at her, she managed to stop; but confusion had crept into the ceremony, the *santri* hurried the prayers and carried Pua off, Jay after them. Elegant Madame Charwa, more worldly than the others — she was the local representative of the yam and pepper cooperative in Surabaya — walked Hanna back to the hut. "One acts as one is trained. Your friend was severe with you. The two of you are not alike. Despite your mutual affection. He is less *djava*." (*Less Javanese,* which meant "less human.") A peculiar criticism to which Hanna was too far gone in love to attend. Her fear was that she had offended Jay; he would see how badly she acted, how silly she was, and would stop seeing her.

But Jay returned full of what he'd sought. The Javanese temperament suited his own. *Iklas,* the disciplined unfeeling which the funeral *slametan* was supposed to induce, had less assertive snobbery than British "indomitability," less military callousness than Spartan-Roman stoicism. It was an attitude that would do for much of life. *Another mask for his fragility,* she would write in her diary account of these memories.

In their second Indonesian winter, they took three days off and were married in Jakarta. Her parents sent a hundred dollars—probably their vacation money—and Jay's father, a cultural affairs officer with the State Department, wired them twenty-five through the embassy.

They returned to their assignments, still seeing each other only one day a week, until, at the end of the tour, they took a four-day honeymoon in Bali. It was the first time they had been together knowing they would not be separating.

Which may have accounted for their first deep uneasiness with each other. *He didn't know what marriage would mean,* she wrote in the diary.

Even less than most people. Companionship itself is hard for him. He didn't go into the Corps for adventure or idealism or experience. He went in to be a foreigner, the way he was when he grew up. He was escaping intimacy; then he was trapped by it. Maybe he opened to me in Java because I was a foreigner too. Of course, he needed me physically.

Like many secretive, baffled men, Jay was an intense lover. He relished the depth and special silence of the sexual waters. Lovemaking was his release and his attainment. He was a generous lover. Only during exam weeks did he lose sight of her. Then he labored grimly in her body to unlock himself for his work.

He never talked about sex. It was one of the first things that turned him against her new friends. When she told him what they'd told her about their sexual problems, he said the reason they had problems was that "they liked problems more than love and they think frankness certifies authenticity. Nothing is more of a disguise than that kind of openness."

"I don't see how honesty can be dishonest."

"Too much light blinds. Those who feel love can't talk about it."

She was unwilling to certify this self-praise. He was not malicious; he had the assertiveness of those who fear uncertainty. Why make him still more uncertain? "I passed your pal Vanessa in the library. She was chattering like a maniac. Why is she so noisy? To convince herself she exists? There ought to be a bank for shallowness. Your pals could deposit their daily slivers of self. After a few years, they might have enough for a genuine moment or two."

"I think they're genuine."

"You have a certain solidity which gets reflected in them. You supply what you think you see in them."

Even for this rare compliment, she could not betray her friends. "I wish I had enough for myself, let alone to pass around."

At first, her friends said he was beautiful. Then they decided there was something wrong in his looks: not the features, not the snow and strawberry complexion, or — when they knew her better — "that beautiful tight ass." Maybe the eyes, which looked "like mud with fog caught in it," said Wanda, or the extra centimeters of forehead, which always caught light. "That portable nimbus of his. What a strange saint."

What really got them was his distance, his conspicuous restraint. Wanda said he looked at them as if they were sick and he the only available suppository — "one that isn't all that happy about being inserted."

Jay converted them into caricatures: Wanda was Mount Fat, Clover Callahan was Mouse, Vanessa was the Tongue, and Nora, who had nothing on which he could fix, became his own incapacity to fix her, the Slitherer.

"What's that mean?"

"She has no fixity. It's why clothes are so important to her."

"They are to me too. I just don't have anything to spend on them."

"It's different. She has nothing underneath. She's a flag without a country. She's slither. The Guccied Slitherer." Proclaimed with a discoverer's triumph.

"And you're the Archimedes of slander," said Hanna, but under her breath.

Still, abuse was better than silence. Most nights, silence piled around her. It was like the first months in Java, except that there she knew her tour would come to an end. Jay would study five or six hours without saying anything. Or he would call out, "Why are there no apples?" in such despair that the question was almost metaphysical—amazement at nature's astonishing omission of such an item.

Jay would not discuss their relationship. "It works or it doesn't. Ours mostly works. Discussion kills." He pointed across the Midway to the Gothic stretch of the university. "There's discussion for you. The mausoleum of the real."

The most assiduous of graduate students, never missing a class or an assignment, he hated the idea of the university. "For scholars, the world exists in order to be explained," he explained. He hated anthropology, his field, its "patronizing tolerance." Morgan, a young assistant professor, *la plus noire* of his bêtes noires, had made fun of the green revolution. "Of those thousands of hours you and I put into the paddies. Because the new seeds require petrochemical fertilizers, and oil prices are ruining them. As if we were responsible for oil prices. The world's just a collection of props for his notions, mutters his structuralist honey while eighteen mammary glands quiver at him. What are we doing here, baby? Five hundred million people turn into compost while we pay thousands to listen to theoretical snot."

Jay had grown up inside the coziness which compensates foreign service officers for living abroad. He had lain on a couch while a servant five times his age bent down to serve him iced drinks. At prep school, back in the States, he'd turned against his class. His senior honors thesis on American writers was a fiery tract.

Like Henry James, who wrote, "Everything costs that one does for the rich," Fitzgerald saw the rich up close, saw the murder in their charm, their totalitarian need to wipe out individuality and talent. All great American writers have known that, the Hemingway of A Moveable Feast, *the Melville who created in Captain Ahab the warning not to convert nature into commodity.*

The headmaster had written an amused alert to Jay's parents: "One of our brightest boys, though he needs more steering than we've been able to supply. Maybe Stanford will do better." But Jay's parents were pleased with him; his visits to them in Brussels or Karachi were affectionate and brief. He visited less often while he was in college. When his mother died in Bangkok, he wrote his father that he would attend a private service, he didn't have to travel around the world to mourn her. Hanna, thinking of this, wondered when "love had died in him."

Does he love me? Do I love him? I don't know. Know only that my world is too Jayed. *I used to be confident, happy. If I had to draw myself now, I would draw a zero. Except zero's useful.*

2

"I don't see why you miss the jungle," said Jay. "You've got your pals."

There was something in it. Her friends were messed up and somehow overgrown. Each day she saw how troubled they were.

Clover, Wanda, and Vanessa suffered terribly. Yet they were remarkable, gifted girls.

Clover was a math whiz who'd published a paper on set theory as a college sophomore ten years ago.

Wanda was a physical monster with Leonardo-like gifts: she sculpted, embroidered, made furniture, repaired watches, radios, toilets, played the guitar, painted, made beautiful lithographs.

Vanessa couldn't look a dog in the eye, but in class she scorched inferior analysis and leaped from language to language as if Babel had never been. The intellectual blaze burned connectives from her speech; she spoke a code it took weeks getting used to. In the Grotto, where they met for lunch, she felt less pressure. The light, submarine and bluish, did not make her feel "onstage"; she was coherent, fluent, sympathetic. Her talk, all their talk, wound in and out of anger, bafflement, flight, odium, fear, and disguise, but its mode was farce. They sat in a corner on facing benches, eating thick, meaty soups and talking out each other's troubles. Trouble was their subject, their poetry.

Clover would have been beautiful except for a dermal scurf that was the facade of a wintry interior. Until a breakthrough in her analysis, she had thought of men as statues, dignified and untouchable, women as sluttish hunks, stuff for centerfolds. With the analyst's help, she was able to see the relationship between such distortion and her anorexia: she'd starved herself in order to make her flesh disappear. At eighty pounds, she felt monstrous, overblown. The year before, she'd nearly starved to death. Influenza saved her life; she'd gone in for a flu shot and was put in the hospital. Now, stronger, she could see, literally see, that women were worthy and men approachable. Although she still sometimes felt like "a pea in an invisible pod," she also believed in herself and even hoped for some kind of physical relationship with someone. "I used to have nothing but numbers. A freak, like someone who can whistle with her knees."

Mathematics was not her only gift. She had an extraordinary sense for other people's suffering. "She knows before you do," said Vanessa. "It's like the sixth sense some animals have for warm-blooded creatures." Clover was always on call. People who didn't know her well telephoned at midnight, and she went to talk them back to life.

Wanda's trouble lay under more layers than Troy; enormous energy piled fat, wit, manual genius, and a sense of spectacle over it. Caped to the throat, hair in a great bush, Wanda was the center of any room. She had a lovely, subtle voice which spun the gossip of Hyde Park into manic catastrophes. No one had ever been in Wanda's rooms, though she told Clover—who told Hanna—that she had an intimate friend there. No particulars. (Jay said Wanda had only personified a layer of fat.)

Vanessa was married to a biologist who was driven wild by her hypomania. She knew it, was helpless with the knowledge and the condition. "Knowing, doing, different kettles, different fish." Vanessa had a beautiful body, a harsh, ugly face, tiny nosed, huge lipped. Her husband was handsome, and she was terrified of losing him, but driving him away was better than being left by him. She showed him up, interrupted him, read papers which challenged his—and hated herself. She lived on Valium, had nightmares so awful that after them she'd come close to killing herself.

Compared to the other girls, Nora and Hanna were untroubled. They'd been loved, embraced, encouraged. The Grotto patrons took them for sisters. Both were tall and had dark hair which fell over their shoulders. Nora's was thicker and more lustrous; when she was nervous, her hands ran through it.

Nora's small troubles came from excess: she did lots of things well, painted, wrote poetry, was a good athlete—she ran five miles a day at

the gym—did honors work in Romance languages. But she was terrified of criticism and ran away before it arrived. Her plan was to finish
her master's and become a talk-show hostess. "Hard questions are easy
to ask. And Barbara Walters is wearing out." She was also looking into
government internships, law school, Vista, Fulbrights to Guatemala,
museum-training courses, the Sarasota Clown School. "Why not? I
love the circus." No notion outlasted the required follow-up.

Her love life was equally serial. She'd lived with eight or ten boys
since she'd been in school, the last a "beautiful Nigerian" who'd finished an economics degree and just left to work for OPEC. "It's a relief to lose him. He was heading so straight for the future, he could
hardly remember where we lived."

"I envy that," said Hanna.

"I envy you. You've got the toughest decisions behind you."

Hanna said it wasn't so at all and told her how she'd become a prisoner of Jay's moroseness. "He's dear, but he hates life. It's impossible to
reach him."

Nora said every relationship with a man had more censorship than
expression. "The sex is so important, you sacrifice give-and-take for
it."

Hanna said that wasn't what she feared. She did fear Jay. "He's
never laid a finger on me, but I'm afraid of him. Physically afraid.
Anger's burned the fat off his bones, and I think it has nowhere to go
now but on mine. It's not just a few knocks. I'm not that afraid of pain.
It's the anger itself. I guess I shouldn't say it. I love him, he's remarkable in his way. But to be squeezed so is awful. To feel your nature so
reduced. I'd always hoped marriage would give me space, energy, desire. It hasn't."

"Try getting out of it more. Don't bury yourself in him. He's become your tomb. Get out. On your own." Nora told her to come over
for supper, Jay could manage without her. "It would be the first time,"
said Hanna.

"She didn't invite *me*?"

Jay was assembling the evening's fortress: apples, books, ballpoints,
the vaseful of Sanka.

"She thinks I ought to get out on my own once in a while."

"Fine. Just don't come back on a broomstick."

"Meaning?"

The long face tilted, peering over a celestial ledge. "Witchery's contagious."

"Nora's no witch."

"Wait till midnight. I stood behind what's-her-name, Mount Fuji, the one that sounds like a stray. Wanda! In the co-op. She was adding her groceries on a pocket calculator. Batting her pig eyes. Not at me. The groceries. Six bags full. And none for my master or for any dame but you know who. At least the Slitherer has a streak of generosity in her."

"You and I don't exactly keep a great salon."

"All we're trying to do is get out of here quick as we can. We're not the Salvation Army."

"I don't mean to criticize," she said.

"I don't know what you mean."

"It's been my fault too. Our life's too airless. The girls have been a fine thing for me. I feel human with them. You pick at them. I know it's a kind of game for you, your way of being social with me, but sometimes it's too hard."

He opened a book, looked at it, drank from the vase. "OK. I won't say anything about them. If I have an opinion you don't share, I'll shut up. But, Hanna, I can't have those psychotic shrews around here. Sorry."

That night, asleep beside him, she dreamed she was at the top of the Buddhist mountain Borobudur. Out of the stone bells rose old teachers, her sister, her mother, a boyfriend from Oklahoma who had hit her for not making out with him, girls from grade school and high school. One by one they asked her to forgive them. "We're sorry, we didn't know." *"Mai ben rai,"* she said. "Never mind"—and then was ashamed, for it was Thai, not Javanese. Which brought her to a river, a kayak going down the *klongs*. Jay lay dead on the struts, the boat headed for the cremation pyre. She was crying. "The others' don't mean anything without yours," she said, meaning the petitions for forgiveness, and now she would never have his. The body moved next to her. Jay. She moved away. In the channel between sleep and waking, she knew she was going to leave him.

3

The next night, before Jay got home, Hanna left a note for him and walked across the Midway to Nora's. She'd taken a shower, and put on her best jeans, an openwork blouse over a bra that lifted her breasts, and a blue blazer that was the nicest thing she owned.

Nora lived on Dorchester in a large attic room with a kitchen off one side and a bathroom off another. The furniture consisted of mattresses covered with shawls and cushions. There were lots of plants, books, a stereo, and knickknacks. The walls were covered with prints of Matisse flowers and dancers.

Nora, barefoot, wore old jeans and a sweater.

"You look terrific," she said. "Like someone on vacation."

"Going out to dinner is vacation. Without Jay."

They had jasmine tea and faced each other on the mattresses. Through old blinds, sun dusted the room.

"Are you on probation?" Nora's hands ran in and out of her hair.

"It's more like I've dug my way out of a cell. Blind. Through muck."

"No mud shows."

"The mud's in here," said Hanna, touching her left breast.

"That's nice mud," said Nora.

There was something both tense and easy in this pillowed room, a Turkish air. Hanna felt airy, afloat, yet cloistered, marooned. "I feel high."

"Free," said Nora. "Or maybe hungry. You hungry?"

"Just for air."

"It'll have to be tea."

Hanna brought her cup to the stove. Nora looked at her, her eyes, then her blouse, and put an arm around her waist. Hanna put hers around Nora's shoulder. They leaned forward and kissed.

Nora undid Hanna's blouse and bra. Undressed, they lay down, looked at and stroked each other, then, aroused, became more intimate.

It was, thought Hanna, like making love to oneself. There was the sense that Nora knew her body from inside. It wasn't especially exciting. It was a form of reconnaissance. Nora, no stranger in this country, was able to go further.

To be companionable, Hanna pretended thorough satisfaction.

4

It was midnight when Nora drove her back. Jay had read her note, which told him to read her diary so that he could understand how troubled she was by their marriage.

"I don't think I can live with you," said the note. "Not now. It doesn't mean I don't love you. Whatever that big word means."

Jay read the diary, more and more infuriated by what he regarded as its insensitivity. "Why couldn't she have opened up to me? It's those damn creeps. She had to find something, to keep up with them. If they're not in a mess, they don't know they're alive. Is life supposed to be paradise?"

He found a few dollars and ran down to the all-night liquor store on Sixty-third Street, bought a quart of vodka, and by midnight had drunk half of it.

Hanna came upstairs and saw him marooned in his sad, magic circle (the silvery bottle filling in for the vase of Sanka). "Well?"

"I'm potted."

"You read the note?"

"You bet."

"And the diary?"

"I followed all instructions."

He sat in liquorousness like a fish in an aquarium—apparently the same but altered by the tiny ambience of his new situation (of which the booze was but an element). Yet he looked beautiful, wounded, extravagant, baffled, and—to her surprise, for she'd had some experience of liquor—sexually excited. Even more surprising, she felt a responsive excitement. The signals crossed; discussion was shunted to the side.

For the second time that evening, she took off her clothes. They did not even bother to go down the hall but made love on the floor beside the apple cores and vodka.

Yet, Hanna told herself, half an hour later, awake while he snoozed off beyond troubles, she was in the jungle with Vanessa and Wanda and Clover. Energy, talent, and hope warred with her life; no relationship and no institution could help. She had the isolation of a pioneer in the circumstance of a soap opera. The only ax she had was the knowledge she was in trouble, that she was down there with the others.

LESSON FOR THE DAY

Kiest, with lots of time on his hands—his wife had a job, he didn't—had fallen for—that is, couldn't wait to get in the sack with—Angela Deschay, a pie-eycd, soft-voiced, long-legged, frizzily gorgeous assistant professor in his wife Dottie's department. Dottie and Angela were soaring together. It was WE—Women's Era—in the universities. Every department had to account to equal opportunity boards in the university and in Washington for its minority-hiring practices. Humanities departments had long since run out of qualified blacks and Chicanos. The few in these fields were more precious than natural gas strikes, but there were still good supplies of women. "Not enough to have a representative or two," rumbled Kiest. "You have to represent the whole miserable spectrum, pouters, grinners, thumpers, grunts. And then you can't fire'm. Fire a slit"—he'd borrowed that term from the misogynist Ty Cobb—"and you've got a fire on your hands. They get a new job Wednesday and sue you for the one they lost Tuesday. Lost purposely, so they can collect double."

The rumbling went on, mostly to himself or to his three- and one-year-old sons, who did not exactly tune in to it. It was just Dad going on.

What else did he have to do? He'd been done out of his place by the world's women. In fact, it was Angela Deschay who filled the slot he'd have filled here in Madison. The slit in the slot. His lust for her had been blocked and then ignited by the injustice.

"What leg can a man stand on?" This to Dottie over the repulsive

Cheerios he bought—of course, he did the shopping—because she detested them. "The one in the middle? That's the one that does us in." Thin, bespectacled, mild, and innocent-looking despite his rage, Kiest threatened her with transsexual operations. On her, on himself. "I'll turn slit and give you a run for our money."

Would she even notice? She rushed off, she rushed in, flew to conferences, interviewed, was interviewed, formed and chaired committees, got job offers, salary raises. At this publication-insistent university, her only postdissertation work was a bloody attack on her own dissertation adviser's swan song book on George Herbert. (So veiled with fulsome praise that only Kiest and the victim knew what went on. Dottie herself didn't know. Her aggression was just hearty instructiveness. "He wouldn't respect me if I didn't point out a few things. He's the last man to want friendship to shackle scholarship.") The tigerish assault was pronounced "brilliant" by senior professors who otherwise couldn't justify Dottie's unstoppable rise.

Kiest foresaw their life: Dottie as chairperson, dean, provost, president; board directorships, a cabinet post, and who knows then? He would be Henry Lucing it after her—with the difference that Henry Luce had been Henry Luce, whereas he had never been allowed to be more than just Kiest.

What had he done? Well, he'd written a dissertation on the great and terrible John Wilmot, Earl of Rochester. At graduate school, he'd done far better than Dottie, and yet he could not find a job within a hundred miles of hers. She'd been wined, dined, grabbed for, prostrated before, you'd have thought she was a fusion of Madame Curie and Marilyn Monroe. She was only an enthusiast, a worker, a prettyish, big-bottomed, straitlaced, no, slightly unlaced girl out of the bleached Calvinism of Dutch Reform Michigan. They'd met at the Yale Graduate School, drawn together in dislike of the critical virtuosi there. The literary pantheon at Yale didn't feature Shakespeare, Milton, and Wordsworth but the versions of them offered by H. Miller, H. Bloom, G. Hartman, and S. Fish (whom Kiest rebaptized as Grinder, Wither, Thrombosis, and Carp). Each day, he and Dottie watched them lash, hash, and hack *Lear, Comus,* Browning, and Blake into puzzles of hamburger. "The texts we live and die by," said young Kiest. "And over in Romance, the Barthes-Derrida swine are fusion bombing Balzac and Stendhal. Who'd dare to write a poem in New Haven?"

Not Kiest. It had never been his ambition. All he'd wanted was a chance to dig into the grand old texts. There were plenty of first-rate meals to be made out of those ingredients.

Dottie was saved by languages. At Olivet, she'd majored in classics; at Yale, this was her redoubt, a pocket of antique resistance to the critical buzz bombs. Fresh-faced, black eyes agleam with untouched availability, she wrote the thick, paratactic, unnecessary-to-read prose that was called wonderful writing in the academy.

He, Kiest, had come out of the Garden District of New Orleans with ever-thinning southern speech. His father had been pastry chef at the Commodore Palace Hotel, he became an early observer, then a master, of aristocratic ways. Adolescent, he found the bookstores in the Quarter and, by senior year, was enough ahead of his classmates to win a fellowship—"they'll change it to 'pal-ship'"—to Tulane and, after that, a fatter one to Yale. Ascent was written all over him. Dottie, with innocent hunger, grabbed him. How could she know she'd grabbed a lemon?

Or did she? Had she known even then she'd need a Kiest at home for kids, for chores? He wasn't sure. He accused her of "unisexing" him. Even then, she knew both the unimportance and the necessity of his complaints. She'd become one of the least passionate twenty-eight-year-olds in America, but, in complaint time, she could slide into sexual parody, so that tumbling on her pale rear, or bouncing the bud-nippled chest, complaint melted away. Being home so much did fierce things to the sexual appetite.

Which is how Angela Deschay filled his head.

The Deschays lived across the grassy street. Angela too was a rising star, not in administration, but scholarship. She published complex articles on revenge, power hunger, persiflage, and dominance in Restoration comedy. Before she'd come to Madison, she'd looked up Kiest's dissertation (thinking that the Kiest on the roster was Mervyn L., not Dorothy M.). They were on the same intellectual frequency. Her husband, Jimmy, was in the divinity school, one of the hip new preachers, full of pop cultural garbage spaced tediously by spiritous infusion of Barth and Bultmann, Troeltsch and Tillich. Eyeglassed, helpful, huge, eager, Jimmy was full of soft causes, soft politics, and frequent soft furies which exhausted, sometimes paralyzed him. "How could she have married him?" groaned Kiest to little Myron, Baby Dan. Madisonians—he knew—asked the same question about Dottie.

He and Angela walked their kids along the lake and talked about the seventeenth century, university politics, and, after a few awkward skirmishes, sex and marriage. She knew his views deeply, they were in his dissertation. Kiest spelled out his own failure in Rochester's. The bitter entertainer, pimp, and jester to the monstrous king was a rioter, hater, *débauché,* an actor and counterfeiter who disguised himself as tramp, porter, mountebank doctor. Hobbesian apostle and poet of Nothing, Rochester knew that the difference between con man and banker was that the banker's credit lasted one day longer; that coward and hero differed because the day the coward had to put up, the hero didn't. His couplets lashed everyone from crowned king to two-crown strumpet. Aged thirty-three, burned out by japes, revels, punks, liquor, and disbelief, he was converted by Bishop Burnet and died in the arms of wife, children, debts, and church.

Kiest, five years shy of Rochester's deathbed age, had had no king, only dream queens, no career of make-believe, only a noncareer of it. His debauches were oneiric. Home, after a first spring day stroll by the sail-white, passionate lake, he put the kids down for naps and took out the two hundred and forty bound pages of his dissertation, *Rochester, the Burning Counterfeit.* Its harsh prose seemed beautiful to him, he mouthed the great earl's poems. Angela's legs and breasts, her thick-glassed green eyes, mop of twiny, glittery, leaf-gold hair, her long back with—surely—its generous dip into the beauteous twins, oh what a woman.

> Naked she lay, claspt in my longing arms,
> I filled with love, and she all over charms,
> Both equally inspired with eager fire,
> Melting through kindness, flaming in desire.

For all her dutiful distance and careful amiability, Angela—he was sure—burned for him. She was the right age, the hot late twenties, and she'd seen around, through, and over her hefty, dull divine.

> With arms, legs, lips close clinging to embrace,
> She clips me to her breast, and sucks me to her face.

Angela, Jesus, Mary.

> The nimble tongue (love's lesser lightning) played
> Within my mouth, and to my thoughts conveyed
> Swift orders, that I should prepare to throw
> The all-dissolving thunderbolt below.

Kiest turned on the bed, piled pillows stiff with Sears floral print into an Angelac body.

> In liquid raptures I dissolve all o'er
> Melt into sperm and spend at every pore.
> A touch from any part of her had done 't,
> Her hand, her foot, her very looks a c—t.

Done 't.

Lips on pillow, Angela's and more, more. Other women. Dottie. Angela and Dottie together, hugging, kissing, grinding into porno flicks. His weapon, abused on the rough florets, clumped with generative sap. Window light poured rebuke: "So, Kiest, this is your career. What a great man you are. Life seized by the throat. Another great day, Kiest. Sculptors are itching to get you down in bronze."

Jimmy Deschay was making his preaching debut. More final exam than ministerial vocative, but no matter, it was a large event, and the Kiests were asked to swell the congregation that was part of it. The sacred tryout was in the First Methodist Church of Springvale, twelve miles west of Madison, fifty feet off the interstate. Kids had been bunched with a single babysitter. Kiest drove the Deschays' nine-year-old Dodge Dart, sitting beside Jimmy, whose terror dominated intense silence. The preacher's hands were in and out of his hair, cut into shaggy bangs like Robespierre's. (Every few months, he adopted another antique revolutionary style: ponytailed like young Jefferson, curled like Simón Bolívar.) His eye sockets, lips, and chin cleft dripped; cheekbones, forehead, and chocolate-kiss eyes shone liquidly. The radiant April Sunday darkened in the car. Dottie made talk but was shushed by the Lord's frightened bridegroom. Angela, bareheaded, jouncy in her orange-flower dress, tried comfort and was likewise shushed. Jimmy needed all lines clear for late words from on high.

Is he trying to drum messages from his scalp? thought Kiest, furious at Jimmy's contagious frenzy. That great Vidal Sassoon in the sky? Damn sheepish shepherd.

In church, he sat between the ladies. What a position. Never, never had human appendages so moved him. Under the flocculent orange balls bent the superb, unstockinged, untanned legs of this scholarly charmer, this—please God—sluttish slit. They straightened for hymns, for prayers, up, down, arms, sides, raising and lowering hymnals, fifty, seventy small contacts. She knew, surely, the warmth he generated, the feel of his suit sleeve, the tensed communication of his arm. The holy place, the holy occasion covered the awareness with unthinkability. But, thought Kiest, she is thinking. She *knows*.

> Rise up, oh men of God.
> Have done with lesser things.

No music reader, Kiest fumbled toward the notes behind Dottie's authority, Angela's warble. Hymnals bounced to the thin tune, hymn-booked arms rocked, parted, touched. Down they sat, arms and sides sending and receiving.

"Here we go," thunder-whispered Dottie.

Jimmy was up, black robed, huge. Sheets of light spread from the great windows over sixty worshippers. An electric moment. "Dear friends," dove Jimmy. "The lesson for the day is Matthew 26:23. 'And he answered and said, He that dippeth his hand with me in the dish, the same shall betray me.'"

Mother Mary. Does the bastard know?

Kiest's thought was not just his. Air spiked between his sleeve and the bare arm beside it. The power of words.

"God," said Dottie. "Something's wrong."

The ministerial tower tilted. From the top, vowels bassooned into each other, "Aarch, eeech, uuueeeshhh." Black wings rose, sank, rose; the left wiped the ministerial brow.

"Jimmy." Angela, hands fisted, sent useless strength his way. "Oh, please."

Whereupon, not God but Kiest came to the rescue. Small and straight, he walked the little nave and joined the stunned divine. Jimmy's face, red as if strangled, widened fishily. "Mr. Deschay," said Kiest to the assembly, "rose from a sickbed against his doctor's warning in order to preach today. It's clear he shouldn't have. With his permission, and yours, I'll read his sermon for him."

The colors of humiliation and terror countered those of surprise, relief. Jimmy touched the shoulder of his substitute, then sent the flock those eloquent gestures which would in future decades be seen in the smaller congregations of southern North Dakota. Back in his seat, hands folded, he gave perfect attention, as if he were the benign appraiser of his rescuer.

Kiest looked at the typescript and gave it his fervent all. "Is this betrayal story the essence of Jesus' last Passover? I think not. Grand as the grand story is, deep as it touches our sense of fair play, the betrayal, necessary prelude to the great sacrifice, is not the ultimate meaning. No, dear friends." His eyes found the thick glass behind which were the astonished, excited, decision-taking green eyes of the stricken fledgling's wife. Rescued from her own sympathy and humiliation less by Kiest's stunning move than by the moronic complacence with which her bedmate accepted it, she showed in her look an invigorated sense of the author of *Rochester, the Burning Counterfeit*. And, sure enough, pondering this new acquaintance, she heard clear substitution in the laborious text: lines from the wicked earl's "Satire against Mankind," surely never before or after heard from this pulpit.

> Birds feed on birds, beasts on each other prey,
> But savage Man alone does Man betray.
> Pressed by necessity, *they* kill for food,
> Man undoes Man to do himself no good . . .
> For fear he arms, and is of arms afraid;
> From fear to fear successively betrayed.

Base fear the source whence his best passions came,
His boasted honor and his dear-bought fame . . .

"So," said Kiest over nodding, scratching, shaking heads, "as Reverend Deschay tells us, the betrayal in the midst of the celebrating feast is the essential savagery of man which, in hours, Jesus will die to redeem. So, on this second Sunday after Easter, do not lose yourself in the savage ecstasy of spring, fine as it may be"—small, wild rustling below—"without remembering that amid your feasting self the unredeemed beast trembles in readiness. And here Reverend Deschay bids you turn to number 29 in the hymnal, 'There Is a Land of Pure Delight Where Saints Immortal Reign.' "

That evening, while Dottie was out with her Sunday play-reading group—playing Regina in *Another Part of the Forest*—Kiest put his sons to bed and then, from his doorsill, sent brain waves of imploration across the forty feet of grass to Angela.

Surely she'd managed to drug her preacher into sleep. The ass had covered his debacle with Kiest's excuse for it; so well had he mimicked chills and fever that he suffered them. The car ride back to Madison had been filled with his sniffles. Kiest and Angela had not looked at each other. That was the sign: she knew, he knew. What more was necessary? Knowledge embraced need, need the invitation to requital. *What was holding her back?*

Gold shadows thickened, purpled. A fat moon sat in the oaks. The lights burned at the Deschays', but that was all. Kiest's expectation became anxiety, then misery. Ten o'clock. He threw in the towel and headed for the armistice of bed.

The phone. "Mervyn," said Angela.

"Thank God."

"No, *you*. Thank *you*."

"All right, come thank me."

Crucial silence. "Papers."

Papers.

Of course. End of term for the full-time assistant professor. Wife, mother, assigner of papers, reader of exams, there was hardly time for sleep, let alone . . . *let alone.*

"I need, I want, I must." The unuttered conjugation of Kiest's hunger. He put what he could of it into "Angela."

"Yes, Mervyn." Slowly, softly. It was something. Then, probably faking, "Coming, Jimmy. Good-bye."

Coming, Jimmy. The counterfeiting slit.

Kiest went into the terrible spring night. The moon hung in it like an ulcer. *What to do?*

Headlights in the oaks, and a professorial Dodge pulled to the curb. Dottie. Hot and rosy with self-gratulation: "Bye-bye. Thanks again. See you next time. Bye-bye."

Kiest slipped inside, doused the bed light, took off his clothes under the blanket, closed his eyes.

"Asleep already, baby?"

"No longer."

"Sorry, lambie. Had to tell you. Zack said he'd do it at the Repertory if I'd play Regina." Off with the square slacks, the fuchsia turtleneck. "If I didn't have to chair that curriculum revision." Into the bathroom, front and rear nakedly abounce, splash, scrub, towel, and tinkle, she never closed the door, and back to the dark bed in her grim, dust-colored PJs. "What a day." The bed light shriveled Kiest's eyelids. "Sorry, sweetie, I've got a special fields on Coleridge at nine. Won't take me long. 'Frost at Midnight.' "

"You said it."

"Want to hear?" A specialist in metrics who couldn't find an accent with a Saint Bernard, Dottie sometimes treated him to a reading.

Why not? The day had supplied everything else. Coleridge was the one romantic poet he understood from inside: idler, dreamer, opium guzzler, fragment heaper, a mothering father, isolated, sex starved, pent up with the wrong woman, dying for another. "Read on."

But Dottie, racing, underlining, scribbling, was almost done and could only cap this day of counterfeit and despair with the final wintry lines: " '. . . the secret ministry of frost / Shall hang them up in silent icicles / Quietly shining to the quiet Moon.' "

THE GIRL WHO LOVES SCHUBERT

Yntema and Scharf didn't like each other, but whenever Scharf came to New York—about once a year—they had lunch. Scharf would have finished his business and seen his few real friends, there'd be an open lunch date, why not call Yntema? They'd known each other thirty years, fellow law students at Ann Arbor, till Yntema dropped out, months shy of the degree.

During school, Yntema had gone with a girl, Marjory Spack, who was, he said, "Not my type. Beagle eyes and bandy legs." He introduced her to Scharf (who married her). A week after the introduction, Yntema took off for New York, found work in the trust department of the Chemical Bank, and prospered.

Scharf was orderly, finicky, conservative; Yntema, erratic, flighty, a lover of disorder. When Yntema asked Scharf what was new, the answer would be something like, "I live like a plant. How different can leaves feel?" That was enough for Yntema. They could get down to his troubles, which were always heavy: perfect matter for his fluent, seductive narratives.

Scharf adored them. (They compensated for his dislike of their narrator.) Familiar as he was with their themes, there was always fine new detail. The themes were Yntema's father and his "endless declension of tarts"; Yntema's doubts of his masculinity, traceable, of course, to the paternal freebooter; Yntema's wives, girlfriends, and therapies (sun cults, tarot packs, LSD, jogging, diets), the sources of his latest burst of "inner peace."

Almost every year there was a new wife or friend. "How's Felicia?" On his one visit to Yntema's West End Avenue apartment, Scharf had had a glimpse of her.

"I'm sure she's getting along. Why?"

"So there's a new installation."

"I'm with a terrific girl. A brilliant, tough girl. I met her at the Midtown Club. Weight lifting. I started lifting in May."

"You're looking very solid."

"Three times a week at the club. And at home, with Walter." Walter was Yntema's eighteen-year-old son. "It's quite a sight, the two of us grunting under iron."

Walter's moods, schools, clothes, analysts, and drug bouts were a subtheme of Yntema's saga. Walter was "an index to his generation," a sociological thermometer luckily found in Yntema's own medicine chest.

Yntema had an abnormally quiet but lyric voice. Its lilt was that of repression: repressed laughs, repressed boasts, repressed feelings of every sort. Marjory Scharf remembered it as "a fake seducer's voice. A meadow disguised as a minefield." Laughter was always swelling in it. Then something held it back, and out came snorts and melancholy honks.

Scharf, who'd run to fat and was gray at forty, marveled at Yntema's looks. For all the divorces, the self-doubts, the expressed and suppressed hatreds, Yntema looked much the same as he had at Ann Arbor. Fifty-one, there were scarcely any lines in his face; no gray hair, just less black, less curl above a face that looked like a mix of Byron and Pushkin.

Over tea and sushi, Yntema said that Felicia's successor, Apple Gruber, was "the girl who loves Schubert. Remember *A Handful of Dust*? The fellow trapped in the jungle by that lunatic illiterate who makes him read Dickens's novels aloud over and over? That's me. Except I only have to listen, and Apple's unfortunately literate. She has this dowser's gift of knowing what I don't. 'Have you read this, have you read that?' 'No.' So it's lecture time. I might as well be back in Ann Arbor with all that rigged knowledge. You know how these Sardinian kidnappers always ask for just the amount of dough the guy's got in the bank. They're in cahoots with the bankers. Who's in cahoots with Apple?"

"You must give yourself away."

"The inner banker. Maybe. She gets intellectual crushes. Last spring it was Leibniz. Our place turned into an institute. Ferney West. Optics, hydrostatics, pneumatics, mechanics, calculus. There was nothing the old kraut wasn't into. *La vraie logique, l'art de calculer, l'art d'inventer.* Monads crawling around. Four months of Leibniz. Until ten o'clock, November 27. We're at Lincoln Center listening to Fischer-Dieskau singing Schubert. And boom, zoom, out the room. That night, the monads get the sack. Boole, Frege, Russell, Peano, all those great Leibnizian logicians who'd battered my head since August, are out. November 29 I come home from work and halfway up the elevator I hear Fischer-Dieskau singing *Die Winterreise.*" And Yntema sang, "'*Manche Träne aus meinen Augen.*' On every chair, scores, albums, articles, biographies. Apple, who's a terrific Amazon—you should see her, she's spectacular, it's like making love to the Brooklyn Bridge— she's—what?—swathed, enshrouded in a cloud of tulle. A golden peignoir. My Viennese Alp. Muscles? They're out too. Hair—which had been tied up in a nice lump—is a blizzard. A red blizzard, halfway to Egypt. On the walls are watercolors, lithographs, woodcuts. The Vienna woods, the Danube, the Prater, Metternich, Beethoven. A week later, Schubert himself shows up. In bronze. Eyeglasses and all. Six hundred bucks."

"On you?"

"Are you nuts?"

"What does she do?"

"Physical therapy for retarded kids. Riding and rowing. Rich she is not. But what there is goes to Vienna. I live in a Schubert museum."

If anything, Yntema's apartment looked like a museum of radical nostalgia. Yntema lived his idea of the thirties intellectual, domiciled, but ready to go underground at the first knock. His building's tiny lobby had a defunct carpet, puce walls, an ancient elevator, dark corridors. Varnish scabs ribbed the doors. Yntema's apartment was the natural bloom of this shabbiness. Its walls were the same heavy puce as the lobby's—there must have been a paint sale around the corner—the chairs and the sofa had long since had it. When you rose from them, clumps of hair rose with you. As for decor, Scharf remembered a swatch of frayed batik tacked between an unframed map of Europe and a Woolworth-framed lithograph of the British Museum reading room. The room stank of pamphlets.

Why did Yntema live like this? Alimony, doctors, girls, and Walter were expensive, but he made lots of money. If ever a place staged an idea, it was this one. The idea was, "The hero of a mental saga needs no scenery."

Yntema was living with Felicia Mellowine, a long-necked redhead he'd "rescued from the turpitude of Gimbels. Decorative accessories. Eight hours a day, no sitting down or leaning on counters. Eighty-five dollars a week." Scharf saw Felicia for about a minute and a half. (Though quite a lot of her, for she wore nothing but a blue dressing gown that had served some of Yntema's more careless companions. He tried not to stare at the navel and nipples which winked through the holes.)

"Who's Lawrence of Arabia?" The voice didn't do justice to the beautiful throat.

"Why?" asked Yntema. He did not look up from his can of Blatz.

"Kojak asked this cop who he thought he was, Lawrence of Arabia?"

"President of OPEC," said Yntema.

"An Arab?" Above the neck, Felicia was mostly pout.

"Say hello to Ed Scharf, kiddo."

"Hi, Ed. I won't bother you. I'm into a good show."

Were all Yntema's women — after Marjory, of course — such washouts? They were so vivid in his stories. Perhaps what counted for him was not the girl but what he could invent about her. The less there was to work with, the more he could invent.

Or was this *his* invention? Was he Yntemizing? Making his own Yntema saga?

After all, Yntema radiated intelligence and self-control. The quiet voice was sane and clear.

"A few weeks ago, Walter and I are lifting away, dripping, concentrating. You don't lift, there's a lot to it. The idea's to put every muscle against its pain wall, then drive through it. You have to concentrate every second. Otherwise you'll break. So we're lifting, and, all of a sudden, I feel something. A glance. A shaft. I've got a hundred and seventy pounds in the air, and I spot the *schöne Müllerin* leaning delicately on the wall. Looking. 'Do you boys know what you're doing?' Remember, this girl has *thighs, biceps,* she bench-presses a hundred and forty pounds. 'Is this what you really want? I mean, what's the *point*? Walter'—Walter's stretched out, he looks like a weather map—'Walter,' she says, 'do you know that when Schubert was eighteen he composed two symphonies, three sonatas, and a hundred and forty-five songs? Does that give you pause, Walter?' Walter's so proud of these muscles, Eddie. You know he's not a big guy, eczema's crawling over him, what does the kid have but these muscles? He's worked like a dog for them. I mean what does Walter have to do with some one-in-a-trillion phenomenon who sneezed music? Push Schubert downstairs, the stairs sang.

"So that's life *bei* Yntema. Not all bad. I like to learn. And the first ten times you hear the *Winterreise,* it's everything Apple says it is. But that's the thing about this girl. She doesn't have the usual appetite. No one who looks like Babe Diedrickson—plus Maureen O'Hara—can have a normal appetite. She can't stop with anything. And with Schubert, it's not the songs she wants, it's what they conceal. What they mean. We had to hear this *Winterreise* till she figured out how it killed Schubert."

"I don't get that."

· "It's baloney. That is, pure Apple. Her Schubert had a terrific life. His family loved him, he had great friends, they had these wine-drinking parties where he sang his songs. He composed every day, studied scores, read poems. He was smart as hell, read everything, classics, Goethe, Fenimore Cooper, discovered Heine. And he knew he was great stuff. Then he read these *Winterreise* poems, full of drivel about a guy wandering around the snow, a kind of lumpen Lear, barked at by dogs and so on. He goes crackers and ends up with an organ grinder. Apple's idea is Schubert took every word of this drivel and turned it on himself: he had no one, no girl, no real friend, nobody to understand what he was about. Except Beethoven, who'd just died. Schubert went to the funeral, and that set him up for his own."

"He killed himself?"

"*Typhus abdominalis.* Same thing his mother died of. But Doktor Gruber, Professor of Viennese *Schwärmerei,* says it's essentially suicide. The virus sits around waiting till it gets a mental cue. Then boom, zoom, out the room."

Within Yntema's stories, there were always others. His saga was not a mere odyssey of bruises. Every bruise meant something. Schubert meant something. Apple meant something. The real story was always Yntema's, and Scharf knew that he discovered it as he told the other. That was why Yntema relished their lunches.

"Are you waiting for Schubert to go the way of Leibniz? Is that where you stand?"

Yntema tongued some saki, very thoughtfully. "Don't you see?" Oystery light from the perforated brass shades touched his eyes, teeth, cheekbones. He was like a little festival of insight.

Yntema had his narrative tricks: he held back, called for the check, went through the rigmarole with credit card, receipt, signing, tip, and it was ten minutes—while they walked up Forty-sixth Street in their topcoats—before Scharf pushed him toward the end of the installment. "I don't see what you think she was getting at."

"I don't either. Yet." Yntema stopped. They were in front of the bank. "At first I thought, She's trying to get rid of Walter. But she likes him. If only as another listener. It's something else.

"Leibniz was a force for her, a mentality, not a person. Schubert's something else: a presence. A person. One she takes to. His fecundity, his modesty, his confidence, even his smallness—he was four eleven!—reproach her. And enchant her. What does that make me? Superfluous. Three's a crowd. The question is, Is she *gunning* for me? Not with a gun. An Apple doesn't do it with a gun. The gun she uses is *you.*"

"Me?"

"*Me!* She uses you against yourself. Like Walter's muscles. *Die Winterreise.* She's contriving a *Winterreise* for me. An internal boot in the ass. And out goes Yntema. Into the snow."

The sun blinds the glass skins of Sixth Avenue. "The U. S. of A., Eddie. Shining, stretching, pushing, remaking. 'Oh say, can you see?' No? 'Then move on. The frontier. Build the sonofabitch over. The Indians? Grind'm.' Apple—Christ, her name's Martha!—she's pure

American. Apple pie. And I've eaten of the apple. I've gotta pay. So that's where it stands. Am I Apple's eye? Or her Indians?"

The annual installment often ended like a serial, Yntema dangling over a sexual cliff. But Scharf was in on it; it existed because of him. As if Yntema had troubles in order to have a new installment for their lunches.

There was some ill will here as well: if Yntema dangles, why not Scharf? Scharf knew that Yntema was more than puzzled by his steadiness. His self-deprecations—"I live like a plant," "I'm a uxorious vine"—offended Yntema as patronizing superiority: "He can afford self-deprecation."

Scharf was happy. He loved not only his routines but the idea of them. That fact was beyond or beneath Yntema's comprehension. He resented such vegetal contentment as a worldly as well as a Scharfian fact. How could a human being who was neither prude nor dummy restrict himself in a world so rich with possibility? Scharf felt that Yntema must think he was lazy or that his energy was low. A wife of thirty years must be a security blanket, a form of avarice or fear. "And maybe that's right," Scharf conceded. Still, the concession didn't disturb him. The fact that he could imagine Yntema's views protected him from them. Which was his equivalent of Yntema's technique: surviving trouble by recounting it.

Scharf got back to New York a year from the next January and didn't call Yntema till his last day there. Yntema's secretary said he hadn't come to work.

"All these years I've known him, he's never missed a day," Scharf said, not quite to himself.

"I'm afraid he's missed quite a few lately."

It would have been the third time in a quarter of a century that they hadn't gotten together. But there was a blizzard in Chicago, no flights were going in. Scharf called Yntema's home from LaGuardia. Any chance of their getting together, he'd tried him yesterday at the office.

"Why not?" said Yntema, thickly.

"You don't sound well, Sidney. Can I bring aspirin? Di-Gel?"

"Bring a few cold cuts. You know Zabar's."

The abruptness, plus the canceled flight, the changed venue of their get-together, and then the snow, which started coming down as he rode back into town, pushed Scharf toward depression. The ride was slow, the air heavy. Still, after checking back into the Westbury, he felt better. He taxied to Zabar's and hauled off twenty dollars' worth of corned beef, pastrami, Swiss cheese, and kaiser rolls.

Yntema's lobby sported a green-mold paint and, in place of the defunct carpet, a corrugated rubber runner. The elevator groaned worse than ever, the corridors were as grim, and the front door sicker of varnish than it was three years ago.

Yntema too was in bad shape. He limped, his eyes were dull, the black curls were stippled with gray, and his arms and shoulders seemed at odds with his T-shirt.

The living room was also the worse for wear. Neither map, lithograph, nor batik swatch festooned the puce walls. The room looked as if it had been in a fight. A leg of the coffee table was taped, there was a purple stain on the unhappy sofa.

Scharf followed limping Yntema into the kitchen—another piece of misery, though not a battleground. They unloaded the delicatessen onto poorly cleaned plates and took cans of Blatz out of the only icebox with a spherical motor on top that Scharf had seen since World War II. "I've seen better days," said Yntema.

"I can see that." The room, Scharf realized, was bare of music. No scores, no albums, no bust of Schubert. "Apple taken up another subject?"

"Did she not, Eddie. Very bad scene here." Yntema's pitch was odd, and there was something askew in his face. "Not pleasant."

"Bit of a brawl?"

"Hell of a brawl. The bitch did for me. Christ, it's hard to manage these rolls." His teeth squirreled around the kaiser roll.

Scharf looked closer. The fixity, the evenness, the whiteness of the teeth. Proud-mouthed Yntema had a denture. Still, he wolfed, pastrami bits falling on his jeans, the chair, through the slit in the Blatz can.

"I'm glad I stayed over. I wanted to hear how things were going."

To his surprise and pleasure, Yntema let out a considerable—

unrepressed—laugh. "Hear? Look!" He spread arms, pastrami in his left hand, beer can in his right. "*Yntema Bound.* Act five."

"She really gave it to you."

"Nose. Teeth. Concussion. She threw the goddamn bust at me. Which I'd tried to bust. If I'd have been two feet closer, she'd have killed me. What an arm. She got my ankle with the barbell. There's lots of Blatz." He hoisted his empty, and Scharf brought him another, thinking, There's no pleasure seeing him so low. Which surprised him.

Was it that he was actually *seeing,* not just hearing about it? It was just bruise, not storied bruise.

Story did come out, at least story matter. Slowly, and with little verve. "Felicia started it."

"She came back?"

"Not to me. I saw her. On the street. Recognized her neck."

"Not *cut*!"

"Mink doesn't cut. And that little red nut of a head under more mink. Standing outside Armando's. You and I ate there, five or six years ago." Scharf nodded. "I called her. She turned, saw me, her mouth flew open, and she got red as her hair. I thought she was going to pass out. I had no idea. Then I see the old bastard coming out of Armando's."

Yntema looked at Scharf, who picked it up. "Your father?"

"Dr. Tart Eater himself. I don't know how she found him. Or he her. I don't want to know. But there he was holding on to the mink. He saw me, started to say something, I saw his mouth twisting for it, but she pulled him off. Five years ago, he'd have kicked her into the gutter. Now he's a thousand years old; he just got pulled off. What a moment. I leaned against the menu board. Asking myself, What does this say about my life? My choices? Am I just a continuation of that pig?" Yntema's voice had more lilt in it now, and some dental clicks as well. "Every time I've thought he can't go lower, he does. 'Pitched past pitch of *pitch.*' And what about me? Where did he pitch me?"

Scharf pointed to the battered room, to Yntema's face, his ankle. "I still don't see the connection."

"I took off, just walked uptown. I got home. Apple was out rowing her kids in Central Park. There was this"—hoisting the salted curls toward what was no longer there—"Viennese merde all over. Spectral merde. Musical merde. Bronze merde. I was so low. I felt like I was being played, like a record. Then I just let rip. I hit Franz Peter with the barbell. Right in the eyeglasses. Bashed them into the nose. Knocked a chunk of it off. I flattened him, then flattened his albums. Crazy, just crazy. In my whole life, I never got a drop of beer on a library book. That afternoon I tore them up. Scores, articles, books. Terrible."

"You didn't knock your own teeth out."

"I needed help there. You're sitting on my blood. Or hers. What a battler. But I busted her too. She came home to the wreckage and went crazier than I. Threw her damn Schubert at my face. When I came to, the two of them were sitting on me. Then the super came. Pacified her. They must've heard the racket on Broadway. A woman scorned is nothing. Smash a god, that's when you get fury. Imagine where I'd be if she'd been lifting weights all those months. As it was, I was two weeks in Lenox Hill. I just got off the crutches."

Scharf had to spend another day in New York—O'Hare was still closed—but there was no question of seeing Yntema again. He felt that he'd identified a body; the saga was over. Oh, Yntema was off crutches, there'd be a few more turns, more spills, another girl; and another, but what counted for Scharf was over. Ulysses had come home. To nothing worth singing about. (The only songs that survived here were Schubert's.)

That afternoon, Scharf, about to pass a record store, went in and bought the Fischer-Dieskau recording of the *Winterreise*. For some reason, he didn't bother working out, it seemed the right coming-home present for Marjory.

A SHORT HISTORY OF LOVE

"We've been together four months now and—it's really silly—but I don't even know your name." He didn't say anything so she went on. "I'd never even noticed something was wrong till a day or so ago."

"Oh?"

"It's not been necessary really . . . and then all the usual ways of knowing haven't mattered here."

"What do you mean?"

"Letters and things. You get the letters in the morning—if there ever are any—nobody could write me so I don't care—and then you must come home just about the time of the afternoon mail."

"I do see the postman quite often."

"And you take care of us at the stores, the passports and identity cards. You know my name, don't you?"

"It's Rose or something, isn't it?"

"That's it. Rose. A rose in an open plain if that's possible. Just two things, a plain and a rose, and they differentiate nothing else but each other. The plain nourishes the rose, and the rose gives meaning to the plain."

"That's quite beautiful," he said.

"Is it?"

"Yes, yes, it is."

"That's what I mean . . . the kindness of you. I know that you're the one for beauty. You're the one that makes beautiful things, knows what's beautiful in the room, in the park. Of course, I don't really know if you make beautiful things. I said that because you must. Do you?"

"Well," he said. "I don't really make things."

"I don't know what you do."

"Don't you?"

"We talk about the office and have jokes about Feldman and Gordon, but you're apart from them as if you weren't in the same office, or even had an office of your own. Designing things. A small office, a sort of grand closet filled with things you've made over the years."

"I can't say that it's like that." He raised an index finger to his head as if to push back a hair, but, being bald, the gesture only stood for a time when he had hair.

"I like it," she said, "your being bald."

"I don't mind it."

"It was one of the first things I knew about you. There was a shock right at the start. Your eyes were so bright one expected a tumble of blond hair when you raised your hat—and then there was nothing."

"You're a generous metaphysician."

"Metaphysician?"

"I used the word badly," he said.

"You do nothing badly."

"You're kind."

"No. No, I'm not. I don't even know if you mean that. Like you telling Grimm what fine work he did, and he kept on, never knowing how ridiculous he was."

"He wasn't all that bad, was he?"

"He botched everything. Yet he kept going on what you told him. I'm afraid that I'm doing the same thing."

"I do hope you won't think that, Rose. Even if Grimm were completely without gift, that would have no bearing on us."

"No, I suppose not. Actually, I love you for telling him what you did. He was so small and lonely. Where did he come from?"

"I don't know. I'd imagined he was English."

"Yes, like you, I think." He said nothing. "I said that of course to find out. I've thought you were English, but you might as well be American or Dutch."

"I was born in Sydney," he said.

"Sydney. On the other side of the world?"

"Yes, I suppose it is."

"But that's incredible . . . though I don't know why. You might tell me that you were Zeus, and I wouldn't have much more reason for saying 'incredible.' How did you come here? I mean, in a boat . . . and when . . . why?"

He went to the sink and ran the cold water, saying something which she did not hear.

"When? I couldn't hear you."

"I've been here for a long time. The business in Sydney was something temporary for my father. We came by boat, I believe."

"You believe?"

"I was very young. There was some sort of transition that I associate with the ocean."

"I came by boat. Six years ago. You know where I'm from, don't you?"

"It's America or Canada, isn't it? It's been weeks since we used the passports. The trip north."

"Yes, the trip north. The most beautiful, the only beautiful trip of my life. There was nothing wrong, not even the trains. We brought nothing and found everything. Those hills and the fishing villages. Was it Sondeheym where the rocks were and we drank that green wine and opened the oysters? It seems farther away than sailing from New York. I wonder if we'll ever take another like it?"

"We were very lucky. Perhaps we shall be again. Would you care to see the radio concert tonight?"

"You said that differently. I don't know why, but you've never said anything like that before."

"We're both tired. A concert might be the thing to revive us. They're playing Corelli and some early Germans."

"What's your name, darling?"

He looked at the window, then turned and washed his hands in the sink. As he wiped them on a dish towel, he said, "It's Angus, my dear. Angus Page."

She began to say, "How inappropriate," but then, looking at him, the long bare head and the thin artist's hands in the white towel, she seemed to see the name issuing from him like fog, and she raised her hands as it moved toward her, gray, lethal.

ORVIETO DOMINOS, BOLSENA EELS

The wind in Edward's lungs, stored up so long, now had American sails to fill. The white Fiat beetle was rattled as much by this release from his Italian captivity as from the ninety kilometers of the Via Cassia it consumed every hour. Vicky, however, was not much of a sail. Most of her morning's strength had gone into evading the group. Once they were off in the blue bus, she felt like taking to her bed. After all, they'd had lots of warnings about being picked up, and though Eddy was an American, he *was* twenty-five, a man of the world, and clearly capable of international designs. But wasn't this secondary? After all, she'd come to Italy to see and learn, and Eddy both knew things and talked wonderfully about them. It was he who'd shown her that the Moses statue in San Pietro in Vincoli was not "the sign bole of hanker," as the guide put it, but something more complex, witness the hands, not "clenched in hanker" but only stroking the beard reflectively. Though Eddy admitted at dinner that it was Freud who'd first pointed this out, he had, after all, read Freud, whereas the guide had probably never heard of him, unless a plaque on one of the tours indicated that Freud had gone to the johnny somewhere in nineteen aught two. Anyway, if you started to ask the guide a question in the middle of his lecture, he'd wave you away, afraid he might pick up in the wrong sentence and leave the group without the hot news that the Sistine's *Giudizia Universale* was painted thirty years after the ceiling.

And then it was so much nicer having your own car. Eddy hired the Fiat 600 right after she'd agreed to come with him. He did things right.

Though she could just see her father, laid up in bed after a fall from Sugar Belle—and thus with lots of time to stew—getting the news from the group that Victoria had gone off to Orvieto for a night of God knows what with a strange man. Not that there was going to be any funny stuff. A little woo pitching, fine, but, though she knew she must be passionate from the way she'd felt hundreds of woo-pitching times, Vicky knew also it was wiser to save *that* for when you had nothing else in life but diapers. In the flower market, just across the street from Portinari Drive-Yourself, Eddy had picked up a still-creamy lily from one of the unsold hundreds thrown there by the vendors, and she had its curling flake in her wallet as a good-luck charm against the possible evils of the expedition. It was going to go all right.

"I'm sorry, I didn't get it, Eddy. I was thinking about the darn group. Will they be surprised. They were going to Orvieto Thursday, though they never make up their stupid minds till it's too late to plan right. Last Wednesday, we were all set for Naples, bathing suits, towels, everything, and where did we end up but in Cerveteri and Tarquinia looking at Etruscan tombs. Not that they weren't great, but we didn't use our suits till Saturday. At Ladispoli. The sand was as black as your hair. Which is great for hair, but creepy to walk on. You had the feeling every dirty foot since the Etruscans had dragged itself on the beach."

"It's probably just the composition of the rock. Even the Tyrrhenian's forceful enough to launder a beach."

They'd planned to eat lunch in Viterbo, but Edward was so hungry that they turned off the Via Cassia at a place called Caprarola to find food. He pulled out the Baedeker and, to his amazed delight, saw that the little goat town was the site of "one of the most magnificent châteaus of the Renaissance built by Vignola in 1547 to 1559 for Cardinal Alexander Farnese." He read this to Vicky as if talking about an ancestor, so happy was he to have stumbled upon what few tourists would see, his Baedeker being sixty years old and this road fit for little more than goats and Fiat beetles. Theirs crawled down the hill in second, and, sure enough, high on the town, like a beautiful forehead, was a gray palace.

"Let's eat first," said Edward. "Though I'll bet there isn't even a trattoria in this metropolis."

Which seemed to be correct, though down at the bottom of the hill there was a café. They bought four gorgeous chocolate cakes shaped like the funny Etruscan tumuli at Cerveteri. Edward ate three of them.

Then they drove up to the palace courtyard, where, to their surprise, five large cars were parked. "Maybe the Farnese still live here," said Edward. He got out and ran around to open her door, getting what he wanted, which was a good view of her legs, which he had so happily stroked the night before and with which he planned to be in more intimate contact tonight in Orvieto.

The cars were not the property of the Farnese but of an outfit called Royal Films which was, right then and there, making a film about Napoleon's sister, Pauline. In fact, said the lady custodian, La Lollobrigida was in the garden at this very moment, with about a hundred other people, the implication being that they were trampling the lawns entrusted to her care by Rome. Edward's disappointment at this invasion of his discovery was mollified; he bought the tickets of admission ravenous for a view of the Lollobrigida.

For an hour, then, he and Vicky leaned against a wall while propmen arranged shrubs as a background for the cameras which finally ground away at a woman in green velvet and gold plumes cavorting on a tranquilized stallion over the undefended lawns. Edward's eyes strained with avidity, until a Napoleonic extra said the cavorter was only the Lollobrigida's *contrafigura;* the Lollobrigida herself was off in a corner where, indeed, Edward and Vicky saw her in a duplicate of the gold plumes, probably pining for nice company. But it was lunchtime, too late to satisfy her. Not until they were back on the Via Cassia, Edward's stomach thunderous with hunger, did they realize that they hadn't gone inside the château.

In Viterbo, they ate in a vaulted trattoria called Spacca. "It means 'split,' I think," he said. "I'm ready to," and staggered out under the weight of *lasagna al forno, vitello arrosto, piselli, patate, formaggio,* and *frutta.*

"How is it you're not fat?" asked Vicky, aghast at his large body heaving for breath under the black sports shirt, his head sweating from the working interior more than the roaring, stupefying one o'clock sun.

"Nature. I don't help it. It's great camouflage for gluttons. I'm really pretty hard," and he suppressed the afterward, "You'll soon see."

He asked directions for the Duomo, and they drove the closed-in, cobbled streets of the medieval quarter until they saw it in a fine little piazza, flanked by a palazzo with a Gothic loggia and a half-zebra-striped campanile to the left. They parked in front of the palazzo which, said Edward, was where the people of Viterbo locked up the cardinals in 1270 to see if hunger would force them to end two years of indecision and choose a pope.

"Did it work out?"

"Gregory the Tenth. Hunger's a great persuader," and he helped her out, filling up again on her legs. "We're parked right where Hadrian the Fourth, the only English pope, Nicholas Brakespeare . . ."

"It rhymes."

". . . made the Emperor Frederick the First hold his stirrup."

In the restaurant, Edward had reread Baedeker in the toilet and was more primed than usual. Though for sightseeing he was always primed. It was serious work if you did it right. The night before, he'd looked up the appropriate quotations in Dante and written them into the end pages of the Baedeker, starring them to correspond with the text. This was, in a sense, payment for Vicky's companionship, the entrance fee to what he would later guide her to, the self-discovery of lovemaking.

An old lady sitting on a chair outside the Duomo drew a six-inch key from her dress, opened the door, and led them inside. It was the first Gothic church Vicky had seen in Italy, and, after three weeks of baroque Roman churches, where every chapel, every inch, seemed to be straining for independent beauty, the stripped-down high proud nave made her feel high and proud herself. Edward too was hushed and forgot about Guy de Montfort stabbing Richard of Cornwall's son as the consecrated bread was being elevated at the altar. He followed the old woman, listening to her devoted, unmechanical talk about the dates of the church and the Mantegna frescoes—uncovered by the bombing in '44—which looked like broken bodies issuing from graves for the Last Judgment. A believer in nothing, Edward was still a lover of churches, though like the Romans, who, the man at Portinari Drive-

Yourself had told him, "manufacture the faith which is believed else-where."

On the way out of Viterbo, they stopped fifteen minutes at the Museo and looked at the Etruscan sarcophagi and pottery. "They're so calm about death," said Vicky. "Maybe that's what they lived for, to teach other people how to die."

Edward, a little annoyed at the rhetoric, said there were too many signs of the good life found in their tombs and pointed to what she had missed, a couple playing with each other's nakedness, etched finely on the black back of a vanished mirror. "It's when you live to the full that you can die well," he said, preparing her for the evening with this rhetorical turn of his own.

Which she suspected, but the way things were, seeing so much commemorated life, she could take in stride what was to come. She would be calm and intelligent, equipped, like an Etruscan, with her curled-up lily corresponding to the little plate they carried in their stone hands on which there was a piece of stone fruit for the death god.

They'd planned to swim in Lake Bolsena, partly because of some-thing in Dante, but Edward had missed the turnoff because he'd fol-lowed a sign to Montefiascone, and they'd gone up for a bottle of what Baedeker called "the best muscatel in Italy." The bottle had the "Est, Est, Est" motto on it, said Edward, because of a valet who'd been sent ahead by his master to test the best wines and mark "Est" on the inn doors where they were served. At Montefiascone, he'd written it three times, and his master stayed and died there.

It was a happy indirection: the main road to Orvieto could not have been more beautiful. All along the way there were trees soaked with gold pears and violet plums, trellises with huge blue grapes, and, every kilometer or so, an arbor flooded with ambrosial magenta flowers, the like of which, said Vicky, she had never seen. They were haying in the fields, and oxen drew wagons full of the golden stuff along the road. Now and then, they passed country versions of the papal loggia where people talked and drank among white hens out of the sun. Vicky felt queerly ashamed to be so free, so easily motorized, with no mission but sightseeing and the vague expectation of love. The countryside felt in-timate to her, familiar, filled with what she had little experience of, but much feeling for, the gathering of what had been sown, the harvest of labor, not the easy-moneyed harvest which brought the best, or at least the most worked-at, transported, and refined products, to expensive mouths.

Edward, too, was half enchanted by the heat, the wine, the sense of this blond girl feeling it with him, driving easily through the flaming hills cultivated to the last inch by a people articulate not in the mouth, but in gesture and posture. Half an hour from Montefiascone, round a turn, a couple of thousand feet up across the huge valley, they saw the little walled city, sunstruck. Orvieto. It disappeared as they drove around the road and reappeared at the next curve, disappearing and reappearing at the snaking curves.

Down the Fiat beetled, then up, until it crawled through the medieval, the Roman, the Etruscan walls into the skinny, cobbled ways, going in second, dodging men, women, children, past open stores, into and out of little piazzas, by chocolate and gray palazzi, and then, following the arrows, arriving at the Duomo in front of the astonishing facade, gold, blue, rose, all the colors of the road and fields, sculpted, assembled, "the most beautiful polychromatic monument in the world," said Baedeker, a gorgeous face for the tremendous black-and-white-striped body roaring in back of it.

"My God," said Vicky.

Among the other tourists, cars, buses, and postcard shops, they stared at the dazzling front. Edward read out the description in Baedeker, the commissioning of the church by Urban the Fourth after the "miracle of Bolsena," the appearance of drops of blood on the bread consecrated by a doubting Bohemian priest. "Twelve sixty three. The Feast of Corpus Domini."

"What, Eddy?" Dreamily, for what was there to say before this marvel with the incredible face and black-and-white body. The black and white extended beyond the cathedral to the steps which led to the piazza and to the doorways of the shops.

A great bell sounded in the square, five-thirty. On a tower, a bronze man was striking a bell with a bronze hammer.

"How darling," said Vicky softly.

"What, dear?" asked Edward, touched.

She pointed to the bronze man. "Isn't this the nicest place you've ever seen, Eddy? I think I could live here forever."

"It is especially nice," said Edward. "Let's go see the Signorellis while it's still light," and he took her bare arm against his own half-bare one and walked up the steps and through the central portal.

Inside, Vicky again felt the breath of wonder. The interior seemed huge, a divine, airy structure, great columned, uncluttered, leading far off to the beautiful choir. They walked slowly up the marble pavement and saw, in the right-hand chapel, people looking up.

"I thought it would be bigger," said Edward, who had a book of the Signorellis back home in New York. They went in, and he sat back under the portrait of Dante, his head against the signature "Mario e Domenicho '48," took out black-and-silver opera glasses, and studied one section of the frescoes at a time, smiling when he saw familiar figures, the young man with arms on hips, the prostitute with hand out for money, the woman riding the devil's back toward the pileup of the damned. Perhaps the same prostitute. The damned were twisted, their bones showed, their tendons and muscles were knotted; idolaters, lusters, killers, sloths, gluttons, doubters, whipped, choked, and wrestled by devils. Across the room, the saved were arched toward heaven, their bodies full, strong, easy. Edward's favorite sections were those filled with the colors of life, the prostitute's blue shawl, the blue-and-yellow-striped pants of young men, the plumed hats, the bulging brown money sacks. (Edward's book was only black and white.) On the side of the left wall was Signorelli himself, standing in black with the church's treasurer, thoughtful, perhaps surprised at what he'd created. Never in his life had Edward been so absorbed by painting. He even forgot about Vicky, who, though very happy in the lovely chapel and particularly taken with the sweet blues in Fra Angelico's sections, was getting neck weary. She sat next to Edward, who, after a minute of not noticing her, put a hand on her knee and said it was wonderful, wasn't it, to which she assented.

"Michelangelo owes this man more than Piero," he said. "Fresco perspective, foreshortening, arranging all these figures, making some seem sculpted, some painted, all that."

"I think the light will be better in the morning."

"Ten minutes more," said Edward. "Why don't you see what's in the other chapel? And tell me, so I don't have to see it." And his eyes were back in the opera glasses.

As it turned out, Edward did not see what was in the other chapel, and did not see Vicky again either, except for the thirty seconds in which she ran in, breathless and wild, to whisper, shatteringly, "It's the group. The group! I had to tell 'em I came on a bus, and I've got to go back with them. Now." And then, as his insides broke up, she blew him a kiss, and he watched through the opera glasses as his lovely blond girl joined the bunch of weary sheep following a female guide up the great nave and out of the central portal.

Head in his hands, Edward shook it back and forth until he realized that he was becoming an object of touristic concern. He clicked shut the glasses and headed out after them. Maybe she'd get away. But where would they meet? The car? Or in the Signorelli chapel? She'd said the morning light would be better. But the night? The night. He ran into the piazza in time to see the fat, idiotic backside of the blue bus waddling off down the street. "Holy God," said Edward. "They're probably off for Siena." He touched some holy water to his perspiring head. "No. Not that. They're off to a hotel, and she'll be back. Yes."

With this, Edward felt a little better. Also hungry, nervously hungry. He asked one of the piazza loungers if there was a decent hotel nearby and got directed to a small *albergo* down the steps from the left transept of the Duomo. It was a fine little tower, three stories high, with a small garden at its front steps. Edward got a room on the top floor, gave in his international driving license, said he had no luggage at all—neither, unfortunately, had Vicky, except her bathing suit in the dashboard slot—washed, then lay back on the beautiful double bed, the *matrimoniale* which would have staged his night's paradise. Outside was the upper-left transept of the Duomo, topped by a small bell and peppered with five gargoyles; beyond, in haze, were the violet hills of Umbria. It was the nicest hotel room he'd ever stayed in, eighteen hundred lire, three dollars' worth of irreplaceable niceness. Maybe he could make it for a night without Vicky. After all, he'd lasted twenty-five years without her. Considering that seven weeks ago he'd been at a desk thirty-five floors up in the thunder of New York, his head screaming with burdens, he had been pretty lucky, with or without her. He dressed and went out to find a restaurant. People were going home along the mocha streets, and Edward walked among them, taking the wall against the cars, bikes, and Vespas which maneuvered along the road. Dusk came in like a man happy to be home from work, lights flicked on in houses.

Orvieto. It had been a great city in the Etruscan League, Volsinii, and it did not die with Etruscan calm in the harsh face of Rome but stayed great for centuries, though limited by what had been its strength, its wall-cinctured hills. Now it had nothing but lace, wine, postcards, and fifteen thousand people walking the chocolate corridors, smiling. Mostly smiling. The people at the *albergo,* the *padrona,* the waiter, the maid, all smiled. Did the town make for sweetness?

Edward was back at the Duomo, beautiful in an evening gown of spotlight. Its steps were crowded with soldiers—Orvieto must be a base—mothers and children, young men. Edward went across the piazza to a restaurant terrace which faced the facade and ordered a mezzo-liter of Orvieto, pasta, eggplant parmigiana, and roast beef Bolognese. At the other occupied table, three soldiers gorged while he waited tensely for his own parade of marvels, which, when they came, he consumed in a frenzy of moonlit bliss. It cost two and a half dollars: maybe one could spend a life in Orvieto. Did the Duomo need an up-and-coming, an up-and-been PR man?

After dinner, he heaved himself down the piazza and across a strip of pines to the city wall and sat on it, looking out over the black basin of valley, barely defined by ten or twelve lights, a couple of which were moving, cars Edward tracked in and out of winding roads. Orvieto's perch didn't seem secure to him, though God knows it had lasted two thousand years longer than New York and beaten down God knows what invasions of the high walls on which Michelangelo had probably sat absorbing Signorelli's frescoes.

A group of soldiers came along, singing, saying something or other about *ragazze.* Edward walked down a cobbled street into a square, passed a hunchback sitting on the edge of a street fountain, went down another street filled with the blast of a television set, came into a large square made by two palazzi, climbed a staircase past an old man sleeping against the wall, and looked out from the balcony on the otherwise empty square. To the left, eighty feet in the air, two white faces of a great clock showed ten minutes to ten. Three young fellows ran up the stairs, shoving each other. On the balcony, they played some sort of hide-and-seek, though there was no place to hide but behind one's own knees in the dark. Edward heard some loud talk, turned, and saw a huge spool of film feeding a movie projector. He understood only isolated words, "*strano*," "*amore*," "*mangiare*," "*dispiace*." The old man was still propped against the wall. A white cat walked by, striped by the bars of the staircase. Edward walked down two still streets, then, in a third, saw fifteen faces, mostly old ones, craned toward a boxed light in a corner of a bar: Edward recognized the mock-heroic tune which introduced *Carosello,* Channel One's evening commercials. Further up, four soldiers and two girls giggling. More streets, the same streets, and, now and then, the voices of *Carosello* crashing out of a window.

Back at the Duomo, there was no one in sight, but Edward heard music. He walked to the left transept and saw ten young men, four of whom were sitting on the black-and-white steps playing an accordion, a guitar, a cowbell, and a rattle. The song was called "Domino, Domino," and Edward thought the words were something like, "Domino, Domino, you're the one thing I have in the world, dear. Domino, Domino, there is nothing but you in the world, dear." In the middle of the song, the ten-thirty bells from the bronze man's hammer sounded, filling out a guitar chord. The six men around the musicians, mostly in sport shirts, were motionless, their postures as fixed as those in the frescoes fifty yards away from them. Edward went to the staircase that led from the piazza toward his *albergo* and sat in the shadow, listening to the songs, looking at the stars behind the striped church, the Great Bear, the same stars in the same position behind the striped body for seven hundred years.

The music was soft, but very clear, the only noise in the square: "Jealousy," "*Volare,*" "Begin the Beguine," "*Il pleure dans mon coeur.*" Two of the young men broke the circle with ciaos. Then two others. "Don't leave, boys," said Edward.

What else was there? Walled up in the little town, the three movies seen, tired of *Carosello,* without girls. Not unlike New York, really, except that there the noise disguised the situation. It was clearer in Orvieto, pathetically clearer. That was the difference. With another: in New York, there was no Duomo, and no Signorelli chapel saying, "It's been done, boys. We've reached it. Peddle your postcards, and go home." The town had stopped around "the greatest polychromatic monument in the world" and the "great milestone in the history of painting in Italy."

And what did Maitani's facade and Signorelli's frescoes have to tell the boys? That they would be judged, here and now, before and later, playing "Domino, Domino," peddling postcards, driving Fiats, judged with everyone else according to the absolute, black-and-white standards of the *Giudizia Universale*. If there was a harmony of black and white in the universe, as in the body of the great church, it did not matter who would be judged only black or white. Their harmony was beyond individual fate. Bell, accordion, rattle, guitar, the notes watered down and moved single file, like the cranes in Dante flying toward the Nile. The white faces of the clock showed 11:21 in the Roman numbers which could tell little more than time, lacking the power to express complex equations. The black-and-white body could not sustain worldly life. The musicians, the soldiers, Edward, needed Vickys, love, opportunity, cars, chances to get out of the walled-in city. Unless they were the one in ten million already wise, ready to be judged on the selling of postcards. Signorelli painted himself in a black cloak, and showed his white hair streaming out of a soft black cap. The rest of his picture was finely colored, hotly for life, mutely for afterlife, but all colored. Signorelli worked in this little hill town, on his back, straining his neck like the wall-curved figures of his frescoes, three, four, five years, needing nothing else after his days but bed, a bottle of the local wine, maybe now and then a girl. One in ten million.

When the guitarist got up, so did Edward. He went to his room, washed, and got into the *matrimoniale* as the great bell sounded midnight, followed by two dings of the cathedral bell, unsynchronized with it. "Vicky," said Edward. His body felt hollower than any bell. And hers? Was it waiting in some Sienese *albergo* for his body clapper to sound it?

A bad night. The watchtower clock, the bronze bells, and his need, unslakable by pillow. He didn't sleep till two-thirty and then woke at six to the sound of a man delivering bread on a Vespa.

He got out of bed at seven and went over to the Duomo to see if Vicky was in the chapel. It was closed, and Edward refused the porter's offer to unlock it. He went down the street to a bar for an espresso and pastry, paid his bill at the hotel, and drove dangerously through walkers, loungers, soldiers, children, down the mocha corridors, following the Duomo arrows in reverse, spun out of the great chocolate walls, around the hill, and out toward the Via Cassia for Rome.

Five minutes later, he was on the other side of the valley, looking back at Orvieto, small, contained, pathetically beautiful. "I won't see you again in this life, sweetheart." He drove off, his insides thunderous for food, and stopped at the first trattoria on the road, where he ate six rolls, with butter and jam, and drank two cups of *caffellatte*. Then, replete, he was back in the white beetle heading toward the Lago del Bolsena, where he'd take a swim before going on to Rome. Two nights ago, for Vicky, he'd written down the quotation from *Purgatory* XXIV about Pope Martin of Tours, transformed by diet more than any other of the canto's gluttons:

> *Ebbe la santa Chiesa in le sue braccia;*
> *Dal Torso fu: e purga per digiuno*
> *L'anguille di Bolsena e la vernaccia.*

He, the one from Tours, had the Holy Church in his arms and now, in Purgatory, did without his beloved Bolsena eels cooked in white wine.

Edward was directed by a man on a donkey to the lake turnoff, went down a kilometer of brown dirt to a tiny beach where there were eight wooden cabanas under an arbor of the ambrosial, magenta flowers Vicky liked. He took his Hawaiian trunks from the slot, got a cabin for fifty lire, hung his shirt, slacks, and underwear over a sign about swimming three hours *dopo pasta,* put on his suit, which his sister said made him look like a pineapple, and walked into the marshy, leguminous lake. Off to the right was the island where, Baedeker reported,

> Amalsuntha, Queen of the Goths, the only daughter of Theodoric
> the Great, was imprisoned in 534 and afterward strangled whilst
> bathing by order of her cousin Theodatus, whom she had elevated
> to the rank of co-regent.

Edward went in the water and swam his perfect, boy's camp crawl, fifty feet out, or forty beyond the furthest Italian swimmer. To his left was the other island, where Baedeker placed King Donough O'Brien's surrender to the pope in 1064. "That's not for me," said Edward. He headed for Amalsuntha's prison. Not more than four strokes further, he felt a fire shoot through his stomach. He grunted with pain, clutched his stomach, and doubled over. Cramps. Sweat poured off his head. He stopped moving, sank, moved a foot and an arm, tried to turn over on his back and failed, sweat pouring into the lake water, his head ripping. He let himself go all the way down, knees to his chest, was cooled by the water, touched the oozing bottom, stood on one leg, then hopped a step toward shore, doubled up again, sank, touched bottom, hopped again, sank once more, aching, straightened, and hopped once more, nausea rising in his stomach and throat, irresistible. He turned his face from shore, toward King Donough O'Brien's island, and vomited into the lake. His throat loosened, soured, he sank in the water, the pain lessening. He kicked, slowly, moved his arms, slowly, and slowly, his insides rancid, walking, hopping, swimming, his body emptied of pastry, rolls, the rotted gluttony of the days, he made toward the little beach.

After an hour's rest, he took off his trunks in the cabin where the ambrosial odors of the magenta flowers overpowered his own rancid ones. He removed the sport shirt and slacks from the sign about not swimming till three hours after eating.

"Signs," he grunted. "I ought to pay attention to these damn signs."

VENI, VIDI . . . WENDT

1

From Los Angeles to Santa Barbara, a paradisal coast bears the permanent exhaust of the automobile: shack towns, oil pumps, drive-ins, Tastee-Freez bars, motels, service stations. At Ventura, the coast turns a corner which sends the Santa Ynez mountains east-west and lets the sun hang full on the beaches for its long day. A hundred yards or so off the highway there are a few sandy coves almost free of coastal acne. One of them, a mile north of a red boil of tourism called Santa Claus, is Serena Cove. A wooden plaque over the single-gauge railroad track gives the name. Cross the track to a cyclone fence. Behind that, in a lemon grove, is an amber villa shaped like a square head with glass shoulders. This is the Villa Leone, for which our place was the Changing House. (The villa has been turned into apartments.) Our house was—is—low, white, and gabled. It has one grand room windowed on three sides, three bedrooms, a kitchen, and three bathrooms, two of which function. It is hidden by odorous bushes, palms, live oaks, and great, skin-colored eucalypti, some of whose sides have been gashed by lightning. A wall of honeysuckle ends the driveway; behind it, the south lawn leads thirty feet to a red-dirt bluff covered with vines threaded with tiny blue flowers. They hang to the beach, a half-mile scimitar of ivory sand. Three other houses, hidden from ours by palms and trellises, share beach rights. You see them from the water, glassy monocles snooting it over a subdued sea.

Actually not the sea, but the Santa Barbara Channel, which is formed by the great private islands you see only on very clear summer days. The islands are far enough away to preserve a sense of the sea, but, like a lido, they break waves down to sizes which keep you from worrying about small children.

We were there ten summer weeks, in the last five of which I wrote the first version of an opera. I've never had an easier, less-forced time, and although, now, back in Chicago, I see that what I did there on the coast was not much more than take out the ore, and that I now have to build the factory and make the opera, at the time I didn't know it. During these weeks I never turned back to see what I'd done. Day after day I coasted (yes), writing away, feeling the music and story come with an ease which, till then, I'd never known.

Everyone seems to know that opera is on its last legs. In fact, music itself isn't doing too well. A fine songwriter, Ned Rorem, says that the Beatles are the great music of our time; I suppose they are more inventive than most. Our best composers spend a lot of time stewing about audience teasing and other art-world claptrap. Only Stravinsky seems like a wise inventor who happens to use music instead of words or mathematics. And he is enjoyed more as a Dr. Johnson than as an enchanting musician. A man like me who's spent himself writing a musical drama is led to feel his work has no public significance, that, at best, it will be endured by a few friends and an occasional audience bribed by free tickets and a party in honor of the composer. ("Honor" because he endured the long boredom of working out what bores them only an hour or two.) An "enforced loss of human energy," wrote Mr. Khrushchev about armaments. Of course, writing music is not enforced (though one must pass time doing something), and music is a few wrongs up from armaments.

Though down from political action, as the hierarchy of 1968 had it; and I was influenced by such misestimates as well as by my inner tides. I lent a very small public name and an equivalent public gift to the better-known victims of institutional brutality. Last spring, I marched in the Loop, collected fourteen draft cards, made a speech in the rain beside a Meštrović Indian, was photographed, televised, went home to look at myself on the local news, and had bad hours waiting for the FBI to turn me into the local Dr. Spock. In short, paid the debt to my consciousness of being in so frivolous a trade.

On the one hand, I dream of my own Bayreuth, the Wendt Festival, with, not mesmerism and fruited myth, but classical wisdom and common sense made engaging and novel by the least duplicitous of contemporary musical lines. On the other hand, I feel the shame of luxury, of a large—rotting—house, of privacy and silence, of a livable salary and easy schedule, of an entrée into the little circles in which I whirl—college music departments, two-day festivals in Mexico City and The Hague, occasional mention in a newsmagazine's music section.

For this opera, which, with luck, will be given a truncated radio performance in Stockholm and a workshop run-through in Bloomington, Indiana, I'm trying to do, I suppose, what writers do in prefaces (or what my uncle Herman did fifty years ago as advance agent for Barnum). I'm writing an account of its genesis or composition to serve as a kind of a trailer (which, as usual, precedes what it "trails").

Any thoughtful man who types the solitary "I" on the page as much as I have these past weeks must consider its perils. This is a great time for "I." Half the works billed as fiction are just spayed (or Styrofoamed) memoirs. This week's literary sections are on Malraux's *Anti-Memoirs,* apparently an unravelable mixture of real and fictive "I's," pseudonyms, noms de plume, and noms de guerre, mixed in with fictional guises and life roles (in which "the man" tells Nehru that he is a "Minister of State" the way that Mallarmé's cat becomes *Mallarmé's* cat). I suppose this need to multiply oneself is one of the billion guises of libido. (Professor Lederberg found gender in bacteria; perhaps gravity itself will turn out to be the lust of particles for each other.)

That genius Nietzsche, whom I still read in a Modern Library Giant bought at fifteen after reading Will Durant's *Story of Philosophy* . . . No, I'll begin again; I'm not writing autobiography. Nietzsche asks, "Aren't books written precisely to hide what is in us?" Granting the exceptional concealments of his time, isn't this still the case? I know the authors of some of the frankest books ever written. The books are mostly trailers or self-advertisements, letters to women saying, "Here I am, come get me" or to parents saying, "This is the reason for my condition." Or sometimes, they're just brilliant drugs of self-assurance.

Every book conceals a book. But as the great old fellow (F.N.) says, every thinker is more afraid of being understood than misunderstood. Wants uniqueness more than love and gratitude.

In Nietzsche's day, the pose was to be *simply* grand; in our time, to be *complexly* grand. The good artists I know are more credulous than *smarter* people. (So you hear stories of their naïveté or—its other face—mean shrewdness.)

Writing your own story, you can report, pose, and judge all at once. Not as blissful a cave as music, but not bad at all.

So here's my little *Enstehung des Walpole's Love* (opus 43), my yet-to-be-finished opera. I pray it's not a substitute for it. (In fact, I'm willing to send a Xerox of fifty pages of score to anyone who sends ten dollars and a self-addressed, stamped return envelope to Holt, Rinehart, and Winston, Inc., 383 Madison Avenue, New York, NY 10017.)

[Owing to personnel changes in our office, Mr. Wendt's invitation must be considered null and void. H., R., and W.]

2

I don't begin at the beginning, but with my then-seventeen-year-old son, Jeff-U. (For Ulrich; I'm Jeff-C, for Charles. Ulrich is the great-uncle from whom I inherited not the two hundred thousand I expected, but fifty.) Oedipal miseries were, I thought, ruining my summer. They were at their worst when Jeff-U invited his friend Ollendorf to stay with us.

I was not anxious to have Ollendorf around. The presence of an outsider inhibits me, if only for a time and from walking around in my skin. Though notches up from the loudmouthed adolescent ignoranti who fill up our Chicago house, he would be extra presence, an absence of dear absence; he'd be swinging baseball bats against the vases, tackling Jeff-U into Sackerville's stereo; I'd be forking over six hundred for that in addition to the hundred and eighty-five it cost me every week just to hook our trunks up in Sackerville's place. (Which turned out to be Donloubie's place.)

I did not want him.

But there was small recourse: Gina, my almost-sixteen-year-old, had had her amical quota with Loretta Cropsey.

I laid it on the hard line. "He can come if you, one, specify dates—ten days and not an hour more—and, two, he's got to fly into Santa

Barbara, which means the three-thirty out of San Francisco. And arrival day counts as day number one."

Since Jeff-U daily stretched his six and a sixth feet of unemployed body upon a bed from 1:00 A.M. to 1:00 P.M., it didn't strike me that Ollendorf's afternoon arrival constituted an important loss of a vertical day. "Besides which, it takes half an hour to get to the airport. And before that you'll have to work your way into a T-shirt. Even shoes. Maybe even a pair of socks. Not matched or clean, of course, but you can see there's more Ollendorf to the day than his arrival at the house." (Not that Jeff-U wore the same piece of clothing three consecutive hours. Except for dress shirts, which I told him to pay for himself. Since which the San Ysidro Laundry had been deprived of his custom.)

It turned out I won't let him pick up Ollendorf anyway because (1) he could drive only our New Yorker, Sackerville limiting the Volkswagen to "licensed adults," and (2) "I'm not going to burn a quart of fuel to fetch your effing pal when I'm up at Goleta anyway." (I rehearse the chamber group Mondays.)

He wished to telephone Ollendorf. "Sixty-five cents won't kill you."

"*Kill* me?"

"I paid for most of the calls."

"Not the tax."

"Here's a buck," fingering the besanded back pocket of the early afternoon pants for one of the crushed bills which remain from spring poker triumphs and his grandmother's indolent generosity — substitute for the physical birthday presents which would force her into the dangerous byways of Fifth Avenue.

I take the buck. "This covers about ten percent of them." If it's but a week of weeding nasturtiums or washing windows, I am bent on seeing his hairless arse erect before 1:00 P.M. Without myself having to chain and toss it into the local office of the California State Employment Service.

Of course he knows what I'm about, knows I bait him, but though down to fourteen bucks (if I haven't overlooked some of the pockets or the change which overflows to every couch and bed in the house), he throws me another bill. Which I don't make him pick up or unroll; because if his theatrical arrogance caused him to toss a five instead of a one, he will be down to nine bucks. (I didn't unroll it until I was in the john: I have theatrical bouts as well. It was, unfortunately, a single.)

3

Every other weekend, the cove fills with the land-bound children of my Los Angeles relatives and summer colleagues. (Especially those unable to keep progenitive tools from progenitive work: George Mullidyne has six, the odious Davidov has pumped five into the beauteous Patricia, and even the emeritous Krappell manages to churn junior Krappells out of his third wife.) They turn our half mile of beach into a sty.

I buy twenty-four cans of pop at a crack; they don't last an afternoon. The be-Pepsied urine threatens the brim of the channel and, for all I know, brings on the underground coronaries which the *News-Press* attributes to "settling of the channel fault." The last of these, 4.5 on the Richter scale, had our chairs leaping around for half a minute and, up the coast, severed an oil pipe which poured a hundred thousand lethal gallons over the lobster beds of Gaviota. (Note: Winter '69, after the rig across the way leaked millions—I hadn't seen anything.) But I found a local grease called Gorner's which looked but didn't taste like pop. Two giant bottles last a week. (The better mousetrap.)

Three days after I made the first sketches for *Walpole's Love,* my aunt Jo, her son, Sammy, and his three children, Little Lance, Indian-colored Sabrina, and my favorite, the Golden Triangle, Mina, drove up from L.A.

Sammy's a cetologist at La Jolla. He spends his life in a bathing suit taping the conversation of whales in the green-and-silver tanks of the marine biology laboratory. Whales, it seems, are the wisest of creatures, fearless, sensitive, cooperative. They tend their distressed kind, nudge them to the surface, and skim their pallid flanks for circulation. (Such stuff goes well in Santa Barbara, where the daughter of Thomas Mann used to escort a dog she taught to type to parties where parakeets supposedly chirp *Traviata.*) In such pursuits, Sammy has grown whalish himself. A pink cigar of a man, he rolls out of his Squire Wagon with children, mother, and fly rods. (At the service of the deep during the week, on weekends he murders there.)

Mina is Jeff-U's age. Two strips of psychedelic cloth hang on five and a half feet of intoxicating flesh. Her vitaminized breasts are those of Hungarian spies; her golden triangle—how I imagine its secretive fur—her pure, thick lips, her winking invitations to the ball I think are meant for me. I have seen her beauty spill over since '64. Even then, she was ready, Lolitable. (We watched that film together on the *Late Show*. How she understood.) But then there was Wilma Kitty (Velia and the children were back in Chicago), I had less reason to act out Nabokov's dream life. But while the earth gnashed hot jaws under channel waters and the Impulse to Lobsterhood searched new stuff, I dreamed madly of opening Mina's Northwest Passage. (One day, driving her east, to Grinnell or to Penn State, at dusk, by Winnemucca, Nev., or Provo, U., we pull in to a desert motel, we swim, Mina, you and I, in a silver pool and come back dripping to our cabin, brassy droplets on our golden flesh. Silent, regarding, we strip wet suits—I have lost ten or fifteen more pounds, my pectorals are weight lifted into buttresses of depilated chest—you walk to me—no, turn from me—flipping suit from ankle, I pull your back to my front, Hungarian breasts within my palms, and you, struggling for me, go belly-down upon the double bed, glorious snow-white rearward twins aquiver for the locomotive rod.)

Aunt Jo is gray, gap toothed, powdery, hard of hearing, repetitive, with our family appetite for the fortissimo monologue. When she, her sisters, and her surviving brother, my father, the Optimist, assemble, it looks as if an Eastern rice village on stilts has been given life. (All are on canes.) They enter, four octogenarians with octogenarian spouses. (The spouses, except my father's, are all second mates: this family survives. Survives and kills.) They surround the children with their gifts, old arms, and puckering lips. "Open, darling, open and see what Aunt Jo (Belle, May) has brought her precious." They vomit triumph, praise, self-adoration. All is right with the world. (Why not? It has endured them.) The cities they inhabit are crimeless, the water pure, the streets immaculate, their children extraordinary, known over New York, Scarsdale, the world, on the verge or aftermath of incredible deals— mentioned in *Textile Week*—their grandchildren are peerless beauties of rare and promising shrewdness. The gashes of their lives (children dead in auto accidents, bankrupt sons, psychotic grandchildren, doomed conditions, stymied lives) are scarred over with such noise. They stagger into the living room, drop into sofas, and, huge voices aimed at the room's imagined center, begin their simultaneous, uninterruptible spiels. Canes gaveling carpets for emphasis and control, voices crashing against each other, they solicit, they demand recognition of their life performances.

Only one mortal thing can suspend their arias: food. Velia's thin, West Hartford voice inserts, "Would you like a bite?" Convulsion of struggle, sofa arms crushed, canes gripped to bone, the gravity of sagged flesh reversed by visions of repast. And commences the Long March to the table. There, stunned moment of formality, who will sit where? Velia leaves them struggling—monarchical whales—but appetite dissolves precedence, they fall to, moaning about the splendor of the vittles; though their old hearts are sunk at the thin New England provision, the cellophaned corned beef, the thin, presliced rye bread staled in the Protestant markets which magnetize Velia, and, for sweets, dry wafers in lieu of the thick snail curls of raisins, nuts, and caramelized dough, or the scarlet tarts, the berries swillingly augmented by terrific syrups. No, nothing is right, but then how should a thin-nosed aristocrat know what keeps old Jews alive? Mouths liquid, they compliment—and so enrich—the sober fare. They live, they eat; the juices flood. This is what ancestral migrations have aimed at. (Children of the Book? Yes, quick. Sons and Daughters of the Schnecken, the Custard Tart.)

Aunt Jo and I sit in Sackerville's beautiful living room, Japanese-free of furniture, windows on three sides, in front, the flowered lawn, empalmed, honeysuckled, grassed to the great bluff over the ocean. The noise is of bird and wave, the Pacific is blue, snowy. Aunt Jo takes my arm, pulls herself up by it so that her lips are at my ear. In a voice that is part puzzlement, part revelation, she says, "The Lord has been good to you, Jeffrey."

The gap-toothed, powdery, great-nosed face tosses back toward the drained cans of pop, the scarlet paradise flowers, the spread and noise of children, and what?—the pretty, apparently undemanding, apparently giving wife. She remembers the commissions from Tanglewood and Fromm, the write-ups in *Time* (three harsh slaps), the full-fledged attack by Winthrop Sargeant ("The complex aridity of Wendt's music, commissioned, composed, performed and—hopefully—buried in the academy"), which she has read as professional compliment. And this is all set in the ocean-cooled, semitropic poster dream of paradise.

"Things look good out here, Aunt Jo."

We both know that childhood friends are dead in the wars, drunk, bankrupt, or, at best, anonymous. She knows the deceptions of the present, this powdery old aunt whose first husband died returning a crosscourt volley from her sexagenarian racket and whose second was struck by a Yellow Cab as he hurried to her summons at Madison and Seventy-second Street.

I press the skin bag under her elbow and lead her where lawn and bluff meet in the line of insane-looking palms (spiky umbrellas, vegetable porcupines). On the beach below, dowitchers snap beaks for red beach ants, waves flush iron gleams. (Their metric genius is something I try and try to figure and employ.)

I hand Aunt Jo into a rattan chair, squat beside her ropy legs, and keep my ear alive. I am figuring a sequence.

Yes, for the other night, after a dismal sixteen months in which my only opus was a setting of Definitions from Hoare's *Shorter Italian-English Dictionary* for Wind Instruments, Radio Static, and Audience Coughs—I tried to be of the brave new laboratory world, and it crippled me—mooning on the beach, watching the murderous oil rigs lit like rubies in the channel, I hit upon Something Grand, Out of the Blue. And, while Velia snored in the double bed, I sat at Sackerville's cypress worktable and sketched the plan, laid down the lines, established a tone row, and worked it all up around a story.

Yes, the opera. In this day and age, surrounded by aleatory gamesmen, vatic pasticheurs of Mozart, phony pholkistes, electronic adolescents, employers of blowtorchers, caged mice, and concrete crapistes, I fell into this antique pit.

And it's no surrealist cop-out, no twigged-out Clarsic (*Carmini Catulli* or miserable Yeats play with less action than a cigarette ad), no neo-Wagnerian Geschwätz but something new, fresh, off the morning paper. Urban dew. In brief, the story's about a police sergeant and a black hooker he woos with precinct and other stories. In particular with the old eighteenth-century story—he's a night-school reader—of the icy bachelor Horace Walpole, blind old Mme. Du Deffand, who loved him hopelessly, and then, decades later, young Mary Berry, whom the old Walpole loved and who milked him of his wit and knowledge as he had milked the old Deffand. Girl and cop conjure between them the characters, who show up on scrims, on a screen, and on the stage (like the Czechs). The musical lines drift with the actors, or, like motifs, fade into other time schemes. No dominant style (the sign of this century), no batting the company into shape. Deffand sounds like Scarlatti and J. C. F. Bach, Walpole like Haydn and early Beethoven, Berry like Beethoven and early Wagner, the sergeant like Arnold Pretty-mount, Igor the Penman, my dear Webern (the musical laser) plus a bit of Elliot C. and Pierre B.; the hooker will swim in every love song, east and west, that can squeeze into the tone row. Yet the lines are never to blur, there are but chordal shadows round the sparse, informative line.

"Sam found marijuana in her drawer last week."

"What?"

Aunt Jo waved at a gold twig in the blue water. Mina on a mattress. "She said everyone takes it."

"Foolish, foolish. Hardly started, they want life to have italics."

"Maybe if you speak to her, Jeffrey. She respects you, you're the artist in the family, she thinks it's wonderful to have a famous cousin." (Aunt Jo received one of the ten *Who's Who in America* my mother bought the year I joined the Kansas morticians and General Electric VPs.)

Gravel scutters—my sequence has dissolved—a car pulls in the driveway. A gray Bentley. Must be a mistake. No.

Donloubie.

Donloubie is the owner of Sackerville's place. He has come on a mission, foolish and remote as himself.

"Murder."

Two days before, this golden corner had suffered its first Caucasian murder in ten years. Donloubie's neighbor, Mrs. Joel, the candy maker's wife, was found under the closed lid of a heated swimming pool (ten yards back from the Pacific).

Donloubie is hunched, muscular, immensely rich, is said to own much of Columbus, Georgia, his wife a goodly portion of Jacksonville, Florida. The Santa Barbara story is they met and married to stretch their demesnes until they touched. Mrs. Donloubie has contrived the Theory of Three. The week before, Slochum, a broker, was found at the foot of stone stairs in a pool of his blood. Now Lydia Joel. "Who'll be the third?" ask the Donloubies. (Slochum was drunk, fell and broke his own neck.) The Donloubies tremble. They alert housemaids and chauffeurs to departure. But can they depart? Their neighbor has been found floating in eighty-five-degree water, gray head bashed with un-known instrument. They cannot flee the coop, despite the fabulous tracts of Florida and Georgia which underwrite their Bentleys and their orchid garden.

Donloubie comes to his tenant's tenant. I am a university professor, the only one he has ever known. The university conjures up for him the investigation of exotic fauna. Can I suggest a way of getting so-phisticated sleuths into the case past the befogged and bungling local officers? "Perhaps your criminologists up there." He means the Uni-versity of California at Santa Barbara. Doesn't he know I am as remote as can be from university life, that I am a summer-quarter visitor, that I know no one but two colleagues in the music department and a few student instrumentalists and composers in the egg? The Donloubies have lawyers, brilliant manipulators of their tax returns and real estate transactions. Is he afraid to let them know his home touches a house of violence, that he himself has been questioned by police?

Donloubie appears on our—his, Sackerville's—lawn with his Japanese chauffeur, who carries a tremendous basket of fruit. Nec-tarines, peaches, plums, Kadota figs, Persian melons, a pair of gold-en scissors agleam within a leathery grapple of dates. Aunt Jo rises in tribute to this gorgeous heap. Donloubie, unknown to her a minute earlier, has *sur le champ* become a Personage of Note, a fu-ture embellishment of her litany of triumph. She receives him, I am sent for a chair and shout Jeff-U off the Angel baseball game to fetch it. (Argument coagulates in his long face. He is invited to stay, his so-cial charm contrives important business with the National Broad-casting Company.)

Donloubie gives a nervous appraisal of this half-forgotten sliver of his holdings, frowns at an active sprinkler on the south lawn, an unshaven quality in the wall of honeysuckle—I see anew with his landowner's severe eye—but he is on deeper business, he hardly knows what. His gray-blond haycock, his reddish eyes, his sixty years of salted tan, his beauteous chestnut sport coat and fifty-dollar Charvet shirt command the lawn.

Did I know, he begins, that Mrs. Joel had had eight housekeepers since the first of January, that she was a vicious, half-mad woman, that Mr. Joel, slavish in devotion though he was, was on the verge of having her committed, that he had begged him, Donloubie, to keep an eye out on her while he, Joel, gallivanted? Yes, indeed, and the blond cock of hair tossed but did not—a wig?—waver in the air, old Joel had greater interests than in, ha-ha, Tootsie Rolls; for a man of seventy-six, Joel was in—if the missus will excuse the phrase—terrific sexual form, that if he, Donloubie, were not an old acquaintance—not friend, mind you—and had he not received a call from the man at the very time the miserable woman was having her head beaten in, he, Donloubie, would look very closely at Mr. Joel's whereabouts.

Fascinating, but where do I fit in?

—Well, I thought you ought to know, for one thing. I feel responsible as your (pause) host.

Very nice, but isn't—

Yes, perhaps, but I was from a city where they—as it were—specialized in murder, and therefore, surely, in its investigation. Then, too, I was in contact at the university with all sorts of knowledgeable types. He was not entirely persuaded about local competence in these matters, and since he and Mrs. D. were friends of the deceased, if one could be a friend of a totally disagreeable woman who so antagonized her servants that they dropped off like leaves—though, oddly, the present housekeeper, a rather genteel woman, by the by, had stayed more than three months—at any rate, as neighbors, friends, and, too, people who both were obligated elsewhere yet felt they could not leave until at least the preliminary matters were cleared up, they wanted to bring in proper investigators. I, surely, or, at least, *perhaps,* could help them find someone, either in Chicago or at the university.

Strange, but it was a glorious basket of fruit, and the man did not summon me to write a dirge for the dead woman—I was once offered such a commission, as if my lyric mathematics could serve an antique ritual—he was clearly anxious to talk, yet nervous about talking to Mrs. Erwin or any of the very few locals he deigned to talk to, or who deigned to talk with him. It wasn't clear how Donloubie—strange name—perhaps a Creole—came to own Columbus, Georgia (if he did). In fact, it occurred to me then and there that his wealth was squeezed out of young girls' thighs and bloody needles in the port streets of Marseilles and Genoa, and that he was damn scared the dumb locals might dig up this history, that even the local rag would publish it, and that, who knows, he would have to give up the Pacific villa he'd chosen to live and die in. I had better try out those dates on the neighbors' cat.

"The missus and I would like you and yours to come for a drink this evening."

Sorry, pressure of society—we are invited to a party—ditto tomorrow—no party—but he is unstoppable. "Monday, then."

"Splendid."

Aunt Jo shines with solution. "Jeffrey, call the FBI."

Donloubie's tan fingers sink to the basket of fruit, grip a melon, raise and jam it against the dates. "Missus. Donloubie learned to dial a phone some years ago."

The cock of hair waves, the red-pit eyes shiver, the mustard sport coat and hundred-dollar beige slacks rise from the rattan. "See you Monday, Professor. A strategy session."

"I'll be there, Mr. D., don't worry."

"Donloubie don't worry, Professor."

"And thanks for the fruit."

"Enjoy it in health. Good day, missus."

The chauffeur is spun from the house, where he and Jeff-U have divided the misery of the California Angels.

I too have had it, the breathy clucks of the old aunt, the local bloodshed, the noise rising up the bluff. "Aunt Jo, will you excuse me a bit? I've got to," and left hand is up to tap the hair above the ear. The composer's aunt understands.

Past Jeff-U and the cleaning Velia into the bedroom, where the Muse has stripped her toga and where, conjuring up the golden body of the impossible cousin, the composer pours generative sap across Sackerville's rough sheets.

The Party

That is, a select company invited to participate in some form of amusement.

Tonight's amusement: musical assassination.

The company: Davidov and Mullidyne, the university musicologists and their wives; Donald Taylor, my old sidekick from Hindemith's harmony class at New Haven. Invited, but not attending: a Montenegrin serialist employed by the Disney Studios; Mme. Hortense Reilly, local alto and graduate of Mme. Lotte Lehmann's Santa Barbara master classes; and Benedict Krappell, sociologist, emeritus, whose musical credentials were playing double bass for Damrosch in the twenties to support—his words—his academic habit.

The inviter/selector: Franklin S. Ritt, an ex–Morgan Stanley broker and active patron of the arts whom I'd met in a Spanish museum five years ago and with whom I have been semiannually afflicted ever since. (Ritt takes no planes and stops off in Chicago changing trains.)

The ostensible purpose of the gathering was to introduce me to the musical high life of the area. As I already knew Mullidyne, Davidov, Krappell, and Donald Taylor, that left the Montenegrin, Miss Reilly, and Mrs. Ritt, a woman of either great discretion or puissant ignorance. Between "I'm so glad at last" and "So sorry your wife," she said not a word.

Of course, in such company, it didn't show.

"They all know your work," said Ritt in telephonic invitation. Stunned by this rare celebrity, I did not sufficiently examine the reticence of the verb.

Velia does not take much stock in human variety and seldom goes to parties. Besides, her small capacity was exhausted by the Angeleno Wendts. "I'm not going. It'll be one more hellish evening cutting down every absent musician in the world."

This is not my line. An exception to the celebrated viciousness of my fellow craftsmen, a good piece from them gets a loud cheer from me. "Perhaps La Mullidyne will have some tidings about psychotic blackies, and you can feel at home."

"That's sweet talk in front of Gus." (Gus is fathoms deep in a game of solitaire.)

"I said we'd be there at nine. The party's in our honor."

"Your honor."

"I regret the dependent state of the second sex, Velia, but you'll have to play along with it till the kindergartners have had their day. You can star tonight: you're two thousand miles closer to hot gossip than they."

"I don't feel like starring. I don't feel like going."

I fear — to the point of idolatry — the unreason of women. "Come on, Vee, it'll put color in your cheeks."

"If I'm so pale, I'd better not show myself. I don't want to humiliate you."

The bee's suicidal aggression is one of the pathetic drives of nature. And poor Vee's.

> *La pauvre femme n'est pas méchante.*
> *Elle souffre, tu sais, d'une détente.*

This in the bathroom getting on a maroon turtleneck (cotton, to spare myself in heat and pocket) and California sport coat, a rose-and-magenta plaid. Large teeth white in the sunlit skin, blue-black eyes, remnants of black hair, I conjure irresistibility out of the mirror. Though who'll be there to resist? Draggy crones, perhaps one with splendid legs and chest, a wrinkled Frau Musicologue who'll drop her lip my way and, *piano piano,* "Call, I'm in the book."

To Jeff-U, in his sixth straight hour before the enchanted glass: "Get your arse erect and go play Casino with Mom." Rage and disdain darken his long face. "I thought you were going to read *The Possessed.* A whole month, and you're still in part one. Gina read *Martin Chuzzlewit* in two days, she's halfway through *Children of Sánchez,* and you can't fight your way off page sixty-five."

"I don't feel like reading."

"Then write. I bought you that notebook for graduation."

"Whyn't you get off my back?"

"Oh, that's lovely filial talk. Once more, and I'll whack the indolence off your bony hide."

Jeff-U is mortified by skinniness. Strong and good-looking, he feels he has to knock everybody dead with perfection. Horrific vanity of adolescence. Now and then I look at Erikson or some other Guide to

Life's Hard Stages and muzzle my particular fury in generic analysis. Not tonight. "You get no back talk from NBC. No criticism, no testing. That's the source of your infatuation with that machine," and I slap the button which blanks the screen. Jeff-U continues staring at it. "*Amour impropre.* Your mind'll sink so snake low it'll be unable to rise. You'll perish an idiot. A McLuhanite bum. And looka the mess here." Moated by a carton of orange sherbet, the butts of four frankfurters, a quarter-filled bowl of tuna fish (he never finishes anything), pear cores, two cans of Pepsi (he must have bought them himself). "What a spectacular bloom of human culture."

"Good ni-ight, Dad," D gliding to B-flat. Softening my heart, transposing the exchange. A dear boy, wiser than his savage pa, and no power-mad know-it-all, no instant-revolutionary pimpled Robespierre shrieker, no louse-ridden Speed lapper, hardly a drinker (innocent fifth of vermouth in his closet, beer to fatten up), not even a bad driver. Only vanity, sloth, and narcissism blot him. "All right. Take it easy," and I pull out the button of the magic casement.

Why does the party count? I suppose for the musical jaws within which lay Patricia Davidov.

Another tale of Middle-Class Adultery (Genus: The Academy; Species: Music). Human beings have comparatively few ways to express themselves. We swim in a sexual sea, we measure our affective lives by sexuality. Patricia Davidov was the yeast of *Walpole's Love.* Or, at least, what happened with her was partial expression of what it also partially expressed.

She was there, a long, golden, big-boned woman, and across from her, the dark-faced, sandal-wearing, tieless, white-toothed megaphone and music hater, Davidov, author of *The Blindness of Donald Tovey, the Deafness of Ludwig Beethoven.* (Democratic hater of titles, Davidov removed Sir Donald's "Sir" and, ignorant lout, Beethoven's plebeian — Dutch — "van.") His dissertation, bound in the black spring binder which constituted its only public presence (i.e., it was never, could never be published, except by a vanity press, which Davidov's vanity would prevent his using), this dissertation graced my desk the entire summer and was returned in a manila envelope, unread, to Davidov's box. Unread, except for certain comic dip-ins, here and there, when this musical wild man lashed the finest noncomposer analyst in English or, yes, emptied the cerebral intestine which substituted for his neural matter upon the sublimities of opera 109, 111, and 131. Davidov's egoism permitted him to struggle against only the greatest. (The drunkest punk takes on the greatest gun of the west. Except that Davidov had not been shot down, could not be, for he was down to begin with, could hardly have reached lower depths.)

We sat amid Ritt's collection. This fantastic assemblage of the abortions, blotches, and illegitimacies of grandeur needs a word. In Ritt's hillside house, an immense stucco garage affair, this insanely penny-pinching prodigal had collected or piled every cut-rate piece of artistic junk his wide travels had brought him near. There were lithographs by the nephews of Matisse's nurse, oils not of Carraci but of Garraci, dreamscapes not by Redon but Virdon, abstractions done by imprisoned Mensheviks, graffiti from Bombay streets, earrings fashioned from the teeth of Göring's schnauzer. The statistical improbability of so flawless a pile of criminal merde bespoke the kind of genius which marks California. With San Simeon, the Franklin Ritt Collection is the prize of California *Schweinerei*.

In this setting, pictures smeared on walls, clumps of sculpture squatting by perhaps ashtrays, within this prison of creative shit, there were its living voices, Davidov and his junior partner in crime, Francis Mullidyne, and their beautiful wives, one on each side of dear old Donald Taylor (tiny, bespectacled, timid celibate who had deserted the musical zoo for his antique shop in the Paseo and satisfied a scholarly itch by writing articles on eighteenth-century France). (It was his article on Madame Du Deffand which launched my libretto.)

The musicological jaws were biting the throats, ripping the flesh, and drinking the blood of every composer living and dead (with the conspicuously humiliating omission of J. R. C. Wendt). Within the hirsute, vibrant nostrils of Davidov, I read a terrible question: What somatic deficit kept Bach from the proper mode of human expression, murder? What sickness glued Einstein to his numbers, defrauded Shakespeare of dirk and pistol? Where had I gone wrong, squirting out musical sperm instead of poison?

Even Donald Taylor, minute and cyclops eyed behind fishbowl

lenses, was forced from timidity to question the Davidovian Scheme of Musical *Schrecklichkeit*. "I don't follow that bit about Schubert, Bert."

Charmer Davidov responded that if it were a pair of tight trousers, Donald would follow it close enough.

A company gasp, except for the impassive Venus whose Davidov inoculation was renewed each night.

Into the gasp plunged the fury of Wendt. "You're a creep, Davidov. Why Ritt here trots you out as social decoration, I don't know, unless to let his guests enjoy a sight of the sewer. As for me, I've had it," and having calculated that a man with a mouth like Davidov's is probably at least the coward I am and that my extra fifty pounds and six inches will pacify if not tranquilize him, I got up, snarling.

Ritt mentions something about seeing his "latest buy," Donald Taylor says he guesses he'll come with me, Davidov manages, "Wait a mo'. Wait a mo' there, buddy. We gotta talk this thing out," two of the ladies are shivering too much to respond to my farewell nods, the other, the long golden obbligato to the malodorous Davidov, puckers and opens her lips in recognition of the farewell blast, perhaps divining that it was she as much as her husband who excited it.

The Bleeding Jellyfish,
or Masters and Servants

with—for bows to antiquity and other concessionary spice—one epigraph from the saint of English humanism, Dr. S. Johnson: "There is nothing, Sir, too little for so little a creature as man" (which has, with its hidden injunction to the objects of Gallupian inquisition to regard the recalcitrance of small things before blowing stacks of utopian fury, more force in the Age of Gallup than in Dr. J.'s hierarchical time) and, for musicians, another from A. von Webern: "Life, that is to say, the defense of a form."

Or The Persistence of Uoiichh

1

Eight A.M., slow getting started, not from Ritt's select company and bargain booze, but from sheer sludge of time, skeins of fat in blood, layers of surrender stacked in the passage from sleep to waking.

Up, on with shorts scissored from denims shrunk in the Carpinteria Laundro-Mat, haul Gus off the morning cartoons and descend the three tiers of sixty-nine pine steps (only this morning do I notice the pretty mathematics) to the empty beach.

Gus: "You better not run on 'em pockmark things."

—'Em pockmarks is bloodworms.

I avoid them, raise heavy, archless feet and clump up the beach trailed by Gus. When he senses a race and goes into high, my over-reacher's need drives my gross pins, and I beat him by a mile. With frequent stops to assure him that I'm watching his progress, really to mute the hard pumping in my not—quite—unflabbed chest, the diaphragmatic tremor after deep breaths. This morning, I look round from one of my markers, a nude, fallen eucalyptus, and Gus is furiously waving me back, his stickpins flailing the terrific morning air. I lope back, Air-Rider Wendt. Gus, gorgeous, blue-eyed, big-mouthed head split between hysteria and joy, points me to his feet, where lies, sits, squats, a frightful purplish glob of what I would elsewhere take for the fecal deposit of a hippopotamus; or perhaps the aborted hippette itself (gluey within the placenta). Vomitous, wrinkled glob. Uoiichh.

—Look, Daddy, a jellyfish.

Shall such things live?

Closer, one sees incipient differentiae, rubbery pincers, a kind of mouth. Gus nudges it with a eucalyptus prong. The thing gathers itself, wrinkles up for a kind of progress. (Is this what our wrinkles spell?) The pincers shift, the ocean rolls closer, a bubbled fringe breaks round the glob. "It lives," I said. "It's alive."

—I'm going to bring it up to Mom.

—She'll collapse.

—You carry it.

—You're out of your little mind, lovey.

—I'll get the bucket.

—Leave it alone. Let it go back to the ocean.

Which almost happens as the next wave, lapped by its twin, floods the creature and brings it homeward a foot or two.

"I'm gonna get the bucket." Since I have a sweet sight in mind, the presentation of this uoiichh to the sleeping Jeff-U, I say nothing. The little pins mill up the first tier of steps.

I regard this miserable presentation of the sea. Wordsworth had not wasted a cubit of his verse on such as this. Yet it by no means deserved the terrible fate Fellini gave its giant, plastic cousin at the end of that rebuke to (and wallow in) grotesquerie, *La dolce vita*. Among jellyfish, it holds its glob high.

The water embraces it. I pick up Gus's prong and urge it seaward. At which, there issues a squirt of thin, pathetic ink. Gus is back, fist round the loop of a metal bucket. "What happened?" A wave comes up, flushes feet and fish. "Help me, Daddy."

Gus puts the bucket edge on the jellyfish's. An inch of glob is on the metal. And then again, squirt, tiny hemorrhage from hidden wrinkles. "Gus, this jellyfish is bleeding. He's in pain."

Gus laughs at this splendid joke, takes eucalyptus prong in right, bucket in left hand, and tries to fork up glob. Another discharge barely misses his foot.

I take the branch, throw it into the water, and detach his fingers from the bucket. "Leave it be."

Oddly enough, no tantrum. But we run no more, ascend with the story of our discovery to awakened Davy, who doffs pajamas for shorts, runs to the beach, and ascends to tell us he can't find it. What relief, the Wounded Vet has made his way home. (*Histoire d'un Uoiichh*.)

2

On the wall of the Davy/Jeff-U bathroom (unusable toilet) there's a painting, "one of a series by Emil G. Bethke interpreting the world of ophthalmology." This Kandinsky cluster of globes—eye, earth, lens, sun—"illustrates the persistence of roundness, a simple derivative of the roundness of the eye, the solar bodies, and the very instruments with which we examine them." I discharge medusa-shaped phlegm into the sink and meet Herr Bethke's globes. ("Medusa," for I have looked up "jellyfish" in Sackerville's big Webster and seen the picture of the rag-of-bone-hank-of-hair creature named by some witty naturalist.) My yellow-brown glob trailing its thin throat reins supports the thesis of Emil Bethke's art.

Roundness. Persistence. Tonal row. Row nothing. It is roundness, circular. A trap.

In Chicago, the department's musical electrode, Derek Slueter, corners me weekly with the latest advance in musical slavery, "Dumbandeafer's Solipsism for Electro-Encephalograph" (a pianist playing while hooked to the apparatus whose record of his reactions to being hooked dictates what he plays).

I say to Slueter: "I compose for liberation, not tyranny."

Secretive, snaggle-toothed, Jesus-bearded boy, he smears game theory, movies, computers, and synthesizers on our departmental head (and budget). The peace of Santa Barbara is, in no small measure, a Slueterless peace.

Yet today, at the cypress worktable, I sink not into the delicate shoals of my dear Deffand's exchanges with the icy bachelor, but into the calluses, cancerous boles, and labia-shaped knots. One week ago, they drove my fantasies, then me, to the Ali Baba Café on Salsepuedes Street, where I slipped in behind the blue-lit teamsters, soldiers, adolescents, iron-eyed, gray-headed ex-sailors and watched the bumps and jangles of Miranda, the Gaza Stripper, almost stiffened enough to ask the miniskirted dank blond waitress what time she finished. In the living room here there is a table made of a stump of eucalyptus. Its almost flesh-colored (Caucasian) gap faces the couch. I have not been able to joke about it. The persistence of need is a prison.

This morning, everything underlines enclosure: the staves I rule on the white paper, the sharps turning keys which fail to open doors, the annual striations of the cypress, the marine wrinkles raised to purplish bars of cloud. The persistence of uoiichh.

3

We sit, the four of us, Donloubie and his missus, Velia and I, in a stupendous room before fifty feet of treated glass within which preen five miles of crescent beach and untold acres of moon-and-oil-rig-lit ocean.

The room is modeled after the Double Cube at Wilton, but "fifty percent larger," says Donloubie, stranding my small mathematics. A crystal mass, twenty feet above us, draws mild glitter from a hundred gold and silver objects—trays, decanters, dishes, whatnots. Soft light seeps from ivory walls indented with bas-reliefs of mermaids, plastery mock-ups of stonework in the Church of the Miracoli.

We're couched on fifteen curved feet of gold and rose drinking some vodka concoction reddened by a raspberrylike offspring from Donloubie's hothouse. A black-tied, hunched-up butler (not the chauffeur) approaches with heaped tray.

"Ooh," says Missus D., "China Chicks." Butler leans with his great offering, I study the crusted containers of herb and dribblings, reach for a couple, and then—they are so small—as the servant withdraws, reach again, causing him to miscalculate, so that the tray tips and one of the tiny globs falls over the edge to the golden tundra of carpet.

—Swine.

Donloubie, eyes like red ice.

I, momentarily taking this qualifier to myself (who better?), flush, swallow, cough. Butler, hide leathered by frequent whips, mutters apology (to me, Donloubie, or perhaps the injured Chick), scoops, large tray perfectly suspended in one hand—had they recruited him from the defunct Twentieth Century Limited?—and begins a second passage of the Chicks. Persistence of roundness. Velia utters profound thank-yous against Butler's perhaps humiliation. His back, in retreat, humps an extra centimeter, hours nearer its grave.

Masters and servants were having and giving bad times in Santa Barbara. The police had arrested Mrs. Joel's housekeeper, Mrs. Wrightsman. Donloubie: "Not that I blame the woman. Joel said his missus threw her dinners on the floor."

Is the floor Santa Barbara's sacred space?

Perhaps to Mona Wrightsman, who, bent there to retrieve her spurned veal chop, there gathered the final fury of a hundred such rejections, from there rose to the vicious spurner, and, there standing, rage and pan still hot, beat and beat again the thin, hated skull.

Home, I read in Roger Caillois's *Man, Play, and Games* of the romantic toys of boys, the practical toys of girls. Had the child Mona been given miniature skillets? And Butler, had he been given by mistake a broom instead of a three-master? (So China Chicks instead of China Clippers.) And Mrs. Joel, who refused meal after meal, not to find what slaked her appetite, but—Donloubie's version—to fill the day's tyrannic quota. What had her Christmas gifts been? Dolls? Which cried when squeezed? Ninety-five-pound Caesar in rose bathrobe and puffy slippers (Mrs. Wrightsman's doll) to be swatted, sponged, stripped, lifted by those muscular arms, carried to lidded pool, dumped, and lidded up again.

Velia, in rebellious connubial servitude, once again determines nevermore to take master talk from Julius Charlemagne Robespierre Wendt, turns her back to him, and reaches bed edge. Wendt, servant, if not sum, of Appetite and Ambition, conjures up from opposite edge the golden spread of the musical Antichrist Davidov's wife and, breathing, grunting, manacled, and sinking, covets, covets.

Names and Games, Tales and Flails

1

News drifts in muted to our still cove. Plains, mountains, and deserts do something to televised accounts of Cleveland riots, political treks, the Politburo in Prague, or even, just north of us, the trial of Newton, the Black Panther. The palms, the waves, the dowitcher trills, E-flat, G, make it all remote.

Chicago devotee of the *New York Times,* here Velia skims the eight-page *News-Press* and reads California history. She likes to snow me with unexpected expertise and hides her sources under pillows, behind Sackerville's pathetic library or her boxes of Modess. A literary Geiger counter, I find them all. I leave no print unread, cookbooks, cereal boxes, Jeff-U's *Pigskin Prevue,* Davy's *Mad.* From the toilet seat I spot behind the blue economy-size box Professor Bean's *California: An Interpretation* and read how this hundred million acres of mountain, desert, parboiled valley, and paradisal cove received its name from Calafia, queen of California (an "island between India and Paradise"), a black beauty who trained griffins to feed on men. Recruited to fight Amadis of Gaul and his son Esplandian at Constantinople, her winged assistants chewed up both sides. Broken, she turned Christian, married Esplandian's son, and took him back to California. All splendiferously rendered by Garciá Ordóñez de Montalva and read by the deputies of Cortés who sailed up the difficult coast the year after downing Montezuma.

Friday afternoon, for the first time in my daily racket encounters with Jeff-U, my arm could not deliver the cannonballs which plunge him into errors, despair, and double faults. My smart drop shots, volleys, slices, cuts, and crosscourt lobs were countered by confident drives. Jeff-U bounced up and down in wait for my patsy service and swung like his dream of Pancho Gonzales: 6–2, 6–1. I walked off with a dry-mouth whistle, asweat from black eyes to limp crotch, drove wildly home on the freeway, neck too sore to check the approaches, honked at by swerving Jaguars, missing the Serena turnoff and forced to double back from Summerland along the railroad track.

Saturday, after three hours of flubbing Walpole's aria at Mme. Du Deffand's death, music which I must repeat when Mary Berry hears of Walpole's death, I was ready for revenge. I hung around Jeff-U's prostrate form, his immense, bony, but well-made back. (Ah, I thought, I have given him something, Velia's back being a less distinguished feature of her body, curved by some displacement of vertebrae into a flattened S.) The back was being tickled for a penny a minute by Gus and Davy, alternately.

"Wanna play?" asked Jeff-U. Cut-rate Medici of Titillation.

The boys said, "Yes."

I said, "Why not?" and we were off in Sackerville's VW to the beautiful court set in the California oak grove of the Montecito park. There in act 2 of the agon, I lost the first set 6–1, went silently into the second, won the first two games, lost the third out of sheer weakness, not having the strength to serve consistently hard, arm aching with previsioned defeat, lost the next four, and then, going to position on the baseline, heard Jeff-U say his finger was blistering, and "Let's quit," meaning, "We've made the point, why continue?" I left the court silent, trailed by the three boys—the little ones having played during warm-up time—and went in silence home. There, before my shower, I sat down at the little upright I'd rented for our room and worked out with terrific speed a perfect aria. I haven't played it over, haven't dared, but I feel its rightness, its place in the score, its power, felt its words (a line of French, then one of English) as the sybaritic bachelor imagines writing a letter to the dead woman who, from the screen, interprets his words in such a way that they drive small, elegant stakes into her heart.

The explosion—to use the word which in the 1960s stands for every exacerbated encounter, chemical or human, mental or physical—the explosion at Jeff-U came out of the void the next day, an hour before he is to call for Ollendorf (who changed flights at the last minute and arrived a day early). "Better put clean sheets on his bed," said I.

"OK." He gets up, surprising me a bit by the speed of his accession. "I'll put one sheet on."

—Better put two.

—He's my friend. I know what he wants.

I get up and follow him to the linen closet. "Take two, please. Your mother and I are his hosts, it's up to us to see things are done right."

—Bullshit.

I take this in stance for a bit. He has gone inside with the two sheets. I follow, notice his bathtub is filled with sand. "I've asked you to keep the sand out of that bathtub."

—That's Davy. He comes in the back way, washes his feet in there every day, five times a day, and the sand just stays there.

"Will you clean it out please before you go?" My words are polite, but, Walpole-like, there is the undercurrent of menace in them.

—Let Davy do it.

"I realize you've had a tough day, a tough six weeks," I say. "I know you're exhausted from having your back tickled, but I want you to clean it, so your mother doesn't have to further twist her back doing it herself."

"Eff-u," says Jeff-U. Despite almost universal literary freedom, I am a child of repression in print and usually refrain from writing out what is a not infrequent presence in my speech. (Let the Edwardian guff of this sentence express my feeling.)

I approach him, eyes aglitter with rage. "You say that to me once more, and I'll knock the living crap out of you."

His eyes show scare, but he forces his voice through it. "You better not hit me. Ever again."

At which, the rage of days touched off, I shove him across the room onto the bed. He yells, his legs, very long legs, sneakered, start kicking wildly, pumping him up. I crowd him, daring more violent response, "You effing bastard" is the response.

I punch his arm hard.

He leaps up, I punch and miss, he gets out the door, and now amazed (for I've never hit him like this), as well as fearful and furious, he calls to the closed door of our room, "Cmere, Mom, cmere, Dad's trying to *hurt* me."

And I, hearing the wonder in this, O brave new world that has this in it, feel my fire flooded, doused, and think, My God, this is Jeff-U, little beauty boy whom I showed off to Mlle. Boulanger in Paris (a picture keeps this memory refreshed), to whom I gave milk bottles in Cologne reciting the *Inferno,* singing the *Well-Tempered Clavichord,* dear companion and confidant, and he is just learning that I am —*was!* —trying to hurt him.

I stride out, whisper in the muted menace voice of Jimmy Cagney (fellow alumnus of Stuyvesant High School, along with Lewis Mumford and Daniel Bell), "Don't upset me like that again, Jeffrey. Never again."

"I'm not upset," he says.

My rage starts up, my tone rests monotonous. "You haven't the emotional richness of a pebble," and go into the bathroom, heart throbbing terribly, mind so swept with self-disgust, disgust at Jeff-U, disgust at my violent failure as a father, I'm unable to speak to him with any ease at all for four or five days, even with Ollendorf there. (Ollendorf turns out to be a jolly, decent boy, who comes in on a happy roar and jokes the entire two weeks he remains.)

2

Velia has accepted an invitation to a "peacemaking" dinner at the Mullidynes.

"Why did you accept?" I yell. "You know I can't see people when I'm working."

Not quite true, sometimes I have to see them. "Is that effer Davidov coming?"

"I assume that's what the peacemaking is about," said Velia, who has had a triumphant version of my squelch, without, of course, its sexual basso-relievo.

The Mullidynes live in the hills on the lip of a desert. Donald Taylor drives us up in Ryan, his convertible (bought from a man named Ryan who never put the top down but liked the style of convertibles). The drive is up the Riviera, Santa Barbara spread out like a cupful of Genoa, then into the strange broken mocha-colored hills nudging and nuzzling each other, the most artful, Cézanne-looking hills I've ever seen (and I was once in Aix-en-Provence for the playing of the *Drang Nach Bach* songs, my opus 9).

All the way, the body of Patricia Davidov rises from those hills to calm the agitation raised by the menacing apparition of her husband.

But when we arrive at Mullidyne's house—a fine eyebrow on a noble hill—the Davidovs are not there. Nor do they come. Had he refused? Or had Mullidyne managed to unhinge his lower jaw? (The evening supplied the answer.)

Mullidyne is quite decent out of Davidov's presence. And his wife turns out to be quite remarkable, very long and soft and smart, a cabinetmaker, fisherman, linguist, mother of an immense, well-mannered, and—tonight—inconspicuous brood, an honest person who does not press for intimacy yet is quickly your intimate. (Life—she seems to say—is too short for anything else.) Finally, a marvelous cook. We have a terrific kidney dish. I see the Escoffier open in the kitchen, it must be number 1339, *Turban de Rognons à la Piemontaise,* "Fill a ring with *rizotto à la Piemontaise* (2258), press into the mold and keep hot." And, after, marvelous melon balls and strawberries from the valley. Says Sandra, in a voice you would expect a rose to have, "I wanted to have valley grapes in hard sauce, but Chávez has called for a boycott of table grapes. I don't dare buy them." Velia, who has just lugged home a mountain of green grapes, receives a punishing stare from me and says, "I'm not a Californian."

"Don't buy them again," say I, though kindly. Velia has a new dress, a Finnish print (she has read the Finns have learned to stain materials a new way), full of blue and yellow balls and great stripes, a kind of sack but better formed, light, but you know (she says) you've got something on, a knockout, it almost restores her looks. (She had them, her legs are very fine, her body thin, but neat; but that's over.)

It is a night for stories. Of a pattern, as I see it four hours later, riding down the hill in the dark, each story so much more final in its way than a tennis match. (Though who knows. The people involved may have emerged from the fierce predicaments in which our memory abandoned them.)

The one that tells for me is about the Davidovs, but its trailer, another account of domestic fury, also stays. It's Sandra's psychology professor at Duke, a man who, infected with J. B. Rhinitis, took to a Jungian strain of it, the so-called "substratum of certain memories which were 'not one's own,'" the apparent ability of some semimesmerized people to "recall" experiences of psychic ancestors, "Bridie Murphys," or "Viennese court ladies." His wife, a student of cell conductivity in frogs, expressed the contempt a lifetime's Scotch-Presbyterianism had schooled her never to express by telling him that she too had strange inklings of an antecedent life. "Oh yes?" he said, from his worldly, husband side. "Were you a cigar butt in Sir Walter Raleigh's mouth?" But weeks later, short of a willing subject, he decided he had perhaps overlooked a local treasure and asked if she were still smoldering in Raleigh's jaws.

"No," she said, "but I was bending over the microscope last week when I had the strangest feeling that I was gathering fernshoots by a river with a name I knew deeply but which now sounds strange to even pronounce." She had never used, and he had never heard, the word "fernshoots" before.

He removed his Roi-tan from the ashtray, inhaled for steadiness, and asked what name that was. "Huai," she said.

"I'm curious, why do you think?"

"The River Huai," she said. "A broad river curling around a kind of cape of firlike trees."

"We can begin tonight," he said and had her lie back on a couch and switched on his tape recorder. There she registered her month's secretive research into fourth-century Chinese history. She was, she said, a Sinic farm girl living near river fortifications worried by Sienpi troops; her father, Li Huang-ti, grumbled in Chinese—she'd spent twenty hours in the language lab, playing the records—about taking his turn as sentry on the wall. (Sandra's account was more detailed.)

The Jungian husband, blank, like most of us, to any Chinese history between Confucius and Sun Yat-sen, had the notes transcribed and taken to the American professor of "Chinese Civilization: A Survey," not at first revealing the extraordinary source, but when told that, yes, there was such a river, there was a repulsion of nomadic invasion attempts in the fourth century, said, "It's my wife," and asked if the strange sounds that issued from her were authentic Chinese. "I've never bothered speaking it," said the scholar. "Though I pick out what might be a few words. But here," and he smudged out a few characters, "see if she knows these characters. I'll transcribe the English sounds for you." That night, the Chinese peasant girl disclaimed ability to read, that was only for administrators of the rites.

So it went for weeks, until a book-length monograph was transcribed from the tapes, the West Virginia farm girl translating more of her feeling into fourth-century China than she had ever revealed on her own. Her husband was enchanted with this metamorphosis of dogged student of cell conductivity into naively sensuous Chinese village girl (raped by Uncle Su-i Chen, taken up as concubine by a weaver from Shang-Chi, dying of a sexually ignited pneumonia)—all mimicked on the green Grand Rapids sofa while he, the rapt psychologist, fell away from all his domineering cynicism and behavioral training. After he submitted the manuscript with full complement of annotation to not the *Journal of Parapsychology* but Basic Books, his wife told him over his four-minute eggs that she'd played this little joke on him, she thought it was the way to lead him back to proper experimental work, some of the books she'd used were in the upper shelf of the linen closet, would he perhaps return them to the library, they were overdue, and his first class was nearer to it than her lab, she would bring him home a nice sirloin for supper.

When she came home that night, he had not left the chair, she drove him to the hospital, and when, six weeks later, he came out, the term was over and she had gone.

Watching Sandra stroke her husband's browless little head (tactile conclusion to this gruesome tale), I thought, Aha, this soft jewel of a woman, this fruit goddess with her great bowl of rose and golden balls, has suffered terrible blows somewhere. Mullidyne is her rock. He must have his facet of tenderness as she must have hers of toad. Soft jewel with toad in head. Such beauteous carats congeal only from secreted poison. Brutal father. Psychopathic mother.

"Tell about Davidov and Pat," she told Mullidyne in her lovely voice and, in white virgin's dress, passed the crystal bowl of strawberries and melon balls. Behind her, a great window showed night squeezing a line of sun-fire against the blunt point of the hill. "Davidov," said Mullidyne, and laughed. "Davidov." And with what one then could see was indeed a bit of forehead, contrived a wrinkle or two of frown.

Davidov, he said, sprang from the bowels of the Brooklyn ghetto. Ugly, squat, an atheist broken from an orthodox cigar roller's home, "saved for scholarship" by the public library, where, each week, he read B. II. Haggin in *The Nation* and resolved to study music, not for love of music—"He's next to tone deaf"—but for love of the destruction he sensed—wrongly—in Haggin's devastating columns. Native shrewdness sent him to the top of Boys' High and into City College. In '42, despite feeble vision and flat feet, he was drafted, pulled like a rodent from New York, and sent, dazzled by fear, to a Kansas army camp, where he stayed, goldbricking and clerking. Knowing he'd need proficiency in an instrument to pursue musical studies, he got a local drummer to teach him the tympani. In '45, he was transferred to San Francisco, and aimed like a broken arrow for the Japanese invasion, but, with Hiroshima and the end of the war, was discharged in Oakland. He walked over to Berkeley, enrolled with his GI Bill, and became the first World War II veteran to get a doctorate in music, his dissertation, *The Failure of Opus 109: An Analysis of Tovey's Critical*

Blindness and Beethoven's Musical Deafness. (The manuscript on my office desk had been revised for a publication that was never to be.)

In Berkeley, he taught two freshman musical appreciation classes. Enrolled in one, and soon auditing the other, was a beautiful coed from the Napa Valley named Patricia Mulholland, the poor, smart daughter of a workman in the Mondavi bottling plant at St. Helena, a cousin of the Los Angeles aqueduct builder. That this long, great-titted, golden beauty with a famous California name should be hanging on every word dropped from his muzzle (my memory has altered Mullidyne's more straightforward vocabulary) so intoxicated Davidov that his lectures became wilder and wilder, more and more notorious. The destruction of every musical reputation past and present fused with the discovery of sexual perversity or ineptitude in nine-tenths of the great composers of musical history. He called the fusion the Myth of the Castrated Orpheus. It had the postwar coeds slavering at his very name. But Pat was there first, and with the most, and, age seventeen, she let her untouched cup run over the parched, violent instructor. With the ferocity of a miser, he whisked her down to city hall, wrote Davidov after her name, and within a month had impregnated her with the first of their five children, two sons who but faintly darkened the generous gold of Mulholland genes, three daughters who stooped under the squat Davidovian darkness. And down the coast they moved to Santa Barbara's new campus, where he took over as chairman—though then but assistant professor—of the music department.

Here revolts began. First, his colleagues protested his tyranny, obstinacy, and musical ignorance to the chancellor of the university, who removed him from the chairmanship and threatened to withhold tenure unless he mended his tattered ways, and then Patricia, who told him that she loathed him more than any human being could be loathed, felt she was married to the devil himself, and was now ready to have affairs on any street corner with any man who'd deign to look by her ever-swelling belly to the great promise of her never-fulfilled-by-Davidov interior.

Under these twin assaults, Davidov, like rotten wood, broke apart. While Pat picked up astonished flutists in his own department, took them to motels, paid the bills, and shed her extraordinary graces on their graceless heads (this from the unbeautiful, browless Mullidyne), Davidov stayed in the hot mesa apartment, warming the bottles, changing the diapers, driving the kids to school, and hiring sitters when he had to stagger to the university to give his but slightly less fiery lectures on the febrile contortions of Handel and Pergolesi. At night, he would call down the list of graduate students till he traced Pat's lover of the day and beg him to release her for the night. Then, said Mullidyne, he found me at Alabama, liked my little article in *Musical Quarterly* on the "harmonic blunders in *Le Nozze de Figaro,*" brought me here, and then, from the moment I arrived, poured into my ear his tribulations with Pat, with the department, with the life he led, he, the great Davidov, who should be shaping the strong intellects of men who would rewrite musical history, transform the flaccidity of contemporary composers and performers, and water this Sahara of the Arts with the kind of criticism which had lifted literature from caveman grunts to the heights of Miller, Dahlberg, and Selby. "I," said Mullidyne, "who had my friend, Sandra, waiting here at the hearth for me, though we were on Anacapa Street then, couldn't tear myself away until Pat would grind up in their Pontiac—exhausted but triumphant—and brush past poor Davidov with, 'Did you remember to put the vitamins in Gloria's bottle?' "

What vengeance. Yet if she hated him, she hated herself worse. (This seemed reasonable to even Pat-lusting me.) "Sash here had to go to her sister's funeral and take care of her kids for two weeks; and Pat was on my doorstep every time I came back from class. 'I've told Bert I'm here, he's not to bother you,' and she'd lie on the couch, shoes off— she has beautiful feet, kind of thick ankles but terrific legs, I nearly went out of my frigging mind. She begged me to run away with her, I should leave Sash—Sash knows this—Sash, she said, was too soft for a man of my mettle, whereas she'd become hard on Davidov's brutality, she was basically soft as Sash but would stand up to me, improve me. And I'd just shake my head and say I wish she were happy but couldn't she make it for her children, if not for Bert. And she said, 'They have his heart. They can think of nothing but what's in front of them. Or worse, what's in front of each other. They live to eat, they lie around, they have no curiosity.' But I couldn't believe it, I thought the children amazingly good in view of what was happening in the home, helpful to their father, sympathizing with him, yet, as far as I could see, not harsh to their mother. And then she'd go, and half an hour later, Bert would call and ask what did she say, what did she do, and I would say, 'Please keep her away from me, she just complains of her unhappiness, she's such a child it's tragic.' And he'd say, 'Just let her talk to you for a bit, it's better than her picking up these bastards in the street, maybe she'll talk herself out of it. At home, she never says anything, she never talked, ever, except dumb-ass women's questions, why this and why that, why's the ground down, why's the sky up, and I'd have to knock the shit out of her, here she'd been my own student, I'd given her a couple of As, I still think she earned them, but she was probably just giving me back my own words and I was so blinded by my putz I didn't see what I was getting into, Jesus Christ, I wasn't made for this, Frankie,' and on and on, till I'd say, 'Bertie, I've got to go to sleep, Sash is calling me and forgive me.' He'd scream, 'You effing pig sticker, you're nothing but a mouse-brain pig sticker, I saved you from George Wallace and pellagra and you can't give me the time of day, you're an effing sonovabitch' and so on until the next day, or maybe two days later, he wouldn't call, but he'd know what time I went to pick up my mail, and he'd bump into me, and say, 'Francis, I was wrong, you and I are the same type, we're both married to dumb pigs, we both know music, we oughtn't to quarrel.' And it would start all over again."

Sandra, on the couch by her husband, smiled as if she'd not heard this story, as if her husband had repulsed the proffered detente with, "Don't say my wife's a pig. Or even yours."

"But she's still with him," said Velia. "I saw them holding hands downtown in the Paseo." (And my heart bumped in fury, at Velia, at Davidov, at Patricia.)

"What happened," said Mullidyne, "was some kind of contract he made with her. He let her have a round-the-world trip, and in the interval, he built her this house on the shore, it must have cost him sixty thousand even seven years ago, and he hardly had a nickel. He taught night classes, lectured all over, though nobody's ever heard of him, he wrote book reviews at twenty dollars a shot, not even taking time to open the books, just pouring them out, on any subject, he did a stint on the roads in the summer—he's still got muscles under that flab— everything, and she came back after four months and she's stayed down there and I haven't been asked once, and though I see her at parties, it's one nod and good-bye, and that's the way its been for seven years. Oddly enough, I still care for him. And for her. He's a brute, yes, but he's got standards. He cares deeply. He thinks, maybe wildly, but how many think at all?"

Snaking down the Marcos Pass in Ryan, Donald Taylor, as if reborn in the foam of these passionate stories, said, "My God, how can Mullidyne take him? How can he go on all these years with all that he knows about him?"

"He has to have his misery vitamins every day. Maybe to have something to amuse that great wife of his," I said, taking a look from mine.

My bed reading in dear Deffand's letters offered a better answer. Wrote the old poison pen about Buffon, the naturalist, "*il ne s'occupe que des bêtes; il faut l'être un peu soi-même.*"

Gradations of Effing

1

That night, stimulated by this storied bowl of untasted goodies, I slept with my dear wife for the first time in a month. A certain, special pleasure, old acquaintance newly met, though with P.D.'s imagined opulence fresh on my mental bones, I was scarcely replete after the short-order feast. (Of course the polar breeze of imagined betrayal gave its own zing of sadness and soft revenge; what a rummage sale sex is.)

In the Tacitean tradition, my Walpole was a great comparer; sure footed, though procrustean. This morning, while the lawn sprinkler makes instant rainbows in its whirl, and there is otherwise a stillness in pine, palm, and fir, it strikes me I want a musical comparison between such elegance of gradation and the rough-hewn, grandly uncertain gradation of my own mind. Music has splendid means of articulating such contrasts. I think my opera may be about the difference between

oceanic passion and terrene order; policeman and prostitute, each a social control for other people's passion, summon up Walpole and Mme.
Du Deffand to control their own. Something like that.

But it's not enough. Judgment and action live on fine-honed distinctions; verbal ones. ("Galba had the capacity to rule, if only he
hadn't." — Tacitus; "Pitt liked the dignity of despotism, Mansfield, the
reality." — Walpole.) Velia and the thought of Patricia offer different
things. What to choose? (Maybe the policemen should fall in love with
Madame Du Deffand. Like the detective in *Laura*.)

I'd waked up choked with such thought; or, not choked, soaked. In
that estuary in-between state, I heard a thickening of line, a gulf of
bass, E C-sharp D D-flat. Pressure: and into mind Voltaire called out
by Rohan's bullies, beaten in the street, Rohan, chaired, saying, "Spare
the head. It can still amuse us," the crowd watching Voltaire, bleeding,
mad with fury and astonishment, the crowd saying of Rohan, "Oh,
that was decent. *Le bon seigneur.*" "Enough," says Rohan. Voltaire, up,
body, long, bemudded, back to the drawing room, where he had been
the light of the company, answering their gaping faces with his story,
seeing them freeze, sympathetic emotion not available for the likes of
him; a solo bassoon, staggering in fifths, a clutch of cello, a slash of violin, and then, orchestral rumbling, a small structure building. From
this day, Voltaire's dazzle will burn, the Revolution is ten years nearer.

Pressure. In the bed, a sense of leg, Velia's. I roll over, leave an in-
terposed valley of blanket; the leg shifts away. Cold, dangerous, selfish,
womb raddled, public minded, hating.

Yesterday, in the San Ysidro Pharmacy, buying wine, I waited by
the magazines till the afternoon *News-Press* arrived with the latest on
the Joel case. By the fifteen-dollar cribbage boards and Japanese television sets for the beach, a barefoot girl, with fantastic legs and rear.
Bare armed, face pale, blond, a little blunted, but with that sense in the
nostrils and mouth that she wanted someone. Her breasts. No great
matter, but there, in an easy flowered blouse. White pants, a bit cozy
for her beauteous rump. Wrenching legs. I looked up from *Scientific
American* and caught her sense of being looked at. She came back, examined the paperbacks. Had she ever gone through a book? She came
to the magazines. In a minute, I turned and brushed her arm. How
old? Statutory rape age. I couldn't tell. Hopefully eighteen, more hope-

fully twenty, but not unlikely, fifteen, sixteen. Too young, even in this new world where anything goes, where anything that can be called love is applauded—cows, leaves, watermelons, Krafft-Ebing sweetened for mass production—like Château Laflute made out of horse blood, cow urine, and the discarded skins of Marseilles grapes. The Revolution's won, we are all privileged, it is not kitsch, mass culture is for real, though it is plain style for all. I stoop for *Life,* my bare arm, tanned beneath short shirt, feathers the fantastic leg. All I need is "Can I give you a lift?" or "Shall we?" or "Let's go outside" or "I'll be in the VW." I have Sackerville's plates, I'll use a version of his name. There is a whole string of new motels, half empty. Or, hell, in the fields, bugs crawling in us. *Life* has investigations of Masaryk's defenestration, and of thalidomide children learning to cope, a crack at American doctors who didn't know about the Heidelberg clinic where the child learns how to zip, walk, eat, and, as they put it, "toilet himself." Why doesn't every doctor call into the World Health O., which has all the stuff on a computer? Like that Hemingway story of the doctor who carries the guide to medicine indexed for symptoms and treatment. *Life* quotes one of the benevolently lethal Rostow brothers: never a time when so great a percentage spent on armament, yet Donald Taylor told me we're almost back at the Renaissance, when the Napiers and da Vincis refused to publish their lethal inventions. Only vacant-minded puritans and bright tinkerers will work on weapons. But there's the rub. I stoop again, the leg is there. I take my seven-buck Château Lafitte and depart. I will not be refused, I will not be arrested. (I know the symptoms and the treatment, I will stick with my disease.)

2

I look up Davidov in the faculty list, dial, but hang up before the tone, then sit by the phone and look at the eucalyptus, a huge salmon, its terrible insides exposed by the old fire bolt. I ring again.

A child's voice: "Davidov residence."

—May I please speak with Mrs. Davidov?

A flash of music, a terrific theme. I leaped to score paper, phone stretched in left hand, pencil notes, De, dom, dom, dom, de, da-da, dada, da-da, dee de dom. Heavenly, and then more, a flood, transpose, shift, work in the tonic, a depth of brass, a figure.

—Yes? Yes? Who is it?

—Pat?

—Yes. Who's this?

Sigh: Defenestration of Inspiration. "It's Jeff Wendt."

"Oh. Didn't think I'd hear from you." Meaning?

—I want to talk to you. Not to Bert. Just you. Think we can manage that?

Pause. "Mmm." I was in.

—Your body's on my mind. I want to see it. I want to see you. I can hardly wait.

—Mmm.

—Can you meet me at the Safeway in fifteen minutes?

—Half an hour.

—I'll be there in fifteen minutes, in a yellow VW. I'll park as far from the store as I can, in the southeast part of the lot.

—I can't figure directions.

—I'll see you. What'll you be driving?

—A beat-up powder-blue Ford station wagon.

—I can't wait to see you. So long.

—Good-bye.

I haven't shaved. I haven't shat. Bowels crucial. At home, I shave, shit, and read at once. Velia has taken a picture of the three-ring activity. If I write a sequel to this memoir, in the new age of freedom, it will be the dust jacket. Here, the plug is too far from the toilet. I first squat. (The equalizer: Shelley, the Kennedys, Bonaparte, Walpole, Anaximander; Thales fell into a pile of it.) I am too nervous to let go. Then shave with my Philips, bought two years ago in Amsterdam after they played the *Quartet in No Movement* and after the only visit of my life to an official whore.

—You off?

—Yeah.

—I need to get a few things at the store.

Christ. The Safeway. "I'll pick 'em up. Give me a list."

Grumble, but she writes one.

Jeff-U has my car keys, he has lost his ninth set. ("I suppose you never lose anything." "You jerk, I pay for what I lose and pay for the replacement. And still I haven't lost a key since 1961." Arbitrary figure. "Or anything else. Not only is your mind a sieve, but your pockets are full of holes. And the main thing is, you just don't give a damn. Well, that is going to change, buster brown, you are going to be paying your own sweet freight very soon.") The keys are in his back pocket, along with a besanded dollar bill, gum wrappers, change, and, Lord love us, a hairpin with a blond hair therein. Nobody but Davy has blond hair in the Wendt family. My God. When has he had the time?

I have lost all feeling in my gavel. I may not be able to do my stuff. Fantastic.

But I'm there, baking on the asphalt lot, fifteen reflective minutes before the station wagon wheels up the ramp an indiscreet thirty miles an hour, whirls down the last row, then the middle, where I am, and finds a place two empty cars away. My God, she's a big woman.

—Hlo.

I lean in the half-open window. It is the east, and Patricia. The alba is the blast of a Jaguar. ("Ah," says Donald, driving into Montecito, "a Jaguar. I'm home." He saw a black Cadillac the other day. "What are things coming to?" There are more Rolls-Royces for these ninety-three hundred people than in any four blocks of Park or Fifth.) "Glad you came."

She has on one of these psychedelic prints which women with small figures can use as camouflage but which a great beauty like this doesn't need. All she needs is a strip of burlap, one single color with maybe one odd streak of another, the rest done by that great corpus delicti (though not, as yet, by me). "Where you wanna talk?"

—See that motel down the corner. That's where.

—Climb in.

I go around. The door is stuck. Davidov hasn't thrown a new car in with the house and round-the-world. She leans over, and it is then, lightly through the glass, that I catch the outline which cements the runny swamp of my belly, stiffens the gavel, the resolve, here in the noon parking lot of the neo-Aztec center (bougainvillea empurpling the latticework, a gnarled oak brought in from the hills to make a jungle nook).

The *patronne,* back from making beds and distributing packets of soap, comes in from her betwixt brunch-and-lunch coffee. "Wife and I have been driving since dawn. We need a quick snooze. Up from . . ."

—Fifteen dollars. You can have number 3, not on the highway.

I sign in "Mr. and Mrs. J. Mullidyne."

We enter the blind-drawn, shadowy room with the double bed. Patricia kicks off her shoes, she is down to five ten, turns around, her face flushed, her pointed nose huffed with breath, thin mouth open. She holds out her arms. I lean toward the burst of orange and purple sun between her breasts and kiss the rough material, wrap my arms around and drive her awkwardly backward to the bed. Our breath would have terrified Mme. Du Deffand. (Did Walpole ever breathe like this?)

A deep kiss, her mouth rich with Filter Blend. Is there no Lavoris in the Davidov compound?

We rise. I take off my blue sport shirt, breathe hard, flex muscles.

She rises, Venus, barefoot, bends for her hemline—she has somewhere unzipped—removes the dress so that, like a great banana unpeeled upside down, her immense, beauteous legs show to the pants, then her waist, ribs, the bra, marvelous, the neck. I manage out of my Bermudas (despite new obstacle). I wear no underpants. She steps out of pants, I kiss her copious rear, draw up my arms, hers are unclasping her bra, I cup the haughty twins, flip off the cloth, she is mine, I hers, *Himmelweiss*. We fall back, we entangle, she mouths my home base, I hold back, agony, she is no novice, fortunate Davidov, this Napa Valley bottling queen. I make my way out, down the valley, hands on the hills, lower over the great hump, into the sweet divide, oh my, why is this not my daily life? What have I done not to deserve this?

What a sight from beneath, great palisades of peach, she bounces, she jounces, I manage with beach-hardened legs to upend her, I am on top, in the holy saddle. (Paul has just issued the decree from Rome. God, I assume this beauty is in touch with Dr. Rock's pill. Upon this rock. Poor Paul, will you go to your last resting place innocent of this huffing sweetness? In abundance, I think of the underprivileged.) And then, as always, and not when called for, the great maiden humming, noising, "Unck, oonck, yeyeye," and there we are. "Og God, maw, maw, maw." I try, I exert, I limp without fuel, she crushes me. Fiat. It is done.

I sink beneath, I work the tongue, oh crushing, those eucalyptic thighs. "Ahhhh," she says. My eardrums.

Done.

We lie. In a minute, I look over. The great body is working, it is gauzed with sweat. I feel a twinge of surge. It grows apace. I wait. It grows. I lean over, I mount. "Hello, Dolly," she says. We wrestle, we throw each other about. I enter, we somersault, we twist, we bite, we hug, we sniff, taste, we hurt, we work it up, we go, we keep going, we are there again.

Basta.

We hug each other. I sleep.

Awake. "We'll take a shower."

I can hardly walk. I am ashamed to be seen, so limply small am I.

We're in the shower. We soap each other's hair, back, chests, the sun breaks on the line of sea, she touches my aching swell, it is tender, retreats, she is back at my rear, I lean into her, we are face-to-face, we kiss under the jerking spurts of water. Wet, we track our way over the polished wood onto the sheets, we work our way, I slowly, she but fed by what has wearied me, though inside, she squeaks, is tight. I come up to the mark, there is a muscular spasm, there is something else. "I love you," says foolish old undergraduate I.

"I love this."

We agree to meet tomorrow at the Safeway. Two o'clock. I will have a longer time to work.

3

It turns out (what I have but suspected and hardly cared about till now) that I am not the only one in the family making the record. Velia's notebooks, which I thought contained merely digests of her occasional course work at the School of Social Service Administration (her premenopausal contribution to urban wreckage), contain personal observations as well. I should have married Roz, the constricted Connecticuter whose bowels would not move for days (what a partner for Igor, the Constipated Penman), or the culturally silenced Cholonese girl in the biology lab in Paris—was it Vo Ban?—who was so mad for navel licking and the presence of oranges in the love bed.

This record keeping, though it is much more than that, is a late and perverse development. It must derive from our reading, in succession (me, as always—almost always—first), the novel of Tanizaki about the couple who leave their diaries open to stimulate each other's jaded impulse.

But what purpose has Velia's epic catalog of my smells, warts, and deformities (hairy toes, unbalanced ass, flabby chest, hawkish nose— black hair rampant within)? And is it intended for me? Or the children? (The notebooks lie all over the house.)

And, astonishingly, there are analyses of the unhappier traits of our (I assume) children: Gus's rages, Davy's stubbornness, Jeff-U's narcissism, Gina's sharp tongue. Are these her notion of the proper Annals of the Gens Wendt?

She is moving the vacuum around, the striated hose leashing the noise box, which, she deeply knows, prevents my work. Barefoot, I sneak behind her and stamp the green circuit breaker. She heaves, breathes fright, turns.

She has on yellow pants bought from Magnin's, a surge of Californianization, but her legs and rear are so thin she cannot fill these glaring funnels. They droop pathetically below her coccyx, jounce, unpressed by sufficiency. Her face is red with repressed fury.

"I can't work with that." Courteously. "I'm sorry."

Her mouth sucks itself in, the cheeks dimple, not in female courtship, but in advertisement of displeasure at male peacockery.

"Translating your charming diary notes into music is a job that needs concentration. I can't simply transcribe them. I need a template. Music can't take such acids. Like the body, it needs solid stuff, proteins." And I pat the limp rear of the trousers. Her *beaux yeux,* a pure hazel, no one has such single-colored eyes as Velia, how long is it since they entranced me?

"You've been reading m-y private notebooks?" That ascension for Miss Berry, end on B-flat.

—You left them on the right—the northwest—corner of my very own worktable. It was the clearest passage to India ever not supposed to be traversed.

—I can't follow that. I don't read your notebooks.

—I don't keep diaries. My notebooks are sketchbooks. If you wash your hands, you can read them.

—I don't open your letters.

—I wouldn't say that.

—I haven't opened them in years, unless I know they're also meant for me.

When a marriage fails, the couple which has opened each other's mail ceases to do so. And vice versa.

She sits down on the golden couch and covers her small face with her fine hands. Her grandmother's ring, weaving bands of emeralds, diamonds, and sapphires, glitters from the third finger, right hand. She hasn't worn her engagement ring for years. (Its diamond came from the navel of the little gold lady on my uncle Herman's favorite ring. I won the ring in a Casino game when I was six. "That's what you call Big Casino," said Uncle Herman, and could not be made, even by Aunt Lillie, to take it back.) Velia says, "What did you read?"

—About the hair in my rump, the cruelty in my voice, the smell of my body.

—I was furious and controlled myself by writing everything down. Everything that annoyed me that day, I mean.

—It was very well written.

—Thank you.

—I myself don't think it's advisable to do this. It's not like taking a cold shower or singing away your miseries. It's more like gastrulation or, let me put it this way. It seems that internal organs are made from material on the egg surface. I mean, if you start showing, even super-ficially, your discontents and dislikes, like that face you made when I turned off the vacuum, or these little body travel notes of yours, the stuff won't go away. It'll seep and steep inside and become part of you. So a bit of care, or even living together as we do will become impossi-ble. You know when we behave decently to each other, even on the manners level, we soon get to care more for each other.

Velia is crying. Noiselessly. Probably was during my physiological analogy. She asks whether it would be all right to go in the room. (The room where we sleep and I work.)

—Let me get my paper and pens out first.

She goes in, the yellow pants so pitifully ugly I can't watch them. They are now curled up, her face is in the pillow. I take up the sheet I'm working on, then put it back. "I can't work this way. I'm sorry I read your notebooks."

She is heaving and humping in the pillow. No response. The situation is transformed, the apparent meek—who were never meek, just quiet in persistence—inherit the earth.

I grab *World Scriptures* and *Ideas of Modern Biology* (source of my analogy) and, in the kitchen, open a plastic cup of boysenberry yogurt, whip, whip the scarlet juice in the low-fat whiteness, and read about the fly-catching feedback of a praying mantis. And for minutes keep from myself Velia's state, holding off from that puritan, Judaic, masochistic analysis which will show me as tyrant, betrayer, and brute and will see Velia as Ariel Calibanized by me.

Mencius's disciple asked why some are great and some little men, and Mencius said the great men follow that part in them which is great, the little men that which is little. Hypocrisy, arrogance, wrath, conceit, harshness, and *Dummheit* enslave; fearlessness, steady wisdom, almsgiving (I gave the Negro shoe shiner in the shopping center a buck while I waited for Pat), self-restraint (I've never hit Velia), austerity (I've lived for months like a monk), truth (*oui et non*), mildness (*non et oui*), vigor (I run on the beach), forgiveness (mostly), absence of envy and pride (not absence, but overcoming)—these are the divine properties which liberate.

"The success of a given population structure is the probability of survival and reproduction, the fittest genotype that which maximizes the probability." (So pills, abstinence, then sheer attrition of sentiment prevent more Wendts; more Wendts diminish the scope of existent Wendts; so lovelessness is that trait which maximizes the survival of the Wendt population.) Walpole, Mme. Du Deffand, and Miss Berry survive by not marrying. (The generic energy went into what makes them survive.)

Behold, thou art fair, my love; thou hast dove's eyes within thy locks, thy hair is like a flock of goats that appear from Mount Gilead, thy lips are like a thread of scarlet, and thy speech is comely, thy temples are like a piece of pomegranate within thy locks, thy two breasts are like two young roses that are twins, which feed among the lilies.

Until the day break, and the shadows flee, I will get me to the hill of frankincense . . . camphire with spikenard, spikenard and saffron, calamus and cinnamon, myrrh and aloes, a fountain of gardens. Awake, O north wind; and come thou, south; blow upon my garden, that the spices thereof may flow out. Let my beloved come . . .

Yogurt and boysenberry, magnolia, bird of paradise and plastic, honeysuckle and Velia, peaches, roses, VWs, New Yorkers, come my life, pasteurized homogenized DELICIOUS served just as it comes from the carton. Excellent with cheese. Net wt. 8 oz. Distr. by Safeway Stores, Inc., Head Office, Oakland, Cal. 94604.

History Is Made Morning, Noon, and Night, or When Nixon Runs, the Grunion Don't

1

Ocean noises, a piper's flatted G. No one in the house, even Velia making safari to the sands. At the cypress table, my four pens, red pencil, point like a shrew's eye, cubes of india rubber, the stylus with which I draw my own staves, the Weyerhausered trees on which I commit whatever will be my residue (I am not what's swimming in the waves below). I usually don't compose at the piano. A defect? I simply hear the music, I trust what I hear, I have never felt discrepancy between the graphite smudges on the stave and the "sound" in my head. Orchestrating or instrumenting, I am somehow up on almost every blown, bowed, plucked, or hammered sound. When I, rarely, "hear" something whose instrumental elements escape me, I just sit it out, going over sections and choirs like a schoolboy till it comes.

Honeysuckle hanging in the nasal follicles, doubling in the brain. Neural rust. Elicits a "shadow horn" (cf. Ives's "shadow violin" in "Decoration Day") I have my orchestral narrative shadowing

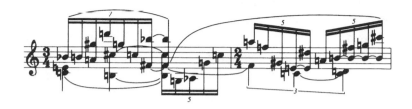

Baritone sounds from horn, bassoon, cello, transforming, as if underwater, a serial current born in the overture foam and never absent, even in the silence which fills a gap in the row. Pacific. Continuity. Humanity. Genes.

Bonaparte's musing aria, "Robespierre, fauve modeste," as secco as a Mozart recitative, a carefully charged *Sprechstimme,* followed by a broken shadow of the row:

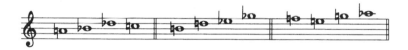

"Giii-nnah." (I can insert that call.)

Three, four hours, I am still fresh.

Hand cramped. No erasures. Confident. I don't look back. This score will go.

2

I drive up 101 (El Camino Real) to get mail and library books at the university. A pretty, wise-faced Chinese librarian, barefoot and minidressed, tells me they've moved the MSS and shows me where. I take out Webern's opus 5 (with the sonata movement in fifty-five bars), Eager S.'s String Concerto with its "motionless measures" (his term) and flutters of wind, some electronic gossip of Stockhausen (*Carée* with its pale glissandi at 67), and the latest *Die Reihe* (to up my adrenalin).

The mail is for Gina (envelopes bleeding impassioned afterthoughts: "Disregard stuff on TP—he just called from H's!!!"), Jeff-U (parietal instructions from Oberlin), an invitation to a McCarthy

"Blow-Your-Mind" during the convention (Chicago socialites in alert modulation; though not quite alert enough), a letter to my mother returned for misaddress (Santa Barbara instead of New York—no further comment today, gentlemen), and *The New York Review of—* Each Other's—*Books* 11, no. 2, minus one of Eager's unearthly/ worldly Swan Songs of an Octogenarian. (My—of course secret— competitor.)

I flip through the *Review,* whose effect is to make me wish to top everything I read there except for the Stravinskys, which are sheer joy. I read H. Morgenthau's harsh entombment of Robert Kennedy (the marble thrown at the corpse's head), admire its Tacitean errors (*capax imperii nisi imperasset*), but, but, last Shakespeare's birthday (April 23) in Indiana, I went on RK's campaign plane and made speeches (for what was not to be) to the Butler and Bloomington music departments. ("We tried to get Irving Berlin," said Bobby.)

On the front cover, a Levine of Hubert Humph-er, knitting with barbed wire, crocodile tear hanging off left eye, fat face squinched half into John Garner, half into Mirabeau.

I feel left out. The music world is fierce but not half so fierce, not a tenth so populous with brains, pens, and venom as the literary-political world, and, of course, not within light-years of influencing events or feelings. We have only our subversive time schemes to insert in half-deafened men (fewer each year).

I don't know whether to leave the *Review* in the men's room (where I've cleared my roughage—alerted by Morgenthau's citation of Cromwell's "I beseech you, in the bowels of Christ, to think it possible you may be mistaken") or to take it home to raise Velia's conversation level and keep her from her catalogs. Or—and this is what I do—take it downstairs for the lovely Chinese girl. (That accursed Exclusion Act which kept this great race of brains and beauties to so dangerous a min- imum that the meeting of East and West will, at best, take place above the dewline.) As she stamps the scores, I ask whether she'd like it.

Her face, scotched a bit at the cheeks (how smallpox must have dev- astated her fruit-picking ancestors), is now alight with sweetness; eyes, mouth, cheeks, even the ears tremble with response. But no words. A shrug: I dunno.

—It's pretty good this week. Gass on Lawrence, Morgenthau on Kennedy.

—I'm an ag sci major.

"That's life," I say. "Thank you," taking up my books, my *Review,* my marbles. I have an abnormally short torso and long legs; the turnstile, which she releases for me, strikes at the testicles, my torso hangs momently over. Ag. Sigh.

3

Twelve-thirty. An hour and a half before my engagement.

In the Volkswagen, zipping past Sandspit Point, ten snooty palms surveying the bikinied beach, I suddenly want to see some pictures. I haven't been to the museum since '64, when Wilma Kitty and I surveyed it and each other in confused simultaneity.

I turn off the freeway onto State and park around the corner from it. In the white courtyard, Greek vases, marble torsos ("after Praxiteles," "after Phidias"), limestone bodhisattvas, beaded, their small sweet breasts soliciting touch (but there are French tourists looking on).

There is a wall of aluminum-and-black-enamel panels, the trick being to arrange the aluminum squares so that the thread differs from section to section, making in-and-out peaks of reflected light, then diving in with a black-enamel cavern; handsome enough, more work than arranging groceries, and, happily, unaleatory ("Arrange the blocks as you wish"). There's a splendid Zurbarán Franciscan (I remember it), Tintoretto lit, brooding, greenishly geometric. At the desk I buy Macedonian gold coin earrings for Gina's sixteenth birthday next week.

The VW is being leaned on by a barefoot Chicano who smiles at me easily, without apology. "Never apologize, never explain," the Balliol aristocrats were taught. Six hippies on the grass are passing—is it called—a joint from pinched fingers to pinched fingers. One is a beautiful girl with a sweeping willow head of hair who gives my long look a second look, pauses, looks too quickly away, but not before I recognize her as a Mullidyne.

4

"How," asks Patricia Davidov, "can you tell that the house has been burgled by a Pole?"

I am making a Greek cross for her verticality. We are between rounds on the second and, it turns out, penultimate day of our affair. "Well?"

"The garbage can's empty and the dog is pregnant." Her head rises from my stomach, and she gets a not-yet-not-ever-to-be-eliminated roll of my side flesh in her teeth, then licks. "Salty."

"Who," I respond, "was Alexander Graham Pucinski?"

"Mmm," she says, arching a long neck northward, till I lean southward far enough to place my tongue within her mouth. Small revival. I slide around on the pivot of my stomach. We are parallel, head to head. "Well?"

—Get in first.

—The first telephone pole.

"Mmm," says Patricia, great knees up, great feet on my rear flanks. "What," she manages, "is a circle, huh, of, uh, Polish intellectuals. Oh. Called?"

"Oh, Patricia."

Three o'clock Augustan sun through blinds. On the wall, sunbarred, a beautiful Japanese print of two ladies, hands on their Frisbeeshaped hats, skirts blown up to show sandals like those by this bed, thongs between first and great toes.

—A dope ring. Now.

So be it.

But, oh, I am feeling it. Whoever hath, to him shall be given, and he shall have more abundance, but the capillaries of my rear bulge sorely, my mouth is clogged with canker sores, there is a drowsy numbness in my chest. By mentality Cyrenaic, I am in body Stoic.

I flop. Patricia encircles me, front to my back, a divine burden, but a burden, a weight. "Had it?"

—Had it.

She plants hands on the sheets and in push-up position attempts a sweet abrasion.

I turn slowly, struggling. Embrace and kiss, deeply sweet. But my legs are weary, my gavel without authority. If I could represent the future in the present, storing away for the hundreds of unsolaced hours the abundance of Patricia, I would even vote for Richard Millstone Nix-no. But nix, but no, Heinz has not yet canned her goods.

5

Full moon. The tide chart says high tide is 9:45. From Miami, Nixon has spooned up the worst of cornball syrups, his plugging history, and received the cheers of the hard-hearted and the surface sentimentalists. The rich dropout, Scranton (of P-ay), leans to Mrs. P. Ryan Nixon and forms the word "terrific," for he can't match such poor-boy sagas. Nixon huddles with the newsmen, faking an intimacy his face can't manage.

From down Padaro Lane, Davy's friend, Willy, walks to tell us that the grunion will come streaming in to lay their eggs at 9:54. We go down the steps to the beach. The moon is there, plowing the water silver, we kick off moccasins and wait, Davy, Jeff-U, Willy, Ollendorf, and I. The waves roll toward us, lap each other, come to pitches, crash, lap each other, fan toward the shore, our feet, the steps, leaving behind bubbles of fringe. But no grunion. No grunion eggs. Perhaps the rigs of some of the men gathered in South Miami have let lethal oil slip into the channel. Or perhaps, when Nixon runs, the grunion don't.

Exemplary Lives and Barbecues

1

Exemplary lives. Stripped of detail by model seekers, the saints, heroes, and witnesses (Kierkegaard's men of significance) are reconstructed by the new democracy of neurosis: everyone afflicted, the race is even. So new Bokes of Governors, Mirrors for Magistrates, Model Courtiers.

Webern. Banal except for his music and his death. The engineer-official father, the parochialism (though he conducted often in London), the poverty, the domination by and idolization of Schönberg, the friendship without (expressed) rivalry with Berg, the teaching and chorale-directing jobs (Jewish Blind, Workers' Chorus), the hated work in the operetta theater at Stettin, a couple of prizes from Vienna, the mountain climbing, the uxoriousness, the absorption in children, then, broken by the Nazis (no funds for Jewish Blind, no Workers' Chorus), proofreader for his publisher, the war, air-raid warden, only son killed near Zagreb, he and wife pack rucksacks, age sixty, take to the roads to see their daughters, cooped up in house with son-in-law's parents, the sons-in-law return from the front, Webern scarcely ever leaves house, timid, laconic, yet, September 15, son-in-law Mattl, working the black market and currency exchange, has found him a cigar, the Americans set a trap, Webern lights up first cigar in years, goes outside to keep smoke away from grandchildren, and is shot by stumbling North Carolina army cook (drunk, trigger-nervous), twice in abdomen, once in lung, stumbles into house, "It's over. I'm lost." Webern's wife denied pension, soldier claims Webern attacked him with iron bar, he shot in self-defense.

Exemplary?

Schönberg, dominating, fierce, teacher, writer (*Harmonie-lehre*, the *Letters*), painter, tennis player, world citizen, late father, excused by Austrians from military service (as was Lehar) after Loos, the architect, spurred by Webern and Berg, appealed; rejected, age seventy, by Guggenheim Foundation for grant to finish *Moses and Aaron* ("I have had some pupils of note . . . My compositions are . . .") though pension from UCLA was only seventy dollars a month; fading in L.A., which, said Mann, in the war was livelier than Paris had ever been (Vera Stravinsky concurring).

Stravinsky's life, looking in from outside, the finest; the intimacy with the best (known) of men, women, whiskeys, food, music, books, places (Vevey—Ravel down the street—Venice, Grasse, Hollywood), visiting the rest of the world, fine wives, children, but then, the mania for bowel talk, the materia medica, the morning headaches, the hypochondria (above the navel, the old seat of melancholy), the jousts with fakes, critics, imitators, thieves; the preference for thinking to understanding (the first continuity, the last conclusion), composing to composition (ditto). Yet in the Rio Zoo, before the anthropoids, he wonders "what it would be like to go about on all fours with one's behind in the air, and with a plaque on one's cage identifying one with a Latin binomial and a paragraph of false information." Is not the good fellow thus bravely exposed in those elegant books of R. Craft?

After my run on the beach in the dankest of all our Santa Barbara days, it strikes me I have been taken in by the charm, the silvery bustle, the off-the-cuff wit. (Glassy the currency of Bobsky and Eager.)

For us, heritors, auditors, watchers, better the laconic failure types (Giacometti, Webern), the mordant and silent (Schönberg and old Pound), the fabling, courteous, twisted invalids (Proust, hiring men to torture rats in his presence), the maniacally narcissistic, vain, jealous, nephew-tortured (Beethoven, Michelangelo), the clipped, snubbed, shunted, but world-relaxed (Mozart, Shakespeare), and finally the old tea leaves, broken spars, drifted seaweed, odd roots, and unforeseen shoots that make up, for better and worse, till death parts one, oneself.

2

Donald Taylor gives a farewell barbecue for himself (he's off to see his mother in Louisville). He lives in the gatehouse of the princely Gossett estate, more or less watching the place while the princes Gossett stay in their château in Normandy. The party takes place in the Orangerie, the company larger and more menacing than I'd guessed it would be: Donloubies (triumphant at the confession of Mrs. Wrightsman, their release from having to depart), Mullidynes, Krappells, a Count and Countess Czaski, he, the piano player in the Hotel Biltmore, infinitely more musical than the musicological jaws. Amazingly enough, Donald has invited the lower half as well. Davidov is in evening sandals (over white socks) and a shirt he wore only twice this week, Patricia is pale but triumphant. Her clumsy beauty contrives a modest slink; to me she is distant, ridiculous. "How *good* to see *you* again." (It's like publishing banns.)

Davidov clumps up darkly, a smiling menace. "Hear you and Pat had coffee together."

"I don't drink coffee." That golden pump has sprung a leak. In order to call for home repairs? (Every story is a minor detail of another story as the librettist of *Walpole's Love* well knows.)

The moon is like an advertisement for the Orangerie. It sits low, reddish, almost full, it lacks only a Gossett gardener to belong exclusively to us. We mill around bushes carrying glasses of gin and quinine, picking limes and lemons, Donald, nervous, tinily cyclopean, stuttering, rallying everywhere with ice buckets, soda, a silver bowl of caviar and lemon. I turn around a jacaranda tree, smell its vanilla and honeysuckle bark, think of Walpole at Strawberry Hill, his editor, Wilmarth Lewis, Jackie Kennedy's uncle, in Farmington. Life's princes. *Crack*. Agony in my ear.

"Lover."

Pat, body shadowed behind the odorous trunk, has kissed into my ear.

"Cheeeristpat," I yell—under control—in whisper.

"Shhh." Lips on mine. She has on a white dress, sleeveless—though the night is cool to chill—cut in the classic female V so her body dominates everything. In the moonlight, she is the lit-up movie screen.

Sure enough, eye never off her, the smirking, tortured torturer, Davidov. "Playing games, kiddies?" Mousing over in sandals.

—Human flesh in moonlight, Bert. You've seen *Figaro*.

"Sloppero," said Davidov. "Why not get out of the cold, Pattie? They're serving up steaks in the house."

—Scat outta here, Bertie, you make me sick, like some private eye or somethin', always trailin' me around, Christ.

Behind silver glasses, a dog's low look. Its fury is driven by his wife's excited beauty, at himself, then at me. "Don't lick his crumby hide. He can't write his way out of a paper bag. Derivative, sloppy, and look at him, the ex–chorus boy."

This is a coward who will fight. I am a coward who almost won't. But am big, even strong, and say with Gary Cooper quiet, Bogart menace, "Be a good idea to cut that out, Bert. A kiss on the ear isn't a week on Capri. And I'm a little sensitive about my work. I know you're a great critic of the art, but I know a little bit myself. I'd just as soon we saved debate for another time." Or some such put-off drivel, the speech, as usual, feeding on itself, hardly related to the heavy breathing, the sense of each of us — I'm sure — that our hearts were thumping our ribs, dangerous to all over thirty-five, especially to three running-to-fat types like us.

Pat, cheated down below, transfers her energy and cracks Bert's cheek, the sound is a snare drum, *thwack,* over the garden.

— Hey.

— Wha' was that?

This through the lemon and lime trees. Pat retreats. Bert moaning low, doggily, on his knees, feels for his glasses. I edge away from Pat's exit toward the servants' garden, feeling my way to a plaster cast of Bacchus and Cupid, onto the Old California porch, past pots hanging from its ceiling, into the warm house, where Krappell, mouth pink with blood juice, delivers to Velia, Mullidynes, Donloubies, and the remote, petite Czaski his old prediction that the Czech filmmakers were the harbingers of the Dubček revolution. "The movie-in-the-round, every man in the driver's seat. The psychological anticipation of the end of serfdom."

Old Count Czaski, small, red faced, a chuckler and man of spirit, says, "Much as I love Charlot, I would have wished they had never brought the cinema to Prague if it had such terrible effects." The count escaped in 1939, taking out nothing but a pair of dueling pistols whose sale in London enabled him to keep his family for a year. Now he is suing the Polish government for his stables and furniture. The countess studies law books, writes letter to U Thant, Gomulka, Ambassador Gronowski, Dean Rusk, the Quai d'Orsay. Without a typewriter, on Woolworth stationery which her spidery script dignifies to parchment. She receives no answers. Only Czaski's Biltmore clientele pays attention to him. Mrs. Sears, a cousin of Woodrow Wilson, drinks brandy Alexanders with him every night after "Smoke Gets in Your Eyes" and the E-flat polonaise. He had complained about the old Baldwin stand-up he was forced to play, and last Christmas, she'd given him a six-thousand-dollar Steinway which he leases to the Biltmore.

Donald's steaks are marvelous. Davidov is vegetarian. One of the world's brutes, he has the habits of a saint. Dark, brooding, he bears his misery into the room, a billboard. Pat creeps after. Thank God for noisy Krappells. Count Czaski tries to immerse Patricia in Polish memories. She says, "Know who Alexander Graham Pucinski is? The first telephone Pole." The most boorish patron of the Biltmore has never told the count a Polish joke.

End of Summer

1

Signs. August 4, summer's height, the sun halfheartedly (cloudily) sweeping the coastal fog out of the cove and lawns. I look out the great glass rectangle of oceanfront and see a single magnolia leaf fall lawnward. Last night, I heard what I thought was a man's voice saying, "No, thank you," thought in fury, Velia's got someone in here, turned over, saw it was Velia herself, talking in one of the strange sleep voices that have for years made the nights theatrical for me. (Gina, too, is a great sleep talker; many a night I have laughed to hear, room to room, these fragments of sleep talk, almost dialogue.)

2

Yesterday, Mina, the Golden Triangle, made her first solo drive on the freeway, stayed with us, and went out to swim at midnight with Jeff-U. Skinny two months ago, Jeff-U has added tan to muscle, his idleness has paid off. He is quite an admirer of his body, hugs himself, partly to articulate the muscles, partly to enjoy himself. And tonight he enjoys another body. They go down bare arse, I watched from my magnolia-veiled window and almost get charged up enough myself to wake Velia up for discharge but don't, and twenty minutes later, when they return and slip around to the back lawn, I shift to the kitchen window and watch them embrace. There is much beautiful mingling, but despite knee raising and other somewhat-educated hints from the Belle

Triangle, Jeff-U remains—as far as the not very good sight of them permits my knowledge—innocent of the triangle's contents.

All is sign, felt prevision of the end of summer, this easy absence from Chicago life where I seldom bother to buy newspapers, have not read the *New York Times* in two months, listen to the distant noise of politics as bird gabblings on morning air. What's the difference, I think. Even that old con man Nixon—whose Cheshire smile passed right through me at Newark Airport a few months ago—has been ground into reasonable enough shape by American life to make him palatable; even the slick little dollie, Reagan, will speak as many right as wrong answers. Though could I think long enough, I'd moan here, just two months from and eighty miles north of the struck-down Bobby. (Of our house of Atreus with its new patents of nobility: books, beauty, sailboats, poems, the public weal. Oh happy oedipal bloom: Ritt has remembered Joseph Kennedy negotiating for RKO, had seen him with local beauties while the gracious daughter of Honey Fitz told her beads and raised the children. Though Lord knows how it worked out for us all. Us all?)

On the campaign plane, late April, yet zero weather, tornado weather in Indiana, Bobby came in after John Glenn (the pure-eyed astronaut elated by his world tour for Royal Crown Cola). Blue suit, blue hooded eyes, mouth latent with smile over squirrel teeth, graceful, dear little fellow, working the crowds like a medieval jongleur, feeling every response as new energy for the old themes. That last day of life, out on Santa Monica beach, an hour south of this one, diving into waves to scoop a son from the undertow, hanging his head, weary football of the lights and American noise, which, that night, would be irremediably punctured. Two months ago today.

Life flies by so quickly, "a field mouse in the grass," sped by that hourly communication of event about which Wordsworth complained in 1800, separating us from every precious thing in our lives. We are so full of the world, this great age of wounding and repairing, moving for movement's sake. Hoping feeling will stick.

An almost impossible time for an artist.

At a Contemporary Music Jamboree in Flagstaff, Arizona, I went to the annual exhibit of Indian arts at the museum. There among the Hopi sand paintings and Navajo rugs, pots, jars, and turquoise pins sat the old men and women who made them. I elbowed through a sportive crowd to a silent, pipe-smoking Indian gentleman who sat on a kitchen chair beside his wooden nameplate, smiled, said how much I admired his work, and then threw in, "It's not easy being an artist in America."

Perhaps his English was poor, the noise too great. The words did not mean the same for him. (Hadn't I said them more or less to have an anecdote for the exhibit?) His look did not differentiate my white-jacketed self from what it hoped to be distinguished from.

3

Mid-August, our beach shakes with autumnal tides which strip the sand and expose more and more of the smooth rocks. In winter, the neighbors tell us, the shore is all rocks. Even now we spread towels and beach seats behind a narrowing sand fortress and still dig out rocks which press on rear and ribs. Television tells us that Kosygin and Brezhnev have been summoned from vacation to a full Presidium meeting, and that night the results of the interruption are announced: troops are marching into Czechoslovakia. Johnson, enormous face grooved by depths nothing in his life or reading prepared him for, returns from a fierce speech to the Veterans of Foreign Wars in Detroit to confront advisers summoned from their own long weekend in Virginia and Chevy Chase. (Johnson advisers, unlike Kennedy's, do not, apparently, stray as far as the Vineyard, though my ex-colleague, Katzenbach, has ventured there, to be assailed in the local gazette by literary sideswipes from the off-season editor-writers from New York.)

For the last ten days, we have new neighbors, the Loves, up from Louisiana, father and eight or ten children by three wives (all absent, he's separating from number 3). The children saturate the length of beach between the felled eucalyptus and the bluff from which it fell. They come in with surfboards, Polynesian bikinis, mattresses, rainbow towels. The loveliest of them speaks Cajun French with me, "*Que voy que zhe zire, cherie?*" and to this cane sugar nineteen-year-old with her flawless Sea and Ski–oiled body, the old music perfesser says, "*Que tu m'adorasse, m'belle.*" She and another of the stepsisters (the tangle of marriages is as complicated as the kelp which meduses the end of the bared tree) are shopping and cooking for the mob of Loves, Williston-Loves, and Freers. "It's lahk the quahtuhmaster caw." Her father, it turns out, owned the beach before Donloubie, was raised in the Villa Leone, and the real estate advice I've passed him ("The bank buys the property, in five years you sell, pure gold") he politely lets fly over his head. He stretches, auxiliary bellies mounting to the volcanic navel, and asks if I've read *African Genesis.* I haven't, but concede the events of the day make me think more of sharks defending territory than modern nations. He hasn't heard the news of the Russian move on Prague, nor of the innocently forked address of our president talking of great powers crushing the will of free peoples; he's given up the boob tube's hourly communications.

The sugarcane turns her oiled belly and says, "Daddy, you doan do nothin' but sleepn read."

"Readin' I enjoy, sleep I need," and he tells me, from his Kremlin-ic isolation, of the good relations down his way between Negroes and whites. One would think the last years had seen him at a permanent eight thousand feet above the delta.

I tell him our smart black cleaning woman is supporting Wallace because he tells it straight and nasty.

—It's best to know whah you stand.

I agree. On the other flank the disturbing beauty peeks a smile out from under her lambent arm. She has loved Bobby Kennedy, she can't figgah out that man Nixon, she thinks after leaving Sophie Newcomb she'll fahn some perfesser to marry and lead a good life goin' different places every summer, she loves travelin', learned maw in Colombia up in the mountains with Indians the term she was on probation, than she's evah done.

Jeff-U and Gina are part of the Loves' night parties; they swim in the midnight surf. Tonight—I say this loudly—I will swim myself, will risk turning pumpkin, rat, or tubercular; my hope is to draw my sugarcaned left flank down from her party to a strange once-in-a-lifetime moment with the transient perfesser. Why not? Twenty-one years separate us, but in this smorgasbord age of kinky love, what is this but digested bread and water? (In Jeff-U's new *Playboy,* Kinsey's assistant, Pomeroy, tells of a "mild-mannered man" who'd had relations with seventeen members of his immediate family, including father and grandmother, and had gone on from this good training to most varied experience among the world's flora and fauna. "What's your preference?" asked Pomeroy. "Women" was the rapid, surprising answer. "But," reflecting, "the burro is very, very nice.")

That night, the house quiet, I flip on Sackerville's playful outside spotlights and make my way down the sixty-nine stairs. It is dark below the reach of the shore light, I feel along the banister, and, on the newel, brush Love's bourbon glass onto a surfboard. It cracks, my big toe steps, is cut, bleeds. I howl, furious, but take off my trunks and run off the pain along the shore. The tide is starting to flow back, but the beach is still wide enough, the lights and waves oil it to lubricity, I run five laps and plunge in. The water is rollicking, warm, intimate. I lie on my back, rock, stare at the starred gauze. The shore outline is a recumbent dragon, no, a turkey. I try not to await, but I await another body on the steps, removing the Polynesian strips from the generous doves and happy wedge. I wait, I roll, I loll, swim, and, by God, I hear hum-bump, hum-bump, and make out a figure on the steps, a girl, the legs buckling in, the hips swaying. I swim up, "Hi," yell I. "Hi thah."

"Who's that?" calls Gina. "Dad? You swimming too?"

Something in the region of my heart dives through something like my intestines, slaps my bare gonads, sinks in my bowels. "No, dear, I'm just cleaning off my rump. Throw me my trunks there from that stump." You clump.

Upstairs, I sit in the—except for the colored-television light—dark and hear that President Svoboda, broadcasting from a hidden radio station, has asked the Russians to release Premier Dubček and leave the country. There has been scattered fighting, the people in Prague, filmed by their television cameras, gather in the squares, sit in front of tanks, the iron muzzles wave over their heads.

While Velia snores, I read in a Sackerville anthology Dr. Browne's vaunting cliché that the world he regards is himself, "the Microcosme of mine owne frame . . . my life, which to relate were not a History, but a peece of poetry . . . that masse of flesh that circumscribes me, limits not my mind."

Dumbhead boast.

Gina, back up, watches the *Late Show,* one cell of the electronic plasmodium. Some cosmos.

Outside, magnolia leaves and canary-headed flowers on the vine against the window lit by the reading lamp. Beyond, night and ocean, *what lasts,* extinguished by reflections of the room, the electric clock radio, the sleeping Velia, my work papers, india rubbers, pens and ink cones, the anthology (plasmodium for Dr. Browne), score paper, stylus, my own bulging head, bed, ashtray, cigars, wallet, checkbook, maps, and, source of the reflected deception, the lamp itself.

4

I am to meet Pat at the Safeway parking lot again. The "scene" with Bert has intervened since our rendezvous making, yet, last night, no signal passed between us, no note of cancellation. We parted without handshake or acknowledgment. But, a man of my word, I will show up on the asphalt, ready, mind and body.

I do. I wait. Ten minutes, twenty. Five minutes more. No Pat. I turn the ignition key. The state is restored, family, morality, ultimate sense. But now, my need is large, pressing. I pull up two parking places from the exit, go change a dollar into dimes, and telephone from a glass booth by the market.

"Hell-O." Bert.

I must hang up, but a lifetime of nonwaste and, yes, straightforwardness inhibits. I cannot even disguise my voice. I but soften it. "Hello."

—Oh, it's you. I suppose you're making a shack-up time with Patty.

—Whatinchrisname you talking about?

—Fuck you. Stumblebums his way through elementary harmony and thinks he can fill every hole in California.

—You miserable dungheap, Davidov. Waddy think your wife's legs are gaping for if you weren't such a hopeless dragass and shitmouth. "Don't hurt me," "don't hurt me," and the next day you're coming on like Mussolini. Christ, I can see why these rubes around here won't give up guns, lice like you rushing around waiting to be crushed.

—You want to try a little crushing there, Wendt? You just wanna try something?

I am blowing sky high. This glass is fogged with my heat. My glasses (I use them for driving but haven't taken them off) are fogged by it. The physiology of rage.

There's another element. At the newsstand, I bought this morning's *New York Times,* thirty cents, flown in the same day. First time this summer, a treat to remember what the great world's about. And what happens? Agony. There's a big We're for McCarthy ad, painters, writers, musicians, entertainers, the "health professions" (to spare the feelings of dentists and veterinarians), and lo and behold, I, a McCarthy supporter now, haven't been sent it, have been sent an Artists for Humphrey (but that's because they can't get many), but apparently they have enough Musicians for McCarthy not to need me. Half the lousy composers of New York are there, there's even a Wendt I never heard of, probably some stage designer, but me, am I fallen this low, that on a list of a thousand artists, I'm not there? So I sat cramped in the miserable VW, my body steaming for Pat, my head raging at exclusion.

And so stayed in that glass booth by the Safeway market ready to tear Davidov's guts out, wrong though I am. And challenge him, "Here I am, you sac of envy. Creep. Come and get me." Though don't tell him where; nor does he ask. He comes back with throaty gurgles, and I say, "Spit it out, Davidov. Cough it out, you slime."

Three feet away, I see, waving at me, out of some Hal Wallis movie of the thirties, Gus, Davy, Gina, Velia, and Jeff-U. Fog, sweat, my face parboiled. The fish is hooked, cooked, and yet alive. Davidov breaks through his gurgle and splits the phone with a yell. An unearthly yell, they must hear it outside the booth, I have to hold the receiver a foot from my ear. I grind my mouth into the speaker and say, "Davidov, if I see you, I'll turn you over to the De-Lousing Squad. I'm taking to the Public Prints if you ever dare drop your pissy pen on a sheet of paper. I'll expose you to the chancellor, you watch your step or I'll shoot the guts out of your fat head. Tell your wife to zip your prick to her arse, I have had it with her, I wouldn't touch a cunt you touched with a revolver. Fuck you eternally," and put the receiver gently back, emerge from the glass tank, sweating triumphantly.

"WELL, what was that all about?" asks smart-eyed, rather pretty Velia.

—I forgot to turn in a report on the chamber group it's the deadline I was cussing the secretary for not reminding me I told her fifteen times I needed cigars from the market here I couldn't go up to the Havana Nook. This town heat is killing me!

"It's not hot here," said Velia. "You're just overagitated by little things."

Bye Bei Wendt

1

September 6.

House empty. I'm orchestrating scene 7. The sergeant is telling the girl about Walpole and Mary Berry. It is his first sure sense of his own love. Dry recital, but I want caverns of love music under it. There are woodwind choirs, all breathy, then a solo cello breaking into, stopping, breaking into, stopping, and finishing out the declaration. When the girl speaks, I have Miss Berry's music in back of her, but in plucked violins, flute, vibraharp, wood percussion. The sergeant is shadowed by Walpole, by Napoleon (who read the letters to Madame Du Deffand en route to Moscow), yet is held in by commentary music and by the tone row spine shifted from choir to choir, instrument to instrument.

An hour, two hours, more. I keep lighting and relighting the Muriel blunt, chewing sour cherry gum, tossing my neck, working with Jeff-U's wrist strengthener. My scores are neat. It is a crucial condition of getting played in our time. A slob elsewhere, I am a beautiful scorer, copyist. I love these notes, I make quarter rests like a cinquecento Flamand, I rule my crescendos into beauteous horns, I rank with the better calligraphers, if not composers, of midcentury.

The telephone. Ignored. It persists. The house must be empty. I've worked long enough.

I answer it. A boy for Gina. I shut up shop, brush the amoebic curls of india rubber into my wastebasket (*Embarcation for Cythera* in rounded tin), put my pens in the red earthenware jug from Arezzo (bought at the museum there after a joint concert with Dallapiccolo), add my score sheets to the flattop snowy mountain. The phone shoots off again. And again for Gina, Loretta Cropsey. I tell her Gina's at, I think, the Point, hang up, and hear from the first floor Gina calling, "Hi."

She comes upstairs, I go to her room with her, deliver messages, cannot say who the boy was—"Dad, I've asked you to get the names of callers"—lie on her bed while she cuts up skirt material and pins it, puts on Aretha Franklin, "Love Is a See-Saw," a very good singer, the music wretched, stiff stuff, put Gina's shell ashtray on my bare chest (I have a convenient cavity), smoke out my Blunt, and listen to her morning picaresque. Gina gives the lie to Beast City, she wanders everywhere, speaks to everyone, gets invited for coffee, tells them easy lies, "I'm from Omaha, my parents are French, my father's a mechanic, wounded in the war, I'm a first-year student at UC," and so on. The day's bag is, "I went to the Point, it was beautiful, I swam, read *Portrait of a Lady*" (my birthday gift to her, along with the earrings), "a well-dressed Negro, quite good-looking, about twenty-five, asked me what I was doing out of school, he was a truant officer. I told him school hadn't started for me. He wasn't a truant officer, he recruits people for jobs. He said he only liked to swim with flippers, and someone had taken his flippers off his boat, would I have breakfast with him tomorrow and go swimming." I am shaking my head, but with Gina in front of me, this pure dear fruit of girl, what is there to say? We are surrounded with rapists, head crackers, she wanders on like a nymph in a pastoral. She went into the shelter with the recreation director, a bored physiology student, "quite good-looking," he was working on heart banks, enter a policeman who "asked me if I was a hippie," said he hated them, had been at the convention last week, he hated Paul Newman, but when Shirley MacLaine had walked in he'd said, "Come on in, honey." "You sure you're not a hippie?" She'd played chess with the physiologist, had been beaten in ten moves, "he was very bright," then ran into Ollendorf at the Unique and was driven home. "A great day."

2

Saturday, September 7.

I wake at seven-thirty, eyes amid the darkening green of the Tree of Heaven, a trimmable branch of which loops over the second-floor porch and, in a stiff breeze, scrapes the window screen. There is no breeze, the day has the pure deep gleams of an early fall day here. Shall I put on sneakers and run in the backyard? Or down toward Dorchester, dodging the glass bits, the dog shit, the paper bags and 7-Up bottles left by Friday's school lunchers? No.

But I go barefoot downstairs, open the door to the empty, tree-caverned street. I do ten quick bends in front of the rubber-banded cylinder that is my day's key, the *Chicago Sun-Times.*

Inside, I fill the coffeepot with water and Stewart's Regular Grind, plug in, slide off the rubber band, make a pitcher of orange juice, a glance at the Cubs (the team's Methuselah, two-years-younger-than-I Ernie Banks, has hit his twenty-ninth homer, his biggest total in eight years, good sign for us oldsters). The first page gives Mayor Daley's rapid-fire defense of his elegant behavior at the Democratic Convention, with illustrations of black widow spiders, razor-bladed tennis balls, and the dented police helmets victimized by these occult and more-than-occult weapons. (Chicago-loving Dick, so monolithic of conviction he will not grasp that television did not register him as the sow's ear without some help.) Onto the whirl of yesterday, I could be reading the Fugger News Letters, the variations would be in detail only. (Viva detail.)

Two cups of coffee. I weaken during two and spread pumpernickel with saltless butter and ruinous peach preserves.

Upstairs, Gus and Davy watch Saturday's horror cartoons, Gina is at Loretta Cropsey's for the night, I wash, shave, and climb another story to the study, why don't I call it "workshop"? There sits the pile of worded notes (noted words?). Slag?

Will some twenty-second-century genius, brooding over "the pastoral, thoughtful, tolerant twentieth century," think of Walpole's farewell aria to Miss Berry and hum its pathetic, chromatic, synthetic loveliness as he plugs in the universal music computer and tunes in on the tonal events of Galaxy Scribble?

I proceed with orchestration, do three pages, rather joyfully, working with end-of-spectrum instruments, double bassoon and piccolo, these bearing melodic burdens while strings and brass police the side streets.

Down the hall, Jeff-U's door is shut. Last night I would not let him take the car because the night before he'd gone to Arlington Park, lost money (his affair), and kept the car until 2:30 A.M. (mine). I was waking at each sweep of car light down the street and met him in fury at the door. We had harsh words, rare these last weeks.

He is stretched out endlessly in bed, feet and neck out of his blue quilt, just the way my father, grandfather, and I sleep; unblanketable Wendts.

I lift the hand weights ten or twelve times, regarding the musculature—already softened in the two weeks since our return, or so it seems to me. Jeff-U's pants, shirts, underpants, socks, weights, magazines, and papers litter the room. At his graduation last June, I tried to persuade him that high school essays on the economy of Chile were not immortal witnesses to his intellectual power, but here they be; his slag. Posters of Einstein and—in color—the Bernini Vatican Piazza dominate two walls, the rest have a Dürer rabbit, an ink sketch of Arezzo by Maniera (which he gave Jeff after I played at the concert in '63, Jeff-U's first appearance at a Wendt concert), and a panel of a Tree of Jesse from either Chartres or Lincoln (stained glass is his forte, not mine).

"Please don' lif' weights here now." Mumble from the bed.

—Sorry.

I sit on his bed and pat his head, a harsh tangle of brown hair. I rub that a bit, his skull is narrow under the hair. He loves to be rubbed and tickled (another Wendtism), and I rub his shoulders. Unblemished, soft skinned, very strong, tan. The little boy who's spent seventeen-plus years in Wendt houses and in one week leaves for college. Yes, a classic scene, but I surrender to it, I play my part. (We fit into such a small repertory.) Back against the wall, I rub his shoulders. *Der Rosenkavalier* flies up from WFMT below. I stare out, through and above the trees, and remember life with Jeff-U, the frightening announcement by letter from Velia—would we have lasted that first year if it hadn't come?—the room in—was it Cherbourg?—she on her way home, I to stay to finish up with Boulanger, the long birth, twenty-six hours in the American Hospital, the noise of carnival drunks below the window, my first sight of the brilliant bright eyes, the heart-wrenching child, how many thousand hours playing, reciting Dante, whistling Bach while I held the bottle for him, teaching him to throw, to bat, to serve, driving with him around Italy and England, with Gina, with Davy and Gus, with Velia, the boy becoming himself, thinning, hardening, his will becoming his own, his lies, his sweetness, swimming in the Neckar, not wanting to go away, staying always with us, no camps, no schools away, reading *I Promessi Sposi,* saving ball cards, climbing in the Dolomites, life, middle-class-American-Wendt life, one of the earth's three billion, one of its hundred million lucky ones, one of my four children, my one and only, unique at least in this, Jeffrey Ulrich Wendt. So long, my dear boy, fare thee well, dear heart. The *Rosenkavalier* dies away, my hand rests on his shoulder, I pat his blanketed rear twice and leave.

—Thanks, *mon père.*

STORY MAKING

1

Story making?

No.

Notes for a story. ("The 'I' Colder Than a Lens.")

Instead of a return address, the envelope said, "I suppose you've heard Jean L.'s been killed in an auto accident."

I hadn't.

At forty, the death of friends is new enough to thrill as well as grind. Jean wasn't much of a friend, ever, but she was the lead role in friend Al's comic serial, and I'd been around in person for some of the episodes. (1) One of their premarital reunions occurred at my thirtieth birthday party. (2) One night I unlocked my own Wanamaker's Basement of schmutz for this future Gimbel of it and they sent me a congratulatory telegram. (3) After divorce and long silence, Jean's daughter ran off one night, and she telephoned Al in London while I was staying with him. In fact, there were seven or eight expensive telephone calls (Al flushed with anal release during the binge).

Most people love stories, but few live and fewer try to live story lives. Jean tried. That her finish was as it was (chosen by or inflicted on her) shows the depth of her attempt. Al had written and published her story the year before. In its end, the Jean character gets run over. Now, a year later, he was doing the best work of his life, farming his analysis for Joe's magazine, and, one night in Central Park, Jean had taken his prescription.

This was a season for the famous to live story lives. King was assassinated in April. Everyone had seen the Jesus motif working its way in him, the only question was when Judas would show up. A few days before that, the presidential sheriff turned his back on the never-say-die Alamo story and abdicated like the impotent, playboy king of 1936 (the martyr's crown read "Country" instead of "Love"). Then we had the McCarthy-out-of-the-West campaign, and in sports a couple of comic disasters: the Masters golf champion, a smiling gaucho, signed the wrong scorecard (prepared by his amiable Judas, Tommy Aaron) and didn't get to wear the green coat; a month later, an even more innocent champion, a horse named—as always, in these cases, auspiciously—Dancer's Image was disqualified in the derby because he'd been fed a painkiller the week before. ("How can you tell the dancer from the dance?") The day I first wrote this, that pop genius of publicity art, Andy Warhol, was shot by a female not-impersonator but actress and, said the morning paper, "has a fifty-fifty chance of recovery." "Oh, no," he'd cried, unable to keep the cool in this new medium.

Jean had only a few lines in the *Times* contributed by her seventeen-year-old daughter, who'd deformed the truth by either dreaming or intimating that Al had adopted (or married) her. At least the name Millie Peters was augmented by Al's last name. Years ago Jean had accused Al of putting it to Millie or wanting to. Millie got hers back: she brought her boyfriend home to sleep with her in the front room while Jean massaged her ache alone in the rear. Motto: Live a story life, and others will live it with you.

Nembutal, Al's and my agent, told me Al had gone away. "He's in the country." Brooding? Mourning? A writer knows: he was writing it up. You know about writers. Mother drowning in her lung fluid, they are noting the color of her iris, the expression of the nurse.

Agents, however, are people of feeling; the throb of death agitated Ma Bell's wires. "It was very late. She was lushing with this little spade faggot. Four A.M., they drove through Central Park and hit a wall."

"Did you go to the funeral?"

"I hardly knew her. He didn't want me to."

"He went?"

"He went."

Nembutal is a dear girl, tired, smart, restless, troubled. Her ambition: to "have" all the writers who count. As clients. As confessors. Anything else, I know not. I'm neither good client nor good confessor. Writers are leading suppliers of personal guff, and in these confessional days, they have to try out their material. Nem had heard it all, at least all the narrative material, complaints, boasts, Tolstoyan plans. She holds up well. She tries to please, she mostly pleases. Her weight goes up as her miseries do: you always know how she feels, a terrific disadvantage she counters by doing more and more business by phone. She is one of the world's telephonic masters. As all McLuhanites know, literary men hate the telephone. That is, till their literary life is over and they're crouched by the receiver waiting for good news from their Nembutals. "Bulgaria is translating *Vertical Vickie*. Not a great pile, but you're in their book club series with John le Carré and Robert Ruark. They haven't even done Faulkner yet." Nembutal is a champ agent, friend to all her boys (no girls), and now famous in the pages of *Esquire, Time,* and other pillows (*Sicut, mes vieux*) of society.

We went to a miserable cocktail party at Rizzoli's bookstore on Fifth Avenue. She was the star. Her hand got kissed, the dim bulbs of literature flashed thrillingly as she passed.

She goes a little far sometimes. One fading, litry girl with terrific legs in a miniskirt kneeled by us, giving herself every benefit. Watching me take in the show, Nembutal asked if I wanted to take Min home. Such is the expert pain of a good agent, but I am timid, inhibited, and orderly (though inwardly, of course, fierce and disorderly). I stray—pitiful concession, this "stray"—infrequently, and this after consumptive Long Marches. My few remaining spurts of pleasure shall be unprinted, unscheduled, unaided. (May classic prose hedge and conceal me. I am not my subject. My personality is too little confident. I'm writing about Some Thing. A treatise.)

The next installment came from Joe. No. From Laura and James, the night before I saw Joe. Laura used to type for me; James is an actor, one of the best and brightest, but unlike half the members of the Chicago group he worked with, hasn't made the marquees. He's done a few pictures, had a few stage parts, but supports himself by commercials.

He's a great straight man, the firm presbyter's face flicking its Calvinism with a lip curl and blink. Laura is writing an art dissertation and
teaching part time at Columbia. During the Great Student Rebellion,
she organized a confrontation with the pedagogical gods. "Imagine,
we called each other by first names. 'Meyer.' 'Laura.' " They live in an
apartment on a Hundredth and Central Park, the unstiffening upper
lip of white burgherdom. Beneath their glassy porch, the shots, sirens,
and screams of lower Harlem. "It's Puerto Rican Independence Day."
True, but as they hadn't noticed this little civic riot, it was no feat to deduce their habituation. "The dog didn't bark, Mr. Holmes."

Four floors below lived Joe's first wife, Rachel, an ex-beauty out of
Lugosi movies, a Gale Sondergaard. She and Jean shared the fate of
being discarded by the risen Jewish stars of letters. Naturally, they detested each other, denying commonality, but knew each other's every
move, measured each other's triumphs (which were the triumphs of
the ex-husbands), gloated over failures: "Did you see Sheed's panning
of Al's book? Murder." Jean was way ahead. Joe had written the first
article on Al, his magazine shone only when it published him. This
deepened Rachel's hatred of the lot of them. Now, though, at last, she
was on top. She reported Jean's death in spades. "They were zapped on
speed. Every night for a month. Jean's luck they didn't run over Caro-
line Kennedy." James shifted, in a way, to female castrators, pointed
out the theme of all the Elaine-Mike sketches, Mike was always choos-
ing such stories. "Such was the talk of their circle." Stendhal, *Journals.*

Joe broke a lunch date to lunch with me. "You're on." Dark, curly
headed, half romantic hero, half gloomy goof. Everything, including
high spirits, is muffled in moral gloom, he is the fading coal, but nice
for that. There's some suggestion of warmth, his values, especially in
the somber ranges, are true (*mine*), his job is done well (though taste is
fooled by that old spice, Novelty), he's a good father—off to buy his
twelve-year-old a Nehru suit because the school hero wears one—
comfortable even in the turbulent gloom of sidetracked ambition and
urban problems. He is *responsible,* he is *relevant* (May 1968), he *keeps up,*
and let me tell you, this is no bad thing. Let Edmund Wilson sink in
the old scriptures, doddering old Ezra P. is still asking, "What's New?"

He had been to the funeral.

"There she lay, all the bitchery washed away. And it hit me. Here we were, all of us who'd been young together in Chicago. Al looked deader than Jean. Expressionless. We were seeing ourselves in the coffin." Velvet curtains, an oboe solo, the story out of the Lux Radio Theater.

Two days later, Al himself. We met a block from his analyst, soon to be a national joke, American fucklore ("fucklaw," to do a better Grim Cherse) of the late sixties, our own Marcel Putz. ("Every man must bare his crotch." This from my pal, Literary Man Number One.) The pancake house, his usual postanalytic pick-me-up, was closed. Decoration Day. We went to the zoo cafeteria and drank coffee while the hyenas woke up. Eight-thirty, no one but animals and the sanitation men picking up from the night's love shift with spiked poles. Quiet, cool, the windows of Fifth Avenue still asleep. As pretty as New York can be in daylight.

"Who has to make anything up? There it is. Smashed up right over there. Except this time, her victim gets off with a scratch. He was at the funeral with her successor, a five-foot lump of anthracite."

Al had met Gelfman in the street two weeks before, had told him Jean had smelled his new money and was going to drag him into court, he wished she were dead. "I'd never said it before. What held me back?"

"You were busy thinking how to do her in."

Willpower. Churchill, on his deathbed, said he wanted to die on the anniversary of his father's death, went into a twelve-day coma, and died within an hour of his father's death hour. "Two weeks after I said it, she was dead. Is that something?"

"The Great Nutcracker."

"They ought to put her monument next to Simón Bolívar's. Here's the Liberator, here's the Enslaver."

And so on. The black eyes hooked on my reactions, I had to overreact a bit. I mean, he's a good fellow, but the universe is a little wider than he provides. One listens, one agrees, one enjoys, but now and then, one's eye looks at the watch.

I had to get my stuff, pick up my daughter, catch a plane. Al walked me to my parents, I let him gather another sample for his great study of the Jewish Parent. His presence intensified the sampling: my mother took my raincoat and refolded it for the bag. Said Al at the elevator: "They know how to fold. They are Great Folders."

2

The night before, I'd taken daughter to the most spectacularly public literary man's house, a glass ship of a place overlooking the premier view of New York, the innocent, lighthoused tip of Manhattan, a fishing village with a few boats and water lights, the dark fist of Wall Street, the soft triangles of the bridge, beyond, the noisy jewels (*on peut essayer*) of Midtown.

This literary bass drum, once the most decent of men, had forced himself out of timidity and the imaginative life to make up for a decade of submergence. (I knew him first just before the new self had been launched from an ingenious assemblage of literary exercises.) Now, leather-thonged across a beary, beery belly, he turned his house into a hall. He was giving a party for the Red Guard of Columbia. The *Times* people were there, critics, the pink-shirted, squeaky, typewriter-revolutionary, McGraw, underground editors with sleek assistants, a fighter nursing a frayed tendon, the School Gang. Drum pounded itself, "HOOOMF, HOOOMF," got attention, and introduced the first Scholar. Tedious nobility. Said Drum, "Great doers and great bores." The veterans of antique revolts (Peekskill, *Partisan R.*) presented these titles of revolution and challenged the boys to "state your positions." Which, slowly, they did, inflating hand-to-mouth inventions into systematic hatred. Turning themselves, in other words, into reportable characters. Drum felt the catastrophe and, *chez lui,* had to stand it, perhaps augment it. I took daughter off.

3

So there we are: two ways of pressuring event into story. One (Al), finding a life simplified by rage or mania into almost-story (Jean's), exaggerating a bit and scribbling. Two (Drum), contriving an event and, at the typewriter, buttering it with that interior he scrupulously kept (he—wrongly—thinks) intact throughout.

4

The minor, low-living burgher, with difficulty still married to the same wife, deprived of fifty-dollar-an-hour self-revelations, never penis-threatened with a knife, never easing the needy wand in the family steak, fantasist but not solipsist, story searcher but, usually, small-time inventor, flies back with daughter to Chicago.

There, a taxi strike, but, with luck, into scab cab, driver a three-hundred-pound, joyously coining black man who drives the thirty cabless miles in twenty-five minutes, turns off the Outer Drive at Forty-seventh, whirls left for a turn, and smashes a car coming north, daughter and I slammed to the floor. Amazingly, OK. A funereal mountain tells us we don't have to pay for the ride.

"You'll need everything you can get," says Generous Fare, giving five (saving three).

MY EX, THE MORAL PHILOSOPHER

1

My room in the Hôtel Saint Louis was so small it felt like an overcoat; when I went out, I felt I should check to see that I wasn't wearing it. But the little hotel squatted in the Marais, one block from the Seine, three from the Place des Vosges, four from Place Bastille, and you took its *petit déjeuner* in a bluish-yellow cave which preserved the stony mystery of a fifteenth-century storeroom. Bliss. I was usually the earliest, sometimes the only, breakfaster. I'd take my constitutional — two blocks to Rue Charles V for today's *Figaro* and yesterday's *Le Monde* — and anticipated the warm, soft-flaked croissants buttered and jammed not from the plastic tomblets served in many so-denominated three-star hotels but from unpackaged slabs of *bon beurre* and rosy gobs of jam which still, forty-eight years after my first Paris breakfast, sing the joy of life to me.

Two years to the week before I read of Rowena's absurd death in the *Times,* I was in the cave hoisting a second coffee-soaked croissant to my mouth when I saw her picture in *Figaro,* not as I'd known her thirty years ago but as the fox-sharp, worn, and trenched ex–not quite beauty she apparently was now.

2

I'd been married to Rowena for 287 days: my lawyer counted them when he arranged the settlement I'd resisted and didn't stop resenting until a year or so after her fourth post-Dortmund marriage. Née Hardy, Rowena had kept the Jewish name of her first quickie husband, Herschel Plotnik. Affixed to her blond, bold, WASP-pure self, Rowena, as I saw it, got academic and public points for sticking to it. My thought was that she thought that if she dropped Plotnik and resumed Hardy she'd be accused of a Heideggerian betrayal. One of her early papers denounced that peasant genius's "debased morality," a high — or low — light of which was his dropping the dedication of *Being and Time* to his Jewish patron, Husserl. (The only humorous note in Rowena's oeuvre was her citation of her teacher Abendschlimmer's characterization of this ignobility as "being on time.")

The *Figaro* article dealt with the lecture series Rowena was giving at the Collège de France. It described her as "the distinguished, prolific, ubiquitous and beautiful moral philosopher, feminist critic and classical humanist."

My 287 marital and fifty or sixty courting days hadn't prepared me for Rowena's academic celebrity. When we met in New York, she was an instructor in comparative literature at Columbia, thrilled that her dissertation, *Eros Betrayed*, had been accepted for publication by the Ohio State University Press. Back then, her self-confidence was flecked, if not with modesty, at least with touches of self-doubt. There was very little sign of that condescending arrogance for which she'd become known. (Abendschlimmer used to talk of the "R. H. Plotnik Foundation for Indulgence and Condescension." "Did you get your Plotnik? Yes? How much was it?" "I got a faceful.") Back then, we were both working hard, I to get free of the newspaper so I could write my own pieces and books, she for tenure and intellectual glory. When she wasn't hidden in a pile of books, she was at the typewriter, clacking away. Minutes after amorous sessions, I could hear what I called the "postcoital clack."

3

I'd met her—no, run into her. Still not right. She ran into me. It was in Central Park, where she jogged around the reservoir every morning between clacking sessions. (And jogged till the last hour of her life.) Having Rowena run into you was, I learned, a well-known hazard of New York jogging. She was nearsighted and wouldn't wear glasses or contacts. The world had to come to or dodge her. By temperament and training, she expected others to give way, but sometimes *the others* were inanimate, which meant she ran into trees. If the others were animate but inhuman, there was also trouble: dogs and squirrels were kicked and, occasionally, revenged themselves by nipping Rowena's ankles or muscular legs. (The year before she ran into me, she'd had an encounter with a Doberman which brought her to Mount Sinai Emergency for abdominal rabies shots.) In addition to myopia and social *je m'en foutisme,* the jogging Rowena was "listening" to the piece of music she'd decided to play in her head that morning. When oak tree or Doberman struck, she'd been lost in some internal *allegro maestoso.* When I was married to her, she was going through the thirty-two Beethoven piano sonatas. The sonata du jour would be on the hi-fi as she pulled on her leotards and clipped a comb in her hair. Jogging, the interior pianist took over.

Anyway, she ran into much of me, knocked me not quite down, suggested that I look where I was going, then, noticing, I now think, my wedding ring, made the "peace offering"—were we already at war?—of coffee. What struck me about her that first morning— other than her knees and fists—was the density of her blue eyes, a fusion of puzzlement and absorption. (I didn't know about the myopia.) This vulpine Atalanta was hungering for your soul. In the Madison Deli, she poured out her history and plans. "I'm an aristocrat who's spent decades squeezing blue blood out of my veins." (I didn't then recognize the Chekhovian adaptation: the great Russian had squeezed serfdom out of his.) "If my dissertation makes the splash Professor Abendschlimmer believes it will, I'll have a choice of tenure tracks around the country." Much more about the academic territory ahead, then, "For me, philosophy isn't a technical Sahara. I want to alter things." "You want to be a public intellectual." "A stupid redundancy," she said.

So much for my contribution. I suppose she found out what I did, but my memory is that I said very little. It did turn out that we had common friends including Elinor Patchell, my wife's sister. I was treated to thumbnail sketches of their inadequacies and the improvements Rowena had tried to install in them. (Of little Elinor she said that she'd spent hours steering her to German and French sources which "the poor twit should have learned as a freshman.") I listened to all this as if it were coming from the burning bush.

A week later, more or less deliberately, I jogged alongside her in the park. More coffee, more sketches, more revelations. (She'd just sold her jewelry and given the money to Amnesty International.)

A week or two later, the four of us, Jean, Elinor, Rowena, and I, were invited to a dinner at Professor Abendschlimmer's. (Had a Rowenian flea been put in his ear?) When Jean and I got home, I mentioned the dense blue look. Jean said, "She may look densely at you, she didn't even see Elly or me, didn't ask us one question about our doings, and when Elly said something, she smiled at her as if she were the house cat. Then you sat on the couch with her, and boom, she opened up, mouth, blouse, thighs, didn't you notice?"

"No."

Of course I'd noticed. There was this large, lean, twenty-five-year-old with this cascade of gold-streaked hair falling about her ears and neck, chest bobbing in counterpoint to Dietrichian proclamations, blue eyes drenching me with God knows what invitation. It was like hiking hours in a forest, then, suddenly, seeing what you'd come to see: "Dr. Livingston!" (Or, in this case, "Mr. Kurtz!")

4

A couple of days into the 287-day marriage, I discovered what a scholar of makeup Rowena was, how much time, study, and application went into her "I don't have time to make myself appealing, take me as I am" look.

Before that, adultery weighed on—and, I guess, sweetened—our sessions. Adultery complicated Rowena's moral position, deepened her as a thinker and person, drove her to subtler descriptions of moral life. "Pleasure and pain are different sides of the sculpture. Sensual pleasure, moral pain. Jean's pain is mine. Even when she doesn't understand it, I understand—and suffer—for her."

Suffering Lover was a Rowenian role. "Living the serious life isn't easy. I hate lying, even to let somebody down easily." (This sentence was the prelude to her revelation that "travel sickness"—her reason for never going out of town with me—was the Princeton philosopher she was banging and blowing. Speaking of which: "Not blow *job*," she early corrected. "If it's *work,* don't do it.")

Even in those first weeks, my head ached from the mixture of passion and pedagogy. I headed home to Jean and little Billy, soggy with guilt. When Jean caught on and took off, there was no philosophic baggage to carry, just—just!—outrage, anger, pain, and exhaustion. Unpretty, but preferable to Rowena's high-wire vocabulary. That vocabulary! I remember the verbal contortions after she decided that her dismissal of feminism—"the clichés of ugly women under Ms. Steinem's meringue"—was a foolish mistake and that if she didn't get on its express train to celebrity and prestige, she'd spend years on suburban locals.

5

Figaro gave the title of her lecture series in English, Love's Intelligence (*par l'auteur de* Eros Trahi), and listed the four lectures in English with only a few of those French errors of contempt for foreign tongues:

    I. Love's Spontanity and Surprise
   II. Virtu and Pompicity: Serious Love, Serious Life
  III. Love: Fatal, Fetal, Fecal
  IV. Bombastique Purity

I no longer think it odd that people attack in others their own weaknesses. We brood about what we're not, what we don't have and can't do. I don't think that the saying "If you can't do, teach" is right. Rowena quoted Aquinas (I assume correctly): "Teaching is an active life." Well, it isn't day-trading, football, or serial killing, but, yes, it's real work. Still, as forgers are not as good as the painters they copy, so professors are not usually up to the great texts they profess. Journalists don't—or shouldn't—pretend that we're as accomplished as the people we interview and rake over our resentment. Reporting, like forging and teaching, is a craft, not an art (although, since the *Times* let Maureen Dowd off the leash, not a few of my colleagues have come to regard themselves as not-so-miniature novelists and historians).

Where was I? Oh yes, Rowena, the professor of moral philosophy.

I'd skimmed a couple of her books after finding my own name in the index. And why was it there? Because Rowena liked to illustrate subtle analysis with "living examples . . . I want to be down in the dusty arena, not preaching from moral Mount Zions." For demonstration, no name was more fully indexed in her books than "Plotnik, Rowena." There it was after Parfit, Plantinga, Plato, and Plotinus, among Pater, Paul, Proust, and Putnam. Unindexed, but otherwise ubiquitous, were Suffering Rowena, Passionate Rowena, and, foremost, High-Minded Responsible Rowena, Moral Philosopher Rowena; Rowena loving X, remembering Y, caring for, that is, improving Z.

Rowena, the Great Scholar, cited articles, reviews, conference papers, and books by "Plotnik, Rowena," a lecture "given in Melbourne and revised in Canberra," "a conference paper presented in Cambridge to an unusually responsive group," "a review article of my early work on counterfactuals in *Ethics,*" "a particularly thoughtful critique by Davidson's best-known student from which I've greatly profited," although, "as it turns out, it seems that a review of my journals reveals that I'd sketched out much of what he suggested, I remain grateful for his generous attention." This is the Rowena who approached speakers after their talks, congratulating—by revealing her "almost-total agreement" with—them, then, opening her rucksack, depositing a pile of "related" Rowenian offprints. Few heterosexual males were immune to the flattery of this vulpine blond a quarter inch of muzzle away from beauty; and not a few found themselves—sometimes within hours of their presentation—propelled by her muscular legs into more intimate awareness of her powers. That this physical and psychic prodigality did not advance her more rapidly in the profession was due

to the cruel telegraphy of academic gossip. It took Rowena years of—
to her—incomprehensible setbacks to realize that she'd better turn
down the burners.

6

The moral significance of love was Rowena's great theme. She was
devotee, practitioner, and explainer of love: "I was so lost in passion, I
couldn't work ... I lay across John Krylchek's belly thinking about
Hume ... My ex-husband, the journalist, Eddy Dortmund, looked at
me disconcertingly; he had no idea what I was getting at." (Maybe not
then, Rowena.)

In copulation, Rowena lost herself—or at least her partner—in the
topology, mechanics, and acoustics of love. There were strategic
scratches, programmatic bites, timed slaps. One was here, there, on the
edge, on the floor. There were hums, screeches, arias, moans. A museum, a parade, a curriculum. It didn't, however, take long to graduate.
Within weeks, I realized that this *professeuse d'amour* was so deeply
self-directed, self-involved, self-important, and self-centered that,
fucking and being fucked by her, I felt not a tithe of what I felt with
Jean (and other women I've known). Rowena had flickers of attentiveness, flickers of pleasure, flickers of amusement, flickers of excitement,
but not a second of whatever it is which gives as it receives, receives as
it gives.

7

Collège de France lectures are open to the public. I walked over to
the Rue des Écoles, beating my way through clouds of Gaulois fumes,
and sat in the back of the auditorium. It is a high-backed shell of a
room, and the back, where I sat, was not far enough from the podium.
My row was just about eye level with the speaker. It didn't disturb
me, partly because I thought it unlikely that Rowena would recognize
me. The fifteen or twenty pounds that I've put on since I last saw her
at her lawyer's office had gone not just to my middle but my cheeks,

and my mustache and head were now gray. Besides, Rowena was myopic.

When she entered, I turned away, just in case. The lights were on during her talk, and we were on the same level, but I didn't believe that she'd see or recognize me from the podium, and if, by some Rowenian power, intuitive or pheromonal, she did, what of it? Why not give her the small pleasure of an ex-husband's homage?

The lecture was "Love's Spontaneity and Surprise" and dealt—as far as I followed—with the mental agility which love energized, the on-your-toes readiness to deal not only with a lover's least word and gesture but the enlarged attentiveness to the world which love supplied. "For lovers, everything is surprising, but nothing is a surprise . . . Spontaneity, a freshness, an originality of both action and reaction, word and audition, is the genius of love. It is the reason so much art, so much insight, and so much invention occur in love's zone." This is what I jotted down as Rowena semisang the words in the hoarsely melodious voice that had not much changed since I'd first heard it thirty-odd years ago. Its cadence and paratactic balance seemed to mesmerize most listeners, so that even those who understood as little as I did of her talks often said that they'd been enchanted by them. I, though, had long ago broken the spell of Rowena's voice and syntax. Then, too, I was busying myself with the contradiction of her paean to spontaneity and her own nature, the least spontaneous, most doggedly, nervously, even fanatically unspontaneous I know.

Years before the answering machine appeared on everyone's table, Rowena had found ways of avoiding the surprises of telephone calls. Anybody who was in her apartment knew that it was his job to pick up the phone and screen her calls. And her friends and relatives also knew that Rowena was to call them, not they her. So with doorbells: even the UPS man knew he should leave packages at the door if no one answered the initial ring. Rowena would no more go to the door without her makeup than the queen of England would open Parliament in shorts. Rowena would not participate in a seminar or conference unless the papers or questions were submitted beforehand in writing. As for any spontaneous or surprising movement from her night's partner in passion, Rowena would check it with, "Keep that for the baboons."

In the middle of some section to which I was not paying attention, I heard my own name and saw Rowena's sleeveless — still rather beautiful — arm tossed over rows of heads and heard something to the effect that "The attendance of those we used to love, and who loved us, has the force of involuntary memory, the vividness of that past which is, as Proust and Faulkner taught us, not only not past, but more vital, more pure, more profound and powerful than the confusing, buzzing, encompassing present." And then, blowing a kiss with her fingers across the swiveling heads, she said, "Thank you for being here, dear Eddie."

Even as I shrank from the exposure, I knew that somehow or other, she'd been prepared for either my presence or that of someone else from that past which is not past. Had someone told her I was in Paris? Had she, or a friend, seen me in the street? I had no idea. All I know is that she'd supplied her audience, all but one member of it, with the "spontaneous" intimacy that guaranteed the success of this initial lecture. The rest of the talk I did not hear. I was sunk in anger, then in debate about what to do about it. Should I leave immediately or should I just go up to Rowena, wait for her admirers to disappear, and take her for an aperitif and whatever might follow?

8

The arm, not quite so lovely up close, shorn gray bristles in the pit and flaps of unsustained flesh where there had been fullness, was flung my way and ready for embrace or a handshake. "Eddie, what a fine surprise. How good of you," and, as I shook limp fingers, "If I'd known, we could have had a Cinzano. Give me your number."

"What a shame, Row," I said. "I'm on assignment."

"Here?"

"Afraid not. This was pure self-indulgence, a nostalgic detour."

The blue eyes, not quite so dense under the dyed gold mop, took in the lie as I intended they should. "Ah yes, self-indulgence," she said with a lilt of melodious menace. "Another time, another place."

9

That was the last time I saw Rowena, although, as I said, two years later, I did see her picture within the obituary headlined "Philosopher Plotnik Struck by Bus after Jog in Central Park." That the most spontaneous event of Rowena's life was its final one moved me more than I'd have guessed.

THE IDEAL ADDRESS

1

Everybody close to Winnie's center was in motion.

Fred, no kid anymore, was doing what he'd been doing for three years, crisscrossing the country, following—he told her in collect calls from Phoenix or Fargo—"leads." That is, friends—often met the week before—who had houses to build, acres to plant, jobs to offer, places to crash. Then it was arrival, and weeks, or days, even, *hours* later, departure. For every amical ointment, a fly. "Ma, the guy lies around all day getting wasted. Good drugs is all there is here. It's one bad scene." Failure of mission reported to Chicago, Fred would be on the road again, thumb cocked, life's accumulation in his rucksack, the Ideal Address summoning him from a few miles, a few states away. "I'm down to twelve bucks. But I don't want anything, Ma. This low, I'll have to stick somewhere."

Twenty-four.

At twenty-four, Winnie had two children, two degrees, and supported four people selling South Side Chicago lots. Supportee number 4 was the Greater Frederick, rounding the last turn of his eight-year doctorate. The Great One had passed to his namesake blond charm, the gift of living off women, and—might as well face it—a deep tract of sheer dumbness, a power of self-delusion from which contempt or dislike washed easily. (The Fredericks couldn't be snubbed.) "Stick anywhere, Freddy. Build up a stake before you move on. You have to eat lots of dirt before flowers bloom in your face. The planet offers no perfect situations."

"I stuck New York, Ma."

Six months in the *Newsweek* morgue, long enough — to the day — to qualify for battered New York's unemployment compensation. Eighty dollars a week, which, with his girl's salary, gave him the life of not Riley, but Oblomov.

An Oblomov who discovered the offtrack betting parlors. And won. Spectacularly. Twenty-three thousand dollars, fourteen on one daily double. "You know the way accountants look at a sheet of figures and see the shape of corporations. Ma, I look at those dope sheets and I *see* the race."

Close to six and a half feet, a hundred and ninety pounds, the green eyes glistening with this *Dummheit*. Yet, the pudding had proved out: twenty-three thousand dollars. "Freddy, now it's time to take the journalism course. Go up to Columbia."

"It's not time for that, Ma."

"Look, Fred, it never hurts for anyone to talk to a counselor. Why not spend a few bucks and get your head cleared? Find out what you'd be best doing, why you're not doing it."

"I'm doing it."

She sensed he was going to stick the money in a hole, not report it to the IRS. "Fred, the tax men are everywhere. They get reports from the OTB every day. Don't conceal anything. Every dollar lights up those computers in Virginia. Don't wiggle."

Was she trying to subdue the divinity of idleness, she who'd burned offerings to its opposite number since she was nineteen? All those mortgages and leases smoking in the golden nostrils.

Fred went to Aqueduct, he'd never seen the track itself before; the actuality needled his balloon. "All these bums in funny hats coming up to *me* for tips. I'm standing around in my Kenyon sweatshirt, and they're asking *me*." It was another sliver of his pride that no one in New York dressed as badly as he did. In New York! It was like the man in Chekhov who was identified as "Lubov, the one who lost his galoshes at the Balanoffs'."

A month later, in a manner hidden from — and hardly credible to — her, Freddy was down to seven thousand dollars, six of which he put into a mutual fund. "I've been studying the Street, Ma." (Hc watched *Wall Street Week* on the educational channel.) "What baffles people?"

With the seventh thousand, he "cleared the post," left girl, apartment (the lease had two months to go), and a phone bill, which she, his permanent address, paid. And headed—*tailed* was a better verb for Fred—west. "I might have a day with you in Chicago, Ma. But Jack's in a hurry. He's got a pad in Sonoma County, he says there are millions of jobs in the wineries. And it's more beautiful than the south of France."

He did stop for a day, but she was just moving in with Tom. Fred never liked her boyfriends, and he missed the old apartment, so he and his two pals (the third was picked up in Ohio, a Marx-bearded dreamer who ate one of Tom's plants) stayed only a night. "There's no place in Chicago for me anymore, Ma."

"It's a big city, Fred. You can go down to Hyde Park with Dad."

"Dad doesn't see where I'm at."

Fourteen inches shorter, plain and dumpy as a muffin next to this green-eyed giant, Winnie couldn't bring herself to ask where he was. He was so hugely *there*. Besides, she had all she could handle now with Tommy.

2

The reason she'd moved in with him after twelve years in her own place was his desperation. A month ago, he'd been "dumped" by his analyst and had imploded, collapsed. He couldn't get out of bed. The black pearl eyes which sat out on his gold cheeks dropped tears down them. "Why did he do it to me, Winnie? What did I do wrong? Was it the writing? He knew I was writing the book."

Tom was finishing a doctorate, writing on the nature of evidence in psychoanalysis. One section recorded his own reactions to fifteen analytic sessions and was to be followed by Dr. Culp's notes on the same sessions. It would be a unique document, real material for students of the profession. But Culp slammed the door. The impassive, lunar face which had dominated Tommy's dreams for two years burned with rage. While Tom was on the couch, Culp called Dr. Fried and told him he thought it was time to turn Mr. Hiyashi over to him. Tom fainted, was revived, staggered up the hall, and found two doctors and three cops—"with guns, Win"—would he sign himself in or did he prefer to be committed by Culp? "You were signaling you wanted to be hospitalized," Culp said when he finally agreed to talk to Tom.

Winifred got Tom out. She went to Professor Klugerman, he found someone to sign for Tom, then gave her the word on Culp: Chicago was littered with his wrecks, he'd been a promising young man, but his own problems had ruined him; he was OK when the transference was rosy; when it got rough, he abandoned ship, hospitalized the patients, and told them he couldn't work with patients who'd been hospitalized.

Psychoanalysis is the best-protected fortress in the world; its stones are invisible; even with a Klugerman on one's side, a malpractice suit was next to impossible.

Anyway, Tom was too low to think of litigation. For two years, all the feeling in the world was held by the four walls of Culp's office. Now he'd never see him again. "Analysis may not have the power to cure, it sure has the power to hurt." Tears dropping on the gold cheek flesh. "I can't think of anything else, Win." Even now, two months after Winnie had moved in, five weeks after he'd started with Dr. Fried, Tom's head was a Culp museum. He parked near Culp's house, gawked at his wife and children, took pictures of the garden, the cars. "Win, yesterday I wanted to steal his garbage. A big sack of garbage, and I wanted it."

"Oh, Tommy."

"Maybe because I was his garbage. And I gave him all mine. I gave him all the crap in my head, and he told me to get out. He's supposed to take it. An analyst is an incinerator. No, a recycling plant. But he cycled me out. How would you feel, Win?"

"I know, Tommy, I know," stroking him, the handsome little black-top head, the beautiful little shoulders.

She knew a little anyway, she'd been dumped as well, and not by a passing stranger. The Greater Frederick had finished his dissertation, acknowledged "its essential ingredient, my wife," and four years later, just starting to make enough money so she could stop making it and concentrate on her poetry, he discovered that "everything on this earth

has a term," they "had had the best of marriage, the worst was coming," it was "time to think of 'fresh fields and pastures new,' old Win."

Of course he'd been plowing the new pasture for a year. Stroking
Tom, Winnie remembered her own obsession with Rosanne, looking
her up, what a shock, a scrawny kid, rearless, breastless, with a nose
that hooked wickedly toward her teeth. A classic Frederickan delusion. (Line up, Rosanne.)

Eight years they lived five blocks apart. So the move to Tommy's
had the relief of that separation as well. And maybe some of the relief
of Freddy's moving; moving for its own sake, though she believed
what she'd quoted at him from Donne, "For there is motion also in
corruption."

"Corrupt, Ma?"

"No, Freddy, it's just that motion isn't necessarily healthy."

"You could sell it to Weight Watchers. I always lose five or six
pounds a trip. You should try it for that alone, Ma."

She didn't need that. Her weight was what she had. "Lose enough,
you can fit in an envelope, mail yourself to yourself. You'd never catch
up. Ride round the earth for the price of a stamp. Need the dime?"

"You're some punkins, Ma." Harshness slid from him. (He always
gained his five pounds back.)

The move did occupy her, and it blurred some of Tom's first shock
and the brevity of Freddy's stay; and then Nora's hysterectomy, which
came ten days after Freddy left.

She had "never been close" to Nora was what she told friends, what
she thought, but of course that was too easy. Nora had been in her belly
and at her breast, she'd loved her wildly, as she'd loved Freddy. But
when Frederick took off, Nora, though she stayed with her mother,
took off too. Eight years old, and Winifred would see the green eyes
flashing chill at her, the unvoiced indictment: "You let what counted
get away, you weren't good enough to hold it. Are you what I have to
be? Is that what a girl is? Someone left?"

But over the phone, Nora wept, she was never going to have her
own child, and Winnie took off for Denver and held Nora's blond
head on her breasts, she mustn't worry, she and Francis could adopt
ten babies, it was the right thing to do in this 1970s world, the hysterectomy was a sign her system would have trouble with babies, she

would have all the joy—and almost all the difficulties—of children, the genetic part was insignificant.

She stayed two weeks, doing chores, keeping cheer, even had the first good talks of her life with Nora, it looked as if at last they would be friends. But toward the end, the new grievance must have revived the old, she looked up to the green eyes flaming at her. "You don't know your own nature, Mama."

"Maybe I'd run away from myself if I did."

"No. If you knew where you were, what you are, things wouldn't happen *to* you all the time. You'd happen to them." Nora, white as a bathtub, with only her green eyes for color.

"I'm not much on all this knowing thyself. That's what our Fredericks are after, or say they are. 'Where's the Great Phone Book in the Sky with my number in it?' What's the point, Nora? Look at Tom." Nora never wanted to look at Tom. "Ten years on the SS *Couch,* and what's his America? Shipwreck. 'I'm too busy for that,' as Pat Nixon told Gloria Steinem. Right on. And if you want better authority for burying the self, go to Jesus. Or Buddha. Or Jane Austen. George Eliot. Did they squat around asking who they were?" But Nora would write no book, adopt no child. "I'm just dodging, Nora. You're right."

It was time to go. Francis took her to the airport. "I can be back in hours if you need me, Francis."

"You're a brick, Win." Endless, vague, unbricklike Francis.

3

Solid, maybe dumpy Winnie, yes, a bit of a brick, but, on her own, had put two children through Lab School and college, had moved more South Side noncommercial real estate than anyone in the city, could have had her own firm, been a rich woman, if she hadn't hated being a boss (firing people, fighting the IRS). She was a brick and then some, a lot of bricks and some windows, doors, and not a bad interior, ask Tom, ask a few discriminating human beings.

But in need of tuck-pointing, chimney work.

Mornings, waking up next to Tom (unless he was out casing Culp's garbage), her head was full of nutty projects: she'd form an Effluvium Corporation, market the leavings of the great (Picasso's shaved hairs, Elizabeth Taylor's sweat, a bottled ounce for eighty bucks); or she'd discover Jesus' *Autobiography. The Word first? No. Words come from throats. I was born in almost the usual way. In a backwater town.*

Breakfast up here was nice. Tom's place was across the street from Wrigley Field, and in the morning, or on days there was no ball game, the neighborhood felt as if it had fallen out of the present tense. The streets zoomed up to the great oval and died; the silence was spectral. There were lots of Koreans and Japanese around—they'd come from California after World War II—the small business streets had a special feel, old ladies bowing to each other, Shinto shrines and rock gardens behind standard Chicago three-flats, the kanji script on the hardware, and grocery stores suggesting intense messages from the clouds.

Ball game days, the morning silence thickened into noise, vendors wheeled their carts, the pennant men and car parkers warmed their throats for the crowd as it poured in under the windows.

What was that crazy mass they celebrated in the oval? (The little white grail pounded and pitched.)

She sat in Tommy's "greenhouse" room, doing her accounts, reading poetry, or just dreaming of something happening, something working, Freddy settling in, Nora taking care of a baby (knowing what feelings you couldn't allow yourself in the depth of that dependence), Tom shifting the hump of trouble from Culp to Fried.

A stillness in others so that her own motion would count.

She didn't want ease, she was even tired of not being tired, of trouble washing too easily out of her system. (Inside, she was brick.)

She wasn't ready to hit the road. (What road was there?) Down the street was far enough.

> . . . Green Chill upon the Heat
> So ominous did pass
> We barred the Windows and the Doors
> As from an Emerald Ghost—

That childless lady in white who never left her room.

The Doom's electric Moccasin . . .
The blond Assassin passes on . . .
imperceptibly . . . lapsed away

For Emily D., the motion of the world was sinister.

But poems didn't do the trick today. They handled too much, stood for too much. (As the accounts stood for too little: Illinois Bell Tel., Consolidated Ed.)

The Oval burst. Home run.

She'd left home, but not arrived. Hidden in Tom's green world, little insectless, birdless, snakeless jungle, so much less jungle than his mind.

Or hers.

Born? In the usual way. Not knowing. Daughter, mother, but alone. Without ideal address.

A COUNTERFACTUAL PROPOSITION

Patchell's gloom was nearly always tinged by his desire to return to Europe. At times he thought the desire roused the gloom, but in the quieter, almost happy moments of resignation, he recognized that the latter was the consort of his static condition, his internal limpness. Remembrance of his European past infiltrated half his hours, slipping perhaps from the pages of a French novel or even from an overheard French vowel sound; and then remembrance melted him to regrets from which he could barely be reassembled.

What reassembled him mostly was more immediate regret, regret for hours, days, and weeks without women; not women in general, but the particular women who surrounded him each day, drawing him into fantasies which could be released only at the cost of the small dignity in which he'd cloaked himself here at the college.

Almost every night Patchell laid down his book and took transport to Paris, to the streets and to the girls he'd found there three years before. After twenty minutes or so, he came back across the ocean to the girls whom he saw each day at school, the thousand careful bodies with whose minds alone he was entrusted, minds which he dreamed of easing out of the flesh towers they inhabited so that those towers could be taken without outcry.

Patchell would go to bed and squander his huge need until his body knew a relief it could in part share with his mind.

The next morning he would walk slowly among the thousand blossoms, each lifting as he passed their coy offerings, proffered with the foreknowledge of impossibility and, therefore, proffered with more ease here on the nunnery greens than would have been possible in the distinguished streets and suburbs of their general frequency. The thousand elliptical variations bound in their hundred hues bobbed round him in a sensuous dance in which he dared not take a sensuous step. The wind clapping the flag against the white pole, the cold sun on the long greens, the gorgeous diamond gray buildings setting the huge interior emerald, and, below, the contained blue of the Sound stiffened his awareness until he stepped into a classroom and began to talk of fallacies and dyslogisms.

In the middle of his second year at the college, Patchell's reveries condensed around the most beautiful of all the girls, Twyla K. Digges.

Twyla was a bright girl who had found in her own beauty the only proper object of intellectual contemplation. Her happiest hours were spent with this object, regarding it and exercising it. Twyla did not exercise to keep her fine body, for her body held to its marvelous beauty with an ease that neither food nor sloth could impair. She exercised between the two bureau mirrors of her room to watch what she loved most and to conjure up in the intoxication of motion that particular juxtaposition which, she knew, could alone complete it. Naked, she saw more than the lovely stems and fruit of her blond trunk; she saw, in passionate conjunction, the hard, imperfect male wrapped and perfected, drained and absorbed.

When the exercise period was over, Twyla would lie down on her bed, moving her palms over her ribs and breasts and then over her extended legs, imagining that the palms were someone else's and that the muscles were male tenants of the skin which contained and was possessed by them.

The exercise periods lasted twenty minutes and, except for the spasms of oblivion, were ones of fear that someone would surprise her, Doris coming back to brush her teeth after her boiled egg or one of the girls who filled what Twyla thought of as the cages of the corridor crawling out to prowl and nose and burrow.

Twyla had never used that prerogative of a beautiful girl which permits her to make almost any friend she chooses and to any degree she chooses to make her friendly. For her, friendship meant a subversion and suspension of her beauty, at the least, a forgetting of it, and Twyla would have risked muscular paralysis sooner that this. The so-

cial terms she made were hard, and although she was social enough so
that the terms were hardly noticed, neither were they ever met. She
was as alone as one could be in a woman's dormitory in a woman's college. She was alone almost as sculpture is alone in its own space,
hemmed in by its observers or by the neighboring solitaries of other
sculpture. And just as the fixity of sculpture spawns, without emotion,
the motions of feeling in others, so Twyla's beauty generated in its lu-
minous passivity vast murmurations of desire.

She walked along the corridors and swards like a magnet, distort-
ing all other purpose along the selfless but tyrannical space of which
her movements, groomed in the bureau mirrors, were as halos.

For Freddie Patchell she became disease and mania. He waited
each school day at his office window in the basement of the Humanities Building to watch her entrances and exits, walked past her dormitory in the evening a hundred times in hopes that she would pass a
window, went down each Sunday to the Congregational Church to
adore her during the pastoral admonitions, and followed her back to
the college walls, outside which he stood like Satan on Niphates gaz-
ing with miserable stupefaction at the paradisal splendors.

The mania was remarked a week after its inception, and it became
one of the major topics of the college trivium. The notice of it was
quick and general because it was simply the most patent symptom of
the campus epidemic; comment on it was a convenient way of in-
dulging in the favorite topic of oneself.

Patchell, however, knew no relief in either action or commentary.
One day, however, he discovered a kind of relief. Doris, Twyla's roommate, was enrolled in his Introduction to Philosophy class, and her
pimpled, swinish features soon seemed to him suffused with gorgeous
reflections. Each day he would prepare for her one special question, the
amorous seed of which would burst so in his body from her answer
that he could barely contain his ecstasy till the end of the hour.

"And what did we say yesterday about the nature of pleasure, Miss
Druse?" he would ask.

"Either the conscious satisfaction of a need or the elimination of an
obstacle to such satisfaction."

In more remote territory, he would turn away so that Miss Druse
could poach the answer more easily from her notebook.

"What is a counterfactual proposition, Miss Druse?"

"A counterwhat, Mr. Patchell?"

"As in Newton's system," he would say, turning his back.

"A proposition which though apparently valid is insufficient and is revealed to be so when it contradicts another proposition of the same system."

"Beautifully put, Miss Druse."

"Just following your lead, sir."

Exquisite, he thought, blushing at the exposure, and he put his hand to his belt to see that it was fast. "That's all for today then," he'd say, and he'd run down to his office to wait for the true antidote to his poison.

One would not think it could continue so, but it continued a year and a half. The second summer was for Patchell an unrelieved agony. The thesis which he was supposed to be finishing at the university rotted at his touch, and his parents wore themselves out watching with respectful joy what they considered the grueling rigors of the philosophic mind.

He went back to college in the fall three weeks early as a monarch returns from exile. Walking the familiar maze of his desire, he eased it for the first time in months. The last week before the opening of the term was a richness of expectation which amounted almost to fulfillment.

His first view of Twyla, getting out of a taxi in front of her dormitory, seemed to him almost rehearsed.

"Hullo," he called to her. "Good to see you again." He had never spoken to her before.

"Oh, hello. It's nice to see you too."

He went to the taxi and took her bags. "May I help you?"

"It's awfully kind of you, Mr. Patchell, but please don't bother."

He took up the leather siblings as if they'd been his offspring.

"They're fine suitcases," he said.

"Thanks. Thank you. They're my sister's."

"I mean they're not heavy," he said, sweating a little at the palms and neck.

"I see," she said. "I live on the third floor. The janitor can help me if you'll just take them inside."

"No need to trouble him," said Patchell. "A man feels of use today."

They walked upstairs without speaking. They passed two girls who said, "Hello, Mr. Patchell," rather breathlessly, and then, "Hi, Twyla."

In her room he put down the bags and closed the door. "Do you mind if I sit down a moment? I think I picked up some gravel in my shoe."

"Of course not," she said. "Thank you so much for helping me." She took off her topcoat and smoothed her suit.

"We've never spoken," he said, "but I've seen you in church. In fact, Sunday is less damned for the sight of you." He took off a shoe and shook something out of it. She stared curiously at his foot. There was a small hole in the sock and this struck her as a most intimate exposure.

"I hope the housemother won't mind your being here," she said. "Though I guess it's all right for professors." He was too tall and thin, she thought, and probably not very strong. Also he had what struck her as dangerously dull gray eyes.

"Do *you* mind?" he asked.

"No, but my roommate might come—" and here, looking up to see herself in the familiar bureau mirrors, she made a decision. "No. She usually comes in on the evening train."

After a pause, he asked, "Which room is yours?" and he nodded toward the two small bedrooms which slanted off the living room.

"Which do you think?" she said smiling.

"It doesn't matter," he replied in the manner of his dreams, and she responded as if she were dreaming with him.

"The one on the left," she said slowly.

He stood up, took two steps toward her, and waited till she looked up. When she did, her cheeks were red and her lips trembled. He bent over her and put his lips easily on hers. They shut their eyes and stayed together, lip to lip, for nearly thirty seconds.

After that they looked at each other for another thirty, fifteen to survey each other's position, and fifteen to maintain their sense of discovery. She put her hand to his cheek, withdrew it, and then put it back as if she were gauging a fever.

Then she went to the door, locked it, and came back to him. He took off his coat, lifted her to him, and lay down with her on the bed.

Ten minutes later the locked door clicked, and Doris, followed by the housemother, Mrs. Pitcher, and the two girls who had gaped at

them on the stairs, walked in, stopped in terror, and dropped her suitcase on her feet. The next seconds held the most terrible confrontation
with the human condition that any of them had ever known. Finally,
Patchell's hand drew up the bedspread, a gesture which released first
Mrs. Pitcher's voice, which said, "And school hasn't even begun," and
then her body, which rammed the two girls behind her out of the
room, leaving the immobile Doris with the lovers. "Out, you ass,"
snapped Patchell, and Doris, taking up her suitcase, ran through the
open door.

As he closed the door after her, Patchell reflected that it was probably his last official act at the college, for by this time, he was sure, Mrs.
Pitcher would be talking to President Emory on the phone.

Mrs. Pitcher was, indeed, doing just that, and, although the matter
was exposed from as great a distance as its recent flavor permitted, it
nevertheless supplied President Emory with the richest satisfaction of
her summer. She bit her lips against the threat of surging hysteria and
drove the suppressed force into her furrowing brow, where, already,
action was being instigated.

Miss Emory was a splendid-looking woman of forty-seven who,
though she had been a grotesque until her thirtieth year, had a presence which suggested that she had been a singularly beautiful girl. Her
round, laughing, noble head grew from her brilliant little body with an
assurance which seemed to have necessitated beauty. In discussions of
women who had never married, she was the prototype of the woman
too good for marriage, the woman whose intelligence overpowered her
attractions in the form of scorn for suitors. In her youth, she had been
on the fringe of a famous intellectual circle whose important members
had hardly known her but who now responded to the blurred solicita-
tions of the years by accepting her as a minor, if vague, contributor.
Such acceptance was the cornerstone of both her progress and of the
vanities which drove it on.

Triumphant now, she was a college president admired for her lack
of affectation and her worldliness. It was her consciousness of this latter attribution which diverted the rush of fury which succeeded the
initial impulse to hysteria and led to her preparations for decision. As
she sat, hand on the receiver, planning the campaign, she looked up to
a knock and then to Patchell's gray face.

After a few elaborately immobile seconds, he said, "I suppose that you have heard from Mrs. Pitcher?"

Miss Emory pointed to a chair, and he sat in it.

"A hell of a thing to do, Patchell," she said in her worldly manner. "One hell of a thing."

"Actually," he said, "it was heavenly."

The crudity upset her calculations. "How nice for you," she finally got out. "Worth, I trust, what you knew it would cost."

"Cost?" he said. "I don't understand."

She leaned back in her chair, beginning to wonder about his sanity.

"It's I, I'm afraid, who don't understand, Mr. Patchell. This is a classic, if, thank God, a still-rare situation; its usual label is moral turpitude, and its unvarying consequence is a parting of the ways."

"Do you choose to forget that we are bound together contractually, Miss Emory?"

"We? Am I to understand that you and—"

"I. We two, you and I, the college and I," he said with a smiling patience that led her to make a further adjustment in her estimate of him.

"My dear fellow," she said, "I am sure you are aware that all contracts of this sort contain clauses which cover this sort of moral malfeasance and that these clauses may be invoked at any time, at any proper time. You do think this a proper time, don't you, Mr. Patchell?"

"Let me proceed on a somewhat breezier tack, Miss Emory," said Patchell brightly. "I am not mad about teaching here, you know, and this year's teaching might have an unpleasant quality, absent the last few. But I have no money, and so I must, I would, if necessary, fight for even so pitiful a job as this with all the little wit and power which I have."

"I am not sure of your word 'fight,'" she said. "Do you plan to complement your action with assault?"

"I mean, of course, that I should sue you for breach of contract in the appropriate legal forum, Miss Emory."

She smiled now, feeling the controls firm again. "My dear Mr. Patchell, you were seen by four people in flagrante—may we say— delicto."

He met her smile with his own. "Of course," he said, "I shall expect the girls and Mrs. Pitcher to testify fully and unambiguously about what I shall claim was their hysterical vision. Or perhaps I shall see in it some plot. I'm not as yet sure of my case."

She now understood him, and she cast the first respectful look at a person that she had in years. "Well, what do you want?" she asked. "Certainly not to remain here."

This time they smiled directly at each other. "I am not so sure but that there would be a certain admirable innovation here," he said in the seductive manner of his dreams. Miss Emory stirred a little in her chair and then rose and went across to the window. "But I want, I suppose, two things. A year's research grant in lieu of salary, so that I may work at the Bibliothèque Nationale, and a letter to Miss Digges's father persuading him to agree to her fervent desire to spend this year at the Sorbonne, claiming a heartfelt talk with her this first day as the reason for your sudden intervention."

Miss Emory looked out over her green domain. Cars were rolling up the macadam curves toward dormitories, the elegant girls were waving to each other from doorways; the colors of the place were turning over under the afternoon sun. She looked across at the statue of the headless Nike in front of the library and was, for the first time, annoyed by it. How strange, she thought, that our only statue should be that of a headless female victor. She was even thinking about a possible ground for its removal when she heard Patchell's cough and recalled what she must do.

"All right, Mr. Patchell," she said, turning back to the desk. "That's agreeable to me. You may make a written report of your research next summer."

"Thank you very much," said Patchell, and left the office.

INS AND OUTS

Why not the quite simple effort to touch the other, to feel the other, to explain the other to myself.

Frantz Fanon

1

Holleb knew the meaning of his respiratory trouble, but what could he do? For him, outlet was intake. When some strong reply to the world sailed up to his lips, he drove it back toward the respiratory tract. Summer, winter, spring, and fall, Holleb hacked, spat, and blew. He was thought by most Hyde Parkers to be a drinker. No such high romance. Their sign, his nose, bulbous, rosy, capillary map agleam, had been burnished not by scotch and rye but by a million handkerchief massages.

"Why Dads blow nosys?" The first remembered question of son Artie.

The remembered response of May, the ever-yukking wife: "Brains, Art. Dad's got so much brain, he's got to relieve the pressure. Why Dad's handkerchiefs"—she let no routine drop—"have higher IQs than most guy's heads. There's people running governments today'd swap their minds for one of Dad's blowers."

If Holleb's inner tract marked repression, May's shimmied day in and out with that other form of evasion, yuks. Her big laughs. Wasn't laughter, with tears, the easiest form of human action?

That her laugh capacity should dwindle, that she would actually get up and do something else, was last year's surprise. A note on the pillow; she had not been up to talking it out with him. "I'm taking off for the Coast. See you in the funny papers."

Amazement, fury, relief, suspicion, jealousy.

The suspicion lit on Kruger, the Grove Press salesman whose rounds seemed to include the tiny Book Nook every other week. Though all salesmen went for her. She'd kept her looks, was taken for his daughter half the time, though she was less than a year younger. Up close, she didn't look so young. The laugh lines had trenched her mouth and eyes. But remoteness, a kind of snoot, kept her from close scrutiny. That and the routines. Still forty, he'd guess she was taken for thirty.

Apparently it was not Kruger or anyone else. At least when Artie went out to stay with her in July, the only one around the bungalow was the woman she shared it with, a German geneticist at UCLA. "Kind of a lady," reported Artie. "With these thigh-high silver suede boots. And whiskers, real Franz Josef muttonchops. I mean, they were *there,* you could *see* them. Sideshow stuff."

Sideshow was a category of Artie's mind, though God knows he was a foot, at least, from midget class. Five one anyway. But height had brought him much misery for years. It was the Great Age for Uglies, but shorties still made out poorly. Holleb, at five nine, stooped, slouched, sat, and lay low before Artie's sad smallness.

What also surprised him was that Artie didn't stay out on the Coast. May was his favorite, also a shortie, though bigger than Artie. And she'd made Artie a yukker, they amused each other for years. "Give Mom my love," he'd told Artie, expecting not to see him for a long time.

"You got some to spare?" yukked Artie.

In a month, though, he was back in Chicago. Seems the bungalow had a bed and a couch; he'd slept on the floor, using Gisella's boots for pillows. Beverly Glen, called Swinger's Canyon in Westwood, was full of musicians, starlets, animators, younger technicians, assistant profs from UCLA, but, said Artie, while music rumbled up and tumbled down on them from every side, he, May, and Gisclla sat in front of Johnny Carson and the *Late Show* night after night. The talk was whose turn it was to have the rocker. "Mom wasn't getting too many laughs out there. It was like living inside a fish." May worked in the UCLA Library. "The laugh meter there was broken too," said Artie.

"She probably couldn't adjust to a structured work environment." The Book Nook's famous charm was chaos. Holleb had to go in every few months to straighten out the inventory.

These days, Artie didn't do much laughing himself. In September he'd started college in Urbana. One semester, and he was back in Hyde Park. "I can't finish a book. And those lectures." So he bagged groceries forty-four hours a week at the Co-op. He had six months of grace before he turned nineteen and fodder for General Hershey.

His problems were turning him hippie. He had his own mutton-chops, two brown trunks of hair edging toward each other across his cheeks. And, on top, fuzzy-wuzzy. Perhaps the intent was not to erase the boundaries between men and women but between animal and vegetable. In addition, his chin and what could be seen of his forehead simmered with boils. Little Artie was a beautiful sight.

Holleb said nothing, did nothing. He felt Artie's misery.

The most expressive part of his son was his room. This sight hit Holleb each time he left his own. A trash can of Artie's life, or not a trash can, because that suggested assemblage; a frozen tornado, a planless exhibit of his son's bafflement. Shirts, shorts, socks, pants, newspapers, letters, record jackets, crimped tubes of Dermasil, cylinders of Man Tan, orange rinds, hardened gobbets of toothpaste like marble droppings—for Artie was an ambulatory toothbrusher—what else? Anything. Cans of Fresca and Tab—though weight was not one of his problems—even soil and leaves scuffed from his shoe soles.

Unbearable, though Holleb bore it, and then, one day, cleaned it up, hung up the pants, knifed gobs of Gleem from the shag rug, stacked the books and records, piled the garbage into bags, and took the laundry down Fifty-seventh Street to the Chinese.

If Artie remarked the change, he found no words for it. So, every week or ten days, Holleb cleaned it again. As well, that is, as any room in what May called their "Battered Five" could be cleaned.

Nine years ago they'd sublet the place from Willard Lobz, a singer.

Illicitly, for the university, which owned the place, didn't permit extended sublets. Lobz kept it to save storage on his grand piano and record collection while he sang in Europe. The Steinway was tuned twice a year, the collection was locked up in a cedar chest. They took up most of room 5, Holleb's study.

The rest of the place went to pot. And the university was not to be called when the toilet fell in or wires strayed from the walls. Lobz would "take care of everything." Yes, while he had Puccini up against the wall in Palermo or Bad Nauheim.

Lobz was one of these *beaux laids,* fierce, chesty, full of operatic presence. Leonine, except it was not a lion's head but a monster catfish's, chinless with spears of pale whisker fanning out from enormous lips, nickel-colored eyes, a mat of yellow hair arranged on the great dome in the shape of Florida.

The voice was something terrific. It started below the shoes in a rumble that lasted seconds before words issued. Said May, "We could get the oil-depletion allowance if we bought him." What a diaphragm. What a chest. And an Adam's apple which, said May, he could rent as a box at the opera.

When Lobz appeared in Chicago, Holleb would present him with the latest crisis in plaster or wires. Lobz was an operatic listener. He listened louder than many yelled. The body throbbed with rumble, then moved with gigantesque motion, charged the telephone, dialed with furious strokes of a thumblike pinkie, and then, a great piece of fortissimo lip; his technique, the Multiple Threat. "You got a damage suit on your hands, Simmons. We got hot wires sticking outta the walls here, one of these kids get toasted, you've had it. Ninety-nine to life for you, Simmons. Criminal negligence. I'll take out full-page ads, your name in a black box. I'm sitting right here now with a man on the *Herald.* Don't tell me that, I called you nine times myself, you better get you a secretary knows something beside Polack. I got me a lawyer's itching to crack your skull for a jury, we know what you mafiosi electrics been givin' the people of Chicago." Followed some Italian curses, or perhaps *Rigoletto,* and the phone was crashed into itself; once Lobz cracked the casing. "These jaybirds got to feel the color of your whip, Holleb. Finesse they don't hear. That's why you're getting no service."

Of course no electrician showed up. Either Lobz had dialed Weather Report or he underrated the insensitivity of Simmons Electric; men who service the homes of midcentury cities were no virgins when it came to abuse.

By the time Holleb got an electrician himself, Lobz was fighting Donizetti to a draw at the Sud-Deutscher Rundfunk.

He tried deducting from the rent, but Lobz was a master of epistolary violence; it wasn't worth his static. Holleb wrote the repairs off. There were very few cheap apartments left in Hyde Park, and, for all its defects, the Battered Five was convenient, steps away from the Book Nook, a grocery, the laundry, the few restaurants and coffeehouses spared by urban renewal. In a dying neighborhood, the few live coals were here. Besides which, he could walk to the *Herald* office in ten minutes, it was even closer for Artie and May to school and work. And what could you expect in a modern American city anyway, Arcadia?

2

Holleb was the business manager of the neighborhood weekly. He also wrote a column about anything which struck his fancy. Such freewheeling columns were a Chicago newspaper tradition, from Lardner and Hecht to Mabley, Harris, and Royko. Holleb's dealt with everything from neighborhood gangs to comments on books and university lectures. It was a popular column, Holleb's picture appeared above it, he was a minor neighborhood celebrity.

He was not a bad writer, and though not ambitious, his desk was filled with sketches and notes for longer essays, even books. He'd published one long piece in the *Southwest Review,* an essay on the conventions of newspaper reporting, the subject which interested him more than any other. He had a working title for a book he might write about it, *The Fictions of Journalism.*

Holleb distrusted his profession. May said it was sour grapes because he was at the rim of it, but he didn't think that was the case. The journalistic situation was, if anything, worse on metropolitan dailies. If a neighborhood reporter couldn't get a story about his own neighborhood straight, how could men sent to the four corners of the world without language or social lore come up with anything but bilge? It was hard writing up what one knew. When you wrote up what you didn't know, it was professional insanity. Or so thought Holleb. He went at the subject in frequent columns. One of his favorites was called "Reflections on Malinowski." "What do we learn," it went,

> from the journal kept by the great anthropologist during his pioneer fieldwork among the Trobrianders? Here he is, the European student of language and customs, living month after month cheek by jowl with his subjects, and what fills his notebooks but reveries of lust and murder. How does he divert himself from "the savages"—as he calls them in one of his gentler references—but by reading detective stories. Mostly he broods on his disgust, nay, his hatred for "the brutes."
>
> Shades of his fellow Pole, the novelist Conrad. But this is a scientist, a superreporter, a model for anthropologists from Mead and Benedict to Leach, Geertz, Powdermaker, and Fallers.
>
> Can we wonder at the turmoil of the world when men without a tithe of Malinowski's learning or genius are sent to report the political opinions of Asian villagers? Diplomats or reporters, these are the men whose muddled accounts inform the world's decision makers. (Cf. the *Herald* column of Sept. 17, '63 on Hughes's *Ordeal of Power.*)
>
> Is this what Scripture means by Evil Communication?

May especially disliked this column. "More show, less tell, Billy. You sound like the Court of Appeals. Judgments, judgments. Less schmoos, more delivery," with four or five other variations. Hers was the tenacity of old composers; give her a theme, it was mangled for an hour. A pretty woman with such brilliant eyes, most people couldn't remember their color—blue. She had the stiff nostrils and high cheekbones of snoot, yet she was not snooty. If anything, she was the reverse, crawling before anyone classed beneath her in the organization tables she'd grown up with, janitors, Negroes, workers below the craftsman-shopkeeper class. The word, even the concept "class" was alien to her; which, of course, meant her sensitivity was riddled with it.

"It's no joke turning out quality on a deadline."

"You bet your life. I wonder how Lippmann managed." Her voice was rough, thick, from childhood diphtheria before antibiotics made the disease a strep throat. Without that voice, she might have been a Milwaukee cheerleader, married an inspector at Schlitz. Instead, shy, she read and got a scholarship to the university, where they met in freshman, married in junior year. Twenty years, minus the one in Beverly Glen, an easy year for him once the shock had worn off, once he'd stopped dreaming of running her down in a car. It was relief to be away from that tongue which grew rougher each year. In a long marriage, what is unthinkable at the beginning may come to seem a caress. As in any form of human degradation. The first years, his columns might have issued from Olympus; she quoted them to friends. The last years, he was relieved at her attacks; it showed she still read him.

"Lippmann's got top-level sources. And what's he do but hand down judgments?"

Lippmann, though, was Holleb's model, and Holleb knew how much more Lippmann did. He'd had a fortunate lifetime of observation and literary practice, and he'd worked out comprehensive principles. He, Holleb, only scratched at the surface of things. He had not even put together the little he knew.

"If you don't know what a tree is, you can't describe a branch." Holleb had used this reproof of Erasmus to Dürer as epigraph for one of his favorite columns, "The Question of Coherence." It had come out a month or so before May's taking off. "When do we know," it began,

> that something really counts? When do we know a true conclusion, how to differentiate it from a "Fading into the Sunset" convention?
>
> We force events to cohere for us by stuffing them into old containers, old story patterns. Three meals a day, funerals, graduations, how true are these to the life surge? Isn't our very sense of life deformed by such false stages, false expectations, by violated senses of fulfillment?

It ended, "Readers, don't look in next week for the solution. Holleb doesn't know it."

3

A week before the anniversary of May's departure, a cold late March day, Holleb, having cleaned Artie's room and cooked himself liver and onions, was half dreaming in an armchair by the window when the doorbell rang. Through the speaker system, Holleb asked who was there and heard some response about Biafra. People in Hyde Park were always collecting signatures for petitions, money for causes. (Sops for violent Cerberus.) Holleb pressed the admission button and waited by the stairwell.

A young Negro in a blue dashiki came up the stairs. "I'm collecting for Biafra," he said. He had no can for money or clipboard for petition signatures. Odd, thought Holleb, but he subdued his uneasiness. In these times, it was a white burgher's obligation to suppress suspicion of Negroes. Of—correcting himself— blacks.

The dashiki was some reassurance. When a man wears what sets him apart—and these tunics were still uncommon in Hyde Park—it means self-consciousness has found an outlet. Such a man is not one of those stymied anonymities who are transformed by sudden rage into assassins.

"I'll get my wallet. The situation is frightful."

The fellow followed him into the living room; Holleb supposed it was all right. In fact, he was thinking he would offer him a cup of tea—they might have an interesting talk—when the fellow asked, "You got the money?"

That did unsettle Holleb, but again, he calmed himself; manners weren't the man.

The fellow was about twenty. He had a large head, the hair was bushed in the natural style, though the coiffure wasn't natural. The sides were trimmed low, the bush rose only in the middle, a camel effect. The mouth was large, the teeth were big, though Holleb remembered no smile. The skin was almost fair, a dark gold. Holleb remembered thinking there was less melanin in that skin than in that of some Caucasians, strange in view of the hair. This while he drew out his wallet, said cautiously he never had much money around, and handed over a dollar.

It was then the fellow clouted him with his fist, and something

more, brass knuckles, coins, something that flashed and caused Holleb
to move enough so that he was caught not in the face but the neck. It
was terrific, he couldn't breathe, couldn't call. "No," he must have
tried, maybe "Help," and the fellow punched him again, low, in the
stomach. The fellow's face was near his, bunched in excitement and
cruelty. It was then Holleb must have seen the teeth, heard the heavy
breath, smelled and felt a hot, vinegary discharge from the leaping
body. He was down, his wallet grabbed, he grabbed for the fellow's
shoe, a blue suede, a Hush Puppy, which arced out of his hand and
then drove into his chest. It was all Holleb remembered of that.

He came to on the floor. Artie, kneeling and crying, "Dad, Dad,
Dad," was putting a washcloth to his face. Holleb rang with ache, so
much he could not localize it. It made him distant from the room, from
Artie, from his, yes, tears, from his strange sideburns, from his voice,
"Are you OK?" You poor, poor Dads. What happened? I called the po-
lice. Easy, old Dads."

The apartment, it turned out, had not been so much burgled as as-
saulted. The man had taken a hammer to Lobz's Steinway, the keys
were cracked, the mahogany case was pocked and splintered. Chairs
had been knifed, their stuffing bled into the room. Glasses and cups
had been smashed and trampled; there was a glass icefall in the dining
room.

Holleb spent three days in the hospital and there looked through
thick mug books, page after page of Negroes with records. Local Negroes, local records.

The sergeant, an alert-looking fellow in civvies, eyeglassed, neat,
nervous, pointed to pictures as Holleb turned pages. His tone was studious, even loving. "Got this one with a baby carriage full of hardware
over on Sixty-third. Here's a fine one. Dumped lighter fluid on his
mama and lit up. This one here hoists Impalas. Only Impalas. Fourteen years old. An Impala's missing, he's on the street, I don't think
twice." The pictures which looked so much alike to Holleb were for
the sergeant intimately different. "We been hunting this mother a year.
His trick's carving initials on girls' cheeks."

Holleb's man was not in the books. At least, he didn't recognize
him.

"We'll keep after him." The sergeant got up, a small man with the large books, a CPA checking out company records. "I think we've got a chance. He'll be going up and down the streets with this Biafra. We may well get him. Then, Mr. Holleb, I hope you'll stick with us."

"What do you mean?" Holleb lay in his white hospital wraparound, his sides taped, his face bandaged. With his almost white hair, he looked like a piece of human angel food—but smeared, battered—an odd extension of the antiseptic cubicle with its air of formaldehyde and the terrible histories of the mug books.

"Charge him. See it through the court."

"Of course. Why not?"

"You'd be surprised. People lose their lumps, they lose their interest. They get lazy. Scared. Or, in Hyde Park, they start thinking, These poor . . . these guys . . .—who beat their brains out, remember—they got no chance in life, why should I make it hard on them? And so on. You'd be surprised."

"Foolish," said Holleb.

4

Two weeks later, Holleb was more or less back in shape. There were a few welts on his body, he had a small scar on the base of his neck, but he wasn't in pain. The apartment was cleaned up also, except for the piano, about which he hadn't dared write Lobz. At seven he got a call from the sergeant. "Mr. Holleb, we've got a line on your boy. We think he's one of that nest of dopies that hang out in the Riviera Hotel over your way on Dorchester. We're going to go in there about eleven o'clock, eleven-thirty, so your bell rings late, don't be scared. It'll be me with somebody for you to look at. I hope."

Though he usually went to bed after the ten o'clock news, Holleb waited up in the armchair. Or tried to, for he woke to the humming buzzer. One o'clock. Fuzzy, he put a bathrobe over his shirt and tie and went downstairs.

In front of the glass door, between the sergeant and a patrolman, stood a black man in a violet turtleneck and orange pants, head hung low, regarding his shoes. Holleb, following his look, saw untied shoelaces, strung like lax whips from brilliant black oxfords.

The sergeant motioned Holleb to stay put behind the door, then cupped the man's jaw in his palm and raised it into the hall light. A horsey, huge-eyed face flowered toward Holleb's in terror and imploration.

It was, of course, not his man. This fellow didn't even have a bush, didn't the sergeant remember his description? Besides, the man was his own age, if younger looking. There was a raw cut on his cheek, a puffy, active, furious rose. In a week he'd have a Heidelberg *Schmiss*. No, not his man.

He shook his head. The face in the palm leaked relief, the eyes closed, the dark flesh sank around the cheekbones. Holleb wasn't thanked, he no longer existed.

Upstairs, unable to sleep, Holleb sat in the dark and watched the whirl light of the patrol car raise blue welts on Fifty-seventh Street. It was heading off, east. Were they taking the man home or down to the Twenty-third Street Station to dig out a congruence between his life and their tally sheets? Search long enough, they should be able to come up with something. That *Schmiss* hadn't been earned at the barber's.

They would, thought Holleb, have to do subtler research to line up *his* life with their sheets. He too had a *Schmiss,* though it had been earned on the right side of the law. But his own tally sheet was nothing to carve on granite. Marriage: over. Son: miserable. Apartment: in bad shape. Work: third rate. Books: unwritten. Victimizer: uncaught.

He was able to tabulate it himself, he was at his own immediate disposition, he hadn't inflicted any visible scars, personally. These were his pluses.

Against what, in the morning, he would call better judgment, Holleb suddenly understood and almost forgave his attacker. The dashiki and nutty coiffure hadn't been enough for him. The money wasn't enough for him. Conning wasn't enough. His terrible rage, his fierce sense of himself, had wanted something more. To inflict on a Holleb an unearned pain. To make the secret welts of a Holleb visible.

Holleb knew the weakness of this fatigued exoneration, knew the evasiveness of easy pardon, but tonight, as the sergeant had predicted, he wavered.

Tout comprendre, tout pardonner.

Though who comprendred tout? Of May? Of his victimizer?

Holleb had been abandoned without a word by a yukker, he'd been knocked around by a cruel man. Where did they sit on the spectrum of cruelty? With the farcical basso Lobz? With the poison-hearted Malinowski? But Malinowski described his savages, did not stomp them. And Lobz's basso soothed thousands.

If you didn't have the brain of the one, the Adam's apple of the other, weren't you even more obliged to hurt minimally? To bag groceries, grow sideburns, drive rage back to your lungs and blow your nose the year round?

In this world of opulent expression, where even soup cans were given voice, who was Holleb to advocate self-repression? Were not such chains being struck off in daily celebrations?

It was not clear.

The world, where action was loved beyond truth, beyond the full report, insisted Holleb had to fish or cut bait. He could forgive and forget, remember and pursue. In the great holes between, truth fell through.

It was not clear.

But, as of fuzzed head hitting soft pillow in this early morning, Holleb thought that, yes, if they caught his man, most unlikely, but if they did, he would, yes, probably, reluctantly, see the darn case through.

NINE LETTERS, TWENTY DAYS

Dearest Nancy,

Mother is in the cabin feeling shoddy, and I'm up in the salon resting after a tough loss in the quarterfinal of the Men's Deck Tennis Tournament (Tourist Class). I now feel the way Mother says she does, but it's a righteous feeling, one I've earned, not like hers which seems imposed. Seasickness, like most other things, turns out to be a matter of temperament. The ocean is my cup of tea, I guess. Discounting now, I've never felt better.

We've had fine weather, sunny both days, the nights mild with just the slightest, most inviting sort of snap. My appetite is terrific and the cooks seem to have been informed of it. (Where do people get this nonsense about British cooking?)

The main thing is that the whole day is arranged for you, and arranged in such a manner as to persuade you that you're a millionaire with a choice of hundreds of pleasures. Breakfast, tonic walks, games, morning tea concerts, lunch, movies, "horse races," bingo, a real profusion of possibilities all to your hand, and, most wonderfully of all, apparently—for you forget the past on board—free, free, and so within our notorious means.

There was a contest this morning, answers coming from Shakespeare's plays, and I worked at least an hour on it. (I missed a few. Isn't there one called *Much Ado about Nothing*? If so, I'll miss only four.) We learn the winner before cocktail time. (Our one luxury: one *pays* for drinks. So you see the voyage has dangers.) If I win, it'll be champagne, and I'll hoist a glass to you; it won't be the first time, dear.

I only wish your mother could concur in all this. She hasn't been very ill, and she hasn't been ill very much, but she does say it's terrible when she is. It's so hard to imagine the illnesses of others that this may be more casual than she deserves, but it does testify to my feelings, doesn't it? Or does it in the wrong way?

This must sound like the ocean liner posters to you, dear, but I'm not alone in my enthusiasm. The Irish fellow who beat me in deck tennis echoed Mr. Goodrich's remark yesterday about the nicest part of Europe being the arriving and leaving.

Which reminds me to ask you a little favor, sweetie. I never did get to say good-bye to Goodrich, and I wonder if you wouldn't mind ringing up and doing it for me. I don't want to write to the bank because then everybody else will be expecting postcards, and I'm not going to do that sort of thing. But you know how much I like Goodrich, dear, and he'd really appreciate it. He's not very acute, or even sensitive, but he's independent and not afraid to run against the tide (nautical imagery on my pen), and maybe you already know how fine a thing that is.

I hope the job is not too troublesome and that you're having some fun. Summer jobs are somehow the worst sort—except that they end. If they start making you do too much, just quit. We're the "international set" now, you know. Go out to the beach with Jeannie and get a tan. Take a picnic and hire a dinghy. (More boats.) At any rate, have fun, and if something called *The Careless Affair* comes to the movies, don't see it—that was yesterday's picture.

So, dear, I'll sign off now (more nautical stuff). I'll write you from Paris in three days. Our letters go from Cherbourg so it will be a week or so before you get this. By then, we'll be there—whatever "there" means, as I sometimes wonder.

See you in a few weeks, dear.
Dad

My dearest Nancy,

This is the first morning of the trip I haven't felt absolutely awful and of course it is next to the last one. Tomorrow at about two we are supposed to see France. Your dad is enormously excited as you can imagine. He's walking about the deck now in that twenty-year-old turtleneck sweater he hasn't worn since college.

When I haven't felt that the bottom of my stomach was falling out, I've been able to enjoy the trip. Everything is made very easy on shipboard. The English are very polite without being stuffy. One has as much as one wants and more. The air is good and there is a lot to do, movies, games, etc. Dad has played the horse game which is really a dice game, though stewards push cardboard horses around a track. There have been some good movies too. At night we've even done some dancing and nothing makes one feel younger than that. We were sort of rusty but it was a lot of fun. I danced once or twice with a very good-looking fellow from California who's an oil salesman; he and his wife have been with us a lot. Dad danced with the wife who's been in the movies (bit parts) though she seems a rather clumsy dancer.

Our dinner partner is a miserable-looking old man, a German or Hungarian who doesn't speak English (or French—your dad tried it) and who seems to be going back to relations in Germany or Austria. It really is too bad to be with him (although I've missed about four meals and have had less to do with him) because he looks very unhappy and tends to dampen your spirits.

Don't forget to write us at the Louis le Grand, dear. We're expecting a letter when we arrive.

Don't want you to slave but I do hope the house doesn't fall over your head. Eat and sleep well.

Much love,
Mother

Dear Mother and Dad,

It's impossible to believe that you'll be reading this letter in Paris, probably looking out the window at the Eiffel Tower between sentences. Never, never has Stamford seemed so "familiar" as now thinking of you in the Tuileries. (I'm not even sure what that is—or they are.) I hope you're just having one-fifth the fine time I'm imagining for you. Please see everything and yet relax. I'm going to go to the worst-looking movie at the Paramount tonight just because the ad shows Ava Gardner standing under the Arch of Triumph.

Mr. Damon was really obscene this morning. He's about as much a "man of God" as I'm Ava Gardner. He's so mousy—you know—I can't even stand to hear him say "God" or "Love." I've decided I'm going to go to hear Mr. Beardsley at the Congregational. Ellen Andrews says he's wonderful, and tho' Ellen Andrews can't tell a sheep from a worm, it's worth a try. At least it won't be profane. I really mean profane too—your heart just goes up in your mouth.

The job is all right. The floor manager looks pretty beastly and he's rumored to make the girls dramatic offers which he follows with threats. There wouldn't be much life-or-honor debate with me. I really would rather die than have that man put one oily finger on me. The girls are nice enough, most of them pretty usual. They only talk about men and clothes and movies. One of them is in college—St. Olaf's or something in Minnesota. She's just like the others. They think I'm sort of a snob, and, for the first time in my life, I guess I am. There are just more degrees of snobbery than are imaginable. At Smith they think I'm a bum disguising myself as an intellectual. ("They" isn't general of course. I'm far from being "that poor girl on the third floor" type.)

I'm reading something wonderful now, *The Life of Henri Brulard* by Stendhal. I read *The Red and the Black* last year; this is his autobiography. Funny thing, I feel both very much like him and that he is like nobody else.

I've decided I'm going to read only European books while you're over there.

Went to the beach last Sat. with Jeannie. We still look like a vaudeville team in bathing suits. We had fun even though no matter if it's as calm as a flapjack or not, she displaces enough water to shake me like a match. Took a jar of pickles, one of olives, tongue sandwiches, and a thermos of coffee. Nobody talked to us though Sara Clough and her brother (in Harvard Business School and—unlike his sister—quite bright) deigned to tell us about the weather. The prettier she gets the more I detest her, and I really don't think from jealousy. She is just a damn prig of the worst order.

So that's all from Stamford. It seems too peculiar to be writing *you* about what goes on *here*. Peculiar and yet good. I am so glad you're away—that sounds awful—I of course mean from *here,* not from *me.*

Please concentrate on having the best time you've ever had.

Much love,
Nancy

Dearest Nancy,

Your letter was here when we got in, and it was just what we needed. I reread it now and then—as tonic, for we have been on the run.

Paris, and maybe you know this, is split up into twenty—I think—districts called arrondissements, and Mother has managed so far to get us through five of them with the help of the guidebooks and the delightful Paris transportation, rollicking buses and the fierce little subway, called, to one's surprise, the Metro. We've even splurged on a few taxis; one doesn't feel like accounting for things here.

Mother's energy is quite amazing. She has, however, tired me out and I am sort of meandering along today while she is off to the Père-Lachaise cemetery. I'm in the hotel now, and after, I'll go see the delightful puppet show in the Tuileries (the park which goes from the Louvre to the Place de la Concorde) and then walk down along the river and drink a little wine.

It's a place one could be so happy in. Even the trees seem sensitive in a tactful, easy way. They set off the whole place along with the avenues and the wonderful buildings, all of which are of a manageable height. If you were here, dear, you would help me see so much more. I'm almost sorry, despite our elaborate definition of this trip and what it was to be for your mother and me, that we didn't listen to our normal impulses and bring you. There are many things that I'd forgo to have it that way—but enough of this.

I started this with the intention of making it a long letter filled with descriptions of the Sorbonne and the Panthéon, but I somehow feel I'd better save all this. It's the feeling I wish I could send you, like a packet of scented soap or a pine-needle pillow, something that would go straight to your senses without a thought. Am I making too much of it? I wonder, but even in the rush from important spot to important spot you catch this air, in the streets or in the faces, which seem both older and younger than those back home. It's even in the ceremony with which the most insistently paltry demand becomes almost an agreeable and important one. Gawking, this all is, but honest gawking, whatever that will mean to you.

Incidentally, there's very little of this "Want some dirty pictures" side to it though certainly the two approaches made me, one by a drunken, bearish prostitute and the other (really others) by the dark money marketeers near the American Express and the Rue de Rivoli, were more blatant than anything one would encounter at home. That of course gives a kind of spice to it all. "I'm someone," you say. "They want me," and it's nice to be mistaken for a rich American (and "taken" for one sometimes, too). I suppose in their terms, though, even *we* are rich.

I'd better be getting my walk now before Mother comes home. I'm going to read your letter again by the river. I can't tell you how much I admire the way you take things.

Good-bye now dear and much love,
Dad

My dearest Nancy,

You can't imagine what it was like for me reading your letter about Stamford while I was away from it. The last time was when Mother died, and you were hardly literate then. I'd almost forgotten what it was like, being away—I don't count the summer weeks in the Thousand Islands somehow, because even the easiest fishing is work for me. I'm not even sure I'm up to the real thing. When I read in your letter about Mr. Damon and Jeannie, I get so nervous about looking out the window and seeing, not the Jebbs, but the back of the Hotel Continental (we always do manage to have rich neighbors) that I'm not myself for an hour. And about the store, dear, though I know that you tend to see things in more dramatic ways than I do, I most definitely do not want you to continue in any atmosphere of that sort for even the shortest period. Use your own judgment of course but judge on my standards. I don't need to say anything else about it.

It's hard to think of anything quite so far away now, though of course, as you see, I do, but I've been seeing such an enormous amount here that I'm almost dizzy. I've bought postcards of practically everything and written the most interesting facts about the buildings on the back, so when we get home, we'll have some real sessions.

As a matter of fact, for the past few days, I've been going by myself. Dad says it's our differing metabolism rates again, so during the day, he wanders around here, and I get on these horrid buses and go hurtling off to the remotest corners of Paris. I usually get back here at six or so and then we have dinner, often at Webers, which is a very famous café-restaurant right down the street from Maxim's. (I hum the *Merry Widow* song every time I go by that.) We've seen some movies at night and we've been twice to clubs on the Champs-Elysées but these are simply outrageous in every way—you *must* drink champagne and I mean must—there's a bottle on the table a second after you sit down—so we usually sit outside a café for a while and then tumble into bed. At least I do. Dad has taken to wandering around at night, walking along the river and so on. There's no telling him it might not be the safest thing to do. I'm not too worried about adventuresses, because there just don't seem to be any around, but there is something about this town which is not quite right on the face of it, something unhealthy and kind of anonymous. That's silly but you'd see it, dear. It's not just the horrors who sneak up to you with offers to change your money or to sell you pornography—a man came up to Dad even when I was right next to him—one almost expects *that* here. It's this something in the air.

It's probably the August weather; that's enough to account for all the Frenchmen being away from Paris now. There does seem to be a larger proportion of tourists—and especially American tourists—here now, than one would have imagined. Maybe it's just the contrast between these old streets and the modern look of the Americans walking through them that makes the proportion seem big.

To think that in less than two weeks we'll be sailing back. I just don't know what I feel about it. I do think Dad will be glad. He misses his young heiress, I know that, and of course I do too, dear, and I will be so glad to come back to that. But I'm afraid I'm going to miss the luxury of these weeks. Day after day of no cleaning or washing or dinner making. I once thought my mind had just rotted away and that I wasn't much good anymore for anything but doing things in the house, but it's not so. I'm not pretending to be in ecstasy every minute, but in my rusty way, I do feel liberated. It's like getting out of Miss Masters again. I hope you'll know *this* feeling, if you were spared at least the necessity of that one.

But now, Good-bye and lots of love,
Mother

Dear Mother and Dad,

Your shipboard letters came yesterday and I've been reading them ever since. In fact, the oily Mr. Ribner came up to me as I was peeking in my pocket at the English stamps—you see what I'm reduced to—and said in his most charming manner, "Pocketing your percentage prematurely, Miss Wheeler?" They say maniacs talk alliteratively, and I really suspect this beast's sanity. Anyway, it's one time in my life that I'm grateful for my plainness. Even so, I've had a look or two from that fish which would make a rhinoceros wonder if he hasn't been transformed into a swan or something.

At any rate, I do carry the letters about and they are, except for the mention of *mal de mer* (!), happy witnesses of happy times, and that, as Mr. Ribner might say, is my pleasurable percentage.

I called up Mr. Goodrich, Dad, and he whispered a thanks. He always sounds as if Mr. Amos were peering over his accounts or something, but he is a wonderful person and I loved talking to him if only because it was a little like talking to you. He says all goes well, and he never passes your desk without thinking of the Arch of Triumph. He also said Mr. Amos makes his joke about "having to check old Wheeler's accounts" about four times a day.

I haven't done anything since the last letter but see the Ava Gardner movie with Jeannie, who, of course, loved it. About all it showed of Paris was the Eiffel Tower and the French flag. The rest was filmed on Catalina Island I suppose.

It's been boiling hot and the house has assumed its summer "stovey" quality. I almost prayed Sunday that God would make the old oak grow back again, even taller and shadier than before—either that or a hurricane, just a little refreshing one this time. I'm ashamed to say that I was just too lazy to drive downtown to Mr. Beardsley but, surprise of surprises, the heat had given Mr. Damon the strength it had drained from everyone else, and he almost looked God in the face. The church was practically empty, which had a good effect on him also, I suppose, for it kept him from glancing apologetically at the Cartwright-Clough gang. (I mean they weren't there, except for John Clough, who nodded to me.)

It's really too hot to go on. I'm not being very amusing anyway. I can only think that when you get this you won't have much more than a week there, and that makes me very sad as well as happy. I don't need to explain why.

Do have a wonderful last week and a wonderful time on the boat.

Love and xxx,
Nancy

I must reopen the letter to tell you that John Clough called. He wanted to know whether I'd seen the Ava Gardner movie—he was on his way—and, after a frantic debate, I said, yes, I had. He'll try me again he says. (T-r-y!?) He seemed nice but I don't know. Why should he want to see the Ava Gardner movie, or did he think it suited my taste, and why didn't he suggest another movie—too reserved? Oh well. It's given me hope that my lot won't have to be a Ribner. *Au revoir encore.*

N.

Nancy dear,

There just hasn't been time. A week after you get this we'll be home and all the bags we packed one way or another for six months will be all unpacked in a couple of hours. And the awful thing is that it worked. Everything has developed as we'd planned. Mother's gone around with a strange kind of shine in her eyes. She raves about buildings and pictures, and all her committee tenderness about people turns out to be personal tenderness as well. She looks and pities and adores.

I'm afraid it's I who fail. I've felt Mr. Amos's eye over my shoulder too. I think, Maybe my accounts are in bad shape. Did I transfer the Benson money? Will I have to? . . . Et cetera, et cetera. And then you write about the house, so that I can feel its so-special heat closing in on me inside Paris's own heat. I walk around alone at night sometimes and think, If I could only stay. Maybe I should have robbed the bank. Did you know Goodrich and I had a parlor game in which we'd devise elaborate swindling schemes, transfers of funds into seven currencies, intricate pass entries that CPAs would have to work on for years, multiple discounts that kept us up hours debating? Maybe we were wrong not to do something. Once I think the only thing that held me back was the fear of hearing Mother harping forever about your ruined future. Now I don't know if she would not have gone ahead with something far beyond my own respectable terrors.

For the past few days Paris might as well have been Catalina Island for me too. Twenty days is just twenty days, though John Reed might claim it's twice as much as you need. But the Bolsheviks had eighty years to prepare, and the only preparation we've had has been a dream, and a dull dream at that.

It's a state I'm in, of course, like the time the hurricane took our single, our wonderful oak, and left the forests of the Jebbs and Cartwrights practically intact. I remember wishing I were a Calvinist so that I could believe that everything did make sense, the whole direction of my life, with the falling oak as its inevitable marker—but it was too magnificent an oak to stand for anything about me, and probably the reason it fell was that it was just too magnificent to shade our little stove of a house—so kerplunk.

You know what I did yesterday? I called one of the black marketeers over and asked him to have a drink with me. Really. He was very stupid and spoke worse French than I (most of them seem to be Arabs or Spaniards). He couldn't understand that I didn't want to exchange money. What I wanted to ask him was couldn't I join his gang. (They all work in gangs.) He kept raising the price, "430, 435, 440," always thinking my noes were attempts to drive him higher. He even paid for his drink, and said "450 *dernière chance*," and I shook my head. Wouldn't you think they could use an honest-looking American? But I've quit applying.

I feel better now, writing out this gripe. But there it is, honey. Don't expect to see us all rejuvenated and close to each other. Mother will be freer and brighter perhaps, but I will be quieter and duller. The distance between us will be the same. I guess it's up to you to have the good times. It hasn't been in the cards for us. The trip didn't belong to us.

I hope the Clough boy calls again. You'll be surprised, though, how many others there are going to be.

Love and kisses, dear,
Dad

Nancy dear,

We're going to pack tomorrow and just right. I've reached the peak, and with one more step I'd be over. We've been to Versailles, Fontainebleau, and yesterday I went down to Chartres. I'm almost sick that we haven't been out of France—wonderful as it's been—money or not. But we'll be back, I know it, and next time with you. Life holds too much more than what one's been led to expect.

You can't imagine what I did. I went over to the ECA office yesterday (it's in the old palace of Talleyrand) and dallied with the personnel people about a job, and do you know, I'm really going to consider it this coming year. I think Dad could get something and it's certain that I could get quite a good secretarial position (if I learned to type). Of course it's too absurd to think about—Dad would lose tenure, pension rights, almost everything, but we could rent the house for more money than it's ever been worth to us; we could save over here, even keep working for the government, I don't know precisely, and I don't care precisely—but I did think of it, and that alone makes me wonder.

What would Dad think? I'm not going to tell him till the boat, for we have to let a sensible, normal year intervene anyway. Can I even go so far as to say prepare to give us your opinion?

I'm so primed to tell things that I don't dare begin or I'll have spilled out everything I'm saving for home. So there, too, you must wait.

As for the Clough boy, dear, I'm just as glad you don't see him. His mother is the dullest, smallest-minded woman I've ever met. Can he really have escaped that? Of course he has if you say it, but I cannot believe that he has some real life of his own. The Harvard Business School is so much the expected thing.

Enough of this maternal interfering!

Where shall we all be in a year, two years? For the first time since I can remember, I've thought of something like this—and with excitement.

It has been a fling, a great, shaking fling, Nancy. Shall we ever get over it?

We'll see you before we know it, dear. Stop work now and be all rested up for us. Until then

Much love,
Mother

Dear Mother and Dad,

Will this get to you at Le Havre? I do hope so. I'm so excited about my little scene and its aftermath that I can hardly write.

Yes, a scene, a real Ava Gardner scene. Just this morning. What happened was that John Clough saw me as he passed the store on his way to the Sport Shop. He came in and we talked for a few minutes. No customers were around as it was very early. All of a sudden out of nowhere Mr. Ribner appears and whispers to me, "Is the gentleman buying a fifteen or a twenty denier, Miss Wheeler?"

I was terribly angry but so startled that I couldn't think of an adequate answer. "It's just a friend of mine," I said.

"The company prefers its clerks to conduct their clandestine affairs outside, Miss Wheeler." Just exactly that? He *is* mad! But I must be madder because I suddenly raised my hand and slapped that oily leering face as hard as I could and then ran in the back for my coat and ran out. John caught me on the way and held my arm. Mr. Ribner had gone back in the office and all the girls called to me as I passed the counters, things like "Good shot, Wheeler" and "That was the college try, Nance." It was just fantastic. And then John said, "Let's drive into New York and celebrate," and I said, "I'd love to more than anything in the world."

And we did and I've had a marvelous time. It was a lovely lovely day and the Parkway was glorious and we went to the U.N. and that was wonderful too and we ate and had drinks and went to Cinerama and bought scalper's tickets for two dollars apiece for the worst seats in the house but I loved it, especially the European part, and then we went to the Plaza for tea and had dinner at King of the Sea and after we went dancing at a gigantic outdoors place on the Hudson and now it's 2:00 A.M. and I've just come home very happy. He is the nicest human being I've ever met. He's bright, considerate, literate, unambitious, and secure. I think he likes me.

You see why I want this to get to the boat—not that I'll be married when you come home or anywheres near being almost close to being engaged—but to show you I've had a time too.

Now you'll think the real reason she wanted us to go was to get us out of her way. God—Freud—knows.

I'll see you wanderers soon down at the boat. I think old John will drive me. What do you think of that, hm?

Love and love,
Ava

IN A WORD, TROWBRIDGE

Her name, a famous name for—as she saw and felt it—a nonentity, was what the policeman who called the ambulance heard her saying: "Trowbridge." The name that made her something before she was anything was what she said when she could say nothing else. The mugger had clubbed her behind the right ear. The two syllables full of rectitude and connectedness, were, apparently, what sustained her. Her identity, her stake in the world. What her mother claimed she took too lightly. (Though she'd kept the name *she'd* grown with, she'd married in part for that name. Her own fame was underwritten by it, as a great corporation looms behind its subsidiaries.)

That Charlotte had been born with the name provoked her mother. That she could "drag it into the mud" was a disgrace. Her "slovenliness, imprecision, ignorance, and carelessness," bad in themselves, were monstrous because she was a Trowbridge. Once, an unforgettable once, the maternal indictment was "ugliness." Torrents of babble about cuteness, prettiness, even beauty did not annul that. Her long Trowbridge jaw and nostrils, her hyperthyroid eyes confirmed it. The sense of ugliness lit her victimage, spotlit her head for muggers.

She was the Trowbridge who served as a subject of parental anecdotes, parental pride in the fact of parentage.

Charlotte Trowbridge.

A moniker out of nineteenth-century arrogance. Nineteen letters, enough for three names; French topping of Anglo-Saxon assertiveness; a scoop of New England pride in plainness. "Family," it proclaimed. "Old American stock."

Part of what sustained her father in the fugal wildness of his life: monumental idleness and monumental frenzy. The Great American Painter of His Time. His gallantry, foolishness, purity, jokes, his proclamations and marching for causes; his famous refusals. "I prefer not to." The Great Novelist said he "was carted around like a piece of the true cross." All that uprightness and, on the nightside of his life, the careening on the razor's edge, fights, binges, arrests, outrages of every sort; his public abandonment of Mother; marriage to the French actress; fathering the doomed twins; leaving them all for the Swedish premier's wife; getting arrested with the Los Angeles drug gang whom he painted into his Last Judgment as angels while his wives and children struggled in loony abstraction between Hell and Purgatory. Finally, the return to Mother and the pathetic death on the Eighty-first Street platform of the Independent Subway station, embracing and sliding down the iron pillar, curled in a great heap, ignored for hours until the old woman — who claimed she heard his last words — called a policeman. " 'Take it,' " she said he'd said. " 'Take it.' " "But the strange thing," wrote the *Times* reporter, "was that nothing appeared to have been taken. Henry Trowbridge died with his watch and wallet. No thief or mugger had touched him."

Take it.

His words. Charlotte's would have been, "You can't take it." Or, "I don't have anything to give." Like Mother's. Mother had grown up poor in a house full of sisters who had nothing but each other. Anything received or taken was held on to desperately. The crime of crimes was theft. Under it lay the fearfulness of starved egos. No prosperity repaired it, no praise, no prizes displaced the sense that others wanted what you had and were. So Mother would do anything to keep whatever she had, money, reputation, power. She served on every committee which distributed memberships or awards. If she could not win prizes herself, she could at least control who got them.

Take it.

Father gave, and gave easily, time, money, self. He'd been given the adoration of a brilliant, resentful mother, was deferred to by a shaky father, relished the large stage of only-child-dom. Huge, strong, willful, awkward, he was a bully, a leader, smart, energetic, good-looking, self-confident of his place and power. All this until his system trapped itself. He "paid for" the power with terrifying mental storms. A month of ecstatic ebullience became two of paralyzing fatigue. "To tie a shoelace," he told ten-year-old Charlotte, "is as hard as painting the Sistine Chapel." In the sixties, the Danes came up with the lithium salts which planed off the heights and depths and gave him an extra decade. Meanwhile, his escapades and his talent made him the best-known American painter of his time.

"Take it." Because he'd grown with love at the top of the world, country houses, town houses, classes in everything from carving to the fox-trot. After a year at Yale, he declared himself a painter and took off for Paris, Arles, Brittany, the valley towns of Idaho and Montana. He created what made his name count for more than property and family history. And it was then that he began to feel for those whose rights were concealed by all they lacked.

Take it.

He gave to the tyrannized, the insulted, the bedeviled, the wounded, the nameless. He fattened the American myth of the noble democrat. It went back to Saint Francis, to Gautama, up through the patriots of Massachusetts and Virginia to the Roosevelts and the latest, thinnest White House version of it.

What was not so conspicuously American was the erotic give-and-take, the women in and out of his life. When mania charged his system, he took off, emptying bank accounts to buy up the world for these transient enchanters, his muses, his subjects. Painted onto the walls and canvases of contemporary culture, they became her mother's public humiliation. What was worse were his public apologies to her.

No wonder that neither Charlotte nor her mother could have said, "Take it." She could not give *anything,* let alone the most private part of her self. So she was withering into what Mother couldn't bear (though she herself hadn't married till she was thirty-five). For Mother, though, it had been independence and a self-advertised sexual free-for-all. Charlotte was simply a spinster, like her great-great-aunts. Not a virgin, not lesbian, neither self-sufficient nor independent, but alone, a large, clumsy, half-pretty offshoot of two famous Americans, one a proclaimed genius, the other an efficient, useful caretaker and servant of the arts.

It wasn't until the huge biography of her father came out that she learned why she'd been destined for spinsterhood. More, why she'd been meant not to exist.

"I won't put this madness into a child," he'd told friends. The biographer said nothing about a mistake, they'd not married because she'd been started; it was two years after their marriage and a dozen before the lithium, so *why was she?*

Welcomed, cheered, a famous baby, alluded to in hundreds of letters—her infantile doings documented like a king's—painted as often as an infanta or the Picasso and Renoir children, by age five, she had a niche in cultural history, was a subject of dissertations.

Not a hint that a girl was less welcome than a boy, somehow she knew that. First destined not to be, then to be an only male child, and, finally, an unfruitful woman. Not only the name but the line of Henry Trowbridge and Vanna Peete would stop with her. Trowbridge cousins could, would, and did perpetuate the name that festooned streets, but she would exist only to entitle her parents: *father, mother.* Still, Father would say, "When you have your children." Grandfatherdom appealed to him more than fatherhood, fattened his large, if ironic affection for continuity, transmission, the variation of features. He would have relished seeing refigurations of himself and his parents. (His paintings were full of familial variation. A cover story in *Vanity Fair* called him the last portraitist.)

But his drive to her motherhood was stopped by Mother.

At first, it was the standard mother-daughter cut down. Her few friends suffered similar cuts and, by adolescence, recognized the sexual rivalry. Here, though, there was intellectual rivalry as well. Not since her father had raved about a kindergarten drawing, which he'd framed and put into his studio, had she known anything but dismissal of any accomplishment, drawn, written, played, thought out. At best, there was laughter or the patronizing dismissal of "charm," "amateur ease," "sweet," maybe "moving" or "touching." What counted was the annihilation of whatever gift the child of two artists would more than possibly show. It was a systematic refrigeration which she felt in her whole being.

And there was an erotic complement. Anyone who hugged or kissed her was eyed like a rapist; even Father could be made to blush for a hearty kiss, a second-longer-than-necessary embrace.

"I don't think you have the legs for that dress." "Your shoulders are too defined for décolletage." "You're developing a pubescent paunch." "I don't think boys admire aggressive charm."

Or life-lasting touches, twists, slaps, looks. The clearest messages she ever got.

What she also learned from the biography was Mother's self-advertised bed-hopping. Not only the easiest lay in American Bohemia but the readiest recorder of sexual performance. With—and Charlotte knew this deeply—about as much erotic feeling as the recording typewriter. Mother was the sort of woman who looked as if she'd once been beautiful. Father had met her when they were both thirty-five—no, Mother was two years older, a preserved secret—she'd just started looking pretty, her legs halfway between youthful stems and the soft trunks they were now. She'd also just painted the only good painting of her career and begun writing the art criticism that became the source of her influence. For the ambitious, uncertain, shrewd, troubled, gifted painter, she was an attraction, a catch. Mother's father had walked away from home when she was eight, she had no sense of or need for a man around the house. She'd made it on her own in difficult New York, she was proud and independent, but there were also fears that things would not last; she never trusted the affection of others; besides, if she wanted a child, it was time to have it. Henry was funny, attractive, learned, gifted, he could make money and had some coming to him; and there was that tremendous name that automatically earned what almost no achievement could—since achievement was its contradiction. (Achievement represented present and future, the name the past.) "So, Charlotte, despite his rough times—I had no idea how rough they were, how rough they'd be—I married him."

Charlotte lived seventy blocks south and four east of the apartment in which she'd grown up. Not all that far by cab or train, but too far for mother and daughter. How often Mother thought of her now she didn't know. Once in a while the phone would ring and be hung up at her "Hello," Mother checking to see if she were alive, not caring to speak to her. She lived on Twelfth Street west of Broadway, an old brownstone neighborhood publishing companies were just moving into. It felt like the New York her parents knew in the thirties and for-tics. She lived above a Vietnamese cleaner-tailor, below a charming gay retired schoolteacher who was writing a novel about eighteenth-century New York. Which she'd agreed to read. (It "revealed" a totally homosexual society, from Washington and Hamilton to pirates and scullery maids. Felix said, "It is completely researched.") In return for the reading, he gave her his sister's dress, the only really beautiful one she'd ever owned.

Wouldn't you know it was the dress she wore the night she'd been clubbed? The taxi stopped a block from the entrance, a standard precaution. Her young man was up to a verbal grab and suggested another date. She went off with relief toward a warm bath. She walked the block without fear or thought, "Call soon" just off her lips and a touch of lips on them, in mind, the relief which sealed her all-but-technical virginity. (Twenty years before, a Trowbridge cousin had fucked her twice.) In the penumbra of the streetlight, her head was crunched, she was gripped, thrown, kicked, and, while out, robbed. Left in a heap like the one Father made in the subway station an ocean from his official wife and the insane twins who divided the trust with her. She must have lain in her heap about as long as he'd lain in his before the policeman who called the ambulance had been called by the early-waking novelist off for his morning Egg McMuffin.

Swathed and befogged, a floating zero, a vague pain zone, she lay in a white room at St. Vincent's. "Trowbridge, Trowbridge." (Enough to get Mother down, her blue eyes terrified—at last—with the fear that she might lose what she'd more or less thrown away.) She reclaimed Charlotte, who came slowly back into what made her Charlotte. She was visited by Samantha, who'd been at Miss Hewitt's and Brearley with her, by Tiffany, who'd roomed with her at Bryn Mawr, by Eliza, who'd worked with her at the Whitney, and Andrea, who'd been her boss at Sotheby's. So life was reassembled, Mother guiding, directing, interpreting.

Then it was time to leave the white room. The beautiful, ripped dress was pushed into the overnight bag in which Mother had brought a schoolgirl's skirt and blouse. She was left off at her own place under Felix and above Le Tho Cleaning and Repair. Her place. After all, she was a Trowbridge, strong enough to either add something to the name or to resist the subtraction willed on it by others. "I'm just the age you were when you married, Mother, when you and Daddy began doing the best work of your life."

Not that she was setting up a rivalry. Success was less important than resolve. Success was transient and problematic, resolve was a way of existing. No point in continuity if it wasn't inspired by that. If you had the confidence of your name, you were even prepared to lose it. That too was not out of the question, so maybe, Mother, you'll dance at my wedding, clumsy at that as you, Daddy, and I always were at it; anyway, be prepared. I say that giving you more than you gave me, which doesn't mean I don't care what happens to you. On the contrary, but the terms are altered. It's time for the old to be old, the young to be whatever they are—it passed me by—and us middlers to do whatever it is we can, which, the way I feel now—tossing the bag strap over her shoulder with the ease of a climber—is plenty.

COOLEY'S VERSION

1

Professor De Witte, head bent low, took the Widener steps two at a time. Still he managed to keep his eye on a stubby, redheaded man standing by a pillar, staring into the Yard. After waiting a few seconds to be acknowledged, De Witte pulled a handkerchief out of his back pocket and blew his nose loudly. The young man kept on staring ahead.

"Ah, Cooley," De Witte called.

"Good morning," Cooley said quietly.

De Witte headed for the pillar and stood there puffing and leaning over Cooley's head. "I've news for you, Cooley. I was talking to this publisher fellow, Simonfreed, in New York last week. He was looking for a translator and I gave him your name. He's found some woman scribbler he thinks is better than Mme. de Lafayette. He's going to send some of her stuff along to you any day now."

De Witte waited for a response and again got none. He grunted, whirled, lowered his head, and charged the revolving door into the library.

Cooley had not withheld a response intentionally. De Witte's words had absorbed him beyond his power to make even those simple gestures which composed his social life. What's it all about? he asked himself. Is this the way he thinks he's going to pay me for doing his Villehardouin? Damned fool. It's probably a children's book. He kicked at a cigarette butt and missed, then slid it deliberately down the stone flight.

The next day he hurried to his mailbox. The only thing in it was the faculty announcement he'd left there unread the day before. For the rest of the week, his heart and feet quickened as he moved down the hall toward the box, only to slow depressingly at its emptiness. The second week went by and he'd nearly forgotten the whole thing when Spencer came into his office carrying a small parcel.

"This was in your box, Cooley."

"Thanks," said Cooley. "I saw it. Someone's going to pick it up there this afternoon."

"Oh," said Spencer. "Awfully sorry. You're just two boxes down from mine on the left and I thought I'd bring it in. I'll take it right back."

"Never mind," said Cooley. "I'll carry it over to him." He took the package from Spencer's fat palm and nodded coldly to him as he went downstairs.

Cooley walked through the Yard among the falling leaves, holding the package tightly. He walked quickly until he reached Ellery Street, then jogged around the corner and up the stairs to his room. There he worked the string off the package and took a white paperbound book out of the wrapping.

Mal-en-point was the title. Under it, in smaller print, "Delphine Trèves," and at the bottom, the florid signature "N.R.F.," with the neat endorsement "Gallimard."

He opened the book, fingered the uncut pages, then, sitting down in his armchair, reached for a kitchen knife on the desk. He cut the pages slowly and pleasurably.

He began reading a little after five o'clock and continued straight through supper till nine-thirty. When he finished, he leaned his head on the back of the chair and shivered a little. "Unbelievable," he said softly. "Unbelievable." He was very hungry. He laid the book on the desk, put on his topcoat, and walked downtown. He was conscious of feeling exalted and allowed the sharpness of the air to heighten both this sense and his consciousness of it. His mind went over the novel as a woman goes up and down the stairs and in and out of the rooms of a new house.

2

He had not been prepared for *Mal-en-point;* he had, in fact, given up the expectation that he might someday find something like it, a person or book which would bring integration, expansion, and exegesis of his sensibility. The reading of Delphine Trèves's novel had meant for Cooley no less than a communion.

His exaltation continued for days. Separate from it, however, was the thought of translation. The reading itself had satisfied him completely.

It was accident which set him to work on it.

Spencer came into Cooley's office one afternoon eating a peach, juice running down his chin and neck into his collar.

"De Witte tells me you're translating some contemporary whorestew," he said. The junior members of the faculty had the habit of asking the chairman of the department what their fellows were "working on," usually after assuring themselves that nothing was being worked on at all.

"That's right," said Cooley. "Something in the line of Laclos."

"Are you trying to call *Les Liaisons* whorestew?" cried Spencer, spitting the pit into his hand. He was engaged in reading memoirs of the period to establish a key for the novel.

"It's one of my favorites," said Cooley, and though he still had papers to correct, he walked out.

The sight of Spencer's jaws mangling the peach upset him. He was affected the way a mother is by the sight of a mongrel nuzzling her child. The impulse to translate was protective: it was as if by rendering the delicate brilliance of *Mal-en-point* in English he could snatch it away from Spencer's jaws and judgment. Home, he went straight to his desk, snapped on his green eyeshade, and translated the first chapter and a half of the book.

It was finished on New Year's Day, a longer job than he'd anticipated. The first draft had taken no time at all; it was almost a matter of typing directly from French to English. When he went over it, however, difficulties cropped up in the phrasing and even in the entire cast of scenes. Hammering out the textual ambiguities to fit the delicate movements of authorial intention had taken his finest efforts.

For a month after he dispatched the manuscript, there was no response, and Cooley was beginning to feel that the enriched isolation which had originated in the reading and terminated in the final sentence of his version was complete, that the by-products of typing, checking, and dispatching the manuscript were the illusory deposits of an activity which his commitment alone had exhausted. Then he received two letters, one from Simonfreed and one from Delphine Trèves. The first was a warm, congratulatory note which concluded by saying that the book would be published in the spring. The note from Delphine Trèves, although a good deal more sparsely written, was, nonetheless, a positive appreciation of his accomplishment, coupled with the implication of her own. It struck him also as an invitation to enter into personal correspondence. Only when it was too late to answer did he regret not having done so.

He did not hear from her again for six months. Then, in the same package in which he received her second novel from Simonfreed, he found a note addressed to him through the publisher's office. Written in an even sparer manner than the first, it treated of technical difficulties which she felt lay in the new book. He answered this, as he answered the similar letters she sent with each succeeding work, in English, with equally technical comments.

3

Her first three novels were neither widely read nor well received. Except for admiring notices in some of the smaller quarterlies, they were usually reviewed along with other foreign novels which they resembled in neither scope nor quality. It was only after the publication of his fourth translation (five years after the first) that her work began to receive the attention which was to be its permanent lot.

The critic who had praised her work most highly in one of the smaller journals wrote an article on recent French fiction for the largest of the literary weeklies in which he gave prominent place to her work. Cooley found the treatment of his author a bold one, but it was, nevertheless, this treatment which set her literary tone over the country. Its account of her "impassioned quietness" did more than set the tone of reviews; it aroused popular interest in her novels.

It was in these first months of her popularity that Cooley sustained his shock. During the Christmas vacation which he spent each year at his aunt Margaret's apartment in New York, his aunt said, coming in, "There's a big Christmas display in Brentano's, Calvin, and your girl takes up the whole window."

"My girl?"

"The Trèves woman. They've got a big picture of her sticking in the window. Lord, she's a monster, isn't she?"

"Yes," he said. "I passed it yesterday."

The next day he got up right after his aunt left and hurried over to Fifth Avenue.

There in the window, framed with his own rendering of her lucidities, her giant image glared at the street. He almost shuddered in disbelief. There seemed no possibility that the gross lips and pendulous cheeks swelling under the steamy eyes could make up the physical instrument of the brilliant spirit he had let out into the American air. Was this, he asked himself, the end product of his five years' absorbed transmutation? His aunt's words came to him like an announcement over a loudspeaker and rooted the factuality of his horror.

Standing there, his eyes fixed on the picture, he wondered if he hadn't been mistaken all along. Did she, did all the books in the window, belong with Spencer, De Witte, and all the other vulgarities which cluttered up his life? Were the texts he'd hammered out the revelation of a vileness which issued only in ambiguity? He walked up the avenue reeling with terror.

A week later, back in Cambridge, he reread her books and found what he was looking for. It was like a nation receiving a declaration of war from a supposedly friendly neighbor; it searches its files to dig the deception from every treaty and dispatch. So Cooley searched, and so he found himself "taken."

4

The morning he was to meet Delphine Trèves, Cooley rose at ten, washed, dressed, then reached outside the door of the apartment to lay on the pile of seven *Herald Tribunes* a note canceling his aunt's subscription for the month. He cooked the eggs he'd brought in with him the night before and listened to the violinist in the next apartment practicing furious scales. Usually the music enraged him. This morning, however, the passion of senseless repetition soothed him.

At eleven-thirty, he left the apartment and walked toward Fifth Avenue. In the elevator, straightening his tie in the mirror, he had an attack of nerves. When he entered the office, however, and saw her across the room with Simonfreed, a plump woman of thirty in a dark suit, a feeling of serene confidence welled up in him and he advanced to meet her with what he felt were giant strides.

She rose and took his palm out of the air like a derrick sweeping up dirt. "A long-awaited pleasure, M. Cooley," she said simply.

The caked syllables of his academic French cracked magically under her words. "Entirely mine, Mlle. Trèves." He squeezed her hand with all the firmness he could muster.

"It's strange, this meeting, isn't it?" she said. "We've done, after all, so many things together."

"I've thought continually about it," he said. "I suppose it's because you have so many others while I, in a sense, have had only you."

"I know," she said, touching his elbow for a moment with her great hand. "I knew you did no one else. The German translator is in the eleventh volume of Bossuet. He does me for *Trinkgeld*. You've really been my greatest compliment."

Simonfreed, bald and spectacled, bent to their level heads. In good French he told them of a reserved table in a famous restaurant around the corner. They went downstairs, Delphine Trèves in the middle, wondering at the speed of the elevator and the spectacle of the avenue. They walked to Forty-third Street and descended a flight of cellar steps to a dark-paneled, white-tabled room.

They drank aperitifs and a fine Bordeaux, something Cooley had never done at a meal in his life. But his wonder was all for her. She ate like a griffin, soup, rolls, mutton, potatoes, salad, cheese, and ice cream; she drank four cups of coffee and eight or nine glasses of wine. Meanwhile she talked brilliantly and continuously in English and French.

It ended with her tipping her fifth cup of coffee into Simonfreed's lap.

"But impossible!" she cried and scooped up a handful of tablecloth to jab at his trousers.

Simonfreed held her off. "It's absolutely nothing," he stammered. "Don't bother at all. There's another suit in the office and I have to change anyway." He rose and initialed the check. "Why don't you and Cooley walk around the city a bit?"

Delphine Trèves got up. "Good," she said. She went up the stairs ahead of them and turned at the top to shake Simonfreed's hand. "You forgive me."

"Of course," he said, and though he'd planned to walk with them a few blocks, he shook hands with her and said, "I'll call you later."

Delphine Trèves caught the exciting air of the avenue at once and said little during the walk. She stopped for a second at the bookshop in which, Cooley told her, he'd first seen her picture and again in front of the mannequins in Bergdorf Goodman's. They walked slowly, her suit skirt limiting her stride. The sun was hot and she removed her jacket. A thin white blouse brought into emphasis her bulk, and he felt suddenly reduced, as if the wind had blown sails to fullness over him.

At the junction of the great hotels at Fifty-ninth Street, they entered the park. Past the horse lanes and the zoo they moved, deeper and deeper into the complex park, until, at the edge of the central lake, they sat on a bench under the trees and watched the rowboats struggling out from the little pier.

"We must do this also, Cooley," she said. He went to the pier and bought an hour's ticket. Their boat looked clumsy and leaky. He got in and felt his shoulder gripped fiercely as she floundered into the boat. The pain did not prevent his rowing round the bend into the middle of the lake.

There, hemmed in by the apartment houses, moving among the grimy ducks, he stared at her great breasts. Something about them as they shifted under her blouse, as if in sympathy with his exertions, gave him the feeling that he could go through with what he had intended. His face bulged with the thought of it.

"Your first sign of strain, Cooley," she said. "You have remarkably fine organization. You don't look at all strong yet we've been moving beautifully." She laughed bearishly as his stroke missed the water, and before he could say anything, asked quietly, "Have you never written, yourself? Have you always held yourself within translation?"

With what irony he could summon in French, he replied, "My temperament is rather precisely suited to translation. I prefer to work on brute matter one degree removed."

She let a hand trail in the water and slapped it to her forehead. "Do you think that I am not more brutal than what I work on?"

He pulled hard on his right oar to avoid collision with a boat whose oarsmen were splashing water at each other. "Do you want to get rammed?" he shouted. The boys remained oblivious.

"You are diverting your strength, Cooley. Why don't we go in before we are responsible for a disaster?"

He turned the boat around and headed for the pier.

"High school boys, the two last in the class," she said thoughtfully. And in English, "My books are made from that. Do you like the *Ad Magistri Vocem*?"

"I'm doing it now," he said. "I like it very much. Where does the title come from? I've lost my Latin."

"I never had any," she said. "I found it in Montaigne, translated in the notes. It's Martial, something about everyone knowing his master's voice. Works well, don't you think? The bishop thinking he's answering his call?"

"Yes," said Cooley, who had not seen it all. "Yes, it does."

He was not disturbed at missing it. His thought was that Delphine Trèves had altered in the last few minutes. It was as if speaking English had made her unsure, made her lose her balance. Cooley noticed a tightness in her movements, noticed it triumphantly as the register of his power.

Back at the pier he took her great arm and guided her across the struts.

The sun had begun to set. Composed now, he strode beside her along the ways they had come, touching her elbows at the crossroads, leading her out of the park. Across Fifty-ninth Street and east from Fifth Avenue they walked, the streets darkening, the evening traffic raging with animal menace in the streets. They moved together down the avenue toward the apartment of his aunt Margaret.

5

The Bar Harbor Express from New York to Boston was the only train ride which Cooley anticipated with pleasure. The gulls on the rocks and the subdued white towns give character to the trip. A gentlemanly loudspeaker announces the stations, and the conductors are fatherly.

The ride, the day after the meeting in New York, seemed to Cooley the shortest he had ever taken. He was feeling extravagant and bold, yet he hoped that the trip would dull the feeling and help him regain his equilibrium.

Under this was a more uneasy feeling, one which forced itself on his consciousness in a theme from a Bach partita. Through the wall which separated Margaret's apartment from the violinist's, the theme had attacked his evening with maniacal reiteration. Its force had carried him blindly through the terrible insistencies of the night; now the memory of its mechanical ecstasy survived the other.

He concentrated on the gulls, the stations, and the passengers, in an effort to ignore it. With each announcement of a station, he became more at ease. The familiar beauty of the scene was more important to him than it had ever been. He was close to tears.

By the time he reached Ellery Street, he was worn out.

When he awoke, it was dark. He switched on the light and rubbed his eyes. He realized he'd been dreaming about Delphine Trèves. He tried to bring back the dream but could only remember that it had not been unpleasant. He looked over at the little shelf of paperbound volumes and at the one above of his hardcover American versions of them. The juxtaposition pleased him.

6

Two days later, postmarked from Washington, the first step of her tour around the United States, came this note:

Dear Cooley,

I have known you a much briefer time than I have my German
translator (a Swiss named Burger) or my Spanish translator (a very
interesting man, a doctor of medicine named Fuentes), yet our
relationship has become, swiftly and intensely, the one I have
always felt to be the perfect social version of the interactions of our
work. With the finest souvenirs,

Delphine Trèves

Cooley was at first unsure of the letter, yet, as months passed and
the memory of the day in New York faded, he came to regard it as the
most stunning emblem of his life, one which never failed to reassure
him amid the ecstatic convolutions of her later books.

ASSESSMENT OF AN AMATEUR

I stopped drawing large drafts on my future when I was just shy of thirty—the usual age, I think, for those with the artistic temperament. For that, I suppose, is what I had, a disposition to take the world at the hands of people who'd made some sense out of it. Before my Paris days, however, I did not differentiate my disposition from my talents, and I thought, in what I know is fairly common fashion, that the disposition promised almost anything ambition could imagine. Not in the arts, as a matter of fact, for not even in music—the art which I knew best—did I ever feel that I had either the physical capacity for performance or the sheer mass of technical training necessary for composition. Nonetheless, it was my accurate, if amateur, feeling for music which, thought I, augured well for brilliance in some lesser field.

It was going over on the boat that I met the real instructor of those years, the pianist, Dave Higgins, whose name you probably know if you are as up in music now as I was then. Geographically, Higgins was, in my then unrepentant New Yorkese, almost ultimately provincial. (I am not absolutely sure even now whether he came from Minneapolis or Milwaukee, and for the reason that I could not, and perhaps cannot now, distinguish those two towns.) Higgins was a professional artist, the only one I've ever really known, and it was the observation of his career in Paris that marked, I think, a turning point in my own self-knowledge. This was due, I believe, to the fact that it demonstrated one of the few tenable distinctions in the social world, the one between the ways and means of amateurs and professionals. At any rate, such distinction serves me in reflecting about Higgins and myself.

He and his wife, Elizabeth, were for over a year almost my only friends in Paris, as I was theirs. Indeed, much of our spare time was spent at each other's apartments, and, when Elizabeth got massively pregnant and stayed at home for days at a time reading the *Milwaukee Journal* forwarded by her mother four times a week, Higgins spent at least half of every day at my place in back of Gare d'Orsay on Rue Verneuil. I had a fair-sized apartment, a better piano than he, and a very sexy neighbor across the courtyard, a small, ravishable blond whose husband worked nights, and whom we constantly threatened with invasion. Wordlessly, of course. We leaned out the window drinking cognac and exchanging leers with her, but it never got beyond that, although, as Elizabeth's "time" drew near, Higgins's threats grew more verbal, if equally hollow.

Higgins's visits to Rue Verneuil usually revolved around his borrowing money; he was "on" the GI Bill, while I was "on" the somewhat more luxurious provisions of the Fulbright Act. He paid for the loans, I suppose, by attending to my musical insights and two-fingered performances. That first winter I was analyzing Beethoven's opus 2, number 2.

"Listen to this figure," I'd say, hacking out a few measures from the stretto in the first movement. "Hear what it's doing?"

"I need three thousand francs," he'd reply.

"In the wallet. Listen again," and I bent to the figure. "Pure quartet writing. The Dutchman was no more at home in the pianoforte than you were in Minneapolis."

"Manitoba," said Higgins, fingering the franc notes.

"Did you ever hear Backhaus play it? He doesn't even suspect what's going on."

"Maybe he sees it another way."

"Exactly."

"What a loss to music when you took up the electoral college, Bucky." "Bucky" is a fond idiocy of my family; the proper reduction of my name is Bill.

"I guess you're just a mechanic, Higgins. A fish with gills, but can't tell sea from Siam."

"Come buy me a drink," he'd finish, and we'd go down to the corner bistro where I had an account.

Practically the only entertainments we went to in Paris were concerts. Indeed, the day Elizabeth went to the hospital to produce Danielle, Higgins called to see if I wouldn't buy her ticket to the Gieseking recital that night. Since I had lent him the money for both tickets, I said that I'd resume possession of one of them.

"Usurer," said Higgins.

"All right. I'll buy it at half price," I said, the thought of Higgins's new hostage to fortune tugging at my bachelor heart.

"I'd rather give it away," said Higgins, whose principles were of iron.

"Done," said I.

But I paid all. We went, and had a bad evening, for we ran into a couple of American music students who were studying with Marguerite Long at the Conservatoire. I'd known one of them in New York, a grape-headed cretin who'd been kicked out of Horace Mann for peeping in girls' washrooms.

The introductory matter was scarcely over when the cretin asked for Higgins's credentials: "Whom'd you study with?"

"I'm at the École with Cortot and Gentil."

"I guessed that," said the cretin. "I mean in America."

"Tarnowski," said Higgins. "He formed Horowitz."

"Lots of people formed Horowitz," said the cretin.

"No compliment to a teacher," said I.

"Ohhh," said the cretin, the long belligerent vowel in all its American impurity drawing the eyes of half of Salle Pleyel our way. "A Horowitz hater, eh?"

"Not at all," said I. "The finest player piano yet patented."

We were treated to another vowel.

"I think he means that Horowitz restricts himself to playing virtuoso works," said Higgins, whose acute sense of good form gave him diplomatic airs.

"Let him play the opus 111, and we'll see," said I.

"Ah, ah," noised the cretin. "A Schnabelite. At least Horowitz admits he doesn't understand Beethoven."

"Exactly," I said. "When he learns to understand some music, let him play in public."

Defeated, the cretin turned flanks. "And whom are you working with?" he asked. "Czerny?"

"André Siegfried," I said coolly. "I'm at the *Science Po'*."

"Ah," said Grapehead. "The amateur hour. That does explain things."

"A mortal blow, Bucky," said Higgins, and drew me back upstairs.

"Shove it, Higgins," said I, but the scratch festered.

When Elizabeth returned with Danielle from the American Hospital to the new apartment they'd taken on Rue Nollet, Higgins declared to her that he was renouncing thoughts of a great career.

"That'll be for the child," he said. "I've come far enough trying to be a musician. Coal miner to pianist in three generations is enough. Let the girl be a saint or a genius and the bloodline will be fulfilled."

An hour later he repeated his renunciation to an Englishman we sometimes sat with in a bar near Place Clichy. The Englishman's response was, "You couldn't expect to give recitals with the name Higgins anyway."

"Why not?" asked Higgins.

"Not in England," said the Englishman. "Couldn't even tune an instrument with a mouthful like that." Cleaning his ear, he added, "With some influence, you might be able to move the piano on the stage — but that's the limit."

Higgins, reflecting that he had just grafted the name onto another human destiny, was somewhat miffed. "How about Shaw?" he put in. "He has a Professor Higgins."

"Yes, Shaw," said the Englishman. "Trust Shaw to do something like that. Of course, remember he wasn't a professor of literature. Didn't have a chair, you know."

"Rot," said Higgins in his English vein, but he was not unperturbed. "I may have renounced greatness," he said back in his apartment, "but I've renounced it, not it me."

The little interchange seemed to him somehow typical of the kind of cross-grained antipathy he had been confronted with in Europe. "Things like this puncture a professional, just like the sort of remark your friend made in the Pleyel punctures amateurs. And to think," he went on mournfully, "that Europe started out so well, too. Elizabeth and I tried eight months in Milwaukee and were as barren as mules. Then, two feet out of New York Harbor, we hit it off."

"Midocean, at least, you damn Celt," said Elizabeth.

The voyage over had been a triumph in other ways: Higgins had been the star of the Tourist Class Amateur Hour, had been invited to use the Steinway in first class, and had received a bottle of champagne from the third mate. His troubles began the third week in Paris after he'd enrolled in the École Normale and had taken his first lesson with Professor Gentil. After it, he'd staggered to the Metro, stumbled home to Elizabeth's arms, and groaned, "Rub my temples. The man's undone me." Undone was it, for Milwaukee's best had been told that he would have to make a *recommencement total*. For three months Higgins played nothing but Cortot exercises and, once a week, submitted his wracked hands to Gentil's inspection. "*Ça viendra. Lentement, mais, ça viendra. La semaine prochaine, M. Ekan, à la même heure*"—this the lesson—and Higgins would rush his aching temples home to his wife's ministering fingers. A terrible time, even to watch, and the climax came in a feverish night, near the termination of which Higgins, scarcely breathing, told Elizabeth to get the doctor, who, in turn, after the French ritual diagnosis of *crise de foi,* told her to call the priest. Extreme unction was pronounced at six-thirty, and, two hours later, Higgins rose and drank a demiliter of red. The crisis was over, and from then on, his confidence seeped back, although tempered by the European reappraisal of his career which laid the groundwork, I suppose, for the grand renunciation after Danielle came.

It was, I know, the renunciation, following hard as it did upon his ascent from the depths, that was for me the instructive act. Higgins's sacrificial speech opened up for me the pleasures of comparative triumphs, or even, indeed, comparative failures, and with this bittersweet wisdom I have since been content.

This was not the case with Higgins. Renunciation is the act of an amateur; for the professional it is but an exercise in depth. While I hourly handled my new doubt, Higgins took on the world again, a world which entered in the guise of a seventy-five-year-old woman named Mme. Souchay who lived with a Methusalean brother on the *deuxième étage* just above the Higgins's dark flat. Under the camouflage of age, Mme. Souchay concealed the untamed heart of a former student of the pianoforte, and, as Higgins graduated from the more complicated Cortot finger exercises into the less mechanical items of the repertory, the heart of this *ancienne élève* began to throb with the terrible memories of her musical capitulation. The first evidence of the throbbing took place during a practice session of the opus 57 berceuse: it consisted of the divers thunder of stamping feet and a pounding cane. For Higgins, however, as for all music students worth their salt, this could be taken—after some surprise and annoyance—in stride; it was a professional hazard. The second manifestation was somewhat more disturbing. It consisted of miserable repetitions on Mme. Souchay's desiccated piano of the works Higgins practiced—while he practiced them. At first this led us to expensive adjournments to Rue Nollet bars, but, gradually, Higgins accustomed himself to the monstrous accompaniments; indeed, he would even play the first bars of the piece he was going to practice a few minutes before beginning the actual session so that Mme. Souchay would have time to hunt out the music and start playing it more or less along with him.

The third stage of the war was a personal appearance. I opened the door one day to a gentle knock and bowed, in amazement, to a minute old woman in a long black dress, whose eyes looked at the floor, or at my socks.

"M. Higgins?" she said.

I informed her that I was not M. Higgins but that I would call him. He came, quivering bravely as a West Pointer at his baptism of fire.

"*Je suis M. Higgins,*" he said in a French that could have passed for almost any of the Romance or Slavic languages.

Hearing it, Mme. Souchay reverted to her somewhat untuned English. "I must wish, M. Higgins, that you desist in the pianoforte for some weeks. Reasons of crisis. My brother, I am afraid, is yesterday dead."

Whatever this meant, it might not have been true—we never learned—but Higgins's answer overrode detail. "*La mort est triste, Madame, mais la vie continue.*"

With this he closed the door; nor would he allow my trembling hand to open it to the powerful knocking which ensued.

Mme. Souchay's final attempt to put down her past involved calling in the police, and here Higgins's triumph was complete. The law permitted instrumental practice from 9:00 A.M. to 10:00 P.M., and Mme. Souchay was cautioned about interfering with the practice of art. Such is the wisdom of France.

The warfare did, however, have its victims—discounting the questionable case of Mme. Souchay's brother. In fact, as in most wars, everybody was victimized. The first to fall in the Higgins household was Danielle. She had serenely stood up to, or rather, slept out, both her father's playing and Mme. Souchay's stamping, but the temper of warfare brought her low. Pursuing the insistent demands of babyhood led her to frequent clashes with an exacerbated father, clashes which, naturally, fed on their own violence. The central instance occurred one day when Higgins and I were discussing Cortot's edition of the Chopin berceuse. To the bizarre C-flat breaking upon a simple stretch of D-flat, Cortot's exquisite *plume* had noted "*une ineffable blessure d'une dissonance heureuse.*" With an intuitive feeling for the text Danielle unfurled a shriek which shook the pages of the score in Higgins's hand.

"Silence, you miserable hellhound," he returned, whereby the shriek was compounded by a slap on Higgins's cheek, a blow which, in turn, resulted in a marital struggle that ended only with the ripping of my shirt (the one I—not Higgins—had on).

"Oh," said Higgins, head in hands. "May God curdle my seed."

With this, I yielded the apartment to a triple forte discussion which, I was informed on my next visit, had led to major decisions. These were: one, that Elizabeth and Danielle were to return to Milwaukee to wait out the year, and, two, that Higgins would work for a lower degree so that he could finish in four instead of sixteen months. The decisions made for weeping and tranquillity and, I believe, the launching of a companion to Danielle before Elizabeth boarded the plane at Orly three weeks later.

With the departure of his helper and heiress, Higgins's presence in the Rue Verneuil increased tenfold; my couch felt his weight about as often as his wifeless bed, and my fattish Fulbright check began to seem the grudging handout of a pauper government. Worse, my visions of European travel disappeared in the cognac bottles which Higgins emptied in the eyes of the little blond across the way, and with them, somehow, trickled out the last of my small passion for the arts. Professionals, however, must be permitted to make the rupture with amateurs. This remains an article of my creed even now when the memory of my rupture with Higgins reminds me of a life unsweetened by any body contact with the Muses.

The rupture took place on the Concorde Bridge. ("The rupture heard round the world" was, for months, my witty term for it.) Higgins and I had picked up our April checks at the embassy and were walking back across the river after a few aperitifs on Rue Royale. When we were in midbridge, the streetlights came on.

"Pretty," said I. "The first time it's happened to me in Paris."

"So what?" said Higgins. He was usually truculent after getting his check.

"It probably won't ever happen again," I said, pensively. "A unique experience, a minor landmark of a vanishing youth."

"It'll happen a thousand times," said Higgins.

"Probably not to us, not on this bridge."

"Nor in April, nor in 1952. Nor with you reeking of bunghole sentiment." And then, with gratuitous elaboration, "What a consummate amateur you are in everything, Bucky."

I said nothing. Or rather, I could think of nothing masterful to say. Higgins, however, found the theme a fruitful one. "You amateurs are a cursed race. You aren't alive to the past; you can't perform in the present, and consequently, you have no future. Barren, sterile, fruitless. The amateur loves without contact, loves what he cannot—"

"Enough, Higgins," said I severely, "or you'll grub from your own check tonight."

Higgins, artistic to the fingertips, stopped, drew my check from my coat pocket, and, with his Cortot-toughened fingers, ripped it into sixteen yellow fragments which he dropped, one by one, over the rail while I watched them float down the Seine with, I suppose, almost admiring incredulity.

"Well, Higgins," I said, gently. "I'll see you in Carnegie Hall," and, with that, which for months I regarded as the most felicitous sentence my voice had so far uttered, I moved on, leaving him—I imagined—crushed.

I, on the contrary, was not crushed. Even on the bridge as I walked away from him that evening I remember feeling more elated than injured. Not only with my remark, of course, although that seemed impressive to me at the time, but with my release from the strain of association with the rigors of professionalism. Something like that. There were two ways of looking at the world and two ways of comporting oneself. One couldn't go both ways, and that was that. I had a marvelous dinner, got drunk, and slept fifteen hours.

Actually, Higgins and I had one further contact. In June, he wrote requesting a loan of fifty dollars which he needed to "clear the post." It was a polite, a coldly polite, and extremely well phrased note. I devoted two hours and four or five practice sheets to framing a suitable reply. It went: "Dear Dave: I enclose fifty dollars ($50.00) which, I trust, will see you to Milwaukee and, I sincerely hope, further than that. Truly," and I signed my full name. The money—all of it—I have looked upon as a fair price for an education.

DYING

Dreben's first call came while Bly was in the laboratory. Mrs. Shearer's pale coniform budded with announcement: "He says it's urgent."

"Can't come." Watching the smear of kinetin coax soluble nitrogens from the right leaf bulge, a mobilization of nutrient which left the ravaged context sere, yellow, senescent. "What kinda urgent?"

"Wouldn't say. An odd one." Her bud, seamed, cracked, needful of a good smear itself, trichloro-hydroxyphenyl, petrolatums, lipids: a ChapStick; or lipstick to mask its aging.

"Get the number." Eyes on the ravenous patch of leaf. Molisch, Curtis, and Clark had shown that mobilizing forces were strongest in flowers and fruits, less strong in growing points, still less strong in lateral buds, weakest in roots. Bly was checking on partial senescence, revving up one section of a tobacco leaf at the expense of another.

Two hours later, he drew the yellow message slip from his box. Name: F. Dorfman Dreben; Number: Bl 6-4664; Message: Please return call; Message Taken By: LES.

He knew no Dorfman Dreben, needed nothing from Bl 6-4664. The yellow slip floated toward the wastebasket.

The second call came that night while he read one of President Kennedy's favorite books—he was going through the *Life* magazine list one by one—*John Quincy Adams and the State of the Union* by Samuel F. Bemis. "Professor Bly?"

"*Der spricht.*"

"Professor Bly?"

"I am Bly."

"F. Dorfman Dreben, F. Dorfman Dreben Enterprises. I called you at two-forty this afternoon."

"My boss wouldn't let me go to the phone, Mr. Dreben. What can I do you for?" Bly held the receiver a foot away, six pockmarks in the auditing cup, six at the center of the speaker's circular rash. A great machine. From the solitary six, as much of F. Dorfman Dreben as could be electrically transmitted from voice box A to eardrum Y appealed. "It was your poem in *Harper's,* right, Professor?"

The forty-fourth poem he'd written since high school, the eleventh since his appointment as instructor in Plant Physiology, Division of the Biological Sciences, University of Chicago, the seventh reproduced for public satisfaction (cf. *Raleigh News and Observer,* December 1954, "Blackie! Thy very name meant life!"; *Wake Forest Lit,* "Sonnet on Your Easter Bonnet," fall 1956; and four others in the same publication) and the only one which had brought him money (thirty-five dollars) and fame (notice in the *Chicago Maroon;* a call from the University of Chicago's public relations office resulting in six lines in the *Chicago Sun-Times;* four comments from students; bemused, pleased, uneasy, mocking, even stupefyingly joyous responses from colleagues; one letter from a lady in Milledgeville, Georgia, declaring the poem "the most beautiful I have read in years," requesting a manuscript copy for the Milledgeville Pantosocratic Society; and, today, one, then a second, call from F. Dorfman Dreben, F. Dorfman Dreben Enterprises). "All mine."

"A great poem," said the six pockmarks. Seven lines unrhymed, iambic tetrameter with frequent substitutions, title, "In Defense of Decrepitude," epigraph, "A characteristic consequence of senescence is the occurrence of death," theme, "Oh death, thy sting is life." "Which explains, besides congratulations, my call, Professor."

"You're too kind." Two cubed plus four squared equals my age, the square root of 576, a dayful of years.

"Not kind, Professor. Needy. I need your help."

You? And I, and my tobacco leaves, and plant physiology, students, the university, *Harper's,* girls — mostly unknown — children — unconceived.

"Though perhaps it will be of help to you too, Professor. Your helping me."

And the greatest of these. "Explain, Mr. Dreben."

"Easily. Here is our situation. My mother, may her soul, lies on her deathbed. A week, a month, who knows, a day, will no longer be with us."

"I'm very sorry." His right eye, nose bone, and right cheek leaked — not sorrow — upon a curl of purple violets (*V. cucullata*), filling a six-by-eight print, glassed over, above the phone, a retreat of flesh toward hollow, though not sorrowful, limpidity. He was mostly eye. Bly the Eye. Eye had mobilized the nutrient that might have fleshed his flesh, made him at twenty-four husband, father, householder, mortgage payer, assistant professor of plant physiology ("Get a loada Bly. Claims he looks like a violet.").

"Thank you sincerely, Professor. I can tell you're a man of feeling. It showed in the poem, and that's why I call. Because more than a man of feeling, you're a master of words." No. Master of Science, Doctor of Philosophy, but no M.W., except honorary, University of Dorfman-Dreben. "We are in need. Sister and I. What we want to do is to put on Mother's stone, already purchased, a short verse, original in nature, only for her. For such a verse, we are inaugurating a contest, prize two hundred dollars. I am officially inviting you to enter the contest with a verse suitable for permanent inscription." The *cucullata* smeared its fuzzy purple into his small jaw, bruised his neck. He was being mobilized for the assault on stone. Bly the Eye reporting. M.W., O.N. (Original in Nature). "A month ago, I wrote this Robert Frost. Saw him on the inaugural day. One month and haven't had a line from him. Not even a no. Once they get into politics they're through."

"Through?"

"Poets. Two weeks ago, I wrote Sandburg. Same result. Negative. They're not interested in a businessman's dollar. I tried writing one on my own. Failure. My sister tried. Also. Then my sister saw your poem in *Harper's*. 'Right in Chicago,' she said. 'A sign.'"

"I was in politics," said Bly. Treasurer of the Arista, Binyon High School. John Quincy Adams, defeated by Jackson, turned to poetry. *Duncan Macmorrogh* or *The Conquest of Ireland*. Epic in four cantos.

"If my mother could have read it, she would say, 'This is the poet for my stone.'"

Bly's mother, "Mother Bly," as his sister's husband, Lember, the John Bircher, called her, had carried the sonnet "Blackie" around in her wallet until its shreds had married those of the Brussels's streetcar stub, souvenir of the European week which was the product of her mother's death and legacy. He had sent his mother neither a copy of *Harper's* nor notice of his poem's presence there; evil communication corrupteth good parents. The viper generation that sent no sign. But he could use two hundred dollars, no doubt of it. The summer at the Oceanographic Institute at Wood's Hole was stale for him. He wanted his own week in Europe. He wanted to marry—girl unknown— though he had his nourished eye on a couple in Plant Physiology 263. A new suit. A car.

"Just a short poem, Professor. Maybe four lines. Rhymed."

"Rhymed'll cost you two-fifty."

The pockmarks paused. "Who knows? I'll expect to hear from you then? F. Dorfman Dreben, 342 Wacker Drive. Bl 6-4664. Any time, day or night. Messages will be taken. I'm very grateful."

Bly sat down under the violets, took up the telephone pad, and wrote nonstop:

> Claramae Dreben droops like a leaf.
> Her chest is still heaving, her boy's full of grief.

He pushed the eraser laterally on his forehead, once, twice.

> When she is nothing but dried skin and bone
> Two hundred smackers will carve grief in stone.

Two errors, "Claramae," odds against, one in two thousand, and "Two hundred smackers," which would not buy Bly's rhymed lines. No, a third error: the whole thing.

Bly threw the quatrain under the couch and picked up *John Quincy Adams,* who was thinking of going into Congress despite his son's assertion that it would be beneath an ex-president's dignity. An hour later, in bed, he thought first of the kinetin smear and the alpha aminoisobutyne acid he would apply to it tomorrow, then of Miss Gammon, a wiry little number in Pl. Phys. 263.

He didn't think of Dorfman Dreben until the third call, five days later. He was home eating the Tai Gum How he had sent up from Sixty-third Street twice a week. "I called you last night, Professor. Failed to get you."

"Forgive me."

"F. Dorfman Dreben. Mother is sinking."

"I was out, Mr. D." The weekly meeting of the instructors in zoology and botany, papers read, discussion, a good meeting.

Bly sat down under the *cucullata,* the Tai Gum How crawling with porcine force up his stomach cavity. "Mr. Dreben. I must have led you astray. I'm no poet. I've written very few poems. Even if I were a poet, I couldn't take the time to work on a poem now. After all, I didn't even know your mother. Not even her name."

The pockmarks were silent. Then, softly, "Clarissa, Professor. A beautiful name."

Bly got up. Almost one in two thousand. A sign. "Yes."

"You are a poet, Professor. No doubt of it. We are not looking for epics. A simple verse, original in nature. Any minute will be her last. I could feel so comforted telling her her resting place will be honored."

At lunch, a joke about the Irishman on his deathbed, sniffing ham cooking in the kitchen, managing to call to his wife for a piece, being refused. "You know better than that, Flaherty. It's for the wake."

"A simple verse at fifty, maybe sixty-one dollars a line. That's not a bad rate in any business."

Cottonwood brushed against the wire screen, the fluff comas breaking off, falling. Behind a violet shield of cotton cloud, the day's sun bowed good night. "Maybe I can try, Mr. Dreben. But listen, if you don't get a note from me this week, you'll know I couldn't do it. I'm not much on elegies. Not exactly a specialty of the house." Tai Gum How / Hot off the sow / One man's meat / Another man's Frau. Dermot O'Flaherty, Epic in Four Graves.

"You'll try then, Professor?"

"I'll try, Mr. D. If I send it on, please remit the two-fifty by certified check. Also, my name is not to be signed to or be associated with the

verse. The dean might not approve. And finally, we must never com-
municate again."

"Wel—"

"Not au revoir but good-bye, Mr. D. You either will or will not hear
from me within a hundred and sixty-eight hours." The pockmarks
chattered as the receiver plunged.

That evening, Bly sat back in his easy chair and thought about
dying. In some ways, he was an expert. There was dying en masse, an-
nually, dying deciduously, dying from the top—tulips, spring wheat,
Dean Swift—dying from the bottom—he, Bly, nearly died there
from the need to live there five or six times a week. Molisch in *Der
Lebensauer der Pflanzen* showed that the century plant (*Agave ameri-
cana*, L.) is a centenarian only when it can't become reproductive for a
hundred years. "The most conspicuous factor associated with plant
senescence is reproduction." The nutrient was mobilized into the fruit,
and the rest suffered. Clarissa Dreben had conceived and spawned F.
Dorfman, and who knows if it didn't kill her? Filial sentiments of a
matricide. He, Bly, would at times have sold ten of his dayful of years
for a few hours with even Mrs. Shearer's dying buds. People dying,
Drebens dying. What to say? "Nuts." (Indehiscent, polycarpellary,
one-seeded fruits, woodily pericarped. "Fine examination there, Bly.")

He picked up *The State of the Union,* then put it down, ran around
the corner to the Trebilcocks, and suggested that there was still enough
light for a quick badminton game. He and Oscar tied the net cords to
the apple trees, laid out the boundary stones, and whacked the birdie
till the dark wouldn't even let them guess where it was. He told them
his assignment and, telling it, laughed at its absurdity. The next day, he
told it at the physiologists' table, elaborating it with echoes of the Flaherty story. That was it. May passed, and thoughts of the dying Clarissa died with it. Teaching, the study of senescence, the preparation of a
paper to be given at the June meetings of the American Association of
Plant Physiologists, and then Phyllis Gammon, drove the drebenitis
from his system.

He had traversed the difficult teacher-student chasm between
"Miss Gammon" and "Phyllis." There'd been coffee, then Tai Gum
How, then intimate conversation, then amorous relations with the
wiry young physiologist from Cumberland, Maryland, who herself re-

marked about, and thus arrested, the humorous notice of hot gammons and Cumberland Gaps. A girl after if not Bly's heart at least his mobilizing centers. Even the thought of sacramental union entered his orderly mind without disordering it. Not that there had to be a crash program. Phyllis was no raving beauty, no sexpot. Her discernible virtues were not those prized in the Bedsheet Derby. She was his, more or less for the asking, a splendid alteration in his life.

He was playing badminton with her at the Trebilcocks when Dreben showed up. A June Sunday that squeezed heat from the stones and thickened the air with summer sounds. They played in shorts, Bly shirtless, asweat. The apple trees were misty with green, their branches wild with the coming weight of the rosy balls busy now sucking nutrient from the sap. The yard ran with children, four Trebilcocks, five Grouts, assorted derivations from China, Ireland, the Baltic, Africa, a running sea of life, rising in the trees, covering the flower borders, drifting through the jungle gym and miniature geodesic dome in the yard. Bly and Phyllis—a little wiry for shorts but a great pull on him—whacked the feathered cork over the net while Trebilcock and his wife poured a gallon of Savoia Red back and forth toward their glasses. Bly and Phyllis swigged away between points, so that by the time the dark, bald, bespectacled man in the houndstooth winter overcoat strode through the yards, through the quieting children, Bly was drunk enough almost to disbelieve his presence. "Professor Bly?" Bly saw the black eyes scoot up and down behind the spectacles and the thinking, This? A professor? A poet? A sweaty squirt slapping a piece of cork at a sweaty girl, boozing on a run-down lawn. What gives?

"Yes, I'm Bly. What can I do you for?" though he knew it was Dreben.

Hand out of the houndstooth sleeve, shaken by Bly. "F. Dorfman Dreben, Professor. You remember. A month back. Excuse my bothering you here Sunday. Your landlady directed—"

"Over here, Mr. Dreben," and Bly led the man by the houndstooth elbow to a corner where a rickety bench leaned on an elm. "You want to talk with me about the poetry, even though I told you that silence meant inability to bring back the bacon." His bare chest, both narrow and puffy, a snake of hair winding sweatily down toward his shorts, did not enforce the harsh chill of voice, blue eyes, nostrils shivering with hauteur.

Dreben's rear sank to the bench, the dark, bald skull lowered to the houndstooth sternum. In the Renoir blaze of yard, he was a funereal smear. Sobered, easier, Bly said, "I'm sorry, Mr. Dreben. If I could have done the job, I'd have done it. Has, is——?"

"Two weeks ago. Smiling." Spoken to his bright oxfords. "She rests under two thousand dollars' worth of granite. Bare. Waiting the expression of our love." The head was up, spectacles catching the gold thrusts of light.

"What can I do, Mr. Dreben? I don't have time. I'm a full-time physiologist." He spread his hands, or rather one hand and one badminton racket. Then, blushed for the latter, and for the guzzled Savoia, for the lawn, for Phyllis, for——as a matter of fact——life. "Except for sheer physical relaxation, every now and then, I don't have the thinking energy for poetry, and poetry takes energy and time. Took me eight works——I mean weeks——to write the one you read."

The head, a darkly golden Arp egg, appealed. "Please," it said. "We know you're the one for us. Two hundred and fifty dollars, a prize in a contest, permanent commemoration on granite."

He'd almost forgotten the gold. On the grass, wiry legs folded against each other, strong knees raised toward an assuredly pointed dickey, straw head apple-rosy with its own and the sun's heat, his hot gammon. Two hundred and fifty would give them a hot little week or two up on the Michigan dunes. "In the mail by Tuesday, Mr. Dreben. Something will be in the mail. You send the check by return mail."

Dreben was up, houndstoothed arms churning, off. Not a word. Was silence a contractual ceremony? At the net, he ducked, head deploying for a half-second stare at the three staring guzzlers, then sideswiping half a dozen racing children, he disappeared.

Five hours later, in Michener's Book Store, Bly skimmed a volume on burials and funeral customs. He learned that in common law, one is responsible for persons dying under one's roof; that corpses were considered sinfully infectious by Persians, who placed them in *dakhmas,* "towers of silence," where birds defleshed them; that West African Negroes wear white at funerals; that the Roman funeral dresses—— black——were called *lugubria;* the Patagonians interred horses, Vikings ships, Hindus and Wends widows, and the Egyptians books with their dead. Books, thought Bly. This was about where he came in with Dreben. Though for the Egyptians, the books were for the dead's guidance, whereas his poem was for display, the display of expensive devotion which could summon something "original in nature," a freshly created object to bury with a freshly uncreated subject.

Bly walked home in the hot streets, past the humming student taverns, the boarded storefronts, the wastelands of the Land Clearance Commission, the crazy blue whirl lights of the police cars, the cottonwood elms sighing in the heat. Life, such as it was, mobilized in the growing points. In Michener's he'd been down where the forces were weakest, in the roots of custom, history, meaning, the roots of death, where only an odd Dreben, dark in his houndstooth winter coat, mobilized for them.

Out of the gashed window of what had been, three weeks ago, a Tastee-Freez bar, the idea for his mortuary poem came to him.

"Systems in internal equilibrium approach states of perfect order as the temperature lowers toward absolute zero." The third law of thermodynamics which Oscar Trebilcock was using as base for research into frozen protozoa; out of the defunct ice creamery it slipped and made for the granite above Clarissa Dreben. "Yes," said Bly, Master of Science, to Bly, Master of Words. "Death is perfect order, life disorder." Dodging a lump of dog dung in the cracked pavement, Bly, the Word Master, thought,

> Clarissa Dreben, know at last,
> Your disorder's been and past.

He stepped off a lawn signed NO DOGS—GRASS CHEMICALLY TREATED and finished:

> Showing others why they die,
> Under granite, perfect lie.

A great breath in his small chest and a proud look at the prinked-up sky. He'd done it. He ran up the block, up his stairs, called Phyllis, and recited it to her. Her response did not dampen him; she was no flatterer. He typed it out on Department of Plant Physiology stationery, just stopped himself from putting an airmail stamp on the envelope, and ran downstairs and two blocks to the Fifty-third Street mailbox, pickup at 6:45 A.M.

He must have lain awake till pickup time, drenched in thoughts of gods and death as perfect systems, the former discarded by his mind's razor, Occam's, the latter retained, warmly, the spur to research, poetry, the ordering of disorder. His president's hero, Quincy Adams, filled volumes dodging the subject. That's what one did. One wasn't dragged by the beast; one saddled it and rode elsewhere. He was grateful to Clarissa and F. Dorfman and went to sleep thinking well of them, the sun firing itself through the soot smears on his window.

The next week he gave his senescence paper at the Plant Physiology Meetings in the Palmer House. A minor triumph which brought him two job offers which he brought to his department chairman for squeezing out a raise and promotion. He saw no one but physiologists and Phyllis, the latter at supper, though one supper extended to breakfast.

At the end of June, the Trebilcocks left for their yearly month in Wisconsin, and Bly remembered the Michigan cabin that he'd planned to rent with his Dreben money. It had not been sent, nor had there been any word at all from F. Dorfman. "Call the man," said Phyllis from the bed, where she lay covered with his sweat and her own. He didn't have to look up the number. Bl 6-4664. He dialed and reached a message service, left his name, number, and any hope of getting through to Dreben.

Half an hour later, though, the phone rang.

"Hello, Mr. Dreben. I called to find out why I haven't heard from you."

"Yes. I was going to call. We've been considering the entries until just this afternoon, Professor. We've reached our decision. I was going to call. As I said. I'm afraid that the decision has gone against your fine poem."

Bly held the phone off for two or three seconds, the six pockmarks whirling in the heat. "What are you doing, Leon?" Phyllis in white socks, the bare remainder toward him like an interrogation mark.

He said, "You'd invited other—there were other poets writing verses for you?"

"Two others, Professor. Baldwin Kerner, editor of the Township School yearbook, a fine young poet, and then a dear friend of my sister's, Mrs. Reiser."

"Which won?"

"I have only one."

"Who won the contest?"

"Baldwin. His poem was not quite so forcibly expressed as yours, but it was beautiful and true to nature and Mother. Of course, he knew her."

"Is there a second prize?"

Pause. "Yes. You won honorable mention."

Bly lay the phone on the tiny rubber towers, reached behind him to touch Phyllis, who reached around to touch him. No plant in evolutionary history had ever contrived such mingling. Then the animal spirits mobilized in the reproductive centers, and he and Phyllis faced each other.

LOSING COLOR

The last thing that had color of the old sort was the penknife. Pearl ponds in snowfields. I'd lifted it from a surgical coat in Mulligan's office.

Mother looked youthful. Suppressed fury had given her good color. (Which I did not take in as color.)

Mulligan said, "Why not wait out the hour?" (He'd seen the nick on my wrist.)

The hour was controlled. That is, as long as I was in slippers and pajamas, I'd be allowed in the corridor and Quentin's room. When I changed into the hospital smock, I'd be restricted to the other room.

I wanted as much time with Quentin and Cammie as possible; yet Cammie had left. I'd hardly noticed it.

We'd come here for Quentin. I was an unexpected dividend. Quentin would be leaving soon. In his smock, he looked like a miniature Roman senator. There was new intelligence in his eyes. (Those blue eyes that evoke the evolution of protection from northern ice. Since the rest of us are brown eyed, I'd wondered if an iceman had paid Cressida a visit.)

"All right?" he asked.

"As rain."

"Is rain right?"

"It is what it is."

This wasn't much, but it was all I had. With what was left, I looked at him and received what he returned. I think he knew he was to pass what there was to Cammie.

Mother waited in the white corridor while I changed into the smock. (I did feel the grace of this propriety.)

"It's surprisingly easy," I said.

"Not for me."

Perhaps, but what I could make of her looked vivid.

In the corridor, whitish things moved here and there. I was certainly not their center of interest. (And hardly my own.)

Now Mulligan is at the door. He shows his palms, as if he's apologizing for a poor gift.

What strikes me at the border is its boundlessness.

GAPS

*Thus we see that we can never arrive at the true
nature of things from without.*
Schopenhauer, *The World as Will and Idea*

1

When a gentleman is out of sympathy with the times, he drifts with the
wind. So Lao-tzu is supposed to have told Confucius, who sought instruction in the rites from him. "Rid yourself of your arrogance and
your lustfulness," continued the sage, "your ingratiating manners and
your excessive ambition. They are all detrimental to your person."

William McCoshan, a gentleman out of sympathy with the times,
had no such guidance. And though he did not exactly drift with the
wind, he was a travel agent. (Who had never traveled.) He descended
from a New England aristocracy whose authority had disintegrated in
the rise of an urbanism and federal power managed by the sons of im-
migrants. William had not taken the aristocratic option of waiting on
the sidelines until the rulers invited him into a useless slot. Instead, he
sank slowly until he found a level which supported him. That is, he left
the University of Connecticut in his sophomore year and took a job
with the American Express Company in Hartford. Six years later, he
transferred to the Dayton office, where for fifteen years he was the

assistant manager of the travel department. He married his landlady's niece and fathered a daughter.

What William appeared to care about was schedules. From Dayton, "the cradle of aviation," he sent fellow citizens to Lima and Melbourne, Portugal and Paris, working out for them intricate fusions of tour and pocketbook.

At home, to Elsa, his life's only confidant, he exposed the deeper side of his nature. William, the schedule maker, distrusted the apparent order of things. Beyond human contrivance lay terrible blanks. Planetary schedules and galactic shifts, these bubbles of human dream could pop in a blink. The world's Newtons and Einsteins, convinced they'd uncovered threads of the Real Fabric of Things, were, for William, life's prime dupes. Nothing he'd read infuriated him more than Einstein's remark that God was not malevolent but subtle. If God—whatever that meant—was so subtle, how could such a piece of mathematized dust dare to believe it could touch the least of his contrivances. Closer to William's view of the True Grain of Things was Einstein's wife, also an Elsa, who carried the ashes of her cremated daughter in a sack next to her heart until forced by her husband to give them up. William's own day-to-day truce with Appearance was unmarked by fetish, but such confessional gestures of human incompetence gratified his heart. The world's vacancies had to be stuffed with bilge. The human job was to see bilge as itself, not wisdom.

His Elsa was a true listener, no debater, no echo. Space probes, Korea, cancer, revolution, civil rights, civil riots, William uncovered for his wife the terrible configurations beneath the newspaper facts. The wars of the Chinese periphery were the conversions of peasant societies into industrial markets at the hidden service of the same force that destroyed a thousand of every thousand and one eel eggs. As for industry, it was a less conspicuous form of the diversion he provided his customers; Chartres and automobiles were made to stop people from thinking about actualities. "People start thinking about the way things really are, the only manufacturers who'll stay in the black will be the rope, knife, and gun makers." The Birchers, Minute Men, Mafia, neo-Nazis, and the NRA were far more useful than the planners, utopians, and think tankers. Why? "Because they take care of civil roughage. They're the national excretory system."

William's breakfast seminars came to an end one winter day when Elsa drove their 1961 Pontiac into a low retaining wall and was decapitated by the windshield.

This death, whatever it was, pricked bubble, discharged synapse in some monster's bloody brain, whatever, drove William's fears into the depths of misery. Almost, almost, he had Elsa's ashes saved for his own heart, but, no, that was naked unreason. There was no option but that animal reason which brought food to mouth, head to pillow.

William had never been close to his daughter, Winnie. Elsa had absorbed all the feeling he had in him. Winnie grew, was hugged, grew more, and found her own life. Yet in the months after the funeral, they spent time together, cooking, doing dishes, cleaning the apartment. One day, apropos of nothing, out of the blue, he mentioned to her the possibility of a vacation in Europe, then, on her birthday, reaffirmed it with the gift of a suitcase.

So they drifted into a three-week European excursion.

In July, Winnie and William flew to Milan and took the train to Rome. The idea was to stay in Rome a week, then fly to Nice, hire a car, and drive west along the southern coast as far as Spain. In Rome, though, Winnie ran into one of William's customers, the boyfriend of her best girlfriend, and with the flirtatious power of adolescent treason, encouraged him. In two days they felt themselves in love. Winnie begged William to let her stay alone in Rome while he went off to France.

At first it seemed out of the question. The very fact that months of closeness had not brought him truly closer to her increased William's feeling of paternal responsibility and simultaneously deepened fears about her safety. (Whatever *that* really meant beyond unscheduled change.) Yet, after all, she was not his type, their lives depended on becoming increasingly separate; true responsibility would be to give her her wish.

"All right," he said.

But anxiety dominated the night before his takeoff. He went to his daughter's hot little room and studied her curled in regression, legs around the stuffed cylinder which misserves Europeans for pillows.

Her breasts, oddly full, glazed with silver sweat, rose and sank in her nightie. Looked at quickly, she seemed like Elsa, but her temperament was a sport. This was a passionate girl, fed on wild rock music, on the pointless violence and anarchic farce of American pop culture. He forced himself to touch her forehead. "No," she said loudly, though not to him. "No, no." Her life wasn't his.

At breakfast William gave copies of his itinerary to Winnie and Robert, her friend, told them how to place an emergency traveler's notice in *Figaro,* cautioned them to eat sensibly, not stay out late, and remember they were being treated as mature young people.

A Roman summer day. Tufa walls sweated orange dust, the heat close enough to feel internal. William took off in a bus for Fiumicino. For France.

Twenty years of reading had prepared him for it. But had also prepared him to show no excitement, prepared him not to expect and not to be disappointed. In the plane, he read *Le Monde,* drank 7-Up, and ignored the pilot's invitation to look down at Corsica and Sardinia.

At Nice, a blue Citroën waited for him in the lot.

Two P.M.

William made for Saint-Tropez. Why not? Since Bardot's first films, he'd dispatched hundreds of Daytonians there; he himself was not averse to seeing such things. Who knows?

But what a route. Travel photographers must hang from clouds. How else omit the snack bars, gas stations, motels, bulldozers, house frames, the wads of hotel cement stuck into the hills. Still, now and then the sea showed up between cypress trees and one understood what had brought people here for three thousand years.

At Fréjus he ran into an endless spine of cars. Four o'clock. With this mob heading down the peninsula, he'd never get a room. He broke from the line, made a U-turn, took a side road, and drove southeast for four kilometers.

A chunk of glass and cement rose out of a pine grove. He circled a floral driveway, entered a lobby, and for eighty francs, thirty more than he'd planned to spend, got a room with a terrace, overlooking a slope of pine backed with marine glitter. The bed was large, it had normal pillows instead of the murderous cylinders, and the bathtub was good sized, important to William, who was six feet and liked to loll.

He stripped, ran in place in front of a closet mirror, breathed deep to force an outline of ribs and broaden his narrow shoulders. God knows, he was no body fetishist, he didn't even care about being in good shape, but why should a man provide comic relief on a beach? Why offend? He took a bath, wrapped himself in a towel, and snoozed. When he awoke, the room was filled with an emerald light. France.

2

Next to the hotel was a brasserie with four tables outside under a string of unlit bulbs. A woman, barefoot, pushed a little girl in a swing. There were no diners, apparently no other staff. William went over and asked the woman if one could order dinner. Yes, indeed, though the cuisine was a simple extension of what they themselves ate. What would he like?

The woman was about thirty, high browed, her flesh a gold tan, her eyes deep blue, large, and set back, her nose narrow, straight, wide nostrilled, her mouth full. She talked beautiful French, her manner that ease one thinks to find only in the rich and usually finds only in the beautiful. He proposed *potage,* an *omelette fines herbes,* and wine, but his unsieved thought was, You.

William was used to driving such spasms of desire out of mind, but this inn-keeping princess going off to cook his meal stayed there, the gravity of rump in a green miniskirt, the length of neck where the hair parted into braids at the nape, the solidity of her legs.

It had been six months since he had been with Elsa, and there had been no one else. His dreams, his reveries, his sheets bore the marks of loss. Yes, there was another side of the world. The age boasted liberation, but millions were chained by need, could scarcely admit it even to themselves. And to break out wasn't easy. First, it might involve one with tenacious, ignorant people who could permanently infect tranquillity. Still, one knew there were millions of fine women, needy as oneself, waiting as one waited. Every other story was about them.

But he didn't know them, nor even how to meet them. Dayton was a place like another, bigger than most, there were stylish women there, long legged, sympathetic. But not in his life.

And now to this young Frenchwoman who carried his tureen of

soup and extracted the cork from a bottle of wine with a smile that nipped the tan base of her cheeks, to this woman, if widowed, divorced, separated, if somehow available, he could surrender himself.

The mental release enriched the soup, the omelet, the wine.

William constructed a French approach and two or three contingent follow-ups, and was, perhaps, on the point of resolve when a black hound loped out of the restaurant followed by the little girl running and waving to a vegetable truck bumping up the road, around the driveway, into a space in the pines. A squat little fellow got out, flicked a switch which lit the colored bulbs above the tables, lifted the little girl, cuffed the hound, nodded to William, and went in. In a minute William heard the rage of family argument.

In his room William read the newsmagazine *L'Express:* de Gaulle, *Roi de Quebec;* Castro and Stokely Carmichael in Havana; the pope in Turkey at the Virgin Mary's death house; the film director Godard married to the granddaughter of Mauriac; the death of a ninety-one-year-old poet named Birot, inventor of the word "surrealism." Yes, exactly. The human bubble glistened like a maniac's dream.

The next morning William was on the road at seven, tearing along as if he had a mission. A second's decision brought him past the turnoff for Saint-Tropez. Why break his stride?

There were lots of hitchhikers, and at Cogolin, he stopped to pick one up, a girl who waited motionless with a rucksack at her bare feet. She stuck her head in the window. "Toulon?" Young, perhaps sixteen, with a long, horsy face, yet pretty in a stupid way.

"Yes," said William. "To Marseilles. Maybe farther."

She threw her rucksack in the back on his suitcase and got in. She had on tight, grass-green pants and a yellow sweater. Very well built.

— You going to Toulon or farther?

— Béziers.

— Where's that?

For response, she made an expression he believed peculiar to French girls. The chin went forward, the mouth dropped, the eyes widened. It signified, "Beyond me."

— Maybe you're on the wrong road.

The expression was modified by a shrug and pouted lips: "Could be." He handed her the Esso map of Provence. After a minute she said, "It may be after Montpellier."

—I might not get that far.

This didn't even call for a shrug. Well, she was no orator. Or perhaps questions violated the hitchhiker's code. Still he persisted, he'd picked her up for company.

—You visiting people in Béziers?

The facial telegraphy signaled the unseen hitchhikers of the world that she had been picked up by a real lulu, but as William looked expectant, she said, "My aunt."

—How far have you come?

—Antwerp.

—Are you Flemish?

A shrug, as much perhaps as yes.

—My name's William. What's yours?

Another telegraphic Waterloo, then, "Christine."

Did she like music?

She supposed she did.

Who?

Armstrong. The Beatles.

No, she did not know the names Monk, Miles, or Ornette, nor did he say from whose album covers he knew the names.

Did she read?

No time.

Hobbies?

No time.

Did she swim?

Yes, it was why she came to the Riviera.

—If we spot a beach, we can take a dip.

The telegraphy went wild.

In Marseilles, William pulled up before a wall on which was scrawled in charcoal U.S. ASSASSINS. VIET CONG VAINCRA. JOHNSON = 卐. He reached for his Instamatic and asked Christine if she'd pose in front of that, he needed a foreground object. She made a bovine facial shrug but got out and stood in front of the yellow cement. William studied her through the lens. She was large, very well developed, though her feet were those of an adolescent, soft, large, tan, the toenails faintly silvered. "Frown," he said. "I want to show how America is detested." The Flemish droop hardened into a tiny smile. Well, they were a bit slow in Wallonia, but they came around.

They went to Montpellier, had a sandwich and a glass of wine in a snack bar—William's treat—then drove south toward Béziers. The country turned to scrub and then dunes. The Gulf of Lions opened at their left, a piece of blue plate touched with crumbs of white sail and foam. Long, spiky, wild grass bearded the road's edge, and every mile or two, paths sliced through it to the water.

William pulled up on the edge near a path and said it was hot, he was going to take a swim. Christine's eyes, little blue fish, scooted around in suspicion.

Still, while he changed in the car, she took off her pants and sweater in the high grass.

When he got out in his trunks, she was in a bikini. "I had it on underneath."

She was terrific.

Between the grass and the great basin of water were a few yards of brown sand. From it, Christine hung a probing foot, then dived shallowly and swam a full-armed crawl fifteen yards out. William flexed himself and walked in. The bottom was marshy, the water warm. He swam in her direction.

She stood, the waterline at her breasts. William tried to think of something to say, to do, but settled for a smile, which he directed at her till her eyes opened and became part of her answering smile. "I'll race you," he said. She made her "beyond me" shrug but plunged off, swimming hard. He followed, caught up, and when she kept on, followed again and caught her ankles. She kicked loose and stood up, her eyes bluely puzzled, afraid, excited. He smiled doubly wide and splashed her gently. She flicked water back at him, he splashed her face, she turned on her stomach and kicked water at his. He dived, his nose an inch from the marsh bottom, turned, and came up under her, his chest touching hers and his legs her kicking legs. She was still a second, then pushed off from his shoulders and swam. William, very excited, swam after her. "Surrender?" His voice cracked between embarrassment and desire.

She stood, blushed, smiled, and, for want of something to say, splashed him. At which point he came up to her gently and, without lifting his arms, kissed her mouth. Only for a second. Her mouth stayed open, her eyes shut. When she opened them again, William put his arms around her, kissed her very hard, and felt her kissing him back. They fell into the water. With his right arm around her bare waist, they crawled to the sand.

She was virgin, there was enough obstacle to cause William to discharge on her stomach. Pained, pleasured, absorbed, she turned over, a hand reaching back for his. They lay this way for a few minutes, then William leaned into the water, washed the dried seed from her stomach, and handed her the bikini, the little flag of sexual liberty. "Don't worry about anything. There's nothing inside you."

She shrugged, not a girlish shrug, and followed him through the spiky grass up the slope.

The outskirts of Béziers are blocks of factories and apartment buildings. He needn't drive into the center, said Christine, she could take a bus to her aunt's. He stopped on the corner she indicated and said, "I wish we could stay together for a while, but it's best not to."

She shook her head. "It doesn't matter. Thank you for the ride." She hoisted the rucksack to her shoulders and walked off.

William found the route to Narbonne and drove very fast, relaxed and happy. Ahead, off the road, a truck lay on its side with a line of police around it. Cars slowed to a cortege for half a mile, then spread and zoomed. Christine, thought William. The tight grass-green pants walking down the granular white street in Béziers. Why couldn't two human beings with common needs and common culture (Armstrong, French, swimming) service each other in such a countryside?

But that long bent head walking away down the sidewalk out of sight forever. Out of eyesight.

There was something at the edge of his mind, a buzz of sorts, but not in his mind as much as his chest, a hum of feeling — what was it?

Christine did not walk off with his stuff in her, but her body held what was not just air, not in the clownish human treasury. He,

William, was part of her wherever she would go, whatever do. And she, of him.

He thought he might make it to Perpignan, but when the Narbonne signs multiplied, he felt his fatigue and turned in to Centre de Ville, past walls of aperitif posters into a polygonal fortressed heart of rose and silver, then past shops to a canal flanked with plane trees. He pulled up to a hotel and got a room.

For the first time in Europe, he felt like going to a museum. In Rome he'd gone only to the Campidoglio, where the gigantesque marble feet in the courtyard only confirmed his harsh view of what survived.

The *patronne* directed him to the medieval polygon he'd passed on the way in, he walked over, found a courtyard full of Roman fragments, hesitated, then rang a bell for the guard, followed him up a stone screw of stairs into a huge half-frescoed hall with tiny medieval windows and case after case of museum stuff: Neolithic potsherds, Volgae statuettes, Gallic shields incised with boars, "the oldest Roman inscription on French soil" commemorating the victory of Ahenobarbus at Valadium, and then, what William might have been looking for, a bust of Mark Antony, governor of the Narbonne province after Caesar's death.

Antony's tiny bronze forehead wrinkled with puzzlement. The bronze leaked stupidity. This was the soldier to whom Cleopatra, dolled up as Venus, had come in the barge with purple sails, the fellow who'd laughed at Cicero's severed head. This world shaker was a dope. William's heart trembled with confirmation.

The guard was already asleep, chin on his sternum, huge key in his fist: the new Frenchman, descendant of the men who'd carved the shields and broken the pots, who knows, container of genes that had passed through Cleopatra's royal corridors. The old stupidity, Gaul to de Gaulle. William put a silver franc on the inert knee.

At dusk, by the plane trees, William drinks light beer and smokes a twist of black tobacco barely as thick as its smoke. The wind in the gleaming trees stirs up odd clicks. Mysterious telegraphy. The Canal Robine quivers in its pilings. William thinks vaguely of a grand

French dinner, *pâté, saucissions, moules, mouton, petits pois, fraises, vin de pays.* It will be in his body by nine. Then, alone, he will do what he has sometimes done in Dayton, walk the streets, go into bars, looking quietly for someone with a face unenameled by commercial fury. As usual, he will go to bed alone.

A woman at the next table is offering a dish of brandy to a Pomeranian bitch. William finds himself saying, "I should be glad to take nourishment from such hands, mademoiselle."

The woman looks up. She is fat nosed, scraped; what had seemed blond hair is silver. "Were you addressing me, monsieur?"

"I too have a dog." He puts six francs on the table.

Tomorrow.

Tomorrow he will drive back to Béziers, will cruise the streets. At a corner, around a turn, by an alley, he will spot the grass-green pants, the rucksack, the lowered head.

But the next morning, William drives back to Marseilles, turns in the car at the airport, and flies to Rome.

It is four when he reaches the hotel. Signorina McCoshan is out. He waits by the window. At six there is talk outside the door, then a knock. It is Winnie, and beside her, a flushing Robert.

—What a surprise, Dad. Something wrong?

She raises her face painfully for a kiss. William cannot put his lips there. He smells an unscheduled knowledge.

"I felt I was running out on you," he manages, glaring at them, at their blushes.

THE DEGRADATION OF TENDERNESS

1

Infantile, hysteric, passive, regressive, masochistic, narcissistic, frigid. A sample of what, over the years, I've heard and overheard from male colleagues.

It's changed some since I made my slow way into professional security, but attend any psychiatric meeting, you'll hear a hundred new versions. Lou Andreas-Salomé probably heard it from the Master himself. (She knew the score: "The vagina is 'rented' from the rectum" ["Anal and Sexual," *Imago,* 1916].)

Our professional meetings are like medieval tournaments, "fights to the utterance." ("Utterance" in its medieval meaning of "death" and our—professional and nonprofessional—meaning, "words.") Behind our own doors, the patient prostrate before us, we're all masters. (Young sisters-in-arms can work out a feminine for this.) All of us know what it's like: we've been on the couch, have had our ripostes riposted, our ploys employed against us. Now, faces hidden from recumbent patients, we riposte, we counter, we review.

At professional meetings, on our own, in armor, we try to unhorse each other. (What can outsiders make of it?)

Still, as I say, in the last twenty years, we women have done better. We've been elected, chosen by the chosen. I myself have been nominated. (Lost—to another woman.)

2

Charlie's gone now. He chose to go. (Choice!) And I? Angry, resentful, bereft. The anger's like a madman's gun, aimed at Charlie, at Patricia, at Alfred, at myself, the spectator of this family mess.

Thirty-five years ago, Charlie's first article scuttled the "death instinct" ("Freud's Incomprehension of Aggression," *Journal of Psychopathology* 48, no. 2, pp. 117–24). It analyzed the Master's attachment to biochemistry and elementary physics, his discovery of the ego's need to abolish chemical tension, his contempt for the Adlerian power drive, his refusal to accept aggression as a component of creativity.

Charlie's last articles, "The Father as Clinical Observer I, II," instead of dismantling the Master-father, dismantled his children. If Freud analyzing Freud or Freud analyzing his daughter—my namesake, Anna—was brave, so, thought Charlie, was Charlie. At least until his children's responses blew him out of the water (that psychic Mediterranean on whose deceptive blue the world's Charlies sail).

3

Charlie gone, Alfred gone, Porphyria Ostreiker gone, Patricia in Amman, as good as gone.

4

Zennor, Cornwall
Dec. 1, 1989

Dear Annushka,

I'm thinking of Hopper pictures of people stranded in the corners of restaurants, theaters, towns, staring into nothing while people closer to the center are going about their own business. That's the way it is with me now. Growing up, at least the way we all did, is like Renaissance painting. You're always center stage. Here I don't count, at least not much, and it's fine with me.

What's the theme of *Upstairs, Downstairs* but "If you don't know your place, you get in trouble"?

Isn't that what Daddy did to us? We thought we were the apple of his eye. It turned out we were only its worm.

Too clever?

It seems I wasn't clever enough.

Still, at least partially, yours,
Patricia

5

"The Father as Clinical Observer." Charlie's bid to be as masterful as the Master, trying to make the subjective objective. "Am I that far off, Annushka?"

"Freud exposed Freud, Charlie. You expose Patricia and Alfred."

"But that exposes me."

"More than you think."

"*You* think."

The sidetrack. I refused it. "You understand how the children have taken it, Charlie. Are they so wrong?"

"How did Einstein's children take the Special Relativity paper? That's how I expect them to take it. Did Jean Renoir fold under his father's portraits of him? Look how beautifully he writes about him."

"He wrote! He handled the handler. Patricia and Alfred aren't as—" I said "lively" instead of "gifted." "I'm sure he gives his resentment away every other page."

"It's the risk I took. I must have known I was taking it."

6

We become what we're accused of being. Anti-Semites—as Sartre said—define the Jew. We define our patients by redefining their self-definitions. What I'm getting at is that despite three decades of "being on top of other people" (face hidden, godlike), I'm still the weak-kneed prisoner in the male dock. Which means that I can feel with victims, with Alfred and Patricia and with Charlie too.

7

I mothered them. (Real motherhood would have been unendurable for me.) In part, they used me to punish their mother. (Francine died when they were ten and twelve.) I didn't *love* Patricia and Alfred, but for much of their lives, they stirred me. "The child is an erotic plaything." "Cuteness," "innocence," then, later, "charm" and "sweetness."

My emotional life is—largely—agapean, that is, like Charlie, I'm an obsessional, psychically invested in Truth.

8

Patricia was Charlie's pal, his angel. When Francine died and Annette came on the scene, she faced down her rage, wrote understanding notes: Dear Dad, I'm happy for you. She acted as she looked, the good, dear girl with clear eyes of the softest brown, small boned but not fragile. Healthy, as if she'd just come in from a three-mile tramp in the snow. She looked beautiful in winter. Summers were tough. Too fair, she didn't tan well. (Couldn't take the heat?)

After Francine's death, she was sent to boarding school in Poughkeepsie; then Holyoke, graduating cum laude. She got on a Virginia newspaper and became political: the country was a machine running on the flesh of its poor. She became briefly famous for a newspaper column about William Buckley, "the classic American exemplar of selfishness," with "his facial tics and verbal tricks, his baroque vocabulary of concealment, cloud-chamber smiles and frantic energy. The Reichian armor against Oedipal terror and natural tenderness." Buckley's lawyers made noise, Patricia's newspaper mounted the First Amendment high horse, but then its business office threw in the hat. The hat was Patricia. She was fired, then spent a year helping the Lakota Sioux hold on to a radio station, their only non-Patrician link to the outside world. The next year she passed out soup and sandwiches to the homeless in Cleveland.

Then came Charlie's case.

9

Charlie had been sued for malpractice. Not extraordinary. Of nineteen thousand therapists in Cook County, ninety-eight hundred have been sued. I probably spend forty hours a year in court. Everybody digs up everybody else's business. (The shovels are lawyers.) Charlie's litigation hit the papers.

What happened was this. For fifteen years, the daughter of a well-known actress shuttled from doctor to doctor. The actress was shooting a film in Lake Forest, someone told her about Charlie, and she went to see him about the daughter. The actress was—is—charming, beautiful. Charlie made space for the daughter, three hours a week. The daughter was theatrical, self-dramatizing, moderately ill, a powerful manipulator. Charlie was good with young women, sympathetic, firm, charming, unfoolable. The daughter wanted more time, a quicker cure. An old boyfriend was coming to live with her, she wanted to be better for him. Charlie took her seriously but resisted her pressure and kept his cool. Daughter persuaded mother to bring in her doctor to pressure Charlie. This idiot bypassed Charlie and made direct calls to the daughter. He even prescribed Mellaril for her. Mother brought it to her; daughter went into a spin, tried to get hold of Charlie. It was Sunday, he was in Wisconsin. Daughter threw herself off the roof. The fall was broken by a first-floor cornice; she lived, but horribly, a paraplegic. The lawyers took it to court. The newspapers played it up—the iconography was powerful: Crippled Beauty, Ogre Doctor.

Enter Patricia. She investigated, dug up dirt; stood by her dad. She sat beside him every day of the trial.

He won the case, Patricia wrote a book about it, maybe you know it. Several thousand Chicagoans read it, and twenty thousand other people. Actress, daughter, and doctor were the villains: Charlie and Patricia, the father-daughter team, took all the marbles.

10

Appear on television or in the newspapers, and you become the light-ning rod of ten thousand idling haters. In the eight-week course of the trial, Charlie had to change his telephone number three times. He came close to moving from the house in which he'd lived since his mar-riage to Annette. You can forgive what you understand, but when anonymous haters intrude with regularity, forgiveness and under-standing collapse. You never know when you'll be struck. In those eight weeks, Charlie lost his celebrated cool (the cool in which over-heated patients, friends, and children, too, took dips). I think his expe-rience with the maddened, maddening crowd spawned a desire in him to master it, like an entrepreneur who sees a waterfall or some other source of natural, free power he can exploit.

Then there was Patricia's book, which gave Charlie not just a new sense of her but a reminder of the power of words. He'd read the pieces she'd published in weekend supplements (he'd given her a few tips for the Buckley column), but newspapers were disposable, so degraded, *trayf*. Books were meant for eons. Patricia's book was not a work of high culture, but it was a responsible, careful work. Charlie was particularly taken by the footnoted allusions to psychoanalytic literature. Scholar-ship was both deferential and authoritative. Patricia's scholarly serious-ness altered his familiar, dismissively tender paternal view of her, and—in my view—opened the way to his clinical portrait.

By the time it was published in the *Journal of Psychopathology,* Patri-cia was living in Cornwall with a Cornish fisherman, making ends meet preparing meat pies in a Cornish pub ("the one"—she wrote me—"in Zennor where Lawrence wrote *Women in Love*"). I sent her the article.

11

Charlie's aim, his boast, was candor.

No time for vanity or shame, that fear of self-exposure, which manners mask . . . Freud describes the war between tenderness and sensuality, the necessary degradation of the sensual object in the oedipal grip. This war

*can bring the death of eros. To triumph over it, as my daughter did,
resulted in an act of parricide, a book about her father's indictment and
humiliation. Who rescued him from that pit? The filial author. The
child parents the parent. Devotion and revenge are fused. Eros is saved.*

12

Every portrait reduces, simplifies, diminishes. I was uneasy. Thirty
years before, I'd been in therapy with Charlie. Our collaboration and
friendship, our erotic refusal of each other, my mothering, or *aunting,*
of his children, all make up so large a part of my life that I was not up
to analyzing them. They were a part of my bedrock. If an earthquake
occurred, I wasn't going to shake myself to see if I were in one piece.
Better to be still. So for a while I didn't say anything to Charlie.

He asked, "Your silence means disapproval?"

"I'm not sure."

"Nothing withers like silence."

"I'd thought it was golden."

"Midas gold. Death. Unfriendly."

"Unfriendly, hah. Unpaternal. Unfilial. We're not all brave enough
to risk what counts for us."

"If it didn't count, it wouldn't be worth risking. Since when have
you thought analysis destructive?"

"Always. Destructive of illusion."

"Well?"

"Well yourself, Charlie. These illusions kept us warm."

"What's this 'us,' Anna? I don't believe there are ten words about
you in the piece. Have you seen something I haven't?"

"I'll have to reread it before I say anything."

"Several times. And perhaps you'd better say nothing then. I had no
idea your skin wrapped Patricia's bones as well as your own."

"I'm sorry I can't respond better. I don't want to hurt you."

"Of course not."

13

Every few years I get out my old Greek textbooks and spend a few hours convincing myself that I'm in touch with the great minds of antiquity. The other day, I went through *Oedipus Turannos* and read the great scene of revelation in which the messengers (the *angeloi*) tell Oedipus, "*Smikra palaia somat' unaze hropo.*" "A small touch on the scale sends the old to their rest." Wising up, Oedipus responds to Jocasta's telling him it's best not to keep prying: "The *best*! *That's* what always made me suffer." "*Ta losta! Toi nun tauta m'algune palai.*"

Charlie had the best and ruined it. (It takes so little to tip the scale and ruin a good life.)

14

The portrait of Alfred was to the one of Patricia as Grünewald is to Van Dyck. Alfred's defenses, crutches, props, and poses were exhibited not only in the name of truth, but love! Charlie didn't miss an Alfredan trick.

15

The day he got Alfred's letter, he'd come home early. "I had a canceled appointment," he told me. "I wrote *that* up, then looked out and noticed how beautiful the lake was, all green and silver. The trees too, decked out in those November colors. I decided to go home early. I walked very slowly. I suppose it's an ugly walk, but it's mine, the Del Prado, the brick six-flats, the bakery with the coconut cakes and sugar rolls, the IC tunnel with the murals and Jim's Tobacco Shop, Harper Court with the truants and dope peddlers on the grass. Like the Grand Jatte."

Charlie's street is a hundred-yard block of wood and brick houses behind the bank. His house is a brown-shingled cottage built during the Columbian Exposition. There are ten square yards of lawn with a young oak tree bent at the top, woodbine hedges, and two cottonwood elms which steal sunlight from the oak.

A middle-aged black man in faded green work shirt and pants was raking leaves there. "I'd never seen him." There were eight glassine sacks of leaves "tied up like carcasses on the curb."

"Does my wife know you're doing this?" Charlie asked him.

"Wouldn't be doing it otherwise."

"I was a little embarrassed," he told me. "He spoke so clearly, so intelligently. I went upstairs. Annette told me she'd paid him fifteen dollars for two and a half hours' work. It was too late to catch him and give him fifteen more, and I was angry about it, punishing her for expressing my anality, then punishing myself for letting her. I'd been so happy on the walk, then here was this decent man, my age, walking the streets to make a few dollars, doing my work. I thought of him going home to his children with the fifteen bucks. I thought, Why is he he, I I? The unfairness of it. After cocktails, Annette brought in Alfred's letter. She'd been saving it, guessing it needed an alcoholic cushion."

Dear Dad,

You win again.
   Congratulations.
   Understanding?
   No.
   Brilliance of insight? Yes, but not into what you're sighting.
   Brilliance of style? I guess so. So what?
   Down here, where it counts, in me, bad as I am, dumb as I am, nothing. No light, no help, no justice, and — of course — no mercy.
   I suppose I'd mistake anything, but could I mistake such a mistake?

Your repellent clown of a son,
Alfred

16

Between 4:00 and 5:00 A.M. of the sleepless night, Charlie wrote his answer.

Dear Alfred,

Three California researchers have invented a mathematical way of making sense of the random. They take off from a famous quote of Laplace, "If I know where every particle in the universe is, and what forces are generated there, from then on I can predict everything." They imagine an ideal billiard game in which friction plays no part. If, however, there's a single electron on the edge of the universe which isn't figured into the Laplacean equations, the randomness it introduces will reach the billiard table in less than a minute and cancel the ability to predict the position of the balls.

A family is a bit more complicated than billiards. Life's randomness is infinitely greater than an unpredicted electron. My professional life has been dedicated to making some predictable sense out of it. My hope was that my children had enough confidence in themselves, in me, and in our relationship to understand and sympathize with this goal.

I printed what you call "portraits" and I call "case studies" not in the *Reader's Digest* or the *New York Times,* but in a technical journal with a circulation of a thousand and a readership—judging from my own habits—half that.

Your indictment, your anger, focuses on the fact that I used you and your sister as the subject of these case histories. Who else could I use? The whole point was that this was a father as well as an analyst examining, as honestly as he could, the parental relation- ship. Freud analyzed his children's dreams and experiences, and much of the civilized world is in his debt for it. If I am egregiously comparing myself to Freud, I respond, "What better model?"

Have I violated the "confidentiality" of the parent-child relationship? I have. And I haven't escaped the pain of it. Your letter sees to that.

There is something odd about the act of interpreting, the act of writing. The interpreter, the writer, has a sense of not being there. This feeling is one of the defenses of the ego. Freud called it the *Entfremdungsgefühl,* the "feeling of estrangement." It's the opposite of that other defense mechanism of the ego, déjà vu, in which the ego masks its panic at a new place by imagining it's been there before.

My point is that I did insulate myself from your and Patricia's feelings while I analyzed and wrote about our relationship. An apology for that is inadequate. Try and understand how much of my self-worth is bound up with this effort to uncover another inch of Truth.

Human beings are composed of dark impulses as well as tenderness, affection, duty, high-mindedness, and love of every sort. Everything is mixed up. Illness and health inhabit the same system. The family is the source of nurture and also the deadliest carcinogen.

I am praying—I have my version of prayer—for your understanding, your forgiveness, your love.

Always, no matter what happens,
Your Father

17

Let me try seeing Alfred without the powerful lens of his father's portrait. (Or without my anger at it.)

A Saul Bellow character counters Feuerbach's "You are what you eat" with "You are what you see." After years in the emotion racket, I was tempted to opt for, "You are whom you desire," although in our professional deconstruction, this emerges as "You are the opposite of those you desire."

What I come down to now, my own rule of thumb, is "You are what you are." (The thumb is the least sensitive finger.)

Outside his technical analysis, Charlie pitied and griped about Alfred. "How can a reasonably intelligent boy be so *geschmoggled* by the world?" By "the world," Charlie usually meant "women." "He's just

like those bowling pins which reset themselves after each knock-
down." Charlie thought Alfred unprepared for women. "It was
Francine's death. Then Annette's coldness and fear of the children."
Alfred had gone out with a particularly wild bunch of girls.

18

The one that Charlie couldn't get out of his head was Porphyria
Ostreiker.

Her appearance first. An hourglass punk. Voluptuousness in Nazi
deco. This daughter of Abraham wore T-shirts emblazoned with
swastikas. Her breasts nuzzled those logos of hatred. Her hair, whatever its original color, changed overnight from orange nails to purple
snakes; her eyes were triangled with gold paint. I never saw her wearing a nose ring, but almost any part of her could be spiked with ban-
gles, crosses, crescents, an anthology of devotional horror.

Alfred defended her à la Tocqueville: "It's democracy. Everybody
can look the way he wants, king of his own appearance."

Porphyria's deeds didn't quite match her looks. That is, she wasn't
on the streets machine-gunning children. Nonetheless, from what I
heard, twice read, and once saw on television, she was a minor public
menace. She bared parts of herself on planes or in department stores;
she stowed herself in a bin of tomatoes in the supermarket; she made
scenes at concerts, movies, plays. During an Elliot Carter quartet, she
rose from her seat and tucked wads of cotton in her ears. In theaters,
she opened a laugh box during romantic scenes. She sprayed wolf
urine during a Peter Sellers *Così fan tutte*. "A chauvinist work which
should have been shelved a hundred years ago," she told news cameras
when she got out of jail. At pro-life rallies, she carried posters of starving children inscribed FRUIT OF THE WOMB or pictures of Charles Man-
son, Hitler, Stalin, and Ronald Reagan reading THESE ARE YOUR
CHILDREN.

Why this mistress of surprise attached herself to repressed, studious
Alfred is as surprising as anything else. Tall, stooped, mild, thoughtful,
Alfred was, in Charlie's phrase, "a gull in the garbage wake of that
filthy putt-putt."

19

Freud told Lou Andreas-Salomé that he wished he had five or six disciples like Otto Rank. "He disposes of the negative aspects of his filial love by interesting himself in the psychology of regicide."

Alfred was doing research on Oliver and Richard Cromwell at Washington University in St. Louis. To support himself he repaired typewriters. (This was a year or two before typewriters disappeared from American campuses.) It was here that he met Porphyria, who brought him her Remington Correcto and, as Alfred said she told him, took him back to repair her.

The next spring after the second article appeared, their mad little campaign against Charlie began. Dressed in storm trooper outfits— boots, knickers, leather belts, swastikaed caps and armbands, not black, though, but pink—they walked the block outside his office on South Shore carrying pickets. Alfred's read, "If you're Dr. Grasmuck's patient, get your head examined." Porphyria's read. "Beware! We were Dr. Grasmuck's patients."

It's a quiet block, little traffic, tennis players going to and from the clay courts, children in the playground, mothers, strollers, cars which turn off the small Outer Drive exit. A few people gathered, and more looked out at them from the apartment windows. Charlie was alerted when his second patient, a woman who'd driven down from Evanston, called him from the Del Prado lobby and asked him what was going on; she was afraid to enter the building. He looked out his seventh-floor window and saw the small crowd around the two odd picketers. He only recognized them when he went downstairs.

"Alfred! You gone outta your mind?"

Alfred and Porphyria took off round the corner, pursued briefly by Charlie, who, feeling himself part of an eager crowd, stopped, shrugged his shoulders, raised his eyes to the sky, and walked back with as much dignity as possible to his building. He was extremely upset and spent the rest of the emptied hour brooding.

His next patient, a local painter, asked him off the bat what was going on downstairs. Charlie looked out. There they were again having their picture taken with another little crowd. He opened the window and shouted, "Alfred, if you and that slut are not out of here in one minute I'm calling the police."

Porphyria looked up. The pink cap fell off her Rudolph Valentino coiffure. "Up thine, Strangelove. We have a license."

"The police!" shouted Charlie.

It was a poor session, the painter left in a huff. But when Charlie looked out the window, there was nobody there.

That night he tried to get hold of Alfred. The last number he had for him had been disconnected. He had a number for Porphyria's mother, a St. Louis caterer. "I'm sorry," the woman told him. "I haven't had anything to do with her for a year. She's the bane of my existence. You wouldn't believe what a sweet girl she was through ninth grade. It was after her period started," and so on, till Charlie extricated himself.

The next day they were back again, this time dressed in formal evening clothes. Porphyria's heart-shaped picket read, "To the patients of Dr. Grasmuck: Want a positive transfer? Leave him." Alfred's said, "I am Grasmuck's damaged goods."

Charlie called his lawyer and told him to get an injunction and the police. Police cars arrived, but after camera crews from the local stations. Reporters came up to Charlie's office. He read a statement. "It is profoundly sad when a family tragedy becomes public. The two young people are seriously disturbed. I'm not sure they realize how much trouble their pranks are causing. As a doctor and as a father, I grieve for them."

That night, the local news included old footage of Porphyria's stunts and a statement from Alfred regretting that his father was unfit to practice psychiatric medicine. "I owe it to him to alert his patients." The final seconds went to a demurely dressed and coiffed Porphyria saying gently that psychoanalysis was discredited and that Freud had long been exposed as a chronic liar and fantasist. "Our actions are a form of public sanitation."

Charlie had been made ludicrous. Nothing's worse for a psychotherapist.

Which Charlie knew. He found it difficult to work with patients; one by one, he directed them to colleagues.

"You can't imagine the straits I'm in, Annushka. I'm much worse off than a patient. I see the structure beneath the symptoms, which doesn't relieve them. Knowledge doesn't help. I know I should be able to get out of it, but I cling to it. I won't use the exit I point out to everyone else."

"Charlie, you're not strong enough to be your own analyst."

"I'm embracing my weakness. I need it. It's time for me to shut down."

Christmas Eve he took a long walk and caught a chill which turned into pneumonia. Hospitalized, he improved, then went back to an office barren of patients.

Annette said, "Let's forget it, Charlie. We've got money. Let's go to Italy for a year. When we come back, if you feel like it, you can start again."

Charlie said, "I only love it here. I love only you and the children; you're still here but they've turned against me."

"You of all people understand that."

"You'll turn against me too. You don't know it, but you will. I embrace my situation. I no longer like my life."

20

Alfred and Patricia came to the funeral, heavy with the guilt of those who have had a terrible wish granted, silent with the silence of those who can no longer be absolved or corrected by the one who can absolve or correct. They stayed in their old rooms and, after the funeral, went over their father's possessions. Alfred took his watch, gold studs, and cufflinks, his underwear shorts and shirts. He told Annette he would work on his father's notebooks, "to see if they're publishable."

Patricia remembered that thirty-five years earlier, Charlie had appeared as a walk-on in a film with Edward G. Robinson. (The director had been one of his first patients.) She got hold of a print and, with Alfred, ran the film, studying the crowd and party scenes. They pored over them frame by frame. There were two men that might have been Charlie, but one walked with a walk that wasn't his, and the other appeared through cigar smoke. They settled on the smoker and had a still of him made, blown up and framed.

21

How quickly days die in our northern Januaries. Charlie dead before dawn on the tenth, buried before noon the fourteenth, Alfred, Patricia, Annette, and I, the executor, listening to his brisk attorney read and parse his uncomplicated will the next day. Three weeks later, Charlie's old film image in tow, the children took off, Patricia to Brazil, Alfred back to St. Louis.

A few nights earlier, they'd given me a cassette of the film and watched Charlie's scene with me. Even through the distortions of the small television screen, despite the smoke, the years, and the sophisticated mimicry of the cigar smoker, I saw the Charlie I knew—and cried.

I hadn't mourned Charlie. The tears came from that internal confusion the Master called melancholia, the guilt of an answered wish for destruction. I mourned the part of me that had failed him, at least failed that part of myself that might have made me the mother of some Alfred or Patricia. (Charlie drew me as no man I've known. I only found my emotional ease these last years living with Roberta de Freitas, whose residency at Michael Reese I supervised.) The tears were for the path I hadn't taken, hadn't been invited to take.

22

With Francine's death, the children suffered deprivational reactions. Alfred's was more severe; he showed the signs of anaclitic depression, which I helped alleviate, maternally, not professionally. Yet when he saw that I was the prop and confidant of his father, his deprivation was reinforced. He entered the long, affectless mildness of his late adolescence, then started with the wild girls who diverted him from reintegrating his ego.

After Charlie's death, I could have taken him in hand. I didn't. Clearly I didn't want him around. I won't analyze this. He went back to St. Louis, to Porphyria, his Cromwell studies, and the typewriters. Three blanks. The Campus Shop was now Campus Computers. He took a course in computer maintenance, "but"—he wrote—"it involves more than my mechanical knack. It's not for me." Cromwell, too, disinterested him: his king was dead, and he didn't have the energy or will to rule in his place.

Charlie had left him two hundred thousand dollars. He put it into a Vanguard fund, "which gives me enough to live in a small way. I've got no desire to live any other. As for Porphyria, she's taken off."

She showed up a week after Charlie's death. "I need you," she told Alfred. She wanted to become pregnant, then have a public abortion.

"I was to be the lucky almost-father. I declined. It took her a week to find a more enlightened Seed Donor."

Modern chivalry! A year later, just before he moved to Tucson, where he studied cactus and desert insects, Alfred bumped into her mother. Alfred wrote me:

> Apparently pregnancy transformed Porphy. She married the
> Knightly Donor and, according to her mother, was "a model wife
> and mother." Her last scandal was normalcy.

Not quite. A week ago I read, in a piece in the *Tribune,* that she was organizing a Mother's March to the White House Against the Destruction of the Cradle of Civilization.

I had only one letter from Tucson but could sense that Alfred was losing what little grip he had. Then he was struck down by the Guillain-Barré syndrome. Patricia and I were listed as "those to call." Patricia was unreachable. I flew down. He was in terrible shape, unable to move. The disease attacks the nerve sheaths and paralyzes the body functions. Two days after I arrived, he died.

23

I sent a message to Patricia though the Red Crescent.

She'd worked a year in the Amazon state of Para, working as a volunteer for the Rural Workers Movement against the destruction of the rain forest. By the time I heard about this, she was in a Jordanian camp organizing supplies and nursing care for refugees from Kuwait and Iraq.

Amman
Oct. 14, 1990

Annushka, dear,

A line to let you know I'm all right. The world's one hell after
another. I'm in the city raising money. Can you get some to us?

The secret is losing what gets hurt, yourself. That's easier here.

Still,
Patricia

24

Yesterday, on CNN, as I watched a parade of fury against the United
States in the streets of Amman, thinking, The ugliness and beauty of
mass hatred, I caught a glimpse—I'm almost positive—of Patricia,
her clear-eyed face lit with passion. She was both ugly and beautiful,
the ugliness that terrifies because it shows unleashed destructiveness,
and beautiful with the repose of abandonment. Was I seeing things?
(I'm not going to ask CNN for a tape.) It felt right to me, Patricia part
of a foreign mob crying out against her fatherland.

WISSLER REMEMBERS

Miss Fennig. Mr. Quincy. Mr. Parcannis. Ms. Shimbel. Ms. Bainbridge. (Antique, silver-glassed, turn-of-the-century-Rebecca-West face; at twenty-two.) Miss Vibsayana, who speaks so beautifully. (You cannot relinquish a sentence, the act of speech such honey in your throat, I can neither bear nor stop it.) Miss Glennie, Mr. Waldemeister. All of you.

Do you know what it is for me to see you here? To have you in this room three hours a week? Can you guess how I've grown to love you? How hard it is for me to lose you?

Never again will you be a group. (Odds against, trillions to one.) We've been together thirty hours, here in this room whose gaseous cylinders emend the erratic window light. (Those spritzes of autumn the neo-Venetian neo-Gothic windows admit.) We have spoken in this room of Abbot Suger, minister of state, inventor of Gothic, have cited his "Dull minds ascend through material things." (Not you, never yours.) But did I tell you that I took a trolley to his church, St. Denis, sitting next to a Croatian lady who trembled when I told her that just a week before I'd talked with the little salesman Peter, who'd been, who was, her king? There's been so much to tell you, woven by my peripatetic memory to our subject.

The thing is I want to tell you everything.

Though I will see some of you again, will write many of you letters of recommendation—for years to come—may even, God knows, teach your children (if you have them soon), may, someday, in Tulsa or West Hartford, see you when your present beauty is long gone, I know that what counts for us is over. When you come up to me in Oklahoma or Connecticut and ask if I remember you—"I took your Studies in Narrative course nine years ago"—or twenty-five—I will not remember. If you remind me that you wrote a paper on Wolfram's *Parzival,* that you were in class with the beautiful Indian girl, Miss—was it Bisayana?—and Mr. Parcannis, the boy who leashed his beagle to his bicycle, perhaps I will make out through the coarsened augmentation and subtraction of the years both you and that beautiful whole that was the class of autumn '77, winter '62. But what counts is gone.

Teaching.

I have been teaching classes for thirty years. Age twenty-one, I had a Fulbright grant to teach fifteen hours a week at the Collège Jules Ferry in Versailles. The boys, *in-* and *externes,* ages ten to nineteen, prepared for the baccalaureate exam. Four days a week, I walked the block and a half from the Pension Marie Antoinette and did my poor stuff. I was so ignorant of French, I had addressed the director as *Directoire.* ("I thought you were trying to get a government bureau.") When I entered the classroom, the boys rose. A thrill and an embarrassment to an awkward fellow not born a prince of the blood. "Good morning, boys." "Good morning, Meestair Weeslair." Much sweetly wicked *ritardandi* of those long syllables. "Today we will do an American poem. I'll supply the French translation, you translate into English. Anyone who gets within twelve words of the original gets a present." Five of the twenty-five understand; they whisper explanation to the others. Blue, black, brown, gray, green eyes intensify and shimmer with competitive greed. (Every student is numbered by class standing and introduces himself accordingly: "I'm LeQuillec, sixteenth of twenty-five.") "Here's the poem. Forgive my pronunciation.

> *A qui sont les bois, je crois le savoir,*
> *Il a sa maison au village.*
> *Et si je m'arrête, it ne peut me voir,*
> *Guettant ses bois qu'emplit la neige."*

The next day I collect the English versions.

To whom are that wood, I believe to know it.
It have its house at the village.
And if I arrest, it is not able to see me,
Staring its woods who fills the snow.

"Not first rate, LeQuillec. *Pas fort bien.*" I read them the original. "*Ça vous plait?*" "*Ah ouiiii, M. Weeslairre. Beaucoup!*"

I see LeQuillec's dark pout, the freckles of Strethmann, the begloved, elegant what's-his-name — Persec? Parsec? — who wrote me the next year in Heidelberg. "Dear Mr. Wissler. How are you? I am well. You shall be happy to know I am fourteen of thirty-one this trimester. How do you find Germany?"

Très bien, Persec. I am teaching at the university here. In the *Anglistikabteilung.* Two classes. For the *Hörgeld,* four hundred marks — a hundred dollars — a semester. Not a great fortune, so I work for the Department of the Army decoding cables at the Staff Message Control. I have top secret clearance which enables me to forward the reports of suspected Russian breakthroughs at the Fulda Gap the coming Christmas Day. One week I work from 6:00 P.M. to 2:00 A.M., the next a normal daytime shift. My classes adjust to this schedule. The American Literary Experience. 1. Prose. 2. Poetry. The first assignment, James's *The Ambassadors.* American libraries all over West Germany send me their copies of the book. I give the class a week to read it. The class shrinks from forty to seven. I don't understand, they rapped on their desks for two minutes after Lecture One. Still, even students who apologize for dropping "because of schedule conflicts" come to me on the street, doff caps, shake hands. A girl runs up the Hauptstrasse to me, asks if I will sign a petition. "For Helgoland, Professor." "Fräulein . . ." "Hochhusen, Professor." She is nearly as tall as I, has hair a little like Ms. Bainbridge's, heartrending blue eyes, hypnotic lips. "Forgive me, Fräulein, I don't think I can sign political petitions when I work for the American Army." Unlike students later on, she says, "I understand, Professor." What a smile. "Excuse me for troubling you." "No trouble, Fräulein. It's a pleasure to see you. I love you." (I do not say the last three words aloud.)

I teach the sons and daughters of soldiers whose bones have been left in the Ukraine and the Ardennes. I teach those who themselves fired guns, were prisoners, who received lessons on such scum as I. We read Emily Dickinson, Thoreau, *Benito Cereno,* Hawthorne (some of whose nastier views run parallel to their old ones). I talk of the power of blackness and try and connect it to the rubble of Mannheim, Ludwigshafen, Frankfurt.

The first poems we do are German: Goethe, Trakl, Heine. To show them what close reading can do for poems. They take to such naked delights like literary sailors ashore after months. *Sie sassen und tranken an Teetisch, Und sprachen von Liebe viel.*

American soldiers fill the Heidelberg streets, eat in special restaurants with special money. I live in a special hotel, buy food in the American commissary. *The ambassadors.*

Fräulein Hochhusen helps me with my first German poem. "Will you check this for me, please, Fräulein? I just felt like writing it. I don't trust my German at all."

> *Wir waren einmal ganz neu.*
> *Solange die Stellen brennen,*
> *brennen wir Heu.*

> Once we were utterly new.
> So long as places burn
> we burn [make?] hay.

"It is not exactly correct, Professor, but very, how shall I say? *Eindrucksvoll. Original.* Original. And your German is beautiful, Professor."

No, Fräulein, berry-cheeked Fräulein with the burned-hay hair, it's you who are beautiful. Give me the petition, darling Fräulein. Tell me about Helgoland. Will they test bombs there? And who owns it? Germany? Denmark? I want to know everything. Is my poem true German? Is it a poem? Do you love me as I love you? "You're much too generous, Fräulein. I feel so bad about the petition."

Herr Doppelgut, stooped, paper white, dog eyed, had walked three hundred kilometers, "black across the border," yet manages to get whitely back to see his mother and bring me dirt cheap books from East Berlin. When I go there Christmastime, with my visa stamped by all four occupying powers, I walk through thirty ex-blocks of ex-houses and ex-stores. Ash, stone dreck, half an arch, a pot, a toilet seat, a bicycle wheel, grimacing iron struts. Insane survivals. In front of the Russian memorial tank, a young guard holds a machine gun. From my new language text, I ask, "*Vy govoritny russki?*" Silence. "*Nyet?*" I think I see the muzzle waver. "Robot," I say, yards off. Gray ladies in beaten slippers fill carts with rubble and push them on tracks across the street where other aged ladies unload them. I go back to Thoreau's beans, to the white whale, to intoxicated bees and Alfred Prufrock, to Herr Doppelgut and Fräulein Hochhusen, to close readings of poems. Of breasts.

Yes, I cannot omit something important. In every class, there is another system of love at work. The necks, the ears, the breasts, the cropped hair of Ms. Bainbridge, the go-ahead green eyes of Miss Fennig, the laughter. There are more parts of love than a city has sections, theaters, parks, residence, business, skid row.

I move to Frankfurt. To take a higher-paying job teaching illiterate American soldiers. A tedium relieved only by new acquaintance with the bewildered backside of American life: ex–coal miners, fired truck drivers, rattled welterweights, disgraced messengers, sharecroppers, fugitives, the human rubbish conscripted to fill a quota, shoved now into school for the glory of the army. I have the most beautiful single class of my life with them. End of grade 4. There is a poem in our soldiers' textbook, "The Psalm of Life." *Tell me not in mournful numbers, life is but an empty dream, for it is the soul that slumbers and things are not what they seem.* We go over every word, every line. How they begin to understand, how deeply they know these truths. Sergeant Carmody, whose boy is dead in the new Korean War. Gray-haired Private Eady, who writes his mother the first letter of his life: "I am in Grad Too, Muther. I work hard every day but Muther, I think it is to lat for me now." Private First Class Coolidge, mouth a fortune of gold teeth, a little black man who joined up after being injured on the job—the Human Missile in Bell and Brother's Circus—and whom I summon to VD Clinic every Monday afternoon. "Dese froolines lak me, perfesser." Carmody, Coolidge, Eady, Dunham, Lake, Barboeuf. The class ends on your breathlessness, your tears, your beautiful silence.

Back home then, to Iowa, to Connecticut, and then here, to the great Gothic hive of instruction and research. Hundreds of classes, hundreds and hundreds of students. Themselves now writing books, teaching classes, building bridges (over rivers, in mouths), editing papers, running bureaus, shops, factories. Or dead in wars, half alive in madhouses. "Dear Mr. Wissler. I am in a bad way. No one to write to. There is nothing for me. Help, help, he . . . ," the *lp* dropped off the postcard (mailed without return address from Pittsburgh). "Dear Professor Wissler. Do you remember Joan Marie Rabb who wrote the paper on Julien and Bonaparte in 1964?" I do remember. For it was a paper so gorgeously phrased and profoundly opaque I called in the dull, potato-faced Miss Rabb to explain it. And with explanation — missed connections filled in, metaphors yoked to amazing logic — the potato opened into a terrible beauty. "I married, Professor. A ruffian, a churl. Children have come. Four, under six. I could not sustain the hurt." "Miss Rabb, if you can ever put down on paper what you've told me in the office, you will write a work of genius. But for now, you see why I must give you a C." "You liked the paper, thought it, thought I, had promise. What I have done, with great laboriousness, is to transmute it into the enclosed poem. Will you see if the promise is herewith fulfilled? Have I a work which has at least merchandisable power?" Fifteen penciled pages, barely legible, and when read, wild, opaque, dull. "Dear Mrs. MacIllheny. I look forward to reading your poem when the pressure of the term is over. Meanwhile, I hope you regain your health. With good wishes from your old professor, George Wissler."

At times, very few, thank God, there have been students who've rubbed me the wrong way. (How many have I antagonized? Surely many more, but the standards of courtesy are so powerful, only the rudest and angriest breach them.) "I have never, never, never, never, never in my life had a C before. Is it your intention, Mr. Wissler, that I do not go to law school? Do you delight in ruining my *entire academic record?*" Terrifying calm from the plump, parent-treasured, parent-driven face.

"One C does not a bad record make, Ms. Glypher. Admissions officers know that anyone can have a bad class, an imperceptive instructor."

"Lovely philosophy, sir, but that does not change the C. It does not get me into *law school*."

May I never be cross-examined by Sophia Glypher. "What can I do, Ms. Glypher? Can I change the grading system to accommodate your ambition?" A wicked stare from the not unbeautiful gray eyes. Since you are so clearly intelligent, Ms. Glypher, why is it that you don't see that my standards curve around sweetness, beauty, charm?

"I'll write an extra paper. Retake the exam."

"There are two worlds rotating around each other here, Ms. Glypher. One is the world of papers, exams, grades, degrees, applications, careers. That's a fairly rigid world." (Or unfairly.) "It is as strictly ruled as chess. Break the rules, you break the world. This is the world that's supposed to count. In the other world, there are no grades. In that world, you're not a C student. I don't know what you are. Or what I am." Ms. Glypher rumbles here on the verge of a discourtesy which might draw us into open combat. As it is, there is struggle. (Unequal.) "That world's one without end. I see my job more in that world than the one in which I grade you C." Even as I oppose her, wrestle within her magnetic hatred, I believe this. "In that world, we're equal. To some degree partners. Your accomplishment there becomes mine, mine yours. It's the world that counts."

"But not for law school, Mr. Wissler. I don't object to poetry, but I'm talking reality."

"Ms. Glypher, the whole point is that you aren't. You are so attached to the one world that you don't even see it clearly. The admissions officers happily do. They will recognize your talent even through what you think of as this stain on your record. If you like, I will put a letter in your dossier explaining my belief in your talent along with the reason I graded you as I did."

"I don't think I'll trouble you to do that," says Ms. Glypher in her finest moment. One which tempts me to the drawer where the Change of Grade slips are kept.

Before, within, and after classes, the stuff of articles, books, lectures — San Diego, Tuscaloosa, Cambridge — East and West — Lawrence, Kansas, Iowa City, Columbia, South Carolina, Columbia, 116th Street, New York, Kyoto, Bologna, Sydney, Buenos Aires, Hull, Nanterre, Leiden. Everywhere wonderful faces, the alert, the genial, the courteous (the bored, the contemptuous, the infuriated; but few). And everywhere, love, with the sexuality displaced (except in the instance which became Wife Number 3). That has been priestly excruciation.

Then pulling toward, docking at and taking off from fifty, I became conscious of the love that has been under all the others. I love individuals, yes, and I stay aware of clothes, bodies, gestures, voices, minds, but it is the class itself I love. The humanscape. The growth of the unique molecule of apprehension and transmission. From the first, tense, scattered day through the interplay, the engagements, the drama of collective discourse to the intimate sadness of the last class. How complicated the history, the anatomy, the poetry of such a body.

Miss Fennig. Mr. Quincy. Mr. Parcannis. Miss Vibsayana. Except for your colors, your noses, your inflections, your wristwatches, I can tell very little about your status. (You are from a warrior caste in Bengal, Miss Vibsayana. You wrote it in a paper. Miss Glennie, you were the brilliant, solitary black girl in the Harrisburg parochial school. You gave me hints of it in office hours.) But I know you inside out; would like to give you all As. (Won't.) All that part is clear, though Mr. Laroche won't know that the extra paragraph he tacked on his paper lowered his grade from B plus to B; nor Mrs. Linsky that if she'd not spoken so beautifully about Stavrogin, she would not have passed.

December. The last class. There is amorous ether in the room. (Isn't it what alumni organizations try to bottle?) Don't we all sense it this last time?

"There's a fine book by the French scholar Marrou on the history of education in antiquity. I recommend it generally but mention it in this windup class because it was there I first encountered the idea that there are strikingly different notions of individuality. One sees this also in the first volume of Mann's Joseph series. People hardly know where their ancestors leave off and they begin. That might be straining a bit. Marrou speaks of family identity. Certain Roman families were known for certain sorts of generosity, others for sacrifice. That's certainly still true. Think of American families associated with philanthropy or public service. Even if an individual in the family feels it goes against his grain to go public — as it were" — smiles from Miss Fennig, Mr. Waldmeister — "he is still conscious of the possibility of public life. I don't say that makes it harder or easier for him." Miss Fennig's slim face is alight, her eyes floating green under her large spectacles. She runs her hand through her long hair, in, up, out, back. Mr. Quincy's urchin face is stippled — such pain for him — with hormone frenzy. He tries to sit where he can see Miss Fennig. The brilliant, troubled Ms. Shimbel is about to speak. I wait. She shakes her head. How she understands. (Speaking only on demand, resigned from so much, but who knows, perhaps already launched on some intricate enterprise.)

I talk more. I watch. Mr. Parcannis questions. Miss Vibsayana responds, endlessly, softly, the thousand bees of her throat discharging nectar into syllables.

"Forgive me, Miss Vibsayana, what you say is beautiful, but I'm afraid we must finish off."

Wonderful inclination of eyes, head. "Excuse me, Professor."

"Of course. You know how much I enjoy your notions. How much I enjoy all your notions. It has been a splendid class. For me. There is almost no future I think should be denied you. What world wouldn't be better led by you?"

I don't say that. Instead: "I will have office hours next week. If you have questions about your papers, the course, anything at all, please come see me. And come whenever you like next quarter. We haven't gotten as far as I'd hoped, but you've helped get us quite far. Good-bye and good luck to all of you."

We have no tradition of farewell — applause, rapping, waving. Still, the faces compose a fine comprehension of our bond. There is the sweetness of a farewell between those who have done well by each other. (It does not exclude some relief.)

In the hall, Miss Vibsayana approaches. "May I — I don't quite know how to put it, Professor — but I feel privileged that you permitted me to take this course."

"I'm grateful to you for contributing so much to it. Thank you."

Outside, darkness falling into the white lawns. The paths are mottled with clots of ice. The Gothic buildings shine beautifully under the iron filigree lamps. A half-moon hangs off the bell tower.

Bundles of cloth and fur walk home. Hellos, good-nights, good-byes. Talk of exams, of Christmas plans. Snow like hard meringue. Winter looms. And whoops, heart gripped, I'm heading down, hand cushioning, but a jar.

"Oh, Mr. Wissler. Are you hurt?" Miss Fennig. What an embarrassment.

"No, no not at all." She bends, gives me her bare hand. I hold it and get pulled while I push up. "Thanks so much. My first fall of the year."

"I took two awful ones yesterday," she lies.

"I wish I'd been there to pull you up. Thank you again."

"Are you sure you're all right?" Green eyes, unspectacled, tender.

"I'm fine, thank you. I think it's wonderful that our last day should see me being pulled out of the snow by you. I wish you were around whenever I took a tumble."

"I'll try to be. It almost makes me hope you'll fall again."

"I will, Miss Fennig. And I'll look for you. Good night now."

"Good night, Mr. Wissler. Take care."

You too, Miss Fennig. You too, dear Miss Vibsayana. Mr. Parcannis. And LeQuillec, wherever you are. *Gute nacht,* Fräulein Hochhusen. So long, Sergeant Carmody. You too, Ms. Glypher. So long. Take care. Good night, my darlings. All of you. Good night.

LA POURRITURE NOBLE

Christmas Eve, Chicago was dressed in its climate of martyrdom, deep freeze. Thirty-five years ago, Mottram's internal navigator had brought him to this gelid foreskin of phallic Lake Michigan. Every winter since, he'd cursed the choice. A man's defined by his errors. Mottram came to Chicago with the worst of his, Adelaide Haggerty. He'd not only picked the wrong place but the wrong companion. (He'd shed the companion.)

This Christmas, Chicago felt right to him. It was the right place, and freeze was the right climate for his solitude. Solitude, more, the sense that he'd been abandoned, was, in a way, his present to himself. He and Adelaide—ten years after their divorce they were friends—had waved their daughter Deirdre into the Alitalia flight to Milan. Junior year abroad. The first Christmas in twenty years without her. All in all, a relief. He need go through none of the Christmas hoops. Mottram's father was an Anglican clergyman. For him, Christmas was the hardest day of the year. Even atheist and skeptic parishioners often let nostalgia bring them to the Christmas service. "They come to recharge their contempt," he said. His Christmas sermon was a frightful weight, especially—Mottram learned this when he read his father's diary—as old Mottram was a hive of doubt: self-doubt, religious doubt, polymorphous sexual doubt. Some of this young Derek had sensed. At Christmas, it settled into the rectory; it was in the holly and the mistletoe, the Christmas goose, the wrapped books, socks, gloves, and sweaters the three Mottrams exchanged before Father carted off his sermon to St. George's.

Self-doubt was a Mottram trait. That and hatred for its generator, the Infernal English Class Machine (scoring off the skin of inferior, degraded Englishmen). More than anything else, it sent Mottram to America. It didn't matter that Mottrams weren't near the bottom of the pyramid: clergymen and successful tradesmen could snub as well as be snubbed. Three generations had gone to Oxford, they were certainly not bottom drawer, but this didn't mean insulation from jokes, looks, ironies, exclusions, and, worse, implied, required inclusions. After Oxford, Mottram was apprenticed to a cousin's wine firm. He spent a year in Bordeaux—where an even creakier Machine ground out points—then grabbed the chance to come to America with the firm. Whom should he meet his third month in New York but one of the relatively few American girls savaged by the Machine.

Daughter of a chauffeur to one of the First Irish Families, Adelaide Haggerty grew up feeling invisible to those she'd been taught to believe were everything. Pretty, she felt ugly, smart, she felt stupid. Timid, sex-starved, stuttering Mottram made her feel beautiful and wise. If he stuttered, it was in Oxbridge English. That signaled social superiority to the Southampton chauffeur's daughter. She fell for his phonemes, he for her falling for them. Two months after they'd met at a New York matinee, he was offered a job in Chicago with Sellinbon Wine Imports.

Driving back alone to the South Side—he'd refused a dinner invitation from Adelaide and her husband—Mottram prepared for solitude. At Mr. G.'s he bought lamb chops, grapefruit, Häagen-Dazs, and Constant Comment; at the Chalet a slab of Brie and two bottles of Bushmills Irish; at O'Gara's a sackful of paperback novels. Martyrdom did not include starvation or mental blank.

Christmas Eve. Three-thirty. In his snug bay window, Mottram sat with the first whiskey of the evening. His apartment was the second—top—floor of Harvey Wallop's hundred-year-old brown-shingle cottage. Pinewood Court's two- and three-story bungalows had been put up for workers who'd built the Columbian Exposition buildings in the 1890s. Like Harvey's, some had been modernized or enlarged, others were molecules away from collapse. Harvey, a contractor, had modernized, renewed, remodernized, and rerenewed every inch of his place. The floor gleamed, the ceilings were freshly painted, the porch was solid, the heat and plumbing superb. Mottram was Wallop's ideal tenant: no wife, no young children, few visitors, and a polite sufferer of alterations and repairs. The rent was low, the living easy.

Mottram watched night fall into the street. Lamps shaped like guillotines exposed cruel lumps of ice; now and then shadowy, thuglike nonthugs passed by, homeward, wayward. Some were leashed to dogs, some carried Christmas trees or sacks of packages. Here and there, tapered bulbs were strung on trees and wreaths; but mostly, on Pinewood Court, Christmas was invisible. Which suited Mottram. When the doorbell rang, it was as shocking as a fire alarm. (He hadn't seen anyone coming up the street.) There was no speaker system— Harvey mistrusted them.

Mottram kept the brass chain linked in its slot and opened the door. It was a tall, bearded man in a knee-length black overcoat. He carried a blue denim laundry bag.

"Yes? What can I—?"

"Derek. It's me."

Mottram looked closely and recognized him. "So it is," he said. "Denis. What in—? Come in."

"I walked from the Greyhound station."

It would not have surprised Mottram if he'd walked from West Virginia. "That was intrepid of you, Denis. I couldn't imagine who it was. Santa Claus skips this house. I'm glad," he lied, "to see you. Give me your coat." He took the denim bag, then pointed to the coat till Denis got the idea, removed and handed it to him. It weighed a ton. He hoisted it over the brass knob and led Denis up the carpeted stairs. Denis had wiped his feet on the doormat. "You remember the way. What a surprise. What would you have done if I hadn't been here?"

"Waited for you."

Of course. Denis would have waited a month. The coat was probably full of peanut butter and Fig Newtons. "Well, we'll celebrate, tea for you, booze for me. Herbal, right? There's probably some left over from last time. It's what? Four years? Maybe there are some Fig New-tons. Petrified by now. We'll see. We'll scrape something together."

In the living room, Denis plonked himself in the red leather arm-chair in which he'd spent most of his last visit. "What's that?" he asked. *That* was Mottram's newest acquisition, a five-foot-high ficus tree in a lacquered rattan basket. "It wasn't here last time."

"It came a week ago. From Deirdre. She said she wanted something alive around here."

"Trees should be left outside," said Denis.

"I hope you don't mind if it stays inside."

Denis regarded its thin braided trunks and emerald leaves. "It be-longs outside." But there were other enemies in Mottram's apartment. Indeed, he sat where he did to avoid seeing the painting over his head. It was Mottram's prize, a de Kooning–like swirl of rose and violet, in which lay a spread-eagled nude woman. Mottram had paid more for it than he'd ever paid for anything. "How is little Deirdre?"

"Not so little."

"She's a dear little girl."

Denis did not register much contradiction. "Where have you come from this time, Denis?"

"Missouri. The Lotus Foot Ashram. Outside Kirksville."

"Things didn't go well?"

"Things went very well. A fine place. Could've stayed a long time. No desire to leave. Had to. Not sure why. They gave me a bus ticket. Yesterday. Pulled me down."

"Pulled you?"

"I'd climbed up. A gazebo. Gold weather vane. Held on to it. They got a ladder. Took me off. The bird came too. Bad business. Nothing to do. I took the ticket. They knew I had friends in Chicago."

"Friends? Oh, yes. Of course." On a planet of five billion, somehow he, Mottram, had the privilege of being *the friends* of this pathetic *gilk*.

It was the third time in seven years Denis Sellinbon had come to him. The last time he'd stayed almost a week, the first time nearly as long. That first time, Denis's father had warned him Denis was com-ing. Walter called from L.A., where he and Eileen had moved after selling the business. "Denis is loose, Derek. I'd told him — I hope you'll forgive me—that in an emergency he could go to you. I'm afraid he might show up. He was with some Arkansas swami. If you could possibly take him in for a day or two, I'd be very grateful. Or just get him to a hotel. If he has no money—he usually has some—advance him a few bucks. I'm sorry as hell about this, Derek. I wish—"

Eileen's trombone snort filled the earpiece. "He's no trouble, Der. A good boy. Basically. You know that. Different, maybe. A stubborn bugger, but he doesn't need much. Place to sleep, the floor's perfect. He's used to floors. He eats anything, stale rolls, beans, whatever, it'll be better than what those monks give him. And he's a world-class faster. Let him clean up the place for you. If I know you, it needs it. He's good with brooms. Just watch out for lice in that beard. Get him to shave it. We're off to Tucson for a few days. If you have a problem, put him on a bus. He'll be fine. Look, he may not even show up."

Of course, he showed up. Eileen had told him to. Mottram got that from Denis. Denis had asked her if he could come back home, told her he wouldn't be any trouble. No, she'd said, no way, Dad's heart was on the fritz, Dad couldn't take any excitement. "I won't make any excitement." "You *are* excitement. You go to Derek Mottram. He owes your father everything." That's how Denis reported it. Whatever else he was, he was no liar.

Which, considering his life, as Mottram did, was odd. How could a child of Eileen Sellinbon not become a liar? But instead of small, constant lies, Denis constructed a labyrinth of which only he was Ariadne.

For years, he'd been able to live in two worlds. The Sellinbons sent him to a Montessori school. At age ten, he'd brained a girl with a block and had to leave. From then on, he always had to leave.

Eileen wouldn't hear of a shrink; Boylans and Sellinbons didn't go to medicine men. For loose screws, there were seminaries and monasteries. Priests existed to mop up spilled milk. Walter—the freethinker—had made a mistake not sending the kid to the nuns from the beginning.

In his first Chicago years, Mottram had known the Sellinbon household well. Walter did a lot of business at home, gave tastings and dinners for customers, salesmen, vintners, advertisers. Those first years,

Eileen was under wraps. Even when she showed her crude stuff, Walter's kindness and courtesy compensated for it. But why had he ever taken up with her? Was his inner navigator as punch-drunk as Derek's or Denis's?

Like Adelaide, Eileen had been a sort of beauty. A big woman, but, in those days, both slim and voluptuous. Her hair was the brilliant red of danger signals, her eyes were ice blue. In those days, her mouth didn't look like hell's gate. The thing was she didn't talk much in those days, though when she did—just saying hello, taking your hand, and welcoming you—you sensed her discomfort and aggression. Mottram didn't sense her genius for other people's weakness, her hater's need to display it. The first time she set eyes on him, she'd said, "I didn't realize your Englishman'd be such a dumpling, Walter." In time, her vulgarity became a domestic Van Allen belt against which Walter's kindness and gentleness shattered. Denis would have had to have the thrusting power of a rocket to break through unharmed. How terrified he must have been of her voice. Not that Eileen knew she shouted. She didn't even want to talk; it's just that she couldn't bear others talking. She hated other people's ease. (Why should they have what she didn't?) After those first, submerged, apprentice years, her tigerish self emerged. She interrupted, she contradicted, she overruled.

Only Walter escaped her tongue. Walter was the best of men, a wonderful lover, husband, father, a brilliant businessman. Eileen had been raised in a household of female deference. That part of her which didn't imitate maleness deferred to it. So when the wine men—they were all men in these years—came to the house, Eileen buckled herself into her notion of femininity. That she had no taste for dress, makeup, charm, decoration, cuisine, or—Derek guessed—amorousness did not seem to bother Walter. That his Eileen tried so hard, that she went against what he must have known was her grain moved him. Only when she brought out what had been fermenting beneath did he realize that the business was imperiled by it. Her terrible voice blasted the old give-and-take of vinous dinners. The acme of her ruinous interference came the night a representative of Château Mouton-Rothschild, Alexandre de Bonville, came to the house. It was the night before the signing of their first contract with Sellinbon Imports. An arrangement with the firm of Philippe de Rothschild was very important to Walter. Perhaps it was this which roused Eileen. "I prepared for weeks," she said after. "Read my eyes out. I had Baron Philippe down cold, knew everything about him." No sooner was Bonville in his chair than she let go: "In this house, Alex, your boss is God. *Preemyay nay poos, second jay dikne, Mouton soos.*" This was her version of the famous motto, "*Premier ne puis, second je daigne. Mouton suis*" — "I can't be first, I scorn being second. I am *Mouton.*" Hearing it in her special brass, Bonville reeled, which was but prelude to her recitation of the rise of Mouton, its rejection by the Bordeaux vintners as a *premier cru* "after Phil took over," its acceptance in 1973. She went on to the annual labels, the change of name after "Paulette died, what a gesture," the rivalry with "your cousin's brew. You Jew boys know quality, just like us Sellinbons." Bonville was about as Jewish as the pope, but shriveled in his chair as if he'd been an eight-year-old shtetl boy before a storm trooper. A red trumpet of flesh, Eileen ended with, "That's why we love doing business with you boys. Now, let's put on the nose bag."

They did not put on the nose bag. Bonville excused himself and, after five minutes in the bathroom, emerged with regret: jet lag had caught up with him and was advancing a flu with which he did not dare endanger them.

The contract was never signed, and, from that night on, Sellinbon Imports began to sink. Walter, awake at last to his domestic swamp, began shifting all entertainment to the office. Too late. Three years later, Walter sold out most of the business to Félicien Trancart and moved to Los Angeles. Mottram turned down Félicien's offer to handle Italian, Spanish, and Portuguese wines and retired on his share of the sale and the small means of his father's estate.

The day after Walter and Eileen had called, seven years ago, Denis had shown up. Gentle, polite, he asked little. Much of the next days he spent calling lamaseries, monasteries, ashrams. It was astonishing that there were so many, you'd have thought the Midwest was Tibet. (The month's phone bill suggested a hotline to Lhasa.) The rest of the day, Denis sat immobile in the red armchair looking into space. Two or three times, he went off to St. Thomas's for mass. The fifth day, after an epic call, he told Mottram he'd be off, he'd found a halfway house for alcoholic ex-clergymen in Ashtabula. Mottram walked him to the IC — the Fifty-ninth Street station, as Denis refused to believe there was one on Fifty-sixth. When he got back to the apartment, he found Denis's present, a book of poems and essays by modern Russian poets. Who else in his life would have found, let alone given, him such a book? It was inscribed, "For Derek, who, beneath his shroud, is pure. From Denis. See page 74." On that page, Denis had underlined sentences of an essay by one Khlebnikov.

The word can be divided into the pure word and the everyday
word. One can think of the word concealing in itself both the
reason of the starlit night and the reason of the sunlit day.

This time, Denis had brought a present with him. "I painted a picture for you."

"How kind of you, Denis. I didn't know you painted."

"I paint well. It's to replace —" and he tilted his head to indicate the painting over his head. "I don't think you want little Deirdre exposed to such a scene. And you may have other young visitors."

"Little Deirdre isn't little, Denis. She's twenty and off on her own. To Europe." Almost adding that she might be revealing herself to some Italian contemporary in just the manner of the offensive painting.

Denis had removed from his denim bag a wrinkled square of paper which he unfolded, then shook out like a wet towel. He took it by the corners and held it up. "The wrinkles will iron out. But you can see, can't you?" What Mottram saw was a mess of tepid color, silvery blue with some reddish sticks leaning this way and that. There were also some grayish oblongs against what in a realistic painting might be a stormy sky. "I see you like it. I painted it last week, thinking of you here. Of course, it's abstract. I take Exodus 20 seriously."

"Exodus 20?"

" 'Thou shalt not make graven images, or any likeness of anything in heaven above, or the earth beneath, or the water under the earth.' I believe one is permitted to suggest. Do you see Rockefeller Chapel, the ice-skaters on the Midway? I knew it would please you, and I've used the colors of your rug. It's the size of — this thing." He held the watercolor above the splayed nude. "I see I misjudged it a few inches each way, otherwise we could just slip it under the frame. We'll have to tape it now. Have you got Scotch tape?"

There was no point in fury, but Derek was suddenly furious. The colossal nerve of this intruding nut. How dare he? His mother's son. Still, he managed to say, "I paid more money for that than I've ever paid for anything, Denis. And I've been offered five times the amount I paid. I have an art historian friend who thinks it's a masterpiece. Deirdre appreciates it. It has pictorial value. I'm afraid if we subscribed to Exodus 20, there'd be no artistic culture anywhere in the world outside of Isfahan and Damascus. It is not something out of *Hustler* magazine. Not that I'm ungrateful for your painting. It's very pretty. I don't have room for it here, but I'll find a place for it. I'm grateful to you for thinking of me."

"If you had Scotch tape, I'd show you how nice it looks here. I remembered the colors of the chair and the rug. You see how I've used them, red and pink. Give yourself a chance. You'll learn to like them much more than . . ." Voice trembling as the demonstrative pronoun died in his throat.

When Mottram got up for his six o'clock pee, he saw down the hall Denis's immobile profile by the emerald bush of the ficus leaves. He wore the black sweater, pants, and shoes in which, last night, he'd gone to his room. Perhaps he'd slept in them. Or did he sleep? Sharks, thought Mottram, don't. Instead of standing up, Mottram sat down on the oak toilet seat. What was he going to do with him?

One thing he was not going to do was spend Christmas watching Denis watch, or not watch, him. He had an invitation he'd planned to ignore, had even mentioned it to Denis last night. His "out." "Félicien and Valerie Trancart's. He used to work for your father."

"Blond mustache, brown eyes, three cheek moles. Like Orion."

"Amazing, Denis. You can't have been more than ten when he left the business." Was there a smile flick on Denis's hair-bordered lips? Yes. But were Félicien's eyes brown? Were there moles on his cheek? He'd check that out. "He got your father into those Perigord dessert wines. Montravel, Bergerac, Monbazillac. We put them into Chez

Drouet, Maxim's, the Ambassador East. Cincinnati, St. Louis. We had a good order from New Orleans, the Commodore Palace. Monbazillac alone did half a million dollars for us. Then Félicien tried making it himself, got some Semillon and Muscadet cuttings and planted them on an Ozark hill. They never grew the right mold. *La pourriture noble,* they call it, the noble rot. That was a few years before your dad threw in the towel. Félicien took over half the business. He asked me to work for him."

"Why didn't you?"

Mottram was surprised. Denis was actually curious about him. It was as if the wall had said good morning. "Fatigue. Sloth. *La pourriture ignoble.* My father left me a little money. I'd put it in the market, done all right. And I had the share of Sellinbon your dear dad gave me. I thought I could just make it, and I have. Biggest expense is Deirdre, and that won't be for long."

"Little Deirdre," said Denis.

Eileen's call came as he was serving Denis a poached egg and an English muffin. Nine o'clock, 7:00 A.M. in Westwood, she must have been prowling the floor all night after Denis's call. "Merry C., Derek. I hear Santa arrived. In the Saint Nick of time. You boys having a nice time? Did he bring you a present? Besides himself." And sotto voce, "Selfish little bastard." In normal roar, "A relief I got him settled. I take off tomorrow."

"I'm not sure what you mean by 'settled.' "

"We don't want him riding the rails on Christmas, do we? By the way, you can take him to Félicien's today. I called."

"What?"

"Valerie, that little rat, began some French nonsense, I cut her off at the pass, reminded her what her little hubby owed the Sellinbons, so you boys won't have to be alone with each other."

"Very thoughtful of you. Where are you off to?"

"Paradise. Want to come? Tahiti, Moa-Moa, Samoa, Go-Blowa. Six weeks in a white boat with, please God, rich, rich white men. If I come back with the same moniker, I'll have blown thousands. Two weeks on the fat farm, a suction job on the boobs, I was stepping on them. You should see me now." Mottram shut his eyes. "Young tourist at the Brentwood market asked me if I used to be Kim Novak."

"Were you?"

"Too bad you're such a poor rat, Derek. Well, give that thief Félicien my love. He must be rich as the pope, I'm surprised he wasn't on the *Forbes* list." So, thought Mottram, she's scouting the world's four hundred richest; she's as deluded as her son.

"It's Mother?" said Denis.

"Right. Off on a cruise."

"Off," said Denis. "Always off."

That afternoon, the two of them walked a slippery half mile to the Trancarts' Kenwood mansion. Mottram had given Denis a blue tie, otherwise he remained the arrow of death.

At Trancarts', a mob, neighbors and friends of the parents and three children. There were log fires, holly, and mistletoe; champagne, punch, and Glühwein passed round on silver trays; hams, roast beefs, cakes, and cookies on the huge dining room table. Denis faded into a curtained nook where he sat in a golden armchair; his black-sweatered arms hung down its golden flanks; the bearded head was tilted, as if receiving messages.

Every fifteen minutes, Mottram checked up on him. People seemed to nod or talk at him, he seemed to respond, but blankly. He was not a social creature. The space around him grew as if people had discovered he was a George Segal figure of fleshlike material. Mottram felt a twinge of something. "But why? Let the bastard sink."

Mottram spotted a bottle of Monbazillac you couldn't get outside of Perigord and made it his own. He drank glass after wonderful glass. This was paradise. Pretty women with red cheeks floated in the room on Bach cantatas. Faces, dresses, silver, mirrors, chandeliers, chairs, curtains, couches, the odors of good food, what a fine party. Mottram talked to a wine salesman, an obstetrician, a pretty professor of chemistry, the wife of a football player. The martyrdom of solitude leaked away. Thank you, Eileen, he thought. May you find your match in the South Seas, maybe a nice killer shark.

A woman's terrible scream speared through the jolly haze, followed by silence, as if the whole house had been hit in the stomach. Then another scream, and shouts, laughs. Mottram knew; he could not budge. "Get'm down," he heard. "Right now." The *r* of "right" was French, the voice, Valerie Trancart's. Mottram took four deep breaths, then managed to walk through people toward the curtained alcove.

There was Denis, beyond Mrs. Trancart's outstretched arm, high up the curtain, bearded head touching the ceiling, arms and legs gripping the golden curtain. Men had moved chairs and were now reaching for his legs, but he kicked them off. He was implored, tempted. There was also laughter, hearty and nervous. Everyone found some way to deal with what you were not supposed to deal with Christmas — or any other day — in Kenwood mansions. "Der-reek," called Valerie Trancart. *"Où es-tu? Viens vite. Mon Dieu. Le fou est en train de détruire la maison."*

He was at her side. "Denis, it's Derek. Would you mind coming down, old boy? We've had our joke now. Very good. But we'd better get home. I'm tired." For a moment, he thought Denis responded to him, but if so, his was just one voice among spectral others. "Maybe we'd better get the firemen. Or an ambulance. We'll take him to Billings. Or maybe — do you have a ladder?"

He'd been anticipated. Félicien and a houseboy carried one in and propped it up a yard from Denis. Félicien pointed to the houseboy and gestured toward the ladder. The boy shook his head. As for Félicien, he had the physique of a cauliflower; even if he could get up, what would he do? People looked around. Where was the football player? Not here. Mottram felt the heat of attention.

"Hold it steady for me," he said to Félicien, who held one strut while the houseboy held the other. Mottram, breathing hard, went up one, two, four, five rungs till his bald head was within two feet of Denis's beard. "Denis," he said quietly. "Look at me, old fellow." And Denis, eyes enormous with fear, did look and seemed to see. "Could you manage to slide down, old boy? Then we'll just go home. We'll walk back to the house. Could you please do this?"

For a moment, comprehension and agreement seemed to be in Denis's face, then this small social contract ruptured, and he was back in the wild place that had sent him there. Mottram heard a small buzz-saw sound, then saw what it was. Behind Denis's head a rip opened in the gold fabric, and, suddenly, like a terrible laugh, it went. Denis swung like Tarzan on the gold curtain, swiped Mottram, knocked him off the ladder, and crashed on top of him.

Three days later, Mottram walked around Promontory Point. He'd been pampering his aches long enough. No breaks, no large bruises. Luck and thick Trancart carpets saved him. And Denis, too, had broken nothing of his own. (He'd had not only luck and thick carpets but Mottram.)

And he'd signed himself into W-3, the psycho ward. "To spare you," he told Mottram. "You'll have a ready-made explanation for them" ("them" being the Trancarts, the party guests, all who couldn't understand the "higher reasoning" behind his behavior).

Mottram had been too furious to listen to the higher reasoning (it had something to do with inner and outer facts), although it seemed that he was one of the few people capable of understanding it. Aching, angry, and humiliated by Denis, exhausted by the ambulance ride and hospital processing—thank God Denis had Blue Cross—Mottram was in no mood for Denis's loony flattery. Wheelchair to wheelchair, they waited for X-rays in the emergency room, and Mottram lectured. "There's no acceptable explanation, Denis. You ruined the Christmas of a hundred people. You ruined five or ten thousand dollars' worth of drapery. You're a troublemaker."

"I am. I have been. I may always be."

"You need help."

"All do."

"*You* need medical help. *You* need to-to-to"—for the first time in years, Mottram stuttered—"get closer to the world in which you-you-you live."

"I wanted to get out of it. That's what I was doing."

"Up curtains? Through ceilings? Did-Did you-you think you w-w-were Santa Claus?"

"I couldn't remember where the door was. People stared, expecting something. Wanted me to leave."

"S-S-So you were s-s-s-supplying a demand? N-N-No. You created one. They didn't want you to go till you d-d-did what-what you did. You harmed people. You harmed property. People will have to pay real m-m-money for the d-d-damage you did. You can't."

Beard against his chest, Denis sank in the wheelchair. A study in contrition. No, thought Mottram, he's not contrite, he's working out loony explanations, I can feel the heat of his concentration. It insulates him.

Denis had ruptured his solitude, forced him into—well, pleasure, and then had made him pay through the nose for it. He couldn't disavow him, he'd brought him. (As the hunchback brings his hump.) "They can hold you forty-eight hours, with or without permission. Sign in yourself, and you can sign out when you're better."

"I know these places," said Denis, quietly. "But I'll sign. You'll have peace of mind."

Home, without Denis, was indeed peace. Beloved solitude. Nothing to supervise, nothing for which he was responsible. Bliss.

The third day of it, he treated himself to the walk up Fifty-fifth Street to Promontory Point. The sun was brilliant, the air frigid. Ice quilted the tiered boulders of the shore. The lake had carved itself into a zoo of almost animals. Dazzling, beautiful, solitary. Occasionally a jogger ran by, huffing smoke. Six miles north, the black and silver cutlery of the Loop lay on the white sky.

Mottram was still stiff, but it was the stiffness of years. Age stiffened the cells as it loosened the moral seams. Bit by bit, it seduced you into carelessness till you died in a heap of it. Careless. You didn't care. You took care—of yourself. Loosely: it didn't matter how you looked, what—within limits—you did. You weren't punctilious, weren't dutiful. Want to change a routine? Change it. The only boss was your body.

Mottram's father had been dutiful to the end, had asked the right questions, displayed ministerial concern. His collar bound him to obligation. Essentially, Mottram knew, his father was a cold man. He'd read his diary. Again and again, the old man beseeched the god in whom he hadn't believed for decades for belief, warmth, feeling.

Mottram had, for years now, felt himself turning into his father. First his looks, the baldness, the gray eyes, the pinched nose, the long cheeks and jowls. Five times, seeing himself in shopwindows, he'd said with surprise, "Dad!"

And now he felt his father's inner chill. (The burden of obligation. Martyrdom.) Coldness had sneaked into him, like ice into water.

In the mailbox, a postcard, from Italy. Scaffolding over *The Last Supper*. Deirdre. He poured himself a glass of Bushmills and read in the bay.

Dear Dad,

Exhausting flight. Milan freezing. Hotel horrible. Still, I'm *here*!! I guess there's no point in going to see this!! The Duomo is white. Crazy. Merry Christmas. xoxoxo.

Signorina D.
ta figlia

The girl who owned his father's eyes, her mother's hair, and his two thousand dollars, the person who'd inherit his couch and carpet, armchairs, kettle, paintings, every material thing including what she'd have to see into the earth.

Light from the streetlamps slashed Pinewood Court. Four-thirty, the dark was holding off. The doorbell rang. Startling. What the hell? Down the stairs—legs aching, calling through the door, "Who is it?"

"It's me, Derek. Denis."

"Go 'way. You can't come here. You've given me trouble enough for a lifetime. I don't want to see you again." This is what Mottram wanted to say, came close to saying. Instead, he opened the door, shook Denis's hand, took his coat, hung it on the brass knob, and led him upstairs.

And here he watched him: slumped in the red chair by the fizzy green crown of ficus leaves, almost hammerlocked in the legs of the rose and violet nude, Denis dunked Triscuits in peppermint tea and recited, quietly, his "escape from the medicine men of W-3."

For all the blips in his genetic matter, Denis was as intrepid as Caesar. He'd pulled wool over a battery of psychiatrists, told them he wasn't used to alcohol, had had too much to drink, and then, before he'd known what he was doing, had pretended to be Tarzan to impress a pretty girl. He actually had been sliding down when the curtain ripped off its rings. Many people there had been amused by him, but not he—virtuous, sensible Denis—he was embarrassed and ashamed. Félicien had been his father's friend and employee, he'd never in the world have done anything to harm him. And he would pay for the damage he'd caused, if it meant sending the Trancarts fifty dollars a month for the rest of his life. (Slipping soppy Triscuits into his mouth, bits befouling his black beard.)

"You surprise me, Denis. So-So manip—worldly."

"I know such people inside out. If God stepped out of the Burning Bush, they'd use him to light their cigarettes. If I told them the inner truth, I'd be locked up for a year."

"I don't h-h-have your spiritual resources. I'm ordinary. I live among the ordinary. Why don't you accommodate to us? You understand us."

Denis thoughtfully rotated a Triscuit in his fingers. Part of it fell on him. "It's only those who understand who count for me. My teachers. You."

"I can't teach anyone anything. My life's modest, even poor, but I have a right to it. You have no right to change ordinary people. Even if you're saving us. OK for Je-Jesus to bring swords instead of peace, but there's been only one Jesus. Maybe one too many."

"You're afraid they'll put me away. You're doing your duty. In loco parentis for me. You're a good person, Derek." He sprang from the chair. Mottram, frightened, got up too. "I'm going to show you something." He raced downstairs; Mottram, still fearful, started to follow, but then he was back, carrying a white cube. "Here," he said. He handed it to Mottram. "My book."

That night, Derek read himself to sleep in Denis's book. Or rather, he read at it; the most dogged reader couldn't have read it straight. There were eight hundred small pages—Denis had folded and cut ordinary eight-by-eleven bond paper into quarters—every other one of which was covered with tiny script. Denis had explained the arrangement.

"It's a workbook. Every reader's a collaborator. Across from my ideas, his ideas. Next to my experience, his. It'll be a great success."

"So you have commercial ambitions for it?"

"Why not? Money's filth, enlightenment isn't. Everyone can be reached."

"I thought you only cared for cognoscenti."

"I don't know that word."

"People in the know. Special people."

"The idea's to make everyone cognoscenti."

The modest title was *The World's Mind.* The dedication read, "To my teacher, Satyandi Purush, at whose Blessed Lotus feet I lay thought and life." (Under the dedicatee's name, another had been crossed out.)

As for the book itself, it was written in short, clear (and clearly borrowed) sentences. It began with the human progenitor: "Four and a half feet tall, muscular, and black. Eve, traced via mitochondrial DNA. Two hundred thousand years B.C." Millennia were skipped, and the author descended for a sentence to the pre-Paleolithic. Then the lower Paleolithic: "The Clactonian worked with rough flakes. The Levalloisian worked with large ones." Mesopotamia: "Four thousand B.C. The Al-Ubaid period features simple agriculture and painted pots." That did it for Al-Ubaid. Asia Minor, Persia, India, Turkestan, China, and Siberia took another two pages. Ancient Egypt, "known as *Kemet,* the Black Land," was given a page of its own.

Modern history got personal. So the French and American Revolutions were important because Sellinbons had "come to tame the Indians." The famous mixed with the unknown, the private with the public. "The most important person in Nazi Germany was not Adolf Hitler, but my teacher Herman Schlonk." This was the only reference to either Hitler or Schlonk. An account of Philippe de Rothschild's life took up four pages.

Here and there, the book burst into reflection. So there was a discussion of leisure, an appeal to tycoons and politicians "to take more of it" so that they would "have less time to make trouble for the rest of us." Some pages were just lists of names, "Einstein, Mendel, Darwin, Faraday, Dr. Peabody, Whistler, Hudson, Chevrolet, Mayor Bradley."

A history? thought weary Mottram. No, a listory.

He was too tired to turn out the light, but when he woke hours later in the dark, he thought, Odd, I could have sworn. He stumbled to the bathroom, not noticing what he did when he awoke again at eight-thirty, that Denis's book was neither on the bed nor on the floor. He looked under the blankets, beneath the bed. Nothing.

The explanation was that Denis was gone too. Mottram found his note on the kettle.

Derek. Was tempted to wait for good-bye, but the bus leaves at nine, and it's a ninety-minute walk to the station. What is good-bye between friends? I'm off to Brother Bull's Lamasery, near Oconomowoc, Wisc. Long talk with him last night. Seems right for me. A black man. (Blacks are the only Americans who still feel.) You're one of the few whites that has a good black heart. I want your opinion of my book. It will be a useful guide for school-children, and high school students can use it to prepare for the SATs. I put the ficus plant outside.

Denis

Mottram, part of whose frost had melted at this letter, finished it in fury. His plant. Deirdre's gift.

And that was nothing to his rage when he saw Denis's horrible watercolor Scotch taped over the nude. "I'll kill him." He tore it off and stomped on it. That filthy, cretinous Eileen spawn had bombed his life. Where did he get the goddamn nerve? Taken in like a crippled dog with nothing in the world to recommend him except the memory of his father, and he repays with destruction. Bitch son of a bitch mother, crawling in like the hound of death and pawing my sacred things. Where had he put the plant? Good God. Talk of exploitation, talk of power plays. These innocent killers, tuning up their harps while they rifle the eyes from your skull.

The ficus tree was freezing on the porch. Mottram ran down in his slippers and carried it in, the cold pouring off its bright leaves. The monster had killed it. "My poor ficus," he said. "I'll never forgive that bastard."

———

Two days later, the day Mottram did the laundry, he went to get Denis's sheets. Ripping them off—Denis had made the bed—he saw something fly into the air. It was a hundred-dollar bill. Incredible. The fellow couldn't even hang on to his few dollars. "I'll send it to Deirdre." Serve him right. But, of course, he put it into an envelope for Denis. When he got an address, he'd send it on. (Not to Eileen, she'd confiscate it.)

When a letter did come, four weeks later, he'd almost forgotten it.

The Lodge
Melvin, N.D.

Dear Derek,

Snow is part of my nature, but there's too much here at the Lodge. We're vowed to silence. At meals, the thoughts of Swami are read. So quiet. You hear the riprap of the river over the stones. Good for this restless soul of mine. Brother Bull's was good, but irreconcilable differences. I wish I had money to send you, but have only seventy-seven dollars. (Swami asks for the rest.) Please share it with Félicien. The author of Ecclesiasticus, Jesus, son of Sirach, says (approximate rending), "The world is a composition of fury, jealousy, tumult, unrest, fear of death, rivalry, and strife" (the Jerusalem Bible). I read the Prophets, Bantam Shakespeare, and Kahlil Gibran (a Lebanese man who loved strong coffee, cigarettes, never married, and eked a living from sketches and writing). If you need music, train your ear on wind. Practice drawing the light coming through the frost. One day you and I can tour the U.S. Like Steinbeck and Charley. It interests me to know if it is all there.

Your friend,
Denis

Mottram was a poor dreamer, but that night he dreamed vividly. He was going into a church with Adelaide but was stopped by a powerful detergent smell in the nave. "Varnish?" he asked. "No, it's

george," said Adelaide. So they waited outside, but inside was a full
congregation. There a child cried. It was little Deirdre. Who was also
little Denis. He/she ran into his arms, weeping, and he told her/him,
"I'll never leave you." In his body, he felt her/his sobbing relief.

When he woke for his six o'clock pee, the dream was with him. He
asked himself what "george" could have meant. It was somehow important. As the yellow stream clattered into the bowl, it came to him.
"George" was his father's church in the country which, so many years
ago, Mottram had left for good.

RIORDAN'S FIFTIETH

Riordan's fiftieth birthday. For three years, it had been waiting for him; and here it was, a day like another, up before everyone, a cup of instant, a corn muffin with marmalade, the six-block walk to Stony Island, the ride to the bus shed. He said nothing about it; but every other minute, it was there. Lucky he didn't drive Big Bertha up a lamppost. And thank God he had route 12, a bit of air, a bit of green. When Lou Flint was fifty, three years ago, his missus turned the apartment into a parade float, there was everything but *Playboy* bunnies, and, all over, paper banners with "Half a Century of Flint" on them. The old lady had come on with a cake in Flint's own shape — what a shape, not far off a normal cake. And half the boys from the shift were there, there must have been forty, plus wives, it looked like Randolph and State. What a racket, what presents, and they'd drunk till time to go to work, there must have been fifty collisions and a thousand road fights that day in Chicago.

That was the way to pack it up.

And here he was, Teddy Riordan, fifty to the day, and on his way home he'd had not one greeting and didn't know if his own kids had been told but knew if he got a greeting out of her, it would leak out of the side of her moon face and make him feel, "Who're you, Riordan, that anyone in the world should care you've weighted the planet fifty years?" The twins, ten years of Riordan spunk, would think it no different from any other day. They wouldn't remember that even last year they were making crayon pictures of cakes and missiles for him.

"Happy birthday, Dads," and big kisses, and she'd stirred herself enough to come up with a store cake, and Bill had carried it in, and Joey had cut it up for them. She had refused her piece, though had not refrained when he was off on the route the next day, oh no, had put half the cake in her gut, and when he'd asked for a piece that night, she said it had gone bad, they made it with month-old eggs, she wouldn't buy any more A&P cakes, you bet your life, and, anyway, wasn't he a little long in the tooth to be stuffing himself with chocolate night after night, a coronary would clout him on the route, he'd kill a busload if not himself and be hauled off for prosecution in the courts, he'd damn better watch his weight, he wouldn't be able to stuff himself back of the wheel. This from Mrs. Fat herself.

Not a civil word to him for a week, and then, in front of the kids, this mouthful of sewage if he bothered to answer would make him so wroth he'd haul off and fetch her a clop round the ears.

What had happened? Where had his tranquillity, where had his life gone?

Was she right, had it been a mistake from the start? One of her wild remarks that rang true. Four kids late. Why hadn't she stopped? God knows she had stopped the last years, he never even looked at her now, not that that slop of rump could get a rise from a three-year-old bull. A slob and a bad-mouther, this was what came of her, and the poor kids, living under this terrible roof with her leaking acid over them every day of their lives. No wonder Stan and Susie got out quick as they could. As if any other man could have stood her as long as he had without falling into a bit of comfort and sympathy. He hadn't moved a finger that way. Day after day, twenty-three years watching the birds climb on the bus, every shape and color of woman, legs climbing the steps, the skirts over the knees, let alone those skirts, where, practically in his eye, were thighs and more. And he had nothing but smiles and didn't know where to turn, only looking in the rear mirror and trying to steer.

What was it all about?

If the Cubs were warm in the race, at least there was something to look for; and in winter the Bulls and the Hawks, in the fall the Bears. All these animal teams he'd invested his heart in.

Not enough.

The folks were dead on the highway ten years now, Sis moved off to Detroit, and now the kids, Stan in the army, sure to go on to the lousy war, and Sue downtown calling up once a month, unable to hold her rage for his not sending her to college, her mother's tongue lashing him, who had been so dear a little girl, never a pouter, always fetching and kissing. As if he were Rockefeller. And she wouldn't even try the night course at Loyola or Wright Junior. Beneath her. No, above her, she never brought home the gold stars, the nuns said she was a dreamer, wouldn't concentrate. What did she dream about? The Beatles and worse. How did they fit her for college, even if he'd had the wherewithal?

There was a spoilage in this family. Maybe it was him. That was her view, he had that clear, though God knows short of lying around with a can of Schlitz watching the game, what was his life of luxury? Who had he made pay? Stan and the twins liked the games just like he. Every summer, he took them off in the car for two weeks, Colorado, Texas, Vermont, they'd seen the whole country, thirty-nine states they'd been in. And stayed in the best motels, it cost God knows what over the years; added up, it would have sent Susan to college, Stan too. But what were they to do, all those years, live like clams in the dark? You had to get out of the city. God knows he couldn't blame the blacks down in Woodlawn, Kenwood, Lawndale, penned into those streets summer and winter, year after year. He might bust out and club a few heads himself given that.

So here he was, fifty, Susan a stranger and Stan in the army because he wasn't in college, and it was a rotten war, not the way it was in Korea where if you weren't gung ho you were daft, and if you froze to death in the hills, at least you knew you were keeping the Chinks from running the Pacific, and he hadn't lost so much as a fingernail. Perhaps better off if he'd come back minus an arm. Worse men than he were pulling ten thousand a year toting up figures at desks or bossing their betters in bottling plants and the white oil drums down in Whiting. Ten and fifteen thousand, and here he was, twenty-three years behind the wheel and finally making eighty-four hundred with three weeks in the summer. Plus the dread half your time you'd be hit on the head for the fares. He'd been damn lucky there, held up only twice and never been touched, knock wood. Now the fare box was locked, and the signs were up the drivers had no money, but there were heads and lushes all over, they stumbled up the steps with their dollar bills, didn't know or couldn't read, and one of these days, out on route 10 or 11, one of them might slice him up for his shoes and his cap.

Not even the boys in the pool knew of his birthday. No loner, he just didn't shoot off his face. And wasn't close to anyone now. Two years ago, he'd dropped out of the card game. Elly could have made a scene if they'd come to the house; he'd said she'd taken sick, he had to stay and watch her. So no one said, "Happy birthday" and "Keep it flying, Teddy." They talked as they always did. It was the vote for Manager of the Year, and they'd passed over Weaver. "He only won a hundred and thirteen games and cleaned up the Reds in five." This from Powers. And he'd thrown in, wasn't that the way it always was, they always passed over the ones who did their jobs with their mouths shut and picked some flash with the bankroll behind him. "Like Durocher," said Powers, who grew up behind Comiskey Park and hated the Cubs. "No," he said, "Durocher took an armful of bums and kept them contending five years. He's loud but no bum." No point knocking good men. Though God knows Durocher showboated and mouthed.

The best of the day was the half-mile walk from Stony. Not the neighborhood it had been when they'd moved eighteen years ago, and, true, it got worse each year. But it wasn't as bad as Elly's complaints that he'd kept them here while the blacks took over, knocking everyone over the head, and she scared to walk to the A&P except in broad daylight and then with her heart in her mouth. Maybe, but at six, with the night coming on, it was quiet and out of the stench of downtown, the air was breathable when the wind was up, they were close to the lake, what he'd've given for that as a boy, and there were a few trees. Walking, he rolled. Cramped on a bus seat eight hours a day didn't slim you, and he started low to the ground as it was.

The streets still, small lawns in front of the stone three-flats, and, every now and then, a little home, the sort they'd aimed at for years, and if there hadn't been Stan's teeth, the surprise of the twins, and the summer trips, that would be what they'd be living in now. Which might have kept her happy. Enough anyway to let him walk home tonight to a cake and his kids singing "Happy Birthday" over the can dles so he could know he hadn't spent fifty years for nothing at all. So he was visible to someone. After all, his job was decent, he serviced more people in one week than most people in fifty, people of every type and look, and he went all over the city of Chicago, every four months taking the worst of its air—route 7, where you moved up State on a Wednesday at noon at a mile an hour, the fumes of the tailpipes making hell in your lungs. And for eighty-four hundred a year while hamburger was seventy-five a pound. Oh Lord, this was wasting his mind on complaint. Here was a nice October night, the leaves falling, quiet in the streets, the air decent enough, he had four fine kids, he'd lived fifty pretty fair years, why fill the head with such garbage? Fifty years old, and inside no difference, no pains, maybe stiff in the back after the route, quicker to hit the sheets at night, but the same, and God knows if some decent woman, a widow like Mary Sears or a decent little catface spinster like Helen Whatshername—how long since he'd seen her, Easter Sunday at Holy Name—would say, "What about it, Teddy?" who knows if he mightn't take up the stakes and start for fresh. A woman, a real woman with sympathy and a body for his loneliness, and no more gaff and meanness. This sniping life while the boys looked on and ran off to the television to get out of the way.

Bad thoughts, and, at his corner, there was lead in his heart, his key was lead, and his legs, and up the stairs past the college kids and the widow, and then, ah well, his own door, scratched, the pattern of scratches as close to him as his signature, and the noise of *McHale's Navy* from the machine and the light from it as he passed to hang up his jacket, and her kitchen noise. "Good evening, Elly," he called toward it, and maybe there was a "Good evening" back at him and maybe not, and into the living room with Joey and Bill in the armchairs, and his hands on their heads. "Hello, boys, how goes it today?" and got his "Hi, Dads" from Bill, the plugger, and a colder "Hi" from Joey, Elly's product, who rose to affection only when food was in his mouth. Though he loved them both equally, they were dear boys, he couldn't take offense at Joey's coldness, the boy didn't know what he did or why, and now and then, out of the blue, the boy would pop up and kiss his cheek. They were good boys, he hoped he could get them into a decent trade, or, who knows, maybe college. If the present crop of wild ones didn't burn them all down by then. What a world.

Washing up, his face looked strange. The eyes seemed loose in the sockets, and his face thinner, maybe it was the new fluorescent which trimmed it down. A pug's nose, a chin like a boat keel, and what was left of his hair a rubble color, ash and brown. No face for the movies. Just Theodore Riordan on his fiftieth. His own birthday cake.

Too late for the TV news, he lay on his bed and listened to WGN. The usual garbage. They'd caught a hippie nut who'd killed a whole family out in the redwood country of California. The nuts of the world were everywhere. You were as safe in the middle of Chicago as any-where. Nixon mouthed some guff to the United Nations, so fast you could hardly follow, if he wanted to speak why sound as if he didn't, the man was a phony, and this Agnew a showboat and mean to boot. And the wars, Arabs and Jews, and another forty boys dead in Viet-nam, and this the lowest count in years. But if one were Stan. Hun-dreds wounded, and they didn't tell you if it was sprained ankles, lost legs, or worse. Maybe Stan would call. Last year he'd come home late, but in the morning he'd had a funny card from him. Signed, "From a fellow fan." There'd be no chance Sue would call. She would remem-ber and make a point of *not* calling. Or she'd call tomorrow and not say a word. Elly had handed her tongue on to Susan. Poor thing, poor girl making life miserable for herself. Selling shoes was a decent job for a girl without training, why wail you'd been given the short end of the stick? Seventeen, she had years to look around and try other things. Her mother's daughter, and God help the man who fell for her apple head, though God knows he still loved her and wouldn't want her to spend her life alone selling shoes. Why was she such a weight on him tonight? What had he done to turn her from him? Was it only college she'd wanted?

In the morning, he'd climb in the bus, and Harry would give him the finger, and he'd come out of the pen, the great swiveling bus, and there would be that release, the roar and out in the morning. That's how the bus is. Years of it don't add up enough *to send you down to Loy-ola, and you didn't have the grades, my girl, for the nuns to set you up. What is it you want from me, darling? I wish I could give it to you yet.*

"Supper. Wash your hands, boys. Let's go."

The call that used to cheer his heart. He'd come into the roast after his day, the table set and the kids, four or two, and there'd be talk over the meat, and they'd pass round the chunks of potato and scoop out the beans, there'd be gravy for the beef and brown Betty or ice cream for dessert, and coffee, ten or twelve colors on the table, and noise, and sometimes Sis and her husband, and sometimes no children, only friends, and, years before, Mother and Dad.

And now what was there for the twins but a house of gloom. No one came, and even Stan and Susan were gone. Elly would not have his friends, saw only her pal the Mouth during the day. What idea of life would Bill and Joey have? That it was a tunnel of gloom, best out of it quickly. With dinner a call to a graveyard of feeling, to argument or silence, the only noise that of plates or "Pass this" or "Mind your manners."

Tonight at least there was noise.

Joey said Bill hadn't washed, Bill said, "You're a liar," and he'd come in with, "I'll take a look, and don't let me hear such stuff in your mouth, you're brothers," and Joey said, "You're husband to Mother, why do you fight?" and after a breath he got out with, "Older people have their differences over the years, and we're not the same flesh and blood, let alone twins, and keep respect in your mouth or I'll slap it there," and Elly said, "Let's forget talk of slapping, the both of you wash up your hands, you too, Joey, I can see the muck on them from here," and she sat down and put a breast of fried chicken on her plate and handed the platter down to him without a word.

"How's it go?" he tried.

"It went," she said. "You want to break down and try the peas?"

On his birthday, she cooked the one vegetable he hated. "I haven't eaten a pea in twenty-five years."

"It might be the making of you." Bare arms, red, chafed, and the moon head with a tent of brown fluff, some sight for a man, yet her skin was clear and the green eyes. Years ago, years ago it had been a face. Now bunched with anger, the nose, mouth, and chin crowding the middle. What waste.

The boys were back, Joey scowling. He asked them how school went.

"Same," said Bill. "Joey got throwed, oh well, never mind."

"Where did Joey get throwed?" from Elly.

"You mousefink. I'll get you, finko." Joey hot, and, before the other mouthed back, he said, "I've had it from you two. One more little love song tonight, and I'll haul off and clap you for good."

A grumble from Joey with "You and who else?" somewhere inside, but he took it as grumble. God knows he didn't want to break heads on this of all days.

"You can imagine where he finds his words," said Elly. "He don't need to read up in the dictionary. You might check your own mouth once in a while."

"Come on, Mom," said Bill. "Let's try it in peace." His plugging boy, a peacemaker at ten. Joey was into his chicken leg, grease over his face, lost. As if in a different part of the universe. Oh, life was a raw, strange thing.

"It's not me wants war," she said, and held up a forkful of peas in toast to him. The actress. A hundred and eighty pounds of ham.

He put his fork on the plate with a noise, lifted his fists to the table, felt the silence, and said, "Boys, you know what?"

"What?" said Bill. Joey stopped jawing the leg.

"Your dad's at a milestone today."

He could feel thunder down the table, could feel her darken, feel the resentment, he was putting one over her, she who should have been springing surprise for him. But that wasn't what he wanted. He didn't want that.

Said Bill, "What's a milestone?"

"A milestone. It's something that's important. You know on the turnpikes, they have the signs giving you the mileage every mile. They used to be on white stones. Well, I'm at a big white stone today, I thought you'd like to know."

"You been fired, Dad?" said Joey, scared, the chicken leg shaking in his fist.

"No. I'm fifty years old today. It's my birthday, and a big one, and I'm going to take everyone over to 31 Flavors for dessert, and you can have three scoops or four, whatever you want."

"Yay, Dads," said Joey, and out of his chair with the chicken leg and kissed his cheek.

And Bill came up, and said, "Happy birthday, Dads. Wish I'd knowed, I'd made you a card," and kissed the other cheek.

And from her, "It slipped my mind. I thought it was next Friday. I had a cake on the list for it. Well, here's looking at you," and she hoisted her coffee. It was something anyway. At least, for a second. "And may the next fifty see you try harder."

"Thanks, Elly. The first fifty's the toughest."

"On who?"

There was no stopping her. It was like a child in her. Maybe the change of life would ease her. Let it pass tonight. What counted were these two, throwing them a lifeline, giving them a boost. Too late for her. Maybe for him.

She didn't go with them, but till they went, there were no more slams, and the boys didn't fight, they felt something, and it was good to get out in the dark, the day had counted for something. Back in the car, he told the boys of Mother and Dad and how they'd come so close to seeing them born and how loved they'd have been, and when they got back, Elly said, "Stan called to wish you returns of the day, he says he's fine," and there was a Hawks game at eight from Maple Leaf Gardens, and Hull got the hat trick, first in the year. It was enough, more than he'd expected.

The moral was "Keep looking and waiting and maybe push it a little here or there, there's enough somewhere to celebrate," and maybe she was right, God knows, he could push harder the next fifty.

ZHOOF

1

The man was Powdermaker's age, fifty, but grayer, eyeglassed, sharp faced, somehow not American. Somehow? Yes, there was some indrawn, hard-knot quality in that face, something older than the rest of him that said, "This is what we are, what we've been, what we'll be." It felt European to Powdermaker.

Retrospection? Well, yes, he was looking back, but Powdermaker prided himself on looking back clearly. He was no sentimentalist, no rhetorician of memory. For instance, he was systematic about classifying novelty. He located new faces on the spectrum of those he knew well. This man looked like Eph Weiss, the photographer. Not quite as sharp or as innocent as Weiss. Eph looked like an innocent fox, much of the innocence sitting in the don't-tell-*me* green eyes. This man's eyes were lighter, more rigid, stony. "Maybe I'm going overboard here."

Initially, the fellow seemed all right. (Which made what happened worse.) "A man of the world. Like me." A comfortable, thrifty burgher in a sport coat off the rack, slacks, a dress shirt open at the collar, all more or less in synch, soft blues, soft greens. If anything, Powdermaker should have liked him.

Yet he was sure he hadn't. He remembered liking the wife. She had gotten out of the compartment at Chiasso to wait for the dining car. In his narrow, proud French, Powdermaker had talked with her about the weather, the train, the whereabouts of the car, and then, in his even

357

narrower Italian, asked a workman standing in the rail bed when the diner was coming. The man pointed up the track, there it was.

It was then that the husband, standing at the compartment door, told his wife to come back on the train, he didn't want her on the platform till the car was linked up. Powdermaker remembered his surprise at the order, its specificity and sharpness. She must have been used to it. She said something which Powdermaker didn't get and stayed where she was, or, rather, walked further up the platform in the direction of the car coming their way.

Mostly, Powdermaker was hungry. The only thing he'd had since breakfast was a limp, Daliesque burger in the Wendy's across the street from the Stazione Centrale in Milan. The restaurant in the Excelsior had closed at two, and everything else within blocks of the station was closed. (It was the Sunday of the Ferragosto weekend.) Wendy's, at least, was air conditioned. Back in the station, he took his bag out of the *deposito* and ate the sack of gingerbread cookies he'd bought a week ago in Nuremberg.

2

It was his first time in Nuremberg. That's why he was there. Also, it was the last town in which he could leave his Eurocar without paying a drop-off penalty. The People's Express flight had landed in Brussels, and, twenty minutes later, Powdermaker was on the E-40's boring green fields flagged with some of the bloodiest names in European history: Liège, Malmedy, the Ardennes. At the border, he took a small road to Aachen; woods, hills, Teuton quaintness. The ancestral land of the Powdermakers—Pulvermachers—was not one of Powdermaker's favorites. For one thing, the language was too tough, the verbs waiting in ambush to shoot down the piled clauses. Outside of simple declarative sentences, Powdermaker was lost in it. Oh, with much flipping in his pocket dictionary, he could read the newspaper and order dinner, but that was it. His accent was good—he had that knack in all his languages—but when waitresses, salesmen, or desk clerks opened up to him in idiomatic German, he bowed out. Annoying. There was much that was annoying here, but, as everyone said, things worked: the water was hotly fluent, the radio full of Beethoven,

Mozart, the Bachs, the windows kept out street noise, the air conditioner labored in silence.

In town was the rebuilt church in which Charlemagne had been crowned and the rebuilt Rathaus, whose staircase was lined with pictures of Adenauer, De Gasperi, Schumann, Roy Jenkins, and George Marshall, the rational, decent champions of Pan-Europa, men after Powdermaker's heart. Across the street from St. Follain, "burned in the seventh century and again in 1944," Powdermaker took a picture of an immense wolfhound drinking from a pool surrounded by seven fat-bellied, bronze sacks of greed, bronze hands in each other's bronze pockets. One bronze fellow, a thin, browless meanie, was instructing a boy in the secrets of calculation. The sculpture's title was *Kreislauf des Geldes.* Powdermaker checked *Kreislauf* in the yellow dictionary: "circulation." The Circulation of Money. Germany mocking itself, as it had after every catastrophe it had inflicted on Europe. Mockery was the outlet for national ferocity. Or so—in the manner of Eph Weiss— thought Powdermaker.

3

The autobahn was another outlet. No mockery here, and no speed limit. Powdermaker floored his asthmatic Opel past sluggards and was himself flashed, honked at, and passed by Mercedes and BMWs. In an hour, his stomach was an iron knot, he was soaked with sweat, his tie and belt were loose, his moccasins off. *Gott sei dank,* the radio played Bach and Mozart; otherwise, the autobahn would be a river of blood. What was the ratio between German music and German ferocity?

4

The thirty-pfennig tourist pamphlet began:

> Certain thoughts always spring to mind when Nuremberg is mentioned: bratwurst, *Lebkuchen,* toys, Dürer, the Christmas Fair, and the famous soccer team.

These were not the thoughts that sprang to Powdermaker's mind. His thought was the album of *Die Meistersinger,* a print of the walls, towers, spires, castle, the Virtue Fountain and Pegnitz River of medieval Nuremberg.

Now, on this infernal August day, there it was: St. Sebaldus, the Lorenzkirche, the Schloss, the Rathaus, "the wonderfully preserved fifteenth-century gentleman's residence" called the Albrecht Dürer Haus.

Three o'clock, the day boiling in gold. Powdermaker walked up the König and Kaiser Strassen, past fountains, bridges, churches, past flocks of unisex punks in hot black clothes, orange spiked hair, eyes agog in mascara moons. Here and there—punctuation in this reconstituted Hans Sachs town—were tramps, often with bottles in their hands; they soliloquized, boozed, bummed smokes: failure in the marrow of the insistent commerce of bargain tables (patrolled by tense, intrusive clerks). Powdermaker paid four marks, two dollars, for sixteen green grapes which he popped against his teeth and palate.

In the Hauptmarkt, a fellow in top hat and a girl in tights clog danced for an unsmiling crowd. A white poodle carried the hat around for coins. By a baroque fountain which jetted water from the bronze nipples of haughty ladies, a girl with an angry, pocked nose played the violin for no one. She played Vivaldi, terribly. Powdermaker crossed the square to listen, paying tribute to the idea of public music and to her isolation. When she scratched out the end of a movement, he dropped three marks into the violin case. She did not thank him. He walked down the Kaiserstrasse and browsed in a bookstore; he liked to have a souvenir from every foreign town. Hot in a saleswoman's impatience, he bought a cheap yellow paperback, *Lyrik des Exils.* Looking at it, he almost bumped a bearded man in a filthy brown suit. The man carried a wine bottle. To Powdermaker, he said, *"Erst brennen Sie uns, dann liefern Sie uns."* [First you burn us, then you ruin us.] In his blue blazer, his Italian shoes, French shirt, and English tie, Powdermaker jumped aside, furious. What goddamn nerve. Miserable, bomb-brained ruin, ignoramus, know-nothing. That he should say this to me, whose cousins could have been beaten to death by his uncles a decade before he'd been conceived.

5

Under chestnut trees was a pleasant-looking restaurant. Powdermaker ordered a *Bauernomelett,* a *Gemüse Salat,* and a carafe of white wine, lit a cigar, unfolded the *Nürnberger Nachrichten,* and relaxed with these sacraments of the good tourist. In the local news, a man celebrated his twenty-third birthday by knocking the books off the shelves of a local bookstore; the police found him in the bushes, laid on the cuffs, and took him off. There was a wasp plague in the Rhineland. In Frankfurt/Main, a woman attended the murder trial of her daughter, a member of the Red Army Faction; the mother formed a group of RAF parents to see that the children were not abused in prison. "For instance, they supply no washcloths. The prisoners must use their handkerchiefs."

"Hast was zu rauchen?" Powdermaker looked up to an elderly, bald fellow speaking to him across the hedge which separated restaurant from street. "I don't smoke," said Powdermaker. The man's face grew red; he pointed to Powdermaker's lit cigar. "Filthy Yankee liar." The indictment went on, beyond Powdermaker's German, a high-pitched aria which roused Powdermaker's neighbors, some to laughs, most to anger. A waiter ordered the drunk to take a powder. The man cursed and shook his fist, then suddenly sank with hydraulic slowness to the ground. A police car pulled up, two uniformed policemen leaped out, lifted, held, cuffed, and lectured the drunk. Bald head lowered to his chest, he was put in the back of the car. It turned Powdermaker around. "To be so singled out. So humiliated."

6

That night, tense and fearful in the *couchette,* worrying about kicking the bunk above, falling out of his narrow bed—he was in the middle of the left side of the double tier of six—holding back internal as well as overt noise and motion, peeking and trying not to peek at the girl on the top bunk, choked with airlessness and human smell, then, opening a window, cold, and covering himself with his blazer, Powdermaker passed a restless, semihallucinatory night.

The desk clerk in the Hotel Veit had been so nice to him—looking up the train schedules from Munich to Milan, directing him to the *Bahnhof* —that it almost overrode the uneasiness he'd felt in Nuremberg. Wonderful what one decent person can do for you. This was a squarish, ordinary fellow with small spectacles on a small nose and gray eyes that seemed to have seen much, suffered much, and stayed decent. Eph might have said, "You never know. The guy's apartment walls could be covered with Jewish skin." Eph's skepticism was as automatic as Powdermaker's benevolence and sentimentality. No, this was a decent man, and if, like all men, he'd done bad things, he was not doing them now.

On the local train to Munich he was amazed how much he had forgotten about Nuremberg. He was alone in the compartment, looking at the woods, the farms, the pretty *Dörfchen,* when he thought, My God, I didn't see the Stadium, the Hall of Justice. I didn't think of them. Unbelievable. For the next few hours, in that train, on the platform, then in his *couchette,* chilled, tense, and sleepless, he went over his Nuremberg lore. There was a lot of it. He'd seen films, he'd read books, he'd been in arguments about the modern history that stuck like poisonous spines to this town. Why had he thought only of Wagner and Dürer?

A decade ago he'd seen the great Ophuls film. It was shown in two evenings at the Art Institute—and he'd left the auditorium shaking like a leaf. The next day, he talked about it with Weiss, who for a month brought him books about the trials, the Nazis, and their state. Nothing was more fascinating than historical monstrosity, and there may never have been a historical monstrosity as monstrous as this one. Nuremberg was its heart. Powdermaker, a man who was bored to death with Holocaust talk, who could hardly bear to hear that word, who equally disliked anti-Semitic stories and stories about anti-Semites, found himself sinking with ravenous pleasure into the stories of Nazism. Awake in the *couchette,* he both remembered and contrived theories about it. Hitler had revived the Spanish craziness of the purity of blood, the *limpieza del sangre. Blood* was the touchstone. The Nuremberg rallies were consecrated by the touch of the *Blutfahne,* the flag bloodied by the martyrs of the *Putsch.* Hitler's speeches and Streicher's stories were full of blood: the syphilitic Jew whose sick blood sapped the national strength; the single cohabitation of Jew with

Aryan which contaminated beyond salvation; the Jewish doctors who raped female patients under anesthesia in order to corrupt the Aryan heritage. The Nazis were terrified that their own blood was be-Jewed. Maria Schicklgrüber became pregnant while working for a Jewish family in Vienna. They gave her a pension even after she married Johann Hiedler and passed her name on to her five-year-old son, Alois. Unlike his peasant ancestors, Alois stayed in school and joined the Austrian civil service. His third wife, his niece Clara, became the mother of Adolf. Alois, a sadistic drunkard, whipped the mischievous and imaginative boy who hated him deeply. A Jewish doctor took care of Clara Hitler and saw her out of the world. In Vienna, seventeen-year-old Adolf stayed in Jewish houses when he was rejected for admission to the academies of painting and architecture. In Vienna too he contracted syphilis and left suddenly for Munich before his preinduction medical exam. He served bravely in World War I, then returned in the ebb tide of defeat to a Munich bristling with every sort of hate doctrine. He met Rosenberg, Streicher, learned the anti-Semitic theories of Wilhelm Maar, and read *The Protocols of the Elders of Zion;* he became his terrible self.

Then there was Göring. For a schoolboy essay about his beloved stepfather, Hermann von Epenstein, he was called on the carpet by the headmaster and forced to wear a placard around his neck which read, "My *Pati* is a Jew." And Hess's pal Haushofer had Jewish blood; so did Heydrich. For all of them, Jew hatred meant self-cleansing and a Jew-cleansed Germany (plus all those shekels). Hitler's speeches, Wagner's music, torchlights, blond sex making blond chains. The Third Reich was turned into a bomb.

It was right that the trial of the bomb makers was held in Nuremberg. Powdermaker could remember the faces of the men who sat in the dock: the pale fat-cheeked contempt of Göring; the black-browed remoteness of Hess; the long, brutal, scarred face of Kaltenbrunner; the bald, obscene, childish fierceness of Streicher; Speer, Rosenberg, Dönitz, Schacht, Frick, Frank, Sauckel, who else? Oh yes, Ribbentrop, Jodl, two or three others. In the Nuremberg courtroom they sat in two rows, Göring at one end of the front row, Schacht at the other, like scornful brackets.

And none of this had he thought of for a single moment during the five hours he was in the town. *Morgenlicht Leuchtend, Morninglight Gleaming.* Walter's prize song which won him the hand of Eva and admission to the Meistersinger fraternity. It was morning now, shots of gold in the pearl interstices of the Italian hills. Blood and beauty, hatred and heroism, bashing, biting, cutting, stealing, twisting, easing the hatred and misery of life on the bodies of Jews, Poles, Gypsies, the old, the weak, the defective, the impure. Morninglight gleaming.

7

In the dining car, the couple sat in the last of four booths on the right side, Powdermaker in the first booth on the left. There was no exchange of words or looks. Powdermaker let others set the social tone; he was content to make a decent impression (and to take his own).

The waiter asked if he wanted a cocktail. "Just wine, please," and chose the second-least-expensive white, then veal piccata, pasta, and salad. Across the aisle, the waiter asked the couple if they'd like to sit in the nonsmoking section. They rose and went into the back half of the compartment. "How about you, sir? Nonsmoking?" the waiter asked Powdermaker. "For me, too," he said and sat again in the first seat on the left as far as possible from the couple; he was not one to intrude.

In retrospect, he couldn't remember if it had been one minute or five before they made their move. He was looking out the window at the little villages stuck on the hills above Lake Lugano.

On their way back to the smokers' section, the couple passed him. The waiter followed, asking if anything was wrong. The woman said something which Powdermaker didn't hear, some sort of explanation. Still he felt nothing wrong, just faintly amused surprise. But it was enough to alert him, so that he heard the husband say, *"Zhoof."*

In a second, Powdermaker had spelled this out, *"jouf"*; and, in another, decided it was the harsh, pejorative version of *"juif."*

He'd never heard or read the word, but he knew with certainty that the man had called him, Powdermaker, the equivalent of "kike." If there was any doubt, it disappeared when the wife said, "Shhh," and something else, and the husband responded, "*Mais il parle italien aussi.*"

Sitting with his cold white wine by the beautiful lake, Powdermaker felt as if his head had been sliced like a grapefruit and put on a plate. Everything cold in the universe poured into his decapitated trunk. His heart thumped, his hands shook the wineglass, perspiration rolled from forehead and cheeks to the white tablecloth. He felt himself flushing, paling, felt what he almost never felt, pure rage. He turned all the way around and stared, no, glared at the man's back. The wife forced herself not to look at him, he saw that, but she transmitted nervous awareness to her husband. Powdermaker's fury was registered, that he knew, and he turned back to the wine with some relief.

Perhaps he'd been wrong. Perhaps the word meant something else or was even part of another word. Maybe it had had nothing to do with him at all. No, he thought, I can't dodge this. When he'd followed them into the nonsmoking section, something had happened to the husband: he could not physically bear being close to Powdermaker. He'd dragged his wife away and given her the one-word explanation, "*Zhoof.*" When she'd tried to quiet him and said, "At least speak Italian," the man said, "He also speaks Italian." (He'd heard Powdermaker talking at Chiasso.)

The waiter brought Powdermaker's dinner. "Bon appétit." He tried to eat, to be calm, to enjoy the luxury of eating on a train moving through beautiful places. This was his last full day in Europe, tomorrow he'd fly back to Chicago. Why should a vulgar hater ruin things for him? He tried to lose himself in the beautiful last daylight, to become translucent, a slice of human scenery. After all, what did anything matter?

No luck.

The food was tasteless, the wine flat, the scenery was scenery. He turned again and sent all the hatred he could summon toward the man who hated him.

If he'd been stronger, more self-confident, even more gifted with anger, he could have walked to their table and said, "Madam, you have the bad luck to be married to a Nazi pig."

8

A year or two ago, Eph Weiss told him, "The reason travel's so important to you, Arthur, is that it gives you the illusion of being someone. It's tiring, you cover ground, and it makes you think you're accomplishing something."

Powdermaker had said, "It makes more sense than what I do here with you."

"You're a lucky fellow, Arthur. You don't see what's in front of you."

As he'd said this from behind his viewfinder, his green eyes aflare over the little porthole, Powdermaker thought, A photographer's point of view.

For years, Powdermaker had lived by filling a gap in an advertiser's gallery: the faintly Jewish gentleman. His decent face could also pass for Spanish aristocrat, Italian waiter, golfer at the second-rank Jewish country clubs. He usually sported good but not tailor-made suits, three-hundred-dollar watches; he drank Jim Beam, had a Piece of the Rock, a Harris Banker's attention, drove a Chrysler, dreamed of a Porsche.

Earlier, his range was wider. Pullover round his shoulders, tennis racket in hand, he leaned over convertibles driven by open-mouthed blonds. The year Manny Echevarria spent in Cozumel, Powdermaker had doubled as a gaucho, a chef, and, mustached and bereted, a Basque fisherman.

Son and grandson of assimilated German-Jewish burghers, his slogans were theirs: Let sleeping dogs lie. Don't cry over spilled milk. His father changed the name from Pulvermacher to Powdermaker. Young Arthur stayed out of school one day of two for Rosh Hashanah and Yom Kippur, but he was not bar mitzvahed. "Such nonsense isn't for us, why spend the money?" As for any Pulvermachers who'd stayed in Germany, God knows what happened to them. No calls for help were made, or, at least, received.

At Wright Junior College, Powdermaker was spotted by the photographer Eph Weiss, who needed a "nice-looking Jewish but not too Jewish model." For twenty-eight years, they worked together. Beverages, cars, garments, accessories, what purified, what amused, what glittered; for these products he posed.

When Powdermaker complained about the emptiness of his life, Weiss said, "We're indispensable, Arthur. We're making the myths the tribe lives by. We show them how to live. Without us, they'd burn down the Pentagon, shoot the presidents. Which they do pretty regularly, anyway."

But Powdermaker felt a professional hollowness. Only traveling fulfilled him: he was taking in the world, preparing for something that wouldn't be just appearance and pretense.

9

At the brief stopover in Bissone, Powdermaker dashed the hundred yards from the dining car to his compartment. It relieved and exhausted him. He felt swallowed by heat. In the compartment, he took off his clothes and sat naked by the window, bent over the vents through which cold air rose. At Lago Maggiore, mountains fell down greenly to the water; blue and white villages clustered around spires. How beautiful and neat Switzerland was; it was what it was supposed to be.

Zhoof. "Am I so clearly that? The eyes? The big nose? My walk? My open mouth—the Whiner's deferential mouth, the Ingratiator's smile? All that helpfulness with the train; damn eagerness to belong? Jewiness. *Zhoofheit.* Whatever the bastard saw, felt. And couldn't bear. Some Yid stuff leaking out of me. The only thing that counted for him. Not tourist, not American, not fellow traveler. Certainly not fellow man. *Zhoof. Disjecta membra.* Garbage."

10

He'd be coming back. Their compartment was three down, they'd walk past. Powdermaker could open the door, naked, and stare at them. The message would be, "You aren't part of that world which obliges me to clothe myself." He'd be in his own compartment, he had his rights. Or did he? There might be some railway code enjoining decency. Maybe he could say, "Madam, would you care to come in and have a nightcap? I can offer you more civilized company than you're used to." Even if ignored—of course it would be—it would make the point. Or would it reinforce their contempt for *Zhoofs*? Maybe a collision: he'd open the door as they passed and crash into the bastard. "Watch where you're going, you old bastard," while he kicked his ankle, kneed him, put an elbow in his eye.

Never in his life had Powdermaker done anything remotely like this. Was it time? He'd been insulted; men had fought duels for less than this. If he could only hold on to his anger, not weaken it with doubt, maybe he could pull it off, *do* something for a change.

11

The year before, Powdermaker had gone through the Guillaumin Collection at the Orangerie. Cézannes, Monets, Manets, Bonnards, Pissarros, the wonderful familiar crew who'd brought such happiness to millions. To Powdermaker, the Cézannes were special, an intelligence beyond beauty. You could look deeper and deeper into them. They touched the essential, they were essential.

Now in the compartment, with the door ajar, not just the compartment door but the one in himself, Powdermaker felt something in that untouched part of himself which had been identified in contempt by the man. *Zhoof*. It stood for the outsiders who had brought the message which linked the transient to the eternal. It said, "You, you by the road, criminal, coward, beggar, weakling, you're an absolutely essential part of what counts." That was the part Hitler couldn't stand in himself and identified in his sadistic father with the Viennese Jew who'd impregnated the upstairs maid.

Powdermaker had spent his life posing and would leave behind nothing but a few images that persuaded people to decorate the surface of their lives. Now, thanks to a twisted fellow, he'd been forced into the part of himself that he'd covered over, one it was necessary to recognize, if not defend. Only that way did you earn the right to be on the same earth with the Cézannes, the deepeners and sweeteners of life. As for the haters, they existed, oddly enough, to rouse the drugged souls of the world's Powdermakers.

12

Powdermaker slept well. He woke to the porter's knock, opened the door and got his passport, put on his socks, shirt, and pants, and walked down the corridor to the bathroom. While he emptied his bowels, he looked at the passport picture, as blank a one as he'd ever taken. Someone was waiting. As he zipped up, Powdermaker knew it was the *Zhoof* hater.

Why hadn't he brought a deodorant? The fellow would smell his leavings: a triumph of disgust. Good, thought Powdermaker. Let him choke. Another repertoire of violence flashed through him: elbow in ribs, knee in groin, door slammed in face. The fellow was probably stronger than he, but he'd have surprise on his side. He could at least stamp on his foot; no, he was in socks, more evidence of *Zhoofheit*.

He opened the door. There the man was, in shirt and jacket, face sharp and blank till it registered Powdermaker and turned icy. Powdermaker arranged his own face into amused contempt and looked into the fellow's eyes. The man drew back into a further state of blankness. Passing, Powdermaker felt him hesitate—could he endure being in a *Zhoof*'s toilet, the wood still *Zhoof* warm? Powdermaker heard the WC door shut.

13

As the train pulled into Brussels's Gare du Nord, the couple stood behind Powdermaker. When he got off, he looked behind. The woman looked at him, flushed, almost pleading. He gave her a small nod, a sympathetic, a human nod. She understood.

MILIUS AND MELANIE

1

They were to meet at the Wollman Rink in Central Park. A stupid idea, his, and in the unbalanced sentiment of reunion, agreed to by her. If they had even heard each other's voices over the phone, they wouldn't have gone through with it, but no, they had transmitted the proposals and confirmations through Tsvević; it had been Tsvević who'd spotted her in his painting, Tsvević who'd told him he must see her again, and Tsvević who had put in the call to Tulsa. "You must transform your emotional *situation*." Tsvević, an intellectual straggler who compensated in ferocity for modishness, was undergoing Sartre; *situation* had nothing to do with its banal English uses; no, it stood for fixity which choice would shatter.

Tsvević gleamed with false wisdom, his dab of nose, popped blue eyes, and ice-colored lips mere service stations for the gray-topped mental apparatus which ran the Language Schools and, for thirty years, no small part of Orlando Milius's life. What counted even more in Tsvević was the maniacally tended flesh whose terrific muscles bulged clothes into second skin. Every morning, in sneakers and sweatpants, Tsvević ran four laps around the Central Park Reservoir, a character known to policemen and taxi drivers going off late shifts and to the thugs who worked the West Side Eighties and Nineties. None had ever held him up: out for gain, there were nothing but gym clothes and flying feet; out for mischief and violence, there were those muscles. Such confidence muscles gave small intelligence, thought Milius, who, seven inches taller and fifty pounds heavier than Tsvević, was soft, had always been soft, and though now stronger, for he walked a lot and lifted furniture at his wife's frequent command, had none of the confidence of size or strength. Milius would never appear in the park after dusk, he crossed streets with caution and swiftness, treasured all uniforms and the pacification they promised. A civic coward. Yet it was he, not Tsvević, who had almost a hero's record in wartime, had worked in the hills with partisans, had, if not shot, been shot at.

But he had not had the confidence to telephone Melanie Booler in Tulsa, Oklahoma. Indeed, lack of confidence had hidden his feelings about her for twenty years, and, even now, when he had at least recognized something in his painting, timidity had slurred identification; she had just looked familiar, an ideal woman, too beautiful and wise for him to have known.

Tsvević had spotted her at once and, great fisher of feeling, had drawn Milius's old longing from him. "That's your Melanie."

Of course it was. Naturally. Melanie. Who else? On the floor in his loft, looking up at the canvas pinned in light, Milius saw her skating inside the smashed cobalt arcs and gorgeous polygonal blots. Once again the pilot had brought him in safely.

Safely, yes, but into harsh country! Up the corridor, Vera's cabbage soup steamed in on little Lucy's flatulent tromboning; and in Milius's wallet reposed the villainous paragraph from the *Times Literary Supplement* clipped out by his London publisher, daggered with a red question mark, and airmailed across the Atlantic.

Now, zippered to the neck in his old orange suede jacket, an overturned keel of black lamb's wool on his gray head, Orlando Milius diverts his nerves from the noon meeting by focusing on the brilliant New York scene. The skating pond blares pink and white; little frozen sea, fleshed over by sweatered, jacketed, scarfed, and capped New Yorkers twirling under the stony smiles of the great hotels, Plaza, Pierre, Essex, and Hampshire Houses. Sunday morning, mid-December, yet a Floridan sun has softened the ice to a green scurf which permits no skating distinction but awkwardness: tots skitter, girls shriek, corpulent swaggerers crumple.

Twenty-four years. She will not know him. Or, worse, he will not know her. The crowds will rush on and off the ice at noon, and they will be lost in the rush. "To the left of the gate by the railing" wasn't sufficient direction. Had the railing even been here? It was surely not where they used to meet. No, they would walk together from Columbus Circle, skates around their necks, Melanie darkly golden, her body, so shy and full, turned military by a thigh-length leather jacket out of which stuck her beautiful, stubby legs, black in woolen stocking pants. Large eyed, quick, shy but never anxious, while he walked in fear that Sophie would catch them in the park, righteous in illegitimate possessiveness, picking them out with that look which boiled needles off pine trees.

When Vera, quieter than Sophie, but with a fierceness disciplined in wartime hills, learned what he had done, the ice under the skaters' blades would not be cut as often as his heart.

Learned?

Was he confusing Melanie and the *TLS*?

No, they were of a piece. There was meaning to the convergence. Vera would spot the common treason. Yet her father, dear old Poppa Murko, would have understood. Did he not want his turgid, scholar's versions of the Chinese tales put into clear English prose? Those beautiful chunks of Ming erotica which he had mined from Zagreb archives. And which now, for the price of a bottle of aspirin, transmuted the amorous encounters of Nebraska salesmen into sensuous pageants. What had he, Milius, done, after all, but clean Poppa's Serbian gunk from these Oriental diamonds, polish them up, and put them into American settings? With no thought of large profits or glory. Just to make enough for paints and canvas, to keep Poppa's daughter in cabbage soup and his granddaughter in trombone lessons.

Yet he was not wholly innocent. No, he had made one mistake: he'd hinted at the Chinese sources of his books, but had never mentioned Poppa Murko. And perhaps a second mistake: he'd yielded to Benny Goss and Americanized the books: Meiling Fan had become Dora Trent; Ch'o Tuan, the eager scholar, was Roderick Peake, the lascivious topologist. "Now we've got us something," said Benny Goss. Yes, Benny, a dagger. Any minute the phone would ring, Benny would see the paragraph clipped from the *TLS,* and, with the rage of the cornered pornographer, he would throw Milius to the wolves. To Vera.

To Milosović and Krenk. Twin canines, he remembered them, sharp, torpid, yet turbulent men, dark and ugly, he could not distinguish their features or disentangle them. Spittle lickers of Mihailović, they'd sold out to the Germans, and he, Milius, had had to cut out for the mountains with Vera and live like a block of ice for a year while Milosović and Krenk drank slivovitz in Gradisti. After the war, they'd surfaced in England with fish in their teeth (redbrick chairs of Serbian studies), and now, behind the anonymous authority of the *TLS*, they did their poisonous survey of Serbian Oriental studies, straying just far enough to include "the vulgarized, baroque renditions of Professor Murko's versions of the *Jou-p'u-t'uan,* the *Ching-P'ing-Mei,* and the *Ko-lien h'ai-ying* made by neither a Serbian nor an Oriental scholar, but by a third-rate American writer, O. Milius."

A day, a week, and Vera would learn that he'd stripped her darling Pop of his rightful possessions, and she would turn him into soup. Ah, Melanie.

Yes, out of his need, as out of the broken polygons of his painting, came the dear love of his life, surely that, his Beatrice, his Laura, his Stella. Yes, noble Sidney's precious star, he knew those lovely poems: Stella sees the very face of woe, painted in my clouded face, how she will pity my disgrace, as though thereof the cause she know, and some heartrending, bull's-eye ending, "I am not I, pity the tale of me." Yes, he was Milius *Pictor,* not Milius *Auctor Plagiarist Thief.*

Dear God, what the artist had to become in America. Poor Edmund Wilson hiding out from the income-tax men to sip his champagne in peace; the poets all mad, spiked on their own dreams, exhibited like Cromwell's head for public delectation; the painters smashed up in automobiles fleeing the ravenous curiosity hounds, poor Jackson, dear Joey. And who flourished but museum directors, gallery owners, publishers? Business actors all, bearing their expensive agonies for cocktail-hour inspection, or, lacking the gift of gab, for fifty-dollar-an-hour confessors. The artists looked normal, jovial, quiet, only occasionally stabbing a wife or doping their veins, the only workers left, and what happened? Milosovićs and Krenks. Mindless teeth, snapping at air, coming up with artist hearts. *O tempora, o mores, senatus haec intellegit, consul vidit, hic tamen vivint. Vivint?* They strut in Bedford Square, shine in the *Times,* these critic-heroes, full of hatred or wild, mad enthusiasm, consumers, editorial powers, dressing themselves in the snot of kings, rejecting, accepting, declining, appraising, and we, weak-willed artists, we follow, we succumb, we bend, we take them at their own worth. Astounding them. And they eat us. Oh, Milosović, oh, Krenk, shoot me here, shoot me.

And Milius, lost, pushed his hand to his head; his hat, little up-turned lamb's wool boat, scooted to the ice, and a tiny skater, unable to stop, ground into it and smashed her tiny nose on the ice; blood and screams flowed over the green scurf, and Milius found himself gripped by fierce hands, shoulders shaken by a ferocious little man yelling into his face, blissful in his hatred, grateful for his daughter's blood so he could bite the world's throat, and Milius, trying to shake loose, called out, "Little girl. Darling. I'm so sorry. Forgive me. How are you? Little sweets, take a soda with me. At the Zoo Shoppe. Come," and he pushed his yellow gloves into the wild man's chest and, punched in the ribs, began to punch back, what was he doing, here on a Sunday bringing blood out of a child, punching, and then a stout, gray-haired woman in a cloth coat rushed between them, picked up the child, thrust her into her father's arms, stooped for Milius's hat, put it on his head, and said, "Orlando. Orlando, dear. Are you all right? It's me. Yes, Melanie."

2

The Obiitelj, the Family, that was Tsvević's name for the fifteen, then twenty, then seven or eight of them who met day in and out at the old Tip-Toe Inn on Eighty-sixth and Broadway or in the creaky three-story brownstones of the upper Eighties and lower Nineties of West Side Manhattan. They used the Serbian name, abbreviated to Obiit, because Tsvević, a Serb, was the organizer. The others came from all over the Balkans, Willie Eminescu from Moldavia, Veronica and Leo Micle from Bucharest, the mathematics student, Panayot Rustchok, from Sofia, and from Pest, their great success, Béla Finicky, assistant professor of Oriental studies at Columbia, who introduced his most confused and beautiful pupil, Melanie Booler, of Tulsa, Oklahoma.

The Americans in the group were usually transients, pupils in Tsvević's Language School, Tip-Toe Inn acquaintances, or sympathetic
types who hung around the Soldiers and Sailors Monument on Riverside Drive. It was by this classical preface to the mausoleum of General Grant a few miles up the drive that Tsvević's pupils met on
weekends, here that Milius first saw Melanie. He had already come to
understand that what held and stamped the Obiit—Balkan core and
American accretions—was failure. Other New York groups, formed
at the same time out of similar drifters, foreign and domestic, somehow acquired the motor power which drove them through the Depression and the war into various triumphs, artistic, theatrical,
publishing, and publicity, but the Obiit foundered in eccentricity,
quixoticism, sheer inability to make headway. Milius had thought
about it many nights. Why was it? Lack of ambition? No. The Obiit
members were full of schemes, personal, civic, worldly, universal,
timeless. Lack of tenacity? Perhaps, in part. But more, it seemed that
American life wasn't ready to absorb these unassimilable bits of the
unassimilated Balkans, these fragments of fragments. The Obiit, like
their native lands, were the shuttlecocks of established powers. You'd
think these people, ancestrally alerted to overreaching ambition and
toppling regimes, could have adjusted to American life. But no, hardly a handful survived—Tsvević, Eminescu, and Milius himself.
Though he had never been a true part of them. He'd come to earn a
living and stayed for Melanie, but always, his persistence, insularity,
and, yes, hardness had held him to his painting, and this in almost
complete isolation from the powerful temperaments already making
themselves known in New York—Pollock, Rothko, Klein, Hofmann,
de Kooning. They were unstoppable, and after the war, they constituted the field, their critics, friends from WPA days, preceding them with
brilliant manifestos, their gallery sponsors alert to the importance of
abstraction in the opulence, anxiety, hedonism, and skepticism of postwar life.

By then, the Obiit were scattered beyond reassemblage. The war
had assigned them, fed them, broken them; even their bodies, oddly
enough, had strange chinks through which certain war and postwar
diseases found ready and fatal admission—hepatitis, lupus, ery-

thremic myelosis. By 1948, ten of them lay in the cemeteries of Queens. Who watching the dark, gorgeous, noisy energy held in the corner booths of the Tip-Toe Inn could have foreseen such decimation?

In 1935, when he first met Tsvević, Milius, aged twenty-eight, was living in a bedroom-kitchenette apartment with Sophie Grindel, a severe, sensuous Latin teacher at Stuyvesant High School on Fifteenth Street. Sophie and the monthly hundred-dollar check from the WPA Arts Section were his support. Sophie had forced him into the project. "If you couldn't daub a barn, you've as much claim on the funds as those bums at the Municipal Building." She got her cousin, Sasha Grindel, a painter by virtue of talk and possession of an easel, to sign his form. "That sulky Dutchman dreaming of Ginger Rogers, and that galoot Hammerslough reading Trotsky while the other bums swipe at the walls. Roosevelt stands in back of them, he can stand in back of a real American like you. Talent or no."

Sophie was no admirer of his painting. He was income supplement, bed warmer, audience, and chef. While she corrected *fero, ferre, tuli, latum,* Milius broiled carp, made matzo ball soup, tried out pasta dishes. Why not? He stayed home. He went out only once on a project, drove Sasha's jalopy through the Holland Tunnel to a New Jersey post office and painted what he thought would be a fit mural for this center of Washington's struggling colonials, an ocean of English red and black out of which coagulated shivery red, white, and blue streaks. Up on the ladder, he bore the catcalls of the Philistine postcard buyers. During Christmas, he did part-time work dressing Fourteenth Street department store windows. Most of the year, he just painted at home or on the walls of friends' apartments. Indeed, it was just learning to use this diseased skin of cheap apartments which opened his eyes to his screen techniques and led him to think out his notions of accident-proof painting. The apartment walls were his Paris and his Provence. Smoke and brick dust now, they were no more durable than the *spaghetti alle vongole* of some Tuesday prewar dinner. Less memorable to that great eater, Sophie. In the morning, when she left, the six square feet above their bed would be a mean green grime; at four, she'd return with her quizzes to a thick garden of color and would barely nod at it. Was this what Cicero, that canny sybarite, had taught her?

Sophie was not harsh or mean, only intense and fierce. Powerful, nervous, silently demanding, Roman nosed as her authors, her features dominated the narrow flesh of her face, the subtle lips whose underflap was gripped by powerful teeth when he had troubled her, straight hair the color of Moselle white wine, full of rich gleams though sparse, and the eyes like hot chocolate, steaming. They'd seen each other first through an Ohrbachs' window he was decorating with sugar frost and holly, she checking out a pile of cashmere sweaters with the volatile, chocolate eyes that soon fixed his. Her underlip drew into her teeth, and, behind the glass, in shirtsleeves, Milius had felt a shimmer of heat. That night he'd gone home with her—there was no nonsense anywhere in Sophie— and, the next day, he'd removed his clothes in a paper bag from his brother's Bronx apartment and moved into her two and a half rooms down the dying street from the high school.

Sophie had no friends, and Milius was too absorbed in painting to visit his old friends in the Bronx. They saw almost no one but Tsvević, a substitute German teacher in the school system who, at Stuyvesant, tried to pick Sophie up. When, one day, he succeeded, he found himself brought home to Milius. A shock, but for Tsvević's disciplined system, one activity could substitute for another without noticeable abrasion. Lust stymied, Tsvević orated, planned, organized. He was beginning to roll out schemes of language schools. Urban man was in trouble, flabby in mind, flabby in body. "Tissues feeble, issues trouble." Tsvević's passion that year was Quintilian. "Perfect Man Is Man Speaking." Exercise would build up the tissues, recitation of great poems and speeches would do the rest. There'd be no overhead, classes would be in open air, *Mens sana in corpore sano,* eh, Miss Grindel?"

Over the next months, they worked out the Scuola Quintiliana; notices were inked on the back of laundry cardboards and put in windows along Broadway. The first meeting was to take place on Saturday, March 21, at the Soldiers and Sailors Monument. The day came, but no pupils. Only Tsvević, Willie Eminescu, and Milius, the instructors. For forty minutes they shivered in a trough of Arctic air, then adjourned to the Tip-Toe Inn to regroup their forces. It was decided to delay the opening for a month, change the name to Mens Sana School, and alter the curriculum to instruction in foreign languages, beginning with words for parts of the body, words which, as the new notice had it, "would be riveted in memory by overt motor activity. $2.45 per week."

Oddly enough, this notice brought out eight men and women on an April Sunday. The next week, fifteen enrolled, and, finally, about thirty people, mostly young men and women whose schooling had been doused by the Depression. They met every Saturday and Sunday for instruction in Serbo-Croatian by Tsvević, Romanian by Eminescu, and in his family German by Milius. The first month, Milius did no teaching but was instead a nonpaying and phenomenally able member of Tsvević's Serbian class. The pupils ran along the Hudson River framing Serbian slogans, bent low to address gruff vocatives to the stones of Riverside Drive, exhaled declensions toward the coppery cliffs of the Palisades.

Milius began his German class in May, four men and women he could not remember and Béla Finicky, who knew German as well as he but who'd been converted by Tsvević to the cult of verbalized muscularity and who thought it a good way to be with his pretty young student from the West, Melanie Booler.

Milius fell in love with Melanie during her first push-up. A modest girl, Melanie was not the sort to suck beauty out of the mirror. Her expressions, untrained by vanity, were striking smiles and laughs, the dark gold head flung suddenly back. Intoxicating. That first day, she wore shorts, sneakers, white socks, a loose white blouse. When she lowered herself for the first push-up, Milius saw her cloth-capped breasts enjoying their little motion. Eye snared tongue; correcting her stance, instead of "*Man muss die Beine* [legs] *ganz gerade halten,*" he'd said, "*Man muss die Brust* [breast] *ganz gerade halten.*" Professor Finicky, at the summit of a push-up, caught the error and divined the source; his eyes fixed hard on Milius, but, too late, Milius was lost.

Walking up Ninetieth Street to West End Avenue, he'd touched Melanie Booler's bare arm. "You are so beautiful, Miss Booler," he said. "I find *ich bin schon ganz entzückt von* you."

3

By the seal pool, an arc of fish flew by their heads. Chow time. The great commas waddled, honked, panted, dived, and then such grace, delight, and marvel. Melanie Dube laughed quietly. The powdered, grandmotherly lumpishness disappeared into smile lines. Under the specs, the periwinkle eyes, within the gray hair, deep gold shadows. (Ah, thought Milius, Melanie in his mind, the seals in water.)

They walked by the wolf cages, the gnus, and ostriches, then north along the chunky feldspar wall which split avenue from park. Melanie talked of Jack, her brilliant son, a wanderer, guitar player, dropout, and CO, Milius of Vera, Lucy, and his books, of which she hadn't heard.

Out of breath a bit, yes, but inside, Melanie and Milius felt musical, joyous. What were years but signs for outsiders? They were insiders, and, an hour later, over English muffins on a couch in Melanie's room at the Hotel Bolivar, Milius, awkwardly, but not upset at the awkwardness, took up her unringed left hand and kissed it.

How could it be? Thousands of hours had not dispersed but only screened his feelings. Anonymous, cautious, sidelined, he felt singled out, magnified. Orlando Milius, hero's name on a coward's heart, oddity cloaked in oddity, he had not looked into his feelings for thirty years. A painter, his feelings were absorbed by the techniques of appearance. No wonder his paintings were strange. Yet one didn't choose the strange, one fell into it. Like birth. (What to do but breathe, cry, suck?) Or the war. There he was, four thousand feet over the iron river, the ocher shack on the lip of the copse, and Vera, Djovan, little Vuk, and Poppa Murko with his wooden trunk of papers. Alone, he had felt all alone, and there was Vera, intense, tiny, her cartridge belt across her breasts, her black hair clipped under the astrakhan, and old Murko, dear snaggletoothed coot, sitting on those Oriental grapes. Ah, it was hard. Old Murko could draw roses from a rock garden. At night, above the icing Sava, he read the manuscripts aloud, and Vera's face, touched by the steaming *raka*, flushed in the sudden, masculine silence. Yes, Poppa knew his stuff. He had learned plenty from the wily Mings, knew his lungs weren't going to last another winter in the hills, and provided for his manuscripts and his daughter. That was the way life went: those who knew their hearts arranged the lives of those who didn't. Was it too late? For him? For Melanie?

For Melanie, no. Not from the first minute, seeing Milius punched and hatless, her sweet Orlando, so blotted a mixture of subtlety and confusion, so intricate and awkward. Despite Dube, dear Dube, as far out of the mainstream in his way as Orlando in his. She'd fitted around his oddities all these years, she would not pain him now. But he floated on those depthless oddities, she was only another one along with the white wool socks he wore to bed summer and winter, the collection of snakeskins, the rooster imitation. Poor Dube. His puzzlement underwrote her week in New York.

She had never tried him beyond puzzlement, but she was ready now. Not that she had ever been one to force things. *Wu-wei.* That's what she had learned from Béla Finicky in Chinese Thought. Let nature take its course. Sails, not oars; the stirrup, not the whip. It was her nature as well. Rivers bit away at old beds and formed new ones. (Did that mean old beds were abandoned?)

Milius walked home through the park at Eighty-fifth Street. Provence. Purple vineyards, silvered olive trees, Renoir gardens, Monet ponds, Cézanne mountains freaked with jets of gold. Oh, such beauty. His hands in the yellow gloves tensed and perspired, he knew the sign, he walked fast, he must get home. At Fifth he hopped a bus over to Second, then ran down the block, stormed up the stairs past Vera's call, "Orlando," and, in the loft, dived for his paints.

But Vera's cry was not to be shut off, and guilt amplified it in Milius's ears. He dropped his brush. "It's happened." At last. She's found out. Down the hall she'll come, a pot of steaming water in those partisan's hard hands. Benny Goss, Milosović, Krenk, Lucy, Sophie, the ghost of Béla Finicky, Poppa Murko, and the lustful Chinese scribes would sup on his souped-down flesh. It was over. Provence? Hah. The butcher's knife. "Orlando," called Vera, and then another cry, "Brat. Brat Lando." Another voice: baritone.

The door whirred. A great slab of man grabbed Milius in his arms as if he were cardboard, whirled him dizzy, kissed his cheeks. Lucy and Vera cooed and leaped at his flanks.

It was Vuk. Cousin Vuk.

He'd flown in today, hadn't Milius been reading the papers? There was to be a reading at Madison Square Garden, the only poet ever to read there. "Not one word publicity, and the house is sold off in two hours. Tickets skulped for fifty smockers."

Vuk the Bard, Tito's greatest export, life's king, subsidized for singing what Djilas was jailed for saying. At eighteen, he had told Stalin to his face he was going out of his mind, and the old iron man, with the Georgian worship of the poet-seer, had taken it deeply to heart. So dissolved the world's miseries in that Shark's face with the wise, ice-blue eyes.

Now Vuk was, as usual, suffering. Heartburn, cramps. He raised his sweater, shirt, and undershirt, put Milius's hand against his rib cage. "Feel, Lando, feel," and in a loud whisper to both protect and excite Lucy, "Weemens is keelink me." Rome, Brussels, London — "incredible" — Paris, Barcelona — "estupendo" — even Dublin, two, three a day. And drawing a pack of Gaulois from his corduroys, "Plus fumigottink mine lunks." The hard, narrow flesh devoured by little Lucy and Vera till the shirt dropped. Then, in Milius's ear, "But waddya hell, us Communist mission is focking capitalists." This the shy rail of a boy skiing the hills with his bag and shotgun, bringing back the snipe. Now, in Serbian, he stuffed them with that great cake which was his life: tiger hunting in Nepal, swimming with La Cardinale at Porto San Stefano, strangling a rabid camel in Kabul, debating Rumlï in Vienna, frugging in a Siberian igloo. And the erotic Niagara roared: one-legged beauties in the Pescadores, tree loving in Zambia, a flower bath in Oahu, and heart-cracking loves with an Israeli sergeant, an Amarillo cattleman's wife, a florist's assistant in Kuala Lumpur.

But Vuk, seismograph as well as earthquake, spotted uneasiness in Milius's laughter. "Enough. Let's walk, Lando. I must get some New York gas to my lunks," and took Milius off to Central Park, where Milius, content to be Vuk's oyster, opened up his troubles.

For Vuk, though, Milius's troubles were unrecognizable as troubles. How could sheer possibility, whether for love or hatred, be anything but good? Vuk was delighted about Melanie; it looked as if one could go on a long time. For Vuk, life was a trail of eggshells. That a shell should suddenly churn with new life was a wonder. "And where is the nymph of yours, dear Lando?" He must see her, this wonder of sixty-year flesh

As for Milosović and Krenk, he would grind them. If he could face Tito, Stalin, Khrushchev, and Mao, it would be an eye's blink to crush Serbian scum into nonexistence. He would read them out of the world in Madison Square Garden, pop them into dust in Chattanooga, St. Louis, Winnipeg, and L.A. He would pull them out of literature like decayed teeth, and he could celebrate Orlando's beautiful erotica — though personally he didn't care much for fancy smut — that was no trouble, but first, they must see Melanie, "your neemph."

Vera?

Vera would understand, appreciate, adore his being refreshed for her. "Like dugs, weemens love sneef of other weemens on bones." As for leaving her, well, that was perhaps too much. Life was no coffin, each day a nail, one must move after one's heart, but leaving, leaving was much trouble. He would not dream of leaving his own wife, she was his mother, sister, lover, nurse, why should he leave her, she knew nothing — hah, thought Milius — about his other focking, why should she, she was brilliant, beautiful, had a life of her own, was strictly faithful to him, who would need any more? With his shark's smile, insistent, innocent, powerful.

At the Bolivar, Melanie was celebrating reunion with Tsvević.

Reunion?

Tsvević was putting it on the existential line: hot coffee and cold turkey. In detail. (Serious advice could not be capsular, look at *Being and Nothingness,* look at *Saint Genet.*) He had hardly warmed up, did not relish the entrance of Milius, let alone Vuk. That a Tito stooge, a ninth-rate versifier, a publicity gorger and narcissist should preempt his platform was a bit much. Seldom calm, Tsvević grew into a frenzy of calm. His sentences lengthened, his face grew polelike under constraint, the madly exercised body quivered inside the grimy tweed. He was disturbed, yes, dismayed by their indecision. Life called to them, the very earth suspended its course so that they could come together again, yet here they were, locked in bourgeois fears, corpses of life.

4

Ah, well, perhaps, but not that afternoon, that dusk, that evening.

For Milius and Melanie are in the Paris Theater swept by the love story of a racing-car driver and a widowed script girl, melting as the difficulties of the thirty-year-old French beauties blot into their own.

While Vuk—at Madison Square Garden—dedicates his reading to that great artist in prose and paint, his old friend and comrade-in-arms, Orlando Milius, assailed on the left by vicious Serbian cannibals, on the right by silence and poverty.

And while Vera Murko Milius lies on a velvet ottoman, head aburst with Leo Tsvević's story.

Tsvević stands in front of her, a sword, vague eye on a print above her reeling head, a Byzantine Christ whose head lies shipwrecked on its reef of shoulder. "Serbian agony," he growls. "Smash these icons."

"Darling Poppa."

"No regrets, Vera. No bitterness. Bourgeois gloom saps vitality. Look up at Leo, darling." Vera looks up. "Liberate Orlando. And you liberate Vera." An iron hand grabs hers, draws her up, they are nose to nose. "You have camouflaged *une mauvaise situation, chère* Vera." His great eyes swim in the red-veined net.

Milius and Melanie drink Cherry Heering in the Bolivar Room, go upstairs, and, in the dark, take off their clothes. Sympathy performs its magic fusion. The clumsy, creaky bodies understand; they are lovers once again.

Ten-thirty, and Milius takes the crosstown bus, in his hand a cellophane sack of chocolate kisses from Whelan's.

In the tiny living room, Vera Milius rises, fierce and silent. The chocolate obols are laid on the ottoman. Minutes eat silence. Then Vera begins, quietly: the historical introduction, the Balkan histories of treason, epic stories, the long fight for national freedom, the wars, the Bulgars, Turks, Austrians, and Huns, the traitors, Djuleks and Mihailovićs, who dog Serbian history. She should have been alert to treason. She should know the grain of the world. Like Milos and Branković, Orlando is infected. That her darling father had seen him as a son, that she should have been his prize was spice on the legend. Yes, even as she was, the years of her fullness given to him, Ganelon, Djulek the Bimbasa, Judas. Robbery. He had robbed his only heir. What price was it to come into the world the child of Milius? Sixty-two years of age, treason took a new turn here. And with what? A sugar babe? A gold digger? A baby doll? No. Beauty she could understand, flesh she understood, but such treason, no. To salt his treason, his rebuke, he took a woman older than his wife, a rag discarded years ago, a Western American woman, with dental plates, white hair, hard of hearing. Was this the madness of abstract artists? That they had no touch with life, the world? Was this the meaning of his treason, that it went against the grain of flesh as well as family? If he'd brought a filthy nag, yes, literally, a horse into his bed, she would have only more clearly seen the insanity of his treason. And he brings me sweets, chocolates, Judas kisses.

Vera, small, dark, blunt nosed, solid, pours her survey on his head. Powerful, analytic, a great moment, and in English, her second language, her father would have been so proud. Justice, intelligence, wisdom, passion employed to describe, correct, chasten. She ended in a great breath, rose, as high as a small woman could, he imagined her with the bandoliers across her breasts, the fur hat, the knitted gloves in the mountain ice, Vera, the great soup maker, enduring here his few dollars, making her own world amid the aliens, back now alone on her mountains, a heroine of family life, out of the sagas. And he, a swine, thief, two-timer.

Milius sat alone in the parlor, heard the toilet flush — Vera allowed herself the privileges of being natural — he crushed a piece of candy, the stain was beautiful, he would put it on canvas. He sat brooding, and, then, bored and tired; but there was only the other side of their bed. Did he dare?

Yes.

He went in. She was, of course, awake. (Could pain advertise itself in sleep?) He took her breaths as whips, undressed, ashamed of his body's ease, put on his pajamas, did not dare empty his bowels, only allowed himself to urinate, ashamed even here of relief, brushed his teeth so his breath would not add offense, crept around to the other side of the bed, undid his pajama string for more ease, slid under the quilt. "Forgive me, please, dear Vera. I'm so weak a man. Please forgive me."

She had often rebuked him for ease of sleep while her ears seined the city's riot. He tried not to sleep before she did, but once again, his body triumphed, and he snored, terribly. Vera then could sleep herself, certified by the criminality of his noise.

5

The next morning brought great changes. Via a telephone call at six-thirty. A reporter, then another, then the Yugoslav Embassy, then the State Department.

It was Vuk. But by mischance. Life had caught up with him. The cake had its worms. He was in Lenox Hill Hospital, skull crushed, sure of recovery, but in a bad way. Reporters were chronicling his New York day. The feature seemed to be one Orlando C. Milius, American painter and author, whom Vuk had visited in the afternoon and extolled at Madison Square Garden a couple of hours before he had been mugged, slugged, robbed, and left for dead.

For most of the day, Milius smoked in the blaze of contemporary publicity. Pen, mike, and camera elicited every available piece of his body, every cent of his income, every stage of his life. By noon, he had watched himself on television and read about himself in the early editions with the happy puzzlement of a child seeing a drop of water under a microscope. "So this is Milius, this mass of warts, this lump of crystals, this strange being who has been given my name." He was described as "handsome and distinguished," "faded and undistinguished," "a youthful sixty," "an elderly man," "a famous painter," "an unknown poet," "a war hero and scholar," "an unemployed language teacher." He could not wait to cart his new lives over to Melanie.

She, unaware of his fame, had sat all day at her window, watching a veil of cobalt sleet lift from the city, seeing the dendrite ache of Central Park trees, daydreaming the strange turn in her life. Orlando, my dearest, no sleet with you. Our autumn is harvesttime in dear New York, sweet nature's town.

Milius, arriving at six, was almost an intruder. She had to shake herself from the day's cocoon, face up to his excitement and great news. The Willeth Gallery had made overtures, his first show in a major gallery; Benny Goss, voice full of gold instead of rage, had planned new editions, translations, campaigns for awards, critical conferences, the literary works.

Night edged dusk, Orlando wore down. Too much. The variety and speed were too much. Their embrace was static, the amorous focus blurred. "We must go out," he said. They studied the movie section. *Blow Up* had just opened at the Plaza. "That's our dish."

In his fine chesterfield, bought years ago in the Gramercy Thrift Shop, riding downtown beside his lovely Melanie, holding a newspaper which carried his own picture, Milius felt like a man whose rich personal life was of public concern.

In the dark of the Plaza, watching the two chippies wrestle each other naked on the purple backdrop paper, Milius had an erection. And simultaneously, a tremendous idea. He would paint screenlessly. He would lay clear, intricate blocks of space events directly on canvas. No subtle schemes of indirection, only direct interrogations of matter, unambiguous shafts through surface forms.

What joy.

He turned Melanie's head toward his and, in the dark, kissed her lips. Nature had its seven ages, yes, but each generation altered their dynamics and duration. He and Melanie were vanguardists of the sexagenarian revival.

Yet, an hour later, eating at a Second Avenue steak house, there was another relapse. The peppered vodka-and-bouillon drinks, the adolescent hamburgers and onion, the noisy, gaseous, glittery night of Second Avenue, were not the backdrop for resurrected feelings or revolutionary passion.

At the Bolivar once again, holding each other, eyes closed against the sad circumstance of their bodies, loving but spent, half querulous, half amused, Milius and Melanie separated in the labyrinth of desire.

6

Artists, Milius knew, were hypersensitive to their cycles, emotional and social, intellectual and sexual. According to Françoise Gilot, Picasso had a daily rise and fall: her job was weaning him from noon blues to the two o'clock assault on canvas. Milius's friend Praeger, the poet-obstetrician, had a yearly cycle: a fine, productive spring; a frenzied, coruscating summer; then an autumn and winter of uncheckable misery. He himself, thought Milius, had an elephantine cycle: his works took years to come to anything, his passions were lethargic as glaciers, his discoveries immense but molasseslike in realization. The discovery in the Plaza Theater had led to a week's thickheaded absorption in paints. Now, his insight come to almost nothing, he surfaced for air. Melanie was gone, gone and he'd hardly noticed. His last hours with her were more nostalgic than amorous, scarcely a backdrop for his painting. For a moment, he couldn't remember if he had taken her to the plane. He hadn't. He had moled it in the attic, refusing phone calls, not speaking to Vera or Lucy, forgetful that he had been, unaware that he was no longer, a public figure. Now fog throttled dawn light at his attic's glass wimple. Worn-out, stained hands on his long face, Milius was carved by his ache for Melanie. Seven-thirty. He'd been up since six.

He put on his chesterfield and astrakhan, kept on the lumberman's boots in which he painted, and went out. He walked by the great, silent museum which showed no Milius, into Central Park, up and down the unshaven little hills, across the empty bridle paths, between great rocks befogged into Rhenish ruins. He walked northwest to the reservoir and waited. A runner passed, another, and then, chugging slowly, lined, gray, pullover limp over his knickers, Tsvević. "Leo," called Milius softly.

Tsvević stopped, took breath, stared in fright. "Who? Where? What's up? Oh, you, Lando." He jogged in place, panting, eyes popped and veined. "Something wrong?"

"I'm so restless. I had to get outside."

"All right. I'm finished. Let's go home."

For years Tsvević had had a woman friend who cleaned his apartment. She'd died a year ago, and Tsvević had not touched a broom or picked up a newspaper since. The place was clogged with candy wrappers, socks, shoe rags, empty tubes of Bufferin, exhausted inhalators, copies of *Horoscope* and the *Balkan News-Letter;* the rugs were plots of dust; months of burned toast and bacon fat hung in the light motes.

It was a little better in the kitchen. Tsvević brewed tea, cleared the table, poured into dirty blue cups. They sat at the window which gave on a coppery well of light in the apartment house courtyard. Tsvević regained confidence. "It's worked out badly, Lando. Who would have guessed that Titoist monkey would turn you into a public freak?"

"A freak? The picture in the paper? That was nothing, Leo."

"You're wrong. It was everything. Kings have lost thrones with less exposure. You're fortunate you lost only Melanie."

"Melanie didn't leave because my picture was on television."

"Your picture was on television because of the dislocation in your life."

"What are you saying, Leo? Make sense. Don't talk like a foolish mystic."

"Mystic? We mustn't be so quickly contemptuous, Orlando. The world has mysteries beyond the scope of J.-P. Sartre. Have you not read Teilhard? Matter has its mysteries, and the spirit is not insensible. All conditions are enchantments, Orlando. The mistake may have been in forcing the situation. Acceptance, Orlando. Our lot is good." He tossed his soaked tea bag toward a garbage pail; it missed and spread its tiny leaves against the porcelain side of the stove.

7

Nine-thirty. Milius walks across the park as he had come. The Queens factories have sent their fumes into the risen mist; café au lait. The rocks are lit in the hollows where the crystals mass. At Madison, Milius goes into the drugstore and changes ten dollars into quarters.

In Tulsa, it is only seven-forty. Dube answers the phone. "Hello-o." Milius's throat fills, his heart thuds on his ribs, he can't speak. "What's this?" says the voice. "Jack? Trouble?"

Milius tries to say, "Wrong number," but can manage only phlegmatic clearance. He hangs up, wipes the perspiration off his forehead with the sleeve of the chesterfield.

Two weeks ago, the failure would have thrown him off for a month, if not permanently. Not now. Now he will wait two hours and phone again, person to person. The operator will get Melanie to the phone, then he, Milius, will manage the rest.

ARRANGEMENTS AT THE GULF

In Lake Forest Mr. Lomax scarcely ever went out of his daughter Celia's house. Most of the day, he sat well wrapped up in the upstairs sitting room playing cribbage with his valet, Mr. Graves. After his morning broth, he read half of the *Tribune,* and, in the afternoon, after his nap, he read the other half. The only season he remarked was winter, which began for him when he saw the first snowfall coming down over the lawns. Then he would instruct Mr. Graves to begin preparations for the trip to Magnolia, the Florida Gulf town where he spent the last twenty-three of his eighty-six winters. A few days later, that third of his family whose year it was to see him off gathered round him at the La Salle Street Station and waved good-bye as his train moved down the tracks.

In his last year, Mr. Lomax was annoyed to find that all his family who lived in or near Chicago—and this was well over two-thirds of it—had come down to say good-bye to him.

Later, alone with Mr. Graves in his compartment, Mr. Lomax mumbled, "Like a golf gallery. Goggled at me like a golf mob."

Mr. Graves went into the adjoining compartment to brew some tea, but tea did not settle Mr. Lomax this evening.

He waved Mr. Graves away, saying that he would stay up till nine o'clock.

Mr. Lomax wished to stay up the extra hour in order to consider the annoyance which he had suffered at the station, to consider it with the shame he felt in remembering that he himself had been the cause of it all. Two weeks before, at the family Thanksgiving dinner, he had said something out loud which formerly he would not have permitted himself to think. He had been served and was studying a white cut of turkey breast similar to those which he had for some years pretended to enjoy for the sake of the family. They've given me an awfully big slice this year, he was thinking when his son, Henry, a priggish busybody and alarmist, asked him if the turkey didn't look quite right to him. Mr. Lomax, with the same effort it would have cost him to say yes said instead, "I think I'm going to die in Florida." The consequence of this irrelevance was that Mr. Lomax's leave-taking had been an informal rehearsal of his funeral. Now, shaking his head, Mr. Lomax made sense of the parting remarks which his children had made to him, Celia's "It's been fun taking care of you, Papa" and Henry's "I'm sorry about the business, Papa." As if he hadn't forced Henry out of the firm thirty-five years ago, and as if Celia had not regarded him for twenty years as an immense burden sufferable only because she owed it to him.

"A pretty thought," mumbled Mr. Lomax. At least, he reflected, his bachelor friend Granville had never had to put up with that sort of smallness. Thinking of Granville, as he would see him the next day waiting at the Magnolia station as he had every other year for the past twenty, Mr. Lomax revived enough so that he almost shuddered at the funeral pageant of which he had been cause and center.

It was very nearly always Granville, the thought of Granville, which pulled Mr. Lomax up in these last years. They were so different, they had done such different things, that the comparison of their lives—and this is what Mr. Lomax constantly made—was never exhausted. The comparison had roots in both pity and envy, and, even now, as his mind wandered, Mr. Lomax pitied what he felt must have been the loneliness of his friend's departure from Philadelphia and then envied its self-sufficiency.

Mr. Lomax was rather proud of his friendship with Granville— Granville was an author—for although the latter was not well enough known for Mr. Lomax to be distinguished by their association, Granville's varied learning and energy had been the source of much pleasure for him, in conversation, contemplation, and in Granville's books. From the last, Mr. Lomax had learned a great many things, the history of investment banking and of New England Colonial preachers, the topography of the Gaspé Peninsula and the rivers of California. Granville's latest volume—the third he'd completed since his seventieth year—had come in the mail the preceding week, and, thinking of this, Mr. Lomax rapped on the compartment door for Mr. Graves.

"Is anything wrong, sir?"

"You might try me with another half a cup," said Mr. Lomax, handing him the cup although this was not easy for him, "and I think I'll look through the new book."

Mr. Graves opened a suitcase and handed Mr. Lomax the book and his magnifying glass.

"Never mind the tea, Graves," said Mr. Lomax. "I'd better not stay up too late." He had not wanted to bother Graves just for the book.

As usual, Granville had inscribed something on the flyleaf. It went, "For my old friend, Wallace Lomax, from his 'young' admirer, Herbert Granville." Mr. Lomax frowned. He disliked his friend's frequent allusions to the decade which separated them, for he sensed in them a possible reflection of the uselessness of his own last years in the light of his friend's striking productiveness.

The book was called *Givings and Misgivings,* and Mr. Lomax, who sometimes read little more of the books than was required for acknowledgment and compliment, could not guess whether or not it would absorb him.

After a bit, he decided that it would not. It was made up of disconnected paragraphs of advice and reflection held together by little more than the calendar: there were 365 paragraphs, each labeled, in journal fashion, by a date of the year.

The simplicity, the naïveté even, of this arrangement suggested so much of Granville that Mr. Lomax looked toward the dark window as if to see him standing at the station in his English cap and knickerbockers, and, in this movement, he recovered the ease and self-satisfaction which his departure had taken from him.

He turned to the paragraph headed March 11, which was his birthday. It went:

Nothing honest comes with ease; nothing dishonest brings ease.
The pressures of life are life itself, as the pressure of the blood is
our pulse, the pressure of lungs our breath. Birth itself is the
pressure of new life on old. The people who tell you, "Worry kills.
Don't worry," do not realize that they are saying, "Life kills. Don't
live."

Mr. Lomax read this through twice and then rapped on the door for
Mr. Graves.

"A pencil please, Graves," he said, and, when Graves was gone
again, he made a star by the paragraph and another at the bottom mar-
gin, and, by the latter, he wrote "Nonsense" and then his initials,
"W.L."

If he could have managed the pencil, thought Mr. Lomax, he would
have written a great deal more. The paragraph had seemed to him almost an attack, and he would like to have countered it with something
like, "The words of a man whose sole worry in life has been whether
it's his year to go to Florida or California, who's never done any work
in his life but write books, and never had anything to do with birth except be born."

The imagined counterattack tired Mr. Lomax, and he leaned back
against the chair and closed his eyes. Then he tried another paragraph,
June 11, which was the date on which his first wife had died and that,
a year later, on which he'd proposed to his second. This paragraph
read:

Now that glittering heavens and hot seas warm the blood with
feelings deeper than all memory, do not turn away, feeling
incapable of such beauty. If unfulfillment is bitter, unacknowl-
edgment is bitterer still. It is men who deny the world, not the
world which denies men.

Mr. Lomax shook his head and decided not to write anything after
this paragraph. In a moment, though, he thought of something, and,
taking up his pencil and making the two stars, he wrote after the bottom one, "I wish you could have had one of mine, Herbert. W.L."

When the train arrived in Magnolia the next evening, Mr. Granville in his white cap and knickerbockers waved as Mr. Graves and the conductor helped Mr. Lomax off the train and into the wheelchair.

"Hello there, Lomax," he called. "It's good to see you again."

Mr. Graves wheeled Mr. Lomax over, and the two old men shook hands. "It's good to see you too," said Mr. Lomax. "You shouldn't have come down to the station."

Granville and Bob, the man from the inn, helped Mr. Graves lift Mr. Lomax into the station wagon.

"I took the train down this year, too," said Granville. "Just decided not to drive. My reflexes are as good as ever, but I just decided against it."

"Wise thing," said Mr. Lomax, thinking Granville must have had an accident driving back from California last spring.

When they arrived at the inn, Mr. Lomax went directly to his room without greeting anybody but the owner, Mrs. Pleasants, who waited on the veranda to welcome him for the twenty-third consecutive season.

He slept through dinner and came out at nine-thirty, just as most of the other guests were going up to bed. Those who knew him stayed with him while he had his bowl of soup, talking about their trips down and inquiring about his.

When they had all gone up, Granville wheeled Mr. Lomax out to the long porch which overlooked the Gulf, and they sat there alone.

"Here we are again," he said.

"And very good to be here," said Mr. Lomax.

"Lucky as well, I think," said Granville, moving his head slightly in the breeze and wondering whether it was too strong for Mr. Lomax.

"Not you," said Mr. Lomax. "You have some claim on the years yet."

Granville smoked a cigarette, taking care to blow the smoke away from his friend's face. "Funny," he said, following the smoke off the dark porch, "I always think of you when I think of that. I mean, after all, you're here and well here. That's taken a lot of weight off my shoulders."

"I've got good shoulders," said Mr. Lomax.

Granville looked at his friend, small and humped in the chair, and he said, "Of course." After a pause, he added, "You make me envious too, you know, so I don't know whether you do me more harm than good. I sometimes tell myself, 'Granville, even if you went around the world, married a ballet dancer, and did God knows what, you still wouldn't have lived half the life Wallace Lomax has.'"

"Work and trouble. That your idea of a full life?" said Mr. Lomax. He shivered a little in the breeze. "Never did anything with real thought in my life, and the consequence is I leave nothing worth thinking about behind."

"Children," said Granville, emphatically.

Mr. Lomax grunted. "There were twenty people at the station to see me off, and, except for three in-laws, not one of them would have been alive except for me. But that's all, Granville. Could have been any twenty people in the station, any twenty off the Chicago gutters, and they would have been as near to me as those. As near and as understanding. The virtue of children is a fiction of bachelors."

"Can you mean it?"

"Can you ask me?"

They didn't talk for a moment but watched the moon coming out of the clouds, lighting the palms along the porch and the boats down by the inn pier.

"I don't regret being old," said Mr. Lomax, looking up at the moon for a moment. "I don't think much about what comes next. As for what I've done, I did it without much consciousness, so it was mostly painless as well as wrong. I think a lot about mistakes. That and the Gulf. I think a lot about sitting out here with you, watching the Gulf." After another pause, he said, "I miss you the odd years."

"Thank you," said Granville smiling. "I think of you often then, too."

Mr. Lomax's hand tightened on the chair. "Do you mind my asking why you go way out there now since your sister died?"

Granville got up to put his cigarette out in one of the sanded containers on the porch. "I don't know," he said, sitting down. "It's very pleasant out there. Mostly, it's because I've worried about getting stiff,

I suppose. Old in a bad way. Not like you, of course, but you've had so much more than I."

Mr. Lomax was getting very tired, but he wanted to say a little more. "I told Henry, by accident, that I was going to die down here."

Granville knew that Lomax wished him to say something, but he could not quite make out what. He stared at one of the buoys trembling in the moonlight.

"I'd been feeling that way," Mr. Lomax went on. "It wasn't to arouse anybody—even if I could at my age." After another pause, he said, "I'd like to die when you're around, Herbert."

"That's a funny thing to say, Wallace."

"Well, it is funny, but not really. Old friends are true family, aren't they, and you understand me, don't you? More than they. You meet me in the right way, say the right things, the right way." Then Lomax asked his favor. "If it's not this year, it'll be next."

"I'll come down then, Wallace," said Granville.

They sat for a while looking out over the Gulf. Then Granville wheeled Mr. Lomax into his room, and, contrary to their custom, they shook hands as they bade each other good night.

GARDINER'S LEGACY

Gardiner lived and died in such obscurity that the revelations of the last twenty years seem particularly, if somewhat peculiarly, vivid. And now that Mrs. Gardiner is dead, one wonders whether the revelations were peculiar in a way which will affect our view of her great work. The textbooks have it that she was a simple woman inspired to great deeds by two things, the loving memory of her husband and a heroic commitment to history and literature. Who can say no? One knows that she began almost immediately after the funeral—if one can use a word which suggests a more complex ceremony than Gardiner enjoyed. At any rate, it couldn't have been more than a month after the city put him in the earth that the news of the first two posthumous volumes appeared in the *Times*. And then, within six months, she found *Weatherby's Version* packed away with old clothes in the attic, and Gardiner vaulted from the status of a footnote in the second edition of Spiller and Thorpe to someone who rated a chapter alongside James and Melville and Faulkner.

That first year, it looked somehow unnatural, a hoax of some sort. Someone even suggested that Elinor had written the new stuff herself. (As far as I was concerned, all the better. More would have been forthcoming while she lived.) But such suspicion couldn't last long and didn't. Elinor was, well, no fool, but nothing could have tapped Weatherby from her, let alone the journals and letters. No woman born of woman could have written it, at least no woman whose imaginative power did not equal, say, Sappho's plus Jane Austen's. And no one has yet accused Elinor of imagination. What was there, she saw, and saw well, which makes the final discovery even stranger.

There she sat in the midst of it, twenty years of brilliant commemoration, copying, collating, editing, managing the swelling estate, selecting playwrights and producers for the adaptations, corresponding with translators, scholars, devotees, newspaper people, a mammoth job, an enterprise that amounted to several millions of dollars, and more, of course, to a new image of action, character, and life.

For that's what Gardiner turned out to be, a Stendhal, a Dostoyevsky, someone who'd created a new sensibility. And there she was, giving it birth in the very act that betrayed her. Every commemorative motion, every discovery, ripped off her skin and flesh, broke the bones, ground them down, and blew the dust into space—and there she sat, getting photographed next to the bookshelves, apparently blooming, intact.

Can she really have remembered him? Certainly, the man she discovered was not the one she'd known, had lived with forty years. Surely he must have seemed like someone out of a dark age and she a literary archaeologist stumbling upon and then recovering the singular preservation. But forty years is forty years, and she'd never had anything but him. Hatched in some Dakotan province, pushed into Bismarck and then Milwaukee, slaving like a fellah to keep flesh to bone, seeing nobody, reading nothing, hardly dreaming, one gathered, and then, at nineteen, meeting the unlikely boy ushering in the movie theater—and that was it, until she was sixty and began reading what had happened in the interim. Happened while she kept him alive, working in the twenty cities that they lived in, clerking in stores and offices and markets, money changer in the subways, elevator operator, waitress, railway checker. A long list, now more or less immortal with the rest of it.

And he writing, occasionally with luck, with money, so that it wasn't always grind. She did see half the world, although twice the local embassies had to bail them out. (It's been reported that once in Rome she prostituted for him, but this sort of thing will only come out from now on, now that they have finally stuffed her into a monument next to the corpse of whoever it was they decided was Gardiner.)

Apparently she did the jobs and everything else with relish. He was always, almost always, "nice" to her. Which of course makes it worse. Years ago, in some television interview, she said, "We never quarreled. He was astonishingly acute about my feelings and always knew how to adapt his mood to mine, to work a harmony. I would have done, I did do, everything I could for him because it was what I wanted to do. His will was my will. And yet I don't think that he mastered me as Catherine Blake was mastered by William." (She was almost a learned woman a few years after their marriage. That was something else she got from him.) "I was never his instrument. On the contrary, he completed me, or made me feel complete, made me, I believe, a real person, and, if you'll forgive a possible blasphemy, I had never existed before. He created me." A typical utterance. And this after she had taken the measure of his loathing, knew how he detested her spirit and her flesh, mocked at her with his women, put her remarks into the most disgusting mouths in modern letters, knew that he kept her around him as a reminder of Hell (he capitalized it, for he turned out to be a kind of secular theologian, if one may risk the contradiction). There she was for forty years, "the hair shirt," "the Adversary and the Primal Sin in one," these a couple of less picturesque and vehement examples of his view of her. All of which now appear in the last work of his she put her hand to, the three volumes of his *Elinor,* as she called it, the thousand pages of his loathing drawn from forty years of reflection. Drawn by her from journals, stories, and the first drafts of letters—"He never paid a bill without making a draft of it first," she joked once—most of which were indicated in the earlier volumes by the once mysterious "E" followed by asterisks. The most fantastic of all posthumous exhibitions. Consider the sheer bulk of his hatred. Apparently, he had written about her from the beginning, from the very first meeting. "Dung in the lobby": this the gallant initial entry. He married her "to marry Lilith," and he called the union "the marriage of Heaven and Hell." I suppose that one could trace her public utterances and find that every noble sentiment had been triggered by reading some viciousness of his. There are numerous examples, although systematic study of them would be work for a tough-minded man.

It'll be done, as will everything else to resurrect that barbarous union. Gardiner and his wife will turn on the spit in history as they never did in life. Every pounding which he never gave her will be given, and every one she suffered after, because she never suffered them directly, will be given too. Yes, like Stendhal and Dostoyevsky, he will live next to his works, a sample of conduct as rigorous as a saint's, if dedicated to obscurer ends. One must marvel at him, the superb restraint which never once revealed its source.

One wonders of course about much of their married life. That they had no children doesn't matter. The notebooks tell us what children were to him. (It's reasonably clear that he forced a least ten of the women to have abortions.) The sexual life, however, undoubtedly proceeded on normal lines—whatever it meant to him, and what it meant was in the nature of research. (The chapter "In the Adversary," from his version of Crébillon's *Sofa,* may be consulted here.) As much as we know—and we know a great deal about the sheer domesticity of their lives, about their bed and bathroom, the kitchen table, incidents with carpets and toothpaste, walks, swims, shopping, all transformed by his malicious vision—we will never really know what it was like. Fifteen thousand days they spent together, or fourteen, say, when one discounts the excursions with his women, his eighty-six women, the already famous gallery of his amours, the women who composed a wholly different universe of delights, the forty women of his Purgatory, the forty-six of his Heaven—yes, he was the oddest of American lovers. It will not be so great a surprise if some of these partners deliver up attics of material to stoke the fire of curiosity for another half century.

But no material will ever mean what Elinor's has meant; none will draw up the fog which will forever, I suppose, obscure her contribution. Every penetration of that fog reveals a different structure. It is as if this was what he calculated from the start.

Or could it possibly have been her scheme? One can hardly credit it, but what else explains so much that is dark now, her amazing ignorance of the others, of his true feelings, his immense perversity, she who saw so much so clearly. Elinor was a brilliant human being. Her reconstruction of his work alone marks her a startlingly able scholar, an editor and bibliographer of enormous knowledge, acumen, and sensitivity, an immensely able woman of affairs, a powerful and subtle diplomat. And all this is as nothing when one estimates the emotional complexity behind this mastery. So great is this complexity that I have wondered if it might not have been there from the beginning.

Is it possible that she was the great mover all along, that she made him *living* as she later made his legend? Who discovered whom in the lobby of the theater? What did she bring with her from the Dakotan plain, what instruments to have managed so huge a legacy?

She did not write the books nor the journals and letters. No, but the universe within which they were written, did she not provide that, shape that? And did he perhaps see her rightly all along? "In the Adversary." Was his work perhaps as much report as vision? This is the oddest mystery of the legacy.

A RECITAL FOR THE POPE

1

In 1567, Carlo Lombardo built a palace for Prince Aldo Lanciatore on the site of the Porticus Linucia which in 110 B.C. had been raised by the Consul M. Linucius for the distribution of corn to the Roman plebs. In the late seventeenth century, a master of less altruistic distributions, the papal banker Giorgio Fretch, bought the palace from the Lanciatore family and summoned a pupil of Borromini, Fulvio Praha, to remake the facade into one of the aimlessly turbulent extravaganzas of Roman baroque. For years now, tours of Roman palazzi, on route from the Cancelleria to the Farnese, have stopped to heave a few laughs at the combination zoo, arboretum, orchard, and mythological wood which Praha's workmen churned from the warm yellow tufa rock and its protective stucco, but in the seventeenth century, this blast at Vitruvian chastity excited the cupidity of numerous Roman families of whom the Quadrata were the most insistent. They purchased the Lanciatore and held it in their possession until World War I erased their line.

A month after Mussolini was installed in the Palazzo Venezia, the Lanciatore was bought for a song and his Spanish whore by Elisha Borg of the Standard Oil Company of Indiana, who, converted by the woman, left it surprisingly, not to her, but to the Dominican order, on condition that it be established as an institute where well-bred American Catholic girls could become yet more refined under the tutelage of the sisters and the amorous frescoes of Domenichino, Guercino, Albani, and Lanfranco.

Each June since 1951, eight American girls paid three thousand dollars apiece for a year's board and room, joined in artistic community by two somewhat older Spellman Scholarship students, one of whom always came from Europe. In 1962, the American Spellman Scholar was a poet from Providence, Rhode Island, named Nina Callahan.

Nina knew Dominicans: her brother had joined the order at twenty and, at twenty-one, had been able to let her in on the Dominican strategy of humbling the sharpies and exalting the occasional nulls who'd crept into the fold. The sharpies would find themselves peeling onions in Kansas kitchens while the nulls would be living it up in European palaces.

The four Palazzo Lanciatore nulls were Sister Clara, a withered thirty-year-old blond who ran the kitchen ("into the devil's throat," said Nina to her one friend among the girls, Sibyl Taylor); Sister Mary Pia, a terrier-faced woman whose self-imposed duty was waiting up for the girls coming back from Rosati's and the Veneto hangouts with the local counts, princelings, and other loafers, discouraging manifestations of affection, and insinuating improprieties; Sister Louella, an immense, gentle lesbian whose pleasure it was to see that the girls never learned anything which would further liberate what she regarded as their inordinately free persons; and Sister Angie Caterina, a moronic dwarf assigned to the maintenance of the musical instruments and art supplies which the girls were supposedly utilizing in their direct encounters with the Roman Muses.

The nulls were bad enough to sour Nina's first weeks in Rome, the girls and their luxurious idleness disturbed her slightly more, but what chiefly coiled her insides was the desecration of the real magnificence which had been accumulated behind Praha's facade in the four centuries of the Lanciatore's existence: the plastic Standa lampshades on the bronze Renaissance lamps, the dangling rips in the Licorne tapestry, the peeling Bassano landscape which sweated over an unsheathed radiator, the Lipton tea bags which daily sank in the chipped gold cups, the paperback detective stories which lined the cypress panels under the begrimed cherubs of the quattrocento cantoria, the ceiling's smoked lunettes, the crumbling egg-and-dye friezes, and the courtyard where weeds overran patterns and tumuli fattened in the lawn: a general squalor of ignorance such as Nina, in years of living from hand to mouth in cavelike rooms from Dublin to Vienna, had never encountered.

In her third week at the palace, Nina secured Sister Clara's careless permission to draw on the bulging maintenance fund for supplies and repairs. Before the sisters woke up to what was going on, she had summoned gardeners, masons, plasterers, painters, carpenters, electricians, and a piano tuner, ordered a thousand dollars' worth of books for the library, another thousand dollars' worth of art supplies—there having been not a piece of armature wire or canvas in the studio, which was used exclusively by the girls' dressmakers—and spent two weeks supervising the workmen and cruising the Via Babuino for a few indispensable replacements.

At the very point of triumphant conversion, the sisters' dull awareness was not shocked, but penetrated by the reparatory swirl. Recoiling from the signs of sodomic luxury, they traced them to Nina and confronted her en bloc to tell her that she should let them attend to "the housework" so that she could take full advantage of her unique opportunity to live in splendor.

Shaken to tears, Nina could think of nothing to say but that in Francis L. Callahan's house one never found a paper napkin by one's plate nor month-old stains on the tablecloth. Though even this was not said aloud. Nina had no use for fruitless rebellion. The one response in her stay at the Lanciatore which even hinted disrespect followed one of Sister Louella's rebukes that she was not paying attention to the news broadcasts which gashed their every dinner hour in the interest of "keeping up" both Italian and knowledge of the world: "Sister, my mind is not good enough for current events."

Nina was a pixie of a woman, small, finely built, cup jawed, flat nosed, merry faced; only blue eyes showed the ire which followed such trampling on her passion for rectitude and beauty. Had it not been for one thing, she might have headed back to Paris then and there. But the one thing was a great temptation.

Each September, after the pope's return from Castel Gandolfo, he received the girls of the Palazzo Lanciatore in private audience. Indeed, each girl was alone with the pope for three minutes, and then joined the others for a group photograph. Framed in Standa's rhinestoned squares, the papal photographs lined the central hallway into the music room.

Nina craved those three minutes. She admired, even loved the round little pope, discerned a translucence in his peasant's vulpine face which marked a sympathy of the highest order. He was clearly someone who responded to the finest human notes, perhaps as much or even more than his elegant predecessor, Pacelli (another favorite of Nina's). She could endure eight weeks of the nulls for this.

As if to mark the time, she undertook another reclamation project, that of the chief human rent in the Lanciatore. This was the year's European Spellman Scholar, Červa Grbisz, who'd come from Kraków with a cardboard valise to pursue her violin studies at the Conservatory. Červa's valise contained neither toothbrush, comb, nor bar of soap. Červa was fetid. Her hair was a knot of greasy filth, her teeth a gangrenous yellow, her breath a reek of garbage. She owned two dresses; both bore sweat marks, armpit to hip, bloody purple on the dark dress, grainy chestnut on the light. When she entered a room, occupants gulped, swallowed, took off. It was this which began to perturb Červa enough to consult her fellow Spellman Scholar. Why was it, she asked, that others did not take to her? Didn't Americans like foreigners? After all, she was a Spellman Scholar, chosen for her adaptability as well as her mastery of English.

Nina made a quick, a "Catholic," decision. Yes, she told Červa, she was sure the girls would take to her in time, they were slow to make friends with people overseas, and, by the way, wasn't Roman heat terrible on one's hair. "I used to have to wash mine every single night." She took up a bottle of Dop. "Except I found this stuff in Prima. You only have to wash every other day with it. You take this one. I've got another bottle."

"I don't have no hair trouble," said Červa.

"Try it anyway, I'll bet you'll have the same luck I did."

"Your hair don't appear different to me."

Nina did not give up. With Elizabeth Arden soap cakes, Pepsodent toothpaste — "A new American product, worked out in a laboratory for Roman women" — cologne water, eyebrow tweezers, nail files, combs — "specially designed for the Roman summer" — and then with the dresses, skirts, blouses, and cardigans which the girls actually tossed into wastepaper baskets after dressmaking and shopping sessions, Nina tried, but although Červa relaxed once or twice into taking something, it was only to appease Nina, for neither her skin, hair, teeth, nor wardrobe were exposed to the menaces which so ruffled the little American.

Červa cared for only two things, the Church and her music. She could barely contain her joy in the forthcoming audience. As for the music, she treated the girls to a sample of it during an afternoon tea while Sister Clara lunged accompaniment at one of the Lanciatore's newly tuned Steinways. Face lit with religious and musical fervor, Červa ground a Tartini sonata into such excruciation that only Nina and Sibyl survived in situ; and Nina survived only by resolving to end her futile attempts to gild the weed. It was high time to return full time to her own work.

Nina's work, the core of her life, was the realization of a plan she'd mapped out when she was sixteen. The plan was to become a major poet. This meant she had to study the poetic accomplishment of the race. In eleven years, three in the United States, the rest in Europe, Nina filled almost all time not spent earning dinner and rent money tracking the great achievements of poetry in eight languages. In New York, Chicago, San Francisco, London, Dublin, Madrid, Paris, Berlin, Vienna, and then Paris again for the last two years, Nina scrounged for the eight or nine hundred dollars a year she needed to live by guiding, nursing, and accompanying tourists; waiting on tables; drawing caricatures; playing piano in bars; clerking; helping in art galleries; begging; borrowing; and when really necessary, stealing. Waking without knowing where the day's meal would come from, far from dismaying, cheered and stimulated her. She thought of herself as a citizen of time, not space. Her country was Poetry.

The Spellman Scholarship was another of the things into which Nina fell. Her Dominican brother had sent her name and book of poems in to the selection committee. Although she was the only applicant who had so exposed herself to the public, it was decided to take a chance on her. Nina had qualms about leaving Paris but was talked into thinking the award a sign of special grace and came with an eagerness that only the nuns dimmed.

In mid-July, she went back on the schedule she'd mapped out eleven years before, mornings in the library, afternoons seeing things, evenings writing. The schedule was pleasant habit, not constraint. Nina never hesitated to alter it for friends, concerts, or laziness. After breakfast at the Lanciatore, she walked as fast as the rising heat allowed across the Tiber to the Vatican Library, where she stayed till it closed at one. She was working on a Plutarchan comparison between the poets of the *Greek Anthology* and the early Italian poets from Ciullo d'Alcamo to the *dolce stil nuovo,* using the *Volgari Eloquentia* as a guide. Her interest was in patterns of cadence, syntax, meter, diction, pitch, stress, junctions (she had also studied linguistics on her own), and the relationship of forms to topics. She did research into musical settings, one of her ambitions being to revive the *sagen-und-singen* techniques of the *Minne* and Provençal poets. It was exciting work. Leaving the library was as difficult as anything that preceded or followed it. She walked back along the rattling avenues to where her free lunch sat engulfed by Červa, the sisters, and the two or three girls who'd stood up their midday dates. Then, without siesta, she trolleyed around the city by the *circolare,* getting off at handsome prospects, museums, and churches.

Rome wasn't, however, exciting her as she'd imagined it would. There were wonderful things at the Villa Giulia and the Diocletian Museum, there were fine views and churches, but more and more the transistors and Vespas which blasted her ears combined with the punitive sun to give her massive headaches. Then, too, the imperial assertions of the embassies, the Bernini squares and Bernini fountains depressed Nina: like the aimless contortions of baroque churches, they proclaimed their egomania. It was as if the sisters had governed Rome since Bramante's time.

At night, dinner behind her, Nina's life came into focus. Looking over the Campo dei Fiori, the odors of the day's market still afloat, Nina's mind sought the precise articulation of thought, feeling, memory. In the dark solitude, old accomplishment married novel expression. Not even Červa's violin wrestling devils across the hall ruined her meditations.

In late July, Nina found herself involved with Sibyl Taylor's problems. Sibyl, too, was discontented with the Lanciatore. She trailed along with Nina, buying beautiful piles of fruit and ice cream, discoursing on her problems with amorous Romans. Sibyl was extremely pretty, blond, pleasant, sensitive. Nina, who liked gossip as well as anyone, found her a great relief from the whistlers and pinchers who were the only people with whom she had any words at all when she went round the city by herself.

Sibyl's most recent problem was not with a Roman but an American named Edward Gunther who'd come up to her in San Pietro in Vincoli to explain Freud's theory about the Moses statue. This had led to an aperitif and talk, hours of talk. Surprisingly, Edward had forgotten to take her address, but the next Sunday, he'd shown up at San Clemente, the church to which the sisters took them every Sunday because it was run by Irish Dominicans. Sibyl noticed him when he'd snorted at Sister Louella lifting Sister Angie Caterina like a poodle into and out of her seat. Sister Clara had pinned him with a fierce look.

Edward was large, black haired, soft looking, lively. He'd been in Rome a month longer than Sibyl and Nina, had neither job, function, nor plan. "I'm relaxing a sick heart," he said, but did not invite questions about it. Nina felt some sort of truth in that but also felt it was a smoke screen. For what, she didn't know. In any event, Edward was a continuous instructor about things Roman. Instructing, his face flamed with eagerness, his gestures with illustrative fluidity. Nina interpreted all this fire and liquidity as more than pedagogy. She also realized that it was not meant only for Sibyl. That did not worry *her*. She'd handled far subtler propositioners.

One staggeringly hot day, they drove out to Hadrian's Villa in Edward's Fiat Cinquecento. "Small but the motor's air cooled." They weren't. Amid the ruins, they sweltered and Edward lectured. Quite brilliantly. He'd read up on the villa and knew where in the white rubble everything had been, theater, atrium, the model of Tartarus.

After an hour, the sun mastered the master. Edward led them to a dead pool where filthy ducks cruised sullenly over the scum. He and Sibyl removed their shoes, put their feet through the disgusting veneer and rubbed them against each other's. Nina felt more superfluous than the ducks. She wandered off while Edward, renewed by Sibyl's feet, was engaged in a comparison of Hadrian with "those broken-down artists who become dictators, Napoleon and Mussolini—ninth-rate novelists—Hitler, a tenth-rate painter." She found a piece of shade under an umbrella pine. Heat-misted miles away lay Rome. *Animula, blandula, vagula:* Hadrian's poem to his little jokester-companion. Jokester-companion. That was like her own role here. Those clumsy, at-the-brink lovers, playing footsie in the scum. Or were they clumsy? How would she know? Scholar-priest of Amor, she had heard the sub-tlest confessions of those apt in its words, Ovid, Gottfried, Ciullo, Cavalcanti. *Ailas. Tant cujava saber / D'amor, et tant petit en sai:* To know so much *about* love and know *it* so little. Nothing that she'd read had matched what she'd felt in the occasional Irish arms which held her in automobiles, on dance floors outside the half-mile limit of Francis L. Callahan's honorable home on Water Street. Not that she was a Louella, not that she had hormonic deficiencies, though, worried, she had gone to a doctor at sixteen and gotten a shot of estrogen to see if it would ease her ability to be gratified by the local pawers. It hadn't. There was always something askew, a psychological oxymoron, a gulf between desire and perception. Her body, shaped for passion, if she could believe the Providence locals and transient hotshots from Dublin to Vienna (or, for that matter, the mirror), had felt nothing more than an odd, erratic itch which, she knew, must never become necessity. No Edwards need apply. She had what she had, far more than scum rubbing with a professional mouther. What was she doing here anyway? Here in the ruined villa? Here in Rome? Free grub three times a day? Not enough. She'd survived years without institutional handouts. Kroening, the nutty Swede who'd corresponded with Tolstoy, had given her a cottage in Brittany; Hauch, the Berlin painter, shared his room and food despite her refusal to share herself; Mrs. Mackie had supported her in Dublin on her Guggenheim and taught her Celtic to boot. Best of all, Mademoiselle, whom she'd deserted, yes, it amounted to that, to come here, her neighbor for two years in the attic on Rue de l'Université. Mademoiselle Laguerre. Minute, aged, horribly poor, yet so graceful amid the propped wreckage, drunks, and shriekers of that attic, she was like a Benedictine among the vandals. The ideal citizen, articulate, curious, the happy frequenter of museums and libraries, the thoughtful reader of discarded newspapers, a preserver of all that was handsomest in her marginal past: the two eighteenth-century Limoges cups in which she served tea (cracks away from her guest); the lace gloves, one soiled (and so always carried in the other); the thirty books, read almost to dust. A purer version of Francis L., really, a man whom

Nina had never seen in shirtsleeves, who governed six children by eyebrow and finger motion, by a high unmentioned honor which could have sustained her through two lifetimes of passionate temptations. Mademoiselle and Nina spent fifty hours a month talking about Indochina, books, Debussy.

Three months before Nina left for Rome, Mademoiselle showed her an inventory of her possessions, cups, gloves, books. By each item was the name of the intended recipient, *"en cas d'une éventualité."* Nina was to get the books, the clothes were to go to the old lady who came upstairs twice a week for tea, her money—about sixty thousand old francs—was to go with her fan, a few daguerreotypes, and the cups to a distant niece. With the inventory was a receipt for a cemetery plot and funeral service in the eighteenth arrondissement. Nina took the papers and no more was said. A few days later, Nina came to Mademoiselle with news of the Spellman award. *"Oh, ma chère,"* said Mademoiselle, "I needed no confirmation of your powers, but I am thrilled. It is a sign of special favor."

Nina didn't want to leave. "They don't include the fare to Rome, Mademoiselle." Mademoiselle took fifty thousand francs from a drawer. "I feel so lucky to be able to do this, Nina."

Nina would have gone if only to accept the money. Now, under the umbrella pine, she felt the departure as desertion, and, worse, desertion into the falsity, show, and noise which art and Mademoiselle's life fought to the death. She'd go back, if she had to sell Červa's violin. She'd go back after the papal audience.

2

The Lanciatore steamed with preparations. Sister Angie Caterina's muttering swelled with the excitement she barely understood. Sister Clara attacked swatches of black poplin so that Červa would make a suitable appearance. The girls stunned their dressmakers with demands for spectacular simplicity. Each three minutes with the pope was to be an indelible picture for him.

On the great day, four taxis deposited sisters and students in front of the Vatican apartments. They walked up marble flights, passed glittering salons, the girls ogled the piked Switzers, were themselves ogled by papal secretaries. Then they were ushered into an antechamber whose golden magnificence staggered even these young productions of Grosse Point and Winnetka.

They were admitted alphabetically. Nina came third. The corpulent little pope sat in a green and gold room frescoed by the Caracci. He smiled at Nina's curtsy, held out his peasant's hand for her kiss, asked if she understood Italian, where she was from, how she liked Rome. It was very beautiful. Very brief. And Nina backed out, yielding to Červa, whose fear-worked sweat glands had already gone to work on her new dress.

When the last girl returned, the pope waddled out to pose for pictures. He stood beside Sister Angie Caterina, who raised her eyes to his generous chin and babbled what he may have thought English but which the girls knew was the senseless litany of her ecstasy and terror. "We're ready now," said the good pope to the photographer.

But not quite, for Červa cried out. "Papa, one moment, please."

"Of course, my dear. What is it?"

Červa went over to the sofa and, from under her coat, drew out her violin. "All my life I wished to play for you."

The pope said that there was nothing in the world that would so delight him.

Červa raised her fiddle arm. Horrific stains released their terrible aroma. Then out of the tortured fiddle struggled Gounod's "Ave Maria," perhaps never in the history of performance played with such passionate deformity. The pope smiled unremittingly. When Červa's thick arm lowered from its musical slaughter, he said, "*Molto bello, cara.* I am grateful to you." He waved to the photographer, smiled for the flash, and disappeared.

3

The girls returned to the Palazzo, stunned, one and all, by the incredible conclusion of the audience.

Sister Clara announced that tonight there would be no permission to leave the house. Since the very concept of permission had been the invention of Clara's fury, it spurred a mass exodus. Nina had the sisters to herself.

Around the dining room table they sat, sweating in their wimples. Sister Angie Caterina still muttered the grim syllables which bound her dim memory to the great occasion. Into this low static, Nina said, "Sisters, I'm going to leave Rome tomorrow."

Sister Louella dropped her coffee cup on the Persian carpet.

"Mother of God," said Sister Mary Pia.

"I cannot do my work here, Sisters. I've got to leave."

Sister Clara rose darkly. "Ingratitude," she said.

"I'm afraid so, Sister. I hope you'll make my apology to the cardinal."

"Lord God," wailed Sister Angie Caterina, driven to clarity by the word "cardinal."

Nina went upstairs, locked her door, and packed her bags. For the next hour, the door was banged, scratched, knocked, and implored at. "Please, dearie." "You must." "Young woman, your scholarship." "Give us another try, Ninie dearie."

"No, Sister, what's left of my mind is made up."

Only to Sibyl did Nina open, and that to refuse an offer to get Eddie to drive her to the station. "I'm back on my own. I better start getting used to it," though that was only part of the reason. It was time to shake loose from nulls.

"I'd go pretty slow with that one if I were you," she threw to Sibyl. (Though who could be less like Sibyl than Nina Callahan?)

In any case, it didn't matter. For Nina Callahan, it didn't matter who played *with* or who played *for* anyone else at all in this megalomaniacal city of nulls and Caesars.

IDYLLS OF DUGAN AND STRUNK

1

On a hunch, Strunk took the check over to Dugan in the hospital. "Is this your baby?"

Dugan's head is mummified, chin to scalp; the cola-colored eyes peer over damaged cheeks. "Lire. The rat." He passes the check to Prudence, sitting in the armchair.

She reads. "Six-point-seven billion lire. Who's this princely Corradi?"

"A Beinfresser holding company. What is it in dollars, a million?"

Strunk say he makes it a million two. "No lagniappe."

"Not from your aunt," growls Dugan. "It's nothing."

Beinfresser was his discovery, he'd been after him over a year, and though he'd worked harder and come up goose eggs, he'd never wanted to hook a prospect more than this one. Ten days ago Strunk's girl had shown him how. Well, this was only first blood. The Beinfresser Library. The Beinfresser Student Village. But lire. "If computers fell in love, I'd call it an accident."

"Maybe that's the way the Holy Ghost dishes it out." (The check was drawn on the Banco di Santo Spirito.)

Early spring light off the Midway. April 12. Roosevelt's death day in Dugan's calendar. Lucky it wasn't his own. University aide, ex–White House assistant, casualty of King riots. He was stupid, but maybe now, after a terrible year, he was getting lucky. He had Beinfresser's first installment, he had Prudence—who could also be charged up to Beinfresser—and he was going to walk out of here more or less as he was a week ago.

But was Beinfresser pulling something? Lire didn't leave Italy. Maybe he was just thrashing around—angry that Dugan cornered him—twisting an arm to make a nickel, making the university pay for conversion of his spare lire.

The glooms and twists of fund-raising. Strunk had laid it out for him the first day, three years ago. "Philanthropy's a Circe. Makes brutes."

Dugan had spent four years shepherding fifty midwestern congressmen through three hundred billion dollars of appropriation; he did not take to the chicken feed of university donors. "They don't have to give."

Younger, gloomier, kinder, an endless generalizer, Strunk said, "They smell our interest in their death. Makes 'em mulish. It's not like plucking taxes from Topeka. You're head-to-head with these dollars."

Which was so.

Donors were coaxed over soufflés, in swimming pools. One studied their habits, wishes, connections. One knew one's rivals: strayed sons, forgotten cousins, Boy Scouts, Heart Fund, Bahai. One learned the seasons of donation: seeding, watering, bloom, the stems of resistance turning brittle, dropping into the basket. Even then it wasn't over. In three years Dugan had already been ambushed by devious wills, consumptive litigation.

Meanwhile, despite his pride at taking no guff, he ran errands, commiserated sniffles, confiscatory taxes, the moneyed nature of things.

His first year, he'd gone once a month to the Cliffhanger's Club for cheese soufflé, apple pie, and the discourse of Lynch, the bond man.

Out of Georgia scratch country into the Chicago grain market, then, after World War I, sensing the shift in Chicago big money from goods to paper, Lynch started the first great bond house west of Manhattan. A bachelor without apparent ties, a fund-raiser's dream, he was worth at least seventy million. Gray, froggy, his vague eyes hung from a large, warty head; a real beaut. Subtle, cold, autodidact, and pedant, he was mad for discourse and learning. Yet never bought a book. Uni versity fund-raisers borrowed requested titles from the university library and read them, preparing for the lunches.

In Dugan's time, Lynch was wound up in violence. Carlyle, Sorel, Lenin, Sartre, Fanon, the *Iliad,* and the Old Testament were piled by gold spores of soufflé to be grabbed, leafed through, quoted in refutation. "Got you, Dugan."

Dugan lost himself in dispute and took no guff. A New York street battler, a wounded Korean vet, he had authority in the old bond man's eyes. "Not that your rutting dogfights changed the world that counts."

What counted was dedicated violence, the violence of purification, a strike, Watts, Algeria. "I bring not peace." Lynch was wild about Stokely Carmichael, "a new Lenin," and was driven up to the university to hear him. His Negro chauffeur, Henry, sat beside him, "so you can hear what a great black man sounds like." But Stokely's cold rage roused old cracker blood. Lynch wrote out a question and told Henry to ask it: "Spose that rev-ole-oosh-n-erries is moh crupt den ex-ploiders?" Bird head jeweled with sweat, Carmichael ran sad eyes up and down the little chauffeur. "You're wearing your master's livery, and you ask me such a question. Who wrote that out for you, brother?"

"Answer the question," croaked Lynch. He meant Carmichael, but Henry pointed to his right and said, "He did."

The *Tribune* photographer took a picture, the only time Lynch's face appeared in a Chicago newspaper. This "outrageous impropriety" was his excuse when Dugan popped the long-suspended bubble of his philanthropic intentions. "You see what happens when I stick out my neck. I get smeared all over the newspapers. Can't afford that kind of thing. I'm the diocesan financial adviser. Imagine what the cardinal thinks. You'll have to wait."

Dugan's complexion was curd white, the pallor of repressed fury. The old man, scared, blinked, then covered, asking if they could try Carlyle's *Frederick the Great* next time. "Hitler's favorite book. Goebbels read it to him in the bunker."

"We'd better cool it awhile, Mr. L." Dugan would eat no more soufflés.

A step which, back at the university, he double-checked with his boss, Erwin Seligman, the provost. "Absolutely. Tell him to shove it."

Intense, elegant, baldly handsome, a tongue holder and aristocrat. "I'd rather go under than dangle from that four-flusher's whims."

Said Strunk, "It's the best of flirtatiousness. They dangle their dough under your nose like Elizabeth dangled her stuff for the ambassadors. The whole universe is a come-on. Djever see a two-month-old kid tug a blanket over his eyes?" The bachelor talking to the father, the ex-father. "My God, even flowers do it. Folding with the sun. And rocks. Those winking crystals. The Principle of Uncertainty. Sheer flirtation."

They worked facing each other, their desks by the trilobed, iron-ribbed Gothic window, one of hundreds in the educational Carcassonne along the Midway. "Americans live in a historical rummage sale." Strunk's blue-shirted gorilla arm waved at the useless crenellations, culverts, *contreforts*. "Midway Gothic. And jungle," the arm over the slum miles under the university's architectural eyebrow. "Mies glass, Saarinen concrete, Pevsner topology. And behind, the American behind. With our *rejecta*. And here," the great arm over their slanting nook, "our little museum."

Sure enough. Back of Strunk's head was Dugan's two-dollar Pissarro print, woods, sky, fishermen, towpath, a pond doubling and confusing the rest. Behind his head, *Playboy*'s Miss March, "lasagna-loving, sitar-strumming Lisa Joy Sackerman, M.A. in Slav. Lit." Tacked beside Miss Sackerman's pale watermelons was *The Thoracic Viscera,* lungs, the central clutter, the muscular baggage of the heart, the screw-ribbed pole on top, the trachea, the crewel-stitched pole beneath, the descending aorta.

On their Indiana maple desks, amid bank reports, Olivetti and Dutch Royale typewriters, Florentine blotters, Swedish letter openers, were Dugan's souvenirs, the quartz chip from a Mayan palace, pink limestone from the tower where Roland had supposedly blown out his warning and his brains, a conglomerate sliver from Injon which, with a quarter inch of Pekinese steel, had been removed from Dugan's left elbow in 1951.

"Fossils, sediment, souvenirs, imports, hand-me-downs. Historical junk shop. And what am I doing now? Setting up a transatlantic telecast on genes with Crick, Perutz, Watson, and Burkle. Those little human museums." Strunk meant the genes.

Dugan was on Strunk's wavelength, liked him immensely, and, though he seldom saw him outside the working day, knew he was the one he'd call in a pinch, had, in fact, after his son's death and his wife's breakdown.

They sat across from each other day after day, never quarreled, seldom felt disparity, though Dugan was fifteen years older, a hardnose, an athlete, a fighter, a little man, and Strunk was huge, soft, a pacifist and do-gooder, a fantasist who wanted to alter the world and make himself heard doing it.

Strunk's reveries were violent, formed out of Eric Ambler and James Bond. He daydreamed himself in Park Lane tweeds carrying lethal pencils through chancellory gates, kidnapping presidential grandchildren to force changes in policy (infantile fingers mailed, one a day, with menacing but high-minded notes), organizing guerrilla wars on Burmese borders, convening world revolutionaries, himself and the late Guevara the only white men. Then, tanned and hardened, converting twelve-year-old Thai maidens into sexual H-bombs, riding herd on the aligned golden backsides of Santa Monica, sipping at the True Beloved's clitoral brim.

In daylight, Strunk outlined salvationary schemes, discerned threats to civic harmony, leaking valves, closed doors, defects in thought and state which he called to the attention of congressman, policy maker, theoretician, and physician in newspapers, magazines, letters. A new, unknown Voltaire, demipoet, demiartist, urban dreamer, reader, raised in Manhattan, educated in Chicago, a bachelor who'd not been east of Long Island or west of Oak Park, M.A. in English lit, university functionary, and one-course-a-year lecturer in the English department.

Whereas Dugan, born in La Guardia's New York fifteen years earlier and two miles southwest of Strunk's birth house on West Eighty-second Street, fighter, traveler, ex-father, ex-husband, daydreamed pastorals. His life as violent as a legal, urban, burgher life could be, Dugan had no utopian thoughts. The university was the closest waking life had come to his reveries, and he believed this even after his fourteen-year-old son was stabbed to death on a Hyde Park street.

Dugan celebrated his fortieth birthday in October 1967, "the two-hundred-eighth anniversary of Georges Jacques Danton, French revolutionary figure's birth," said the all-news station WNUS. WNUS remembered Danton, no one remembered Dugan. Burkle, the development office's hope for the next Nobel, told him that after thirty-five, fifty thousand brain cells a year were irreplaceably destroyed. "Not a large fraction of ten billion," but, at forty, Dugan figured a quarter of a million lost cells no joke.

He'd birthday-treated himself to a color television set. Feet up on the old black-and-white one, drinking his nightly bottle of dollar German wine, he watched the shifting Renoirs of the Cronkite news. A scientist found that plants registered human antipathy. Hooked to a polygraph, they sweated anxiety when threatened. What next? Rocks? Matter itself? Unneutral neutrons, shocked electrons? The whole universe a sensorium?

So why not gloom for Dugan? Fifty trillion cells fired into feeling by ten billion (minus a quarter million) neural triggers. "Enough neural combinations," said Burkle, "to register everything in the universe." Let alone Dugan's troubles: the war, the gripping stink of sulfurous air through the window, the cells dying in his four-decade-old head, his stubborn prospects, the birthday without his son, his wife cracked up in Oswego.

2

What other woman would unerringly find the wrong manhole and falling, fallen, be saved, and how but by "dese tings." Her "bosoms." There in the middle of Clyde and Diversey, he, Strunk, and the Burkles walking to the restaurant, and no Lena, or only her head, which was screaming, "Omigawd." A black-matted cauliflower yelling in the manhole. Unlikely. (As it had been from the first day in the Amsterdam Avenue Library. "Scuse me, mister, could I take a look at that book you got there? I never in my life seen such a big book.") Hauled out of the manhole, groaning, she ate her way through clams, ribs, and shortcake, now and then hefting her bruised beauties, "Omigawd." Scene ten million of Lena's theater.

Pain or pleasure, it never ended: chasing rock throwers off the fence, "Don't gimme that racial shit, boy, you're a rat, black or green.

Toss another of them rocks and you get it right inna mouth"; piling the Appalachians' mattresses into the Rambler ("Miz Dugan, you one fiuhn person"), shouting at the subcommittee hearing, "He's a goddamn liar, Senator. Don't tell me, Smalley. I moved you in them five rooms myself, what you givin' these senators that shit for?" With Javits saying, "Now, look here, let's keep it calm, please, Miss." "Miss! There's ninety pounds of son out of this miss, Senator. This man is lying. I moved him in myself. He is just milking you guys. Right, Smalley?" "Hell, Miz Dugan, ahm jis tryin' to git these senators tuh see the kiuhnd of thing, ya know," and Kennedy said, "OK, Van, take down what this woman has to say."

Those first weeks in New York, she was the country mouse, no question, up from Simsbury, Ohio, nine hundred people, five Italian families who got together every month to sing opera, the kids taking parts, the factory money going into the pizzas and red wine from her father's 'storante, people driving over the bridge from West Virginia or even the mystical sixty miles over the hills from Pittsburgh. (When someone had to go up there for X-rays, the families would see him off as if to the moon, he'd return with stories of the terrible roads, the turns, the black fog.)

It was from Pittsburgh their troubles came, Domenico Buccafazzi with the gold watch to be raffled for the Poor Widow with Seven Children Whose Husband Drowned in the Oak Grove Brook, and next month Papa asked him, "Who won the watch?" and it was someone over in Branchtown, and a month later, it was another watch, and this time it was won by a Mrs. DiBaccio, a Crippled Lady in Oak Grove, and Papa said, "I don't believe," and drove the pickup over the hills, and there was no Mrs. DiBaccio in Oak Grove. And one day Luccio, the fruit man, came in the house and told the kids to get under the beds and said to Mama, "Don't go downstairs, whatever." In the street was a black Imperial with curtains down on the windows, and they all knew only They could own such a car, and Papa went into it and was gone three days, they thought he was never coming back, and Mama said to Luccio, "I'm going to the FBI, I'm an American," but Papa came back that night; though not the same inside.

At night, the old people sat in the room with red wine, she would close her eyes on the couch and would hear how the little Oak Grove vegetable man, Cucciadifreddi, who'd Brought Over his sister's son and taken him into the store, had been forced by Them to Show the Sign and shot the boy himself and threw him into the river. She had gone to the funeral with Mama, and when people wondered how such a good swimmer could have drowned, she had said, "But, Mama, he was shot," and Mama had stuffed the rosary beads in her mouth and said, "Where you hear that? Who tell you that? Milena, please don' say tings like dat."

In Tampa, staying with Cousin Franco, who ran a club on the Gulf, she'd gone to a party, there were racks of fur coats, and the ladies' heads jerked toward them every other minute (as they had been gotten, so could they be got), and Franco came not with Cousin Mary but with a pile of hair, mink, and diamonds, Margarita, who invited Milena for a sail on her boat, till Cousin Franco said, "She don' visit." She had helped out at the tables, serving whatever it was that passed for Cutty Sark or Johnnie Walker, when the ladies started grabbing their coats, and there by the dance-floor palms, like a George Raft movie, stood the iron-eyed men with guns out, cursing.

Her brother Louie whizzed through law school and the bar exam. Every week, he'd be taken to New York or Chicago and lapped it up, thinking what a card he must be. He hadn't finished the exams a month when a man whose picture she later saw at the Kefauver hearings showed him a list which said, "Louis Masiotti, Judge of the Circuit Court," and Papa said, "We're moving," and they'd gone north, but one day the man showed up and asked Papa, "What happened to that son of yours? I showed him the list. Is he crazy?" And Papa said, "You know kids, he went on the bum. He is a restless kid."

Lena's cousins from Oak Park invited them to a party, Milena and the Irish husband who'd worked for President Kennedy. They were jeweled and furred and talked about their children. One of the cousins had blue streaks on her face. Two weeks before, her husband had been gunned to death in his bed, the blue marks were powder burns, and she was drinking with the wife of the man who'd made them.

Dugan told Strunk, who said, "Sure, but they're getting these guys now. Giancana has to live in Mexico, Genovese is in the can. With this immunity thing, they can't take the Fifth. Anyway, television is killing it. The kids don't care about the furs and nightclubs and fixing horse races. Watch. In fifteen years, there'll be no Mafia," but when they found Mikey bled to death in the street, though it was the Apostles that stabbed him, no question of that, Strunk believed it was the Mafia and wanted to have all of Lena's relatives hauled in till one of them broke down and confessed.

But by then, she'd started to break; one look at her face zipped Strunk's mouth, and he took care of the coffin, the service, the grave, the newspapermen, got Lena into the hospital, and sat with Dugan till he could manage by himself.

Though, thought Dugan, in a way Strunk was right, the Mafia was guilty, for wasn't it that crazy theater in her blood that not only made her heroic but made her force Mikey into the squad car and ride up and down the streets fingering the boys who'd forced the white boys to climb the ropes in gym and push them off? And wasn't it in the Mafia towns, Tampa, Newark, Buffalo, Youngstown, Chicago, that government rotted and ghettos burned?

Misery fogged his mind. What did the cause of it matter? The kid was dead, one of the best ever, the only thing he'd come close to being lost in with love.

And the second thing, Lena, was as good as dead.

In the cold-temperature lab, Dugan had watched a professor dip chrysanthemums into superchilled nitrogen. Out they came, apparently the same, but crystalline. So Lena went through the funeral, apparently unaltered, only slightly abstracted, but within, the motion was gone. Strunk took her to Billings, and from there she went to Oswego.

3

Dugan discovered Beinfresser in the periodical room. Once a month he speed-read thirty or forty periodicals in four or five languages. The gift of tongues, found out on Ninth Avenue among Puerto Ricans and Poles, developed in Brooklyn College, Korea, Washington. In *Der Spiegel*'s series "The New Breed of Tycoons," he learned that Beinfresser had not only gone to the university but regarded himself as a "true offshoot [*ein echter Sprössling*] of Chancellor Tatum's reforms." It was during the Depression ("a moneymaker's good times are other people's bad times") that he'd cornered the dormitory coal and laundry concessions, made twelve thousand Depression dollars a year, and won a special farewell from Chancellor Tatum at the graduation ceremony: "You're the model of the student this university exists to eliminate."

In 1946, out of the OSS, Beinfresser showed up in civilian clothes in Frankfurt/Main with enough of a stake to pick up the war's usable junk: tires, rifles, mess kits, soap, iodine, antibiotics, boots, condoms, airplanes. He had a workforce made up of DPs, deserters, cripples, quislings, *Staatlosen,* Krupp foremen, undenazifiables. They peddled his goods door-to-door, unfroze the assets in widows' mattresses, socks of gold sovereigns, wedding silver, unworked pig farms. Twenty years later, "this great coiner" [*dieser grosse Münzer*] was "the Daedalus, Ariadne, Theseus, and Minotaur of the largest corporate labyrinth in Europe." *Der Spiegel* listed "a small fraction" of the companies, "Uganda Ores, Buttenwieser Computations, Banque Nationale de Ruande, Walsh Construction Toys, Fahnweiler, Peyton Shoes, Tucson Metals, Weymouth Investment and Mutual Fund, Corradi, Sempler, Cie., Montevideo Freight and Shipping, Foulke-Arabo Petroleum Products, Meysterdam, Wrench Ltd., the Hamburg *Presse-Zeitung,* the Nord-Suabische Rundfunk, and *Peep: A Weekly.*"

With the help of Alfred Somerstadt and Jean Docker of the business school, Dugan followed the Beinfresser trail. Section 60-735A of the 1959 Internal Revenue Code was called by the author of *The Great Treasury Raid* "the Beinfresser Provision," tailored by Beinfresser lawyers to his mutual-fund operations and inserted in the bill by Representative Templeton (R.-Ariz.) "without opposition." Mrs. Docker had done a dissertation on mutual-fund manipulation, but Beinfresser's were beyond her grasp. "He's just another social tapeworm."

Somerstadt was more useful. A jolly little fellow, tycoons enchanted him. He'd written a three-volume work on Diesel, Heinkel, and Bosch; these were the true forces of German history. "Hitler," said Alfred. "What is that *Schwein* but an economic splinter?" Beinfresser was something else. Each day Alfred discovered some other refinement in the corporate geometry. "This fellow's an artist. Not a Diesel — he's no scientist — but money. Money he understands."

"Does he have money to give?"

Alfred's generous lip puffed out that absurd irrelevance. "What's that going to do for him? He wouldn't give a quarter to a daughter."

"He's got a daughter?"

"Of course not. Can you see him putting *Geld* into baby shoes? This man is pure. An economic saint."

Dugan had enough of the celebrant's mass. He needed a lead-in but didn't spot one till Tatum showed up in Chicago for a speech to Midwest philologists.

4

The ex-chancellor was a man who relished distant views and noises—droning, humming—the genuflection of furniture, all heights, pulpits, platforms, theater boxes. He was built to be looked up to. Tall, muscular, his face loomed with northern contrasts, salt-white hair combed into waves, blue eyes deep in deep sockets, cheeks red at the bone points and creviced with years of public sufferance of fools. His voice was rough, scraped, his hands thick veined, a farmer's except for the nails, small reflectors which, as he talked, mooned around for emphasis.

Dugan, a sniffer of snow jobs, had to fight off a giant one. Tatum, like a great clown, made himself life's butt. He told Dugan how FDR had seen through him. "Ickes and I were after the vice presidency. Roosevelt handled us like counterfeit fives." He went back to Chicago, defeat in his face. Failure was infectious. Soon he couldn't handle trustees, other university presidents, the faculty. "Those opera tenors did me in."

The eyes stayed on Dugan's, a weight of assessment. For *Harper's,* he'd written, "Kennedy's death scattered a flock of loyalists over the country, rough Irish trade that cleared the trail of his political flop and called it gold dust."

"Good fighters only remember their losses, Mr. Tatum. That's the way with you. And probably that billionaire graduate of ours, Beinfresser. He's always talking about you."

"Oh? What's he say?" Tatum never objected to hearing himself quoted. Though he had a fine clipping service and had seen the piece in *Der Spiegel.*

"He mentions what you said about the university existing to elimi-

nate types like him. Yet, you know, he thinks of himself as your disciple. You're probably one of the few living people he's showing off for."

"Absurd. Except for an annual Christmas card, atheist Jew to atheist Baptist, I don't hear from him. Just an annual touch of spiritualist
Esperanto."

"Maybe," said Dugan, "but types like him are after some kind of
championship. What they need is someone to crown 'em. Like Napoleon needed the pope. I think it's why he sends you Christmas cards,
makes references to you. I'm convinced all he needs to know is you're
still behind the university. One letter from you, and I'd bet in a year or
less there'd be money for a building. Named after you. The Tatum
Cryogenics Laboratory."

Said Tatum, "I thought whatever the university was like now, it
had good technicians. As usual, I'm wrong. The technicians are just
romantic poets. Mr. Dugan, this man wouldn't notice if my corpse
were left in his bathtub. As for the university, it wouldn't name a ba-
boon's toilet after me. I enjoy a bit of Celtic twilight, Dugan, but at
eleven o'clock in the morning, even my eyes are usually on the objects
in front of them."

"You know your powers better than anyone, Mr. T."

Something went on in Tatum's face, a small anxiety. "Power is
something men understand very differently. I've been around too
many sorts to reconcile them."

"Some sorts are unquestionable, aren't they? Something comes off,
or it doesn't. In public life or private. I was around Washington for two
Cuban crises. I know the difference between bringing something off
and not bringing it off. You can tell the difference in people's walks,
the way they eat, when they joke, how they go to bed."

"Public failure intensifies private relationships, Mr. Dugan."

"Not mine, Mr. T. I can't operate anywhere with failure in my
system."

"I think you'll come to feel differently. Even about the relative failures of your Mr. Kennedy. I think he was a fairly strong man after the
Bay of Pigs. The admission of stupidity is strength. As for that missile
so-called crisis, that was a sporting event, whipped up for personal redemption. Those silver calendars, JFK to RSM or whatever, they were

boys' trophies. Banana-state dramatizing. Look at the Sorensen book, with all its theater talk, 'roles,' 'postures,' 'antagonists.' Crisis was just drama for your sportive ex-bosses. They'd burn up the world for a good show.

"I say the hell with all these strutters. Everyone quotes Acton's maxim, but how many believe it? I do. Stay in power long, and the concrete turns to smoke. You can't handle it. You can't tolerate opposition. And you exhaust your own aides. Look at the married life of a powerful man's subordinates. They're emasculated by him. He sets the schedules, tells them when they can go home to their wives. And if he wants, the wives will sleep with him. In their dreams, half of them do.

"I'm not speaking out of inexperience, Mr. Dugan. I stayed much too long at the university and nearly ruined it. And I was one of the few in America who knew what it was all about, knew, for better or worse—and you know it's worse—it was going to be the center of action.

"The best intentioned become posers and tyrants. You don't want a letter from me, Dugan. You know the rich. You don't pat them at a distance. They want the dogs to come to their hand for the bone. I've got enough trouble finding a little meat for myself."

"That old queen," Dugan told Strunk back at the office. "One lousy letter. I should have beaten it out of him."

5

Leonard Strunk had bad luck with girls. This after an adolescence that, as that tunnel of horrors went, was a tunnel of love. From fifteen to eighteen, Strunk was almost continuously in love, and although he did not "lose his cherry"—as the touching expression of those years went—till his junior year at college, the body hugging, tongue kissing, and digital probation of a good lot of pretty New York and Chicago girls fed masturbatory pleasure, sometimes, blissfully, on the unclothed belly of whomever he'd brought up to his room to tune in on Amorous Brahms. Now, in his late twenties, masturbation remained Strunk's chief sexual relief.

As a good part of Strunk's life was determined by what he read, any shame about masturbation was allayed by select readings in twentieth-century novelists. When Norman Mailer condemned it, Strunk sulked. "Why," he complained to Dugan, "the writer who strokes himself more publicly than any writer since Whitman should have this terrible bug about the most economical of pleasures this old economist knoweth not."

Dugan disliked such subjects, had to force hearty interest.

"When a man's work is done to corral nooky, and Mailer must get plenty, he's naturally going to crow over poor lugs like you beating their lonely meat to Judy Collins. If he ate shit, he'd be knocking hamburgers."

"It's more complicated than that. The guy hates solipsism. That's masturbation. It's why he had to give up fiction, how he saved himself from the loony bin by reportage. See that piece on the Pentagon in *Harper's?* Mailer's our Henry Adams. Explaining America's sewers and cathedrals for the East Hampton feebles."

Masturbation wasn't Strunk's unique source of sexual joy. There was also Mrs. Babette Preester, a thick, sometimes ardent divorcée, secretary to the Committee on New Nations, who shared herself with Strunk three or four times a month after a suitable dinner and what she called "downtown entertainment." (Shows, movies, concerts, good or bad, as long as they got her into the Loop.)

In addition, a student sometimes brought her problems to him in such a way that his fear of endangering a small hold on the English department was overcome, and, at least for the duration of the term, he enjoyed more or less steady sex. There were occasional windfalls elsewhere: a hatcheck girl at the Astor Towers had, to his delighted surprise, winked at him; over Babette's low forehead, he'd made an engagement with her when retrieving his coat, and she'd come to his place on Dorchester a few times, though it was clearer than it was with Babette that she and Leonard shared nothing but each other's parts, clearer that long-term interests could not be realized or envisaged in Leonard's bare-floored, scarcely furnished, book-and-paper-laden bedroom-kitchenette.

Much of Strunk's spare time was spent concocting schemes, plans, suggestions, and criticisms, which were written up in letter form and sent to people of appropriate authority and influence. More and more, the correspondence absorbed his spare time and channeled his large energies. Sometimes, though, he thought his letters might be the static of a mind that was otherwise not getting through. Weren't letters a substitute for real writing? Toil without test? Yet how else be effective? It was better than writing on toilet walls. Though, God knows, more expensive.

Strunk bought stamps by the hundred sheet, and when postal rates were upped he suffered an economic crisis. In addition, he used fine stationery, Pott-sized, creamy rag paper with his signature, O. Leonard Strunk, engraved in six-point golden Mauritius off left center, his home address, in smaller script, off right.

He wasn't vain about his correspondence, nor did he consider it in capital letters as a life's work of commentary and reportage in the manner of Walpole and Grimm. Strunk thought of himself as a small conduit of serious ideas and humane complaints, a Voltaire without genius. Unlike Voltaire, he wrote no intimate letters, no mere expressions of wit, gallantry. He wrote to aldermen about potholes in the street, to the Bundy and Rostow brothers about Southeast Asia, to thinkers and scholars about their discoveries and specialties, and, after Christmas, to the foreign artists who'd painted the finest UNESCO cards. He exchanged letters in French with Papa Ibrahim Tall about the problems of African carpet makers, in German with Willie Fenstermacher, the skiologist of Lech am Arlberg, and in English with Vuk Murković, the poet, about the bards of Montenegro.

In addition to corresponding with private persons, as his account book labeled them, Strunk wrote to newspapers and magazines over the world. His account book was covered with red dirks for unacknowledged and blue skulls for unprinted letters, but it was a bad year that saw fewer than a hundred in American newspapers alone. The *Chicago Sun-Times,* the *Des Moines Register,* and the *Santa Barbara News-Press* regarded Strunk as a steady, and their letters column was instructed to use one Strunk a month.

In the spring of 1966 Strunk began writing to someone who became his single most important correspondent. Miss Elizabeth Schultz had been a student in his Lyric from Wyatt to Berryman and was now a researcher for *Newsweek.* She had begun the correspondence by writing Strunk what she said she'd meant to tell him after the course, that it was one of the finest she'd taken at the university. Strunk had replied in grateful acknowledgment, but, as his epistolary impulse was not so easily slaked, he wrote a longish response. What would interest her? He couldn't remember Miss Schultz by looks or intellect (though his record book showed he'd graded her A). He settled on a disquisition about the functions of newsmagazines, the perils of their simultaneous obligation to entertainment and comprehensive authority. To his pleased surprise, Miss Schultz wrote back an account of the transformation of her research (she worked in the business section) by the editorial and writing staffs and related this to those fashions and conventions in lyric which were, "as you showed us in class," the key to many of the finest poems in the language. So delighted was Strunk that he wrote back an account of structural transformations in neurosis, kinship, language, and religion as he had intertwined them from pages of Lévi-Strauss, R. Barthes, J. Lacan, and N. Chomsky. Miss Schultz replied, after a week "spent on the texts," and her answer generated a full-scale epistle on the relationship of PERT (Program Evaluation Review Techniques) to such other "self-generating systems as musical scales." Miss Schultz slid by this epistolary iceberg, waited ten days, and discussed the attempts by Wright and Breuer to overcome the "tyranny of New York property rectangles, perhaps another system of self-generation." Her gentle caution evoked in Strunk a tender flow of ideas which, in a few days, found epistolary form in a discussion of the relationship of basic forms to basic concepts. ("Is not the triangle inevitability, the pentagon authority?")

In short, Miss Schultz became Strunk's Interdisciplinary Recipient, his steadiest pen pal. In a year and a half, they exchanged more than fifty letters.

Strunk began to wonder more and more about her. One August day he decided he would take his pre-fall-quarter vacation in New York, but the afternoon mail brought him Elizabeth's reflections on Mini Art and the Warhol Strategy, with a postscript which said that she was about to spend two weeks with her parents on their farm south of Little Rock. It was the first personal note since letter 1. His Interdisciplinary Recipient was a farmer's daughter. She, a daughter, could have a daughter. Not now — she was a miss and no East Village hippie mama — but the potency was more than likely there.

That evening Strunk reread the letter and felt the grip of loneliness. What to do? He telephoned Mrs. Preester but was told by a babysitter she wasn't expected till late.

He put on his summer suit, a pale gabardine he'd bought five years ago in Field's basement, and went over to the Oxford Lounge, from which, three or four times, he'd extracted a girl for a horizontal hour in his apartment. Tonight, however, the Kansas City Athletics were at the hotel across the street, and there were no spare girls.

Strunk walked to Fifty-fifth Street, east to Jackson Park, and through the underpass to the lake. Out on the promontory, black girls in bikinis stomped and curled to the isolating music of flutes and bongo drums. Coals under hibachis, beer bottles and cans shivered with fire and moonlight. From the vaporous green lake rose Elizabeth Schultz, long and softly ropy. Each nude tendon, each sweet transit from curve to curve, sped him to her. "Open, open," begged Strunk.

The next day, he wrote to Arkansas.

Dear Elizabeth,

The study of autism (Mahler, Fuère, Bettelheim) reveals the connections between excrement and the sense of self. The autistic child identifies with her excrement; a throwaway, she becomes excremental to save the last vestige of her self.

Elizabeth, I must interrupt the train of thought. It is warm here. Mercilessly. Perhaps it is time to bring up (not as ejecta, let alone excreta) a matter long on my mind. I have been in hopes that you and I might be able to enrich our epistolary mutuality. It would, I mean, be a great pleasure for me to see you. To spend some time talking with you.

I had thought of going to New York now, but you are not there. Before the beginning of the autumn quarter here—that is on Oct. 1—I have several free days. Would you perhaps consider reserving a room for me at a hotel not far from your apartment? Yours is no longer a neighborhood I know well. In my boyhood, it was one to be shunned in fear or approached in trembling. At any rate, perhaps you will think of this proposal and decide what is best. I sign off, then,

In cordial hope, in hopeful
expectancy, but, in any case,
immer dein,
Leonard S.

Postscriptum: Please forgive rude brevity. Much to tell you anon re.
cultures which prize excreta (Shakes's father; post-Mongol Near
East — cf. treatise of Ibn-al-Wahdwa): sewage, drainage-ex-aquaria
(Med. Lat. *sewaria,* sluice of millponds), thoughts of Rome and
Knossos, the Austro-Germany of outcast (*excretum*) Freud,
Protestantism (cf. N. Brown on Swift, Luther), money as dreck in
11th-century Europe. But, dear Elizabeth, all this can save till we
come together, hopefully, dare I say, in new phase of our relat.

Y,
L.

6

The Thursday before his flight to New York, Strunk was too skittery
to write any letters at all, couldn't read, couldn't do more than pack
and repack, deciding which two of four suits he should take, and
which of the two pack, which wear. Strunk shopped with the finesse of
tornadoes, in with a head-low rip, hand riffling 42 longs (though his
arboreal trunk and arms needed extra long), then choice, change, fit,
and out. He had one tailor-made suit. In July 1967, a Lebanese tailor
from the Loop, in deep water after the Arab-Israeli war, took his stuff
up to the Windermere Hotel and offered bargains to Hyde Parkers.
Strunk disgorged a rare hundred and fifty dollars and emerged with a
"Mediterranean blue-green double-vent glen plaid" that made him
look like an Aegean island. Said Mr. Dalah toward the Strunk-filled
ballroom mirror, "Downtown you wouldn't walk out of here for under
three-fifty."

The plaid was cut too squarely for Strunk's hulking shoulders, and
Mr. Dalah had surrendered too soon to his extensive rear, but the suit
was still Strunk's best and thus hung over the closet door for Elizabeth's first sight of him.

That morning he took twenty minutes passing the electric razor over his face, inspecting and practicing expressions, trying for leanness in his generous cheeks, for depth in his puddle-colored eyes, length in his too apish jaw.

No beauty, Strunk, but after all, Elizabeth knew what he looked like, he had not put on more than ten pounds in the years since she'd been in his class, there were still elements of good looks that could be assembled by goodwill. And her letters bore no sign that Manhattan had raised her standards of masculine beauty beyond Strunkish reach; he might pass, especially in these days when even monsters were thought beautiful.

He ran in place, shoulders back, stomach in, great legs high. The razor cord twisted around the faucet, the razor pulled out of his pumping arm and crashed on the sink. The white plastic cracked, the buzz castrated into whine. Twenty-six dollars.

"Vanity," he told Dugan later. "There I was metamorphosing into Gregory Peck, and Matter Itself rose up against me. I ought to tear this up." His ticket.

Dugan said any woman who passed up a hunk of male glory like O. L. Strunk would be too thick to penetrate with human weapons. He drove him to O'Hare for a final buck up. "I expect to see you back totally unhumped. An April carpet."

"Poor thing's probably in a wheelchair."

7

New York.

When he was a boy, Third Avenue was bums, pawnshops, bars. Lexington was the limit of the habitable world. You crossed to Third with fear. Now it was a gold-flecked pleasure tent converging downtown in fifty-story glitter. Here, at Elizabeth's corner, were restaurants, antique shops, tailors, cigar stores, butchers, a mailbox. The box which held Elizabeth's letters. No hand behind any light but one could write those letters.

She lived two doors east of Third above a frame shop, closed but lit. Ten names on the mail slots, girls from Teaneck, Hartford, Greensboro, and Mason City who came down the old steps for buses and taxis to ad agencies, dental offices, brokerages, *Newsweek*. Strunk pressed E. SCHULTZ, 3C.

Telling Dugan as much as he wanted to a week later, Strunk confessed that the first look was a shocker. Here was this girl of questing intellect, of voice liquid with kindness, and, at the doorway, greeting her admired instructor, her mind's correspondent, her future lover, there was . . . Slob. Sheer Slob. And not even the Slob of Inattention—mind elsewhere on difficult matter, Thales tripping on the dungheap—but Conscientious Career Slob. Blond hair wild, hip-huggers uncomplimentary to big bottom, shirt stained, middle buttons misbuttoned so hole showed torn brassiere (a bit of tug there). She wore black glasses, had a yolk-tinged smile. What, he had wondered, was this self-presentation supposed to mean?

The place was not quite in motion but looked as if the order of creation had just been sent in. Clearly the elements had not been able to get into shape on their own. Skirts, newspapers, *New Statesmen,* bridge scores, glasses, packaged-gravy envelopes, cracker cylinders, toothpaste caps, stockings, record jackets, manila envelopes, socks, panties, exhausted ballpoints, piles of anything.

"It's a little crowded here." Said easily, liquidly. "I don't know what to throw out. My consumer mind. But here you are. The best item in the place." With an arm shove, clearing a wounded couch. Then opened a labelless bottle of soybean-colored liquid and poured into glasses which many, less fastidious than Strunk, would have refused to touch. "I tell you, Dugan, at that point, I thought the old leaning tower would fall. Yet, I dunno. Somehow, in the room, she had that wine at her mouth, and there was this sweetness in her smile. Terrific. And she had the loveliest, clear jawline. I love jawlines. And an out-of-this-universe cream-and-fruit complexion. I tell you, she just came together for me. In that sewer of a room. Maybe that was the reason for it. A dung setting for the queen pearl. So I stayed. The whole week. The bedroom wasn't bad. And she's a heartbreaker. I recommend letters."

8

In Geneva, where the Rhone debouches into the lake by the Quai du Mont Blanc, is the Hôtel de Pologne, eight stories of angel food cake limestone, its lakefront windows shaded by purple awnings which, from the excursion boats docked below, appear the proper regal flourish of this most republican town.

Barney Beinfresser occupies the top three floors of the hotel. Six years before, plaster walls were knocked down, and, in the tripled spaces, walls of mirror and satin put up. Persian beds, Murano chandeliers, Roman chests, Empire beds, Brussels tapestries, French fusils, Danish desks, and American business machines were lifted by exterior cables and installed through dismantled windows. Fifty of the prettiest girls in the canton followed to answer phones and press buttons.

As is well known since the rise of capitalism, money will give a cripple legs, a bald man hair, a faded woman skin of rose and silk. Barney Beinfresser's money put gloss in his monk's crescent of black hair, exercised and massaged his flab into muscle, tanned his short body (and, in shoes, subtly elevated it), shaped his face away from his persimmon nose, educated sideburns over his great ears, and polished the very air around him. Girls genuinely lusted for Barney and told themselves — as well as him — that for richer or poorer they would be his.

Barney had horses and Barney had planes, Barney had assistants whose assistants had horses and his assistants had planes. And all this he had earned himself.

After a couple of head-bashing years in which he'd used up the stake he'd accumulated as a student-businessman at Chicago, Barney converted small Yiddish into German and became a denazifier for the OSS, a role which had him, a sergeant, outranking colonels. He worked out a technique for uncovering concentration camp guards masquerading as inmates: a key question, a five-hundred-watt spotlight in the eyes, and a punch under them; his confession rate was tremendous. He lived in a Rhine castle, commandeered cars, concerts, wine, and girls.

Meanwhile, he prepared.

He crated gargoyles off cathedrals (some fallen, some helped to

fall), picked up dinner services of Meissen and Rosenthal china for cigarettes, and trafficked heavily in enemy souvenirs.

He had an OSS colleague, Corporal Vincenzo, who was attached to
the Committee of National Liberation for North Italy. Vincenzo was
in the Piazzale Loreto on April 29 when the bodies of Mussolini and
Claretta Petacci were hauled in from the hills. Before they were strung
up, Vincenzo cut off a few square feet of their bloodied garments and
took pictures of the excisions. These, cut into square inches and
mounted on inscribed plastic with the demarcated picture attached to
the bottom, brought in fifty thousand dollars from collectors in New
York, Paris, and Beirut. On May 1, Vincenzo and Beinfresser just
missed a ride into Berlin, where they hoped to convert the remains of
Hitler into inventory. It was one of their few failures.

In June they drove their crates in half-ton trucks into a Dolomite
village and laid low till October. Vincenzo caught pneumonia, Beinfresser confused the antibiotic dosage, and Vincenzo died. Barney dug
him a deep grave.

Two weeks later, Barney had his first office, a cellar room in the
bombed-out Röhmer section of Frankfurt/Main.

9

March 1968.

Beads of mist from Mont Blanc hang across the Petit Saleve over
the beautiful lake and the gray Old Town. Strunk would have shivered
with historic delight, but Dugan is too busy to shift historic furniture.
His quarry is very present tense indeed, hairy wristed, claw eyed,
clumped with terrific force, empty of courtesy.

Dugan and Beinfresser. They sit in an anteroom of an office Dugan
will never see. Dugan is sure every word here is taped, there's probably a camera in the gold doorknob.

He has opened up with a conclusion: Beinfresser is a distinguished
graduate of the university, his wealth is reputed to be considerable, he,
Dugan, wishes him to become a permanent part of one of the great in-
stitutions of the world. "What endure at universities are the contribu-

tions of the faculty and its graduates. And what houses them. Everything else is transient. We hope a Beinfresser library or laboratory will be a fixture of the scene."

"I'm not much on sarcophagi."

Beinfresser's hands are at ease. Only small movements in the arms under the tan cloth suggest that he is not just waiting for Dugan, that he too is heading for something.

"If the next century's Shakespeare and Einstein walk out of the Beinfresser Library, nobody would call it a sarcophagus."

Beinfresser is annoyed at Dugan's shoes heeling his ten-thousand-dollar carpet. Nineteen-dollar shoes. The universities better get with it. They send men after money who look as if they don't know what it is. But Dugan seems a tough cookie. Why is he hung up with a third-rate enterprise? What's lax in him? Where's he been broken? He tells him a new Shakespeare won't need a new library. "Electronics is making an oral culture. Tribal. Nobody ahead of anybody else. Nobody storing it up in files or banks."

What a nerve, thinks Dugan. The ancien régime keeping the farmers down on the farm. "Anyway, I'm not thinking about plays I'll never see, Mr. Dugan. I'm only at the *Titus Andronicus* stage of my own life. Shakespeare worked with stories, I with money. I can't bury what I work with. You're not talking to the old Rockefeller now. He was," and Beinfresser pointed a thumb past his ear toward the old city, "a Calvinist. 'Money is the sign God knows I've acted right.' Pretty notion, but sheer balls. I may have been a lousy student, but in Tatum's day, even mules like me found out how to read old rocks. I'm no Calvinist. Money isn't sacred to me in any way. It's just what I work with. Not for. With."

Dugan held back from anything but a look of absorption.

"If I give money, it has nothing to do with Band-Aids. When I give it, it works for me directly or indirectly. It buys me something or it puts odor-of-rose instead of wolf in someone's nostrils."

Dugan gave him a cold nod, old man to naughty boy; such a big bad wolf playing Machiavelli.

"I don't hide much, what's the point? I'm not even beating around your little bush. You got in here because I have a feeling. That's all now. A feeling the university and I may have something in common besides my degree. It may be certain studies that can be done that I'd, as it were, pay for. Or some property we both can use. I don't need to tell you the university has a tax advantage over even a well-lawyered businessman. Mostly, it's information I need. Maps. I want to know what's going to happen. And I don't want my maps to change too much.

"The universities are making all sorts of excitement. They're spilling over their containers. That changes the maps. My notion is you've got to get better containers. Things change, but rational men must see how they'll change.

"I've operated in junk heaps and ruins. Better than most. But that's over. I'm miles away from that part of my life. I don't want my factories in smoke. I've had that. I was booted out of Iraq last year without an ashtray. I don't like that. I want to get out before the pot boils. A good university's an information center. Maybe even a generator. I might be willing to pay for a plug-in.

"But don't expect anything by next Tuesday. Don't expect anything at all. And don't dun me. I don't forget. You're on my docket. There's a fair chance you'll profit the way you want to profit. But, let me, as they say, do the calling. This isn't a brush-off, Mr. Dugan." He was up. Dugan, in rage, followed.

"I can't have lunch with you. But there's a delightful girl, Mlle. Quelquechose, who said you caught her eye as you came in. She would enjoy your company. And there's always an excellent lunch for people with whom I do business.

"It's been a pleasure, Mr. Dugan."

10

Living as he had for three years in a place where most people systematically deformed their appearance in the interest of that higher appeal which disregards it, Dugan was exceptionally pleased by those who looked as if they'd studied how to look splendid. So the girl who sat on one of the gold couches of the lounge which spooned off the corridor of Beinfresser's anteroom converted the weight of the moneyman's assault into air. Mlle. Quelquechose was quite something.

A small girl, a pert beauty, hair cut boyishly like Mia Farrow's, a nose that started for blue-blooded hauteur, then buttoned off, blue eyes clear in liquid brightness, a small chin, nectarine cheeks. A miniature beauty, but then, for surprise, for erotic drama, within the red-sweatered suit, an almost Lena-like affluence of breast, and, out of it, what Dugan especially treasured, splendid legs, longer than the short-ish body promised, the length emphasized by the nyloned inches north of knee to red miniskirt. The legs pointed his way, crossed like a man's at the red pumps, and an almost male, a gruff little voice came from the red-corollaed throat, "I'm Prudence Rosenstock, Mr. Dugan."

Beinfresser combed more than the Swiss cantons for his flowers. Prudence was Miss Western Michigan 1962, a model for the Sears Roebuck catalog who'd saved to try it with Galitzine in Italy, hadn't last-ed, and had been found by a Beinfresser man in the Milan Galleria cadging emergency income.

The autobiography unrolled in a Fiat 125, "a nervous car," said the Hertz girl, herself a likely enough candidate for the Beinfresser offices. Beinfresser allowed the girls a thousand Swiss francs and a couple of hundred miles. Prudence suggested they drive into the mountains. Dugan, surveying the map, lit on Vezelay. He'd never been there, never been in Burgundy, and the idea of having the rest of his three days in Europe with Prudence, Burgundian cuisine, and medieval marvels was a powerful draw. Each expectation advanced the other. In fact, allowed it. Dugan was not the sort to enroll in Beinfresser's fuck-now, kneel-later business. He had to have at least the illusion Prudence was part of a Larger Scheme of Pleasure. He would not even let her charge the Fiat to Beinfresser.

It turned out he could discuss it with Prudence. "I may be semi-professional, but it sure doesn't suit me. I'm like a nun there. I mean, I live in the hotel," she pronounced this charmingly in Dugan's ears, *HOE-tel,* "and I go upstairs to the office, and when there's no work, I go shopping with the girls or fix my hair or read, which is OK, I love to read, but," and she tipped around in the corner to coax Dugan's look from the terrible twists of the Jura roads, a marvelous, novel animal in her round beaver collar and toque, a fur bloom on the red suit coat. "I mean, where's the Struc-ture of my life? I mean, what does it lead to?"

She got lots of good advice from her business acquaintances. Lying, bare, in the Gritti or the Paris Ritz, looking out the windows at the Salute or the Place Vendôme, she'd posed the problem many a time and had received numerous if unvaried solutions. "Flowers shouldn't worry about their future." Occasionally a job offer. "Sure, more reception whoring, and I had a year at Olivet, bet you never heard of it, but it's a good school." An occasional marriage proposal, "but I'm only twenty-four, my looks are the type that last, if you don't drive us over the cliffs. I didn't have it as a fashion model. You know they want these pieces of pipe that can fold themselves up six or eight times and still come out taller than me. I used to tie ice cubes against my cheeks. A girl told me if you did that long enough it would make them look as if they had caves in them. These big houses love those caved-in cheeks. The more money you spend, the more starved you're supposed to look. You're thin, you're spiritual. I mean, the human body has so few variations, people go after any crazy detail. Next year they'll be looking for girls with hair on the lower lip."

They ate a lunch in Beaune, which was so regal in detail and strength, they decided to take a room in the hotel, and there, after half an hour to digest and play with each other, they snoozed, alternately cozying each other's backsides in their semilaps.

That night, after hours in town and a dinner served like a mass, Dugan told Prudence *his* troubles. Trouble-telling was a fine superstructure for love. The tongue was an eloquent penis, the ears generous receptors. Trouble-telling preceded every deep relationship, as trouble itself deepened, then ended it. The resistance of flesh to flesh, earth to cultivation, donor to beggar, fact to system, this was proper scenery for the few great human moments. Dugan lay beside the soft beauty in the lumpy bed in the Hôtel de la Poste, muttering his wounds, salving them in her soft bowls, her soft hills.

The next day, in Vezelay, he bought a postcard of the most beautiful of the church's capitals, a dreamy stone man pouring stone grain into a stone mill, an amazed stone man holding a stone bag to receive the stone flour. The guidebook explained: Moses pouring the Old Law into Christ, Saint Paul receiving the purified text. "Like experience," said Prudence. "You go through the mill, so next time you do better."

Thought Dugan, Beinfresser has poured this crude beauty my way, but what we have done together has refined her into what I won't do without. There she curled in the Fiat, gob of American melting pot, white German, white Celt, taught letters in a PWA high school, lovemaking by a second-string guard, Western civ by a nail-biting doctor-al candidate from Ann Arbor, ambition by movie magazines and *The Tonight Show,* found useful by Beinfresser and now found crucial by Dugan.

11

The day's letter from Leonard was hardly more than telegram length, and then that evening, his telegram arrived with more or less the same message but spelling out which plane she should get on this Thursday.

Ever since Elizabeth had read *Allegory of Love* and found out that love, like the spinning jenny, was an invention, she'd felt reborn, for if love was something patented in eleventh-century Provence, then so was every other conventional feeling somewhere or other patented. In Bi. Sci. 2, she'd read in Darwin's *Expression of the Emotions in Man and Animals* that musculature developed for one purpose was used by evolved creatures for another: hair bristling to frighten enemies became, in men, expression of their own fright. Thus she could make the motions of love without being in love. (By 1967, every urban girl in the world knew that.) But more, you could think without having to accomplish anything with thought, could run without going anywhere. You could do anything without having the reasons you were supposed to have when you were first told to do it. Wasn't this what existentialism was all about?

She'd come to define her life by accident as much as anything. The apartment mess, which Leonard hadn't caught on to at all, hadn't started that way. She'd been a more or less automatic tidier, as, in adolescence, she'd been an automatic slob, but one day she'd buzzed up to the apartment a guy who'd tied her up and went through the place like Sherman through Georgia. He didn't get a nickel till he'd raped her. Not the worst, and she naturally took Enovid the way Englishmen take their brollies. A runty, thickheaded, white brute, he asked where the money was. Right in her purse, which she took from the icebox, and handed him one of the two fives. He laughed and left, a handyman paid after a job. She started to pick up the mess but stopped. No. There was no point. Who decided what was Mess and what Order? Let her chips fall.

In a month, the habit of old order was gone; she'd disciplined herself to disorder.

For Leonard, she'd actually compromised. Compromising was something like accepting disorder. Don't buck it. Born a farmer's daughter, with old attachments to natural order, she knew there was no point in making life a series of funerals over old habits. Disorder could include a few of these. Another stage of liberation.

When, in college, she'd spotted her prototype spelled out in novels (the Marquise de Merteuil, Lamiel, Hendricks), she realized her contribution to the new woman could be softness. There was no need to be hard about altering woman's fate. She didn't often feel hard, or mean, hadn't been pushed around enough to be resentful or vengeful. Searching her own feelings, she decided that her independence would be unaggressive, unlike her fictional ancestors', and if not consciously benevolent, at least along her own reasonably gentle grain.

As for Leonard, he cared about everything. He cared who ran for president, he cared who won. He cared for her and he cared for going to bed with her. Old-line, he needed to put the two together; or, at least, didn't bother thinking that they didn't have to go together. He "wanted children," but couldn't separate the curiosity and egoism of having his own from the pleasures of having pretty human miniatures about the house. She said, "I'm for solving population problems by adopting my kids." Which annoyed him.

Which annoyed her. For she didn't like to annoy anybody much, certainly not a dear old wise-foolish boob brain like Leonard. But she had no curiosity at all about seeing what her genes came up with. They weren't her invention anyway. She was just another transient hostess. It would be a grace to retire them. Now that the world's submerged were poking their noses out of the swamps, there'd be genius enough around to pester the whole universe, let alone this planetary crumb. Such, at least, was the view of E. Schultz.

She checked with United and telegraphed Leonard she'd be at O'Hare at 6:46—he was queer for numbers. She had a present to bring him from the *Newsweek* morgue about this Beinfresser he and his pal Dugan were after. The researchers hadn't been able to check this item and hadn't used it, but as a student of medieval literature she'd lit up at it. The source—an Italian World War II partisan—claimed Beinfresser got his start by selling relics of "Fascist saints" to American soldiers in occupied Germany. He'd gotten Mussolini's death suit, cut it into bloody strips, and sold them for a hundred dollars apiece. He had likewise—claimed the source—disposed of a suit of Hitler's underwear and Goebbels's clubfoot shoe. Whatever ghoulish use Leonard could make of this exemplary anality, she didn't know, but, if nothing else, he could see her ease of living as relief from it.

She also brought a bottle of the wine he built his courage with. If the gifts didn't stem from love, at least they came from thoughtfulness and caring. Shouldn't that serve even so antiquated a dear as Strunk?

12

The friendly skies of United buckled in the thermal troughs of early spring. In addition to which, the friendly plane was more than woman's flesh could bear, computer salesmen, grandmothers, rusting hostesses trying to enlist you if they were under twenty, eyeing you out of existence if you spotted them a few years. And the anal supper plates, subdivided by Cornell engineers, packaged by Michigan State. The eggs laid, the hatching Skinnerized, the feathers plucked, the feet sliced by orderly metals, the contentment quotients laid out on statistical maps. Elizabeth hated airplanes.

Leonard's freighted little head rose half a foot above five other greeters. He was working to diminish his grin. She leaned over the rail and kissed it. "Cheers, love." Two hundred pounds of smiling butter.

He drove Dugan's Dodge, badly, a form of disorder she didn't relish. "I hate cars."

Was it the reason he didn't watch the others? Eyes on the pop-pop flashes of northbound lights. The Loop huffed up, the traffic narrowed, slowed.

Leonard aimed for and missed the Ohio Street cutoff, went onto Congress Street at thirty miles per, ignoring horns, glares, fuck-you gestures out the windows. On the Outer Drive, relief. It was the only stretch of road he drove easily, the Magikist lips, the Standard sign, the Donnelly plant, the lit-up Douglas pillar, the Drive motels. Relaxed, he waxed. "It took the 1812 war to warm Jefferson to cities."

Liz, liquidly: "Why so?"

"Saw the country couldn't depend on Europe for manufactures. The anticity strain is deep in America."

" 'Our alabaster cities gleam undimmed by human tears.' "

Leonard turned off the Drive at Forty-seventh, drove past the wasteland fringe of the South Side slum, braked by a field of cinders, and kissed her. "I love your learning, Elizabeth."

Less than most men was Leonard made for automobile loving. Nor did Elizabeth relish the Dodge's mechanic breath, the double-parking yards off the express drive. How much dumbness could go with so much doll? "Preserve it then," pointing at cars screeching around them.

He got his hands on the wheel, started off, gears clashing. (If you can't find it, grind it.) "The Vedas are antiurban, but the city's made for love."

"They do all right in the country. Sometimes with corncobs." Liquidly.

They drove around the high-rise twins islanded in Fifty-fifth Street, turned up Dorchester without pausing for the stop sign, taking horn fire at the rear.

"The Vedas didn't have urban prescriptions. Buddha did. Like Jesus. The preaching was to the cities. And city people got him in the end."

They were not upstairs ten minutes when the phone rang. Prudence, Dugan's new girl, calling to ask them over for a drink.

Odd foursome of love.

13

In the fall of 1964 Dugan campaigned in California, half for the president, half for Salinger. Nothing big, answering phones, pushing noses out of keyholes, pacifying, procuring, buttering, counting, but it got him out of shepherding his congressmen, and his boss, Bronson Kraus, said he could gather the index figures and feed them to the president once a week.

Which he did, taking a day to gather them and five minutes to show them to the president and listen to him repeat them without looking at the sheet of paper.

One day, after the session, Dugan told him that he'd been thinking about a guaranteed national income and would like to do something about it.

The huge executive forefinger rammed Dugan's breastbone. "When ah need a shoe shine, Dugan, ah'll git me the shoe-shine boy."

Dugan was transferred to a closet in the Executive Office Building. Kraus found a place for him with the archives division declassifying material for release. Dull work for Dugan, who hated everything about history but making it. A Chicago congressman steered him to an opening at the university; there he flew, and there he stayed.

But Dugan's three weeks in archives had traced a few grooves in his memory. When he and Prudence drank Bloody Marys with Strunk and his pleasant, ham-flanked, not-unbeautiful slob, Elizabeth, her little Beinfresser item ticked into the groove of an Italian Front cable about one Corporal Henry Vincenzo of the CIC, who, after being seen and photographed in the Piazzale Loreto the morning of Mussolini's death, had disappeared and not been heard from since.

As the others drank, Dugan's groove deepened and widened. Then he leaped up and wrote a letter which released the grip of fury Beinfresser had held him in since he had gone to see Chancellor Tatum at the Drake. The letter, most of it based on Dugan's infuriated guesswork, went as follows:

Dear Mr. Beinfresser:

I want to thank you again for the fascinating talk. I will respect your wishes about not mentioning the subject I broached to you in Geneva. I only wish to tell you that the description of your possible relations to the University Campaign Fund is one which I understand.

I write primarily of another matter which has come to my attention. I've recently been interested in the case of a Corporal Henry Vincenzo of the counterintelligence group which worked with the Liberation Front of Northern Italy (Audisio et al.). There is some evidence that Vincenzo played a somewhat amusing but discomforting role back there. It had to do with the acquisition and sale of some Fascist relics. I need not bother you with the details. What interests me is that the corporal disappeared in May 1945 and has not been heard from since. His family assumed he had been killed by German sentries in the last days of the war, then stripped of his identification and buried somewhere. It occurred to me to write a number of men such as yourself who were in various counterintelligence groups and might have gotten to know Corporal Vincenzo. If something about his habits were learned, it might lead authorities to him so that his family could be comforted about his last days (if such they indeed were). Did you perhaps know the corporal?

Chicago is on the edge of spring. My neighbor's tulip shoots are making their debut.

Miss Rosenstock, one of your former employees, joins me in sending regards.

Sincerely yours,
Hugh Dugan
University Development Office

14

By the time Beinfresser's response came, Dugan was in the hospital. Another consequence of his unhistoric regard for perturbation. For it was he who suggested that they go, the afternoon of Martin Luther King's funeral, to Sixty-third Street; worse, he who had misinterpreted an informative gesture as a belligerent one, had let rage blot out his good sense, and had waged bitter struggle in the street.

It would be too much to blame him for not knowing that Beinfresser's donation had as much to do with these same events as with his clever letter, for Dugan is an old-fashioned man. That Beinfresser is ever alert to those perturbations which alter the values of property and chattel is something Dugan knows only theoretically. (The Beinfresser Computer Center, built largely with federal funds—and supplied by Buttenwieser Computations—began rising on Sixty-second Street in

1969.) But our idyll does not really care for finance, only Dugan and Strunk and the girls with whom they will spend years. Beinfresser may make huge gains in South Side property, but Dugan and Strunk prosper in other ways.

This is an idyll.

A final section, then, about the troubled days after the murder of Martin Luther King in Memphis, which occurred the evening after Elizabeth came to Chicago for her first visit with Leonard Strunk.

15

In the monkish beauty of Strunk's apartment, Elizabeth woke. What was that ahead, Notre Dame? No. Slant light transmuting a window shaft of a Mies high-rise into a medieval tower.

Behind her, in the three-quarter bed of which he took two-thirds, her good monk, who, last night, had labored so sweetly in their common cause.

No common cause held together the troubled city of Chicago. Rumors burned and then blocks.

Sunday, she and Strunk, Dugan and Prudence drove downtown. At Madison Street, beyond the yellow police barricades, clouds of flame-edged smoke swelled, buckled, and broke.

That night the National Guard came into the city. The four lovers watched them—on television—land in planes, take to jeeps and half-ton trucks, then, driving into the city, saw them posted on avenues where stores were shuttered with iron Xs, where other windows showed stalactite jags of glass. Smoke from dying fires snaked, flattened, and floated against the ancient walls, less than fifty years of age, but older than Pompeii if measured by cumulative degradation.

Again on television they watched concentrations of violence that made what they had seen even more desperate: a sibling conflagration in Washington, Robert Kennedy talking in a Cincinnati ghetto about his brother's assassination, grieving men who had been with King, the Memphis motel and the room from which the unknown assassin fired. Black leaders spoke direfully, bleakly, menacingly; the president read a hasty message. He had not had a week of martyr's pleasure after his great moment of renunciation. Undercut, as always, by the world's Ks.

Sunday passed, and Elizabeth changed her reservation. She called her office Monday, said she'd be in Tuesday; but Tuesday saw her head in Leonard's lap, watching King's funeral on Dugan's color television set. Strunk had a Xeroxed copy of King's dissertation on Paul Tillich. "God in the streets," he described it. "Mad the way these myths won't stop. You can see King spotting his death in the stories, but how does Judas know he must take the part?" Great nose and lips gilded with the weird light of the set, the rest of the upside-down head obscure to her.

Dugan, in a chair, hand on Prudence's head, feet up on the green casing of his discarded black-and-white set, pointed to Nelson Rockefeller in the packed church rising from a seat to stand with Mayor Lindsay of New York against the wall. The Rockefellers, said their instant historian Strunk, were quick learners. "And probably the only white Baptists in the church." The sermons, the hymns, the mourners in white ("an African carryover," said Strunk), the smallest King girl asleep against the veiled mother, a bored Senator McCarthy high over his rival, Kennedy, candidate Nixon leaning over to gab with Mrs. John Kennedy, getting frozen, beating a quick retreat into difficult self-absorption: the white-power reef in the mahogany bay within the Ebenezer Baptist Church.

When the casket was put on the mule cart, the lovers went into the kitchen for hamburgers, which Prudence incinerated on the frying platter. "Two weeks, and I can't get the hang of it."

Dugan suggested they go see what was happening on Sixty-third Street.

Strunk thought it would be dangerous, though there'd been comparatively little activity on Sixty-third after Saturday night.

They got in the Dodge and drove down Cottage Grove by the smashed acres of urban clearance. "Better put the headlights on, Hughie": Prudence. Dugan pulled them on. South of Sixtieth Street, every car's lights shone against the sun.

Elizabeth said she thought the soldiers would be out in force. At Sixty-third, under the filthy iron of the elevated tracks, they waited to turn left. A clot of teenagers looked across the iron-pillared, El-shadowed street. The light changed, Dugan went forward and waited for the northbound cars to make his turn. Behind him, a horn sounded and kept sounding. They looked around. "We allowed to turn here?" asked Prudence.

"Why not."

The horn yowled on, they made the turn, and Dugan looked around. A black man of thirty or so leaned out of the window of a scarred Pontiac and yelled something.

Dugan felt his old street fighter's click. Perhaps it had to do with the misery of his last year. Who will say? He stuck his fist out and yelled back, "Who the hell you think you ARE?" And pulled up, front wheels to the curb.

"Jesus," said Strunk. Prudence and Elizabeth could not speak, could hardly breathe, their mental preparation nothing in the dark of this stupid minute.

The Pontiac stopped in midstreet, cars pulled around it, the driver got out, Dugan's size, a lean man in a green sport shirt. Strunk could see a block down the pillared cavern. Guardsmen in olive green, spread ten yards apart, holding their rifles. A comfort, but Dugan was out of the car, in the middle of the street, flecks of light coming through the crossed rails, the teenage boys moving off the boarded stores through the smashed glass on the sidewalks. They circled Dugan and the other driver. While the girls called noes, Strunk got himself out of the car. Dugan and his new enemy faced each other, arms raising into pincers, faces stiff with rage. "No," yelled Strunk. "No more." The Pontiac driver stared at the white whale Strunk. Veins split his neck. Then, oddly, astonishingly, his head snapped toward the iron El tracks and he yelled.

Terror.

Dugan, a statue, absolute marble in the brown street, shook loose and then, madly, struck out. And was swarmed over, windmilled. Strunk, fear and terror drowned by necessity, called, "Soldiers. Police." Dugan was standing, slugging; six or seven others were slugging, kneeling, there was flesh, teeth, blood. And then, from everywhere, people, women, girls, ululating, and the soldiers, up the long street, running, bayonets out. And Strunk was hit in the back, the head, the side, oh God, his insides, his skin, arm, chest, nose, he covered up, the soldiers were there, cars were moving, cars were stopping, and then crashes, smashes, glass, a tavern window, bottles, boys running up the street, and there were rocks and bottles in the air smashing against cars and pillars, and a low boom, and a flower of fire grew from the smashed store, and then a thick twist of smoke, and the street was a blur, though Strunk, leaning on the car, his shirt out, face bloody, saw over his arm a small girl and boy, hand in hand, eyes chilled with fear, still as flowers on the sidewalk, the sidewalks themselves a frieze, noise turned off, and then sirens and blue whirl lights and black policemen and two jeeps and a half-ton truck with soldiers, and men and women flooding east and west in the flare-spiked shade, and the fire bloomed, glass shivered, and a thin, old, bearded black man in a burnoose raised his arms, and Dugan, face broken, body filthy, welted, stained, and bloody, was picked up and put in a jeep and was gone, and the old man said in Strunk's ear, "Better git, mister," and then a rifle butt bent his side, and Strunk saw the scared and scary face of a blue-eyed guardsman behind the gun and got to the driver's seat in front of a whimpering, shrunk Elizabeth and a collapsed Prudence and with unepistolary uncontrol drove wildly through the iron cavern, dodging the pillars, turning north — wrong — on Drexel, winging by glaring incarcerated eyes toward the light, toward the open green and light of the Midway, toward the gray university towers.

DOUBLE CHARLEY

Professional deformity: the dyer's hand, the blacksmith's forearm, the model's complexion, the lawyer's skepticism. And the songwriter's?

"Mindlessness," said Charley Schmitter to his longtime collaborator, Charley Rangel. "Empty mindedness. So your tunes don't bump into anything but my jingles. And vice versa."

Manifestly untrue, but Charley Schmitter never reconciled himself to "this degraded métier." The Greatness of the American Musical Comedy was not an admissible topic at Schmitter's table.

On the other hand, Schmitter gave no quarter to *official* poets. "Glue-eyed narcissists, licking the fat off their own bones so some acne-headed sophomore can have his quota of wet dreams. So some Bulgarian history major can think about something while she mouths his member. 'I wandered lonely as a cow / That chews the cud of Chairman Mao.' Ohhhh, soo-bleem."

Immense, passionate, mad for his own spiels and his own learning, Charley Schmitter couldn't be contained by any métier.

At least, this was the sense of his old-time collaborator. "Soon as he had a few bucks salted away, he could become what he always was, a spieler, a schmooser." This to Maggie Moon, Rangel's off-and-on-again companion. "He's the most profoundly self-contented man in the world." (Rangel himself was no slouch in that department.) "He's got a tolerant, gifted wife, willing tootsies, the constitution of Mont Blanc. And he doesn't need more than ten or twelve thousand bucks a year to pay for his lousy flannel shirts, Gallo Rhine, and egg foo yong. The greatest pleasure he provides himself: schmoos. He only calls now to try it out on me. When was the last time I had a lyric out of him? Seven years ago?"

"Too long," said Maggie.

" 'Starved in Fat City.' His last trip out here. Six, seven years ago. Just before your vanishing act."

Afraid that her irregular life was upsetting Chippie, her ten-year-old daughter, Maggie had disappeared one morning, bag and baggage. For three weeks, Rangel had had no word at all. Then a one-line card from New York: "Chippie had to get away. Love, M." (Which, thought Rangel, was the reason he didn't set "Fat City"; never would.)

That had been dark-night-of-the-soul time for him. He'd lived with Maggie five years, since he'd come back to Chicago. There'd been no commissions coming in, jockeys weren't playing their songs. Only now and then would a "Golden Oldies" play a Double Charley. So he came back to the apartment he'd grown up in on West Armitage above the candy store his parents owned. (It was a Christian Science reading room now.) Maggie had left her third husband, "the Casanova of cotton goods," and was working in the billing office of Roosevelt Hospital. Rangel came in to complain and walked out with an invitation. His own wife had stayed in Santa Monica, was en route to marrying the unit manager of a TV news station. The great sexual switchboard had more links than Ma Bell's system, but, sooner or later, everyone got plugged in, if only to his own opening.

Rangel fell so hard for pretty Maggie, he wasn't bothered by her marital record. "I just kept trying. It was a substitute for B.A., M.A., Ph.D. I'm an expert now, Charley. And you're—what's that Kern song?—'My Man.' "

"Pollack and Yvain," corrected Charley.

For the first year, he'd been so charged by her presence in the same apartment, he thought he couldn't think of anything else. It turned out to be the best year he'd had in a decade. Schmitter caught fire, and Decca took a flutter on a Double Charley album. (Connoisseurs of the forties made room for it between Beatles'.)

A largish girl, especially next to tiny Rangel, Maggie had the complexion of an English milkmaid. Pretty to the point of unreality: a perfect bobbed nose and eyes so strangely lit by every feeling, you could not concentrate on their color—a blue-flecked verdure. When she put on weight—every six months or so—it went to her face and marred the perfection. But such distinctions were only for Maggie and such experts as himself. Passersby still kept looking back for seconds: quite a tribute to a woman clocking fifty.

Back then, though, her beauty and their passion were intensified by what she called "the condiment of guilt."

It was that, she said, that made her take off. Chippie, "disturbed by the irregular life," was stuttering. Rangel told her many children stuttered. "Ignore the stutter, respond to the meaning."

But Maggie, fearful of imperfection, rushed the little girl. "Speak up, speak up." Of course, it got worse. Rangel begged, ordered, threatened. For him, children were sacred. "The look on Chippie when she tried to get a sentence out," he told Schmitter, who'd come to Chicago for a workweek. "It breaks me, Charley. I never hit a woman in my life, let alone the one I loved. But if she gets on that kid again, I may break her nose."

Did that message reach Maggie? In any case, within a week, she and Chippie were off.

A month later, Schmitter telephoned to say he'd seen her, she was working in the billing office at Lenox Hill. "Seems to be all right, Charley."

"I don't care," Rangel had said. "If it wasn't for Chippie, I'd hire a truck to break her bones. Every part of me that loved her hates her. But I've even stopped dreaming of busting her nose. God bless whatever does it."

Ten months later, he saw her in the Art Institute. "I don't believe it." She was gaunt, newly beautiful. "Why didn't you call me?"

"I thought you'd kill me."

She'd been back two months, had an apartment in Hyde Park with a librarian at ITT, Olive Baum. She worked in the billing office at Michael Reese. Chippie was at Kenwood, a good public school.

They began going out again, and then, after a visit from Schmitter and the consequent departure of Olive Baum, she and Chippie came back to West Armitage. Stutter gone, Chippie went to Francis Parker; Rangel paid.

"It's like leaves," Rangel told Schmitter between spiels. "Once the chlorophyll factories start churning out all that green, you can't see those gorgeous reds that'll kill them in the fall. She's back, we click, she's for me, it's green for go."

"Not bad, little Charley. Maybe I can work it up for us."

Rangel knew better than that. There'd be no more lyrics coming his way. Only happiness with Maggie eased the pain of it then.

"Why can't you write your own?" Maggie asked him.

"Did Gershwin? Did Rodgers?"

"How about Porter? Berlin?"

"I don't have it. I can't even work with anyone but Charley."

"It's not too late for that. Get the right tune in his head, push him with a title. Recerebrate him. And you'll have another Double Charley."

Not that easy.

Though every morning, breaking from sleep, ideas dribbled into Rangel's head. Sometimes he got them on the pad beside his reading light. Phrases, rhythms; six bars, eight. The piano sideboard piled with note cards, ideas enough for a Ring Cycle. But songs themselves, finished songs, that was something else. He couldn't work without Schmitter. Didn't know why. After Hart's death, Rodgers found Hammerstein. Weill had Kaiser before Brecht, Anderson and a host of others after. Kern, Arlen, Youmans, almost everyone moved from lyric bed to lyric bed. Without difficulty, nostalgia, or remorse. Only he seemed yoked to one writer. "I'm just a standard thirty-two-bar hack," went his self-deprecating line. "Charley's stuff transfigures me. Without it, I'm dry gulched. No charge in the battery. Pffft."

Maggie's suggestion was, "Try a new style. It's not you that's yoked to Charley. It's your old success. You're yoked to it and call it 'Schmitter.'"

"Anyone else say that, I'd punch his nose. 'Success!' I hate those damn songs of ours. I hear one on the radio, off it goes. Antiques. Claptrap. Unbearable. But I can't feel my way into this new stuff. It sounds like recitative to me. *Sprechstimme.* And not such brilliant *Sprech* at that. As for the seventy-eight varieties of rock, they're demolition derbies for me. Lyric fission."

Not quite. Rangel was tempted again and again by the easy speech—"Nim Chimsky could sing it"—the unpushiness of the melodic line. "Into you before you know you've bitten it. But I can't feel it. Can't write it. It's not my line."

From New York, Schmitter telephoned bulletins of self-gratulation. "We're still a name at the Capers Club. Frunz" — their longtime agent who now took ten weeks to answer Rangel's letters — "overheard Steve Keith bawling out his latest jailbait the other night for not knowing who Double Charley was. Told her to listen to 'Slit Throat' if she wanted to know what a song was."

"Did he tell her he lifted six bars from 'Eat This Heart'?"

"That was flattery too, Charley, you know that." The telephone magnified Schmitter's wavery treble (a surprise for those who knew its immense source). "Did Beethoven sue Schubert for stealing from the 'Kreutzer'?"

"He was dead. Or maybe it killed him. I'da bloodied the little shit's nostrils."

"Nonsense, sweetheart. It's noblesse oblige. Keith has nothing to gain from puffing us. The point is, among cognoscenti, we *still count*."

"He's made four hundred grand from our six bars, he can afford to pamper his guilt. He probably saw Frunz lapping it up in the corner, knew it would get back to us. More points for Keith."

"Bitter, Charley, bitter."

Why not? Could he live on thirdhand compliments? Day after day, he was at the piano, music paper on the flowerless wooden trellis, notes making their way from keys to paper, where they died. In the wordless, the Schmitter-less vacuum, they died. And nothing came from New York. "It's that cretinous broad you introduced him to," he said to Maggie. "She's dried him out. He always said he couldn't work around idiots. And now he pours himself into that mental Sahara."

"She's the sign of his trouble, not the cause. Charley's not young, lambie."

"Sure he is. At ninety, he'll have more sexual charm than Paul Newman. Bulk, bad leg, bronchitis, nothing derails Charley. Age is just a rumor to him. Sickness is for other guys. Stupidity. That's what kills him. He goes home to Agnes to get Olive's stupidity washed off him. I'd finance some babe through a doctorate if she'd play with Charley. He has to have his toke of baby nooky. Look at him."

Pointing. On the wall, in a mosaic frame, was Agnes's marvelous miniature of him. Agnes painted on enamel in the manner of the Persians and Léonard Limosin. Her portrait of Charley had won a prize in Paris. Before that, Rangel had told her he couldn't live without it, and he bought it on time, two hundred dollars a month for four years. There was the great black bramble of a head, the wild mustache ambling into the regal cheeks, Schmitter's bulk jutting over the enamel curve. Beside the figure in the six square inches, a fountain frothed minuscule lilac spray in solar glitter.

That such Flemish genius flowed from the florid, muscular, eagle-browed Agnes had been an art world secret for decades. Only with the Paris exhibition in the midsixties did Agnes Schmitter become the name behind those few, tiny works of refined genius. Till then, she was only what she kept on being, Charley Schmitter's passionate, tolerant, quarrelsome, adoring, bellicose worshipper. For years, she'd shut her eyes to the passionate geniality which poured sexual charm over New York ladies.

Not that Charley ever *came on*. He was just there, waiting with a rub here, a kiss there. His parts bulged in his corduroys. Of them, and anything else that was not controlled by the power of thought, he was magnificently careless. What counted was mental power. "It's why I work with Rangel," he'd said from the beginning. "Not just that he's a top musician. He could be twice as good, and I wouldn't work with him if he were a dope."

Maggie kept telling Rangel Schmitter would revive. "One day, you'll sing him a few bars, it'll be like a quarter in the jukebox. The machinery will crank up again. Olive or no Olive."

Rangel knew it was over, but possibility nagged at him until the last day.

That occurred one month after Charley's last telephonic burst of schmoos. He'd been, he said, reading the poet Jules Laforgue, "the kid Eliot stole the line about measuring out his life with coffee spoons from. Listen to this." And the wavery voice, tinier than ever, read in what seemed to Rangel perfect French, a few difficult lines of verse.

" 'Divers Flutes!' How does that enchant you? 'Mademoiselle who might have wished to hear the wood of my diversity of flutes display themselves a bit.' Can you imagine crooning that to a hundred, a hundred million people? And that's the source of modern mentality as they see it at Cambridge and the Sorbonne. Think Stockhausen could work up a tune for that baby?

"I'm glad we never worked that side of the street. That's for No-One-Caresville. We're down where people eat, sleep, love, and die. In tune with *this* world. We didn't go diving into waterless pools."

On the way to New York for the funeral, Rangel realized that had been Charley's memorial; and—who knows?—perhaps his justification for turning off the spigot while his partner still thirsted.

Two hours before the funeral, Olive Baum called him. (Maggie had given her his number.) She wanted a favor. "Agnes wouldn't let me see him at the hospital." She was crying. "He *wanted* to see me. She *told* me. She had the nerve to tell me. He couldn't speak, could only move his eyelids; and he blinked yes when she asked him if he wanted to see me. She said she asked him twice, and he blinked yes, and she didn't tell me till he was gone. And now she won't tell me where he's being buried. You tell me, please, Charley. You know we loved each other."

"I'll get her to let me tell you, Olive."

Rangel had identified the body for Campbell's; Agnes had been too distraught. In the coffin, ready to go, Charley was de-Schmittered: powdery, Roman, the black bramble head too grand for the wispy neck and the timid blue tie someone had put on him.

The funeral day was rough with January light. An icy day. Tiny Charley sat beside Agnes in the back of the limousine. (He'd always felt smaller next to her than he did next to Charley.) Her face was full of aquiline rancor, her black hair—"I suppose she's dyed it for years"—lay heavily on her shoulders. It smelled musty, sad. The limousine went up the West Side Highway heading for Mount of Hope Cemetery. To their surprise, Charley, great scorner of death, had, for forty years, maintained a plot there.

In the mortuary city, his coffin lay on the iced earth among the small gravestones. Below were the grander slabs, one-room marble mansions. While they stood, uncertain what to do, it began to sleet. Drops pelted the coffin. "Should have brought a Bible," said Rangel. "Or an anthology." No poems came to mind. He tried to think of a line from one of their songs. Couldn't. "I guess this is it, kid," he said. "God bless you."

With the soft sleet and Agnes's tears, this was Charley's service.

Rangel put his arm around as much of her shoulders as it could reach, then wandered down the slope looking at names, some familiar. On one marble slab, he read, "Billy Rose." Across from it was a one-room temple with ugly stained glass. "Agnes," he called. "Charley's in good company."

She looked through the sleet at the little man pointing to the sarcophagus.

"It's Gershwin. Wouldn't you know? Even here, we suck hind tit."

"Make sense, Charley."

Back in the limousine, Rangel looked at the sleet changing to drizzle and fog. The countryside was muffled in rat fur, the Hudson invisible. Rangel tried to think of Charley, the amputation of Double Charley. He took Agnes's hand. "Maybe you should have let Olive see him."

"What?"

"She was just a security blanket. I know that. Still, a sad dummy. Let her go up to the cemetery."

Agnes removed her hand.

"You were the only woman who ever counted for him."

"Hah."

"You were. The only one that understood him, that he could talk with."

"A lot you know, Charley."

"I knew him forty years, Agnes. No one but you better."

"No one knew the big stiff. Everyone knew parts of him."

"It's always like that. But we knew him most and loved him most."

"That's the truth."

"I wish he could have seen that dumb broad. She must have been something for him. At least, it was the last favor he could give anyone."

Agnes, florid, haughty, looked down at him. "That's what it would have been. The great favor giver. The charm distributor. That's where his career went. Everybody got his lyrics but you, Charley."

"I got enough. But Olive could have used one more."

Agnes picked at her heavy hair. (Charley moved away. Its odor was poor.) "She had no more business there than . . . Maggie."

"Sure she did. She was Charley's. For better or worse."

"And wasn't Maggie? Didn't she head out with him too? That was no great secret in New York. Why shouldn't she and sixteen others have been in the hospital room? He'd've found hands for them all. Oh God." Past and imagined wrongs clotted with her new solitude into a terrible bolus of feeling.

While she sobbed, Charley Rangel, arms out to hold what he could of her, felt his own head cracking. So that was the story. The stinking small grain of this world.

At Ninety-sixth Street, the chauffeur made the fat turn off the Drive. Here in New York, Double Charley's last song began, the mean act of betrayal that was Charley Rangel's to set, to live with. "I'da punched his goddamn nose for him," he said. "I'd've bloodied the big bastard's nose."

IN THE DOCK

1

I've cut lots of corners. Dochel's Nail of the Month claims I do little else. Her delicate point is that I've wasted my talent.

I take indictment seriously. Oddly enough, I still want to make gold in my soul. Has tranquillity undone me? I sit on my beloved back porch watching pumpkin-colored leaves fall into the courtyard. I've got the stereo turned up: a soprano sings *"Mein Herz schwimmt im Blut"*; after that, Ella Fitzgerald will sing the Gershwins. I lie back in a lounge chair smoking a cigarillo, drinking an Alsatian white wine. Bliss. Or it should be. But I am ashamed of my tranquillity. I ache with heart cramps I am too Nietzschean to call love and pity for the vague billions who surface in the news, the insulted, the broken, the deprived, the sinking and the sunk, those exalted in the Beatitudes and damned by the Genealogist of Morals as sneaks, counterfeiters, and masqueraders in ascetic pomp.

Ella sings, "You don't know the half of it, dearie, blues." Wouldn't you know. (These leaves will probably turn out to be subpoenas.)

2

Sylvia.

Seldon Dochel, my old tennis partner, wanted me to meet his Nail of the Month. "She's one of your admirers."

"My money or my beauty?"

"She loves your editorials. All that Let's Consider crapola. She thinks you know everything."

"A woman of discernment. That's a first for you. What is she? A chemist? A VP of Ill. Bell?" Since he left his wife, partly to escape what he charmingly called her Gobi Desert loins, partly because his sick daughter's groans and glares were unbearable, Seldon has suffered— and caused his friends to suffer—his woman trouble. "So-and-so is two steps off the street. I've got to have some human response. It was like hammering a nail into the wall."

"You have no patience, Seldon. Court them a bit."

"This is the twentieth century. I don't look like you, a dog's muzzle." His long face glitters, hypomanic green eyes pop toward his glasses. "I should have the cream of the cream."

His new friend is a lawyer. "She did some work for Texas Instruments. Someone lent her an article from your rag. Despite what I told her about you, she still thinks you're the cat's meow."

Of course this was malarkey. Seldon just wanted to guarantee the worth of his acquisition.

I spend enough time with him, ninety minutes a day, six months a year, laced to his furious forehands, feeble backhands, crippled, mishit, or totally missed overheads. Except for an hour after our Sunday game, when we have juice and muffins at the Plaka, I don't see him socially. "Be glad to see her."

"Bring Emma, too."

That's another story. "She's in bad shape," I say. "She's looking for a new place, and she's just started a new course at Loyola."

"All right. Another time. It's you Sylvia's interested in."

A week later, leaning over the little table at the Café Procope, Sylvia said, "Tell me, Cy. Why have you wasted your life editing other's people's words?"

3

Seldon said, "You're going to get on with Sylvia. She's a terrific lady. Sensitive as grass. Knows what you're thinking before you do. And not trying to get her name in the *Penthouse* Forum. Nothing spectacular there, just nice old-fashioned chewing and screwing. Not like those camels I led around the Sahara. She's the reason I've been so sharp lately. The way she makes me feel I could run Borg's heinie out of Wimbledon. Not even your junk can throw me." Seldon goes mad when I dribble shots over the net, then lob over his head after he's made his tankish forward charge. I enjoy seeing him backpedal on his thick pins, windmilling wildly, the yellow ball hitting him on the head. But I have to be careful. Sometimes he'll stop in the middle of a point and glare hatred across the net at me. The big teeth clamp, the veins bulge, he may slap his forehead or his thighs. I've seen him stamp his own foot. He may say, "Your junk is killing me." He walks off the court to the black bag that contains his equipment and analgesics (antibiotic paste, tape, bandages, Valium, cans of cold pop, gut strings with tools to insert them, a carton of high-tar cigarettes). It's these last painkillers he needs. He lights up, inhales to his toes, and discharges the smoke of his hatred toward me. (He knows I hate smoke.) His innards roar. There is no restraint. The air fills with his body's foulness. His day has turned black. What is there for him? A life of abstract wheat and abstract soybeans. What's that for someone who hates the earth and its products? "I'll be death on the floor today. I won't be able to make a bid." Moan. "I can't take your junk. Your excuses. 'Oh my, the sun got in my eyes. My racket's strung too loose. The wind. The noise.' While it was *me* that passed you clean, asshole." The cigarette arcs toward my face, his head goes in his hands. Sob. "I'm sorry, Cy. I'm a bum, Cy. I wasn't raised for competition. The Skokie nerds sent me to lousy fellow-traveler camps. The only games we played were cooperative. We were taught to be afraid of winning. The only way I can beat your brains in is to think of you as IBM."

In the tranquil little Plaka, among fishnets, wreathed harpoons, blue-and-white posters of Delphi and Epidaurus, the Sunday brunchers are familiar: O'Flaherty, the aristocratic bookseller, at the *Hauptisch* with his harem; Mme. De Forsch, the optometrist's widow, waving the tips of her fingers at us; the *New York Times* readers; the weekend lovers; the policemen. Only our table blasts. "I had you in knots today, pal. Oh, you looked ugly. Where was your junk today?" (Seven tables away, I see O'Flaherty look coldly at us. Josepha, our waitress, told me he wants us seated as far from him as possible.) Or, in despair, cursing his life, his ex-wife's omnisexual flings, his daughter's degenerating nerves, the disasters of Pit and Bedroom, Seldon beats his fists on the table, spills our juice into our muffins, wipes his face with our water, belches, groans, and passes his foul wind as if he were the only sentient creature in the place. Once a cop leaned over the partition and told him where the men's room was.

Emma can't bear him. He embodies what she hates, sexual boasting, unearned authority, unstoppable egocentricity, male tyranny. I tell her he's actually the most innocent fellow alive. "Under all that noise and swinger talk, he's really sweet and courteous. He's just got to show everyone he's not the good-hearted patsy he was raised to be."

"I'm not interested. I don't like his mouth. I won't be part of his therapy. I won't meet the unfortunates he drags into the sack."

In her anger, she writes slogans in silver eyebrow pencil on the immense red heart she painted above her bed. "Dochel to the wall." "Dochel, *lupus feminorum*." "*Ecrasez* Dochel." "*Mange merde,* Seldon D." "Dochel *delenda est*."

At the Café Procope, Sylvia, a fierce, heavy-shouldered, sportive, brilliant-eyed woman, informed me very quickly that my life was a series of evasions. Smiling, she took her sport assessing—i.e., damning—my life. Sloth, it seems, was the heart of my character. I, who'd hung from deadlines since I was twenty, should have thrown such facts—and a left hook—into her face. Didn't. (Not immediately. Not exactly.) She told me, "Your work's a form of sloth." As was fatherhood. "You've made a second noncareer of that." We were at my old table, a dozen yards away from where I used to sleep, eat, and work. "Why have you spent all these years doing what someone with half your brains could do as well?" What a question from anyone, let alone someone I'd never laid eyes on half an hour before.

I tried to defend myself. "I can't be wrong about everything." To that her response was, "Wrong again, Cy."

4

I was halfway through a bottle of house Chablis when Seldon and Sylvia showed up under the blue awning. He was decked out, admiral of the civilian fleet, in a volcanic blue blazer and Gatsby flannels. Beside him, shoulder to shoulder, was this powerful, smiling woman in a frothy, lemon-bright dress. In the queer end of daylight, she seemed lit up, bright blue eyes, bright cheeks, bright — Seldon-size — teeth. A merry lady, I thought as they walked over.

Dochel did not so much introduce us as point out two well-known Dochel landmarks to each other: "Cy, Sylvia." As if our names marked divisions of his life — his bed and battlefield — and it was now time in the Dochel Scheme of Things that we be aware of each other.

Sylvia and I shook hands. At least, she picked my hand up, gave it a couple of probative strokes, and let it go. I was already judged. I said it was nice to see her. She said social formula didn't interest her, she did not think of herself as a scenic attraction, I'd better wait before I decided anything was nice or not nice. "A pettifogging word anyway." That took care of "nice." I let this rearrange my notion of what the evening would be like. She gripped the neck of the Chablis. "They shouldn't be allowed to call it Chablis. They can't tell a Chardonnay grape from a Muscat in the Napa Valley." I said I couldn't either, perhaps I shouldn't enjoy the wine as much as I did. She tipped the bottle over the glass pear on our table and doused the small flame coming from the red candle within. "I can't bear coziness." Then, as if to show she could give as well as take away: "Enjoy what you enjoy." I resisted thanking her; after all, I was here to please Seldon. I said, "There's still daylight. I don't know why they light them. Let me get better wine for us. They have decent Italian stuff. Bardolino, Verdicchio, Orvieto."

"I'm here to meet you," said Sylvia. "I don't care what I drink. As long as it doesn't fog my perceptions."

"They haven't fermented dynamite yet," said Seldon.

I laughed, but that was as much a mistake as the small pleasantry. Sylvia registered both by temperature only, five quick degrees of frost in the area between eyebrows and lower lip. She poured what was left of the bottle into our glasses, her own last, and said, "All right, let's get to know each other. Seldon told me you live ascetically. You don't dress like a monk."

I had on my summer outfit, blue pants, seersucker jacket from Field's basement, blue shirt, paler blue tie. "Thank you, I guess. I thought Seldon thought of me only as a backstop for his forehands." This advanced the conversion of Seldon from producer of the show to third-personned scenery. Why not? He deserved it. He'd loaded this cannon, and he was still all grin, Teddy Roosevelt teeth thrust over the table. "I've done my job," said the teeth.

At this point—nine o'clock—the baldies who supply the Procope's music struck up with "Amapola, my pretty little poppy . . ." They usually plucked their way through the tunes of the twenties, thirties, and forties, then worked up or down to the owner Sonny's favorite Puccinis and Donizettis. "Did Seldon tell you I used to live here, Sylvia?"

"Seldon's a mine of trivia." This with an imperial smile, one emperor to another, right past the ears of the described serf: what could such lowlife make of high wit, the judgment of people who knew the world? Sylvia had sensed my opposition—and my resentment—and that made us equals.

Of course it was she I resented. On sight. My *Weltanschauung,* my *Menschanschauung,* did not tolerate such shoulders in women, such arms, such power. Even as I admired the big smile, the handsome eyes, the jolly cannon of a nose, something else worked in me. Desire and resentment fused. I admired the eyes, but felt an excess in their lucidity, felt her will stoking the brightness.

Did she sniff my resentment? Yes, probably. She'd spent her life sniffing male resentment. So I rationalized for her even as I steamed.

She'd turned around, *swiveled,* and there was her rather beautiful neck under the expensive irregular cut of her hair. That too was interesting. The color, ratty brown, but worked by subtle oils till it glistened. And that neck, strong and long but somehow fragile like a souvenir of her gender. I've never socialized with women who head states or corporations, but about those I read or see on television, I have similar feelings, the subtle, imperial, but confused charmers like Mrs. Gandhi, the fluent, frizzy dominatrices of state like Mrs. Thatcher, Betty Boop flirts and scowlers like our own Jane Byrne. Celebrity augments desire. We know celebrated women so well, we have to force ourselves to remember they don't know us. Of course, my lines are drawn: Mother Teresa doesn't rouse me; nor did Eleanor Roosevelt. And physically I draw the line at those rolling-flab fatties Fellini and other Italian directors—it must be southern notions of abundance—use as sexual initiations. No, I'm roused by powerful women like Sylvia, challenged by their—to me—ambiguous anomaly: the fact their bodies don't exist to satisfy mine but—like mine—to satisfy themselves. Face-to-face—face to body—with a Sylvia, my rational, tolerant, ERA-supporting crust disintegrates.

What Sylvia was doing was giving the place the once-over: drain spouts, waiters, lyre-backed chairs; kumquat-colored tables; the royal-blue awning with the loopy script—*Café Procope*—the cedar tubs which the owner's father, my old neighbor Guido, had filled with roses and which now held hardier, brassier-looking, questionably organic shrubs; the waiters in their dollar-colored cummerbunds; the strumming baldies; even the blacktop roof outside my old windows. (Those days I climbed out every evening for a drink at the very table we sat at now, keeping an eye out for the occasional drunk wandering off the café side of the terrace toward my open window—"Men's room's that-away, buddy.") As she swiveled back to us, she said, "I spot eight code violations just from here."

"I'm sure Sonny pays off plenty," said I. "He's made a fine place, though, don't you think?" I went on as her lips opened for "No." "In time, they won't dare make trouble for him. There are a couple of aldermen here right now." Like most Chicagoans, I'm insouciant about the ubiquitous payoffs which oil city life, proud as the next noninsider about the city's reputation: frauds, clout, Rat-a-tat-tat, Fast Eddies, Bathhouse Johns, Needlenose Labriolas, Don't-Make-No-Waves. Chicago's the country's real Disneyland, Oberammergau with real nails. For us, California's just Polynesia on wheels, and the Sun Belt won't hold up anyone's pants. Since Mrs. O'Leary, our writers have been feeding this guff to the world, and to us. Even the best Chicago politician knows he doesn't have a chance here unless he at least pretends to know this old score, winking and smiling, even if he never dreamed of taking an illicit nickel. "There are probably several people here who won't be troubled by checks. In fact, I used to be on that kind of take myself. At least, I had house rates on food and drink. Sonny wanted happy neighbors. He's a good fellow. Though I preferred his father, Guido. He had his barbershop downstairs where the restaurant is. Up here on the roof, he raised roses. Not easy. Imagine what it was like, six months a year, to walk out my window in the middle of Chicago and see a terrace full or roses."

"Yes, yes, very—"

I rolled on: the more from me, the less from her. And those roses were marvelous. "Pure contradictions," I told Guido, out of my beloved Rilke's epitaph. "Strip their petals to discover their heart, and they disappear." Guido may not have appreciated this, but he appreciated my appreciation of his flowers. We sniffed, caressed, admired those beautiful secretive cupfuls of gold and ivory, scarlet and pink. The day after Richard Nixon pulled his festered self out of the American hide, old Guido—a Nixon diehard—fell dead out here. I picked him out of his compost heap. (Winey pomace, fish scraps, and God knows what, I can smell it now.)

"We may see Sonny tonight. I'll introduce you."

"Don't b—"

"Little dark guy, with *eyebrows*. Looks like a pasha. In his way, he's a scholar too. Named this place after the first coffeehouse in Paris. Run by a Sicilian named Procopio. He also told me that Michelet, the historian—"

"I know Michelet. You don't—"

"—said coffee was behind the French Revolution. I suppose he meant it roused the wine-soaked brains of the *lumières*. As good as any—"

"As bad as any. Totally moronic. I hope the man's reputation rests on something better than that." I couldn't keep it up. Sylvia would eventually break through. And I was worn out. I'm a listener, not a talker. My guide, the great Genealogist of Morals, thought women used weakness, invented weakness, to excuse themselves from life. *Erfinderisch in Schwächen*—inventive in weakness—was his phrase. He didn't know women like Sylvia; his Cosima Wagner and Frau Lou were pussycats.

"I told you I was here to understand you, not revolutions, not cafés, not local hoodlums and fifth-rate Frenchmen. Not Chicago, about which I know sixty times more than you, Cy. I don't work shut up in

a room. I'm in the courts, thirty hours a week, and cleaning legal latrines the rest of the time. You can't bullshit me." She propped elbows
on the table, rested her manly chin on raised palms, and tried to hook
my eyes with hers. I was in the witness box. "I want to understand you.
Cy, the editor. Cy, the poppa. Cy, the lover. Cy, the smart guy who
holes up in his nowheres turning out a very fine *News-Letter* read by—
what?—eleven hundred souls?"

"Thirty-eight hundred," said I. "Sylvia, don't waste analysis on me.
There's not enough to understand. I wish there were."

"That's point one, Cy. I don't think you do."

"I don't get that. Why shouldn't I?"

"That's what I want to know. My suspicion is when a man buries
his talent, he's afraid of it. Or he's hiding from something outside."

"Maybe so, Sylvia. I'm not introspective. Still, I think I'm far more
ordinary than you suspect. Maybe that's what I'm hiding. All right,
maybe I'm an ordinary intellectual. But that's it."

"I don't believe in the ordinary. I spend my life quizzing supposedly ordinary people, jurors, witnesses, clients. Not one of them is ordinary. So how could someone like you be? You digest difficult advanced
research, you make sense of it, you write it up for laymen. You run on
a double track, scientific and literary. That itself is extraordinary."

The words were sympathetic, the tone harsh. Like those blue eyes,
fine, but overly keen, impatient, full of thrust and hunger. The nostrils,
too, looked hungry. Air wasn't enough for them. They weren't simple
conduits, but portals beyond which waited an avaricious, maybe even
a desperate, intelligence. I felt my heart knocking. "You're *making* me
seem extraordinary. What I do is simple. I get contributors to spell out
research so I can understand it. Then I put down more or less what
they say. I'm not a scientist, I'm hardly a writer. At best, I'm a steward
of talent. A warder of my sty. I'm not even getting any better at it.
You'd think I'd get more sophisticated, be able to take more shortcuts,
but I don't."

Sylvia seemed absorbed by this. I couldn't tell if it was genuine absorption or courtroom practice. In court, nothing was incidental,
everything was part of the battle. "Perhaps it's time for you to do something else with your life. I think you're wasting your talent. You're
doing what you're doing because of inertia. Or sloth. And for peanuts.

Is your name in the papers? Never. I have to ask myself what's going on. What's with Cy Riemer?"

"You're a quick study, Sylvia."

"That's my job."

Tusks of smoke grew from Dochel's nose over the table. I looked his way. "She's got your number, Cy. No wool over these baby blues." Reaching over.

The baby blues shot him a look that stopped that. "I'm not after Cy's number. I'm interested in him as a human situation. You brought me here to meet him. I assume that didn't mean seeing what color his eyes were."

"Forgive, forgive. I'm just enjoying."

"Enjoy," said Sylvia again, but as if it were "Die."

I was finishing the second bottle of Chablis. (There were no other marines on the beach.)

"I know you have a whole raft of children."

"Only four," I said. "One for each bedpost."

"What's that mean?" Her head on its fine ivory neck base looked Roman to me now, Caracalla's, Caligula's. The ratty, lucent bangs parted in opposite directions on the forehead. I also noticed a crimson wart on the left flange of her nose. Had the interrogative steam worn down her makeup?

"I suppose I mean the four supports of my life. Like 'Matthew, Mark, Luke, and John, Bless the bed I lie upon.'" The sun said good-bye now, plunging behind the six-flats. Little plugs of gold pinged against the glasses and ice buckets. One lit Sylvia's wart. "Does that make sense?"

"Everything makes sense. If you spend time making sense of it. Very interesting sense. I gather your children are more important to you than—I can't remember the name of your young companion."

"Emma," said Seldon.

"I wouldn't say that," I said. "I don't think of affection as a pie to be sliced."

"I'm sure you have more of it than most." The tone suggested I had little or none. "Seldon tells me you hold her hand, cook her supper, bind her wounds, wipe her ass."

Seldon added his ha-ha to this jewel. I said, "I inflict more wounds than I bind. I wonder what I've told you, Seldon. I'm ashamed Sylvia has this view of me."

Dochel made it's-not-my-doing gestures.

"Nothing to do with Seldon. I'm testing the perimeter. I could guess you'd have a mutual-tyranny arrangement with a woman. To reinforce your retreat from life. These relationships are never one way. The weak party offers weakness, the strong strength. Both equally useful."

"You know lots about relationships, Sylvia."

"Not personally, no."

This got me a bit and softened what I said. "You're probably right, there's some soft mutual tyranny in most relationships. But Emma and I are more a Mutual Aid Society. You can call it love, if you need a name."

"The most useless word in the dictionary. You love Chablis, Seldon loves tennis. The question is, Are you doing each other any good or just sustaining each other's weakness? Are you being held back from something better? Most relationships are just excuses for not getting to the depths. Love, as you call it, work, fatherhood. They can all be forms of sloth. Doing violence to your nature. What do you think, Seldon?"

She would have asked the table if Seldon hadn't been there. It was a cushion shot, that's all. The destination was me. Well, it couldn't last forever. In an hour, I'd be with Emma. She'd have saved up jokes from Johnny Carson to tell me, she'd hear my report on Seldon's latest debacle.

Seldon said, "Cy's basically an artist. A bohemian. He likes all this." He waved at the rooftops, the candlelit tables—only ours dark—the light-popped darkness of Old Town. "Shabby cuteness. That's Cy's world. He's a little enclave of high thinking. Not your average fifty-year-old failure. And the little Mimi who warms her hand at his candle is lucky."

I said, "Thank you, Seldon. That wraps me up now."

"Oh no," said Sylvia. She pointed the waiter to our empty bottle. "We're not at the end of the rainbow yet." She was merry; a Cossack merriment.

I tried to look at us from outside. From the street. Here we were, a jolly corner of a jolly constellation of tinkle and glitter. What did it matter in the grand scheme of the night what Sylvia said or didn't? "Come on, Sylvia. What the hell. What about you? Husbands? Children? What's your story?"

She raised her left hand my way. The fingers were oddly fine, long and soft, strangely beautiful at the end of her big forearm. "No ring, Cy. So no children."

"There can always be a slipup. Many of us started as amorous leaks."

"Very pretty. But I'm a careful person. Not a hole-in-the-corner philoprogenitor like you."

Below, the streetlamps popped on, the lit iron musketry of the night. I loved that moment. Usually. I tried to hold it, to keep down what was rising. "I'm sure I did like the progening. And you're right, it wasn't done in public. And the progeny, I love them too. Most of the time."

"You're a lucky man. Maybe I was wrong about you. You've worked out your life. I've certainly met richer and more influential people less satisfied with themselves." I let this go. "Still, the big question is there." And here she put her unringed fingers on mine. I forced down the shock. (Fury? Excitement?) "Why does a gifted man confine himself to the narrowest possibilities of his talent?"

What a question. From anyone, anytime. The fingers were actually holding mine down now. She must have felt the agitation. I could see a sort of rosy triumph in her face. I pulled them away. My heart was in my throat, I was dizzy, I could feel pressure in my chest, my arms. "You know, Seldon. You're my pal. I've seen you taking lots of punishment for years. It's pained me. Though I know you require a certain amount of suffering. But do you need this much? I mean what are you going to get out of this lady? If America were between her legs, Columbus would have turned around." I put my palm over Sylvia's opening mouth. "This is a *mouth*." I took it away as her teeth came down. "It's going to tear you apart, Seldon. It's going to bite and swallow what it wants and spit the rest of you into the street." I managed to get my wallet out, found a twenty-dollar bill, and laid it on the table. "For your services, lady. If anyone pays you a nickel more than that for anything, he's out of his mind."

Confrontation is not—as they now say—my number. When I see it coming, I head for the alleys that lead away from it. As for the wildness of others, I usually swallow it. Why not? Even at Sylvia, I'd only half blown my stack.

Still, half of it had blown, and I remember how infuriated I thought the scarlet fleurs-de-lis looked on the tiles of the café floor. Before I knew it, I strutted the almost unstruttable ten asphalt feet to my old window. I bent to climb through, puzzled at its being closed. In the window, I saw white eyeballs in a black man's face. "Oh, Lord," I called through the glass, thinking even then, I remember, the man would hear, "Oh, Lawdy," and think I was mocking him. It was like one of those Stepin Fetchit movies of the thirties. (Was everything I did tonight a fall into an abandoned tense?) I made excuse-me motions, right hand cupped to heart, left one to the sky, eyes lifted in puzzlement. As I did, there was laughter. Not from the frightened tenant of my old quarters. From the terrace.

It was then I blew. I felt the way lit phosphorus might feel, rage and humiliation burning. I had to walk past those laughers, past Seldon and Sylvia, whom I would not look at, only sensed as I went by them. I don't believe they were laughing, I had done them to a turn. Nor did I look at the guzzling, crowing, ignorant preeners to whom I'd given a little comic moment. What else did they have but vacancy and zero, waiting for someone like me to occupy them, give them point? Zeros waiting to unegg themselves into sheer holes. Only their arrogant shells made them think themselves substantial, shells without even the mineral consistency and tenacity of functional shells. The little bald guitarist and the skinny bald bass player plucked away, sweating in the moonlight. I remember thinking, At least they sweat, they keep time, they know how to read little squiggles on a page; not total nothings. Though what was the point of their old Italian plucks? To let these guzzling zeros hear each other confess their *Zeroheit*. Better the frozen gases in a trillion miles of dark. At least out there there was no pretense. Gas, ice, mad wind, dark. The whole universe, a cough of dark.

That's more or less how I felt as I made my way past the tables, under the awning, down the stairs, round the lit corner to the parking lot, and into my old Malibu.

Sylvia had struck where it hurt. Even so, I might have swallowed it, if she'd not talked about Emma. Loyal, generous, darling Emma. The other side of the sexual moon. I was on the Outer Drive now, heading south, home, or not home, to Emma's. Out over the lake, out of the fumes of city light blurring the sharpness of the stars. That's what I should concentrate on. And the glistening, bronze cylinder of Lake Point Tower. And the bridge over the light-encrusted shaft of the river banked with mystic glass and steel, the murderous S-curve, and then straight south toward the imperial, deceptive—two-dimensional till you were within yards of them—columns of the Field Museum.

Emma was asleep under the silvery slogan she'd looped on the red walls (painted over the cream base into the shape of a great-valved heart or grand, tiny-cracked buttocks): KONG LOVES FAY. Her nightgown twisted about her waist, her mouth was giving out some sleepish Esperanto. I lay naked beside her, home, and happy there in the familiar sleep heat, the familiar fragrance—lavender and mint. My body touched the twin interrogations and gave them the male salute. There was a squirm of welcome from the faraway dream country. I slid off, the lieutenant still saluting, though now, in confused loyalty, it was saluting another body, the powerful, Seldon-occupied, Sieglinde Fortress that was Sylvia.

SYLVAN AND AGNES

1

Sylvan Harmel's problems were "uff course," said his analyst, "uff a piece. You are not a multiple perzonality, Zylfan. You luff on zuh run like you write your zcenarios, flying avay from yourself. Haf you read Kafka? He vas zuh same. Found all his vimmen—*kak smentnyl gnekh*"—*ugly as sin,* but Dr. Kharki often didn't bother translating—"avay from Prague. On facation."

"Not entirely like me," said Sylvan. "I had girls in Hollywood."

"Not zose you vould bring home."

"I brought Agnes to L.A."

"You met her in New York. She came to L.A. on her own."

"Yes and no."

"Iss zat luff?"

Sylvan Harmel wouldn't say that, but Agnes was the first girl who'd stirred something other than a gut grip in him since Heike and Isabelle.

Dr. Kharki laid out Sylvan's withered feelings in the analytic sun like strips of pemmican. "The idea iss to dizinter your incapazity. Uzzervise, *khot v grob lozhis;* nozzing to do but *lie down and die.*" Pompadoured, thick glassed, tiny head crooked over his paunch in a Rushmore illusion, the quasi dwarf Kharki gestured, strutted, and talked as if he were a giant. He basso profundoed, "Feelings. You confuze zuh dry rifferbed wiz zuh glacier. Any day, any veek, a year tops, two, tree,

it will thaw and flood you. Owerflow." A pinstriped stump, the gold-
en Rolex cozy in wrist hair, rose in blessing over the melting glacier.
"Zuperflux. From every plugged schtream."

There by the buffet table in his brother Sam's Columbus Avenue
duplex stood a Truffaut girl, short-haired, a laughing, toothy face,
gaminlike but harder than the Jean Seberg of *Breathless*. ("More
stunned than stunning," Sylvan told Kharki.)

"I'm Sylvan."

"You look urban."

She could have been twenty-five or thirty-five, a face and body—
lean, muscled arms and legs out of dickie and skirt—that had done
and felt plenty. He liked to think he looked the same without being the
forty he'd just turned. A log Kharki couldn't unjam.

In fact, two months ago, Sylvan had quit him. Kharki had taken his
annual weeks in the Caribbean. Sylvan dulled the agony by going off
to Zihuatanejo, first time in Central America since Costa Rica with
Heike and Isabelle. There, parasailing over the Ixtapa beach, he looked
down over the tanning vacationers and saw *forty* glittering like barbed
wire on the waste of his life. "What good has it all done me?" The "it"
was the years of analysis. He phoned Oscar, the brother who'd also
spent decades and a fortune in analysis. "I'm quitting. I can't take it."

"You'll sink."

"No, I'll soar. I've been in the air." He told him about the fear and
then the joy of looking down at the diminished bodies, the blank of
ocean.

"You can't live up zere." Oscar, analyzing Sylvan, took on the accent of his shrink. (About Sylvan's, he was of two minds. He called him
Car Key.)

"Forty years of muck."

"Sirty-nine. You can turn life around in a month. A minute."

"We've been turning on that spit a quarter of a century."

"And functioning. Working. Grooving. The groove ain't supposed
to be smooz. So vork ain't first rate. Ve're both better."

"Yeah, you could be me."

"See. Don't quit. Car Key's getting you over the worst of it. You're
low because he's off."

"No. I'm high. Or was."

2

In L.A., he showed Agnes his mother's dollhouse. Like everyone who saw it for the first time, she gushed at the almost comical beauty, the astonishing carving, the delicate strength of the chairs and divans, the inlaid desks and tables, the inch-wide Tiffany lamps, the miniature Miros and Bonnards (painted by the painters for the house). His mother's odd, stunted genius. Unlike many gawkers, Agnes had no desire to move in. "I've had enough shrinking."

"I've lived in it half my life."

Agnes was a hiker, climber, swimmer, rider, anything that engaged tenacity, strength, physical inventiveness. Which had included, that first hour in Sylvan's room upstairs in Sam's apartment, a fantastic BJ. Sylvan put his hands on her shoulders. She looked up, held his muddled eyes with her own, and, with the fingers which had gripped half-inch ledges in a rock wall, undid his belt. Sinking, she pulled down his shorts and took him to her astonishing tongue. Sylvan looked down at the short-haired, boyish head bobbing away, trying to connect himself to it. "Do you—huff—take this—Jesus—on—tour?"

Industriously, she extracted the goods, then frothily looked up, removed the handkerchief from his fallen pants and wiped off, a neat priest, and said, "I better get things straight. You know who I sleep with?"

"Not with me?"

"Probably, but I make it best with girls."

"That's exciting. For me."

"We'll see about that."

"This is extra duty? Special service?"

"No, pleasure. I like being fucked too, but it's right only with girls. Did you notice the little blond downstairs? Like Madonna without the fishhook nose? That's my friend."

"Yes?"

"Or was. I don't know where I am with her now."

Dressed, weary, he was readjusted. "You're the first good person I've met in New York. Where do you connect?"

"In Manhattan? It wouldn't even be a problem in Noburg, Ohio."

"You say." Sylvan's New York was dark, Hollywood even darker.

The ocean of beauties didn't break on his shore. "I don't see anyone. My eyes are inside, looking at my troubles. All that fucking sun lying to us everyday. I can't face it."

"I'm going out there."

"Why?"

"Fellowship. Girlship. UCLA. Romance languages."

"Stay in New York. At least the sun's reticent."

"No. I'm going in August."

3

That was eighteen months ago. Sylvan was back on Dr. Kharki's couch. Agnes was feminist criticizing the *Romaunt de la Rose* and choking on the "commodification of phalligocentric hegemonization" in the *Curé de Tours*. Once a month, they hauled each other's ashes, talked about each other's lives. "What's the lesbian scene here?"

"Nonstop. How's the movie business?"

"Red lights, all the way."

Sylvan actually had a couple of projects he wanted to work on. Agnes was indirectly responsible for one of them. Leet de Loor, whom she'd met at the UCLA library, had invited her to the publication party for Spear's book on the old director Ezra Keneret, and she'd invited Sylvan, who'd known Keneret and Spear all his life. "Odd to go in this back way," he said. "I like it." His father, their friend, was not there. Other than an occasional funeral, the only commemorations he went to were for himself.

It was there that Sylvan got the idea of doing a documentary on Keneret's forty years in Hollywood. He liked Keneret's films more than his father's. "They're about us," he told Agnes. "He's made millions turning us, his kids, into grotesques." ("What about the ones I made before you were born," his father asked.) "Not that he means to," he told Agnes. "Fires don't mean to burn houses." A documentary devoted to Keneret's subtle, exquisite films, made about real subjects out there, and about Keneret's modesty and tenacity would be, Sylvan sensed, the expression for his own gift. Kharki said, "A perfect vay out for you. Do zis, and uzzer zings vill follow. Zis iss zuh cork in zuh bottle."

And sure enough, Sylvan had another flash. It was the thirtieth anniversary of the Kennedy assassination, and he watched six or seven television programs and read God knows how many thousands of words about the president, his assassin, his assassin's assassin, and every Tom, Dick, and Harry who touched their lives for as much as five minutes. One of Kennedy's sisters had read aloud an essay the president had written—as a boy at Choate—about the difference between boys growing up rich and others poor. "As if he'd conjured up Oswald. His Other." The idea was to do a diptych about the two bright loners who fled—one from sickness, the other from neglect—to books and dreams. Sylvan saw them as creatures of ambitious, injured mothers, absent or too-present fathers. Both had had peculiar failures and triumphs in the military: Kennedy in the navy was a goof-off, a stogie-smoking second-in-command who redeemed a mistake with heroism; Oswald, a sharpshooting marine full of fury and Marxist slogans who'd used his marine experience to get into the Soviet Union. Both had been intimidated by older brothers, both married beautiful women who saw in them a route to better lives, both hungered for fame, distinction, eminence; and both got it. "They're the iceberg and the *Titanic*," Sylvan told Agnes. "Destined to meet as surely as falling apples and the earth."

Kharki worried about this project. "*Knashe v grob Kladut. Like death varmed ofer.* Esk yourself who is it you're trying to kill? I don't like your spending so much time on a fruitcake. *Vy redeem dreck?* Diptych! For zat, you need heroes, saints."

"Michelangelo shouldn't have painted devils?"

"Now he compares himself wiz Michelangelo! From dreck to genius. No stops between. *Rahdi bawga, for Gawd's sake.* I don't call zis healt, Zylvan. Do zuh Keneret film. Zen ve'll see."

Maybe what he should do was work up the Heike/Isabelle material. The rain forest and the beach. The excess of life and the ocean-beaten sand. The third world, a country of the poor using its difficulties—untillable mountains and beaches and people willing to work for nothing—as bait for the rich. All this the setting for his coming to some sort of terms with himself.

A dozen years ago, he was already twenty-eight. "You are a zlow starter, Zylfan." For six months, he'd been living with—"What a way of putting it, Dr. K."—Jeanne Buchanan, whom he'd known from preschool at Sunrise Academy through Brentwood High and then here and there around town as she became a top agent. Usually the only black girl in class—her *café leche* skin lighter than half the Caucasians'—she had cachet. At Brentwood, she was class president, Most Likely to Succeed, the Person to Be with on a Desert Island. Till adolescence, she'd been adorable. Growing, she didn't stop. At graduation she towered over and outweighed most of the boys. Still, she was a mix of self-deprecation and steely don't-cross-the-line. It wasn't till he lived with her that Sylvan saw what that had cost her.

"I can't decide," he'd told Kharki, "if she picked me to get to my father or because I was a loser."

"*Khot v grob lozhis.* Berhauss becauss you are able to say dot. She vants both ends of the schtick."

To his own surprise, Sylvan defended her. "She's been shoved around more than you think."

"Poor zing, but she iss not my patient."

Smart, lazy, ravenous, charming, lusty, frantically ambitious, Jeanne took up more and more space and air, raked him more and more over the coals. Even punched him out. One day he came home and found his stuff in two laundry bags at the door. His key no longer fit the lock. When he rang the bell, Jeanne appeared, a storm.

"I've had it to here, asshole. You've never done anything. You never will. You're a sniveling parasite. Take off." The door slammed. He picked up the laundry bags, walked the driveway to his Honda, turned on the motor, and thought, If it were in a garage, I'd let it run. The radio was on, rockers going mad. Then, in some temporal hole, the pressure dropped. "My God, free. I'm free." His fingers felt the scallops of the wheel; his wrists flexed; the cuffs were off. He breathed air to his toes and drove to Oscar's.

"Amazing. I was just thinking of you. Thought you could use my ticket." Oscar was due to go off in a day to Costa Rica. "Manges called me for *Billy's Trick.* What's with the laundry bags?"

Oscar was confessor, older brother, loyal buddy. He gave Sylvan sympathy, his ticket, his traveler's checks, and said, "Call if you need more, kid. Have yourself a real time. Wipe the bitch out. Car Key too."

4

In the aerial tram which glided through and over the canopy of the rain forest within the green density of the jungle, Sylvan sat next to a lovely German woman. They drew closer, humble yet regal voyeurs. Slowly, stilly, they glided between palms and cashews, silk cotton-woods and orange-blossoming almendrons. Bromeliads stuck out their huge black-spotted leaves, epiphytes draped and bunched in the trees. Animals and vegetables sucked and strained, absorbed and breathed what maintained and grew them. Excreting, dying, they became each other, epiphytes, parasites, symbiotes. The six passengers of the tram car listened to the forest: clicking beetles, barking frogs, cawing potoos, howling monkeys, the buzz and sizzle of insects. Fabia, the smiling, three-fingered biologist guide, pointed with her deprived hand, "See, on that bromeliad, an anole lizard, eating a mantis." Spiders greened on green petals, frogs exposed glassy bellies through which they saw their ugly guts.

"So crowded," said his seatmate.

Sylvan moved, but the woman meant the jungle.

"Yes. All varieties of a few forms."

"God found the right ones."

Lovely, thought Sylvan. They were in a system of vines, a huge tangle. How could anything count here? Or, for that matter, anywhere? Only the whole counted. One dies, another sprouts. Yet in the little metal car beside the German girl, he felt it was being staged for him.

Rain.

"It is the rain forest," said Fabia. She handed them yellow ponchos. The German girl put a golden umbrella over Sylvan's head and her own. He felt the heat of her flank, legs, head.

"I'm Heike."

"Sylvan."

At the center, they drank Imperiale beers. Said Heike, "Come to Jaco Beach. There's room in the *cabina*. Fery cheap. Twenty-one dollars a week. Three ways, seven dollars."

The third seven dollars was Isabelle's, who'd traveled with Heike since they'd quit jobs as programmers in Stuttgart. "We had love troubles at the same time. Two weeks later, we are in Athens. One month, then Cairo, two months, then Dubai. Not good, we take boat to Bombay, three months Madras, Hyderabad, Calcutta, Srinigar, Yangon. Cheap, not good. Singapore, Sydney, Fiji, Moorea. Now Costa Rica, Jaco Beach. You will lofe it, Sylfan."

Isabelle was blond, pretty, friendly, thirty. The *cabina,* twenty yards from the beach, was one large room with one double and one single bed. Heike and Isabelle undressed in front of him. He managed to look as if he were unaffected by such breasts and butts but felt as transparent as the frog as he concealed his distended shorts.

What did they want?

"To be friends. No hung-ups."

Like them, he'd had the erotic door slammed in his face. He held back, so did they.

At beach or disco, men surrounded them. One night tanked on tequila, the three of them embraced, kissed, stroked, and tumbled. They woke in the big bed.

"Nothing is changed," said Heike.

"We're protected," said Isabelle.

"From everything?"

"Oh, Sylfan, are you sick?"

"I wasn't."

"No fear then."

"We've had too much fear."

For the next two weeks, Sylvan climbed erotic Himalayas. Then a fourth person showed up in the *cabina,* a bearded biker. The erotic quadrangle opened for a minute, then crashed. "Not for me," said Sylvan.

The next day he was back in San Jose, the day after, in Brentwood.

5

Agnes knew she'd not be where she was now if it hadn't been for Sylvan. Sylvan's father, brothers, and friends were in the business. They talked it, did it, dreamed it. What they did outside film was drawn into it.

Everything was material. While Sylvan fucked her, she could feel him thinking, How am I going to use this girl-boy with her Romance languages, Dakota hickishness, lesbian horniness? Agnes watched his black, distant eyes watch hers watching him. It diverted her, at least briefly, to his ever-ready cock.

She took down the photographs Scotch taped to her walls, Jodie Foster, Ellen Barkin, Kinski, Harlow, the Crawfords (Joan and Cindy), Holly Hunter. "I can't have changed course. I'd still die for a night with Jodie."

In her first L.A. days, she found herself in the stacks picking up not Leopardi monographs but books on film. Even when she read French or Italian, she thought, What a film this would make. She read a Verga story, "Rosso Malpelo," about a stupid miner who was called Animal by the other miners. "They think I'm a brute," said Rosso. "I'll be one; and the worst I can be." He meets an even worse wretch whom the others call Frog. Rosso teaches him to be unafraid of the bats which fly around the mine. "They're only rats with wings. They love it underground and so should you." Frog dies and Rosso disappears in the mine, leaving behind the memory of his brutishness.

Agnes walked the sculpture garden thinking about the story. They think I'm a brute. I'll be one, the worst I can be. "I am Agnes, that's all I can be." Till now, she'd been a daughter, a fellowship getter, a lesbian. These fit, then didn't. Walking among the bronze shapes, Agnes conjured up Rosso Malpelo, black hair close to his creviced forehead, neckless, thick handed, filthy, lying on the floor in the dark while billions of stars gleamed above. If she had a few thousand dollars and a camera! There were a hundred thousand Rossos in L.A., millions in the world. A film would be their poem.

She told Sylvan, "I should be doing Montale and Dante. I spent thirty-four dollars for Singleton's edition of the *Paradiso* and haven't opened it. I'm not thinking of my dissertation. I'm only thinking about movies."

"It's good you take an interest in my work."

"It's more than that."

"I'm interested in your work too."

"This is different. A turning point. I want to make a film."

"That's the most frequently said sentence in Southern California."

"So?"

"After the sentence is when it gets hard."

"I know hard."

Sylvan looked at her looking at him. "Yes, you do. So now where are we?"

"Close to the beginning," she said.

"The beginning," he said. "Yes. A good word. Why not? Once again."

WOOL

"The last person I'd have guessed," said Keneret, "after you anyway."
Marcia had just read him the story in the *L.A. Times.*

Character reading was part of Keneret's confidence as man and
filmmaker. He'd spent forty-odd years around actors skilled at appearing what they weren't and felt that he was seldom fooled by people, though the feeling was undercut by habitual skepticism: everybody's
fooled, especially those who think they're not. Eyes, gestures, the way
people held their heads and looked at, under, through, and away from
you, clothes, cars, furniture, handwriting, voices—all part of Keneret's
professional life. In his amateur life, what it came down to was who'd
come through for you, who'd break down, when and how, who was
decent and how deep did the decency go; what was the sellout price,
who sold out from love of selling, who from cowardice.

Which didn't mean that Keneret wasn't frequently surprised by
people. Surprise was an ingredient of films and life. In films, though,
at least in Keneret's, surprise was grounded in character.

Zack Wool surprised him. After the arrest, Keneret went back to
what he knew of the man and tried to spot what made sense of the
senseless thing Wool had done.

One difficulty he had was his incapacity for numbers. For Wool,
numbers were crucial. For Keneret, numbers were an injection of
Novocain. He didn't get what they were getting at; and he was afraid
of them. When cameramen talked about f-numbers or the ones on
their scopes, Keneret's mind shut down.

Dealing with moneymen, oddly enough, was easy for him. He felt almost savage exhilaration in dollars and cents, though even here, he relied on his sense of character to find trustworthy partners, backers, accountants, and cost assessors.

None was more trustworthy than Zack Wool, who had done his taxes for twenty-seven years—since his divorce from Elizabeth. (A number whiz—was this part of what divided them?—she'd done them till then.) Zack was conservative to the point of mania, that is to the point of costing Keneret small fortunes. When he griped about it to Marcia, she'd said, "It buys you sleep."

"There are lots of nights I worry what he's cost me."

"You aren't worrying in San Quentin."

Now though: "Something's driven Zack off the cliff. Till now, he's been straight, I'll swear to it. I'll swear on his numbers. They'd be the last part of him to go. They are—they were—his defense *against* going nuts."

It was the numbers with which his clients tried to disguise their losses, profits, charities, costs, their incomes, their *lives* that drove Zack Wool wild. Numbers abused, numbers criminalized. "So what's new?" the most naive movie person would say. Not Zack. Numerical propriety was his version of that foolishness his father called "honor," not quite joking when he said, "The honor code of the Wools." Some code, was young Zack's thought, thinking of his father's life in the feed and fertilizer stores. Fifty thousand sacks of shit which turned your body into barrel staves.

Decades ago, Keneret, in for his annual tax grilling, asked Wool about a sword that hung, tasseled and silvery, on the wall among certificates and diplomas. Zack looked up from heaps of Keneret papers as if he hadn't seen it for twenty years. "Belonged to some old Wool. A general. My dad traced us to everybody but Jesus Christ."

"That's my branch. Looks like the Civil War."

"Mexican. General John Wool. Fought under Zachary—"

"Ah. Your name."

"Taylor. Against the Mexicans."

Under the sword, a brass plaque with sentences Keneret read and then copied into his notebook.

Through our great good fortune in our youth, our hearts were touched with fire. It was given us to learn at the outset that life is a profound and passionate thing. While we are permitted to scorn nothing but indifference, and do not pretend to undervalue the worldly rewards of ambition, we have seen with our own eyes, above and beyond the gold fields, the snowy heights of honor, and it is for us to bear the report to those who come after us.—OLIVER W. HOLMES JR.

"Holmes in the family tree, too?"

"I don't think so. He and Genghis Khan didn't make it." Patting the debris on his desk, "The IRS is not going to be happy with these memos. Is it so hard to date them? How many years have I begged you to—"

"Better sword than pen."

Wool shook this incomprehensibility off. "OK, ancillary costs."

When Marcia read him the *Times* story, Keneret saw Wool's humorless, Buster Keaton face glooming over the white sea of receipts, canceled checks, Visa and American Express statements, spreadsheets. "They have the wrong man."

"They have tapes of phone conversations, a check he gave his contact. A check!"

"He wanted to be caught."

"He turned himself in." Pouring Keneret and herself more coffee from a silver urn. "Could it be drugs?"

"Impossible," said Keneret, but then, remembering when cocaine started taking over the studios, "Who knows." Technicians you'd relied on for twenty years were one day unreliable. Production units dissolved. People looked, walked, talked, for a while acted the same, but weren't. "Twenty-five years with the guy, I don't have a clue."

"Half his clients are probably commissioning screenplays about him right now."

"Something was eating at him, adding up in him, no one saw it, he didn't see it. One day, boom, darkness. Scary. Like black holes and space. The hugeness. And our almost nothingness. What do we know? Think we know?"

At the honeysuckle trellis, a black and orange bee dipped into a beautiful blossom. Keneret watched it dip and rise. Such programmed industry, Zack in his spreadsheets. Keneret's spreadsheets, *Keneret's* accounts. Zack knew him—in some ways—better than Marcia. Whatever could be quantified, he knew. And more, more than Keneret himself, for he understood not only Keneret's numbers but how they linked up with a million others. Wool, the cosmologist and cosmetician of exemptions, brackets, finagling.

But why a hit man? Was it his version of the ancestral sword? Zack Wool and a hit man? Who'd play that? Franklin Pangborn and Eddie Robinson? Fields and Groucho. It was the Tarantino-Mamet world, but Zack belonged in Andy Hardy's.

For ten years, Wool's office was on the top—fourteenth—floor of the Westcloud on Wilshire. He liked looking out the windows to the high, glassy, classy propinquity of Westwood's little scatter of multimillion-dollar high-rises.

Keneret, his second film client, had come to him almost thirty years ago through Wendell Spear, the film critic, his first. Back then, Wool was in the one-room, assistantless office above the frame shop on West Pico. Both clients had followed him to Westwood. "It's a Capra movie," Keneret said. (In these days, Wool didn't understand the reference.) "Not that you've changed. Which meant," he told Marcia now, remembering, "the same soup bowl haircuts, Buster Keaton deadpan mug, the same tedious caution. Now his suits and decor are better, but I've still had only two audits in thirty years, and Wendell one. Wool's been safe as a—safe. And closed—like a book."

"In Greek," said Marcia.

"Not Greek, *numbers.*"

Among pens, pads, keyboards, monitors, files of disks, and piles of forms, Wool, shirtsleeves, white or blue, rolled up on oddly powerful forearms, faced his client. "Wimpy with Popeye's arms" was Spear's description. Wool's face: "The Dead Sea." It skirted melancholy, skirted ease, skirted any expression "you'd want to photograph, except a corpse's." It was the face the two old friends wanted doing their taxes. "Not honesty, really," said Spear. "That would be flattering it. Absence of dishonesty."

"Last month, he grilled me an hour about what fraction of scouting a location I spent in undeductible ogling. Crucifixion."

"The cross is the plus sign."

As long as Wool could remember, numbers had been easy for him. Through grade and high school in Houston, he'd been at or near the top of math classes. At Texas Tech, though, he'd hit the number wall: he wasn't good enough to make pure math his life. He tried accounting, intertranslating assets and liabilities, following trails of depreciation, incorporation, partnership, the sixteen categories of tax law, the rigors of auditing. Working in, through, and around all this was strenuous, occult, and, when successful, thrilling. After he passed the CPA exams, he went out to work for his father's cousin in Long Beach, California. George Wool had a dry goods store. When it prospered, he asked his young Texas cousin to do his books. Wool swotted up California law and the dry goods field. Two years later, he opened the office on West Pico in the room above the frame shop. The clients were local until Spear and then Keneret showed up. Other film clients followed, and five years later Wool was a film specialist. By the time he moved to the suite on Wilshire near the UCLA campus, he was prosperous.

He'd never liked the clients' fudging, fakery, and dodging, the phony smoothness, the irritability, the selfishness, the anger seen and heard as he worked out the mathematics of profit and liability. Those who worked least and made most were—much of the time—the greediest and meanest. Misers are miserable bastards, thought Wool, who didn't like it that his job was keeping them rich and out of trouble. The mathematic structures made to accomplish it, though, insulated him from their greed, mendacity, and anxiety. In his numerical zone of quiet, he felt as snug as his father had among the genealogical charts he studied nights and weekends after heavy hours at the feed and grain store. (All that remained of that—

the sword and the plaque—he hung in the bathroom of the West Pico office.)

Wool passed his early California years in apartments, then, in a spasm of extravagance, bought the glass and cypress house of a bankrupt client. For a couple of years, he tried domesticity; that is, he bought sofas, tables, towels, gadgets, garden tools, and plants, following the tips that Frances LaPlante, his longtime secretary, gave him about what well-to-do West Los Angelenos put into their homes. It was a brief binge of domesticity, after which the house became almost as abstract for him as Hollywood. "I don't have time for it," he told Frances.

"Everybody's got time for a home life, Mr. Wool."

"I sleep and eat. The place gets cleaned, the bushes trimmed. That's it for me. I could do it all from the office, but I like the drive home. It rests me. You've got a husband, a kid. That I don't have time—or the gift—for. Shopping, gardening, finding people to do them, that's a profession. I'm lucky I have you, Frances." To himself, he said, Domesticity's for domestics.

Wool worked for people but was no servant. He'd made his way without sinecures, money, or charm. The sham of family glory had turned his decent old man into a caricature. His own aspirations were satisfied by work with numbers. Beyond them he felt uneasy, restless. They were a sort of family, disciplined and dignified. Everyone had to respect, even live by them. Everything, at least everything that wasn't dangerously contingent, ended up in numbers. The closest Wool got to irony was thinking that the California he knew was more contingent and shaky than any place but a fishing village on the Indian Ocean.

Beside the unpacific Pacific, in the heart of its most celebrated industry, almost everything was up for grabs. Every film was a risk, almost every job insecure. This week's success, next year's failure. Wool's clients were among those who knew and even organized the way things ran, but the paper they or their managers dumped on his desk was as fault ridden as the Pacific Rim. Gifted, yes, technically, artistically, intellectually, personally, but Wool admired none of them.

At Texas Tech, Wool had done a history paper on William Gladstone. Gladstone, too, was gifted; he had brains, vigor, family wealth, education, religious faith, but his diaries revealed a self shaky as a leaf. In the daytime, he ran ministries and governments, wrote hundreds of pamphlets, articles, and books—his speeches filled fifteen thousand columns of *Hansard*—but back home, after family prayers, he cruised London streets for prostitutes. "To redeem them," he wrote, but his conscience, hot as a toaster, knew better, and the prime minister, night after night, whipped himself raw. As much as anything, Wool's memory of Gladstone's self-punishment kept him from shifting to a steadier clientele in a steadier geological place. He stayed where the discrepancy between solidity and illusion was at least acknowledged, where the major industry manufactured illusion.

Wool knew his reputation here: "With Wool you know where you are." "He won't let you fudge a nickel; on the other hand, you won't be audited." "Wool doesn't pull it over your eyes." Was it true? Wool didn't spend time thinking about it: self-examination was not for him. He wrote no diaries, wasn't interested in himself. He scarcely knew what he looked like. Shaving, he shook the cylinder of cream up and down, pressed the spigot, smeared lather over cheeks and throat, made fifteen or twenty strokes with the razor, and that was that. Somewhere there were his eyebrows, gray and black hairs curling toward a lined forehead, gray sideburns, nostrils from which he shaved a few hairs, a chin with a vertical cleft that was hard to shave, gray eyes set back in their sockets. Seeing a long, gray head in a store window, he didn't realize—for seconds—who it was. "Christ, so that's what I look like now."

For years, he'd satisfied sexual need rapidly and alone. Occasionally, cautiously, he fornicated with office temps. Not quite scratching itches, but not companionship. There was no time; he was no Gladstone.

Only now and then was he gripped by sexual hunger he couldn't work off. Usually, he managed to sideline it till tax deadline time. Then, off. Almost every May and September, he spent three weeks away, either in Mexico or Europe, where hotel help often supplied or contained what he needed. Recently, he stayed closer to home. He bought good sports clothes and a Porsche, which he drove up the coast to Santa Barbara. He spent a few nights at the Biltmore, arranging for a girl to be sent in. Or he went to one of the bars on Anacapa Street until his need was spotted, then let things happen. Now and then, at the pool or the beach, risking fair skin in afternoon sun, he encountered what he needed. It usually involved a few dinners, movies, concerts, drives, and very dull histories: mean parents, lost chances, stupid ambitions. Several times there'd been monthlong affairs that dribbled away in uncomfortable phone calls.

A year ago, Wool thought of buying a house or cabin to which he could drive up weekends or in which he could spend his May and September holidays. He went into a real estate office in Montecito, where a friendly woman more or less his own age outlined the possibilities. Her ease, slight formality, and alertness to his scarcely defined want charmed him.

"Would you like to drive around and see a few places?" Her voice was melodious, her hair brown. Laurette Kelilo. In low heels, she was slightly taller than he. A bit leaner, bonier, than he liked.

They drove the hills, stopping to look at houses. She talked taxes and maintenance, cisterns and wiring. Her veiny forearms, large nose, and too-rapid walk dissolved in an easy flow of decorous amiability and expertise. The houses stirred proprietary, even domestic feelings in him. The tax jungle receded.

Sitting by her desk in the Montecito office, Wool eyed her thoughtful, large-nosed face as she wrote up his needs. Not a homely face, a homey face, one that fit in, that effused pleasantness, decency. A straightforward face, an unrepellent brown mole on the left flange of the nose. "There are three places in the hills I think you might like. Could I show them to you tomorrow?"

"Yes." And then, before he'd calculated, "If you're free, we could talk things out over dinner." Actually, as you looked at it, a pretty face. No, it was the person who was pretty, the character.

"I am free."

A direct, honorable person, really almost beautiful.

Wool took in her history with dinner and, later, in bed. This was clearly—he was sure—not a part of her usual sales pitch. Laurette Kelilo wasn't incautious, desperate, or lonely; she was far more part of a community than Wool had ever been. A divorcée who lived alone in a one-bedroom ranch house—"The spoils of divorce, or is it marriage?"—she said, "A job like this is all contacts. You join clubs, churches, you make up foursomes, you fill in at dinners, you volunteer. If I had children, I'd be in the PTA." The last to inform him quickly.

When he drove off at midnight, Wool asked himself questions he'd not asked before: What does she see in me? What have I got that she wants?

They spent the next four nights together.

When he drove back to L.A., nothing had been said about meeting again. He had her numbers; she didn't have to ask for his. They'd had a good time; he was sure of that. They'd been passionate. They'd been friendly. He'd told her about his work, his clients. First in amusement, then in contempt, he described the ploys and dodges he contrived for them. He talked of his feelings about the gulf between them and the fruit pickers he saw bending and straightening in the fields as he drove south. "I widen the gulf; I pave it."

"I, too."

The daughter of an Orange County teamster who'd put savings, energy, and hope into a fast-food franchise that failed when she was in high school, Laurette knew different sides of the class canyon. Some of her schoolmates followed parents from one farm job to the next. She hated their humiliation and, after her father's failure, felt it. Her last two years in high school she worked six hours a day at another franchise, and during her two years at community college, she worked a forty-hour week for a Ventura Realtor. She studied for a real estate exam, got a license, and found the job in Montecito.

Her history, like her body, excited him. Both were surprising—unearned, uninherited gifts. Sleeping with and listening to her gave him the most joyful days he could remember.

Back home, he put questions to himself. Could normal life sustain itself with such joy? Could he settle in with it? With her? And could she take a lifeful of him? Then: Would life without her be what it had been before he met her?

Answers rode up and down his feelings, so tiring that he often couldn't concentrate on work.

What he did was let the fire burn itself out. He didn't drive back to

Montecito, didn't call Laurette. Since he'd neither taken nor posed for pictures, there were no physical souvenirs. The fire died down, and he was relieved. Best to chalk it up to a special, onetime expense.

But the cost-benefit analysis wasn't that clear. Benefits: ready sex, home meals, companionship (touches, exchanges of opinion, common amusements). Costs, financial and psychic: responsibility, dependence, competing schedules, new worries of every sort.

He'd functioned well before Laurette. Why not as well or better—experience was a plus—after? He'd had the pleasure, the knowledge, the confidence that a decent person was attracted to him, yet he was free of the moral, let alone legal, entanglement of a relationship.

Nothing that counted lasted. (Except perhaps memories, which were hollow, like shells. Time pulverized them as it did what they'd contained.)

Wool began to alter. The feelings that had been roused were not pulverized but transfigured. Woolishly.

A few months after he'd met Laurette, he was sitting in front of a monitor mousing up a client's account when suddenly, as if generated by an algorithm, the *meaning* of the numbers stormed from the screen: the games played with the IRS, the structures of a phony corporation, of fictional costs, the disappearing border between the real and the invented. In the blue glass, Wool saw the clients, hideous repositories of trickery and greed.

The glass towers of Wilshire no longer seemed neutral but arrogant monuments to deceit. The steel smirked with it; the glass was dark with devilry.

Forehead against window, Wool felt his brains plummet through his chest, through the floor, fourteen floors, through the pilings, the earth crust, the huge hot plates, the sulfurous lava, the earth core. "Pa," he called. "Oh Jesus, Pa."

In the bathroom, he threw water into his face, then sat on the toilet seat and stared at the daguerreotypes of John Wool and Zachary Taylor. He read words on the plaque:

. . . life . . . profound and passionate . . . not pretend . . . worldly rewards . . . ambition . . . our own eyes . . . beyond the gold fields, the snowy heights of honor . . . us to bear . . . those who come after . . .

Driving home early, Wool heard a southern voice: *Jesus went into the temple and cast out them that sold and bought.* Mrs. Shelman, Methodist Sunday school. *I wasn't sleepin, ma'am, jes thinkin.* Eating microwaved meat loaf in front of CNN's comfortably serious faces, he felt images delinking themselves from the words. Pictures from Sudan and Bosnia were speaking privately, desperately, to him. Helplessness and riot broke from the glass.

He pressed OFF.

Darkness. The fork motionless in gluey meat. Such things out there: a small girl bleeding on a road, screaming; a mob of fleshless people, also screaming. What was it all about? What was *he* supposed to do about it?

Do?

Things were caused, were connected. Patterns, equations.

His clients equaled the streets.

Mrs. Shelman, it's Zack.

General Wool. Oliver W. Holmes Jr. William Gladstone. Laurette Kelilo.

Everything led to *If you do not do, you cannot be.*

He drove to Montecito and proposed to Laurette Kelilo.

"I thought you'd forgotten me." A month ago, she'd started going out with a Realtor from Lompoc. "We decided to merge our offices. Now we're thinking of merging everything."

Wool said he was disappointed but wished her well and drove back to L.A. That night, bitterness seized him so fiercely he could hardly move. Not Laurette but his clients were its object.

The next day he made a call to his shiftiest client. Through him, he found someone else, and then someone else. Layer after layer, the calls descended until they reached Hugo Fenstermacher Gallego, a lump of professional mayhem whose portable office—a hyperengined '82 Buick—contained the hardware that was his business equipment. A mad contract was made, and within a week, the friends and associates of the producer Marcel Slobos were aware that he had disappeared.

An hour after he paid Hugo, Wool called the IRS office in Los Angeles and said that he was bringing them evidence of widespread tax malfeasance. He hauled disks, books, and papers in to an auditor, Gerald C. Whipp, a back-twisted dwarf, "the straightest man I've met out here," Wool told the reporter for the *Los Angeles Times*. Then told more. "Murderer Turns Songbird" was the headline of one tabloid story.

"I hear Joe Hart settled for forty-eight million," Spear told the Kenerets over dinner in Santa Monica. "Thank God for poverty."

"That hit man's still loose," said Keneret. "Who knows who else is on the list?"

"Maybe we should get guns."

"Why not, everything else is crazy. Oscar Harmel called yesterday, did I want to work with him on a treatment."

"You didn't—" groaned Marcia.

"I pled my gray hair."

A month after they found some of Slobos in a Los Angeles dump, Wool hanged himself in the Los Angeles County jail.

OSCAR AND HYPATIA

1

Oscar noticed her in the plane from London. Well, not quite *noticed;* not quite *her.* Night. Most passengers asleep. Middle of row 35, a heaving, huffing knoll of blankets.

When the sun dribbled over the Ethiopian desert, Oscar decided to check it—them!—out.

The middle of row 35 had resolved itself into two readers, a youngish, small-mustached, blue-eyed man in a tropical sport shirt and a blowzy—hair a mess of autumn-colored ringlets—bony-faced, blue-eyed woman. Though the sleeveless blouse revealed enough to pump Oscar's ever-ready heart: breasts pointing east and west, and bony arms, bushy at the pits. "East of Vienna," deduced Oscar. "Lucky bastard."

In the Nairobi airport, he waited by the baggage carousel next to the man. The woman, as tall as Oscar, five eight, wheeled a cart overloaded with photographic paraphernalia, cameras, tripods, lights. Neither she nor the other half of the knoll looked at each other. Maybe there'd been an argument. No, they're strangers. Were, are. A onenighter. Airlines probably have a name for it. Or them: eagles in flyby; power surge over Mediterranean; econofuck.

Several times in his own flying life, Oscar had been overcome by heat coming off an arm, a calf, a pillow-reclining face eager as his own for airy congress, yet he'd never moved, never pressed or touched, never lifted a seat arm, never covered the other body with his blanket, never kissed the face.

"Safari?" English accent, not Oxbridge, maybe Cockney, maybe northern — Oscar's small range of English accents.

"That's the plan."

"Masai Mara?"

"Serengeti. Ngorongoro. Lake Nakuru, for the flamingos. You?"

"Business. Going down to the Seychelles. Doing customs here."

"Selling seashells by the seashore?"

"Marine supplies, actually."

"First trip?"

"Used to live there."

"Nice?"

"Indeed. Africans, Arabs, Portuguese. Very harmonious. No tension whatsoever. Beaches. Fishing. Ninety islands. One does reasonably well down there."

Well as you did last night? Oscar did not ask.

Dr. Siebentaler had told him, "You're not a naysayer, Oshkar, you're a notsayer." It seemed — to Siebentaler — that Oscar substituted pranks for self-expression. The Harmel family prankster: short-sheeted beds, scary faces at dark windows, dog turds in Valentine's Day chocolates. "Distress signals, Oshkar," said Siebentaler. "Zuh false exuberance of younger siblings. Cries for recognition."

Well, yes, *recognition* was part of the Harmel lingua franca.

"Half my patients are children of *Someone*. Zuh serpent in zeir Paradise."

"I didn't notice," young Oscar had said. "Neither serpent nor paradise."

"Zat's why you are zere, and I am here. If everyone's a hunchback, no one is. Your pranks are clear as dreams. Zough exceptionally inventive." Siebentaler's enormous black eyebrows — he looked like young Edward Teller — danced over his minimalist smile. "Yoshua of Nazareth."

The reference was to an "Author's Query" sixteen-year-old Oscar had submitted to the *L.A. Times,* which printed it.

I would be grateful to anyone who has information about or possesses letters written by or about the first-century Palestinian rabbi Yoshua of Nazareth (aka Jesus the Anointed One). Please send to

Oscar T. Harmel
603 Melinda Crescent
Los Angeles, CA 90024

One of his father's PR people pushed the item into gossip columns here and abroad, Oscar's flash of recognition. The item had been framed with twinkling paternal comments, which moved the son from pride to anger. "Why didn't you get my permission?"

"You were after attention," said his father. "You just got more of it."

"He's *your* PR, not mine. He did it for you. It reduced me to nothing."

"Oscar, I don't think your international reputation has been seriously damaged."

A year later, Oscar and his mother moved to Westwood, a twenty-minute drive from the Bel Air mansion. "You *can* live here—if you want," said his father.

"I'll take my chance with Mom. She needs me."

"Your presence or your absence? Anyway, you have the key. It's still your house."

Never was, said Oscar, but to himself.

For a while, he stayed away. Sylvan, the half brother to whom he was closest, would drive down to Westwood. Sylvan was closer to Oscar's mother, Thea, than his own, Norma. Thea was the third Harmel wife. Her marital tenure was eight years, double that of the previous two. With the alimony settlement, she went to design school and bought into a Westwood dress shop. Meanwhile, Oscar hung on to twelfth grade by the skin of his teeth, then made it into and dropped out of Cal State, Long Beach. Which is when Siebentaler entered his life.

"Not my shrink," he told Sylvan. "My enlarger." He didn't add, "Pal, priest, pop," but "He takes out my garbage."

Sylvan was a literal fellow. One source of their fraternity was his dependence on Oscar's showing him the ropes and Oscar's pleasure doing it.

Oscar tapped his forehead, the tanned slope of all Harmel's children. "And puts other things here."

"Such as?"

"Dostoyevsky, Stendahl, Mann, Whitman."

"Who're they?"

"That's what I'm supposed to find out. Authors. That's not half of it. Last week he told me to listen to a record. 'Listen till you see how it's like your feelings.' "

"He's not like my shrink. What record?"

"Some Beethoven thing. Then I'm supposed to read about it in a book."

"Jesus, it's worse than school. Was it good?"

"It went on too long."

"What about the book?"

"Siebentaler explained it."

"And?"

"I didn't know why music should be so complicated."

"So?"

"It floored him."

When he was eighteen, Oscar got a job, assistant gaffer in the production company of his father's friend, Ezra Keneret.

"You could've worked for me," said his father. "A lot of people have learned the movie business from me. Including your new boss."

"Dr. Siebentaler thought it would be better for me to work for someone else."

"Your secret sharer. Fine with me. Ezra has good people. Keep your eyes open."

2

In Nairobi, a week later, Oscar saw the blowzy-haired, bony-armed girl sitting three tables away on the terrace of the Boulevard Hotel. He'd spent the day camcording thousands of flamingos taking off from

Lake Nakuru like pink mist. Running along the shore, waving arm and camcorder like Leonard Bernstein, he'd raised them from their idle predation. That was power.

The girl's table was heaped with cameras, light meters, lens cases. She was flipping through pictures in a shoe box. Every once in a while, she held one up. Her piston-thin, bush-pitted arms excited Oscar. He aimed the camcorder at her. She turned at the buzz, he shifted the nozzle toward the bar, the tennis courts.

The next day he watched her stride up Harry Thuku Road toward the National Museum. He followed. More or less together in the courtyard, they watched a Japanese man in safari outfit, rifle under one arm, a young Japanese woman under the other, standing by the stuffed elephant in the courtyard. Another Japanese man photographed them with a movie camera. Oscar's girl spoke to a third Japanese man standing by. "Film documentary," overheard Oscar. "For personal purpose."

"I'd pay to see it," said the girl.

Oscar saw her next by the glass case which held "*homo habilus,* two and a half million years old."

Not looking at Oscar, she said, "Our gross-gross-gross-gross-gross-*Vater.*"

"You and I are cousins," said Oscar.

3

Hypatia's room on the Boulevard's second floor looked over a garbage-filled stream where colorful birds congregated. From the taupe walls, she'd removed two batiks and, in their place, Scotch-taped pictures of animals grazing, leaping, posing on rocks and termitaries, chewing each other's flesh, crunching each other's bones. There were also full and partial nudes of black men and women, or their knees, earlobes, nose bridges, scapulae, thighs.

"Sculpture," said Oscar.

"Colored shapes. Space fillers."

"Too abstract. Mind?" He raised a thin cigar, bought at the Norfolk bar next door. "I'll blow the smoke away."

"I don't mind smoke. I'll take a picture. *Filmmaker in Smoke.*"

"My father's the filmmaker."

"You don't collaborate?"

"Once. On *The Way You Used to Look*."

"A beautiful film."

"He said I cost him too much money."

"He wants you to work for nothing?"

"He pays well. I was too fussy."

"How?"

"I'm careful. I saw too many reverse shots, poor angles, reflections, anachronisms. I exasperated him."

"His films are beautiful but don't interest me. *He* interests me. Like cigars. I don't smoke, but I photograph them." Here she raised her Leica, counted "one-two-three-four." Click. "Now I have you."

"Do you want more of me?"

The long face stared thoughtfully.

4

Oscar enjoyed the bony, mammary excitement—Hypatia was an active lovemaker—and thought her wonderful. She was neither diplomatic nor contradictory; she was open, exploratory, thoughtful; not cautious, not scared. Her sexual fervor had none of the verbal assault and genital threat which, in his California experience, rose from the terror, hatred, and contempt Oscar associated with *the new woman*.

Hypatia was really new.

5

At dinner, in the Boulevard's dining room, he found out her history: born in Zagreb of Polish and Croatian middle-class parents, she'd gone to Paris as a teenager, then London, where she'd lived three years as au pair girl, waitress, photographer.

"Your parents alive?"

"Father dead; Mother religious and bitter. It's bad to come to the world through bitterness."

"What's she bitter about?"

"Being."

Hypatia hoped to sell her African pictures for enough money to get to the States. "New York, Chicago, Texas, California. Can you help me?"

"Make up your mind?"

Flashing, "I think not. With a job."

Oscar puffed away. "I know a couple of freelancers. Some magazine people. You weren't thinking of my father?"

Another blue flash. Oscar felt more than saw it. "Certainly not."

"My brother's girlfriend's in some new publishing outfit. They might be able to use a good photographer."

6

Five days later, Oscar rose from their bed in the Serengeti Lodge, put on his safari jacket and hat, and walked in the moonlight to the dining room.

"*Jambo,*" said waiter, who was setting out coffee cups beside a silver urn.

"Good morning. *Jambo.* Coffee ready?"

"Five minutes."

Oscar sat by the huge window and saw the first bolt of sun gold crack the night. In minutes, there was a silhouette of umbrella acacias. Into the now silvery pallor, a stork zoomed and nestled on one: its beak pointed skyward. Another flew into another tree. Soon the window became a giant musical score of beaks and globular heads. I should wake her to photograph this, thought Oscar. Even as he said it, it was too late. A different beauty, purple, scarlet, orange, and gold dissolved the other. The plain awoke. Shivery whines and odd calls—hyenas? baboons?—filled the air.

Other early bird patrons came in. "*Bonjour, Madame.*"

"*Guten Morgen.*"

"*Jambo.*"

Waiters carried in bowls of mango, pineapple, tiny bananas, bins of scrambled eggs, bacon, giblets, and fried sausage, racks of toast. There were bursts of Swahili and—Oscar supposed—Luo. He filled a plate and cup and ate in front of the window as day became its normal self.

At the next table, a small man in a sleeveless jacket with brass buttons looked up from his eggs at Hypatia, camouflage shorts and thick boots on her bony legs, safari hat tipped back on the autumnal mob of curls.

"*Belle vue,*" said Oscar.

"*Pas mal de tout,*" said the man.

7

Two hours later, they are standing in the back of the minivan, heads out the sunroof, surveying—Oscar with binoculars, Hypatia with viewfinder—the enormous plain of ever paler greens and shoulderless, lion-head rocks eructated from the ground. Besides Shadrach, the driver who'd picked them up at the Novotel in Arusha three days ago, sits Mr. Yasupa, the Serengeti ranger who, for fifteen dollars, is guiding them through this reserved kopje of the Serengeti. Overhead, deep, thoughtless sky, suspending here and there, a puzzled cloud. Mr. Yasupa, mustached, large toothed, wears a green uniform with dark green beret. With each piece of information he calls up to them— "Marabou stork," "Ostrich," "Hyena," "Zebra," "Wildebeest"—goes a triumphant grin. He is giving them these presents.

Oscar is both excited and peaceful; Hypatia is tense, busy.

Mr. Yasupa holds up his hand like a traffic cop, and Shadrach brakes the van. Mr. Yasupa gets out, looks through his plastic binoculars, then points, "Over there." They take off over roadless plain.

By an outcrop of low rocks, between green bushes, is a tray of grass on which lies a beautiful, open-eyed gazelle whose flank is being eaten by a cheetah whose huge shoulder blades and hammer-shaped head pump away with the exertion. Oscar can hear the crunch of small bones. The cheetah looks up at and through them; its eyes are immense, blank, gorgeous. Beside it, a large cub with a mane of white fluff over its small, spotted coat looks up at the van, puzzled. Its muzzle is bloody with faun gut. So is the grass. Hypatia's camera clicks. The gazelle's gut is exposed like an anatomy text. A large gleaming purplish jewel has fallen out of her on the grass.

"What's that?" asks Hypatia.

"Stomach," grins Mr. Yasupa.

The gazelle's head is untouched. It looks to Oscar like Audrey Hepburn's.

The horizon line is a frieze of wildebeest and zebra. Oscar points Hypatia to them. "It's like an eye," she says. "We"—pointing to the cheetah, cub, and gazelle—"are the eye apple."

They hear the small, deep growl of the cub. Its mother has slapped it off the carrion. Then she sits up, belly heaving, and the cub eats.

A hyena with its strange gimpy lilt approaches the meal. Buzzards fly in. They keep a distance from the cheetah. Hypatia photographs.

Oscar is ecstatic. He feels that he is seeing something absolutely fundamental.

8

The day before, Shadrach had driven them to the Olduvai Gorge. A temple of rock rose from a whale-shaped boulder under a face of flat rock capped by green bushes. Beyond were blue stretches of grass stippled with hills which appeared newborn and tentative. A plaque informed them that there were seven hundred sites, the oldest two and a half million years.

> The Gorge itself was created one and a half million years ago, by a slippage in a fault, shortly—as geologic time goes—before the appearance of Australopithecus.

Thought Oscar, Mankind starts with a fault.

In the tiny museum was a baked clay block on which were three sets of human footprints.

> The oldest survival of human companionship. It is estimated that one was made by a person four feet tall, another by a person four feet six. The third set of steps is overprinted.

The bad seed, thought Oscar.

Under a thorn tree, Shadrach talked to a Masai in gold chains and blanket who presided over a table of key chains, baskets, and beaded neck bands. "Mister want to buy Masai souvenir?"

Oscar pointed to a pair of earrings. "How much?"

"Fifteen dollars." The Masai's English was pure.

"Expensive."

"There's fine work in the earrings. They take a long time to make."

"Give you seven."

"The price is fifteen dollars."

"How much in shillings?"

"Six thousand."

Oscar handed six notes to the Masai and the earrings to Hypatia. "A beautiful gift," she said to the Masai. "Beautifully negotiated."

Back in the van, Shadrach said, "That Masai told me of one hill eight kilometers from this place. Every year this hill moves fifteen feet."

"I'd like to see that moving hill," said Hypatia.

"You cannot."

"It's only for Masai?"

"You need four-wheel drive." Shadrach pointed to a thorn tree which looked like a dervish fixed in midwhirl. "Masai man says put blackbird meat under this tree, this bring rain."

"You believe him?"

"Of course."

They'd been with Shadrach now so many hours and talked so much and long that this irrationality surprised them. Shadrach too was Masai but had committed himself to modernity and, against his father's wishes, gone to school. He was not going to be like his father, who, like the man from St. Ives, had seven wives and, unlike him, fifty children. Shadrach had one wife and one son.

9

For years, Oscar had built up an inventory of sights, sounds, and notions, for what, he didn't know. He filed away the cheetah and Yasupa, and that night, at supper by the large window, across from a table of four bearded Germans who passed around a single cigar and leered at Hypatia when they thought Oscar wasn't looking, he filed that as well. Tonight, looking at her bony jaws chomping deliciously away, it struck him what his files were for. "I want to make a film."

"Why say it now?"

"I'm forty-two years old, and I never once—I think—thought of it before."

"We'll do it together."

10

Three miles outside Arusha, Shadrach pulled off the tarmac road and carried a box across a field to a tin shack, out of which ran a little boy. A tall, beautiful woman in a flowery skirt followed.

"Will you have coffee in my house?" invited Shadrach. "This Django. This wife."

The floor of the cabin was dirt, the bamboo walls were packed with dry mud, the roof was corrugated tin. Inside was a threadbare sectional couch, two kitchen chairs, and—the household pride—a sideboard in which there were five glasses, a can of powdered coffee, a sugar bowl, and a photograph album. Shadrach set out three cups. His wife boiled water, he spooned in the coffee, served Oscar, Hypatia, and herself. His face was tense with pride and fear of shame.

Oscar showed Django a face game, sticking out his tongue when he touched his nose, moving it to the left when he touched his left ear, to the right when he touched his right one. The boy and his beautiful mother laughed immensely. Shadrach showed them color photographs of his wedding.

A girl of eleven or twelve walked through the door without knocking.

"I didn't know you had a daughter," said Oscar.

"She is neighbor."

"What is your name?" Oscar asked the girl slowly. She said nothing.

"That is Lelee," said Shadrach's wife. "She speaks no English."

Lelee clung to one of the posts that held up the roof. Notions of hospitality were clearly different here. Shadrach, conscious of Oscar's consciousness of this, grew tense again. "We go now."

In the van he said, "I wish to go America. You will send ticket?"

"I think you'd be unhappy there."

"I have one client, a music lady. She say she send ticket. She does not."

"We will," said Hypatia.

In Arusha, carts, crowds, shops like huts. People hauled heavy carts filled with tires, bales of wire, bottles. There were a few six- or seven-story buildings, one a block-long conference center, then the Novotel which, when Oscar had seen it six days ago, had looked like a dump. Now it seemed palatial.

11

For that nontimed space time between a sort of sleep and a sort of waking, Oscar somewhat saw, somewhat felt *Kilimanjaro, crater centered. Then a lioness on her back, legs swaying, unprivate privates open to sun and clicking cameras.* Shadrach, Constant Poker, poked him in the side. "You like simba?" *Syntax always that of his listeners, father's, teachers', Siebentaler's,* he said, "I like." Poke. "You see that?" "What?" "One leopard. Chuy." *Curled like a Spanish question mark, the long, black tail of the leopard on a thorn tree branch. Buzzards beaked the flesh off a wildebeest skeleton; a long-beaked old gent looked on, a marabou; in a sun-dappled pool, a ledge of black snout surfaced, a hippo.* Crocodile: mamba. *Hyena:* fisi. *Ostrich:* embuni. *Cheetah:* duma. *A duma sheared the rear half of Audrey Hepburn's body exposing her ingenious guts to the anatomy class. On Gol Kopje, Mr. Yasupa held a filmstrip to the light.* "Film, like the mind, goes backward or forward, makes the little big, a doorknob an eye." *Now he, Oscar, was filming, astride a boom.*

Warm. Baked bread. From a different part of Oscardom. He raises an arm, cups a hand, sees his knuckle, big as Kilimanjaro, touches a stomach, fingertip in the navel crater.

Their breakfast is carried in by a waiter. They eat mango and banana while listening to the bop-bops of tennis rallies from the court below.

Oscar tells Hypatia of a symposium on his father's films in which seven of the speakers were former wives and mistresses. "He loved it. Assessed each wife for me. 'Didi's one major surgery from stardom.' 'I'd like to dip Rosie's cunt in cocktail sauce and eat it.' "

"I will not like your father."

"You'll like him."

"I won't meet him."

"If we do a film, we'll meet him."

"Maybe we should do something else."

"Astrophysics?"

Everything was implicit, as the nut in its husk, the
future and the present, and the harbor.

Calvino

Es steht das Nichts in der Mandel.
[There's Nothing in the almond.]

Celan

1

I hadn't been avoiding Frankfurt. Far from it. I'd wanted to come back and a couple of times came close. A few years ago, I drove by it on the autobahn, so astonished at the skyline — which hadn't existed when I'd lived there with Jean and Billy in 1951 to 1952 — that I nearly went off the road. This time, though, I had a reason to come, at least bits of different reasons.

My life isn't orderly. Half the year, I'm away from New York. A freelancer makes his lance, then finds things to stick it in. I never had trouble finding them, which led me to discipline myself by accepting almost every assignment. How else become more than you'd been?

This becoming life was for Jean and her first successor, Rowena, unbecoming. "Who needs life in airplanes? I'm not accumulating frequent flier miles" (Jean). "You live the exterior life. I live internally.

And I get airsick" (Rowena). Sarah, to whom I've been married since 1980, is in tune with my—what?—shifty drift. Before her pots made her well known and very busy, she'd take off with me at the drop of a hat. As for Jean, after our two German years, she spent a lot of time alone with Billy and discovered that I was superfluous. Rowena? Her airsickness had less to do with interiority than extramarital flight. We were married for ten months.

2

OK, Frankfurt.

I was in L.A. doing a piece on movie interest in the artistic and intellectual figures of the century. Hemingway, Fitzgerald, Picasso, and Stein were as familiar to movie audiences as the Eiffel Tower, but after Beatty made *Reds,* Hollywood wanted to drag up odder fish. Old Burt Lancaster wanted to make a film about old Ezra Pound; Barbara Streisand optioned a book about Jackson Pollock; T. S. Eliot's widow had closed him off (though not to the astonishing royalties brought in by the musical *Cats*), but Lawrence, Joyce, Rilke, Valéry, and God knows who else were floating properties.

At the Beverly Wilshire, I had a call from Lyon Benjamin, assistant to the director Floyd Harmel.

I do much work by phone and deduce more than I probably should from voices. Benjamin's was a staccato tenor. Phrases sounded as if they were painfully selected and more painfully joined to their predecessors and successors. The voice itself wasn't reedy or breathy, but exceptionally tense. "I'm interested," it said. "In a man—who may be—a cousin of mine. Dead in 1940—sixteen years before I came on—the scene. Suicide. French-Spanish border—trying to escape—Vichy *miliciens.* Heart trouble—carried a manuscript—over the Pyrenees. Wouldn't give it up—more precious than his life. Had an American visa—but—" the pause here was theatrical, not laryngeal. I've received assignments from types who use so few words you're suspended in their silence and from others who need ten calls to let you know what they're after. Usually they don't know themselves until they pick up your response to their fumbling. Lyon Benjamin knew. "That day, the Spanish required a French exit visa. Benjamin—my perhaps cousin—didn't have one. He returned to the French harbor village—Port Bou—injected himself with morphine—and croaked."

"That it?"

"The man was—Walter Benjamin."

"Yes?"

"The great literary critic."

"I don't work much in that area."

I heard the intake and expulsion of breath; the living Benjamin was disappointed, or pretended to be. I don't embarrass, I don't get humiliated, I don't mind being seen as a naïf. Benjamin sensed the score. (He did a lot of telephonic work himself.) He started from scratch, even spoke with ease, legato. "I think there's a film in his life. The last intellectual. Maybe that's hyperbole. Still, the man was at the center of European thought. Lived by it, died for it. And no anchorite. Lots of chicklets. Movies haven't handled intellectuals well."

"Zola."

"Different. The Dreyfus Case. Before my time. The film."

"Before mine. The Case."

"You've done film work. I have your bio."

"Very little."

"But not bad."

In my four-decade writing life, I've done three scenarios and six treatments which got nowhere. Not my line. I tend to see lives at their crests, in crisis. The reportorial knack is seeing the gestures, locating the key words, then spelling out what you've seen and heard. Movies go up and down. My two films made no waves, but I appreciated Benjamin's spare appreciation of them. (More, and I would have discounted it.)

None of my work gets much appreciation. I publish articles, not books. Now and then, one causes a stir. There is next to no fan or hate mail. I don't hear about my skill except from editors, and little from them. New assignments are my reviews. I like it this way. Skill hides itself and the "skiller." Invisibility makes my work easier. The better known the writer, the more he becomes the story. Throwing your mug around is a career in itself, a nerve-rackingly contingent one. The more time you spend on the career, the shorter it is. (And the longer the credo, the less credence.)

"*The End of His Rope*'s a classy film. And a fair moneymaker."

"I didn't have a piece of it."

"You'd have a piece—of this."

"This being a film about your cousin."

"Exactly. Mr. Harmel has—a certain amount—of seed money. We cast it out—selectively—if you can cast selectively. One seed in fifty takes. When it does—you have—a Harmel film. An event. Cultural. Popular."

I'm not a movie fan. Films run through me. I might be able to name ten staying films. *The Godfather. Citizen Kane. Ambersons. City Lights. La Strada. My Darling Clementine,* a Bergman or two. Do even these stack up with the top two hundred novels? I don't think so. They're too diverting, you don't have a chance to sink into them. Bodies, beauties, endangered vehicles, guns, Astaire and Rogers. Floods of temptation. Still, in this world of erotic, visual rat-a-tat-tat, Floyd Harmel holds up, makes pictures you think about.

I finished my assignment, did another in Bogotá, then holed up for a week and read at, in, and around Walter Benjamin. His writing was full of the heavy formulations which, decades ago, turned me off academic life, but there were also sensuous, pleasantly perverse, and surprising observations; he was a writer. More, he'd lived more or less as I have, on his wits (at least after his father stopped supporting him, his wife, and son).

There were other similarities. He'd had three important women in his life, although he'd married only one of them. Like me, he'd had one child, a son, whom he saw as seldom as I see Billy. We even look somewhat alike, burly, heavy in the belly, thin nosed, brown eyes, black hair. His was thicker and rode more fiercely from the scalp. He also had a thick black mustache and thick eyeglasses. Unlike Lyon Benjamin, who turned out to be a self-hugging little fellow, pigeon toed, knock kneed, cross eyed, and bald, I could have passed for Walter Benjamin's cousin.

I decided my scenario would center about Benjamin's love affair with a remarkable, beautiful, promiscuous—does this word still make sense?—young woman, Asja Lacis, whom he met on Capri in 1924.

Asja, a Latvian Bolshevik, was an actress, director, and pioneer in children's theater.

In the next month, I wrote Cousin Lyon an outline, then a treatment, got my twelve thousand dollars and a go-ahead to do a scenario.

3

In March 1994 I had an assignment for a piece on the Italian election (the one which brought in Berlusconi). I went to Rome, then spent a day looking over Capri. I flew Lufthansa to Rome so that I could stop over in Frankfurt. Benjamin's postdoctoral dissertation—*Habilitationsschrift*—had been rejected in 1924 by the Goethe University there, and it was in Frankfurt that he'd decided—as, twenty-eight years later, I would—to live as a literary freelancer. He wrote for the *Frankfurter Zeitung* and other newspapers, for magazines, for the radio; he even did graphological analyses. In any case, under a Benjamin tax cover, I stopped in Frankfurt.

I had other Frankfurters on my plate, a couple I'd met at a European political conference in Bellagio. There, on a tennis court set in a grove of aspen and cypress, Jochen, a law professor, and I played tennis every late afternoon for the five days of the conference. His companion, Cristina—for whom he'd left his American wife—twice fished my copy out of the—to me—alien WordPerfect waters.

En route to Rome, in the two-hour Frankfurt stopover, I left a message on their answering machine saying I'd be coming back in a week, would they please get me a hotel room, close to their place, if possible.

4

From September 1950 to March 1951, I'd worked in Heidelberg. My main job was teaching two courses in American literature at the university. As an assistant, I received only auditor's fees (*Hörgeld*), which amounted to less than three hundred marks a semester, so I also worked for the U.S. Occupation Army as a GS-3 in the Staff Message Control. This paid enough to support Jean and me in a room across the

Neckar from the castle (in whose chapel, under tourists' eyes, we'd been married by a U.S. Army chaplain). When Billy was born the next winter, we needed more space and money. I got a job in Frankfurt as a GS-7 teaching illiterate American soldiers (those who hadn't reached sixth grade and had thus been illicitly recruited).

In March 1951 I took the train up to Frankfurt to find an apartment there. Stepping out of the beautiful, battered iron-and-glass station, I saw a fifteen-foot cardboard cutout of Charlie Chaplin, mustache, derby, battered shoes, cane. An advertisement for *City Lights,* a movie I'd been trying to see for years. I did my business at army offices in the old I. G. Farben Building, got the apartment keys, signed for dishes and linen, and filled out a form for Frau Gortat, the maid who'd helped us with Billy in Heidelberg and for whom the army would now pay. Earning thirty-five hundred dollars a year, GS-7s lived well in occupied Germany. That evening, I trolleyed downtown to see the film.

I remember feeling set apart from the audience. We'd lived a year in Heidelberg but weren't used to being part of a German movie audience. (We saw films at an American army theater.) German opera audiences were different: there wasn't the same passive gawking in the dark, more a—not always—restrained passion, rare license for the severely injured, slowly recuperating Germans of those days.

Near the end of *City Lights,* the tramp gets out of jail. Back walking city streets, he's mocked by a couple of urchins. He takes off after them, missing a kick or two. The audience—including this member of it—roared. Through the window of a flower shop, the tramp sees the formerly blind girl for whose successful eye operation he'd gotten the money (for which he'd been imprisoned). He stares at her lovingly. Noticing the odd little man, she comes out and gives him a flower. He keeps looking at her. She touches his hand and realizes that her savior was not the princely millionaire she'd imagined but this tramp. Her shock and recognition are beautiful, and Charlie's answering expression, a mixture of love, pride, and comprehension, is the close-up to end all close-ups, the expression on which I'd like to close my eyes in this world and to see as—if—they open in another.

When the lights went up in the theater, I stayed in my seat, overcome. The German audience, in overcoats, hats, and scarves, rushed up the aisles, faces frozen, even angry. Something had happened to them in the film's final sequence. Until then, they'd laughed as I had. Why weren't they moved by the beautiful conclusion? Was it un-Germanic? Frankfurt was still squatting in wartime rubble. Around the half-skeletal cathedral were ex-blocks of stony nothing. Were the feelings of its citizens also in the rubble? Had they been decimated by bombs and a dozen years of manhandling by another little mustached man?

5

Nostalgia makes everyone a poet. I was in Frankfurt for poetry. There are 86,400 seconds in a day. Perhaps fewer than 2,000 of my daily seconds have been turned into assigned words, although in most of my conscious seconds, there is a pressure in me, so familiar it's as natural as the circulation of my blood. Interrupted, it bleeds. Yes, I wanted to see where I'd been, wanted to feel what I believed I'd feel, but part of this want was the awareness of literary gold in the feeling.

In 1952 I wasn't a writer. I was vaguely preparing to be a professor. The teaching job I had was tedious, seven hours a day teaching soldiers to read, add, and subtract, but the money—free rent and maid, plus three hundred percent profit on four weekly cartons of American cigarettes (which the German mailman picked up and paid for once a week)—was princely. In two years, I saved three thousand dollars, enough to support Jean and Billy if I went on for a doctorate.

If the job was tedious, life wasn't. I came home to wife and baby in an apartment heavy with mahogany tables and sideboards and to buxom Frau Gortat, who cooked and served our sauerbraten and chops. At twenty-three, I felt like a manly provider. Nights, I read, enormously and with tremendous joy. Once a week, I traded Italian for English lessons with a Neapolitan barber at the Frankfurt military post, and twice a month I studied the *Aeneid* with a German Latin student from the university. Somewhere in there, I wrote my first article, a survey of German cultural and political affairs, modeled on Genet's *New Yorker* pieces on France. The *New Yorker* rejected the piece, but on one of the great days of my life, a *Partisan Review* editor, Catherine Carver, wrote that they'd accepted it. I was going to be in a magazine that published Sartre, Eliot, Orwell, Silone, Camus, Auden. The company was intoxicating, although I stayed sober enough to know I didn't belong to it. I thought I might be a little closer to Genet. If I had a gift, it was for a kind of verbal photography. I could report what was going on. I wasn't much of an interpreter or theorist. The interpretations in my *Partisan* article were quoted from the *Frankfurter Zeitung*.

Still, I'd left a door open; I was a journalist. Even before the article was accepted, I'd sensed that was the way for me to go. I did not want to stand in front of students, dropping stale information and opinions into their mouths or wiping up the misinformation and opinions they spat back.

Our German friends worked for the U.S. Army and HICOG (the High Commissioner of Germany) in the I. G. Farben Building. They'd been schooled, and a few had killed, as Nazis, but, as far as Jean and I could tell, they now thought and felt as we did. They were starting over and were in spiritual step with us.

Now and then, we brought them cigarettes from the PX or American gasoline coupons for trips up the Rhine and to the Tannus Hills. This was not the source of their affection for us. If it were, even such naive enthusiasts as we would have spotted curds in it. We trusted our antenna. After all, we were Jews, we should be able to sense racial antagonism.

Our parents, back in America, were less trusting. Jean's father went on about the school battles he'd fought with "Krauts and micks who called me 'sheeny.' " He wrote us, "Anti-Semitism is the daisy in the German lawn. Pluck it out, wake up the next morning, it's there again. Hating Jews is their avocation. They take it up when there's nothing else to do. Keep your eyes open."

"He's from another time," said Jean. "He doesn't understand what's going on." The most we conceded was that for our German friends our Jewishness was a sort of amulet they could touch to cure their old racial scrofula. "Take Götz," said Jean. "Who could be more decent, tolerant, and gentle?"

Götz had been an aide to Admiral Raeder. He'd spent six months in an English prison camp, where, he told us, he'd read Hölderlin and "was turned inside out." He had one of these top-heavy philosopher heads you sometimes see in German university towns, forehead for much of the face, with a strip of hair like an underline. His eyes, very light blue, sat deep in sockets. He went over a Hölderlin poem with me line by line, "written," he said, "in 1804, as madness was sinking into him."

> Why did you spread night over my eyes
> so that I couldn't see the earth?

Thinking of Götz and Germany rather than Hölderlin, I was moved. (Although my insides stayed where they were.)

One winter evening, walking home to Neuhaustrasse from the Farben Building, I realized that I felt at home in Frankfurt. My feelings had leaped over the rubble of hatred to the days when my German great-grandparents lived here. Two nights earlier, Jean and I had gone to a concert. The young Fischer-Dieskau and the older Tiana Lemnitz had appeared with a wonderful pianist (name forgotten) to sing Schumann's *Liederkreis* and a bunch of Schubert songs. The songs were beautiful, not beyond words but through them. Simple, even simpleminded lyrics full of clouds and streams, love and lost love, they were, in their musical outfits, heartrending. Outside, in the chill air, waiting for the trolley on Eschersheimer Landstrasse, I said, "Why should we let those Nazi murderers stand for Germany? This is Germany."

Jean said, "The murderers came out of this *Schwärmerei*. All this moping and melancholy. I know it's beautiful, but it's a veil for the other."

"Maybe so." I'd read about Germanic vagueness, the lack of legal clarity, the forest spirits, brutality, superstition, arrogance, and xenophobia which, since Tacitus wrote about them, have defined Germany and Germans. I knew a little about the other Germans, Goethe, Kant, Nietzsche, Rilke, and Kafka (the last two Czechs, but writing German), the mathematicians, physicists, chemists, and then the two hundred years of music, Bach through Brahms. That was also Germany. Every castle has latrines. OK, if the German latrines were horrible, most of the castle was glorious.

My grandparents had passed down a Germanic credo to my parents: cleanliness, neatness, punctuality, obedience, hard work, doing your duty. My parents had nagged me with these virtues, and I'd mocked them, but they were in me, they governed my habits, my values, the way I dressed, the way I lived. I thought they might be the reason I'd discovered my vocation in Germany.

6

Jochen and Cristina gave me a map and pointed out the route between their apartment and the Farben Building. I went up Bockenheimer Landstrasse to Opern Platz. The morning was cold, sunny, full of crystal flash off the stone, steel, glass, and concrete. Frankfurt was a hard, proud city. It had elected the Holy Roman emperors and was, until after the Franco-Prussian War, a free city. Now it dominated with money. The new towers were banks. Yet the city was *gemütlich* as well as proud, a cozily horizontal city in which the skyscrapers looked embarrassed, out of place. The low, solid, gray-and-chocolate stone snubbed the bemetaled glass of the presumptuous banks. This was Goethe's city, poetic in its burgher heart. And it was my city. Wasn't my assignment here to understand that? The feeling I had for it was a form of love, one I wanted and was pushing myself to get. You were supposed to feel this way. Nostalgia was an emotional pension earned by living long enough to return.

I crossed Eschersheimer Landstrasse, and there was Neuhaustrasse. Fantastic joy filled me. I floated down its hundred yards of umber six-flats rising from tiny lawns. Here and there were basements newly whitewashed, roofs and chimneys newly tuck-pointed, but otherwise it was unchanged. Number 7. Our house. I could see the back garden where Frau Gortat had married Herr Willy. (Jean and I were their witnesses.) Here was the bay window by whose light I'd read *Clarissa* and the *Aeneid, I promessi sposi* and Heine. Here my parents had come to visit us. I saw them, at least saw the photograph we'd taken of them in the garden holding Billy. A dozen years younger than I was now, my mother's curls were brown, her smile lovely.

Forty-three years ago. They'd been dead twenty years, and Billy was an angry forty-year-old who hardly spoke to me and when he did told me how wrong I was about everything I wrote, said, and was. "I love you," went his last postcard, "but I can't have anything to do with you. You're out of touch."

I walked back to Eschersheimer Landstrasse. The English bookstore where I bought Everyman and Penguin novels was gone—a pang—but much else wasn't. The medieval watchtower, fat and confident as a sausage, had been repainted and stood where it had stood for five hundred years. The Hauptwache, which Goethe thought Frankfurt's most beautiful house, was as it had been. One day, forty-three years ago, classes at the army school were suspended so that Americans could redeem their scrip money for new scrip. Germans stuck with old scrip were out of luck. American soldiers came down to the Hauptwache to trade scrip for German marks at a terrific rate. One of my first-grade students, Private Hoover, an enormous black man with a mouth full of gold teeth and a constitutional resistance to the printed word, was dealing marks and scrip with a banker's aplomb. The week before I'd said to him, "Private Hoover, I'm afraid you're not going to make it to second grade." The teeth gleamed. "Thass all right, Mr. Dortmund, don't you worry none bout't. 'Sno blame on you." After Money Change Day, they gleamed again. "Made me four hunnert thirty-one dollar, Mr. Dortmun'." "You're a financial genius, Hoover." Gleam.

I walked through a crescent of half-timbered houses to the cathedral. In 1952, the houses were sheared in half, the rooms agape. Porcelain toilet bowls shone in the rubble. One-legged and one-armed men were everywhere, as were midgets and hunchbacks. By the station was a poster for *Snow White and the Seven Dwarfs: Schneewitschen and die Siebener Zwerge.* Jean and I decided to see it, but instead spent the evening with our landlord—I don't remember how we found the room—Graf Posadowski, a soft-voiced, soft-faced aristocrat who took in our thirty marks and what we were and offered us schnapps in his book-lined study. He sat in the dark in an embroidered armchair. His English was elegant, the phrases treasured and surrendered with regal grace. "I am required to fill out a questionnaire, a *Fragebogen.* Since I am, unfortunately, of noble birth, I am required to put down the names of all the people I know who are equally unfortunate. I have been writing names of dead people for four days." He told us of one such noble cousin. "His plan was to assassinate Hitler. He made an appointment to demonstrate a piece of equipment for him. He strapped an explosive device under his tunic. His plan was to embrace the Führer, pull a cord, and explode. Hitler broke the appointment. Axel made another. That too was broken. Then Axel was sent to the Russian front and perished." The count walked over and poured schnapps into our glasses. "May I request a favor?"

"Of course," said Jean.

"Our German cigarettes are frightfully expensive and the tobacco is suspect. Could you buy for me from your PX a few boxes of Chesterfields?"

Said Jean, "Of course, Your Excellency. We'll find a soldier and give him some dollars."

"No 'Excellency,' please," said the count gently. "Only the cigarettes."

7

I crossed the Main on an iron bridge and walked up Museum Row to the German Film Museum. For Benjamin, film was the exemplary art of the age of mechanical reproduction. A collaboration of humans and machines, its making differed from that of the older, religion-based art. The film artist performed for no audience but the camera, so there was no "aura," no felt look exchanged between painter and viewer. Yes, the painting looked too, as in that Rilke poem about the headless marble torso, when the viewer realizes, "There is no place that doesn't see you. You've got to change your life."

That was going a bit far for me, but I was looking for a Frankfurt aura.

Oddly enough, four days earlier, in Rome, I'd had an auralike experience with a work of art. I'd taxied over to the Vatican Museum at 8:15 A.M. and was first in line to see the Sistine Chapel. When the guard raised the bar, I'd hoofed it like a maniac up and down stairways, through the marble labyrinth, finally into the chapel itself. Except for three guards gabbing in front of the white curtain behind which restorers worked on *The Last Judgment,* I had the place to myself. I walked from one side to the other, then up and down, taking in the ceiling frescoes, the creation of Adam, of Eve, their expulsion, the flood, then the surrounding prophets and sibyls reading—it seemed to me—the stories depicted above their heads. I felt Michelangelo's intellect touching mine. I knew that the ceiling was about making something out of nothing, about illusion, volume, space, destiny, about the human imitation and betrayal of creation.

When the tour crowds came in, I took off. I bought a couple of books on Michelangelo, walked past the crowds swelling each other, then along the high brick wall to the Bernini Colonnade, down Conciliation Walk, around Castel Sant'Angelo, and across the Tiber. When I got to the Campo dei Fiori, I drank a cappuccino in front of the hooded bronze head of Giordano Bruno and read the books. They didn't put words to what I'd seen and thought, but they knew when Michelangelo had painted what, when he'd fired an assistant, how he lived—miserably—what he wrote to his spoiled brothers and father back in Florence. One book included a sonnet he'd written about painting the chapel. With my pocket dictionary, I worked out a version of it. It went something like "I've grown a goiter in this den . . . which drives my belly to my chin, my beard to heaven, my nape upon my spine . . . My breastbone's a harp, the brush drops dripping on my face turn it into pavement. My loins are in my paunch, my ass [cul'] its counterweight . . . I'm taut as a Syrian bow . . . my perceptions are crazy, false: a twisted gun can't fire straight. [He calls to his friend Giovanni de Pistoia.] Johnny, stick up for my dead pictures and my honor because I'm in a bad way. And I'm no painter."

I worked up a lot of fellow feeling for the fellow. Young, early thirties, he thought himself old, ruined, dying. Full of common and business sense as well as genius, full of feeling for which he never found anyone worthy, except, late in his life, the young marchese Vittoria Colonna. He poured everything into marble. Considerate, tender, erotically, fraternally, and filially passionate, it was only the precious marble from Cararra which responded to him. The aura.

The encounter with Michelangelo was why I went not to the art but the film museum. After caviar, I wasn't up—or down—to hot dogs. (The museum was crammed with apparatus and diagrams about human attempts to preserve what had been seen.)

8

At one o'clock I sat with Jochen in the café of the Literatur Haus on Bockenheimer Landstrasse, waiting for Cornelia Snapper, a friend who was writing her *Habilitationsschrift* on Walter Benjamin and who worked mornings as an archivist for the Deutsche Bank.

The café consists of a few black tables served by two casual waiters. I was the oldest person there, although there were a couple of gray or graying beards and heads, one of which was Jochen's. (He is twenty years my junior.) Since he had only come to introduce me to Cornelia and had an afternoon seminar, we ordered (beer and goulash). We were also expecting Cornelia's companion, Eberhard Kurst.

Jochen seemed edgy. "What's *los,* Jochen? Worried about the seminar?"

"My wife." She'd called about their twelve-year-old daughter. "She says Peggy's made a date, she doesn't know what to do. She lets her watch *Beverly Hills 90210.* What does she expect?"

"Is having a date so awful?"

"She should have space for herself now. Some kid could ruin her for years."

"Nothing will ruin a daughter of yours."

"Her mother thinks that's a recipe for disaster. Disaster is spelled C-r-i-s-t-i-n-a."

"I was a pretty good father, and my son's a bitter, middle-aged bachelor who regards me as what's keeping him from doing anything useful."

"Sons are competitive. You've had three wives, so he'll have none. That'll show you." Jochen's bearded face contracted. "I love this little girl. I can't bear what I may have done to her—but I can't exist without Cristina."

"We live one life after another. Our kids resent it, resent us. When are they going to live?"

A girl in a blue denim jacket headed our way. Extremely pretty, short blond hair, blue eyes, a smile in every pore. I got up. "Cornelia?"

"How did you know?"

"Jochen said you worked for the Deutsche Bank. I was looking for a banker."

She kissed Jochen and shook hands with me. "So I look like a banker?"

"Exactly."

"Good, I like to look important."

There is, I think, a Boyle's Law of Emotional Diffusion. In time, people feel more or less the same about one another. If one cools, the other cools. Cornelia Snapper didn't immediately feel charmed by me, as I was by her, but she felt that I was charmed, and this pleased her. We joked, and this pleased both of us. We liked each other.

I am poorly constructed inside; my emotional mortar has never set properly. Sometimes I think that Sarah is its fixative, but then I pass someone in the street, even see someone in a movie, and I feel the mortar crumbling.

Not that I often fall, an antique word that rings true to my antique psyche, although half or more of me believes the encounter is a triumph. In any case, it's never simply casual, insignificant. Even when a connection is made, there is seldom any follow-up, letter, phone calls, even memory. Basically I've married my Sistine Chapels.

Eberhard, a bespectacled, pleasant man in his midthirties, showed up, and Jochen left. The three of us talked CDU, FDP, the breakup of dominant parties in Mexico, Japan, Italy, and Germany, nationalism, fundamentalism, the political manipulation of skin hue, ethnicity, chauvinism and ideology in Serbia, India, Sri Lanka, East Africa, and— Eberhard's phrase—"the Soviet Disunion." Their persistent note was national self-indictment: Germans were "humorless," "myopic," "grandiose," "fascists in the egg."

"I must know the wrong ones."

"You're passing through," said Eberhard. "We put on Sunday clothes for you." He touched Cornelia's shoulder, shook my hand. "I'm off to train more of us. Cornelia will take care of you. Till tonight." We were all going to see a movie called *In the Name of the Father*.

"What can I show you?" asked Cornelia. "Museums? The Goethehaus? Or would you rather be on your own?"

"I've seen all the museums I want to, and if you have the time—"

"Come to my place. I'll give you tea and a view of the city from our roof."

Bless the amalgam of beauty and niceness. I had to fight dazzlement. "Whither thou, thither I."

"?"

"To your place. Is it far?"

"Ten minutes. Up Reuterweg."

"It wasn't Reuterweg in '52." It was against the erotic tide that I mentioned a year before her birth. "He was mayor of West Berlin. Every letter had to have a two-pfennig Berlin-rebuilding stamp attached."

"You must give me German history lessons."

She walked her bicycle, I behind, gauging hers in the blue jeans. Her walk was flatfooted, toes pointing out, a confident walk.

The house too looked confident, a five-story limestone on a street of its cousins. Cornelia lived on the top floor. No elevator and no concession from her to any difficulty in the ascent. Flattery? The door opened into a small kitchen with a table, oven, fridge, and chair. Versailles it wasn't. The other room featured an unmade bed, a quilt thrown back like an invitation. "Sorry about the bed," she said. "Tea first, or view?"

I sat facing the open quilt, repressing poststaircase huffing and newer excitement. "Perhaps tea."

She filled the kettle. "Jochen said you were writing a movie about Benjamin."

"His affair with Asja Lacis."

She filled mugs and sat within two feet of me, tea steam touching her face, whose every pore glistened with receptivity, amusability; she was the friendliest beauty. "I don't think of him as a person, only an idea machine. Germanic. That's why it takes me so long to write."

"I'm the opposite. Ideas fly right past me. I don't know what Benjamin's talking about, or what others mean when they analyze him. This man Adorno says that he was 'in flight from the trancelike captivity of bourgeois immanence.' For an hour I failed to understand what that meant."

"Pure professional German. Anything to do with innerness makes us think we're getting the truth of things. If it's *innig,* it can't be bad."

"For us, 'inner' means someone's putting something over on someone. Inner circle. Or it's dangerous. Inner city."

The pores and blue eyes lit up. "*Bei uns,* 'inner city' means historic, old, the *Altstadt,* the true center. Want to see?"

We went up to the roof. It was windy, cold, glittery. Cornelia brushed hair from her eyes. She pointed to the cathedral, the bridges, the towers, the Farben Building spread below us like a great orange gun turret. "The city's fighting itself," I said. "The present and past don't fit."

"This is all I've known. I don't see what you see. Want to see where I get my name? Look, beyond that small domed church, to the right of the Dom." She hoisted my arm and pointed it. Her hand on my arm roused me. "A little more to the right. There, Goethe's house."

"On Cornelia Street?"

"*Nein,* Hirschgraben. Not even my parents would name me Hirschgraben Snapper. Cornelia was his sister." She dropped our arms, brushed hair from her face. Where do the mistresses of beauty learn their enchanting gestures? "It's so windy. I'll show you her picture downstairs."

There she handed me a postcard of a long-faced, long-nosed woman, hair pulled back over a powerful forehead, eyes closed, the slightest smile on her full lips. "She looks unhappy."

"Postpartum depression. She died at twenty-seven. Two years younger than I."

"And your parents named you after this sad person?"

"The great genius's sister; his only real companion."

"The secret sister."

"Yes. The new archetype, the sister of the great man, history's trash."

Tea and sympathy, as the popular play of the fifties had it. It was about age and youth, a headmaster's wife, a lonely student. I can't remember if she loved him. I too was on a double track, ageless inside except for the knowledge that I wasn't. Bolder and even older seniors than I would have led Cornelia to the open quilt, but fixed in my burly self, I stayed where I was. No risk, no gain, yes, but no loss either. And I had something to lose, the amiable feeling that this genial, arm-touching beauty had for me. Who knows, if I restrained myself, there'd be something more another time. Other times were getting rarer, but I hadn't thrown in the towel. In any case, to advance only to be pushed off, even as gently as Cornelia would have done it, would be unbearable. Need I could bear.

I told her my life, my wives, my interviews, travels, famous and odd friends. A Desdemonish glint lit her face, but I was no Othello. I interviewed Othellos.

9

[Setting: Capri, summer 1924. A small grocery store, wooden bins of fruit and vegetables, shelves of old-fashioned cartons, cans, and jars. A male storekeeper in apron, mustache. Making purchases is WALTER BENJAMIN, *short, solid, thick black hair, eyeglasses catching and throwing off sunlight from the windows, narrow nose, dressed in suit, necktie.]*

BENJAMIN *[pointing at tomatoes and holding up three fingers]*: *Tre pomodori, signore.*

[Enter ASJA LACIS *in white dress, carrying packages. She is* BENJAMIN's *height, dark gray eyes, dimpled chin, pretty, her Italian is almost nonexistent.]*

ASJA: *Buon giorno. Io*—I wish—*je voudrais—ich möchte gern.*

[Shrugs, dropping two packages, which BENJAMIN *picks up.]*

[To BENJAMIN] Sank you, sank you. Merci. *[To the storekeeper as she looks around for what she wants]* Mandeln.

[The storekeeper shrugs.]

Mindahl. Almonds. *Amandes.*

*[*ASJA *waves her hands, shakes her head, drops her packages.* BENJAMIN *smiles and picks them up.]*

BENJAMIN *[to* ASJA]: *Entschuldigen sie. [To the storekeeper] La signora desidera delle mandorle.*

[The storekeeper fetches a bag of almonds, scoops out a long spoonful, looks questioningly at ASJA. *She nods happily. He pours them into a smaller bag and wraps them up.]*

ASJA: *Grazie, signore. [To* BENJAMIN] *Vielen dank', Mein Herr.*

[Close-up on BENJAMIN's *serious but delighted face. Cut to sunlit street.* BENJAMIN *is carrying all the packages but the sack of nuts. Now and then he drops one, they both stop to pick it up, faces close to each other, smiling. Cut to* ASJA's *apartment. You can see her twelve-year-old daughter,* DAGA, *reading on a small balcony which overlooks the Bay of Naples.* BENJAMIN

is seated at a small table set for three with glasses of red wine, silverware. ASJA *brings a plate of spaghetti to the table and, while they talk, serves it. They drink, eat, talk.*]

BENJAMIN: I've seen you and your daughter for days now. You seem to float in your white dresses. Lovely sight. She has such long legs.

ASJA: She's thirteen. She's acted with me twice, once in Brecht. He said she was very good. We go to Moscow in a few weeks to work with Piscator. There are exciting things happening in the theater there. In everything. Why don't you come? Palestine is the past, Moscow the future.

BENJAMIN [*close-up, smiling*]: I do see some future there.

ASJA [*close-up, smiling, touching his cheek, then calling*]: Daga! There's spaghetti and wine for you.

DAGA [*looking up, craning her head to see them at the table, going back to her book*]: Save some.

10

Waiting for Jochen and Cristina, I read the literature section of the *Ef Ah Zed* (the *Frankfurter Algemeine Zeitung*). A momentary shock: there, in an aquarium, nose to nose with a moronic-looking dogfish, was a photograph of Billy.

Not Billy, of course, but, said the article, "the bard of the Fallen Wall epoch of German literature," one Durs Grünbein of East Berlin. Not even, when I got down to it, a Billy clone, but with a similar bell of brown hair and large-eyed innocence.

My recognition system saw the younger, softer Billy, the one who was still, somehow, mine.

Reading German, my spirit eases when I see the indented, italicized lines of poetry set in the solid blocks of prose. Even the clearest German prose worries me, if only because I know that waiting somewhere on the next page is a construction which will ambush me. I'll have to look up five words I don't know, and by the fifth, the meaning will have been derailed.

Line by line, poetry may be harder, but there's less of it, and that less—like a photograph—goes a long way, and you feel you've penetrated essential Germanness. I like reading about German poets. Here was not only the bard of the Fallen Wall but "his ancestors, Brecht, Celan, Rilke, and Trakl," good German company, the suppliers of neatly packaged profundity. And once you opened the package, there was often something special just for you, a sort of high-grade astrology. It was better reading about the poet, for you didn't have to bother with the whole poem, only the lines the critic selected and interpreted. This critic offered a neat line of Brecht, "*Mit kalten Spruchen innen tapeziert*" ("Tapestried inside with chilly maxims"—appropriate enough) and three lines of Celan so clear I thought I was missing something.

> *und zuweilen, wenn*
> *nur das Nichts zwischen uns stand, fanden*
> *wir ganz zueinander.*

I didn't have to look up a word and came out with the following:

> and sometimes, when
> only Nothing stood between us, we found
> ourselves completely beside each other.

Completely beside each other. Billy and I. Cornelia and I. Billy was hung up on the old "I," an "I" I did not want to revisit. The history of that "I" was streaked with feelings another poet had called "savage, extreme, rude, cruel, not to trust." With his therapist's "help," Billy remembered the noise of paternal rumbles with visiting ladies while Mom was off at Grandma's, and a backyard where he dodged a bulldog while Daddy diddled its mistress within. Grünbein's Wall had fallen in 1989. Would my death crumble Billy's?

There were three other items in the *Ef Ah Zed* that magnetized me. (Odd that focus on a subject magnetizes a field and exposes what bears on it.) My magnets were Benjamin and Billy, Frankfurt, poetry and almonds. So there on Grünbein's page were four lines of Rilke on, magnetically, the almond (*Mandel*):

Mitte aller Mitten, Kern der Kerne,
Mandel, die sich einschliegt und versuesst,—
dieses alles bis an alle Sterne
ist dein Fruchtfleisch: Sei gegruesst.

This too I could work up without my pocket dictionary:

Center of centers, kernel of kernels.
Almond, which encloses and sweetens itself—
all this to all stars
is your fruitmeat: Hello there.

This, I thought, could be worked into Benjamin's courtship scene. The idea was that Asja, guided by that occasional scenario writer, Nature, had shopped for this most amorous of nuts. Something like that.

The second item magnetized from the *Ef Ah Zed* came from an account of recent brain research which described a neural shortcut for emotions through the amygdala (Greek for almond: *amygdalon*) before another neural pathway—from stimuli to the cerebrum—worked them into the complexity called feeling. So what passed between Asja and Walter on Capri went from almonds to passion through the cerebral almond. Something like that.

The third item was dissonant Frankfurt history. It came from a new book on the first Rothschild banker, Meyer Amschel, Goethe's fellow Frankfurter. Not, however, one he was likely to know. Frankfurt's Jews were crammed into the filthy Judengasse, from which they could see the bridge—perhaps the one I'd crossed over the Main. On it was carved a sow whose shit-clogged asshole was being offered to the long, dripping tongue of a hook-nosed gentleman in a yarmulke.

11

In the Name of the Father turned out to be less a story of brutal injustice than the transformed relationship of a father and son imprisoned in the same cell. Most unsettling to this father sitting in the dark beside

Cornelia, into whose ear I whispered English versions of the actor's rapid Irish-English.

Afterward, we went across the street to a café, loud with the rock music I cannot discriminate or bear. The four of us—Cristina had gone home to write a paper—drank beer and managed a few sentences of postfilm critique in the musical intermissions. Time for good-byes.

In the street, I realized I'd forgotten my cap and went back to the café. Our waiter, seeing me, twirled it on his forefinger, an expression on his amused young face which I read as mockery. Was it my age which amused him? (What was an old codger doing in such a place, forgetting his hat and who he was?) Or was it another daisy in the German lawn?

Another uneasy undercurrent in this Frankfurt day. On the dark street, I shook hands with Eberhard and then, as Cornelia leaned toward me, I kissed her mouth.

12

[*Setting: Moscow, December 1926. Scene 31:* ASJA *and* BENJAMIN *are in her small apartment. Outside, glimpses of the Kremlin. They've been arguing.*]

ASJA: If he weren't as stupid as the general, he'd have thrown you into the street. I wouldn't care. We're not each other's property.

BENJAMIN: You get pleasure from these morons.

ASJA: Pleasure's pleasure. It doesn't destroy the pleasure I have with you. Pleasure's not something you deposit in the bank.

[BENJAMIN *shakes his head, goes to the window, stares.*]

BENJAMIN: I used to think snow so beautiful. I must have had a warmer coat.

[*Scene 35: We follow* BENJAMIN *to a baker's. Medium shot through glass window as he buys cake and carries it out. We follow him through the snowy streets, back to his small hotel. In the lobby, to his amazement, sits* ASJA.]

BENJAMIN: Why didn't you go to my room? The key is there.

ASJA [*looking at him with uneasy affection*]: No.

BENJAMIN [*opening the box with the cake and showing it to her*]: For you.

[ASJA *touches his arm, shakes her head. They look at each other, puzzled. Scene 39: We follow* BENJAMIN *out of the lobby of the hotel in his overcoat and fedora. He's carrying a large suitcase.* ASJA *is waiting in the street. An old taxi pulls up in front.*]

ASJA: Perhaps I'll come to Berlin in the spring.

BENJAMIN: Let me know.

[*They look at each other. She kisses him on both cheeks. He gets in the taxi. As it takes off, he looks around and sees her staring at the taxi. It's dusk, the suitcase is on his knees. He puts his head down on it.*]

13

From: Lyon D. Benjamin
To: Edwin Dortmund
Date: April 30, 1994

In re Scenario: Almonds. Fulfillment of Section III.b. Agreement entered into February 9, 1994. 678-A-985-439
    Benjamin fever cooled around here. Apparently need higher gradient fuel for the fin de siècle. Another decade perhaps. Regrets.

LB

14

Frankfurt/Main, May 12, 1994

Dear Edwin,

Thank you for sending this fascinating script.

Will the movie have a performance in Frankfurt? If you invite me, I will buy a new dress.

I wish my work went so well. Perhaps like Benjamin and you, I was not created to be a professor. I follow him into the labyrinth but cannot find the way out.

Eberhard suggests we go to Capri in June. Maybe I'll find the way out in the Blue Grotto. It would be much fun to run into you there.

Cornelia

15

"Dear Cornelia," I wrote in my head.

"Capri! Isle of goats. This old one can't see himself gliding through blue grottos munching almonds in your boat." Letting myself go is always easier when my fingers don't have to type letters on a sheet or monitor.

"Something odd. Three months back from Frankfurt, I can't remember your face. I confuse it with the melancholy one of Goethe's sister. Your body, though—which I never saw—breasts, bottom, groin, is something else. *Fruchtfleisch*. Now and then I lay it over my bed partner's familiar, still-loved flesh.

"Frankfurt poetry."

The capitalism of memory: what I deposited in 1952, I cashed in 1994 with the accumulated interest of forty-two years.

A twisted gun can't fire straight.

"This Father's Day, Billy, out of his incalculable blue—or mind— telephoned. I told him about seeing the house in which he'd spent his first two years. His response: 'I hate the past.'

"Cornelia, untouched-by-me darling, better luck with your Benjamin than I had with mine. And better luck with your Germany than Benjamin had with his among the daisies."

THE SORROWS OF CAPTAIN SCHREIBER

1

"An American novel today, mademoiselle?" asked Schreiber, craning around Goupin to see the paperbound book in the pocket of Verité's pullover. They were walking home along the Cher.

"So you see, Captain," and she pulled the book out so that he could see the title.

"*Le Loup de mer,*" he said. "I've never read him."

"London," said Goupin, also looking. He pronounced the name in the French manner. "I'd thought he was English."

"You read a great deal here, I've noticed," said Schreiber.

"We are far from Paris, Captain," she said.

"Thank God," added Goupin, looking at his daughter.

"I wonder," she said softly.

"I had only two days in Paris," said Schreiber. After a pause, he asked, "What sort of books do you prefer, mademoiselle?"

She raised her eyes to him and then beyond to the Cher. "Would you think philosophy, Captain?"

"Perhaps," he said.

"I'll be getting to that soon, I'm afraid. There are only six novels left. After that, history and long poems. Perhaps you have books I might borrow, Captain?"

"Verité!" said Goupin sharply.

"I should be delighted, mademoiselle. I'm only afraid my tastes won't suit you."

"You're right, Captain." She looked down again at the road. "One doesn't broaden one's tastes in a tannery."

"A rather novelistic remark, my dear," said Goupin softly.

His daughter made no response. Her pullover pinched her under the shoulders, and she was wondering if this was what made Schreiber stare at her, the bones bulging through the gray wool as haphazardly as potatoes in a sack.

They came to the side path.

"Will you come over this evening, Captain?" asked Goupin, easing his eyes from his daughter's squally hair to Schreiber's soft, blue-tinted face. "We still have two bottles of Calvados in reserve. What better way to celebrate the arrival of spring?"

"That's awfully kind, Goupin," said Schreiber. "May I accept for another time? The corporal is driving me to Bourges after dinner."

"Good things will wait, Captain. Perhaps it would be all right to invite the corporal as well?" He phrased it this way knowing the Americans were strange about Negroes.

"I'm sure he'd be honored," said Schreiber.

They parted with some ceremony, handshaking and bowing, and then Schreiber followed the beech-lined path to his billet while the Goupins continued on up the Cher road.

Verité always watched Schreiber move off down the path to her aunt's house. He was plump and ungraceful, and she felt that his movements were a mockery of his position as the local representative of the liberating forces. "It's the black corporal who has the soldier's posture," she said to her father, and then blushed, feeling that her father imagined she was really thinking of the other corporal, whom she had nearly forgotten. Without realizing that she said it aloud, she cried, "A German corporal's higher than an American one."

"Perhaps," said her father, "but they do not have the staying power." He found this amusing but did not wish to smile and embarrass his daughter.

She did not have the energy to laugh or to answer him properly. To him, I'm everybody's fool. What's the difference? And her eyes fastened on the dirt under her feet, the road she had walked so many times that she thought now there would be no other for her and that the most she could hope for would be to be swallowed by the oblivion of the habit.

2

Schreiber lived in a two-story graystone house built around a cobblestone courtyard with a garden in the middle of it. There watering the blackberry bushes she raised now instead of sweet pea and syringa, stood a small, square woman with straggly gray hair. When she heard the clacking on the cobblestones, she put down the hose and wiped her hands on her apron.

"Good evening, Captain Schreiber."

"Good evening, Mme. Cassat." Touching his cap, Schreiber inclined his head to her.

Often, before dinner, he sat with her in the garden but tonight, although Mme. Cassat made the smoothing gestures which served as invitation to such occasions, Schreiber walked to the door which led to his room.

"Have you seen my brother, Captain?" she pushed out, smoothing hair, dress, and sleeves.

"Just now, madame," replied Schreiber.

"I must tell him something about the radishes," she said, and blushed. She picked up the hose and, tightening the spout, concentrated the stream on the shoots of lawn. He wouldn't have been allowed in the parlor before the war, she told herself.

Upstairs, Schreiber had started to type. Mme. Cassat listened to the clicking resentfully and, as her husband came out to the garden, almost snarled at him. "What's he chipping away at? All his papers and numbers and ugly American. Probably counting our china."

Actually Schreiber was engaged in other calculations. He was doing a study of the villagers' evasion of censorship restrictions using circumlocutions in letters. He had begun the study as a subsection of his first administrative report on the village but had gotten interested in it and decided to pursue it on his own in a scholarly fashion. He had never before done anything so thorough, not even in law school, but he seemed to have an instinct for research, and it went very smoothly. The books piled on his desk, commandeered from the Library of Bourges and from Army Special Studies, pleased him by their bulk and solemn titles. The typewriter too was pleasing to him; its noise was like the hammering of tiny nails into meaningful junctions.

Evenings, he usually typed out the results of whatever meditations he'd had on the walk from his office to his billet. Then he would read a chapter or two from two or three of the books and type notations on memorandum cards. He typed as if the mechanics of wrists and fingers determined the conclusions themselves. Often the dull, rusty face of Verité Goupin appeared under the little black hammers. Pitiful, he thought as he hammered a comma into one of her brown eyes.

When the dinner bell sounded, he tapped a semicolon and went over to the basin, rinsed his hands, emptied the water into the slop jar, and went downstairs to the dining room.

It was this evening, as Mme. Cassat offered him the usual choice of *fromage à chèvre* or *port salut* at the end of the meal, that the feeling which had often come upon him as he deliberated the choice—the Cassats waiting with ridiculous intensity for his varying answer—became recognizable as the feeling that he was here, now, and for the first time in his life, at home. Before he'd come to France, four months ago in the fall of '44, Schreiber's preoccupation had been writing long letters to his wife filled with bitter analyses of military life and alien manners. Two weeks after he'd been assigned to the village, however, he'd written her that he had time to write only the briefest notes and that she in turn should direct all her letters through the APO to his office. Now he hardly ever thought of the squat white house in Rye or his wife, and he could scarcely remember the color of his daughter's hair.

"Do you think the *chèvre* too soft this evening, Captain?" asked Old Cassat.

"Not particularly, monsieur. It seems quite good."

"One doesn't like it too soft, but when it's hard, it dribbles all over the floor. It's really only good in Brittany," said Cassat, as if reproaching his wife for keeping him here in Cher. He sucked the last curds from his gums, his dentures rattling with the effort, and took up a knife to take the skin from a fine Italian pear.

"Yes, I've been there," said Schreiber, staring at the yellow membrane spiraling delicately from the white meat and thinking of Verité.

3

Tiberius lived with Mme. Verna Zapenskya just above her bakery two blocks from the Hôtel de Ville on the Rue Bulwer-Lytton. It was not his official billet, but there were only seven enlisted men in the village and Captain Schreiber did not worry them with regulations. In return for her favors and domestic provisions, Tiberius gave Mme. Zapenskya the double distinction of living with a noncommissioned officer and a Negro. In addition, her bakery was soon doing a lively trade in American cigarettes, chocolate bars, soap, underwear, and other valuable items from the PX in Bourges.

Mme. Zapenskya and her neighbors dreaded the release of her husband from the PW camp in Germany; as the son of a White Russian officer's *valet de chambre,* he was looked upon as inordinately jealous and vindictive. Numerous offers were available to Tiberius to exchange the comforts of the Rue Bulwer-Lytton for similar but less precarious ones. He had, however, a fondness for Mme. Zapenskya. She had a huge picture of Franklin D. Roosevelt pinned to the wall next to a mezzotint of the Virgin ("The Lady smiles but the American laughs," she said), and Roosevelt was one of Tiberius's personal idols. He persuaded her to add a somewhat smaller picture of another idol, Jack Johnson, and, under this trinity of images, he lived quite happily.

Tiberius had studied French at Bucknell, and, within a month of his arrival in the village, he spoke it better than Captain Schreiber. In this month, he became one of the central forces of the village, a judge of disputes and a counselor of difficulties; he also became Schreiber's most valuable source of information.

One night a week, he drove Schreiber to headquarters at Bourges, and, on these drives, he gave him reports on the village.

Tonight, the most important news was Fougère's decision to close the tannery.

"What do you mean, 'close it'?" asked Schreiber. "It's been there fifty years. Doesn't he like us?"

"Probably that too, Max. In general, he's just had enough. In his pockets and of this place. He's going down to his daughter's in the Midi. 'No coal thieves there,' he says." Tiberius drove carefully over the bridge. "I guess you'll have to get that Goupin girl a job in the office."

"What about the others? There're five or six of them."

"They'll find something. Verna needs somebody. Metayer too. They'll find something."

"I'd like to take the girl in. She's a little slow but very nice. The old man invited me over tonight."

"She had a little German beau last year. A corporal, except corporal's a little higher with them." He stretched his arm under Schreiber's fat jaw, so close to it that the stripes on his sleeve looked like scars on Schreiber's neck. "There's the cathedral."

"We've seen it," said Schreiber, looking.

"They've got a lot of thirteenth-century glass stored away. You ought to put in a request to get it back in."

"I suppose it could still be shelled."

"Things are pretty well wound up, Max."

The major at headquarters worked at night and always tried to keep Schreiber for drinks. Schreiber never accepted, but the major managed to delay him at least an hour with fatuous questions and quibbles. Schreiber was always worn out after the sessions, and he and Tiberius usually went to a bar outside of town for some Pernod to pick them up.

"They're starting to let the GIs out," said Tiberius when Schreiber got back to the jeep. "MPs all over too. Guess we'd better go home."

"He murdered me tonight," said Schreiber. "I could really use a drink," but they drove back.

"Next time," said Tiberius.

In front of his billet, Schreiber said, "She'll have to learn English, you know."

"That's not much of a problem. She's probably had it in school. Maybe you could help her a little."

"We'll see," said Schreiber. "She's a decent girl."

The Goupins were talking with the Cassats in the living room when he came in. Verité was in the corner, head bent over a book.

"Have you heard what's happened, Captain?" asked Mme. Cassat, calling to him from the door. "Fougère closes the tannery in three weeks, and Verité has no job. Like that," she cried, clapping her hands together sharply.

"These things happen, madame," said Schreiber, "and they are always difficult—but it so happens that I may be able to help. If mademoiselle would consider working with us, we've been needing someone for a long time. It's only a question of knowing a little English ..."

"English!" cried Mme. Cassat. "Wonderful! She's studied it for years, haven't you, my dear?"

"That's very kind indeed, Captain," said Goupin. "Very kind."

"I could never speak it," said Verité.

"Nonsense!" cried Mme. Cassat. "Why it's quite simple. I remember it myself, and it's forty years since I've said a word," and she said quickly, in English, "Good morning. Good-bye. What hour is it? Jolly good."

"I've never heard you speak English, Germaine," said Old Cassat. "It sounds beautiful, doesn't it, Captain?"

"Indeed, monsieur. Mademoiselle shall learn it almost as well if she cares to try. I should be happy to spend some time helping her myself."

This statement produced some seconds' silence.

"That would be very generous, Captain," said Mme. Cassat softly.

"You will find me a slow student, Captain," said Verité, looking up from her book.

"You learned German fairly well," said her father evenly, and there was another wordless interval.

"We can begin tomorrow evening, mademoiselle. In three weeks we should be able to do a good deal." Schreiber bowed slightly and said, "Good evening."

"We shall see," said Verité, and stared at Schreiber's back moving down the hall.

4

Schreiber told Verité that the north side of the river lay in an exposed position within two kilometers of the freight yards and that they would do better to hold their lessons on the south side.

Of course, he doesn't mind our being blown up before or after the lessons, thought Verité, but, nevertheless, twice a week she walked with him across the bridge below her house and a mile up the river to a clearing in a beech grove. Here they had the lesson.

Goupin went down to his sister's after they left, and he could see them walking on the bridge, his daughter, a few steps in back of Schreiber, stooping till she was just his height. They didn't look at each other.

"I hope he will be as cautious as the German," said Goupin to his sister.

"This type always is, Axel. Anyway, more can come from it. Willy was nice, but he could bring only trouble."

"I suppose nothing much can happen to her," said Goupin. "Only better. She will have a job, it will give her some amusement, and," he laughed here, "she will learn American."

They stopped talking when Old Cassat came into the garden to talk about prices.

Despite forebodings about her adequacy, Verité learned English very rapidly. Schreiber was industrious and patient. After they left the house, he would ask her the vocabulary he'd assigned at the end of the preceding lesson. When they reached the grove, he corrected, in the last of the daylight, the sentences she had written out. The last hour and a half was devoted to conversation. Here Verité was brilliant. With a limited vocabulary, she could soon say almost anything she wished. She was in a sense more fluent in English than in French; it was as if the feeling of exposure which hindered her in ordinary conversation disappeared in the foreign idiom. Although most of their talk concerned natural objects or typical situations, Verité managed to infuse her talk with more of her own feelings than she usually put into words.

"You amaze me, mademoiselle," said Schreiber as they crossed back after the fourth lesson.

Verité, to whom the word "amaze" was new, fathomed its meaning and made it her own.

"It's very fine to amaze someone, Captain. One considered me amazing only for being so not amazing. I am very disappointing to Poppa." She said *trompante* for "disappointing."

"We are nearly always disappointing to our parents," said Schreiber, hesitating over "disappointing" to let her learn it. "And they to us."

"Sometimes," she said.

Goupin, walking up the road, noticed they walked almost flank to flank now, and it amused him. He waited for them at the bridge and called in English. "Have you learned much this evening?"

"It comes slowly, Poppa," Verité answered in French.

"Your daughter is modest, Goupin. It goes very well."

"I'm glad. Come refresh yourself now after your labors, Captain. We have not opened the Calvados yet."

"Delighted," said Schreiber.

At Goupin's, Schreiber mentioned that his work was decreasing at the office and, since the weather was so nice, that they might hold their lessons more frequently.

"You take too much trouble, Captain," she said.

"An extraordinary kindness, Captain," said Goupin.

"It is you who do me the kindness, mademoiselle," said Schreiber. The Calvados had warmed and exalted him, and after he had said this, he wondered if it had sounded awkward. Later, walking home, he decided that it had but that Verité had understood it even beyond its intention and had not disapproved.

5

"What was it like?" asked Schreiber when he met Verité at the bridge the evening the tannery closed.

"Sad," she said. "I'd nearly forgotten it was going to end. Fougère called us in at four and told us we could go home an hour early. He said he supposed he would never see us again. We cried."

"Europeans have very strong sentiments," said Schreiber.

They walked across the bridge, and, on the other side, Schreiber touched her arm.

"I ask myself sometimes if your wife is sad at home," she said.

He dropped his hand and said, "I don't know. I hear so little. She has much to occupy her time, but she may be sad."

"Americans have not such strong sentiments," she said.

"Some," said Schreiber.

"You are here," she said, "and are one of us here."

They walked to the grove and sat down. There were no longer any sentences to correct.

"The permission to hire you came from Bourges today. A week or two and the money will be—we say, 'allocated.'"

"I understand," she said. "I will enjoy working in your office."

"You'll really be in Tiberius's office, but I come in there often." She looked expectant, and he added, "The work is not difficult."

"Is it interesting?" she asked.

"You file—*classer*—letters. If you read them, it's interesting." She smiled at him.

"Will it go on much longer, do you think?" she asked. They both understood "the war" for "it."

"I don't think so."

They both thought of the war being over and what would happen.

"It could go on a long time," she said. "The Germans are soft alone but very hard together. It could last for years."

6

Two days before the war actually ended, the report was broadcast that an armistice had been signed. Verité was in the office at the Hôtel de Ville—she had worked there almost two weeks—when Tiberius ran in with the news. Verité ran up to Schreiber's office, but he wasn't in. Then, like everyone else in the building, she ran outside.

The streets were filling. Over the village, people ran into each other's houses to announce that the end had come. The bars and cafés and the square in front of the church were filled with people. The priest rang the bells, and the people in the fields, hearing, started coming into town.

Tiberius was in the jeep shouting and singing. Eight people piled in with him, and they passed around bottles of red wine and American whiskey. They kissed each other, men and women, and waved to people in the streets.

Verité started running home. Halfway there she met the Cassats on the way to town.

"What's happened? Is it all over?" called her aunt.

"Yes, it's all over. The war is over."

"We must go to church," said Old Cassat.

"Yes, Poppa. You're coming too, Verité?" but her niece was running up the path.

"She should come," said Old Cassat.

Nobody was home. Verité waited.

In an hour Schreiber came. He had run most of the way from town, and he was gasping and sweating.

"Come," he said.

She took his hand, and they walked quickly to the bridge and over to the other side. They said nothing. In the shade of the trees, they slowed down. When they came to the clearing, they stretched out on the ground and held each other.

They were there about ten minutes when they heard a terrible noise far down the road on the other side of the river. They sat up and stared and soon distinguished the rasping horn of the jeep and Tiberius and the others shouting. They watched the jeep drive wildly over the bridge and turn up the path which led to the clearing. They stood up quickly and brushed off their clothes.

"Come on, Max," yelled Tiberius. "Climb aboard. Let the lessons go tonight."

Schreiber said nothing. He walked over to the jeep and pointed toward town. Someone spilled wine on his jacket. "Get back, Corporal," he said. "Get back on the double."

Tiberius looked at him. "Christ, Schreiber, it's all over," he said slowly. He spun the jeep around and drove back. The horn began sounding halfway down the path. They could hear it for two or three minutes.

They had sat down again, but now he started to get up. She touched his arm, but he shook his head, brushed off his clothes, and held out his hands to help her up. She took them, and he pulled her up and held her hands till they stopped trembling.

"Later, my dear," he said. "They might come back tonight."

7

People were not overly disappointed that the armistice report turned out to be false because the announcement of it was coupled with an as-surance that the real end was imminent. The day after, the bells and cannon were heard from Bourges. In the village there was no celebra-tion. People nodded to each other as if to say, "Well, there it is," and that was all. Those who had celebrated too wildly before kept inside as much as possible.

That night Schreiber met Verité at the bridge as usual, but this time they walked down instead of upriver. They walked for three-quarters of an hour before they found a place where they could be comfortable.

They talked little, in French, about what would happen. Mostly they waited for it to get dark.

They met every night for almost two weeks, staying out till three or four in the morning.

On the twelfth evening, Verité was at the bridge listening for the footsteps. When she heard the steps which were not Schreiber's, she said, "Now it's over."

It was Mme. Cassat. "He said you'd be here," she said. "He gave me this for you." She took an envelope from her sleeve and handed it to Verité. It was one from his office stamped with the legend PASSED BY CENSOR. "He came back for an hour to pack his clothes and papers. The black one calls for them tomorrow, but he left tonight. He gave me the letter and told me to give it to you, that you'd be here."

Verité was reading the letter. Mme. Cassat turned away. "These things happen," she muttered, smoothing her sleeves. She was rehears-ing what she would say.

The note was in English: "They called me today, and I'm going to Germany. I'll be on my way as you read this. I'll get a leave (*congé*) before long. You know what I think about everything. We shall arrange things." It was initialed: "M." She had never called him Max, didn't even know it was his name till she'd heard Tiberius use it. It was this that made her cry.

Mme. Cassat turned around and held out her arms. "These things happen, my dear."

8

Schreiber was assigned to Mainz. He drove there in the front seat of an army truck; twenty enlisted men were packed into the back. They arrived at night and cruised around the center of the city looking for a building they could requisition to sleep in. There was almost nothing standing. Only the cathedral. Here and there smoke rose and water flowed in the streets. Nobody was awake. They saw a few people rolled up on the grass, and, down by the river, there were hundreds more. Women, children, old men, and cripples. Across the Rhine, they could see American barracks. Two bridges stretched halfway across it; they looked like broken fingers.

They went to sleep on the banks.

The disorder upset Schreiber. He tried to think of Verité, hoping her image would compose him to sleep. Instead, he could see only piles and piles of white cards toppling over on hundreds of desks. The vision made him feel sick, and he went down to the river. He threw up in the water, and then he washed off his face. He got up and saw that an old woman had been watching him. "I was sick," he called to her in French. She looked him over and said something in German. He nodded, smiling to her, and then suddenly he felt much better, and he thought how good it was that the war was over.

The next day, they began working, setting up headquarters, contacting troops, registering the populace, establishing market lines. Schreiber worked harder than he had ever worked in his life. He went to bed every evening as soon as he was off duty. Only when the French command took over the town did he have leisure, and then he allowed himself to think about Verité.

He wrote to her, putting the letter sealed into an envelope addressed to Tiberius. In a week he wrote another. His first letter was returned, stamped, to his amazement, ABSENT WITHOUT LEAVE. RETURNED BY CENSOR. Then he wrote directly to her. There was no answer. He wrote again saying that he would be returned to the States in less than six months.

It was nearly two months now since he had seen her or heard from or about her. Mystery revived and sharpened his passion. He began to think of her all day long. He considered taking his discharge in Europe, of never going back to the States, or only after the affair had run the course these affairs must run.

Finally, he requested a week's leave and got it. He waited two days for a ride to Strasbourg and there three days for one to Dijon. He was already a day late when he started for Bourges. In Bourges, for eight cigarettes, he hired a taxi to drive him to the village. It was seven in the evening when he saw the Hôtel de Ville. He told the driver to wait there and in an hour to drive up the road to Goupin's. He gave him another cigarette and fifty francs.

When he saw the bridge, he started trembling so much he had to stop. He sat down under a beech tree and gripped the bark. He held it so tightly his arms numbed to the elbow. Then he got up and ran to Goupin's. There were no lights in the house. He opened the door and shouted, "Hey." There was no one there, but he shouted twice more. He switched on the light and the first thing he saw was a great heap of books piled up in the corner. He went over and looked at them a second, then kicked at the middle of the pile. The books tumbled against the wall. Six or seven of them remained stacked; he picked up the top one, put it to his lips, then dropped it.

He ran out of the house down the road to the Cassats'.

They were sitting with Goupin in the garden. Mme. Cassat was frightened at the running and called, "Who's there?"

"It's Schreiber," he called, and he ran to her at the edge of the courtyard. He saw Goupin sitting with Cassat in the garden. "Goupin, where's Verité?"

"Come," said Mme. Cassat, and she took him by the sleeve to where the two men sat.

He started to say, "What's wrong?" but he couldn't summon the French for it.

Old Cassat said, "Mlle. Verité is gone, Captain, gone off."

"With the black one," said his wife. "No one knows where. Nearly two months."

Schreiber looked at them all and turned away. At the gate, he said in English, "A taxi is waiting for me."

He walked down the side path to the river. He didn't dare look at the bridge.

The taxi would be coming soon, he thought. He wondered if he should wait for it in the bushes, then slip under the tires. I'm thinking of suicide, he thought, over love. In his pain, he was almost proud. He said, "*Un peu ridicule.*"

He wondered how deep the river was off the banks. Not enough, he thought. He started to cry thinking of her, but also because he couldn't do anything to himself.

At the road, he sat under a tree to wait for the taxi. The ground was wet; his legs were cold. It seemed incredible to him that he was here. When the taxi drove up, he climbed in and said, "Back to Bourges." About halfway there he started to cry. He cried all the way back to the city, not caring what the driver thought nor about anything at all.

EAST, WEST . . . MIDWEST

*Alas, we Mongols are brought up from childhood to
shoot arrows . . . Such a habit is not easy to lay aside.*
Chinghis Khan, March 1223

a small thing, lightly killed
Aeschylus, Agamemnon

1

Bidwell, a man like many, woefully incomplete and woefully ignorant
of it, was, this Christmas Day, worse off than usual. Hong Kong flu.
"The latest installment," as his usually quiet, usually uncomplaining
wife put it, "of Asian vengeance." Bidwell's single scholarly contribution to her domestic arsenal: an essay on the pendulum of revenge
which had swung between East and West since the thirteenth century.

"One more trip up these stairs"—carting iced grape juice to his
bedside—"and your Genghis can notch up another casualty."

"Chinghis," corrected Bidwell, part-time historian of the Mongols.
Their second-oldest exchange.

"Historian, journalist, translator," as he listed himself in *Who's Who
in the Midwest,* Bidwell was functioning in none of these roles when
Miss Cameron called that Christmas afternoon four years to the hour
since she'd first shown herself to be what she'd had to be put away for.

Not up to Chinghis, not up to Christmas games, and certainly not up to Miss Cameron, he was reading old letters in bed when the phone rang at his elbow.

He identified the dead voice between "Mis" and "ter."

"Mr. Bidwell?"

"Speaking."

"This is Freddy Cameron."

"Miss Cameron. Goodness me. How are you?"

"Better."

"I'm so glad."

"How are you?"

"Not too great. Got the flu. Can't shake it. Been in and out of bed for two weeks. You get it, you get over it, and you get it again. They call it the camelback."

"I'm sorry." And oddly, the voice, rising from death, was full of sorrow, no formula. Bidwell had her narrow, foal's head in mind, could see it narrowing more in genuine, illegitimately genuine sorrow. He was still the unwilling usurper of feeling which belonged to those who had denied her. These victims of deniers. How many millions had suffered for that *cangue* the fifteen-year-old Chinghis-Khan, Temüjin then, had dragged from yurt to yurt month after month. "Thank you."

"I wanted to talk to you."

"Yes."

"I mean." The pause which asked him to say her piece, but only the wronged dead could make such wordless demands. "See you."

"Would that be right, Miss Cameron?"

"I don't know."

"Mightn't it trouble you again?"

"Yes."

"Shouldn't you ask your doctor?"

"All right. If it's all right with him, will it be all right with you?"

"I think so. Soon as I shake this flu. Though it looks like a bad bet. You're up, you're down, you're up, you're down."

"Thank you. When?"

"When?"

"When can I call you about it?"

"I should be OK in a week or ten days. Maybe two weeks. Say three. You can call me at *Midland*."

"I'm sorry I called you at home."

" 'Tsall right. I'm glad to know you're better. And while we're at it, Merry Christmas, Miss Cameron."

"Yes. You too."

"So long, then."

"Yes. So long."

Thirty feet up on the third floor of the old brick house, Bidwell opened window and storm window, scooped snow from the cotton-wood branch he'd failed to trim that fall, and brought it to his boiled forehead. Could all relief be so simple.

This Christmas week, the astronauts Anders, Borman, and Lovell were looping the moon in *Apollo 8,* but down here, thought Bidwell, down here, even the fish are begging us to let up. Featured in Sunday's *Midland,* the coho salmon loaded with the DDT washed from its plant-louse-killing jobs in Indiana and Illinois. The pendulum of eco-logical revenge. Oil, bled from underwater shale, burst its iron veins and ruined the shores where the stockholders of Gulf and Humble lay on their dividends. Pigs and cattle, murdered for their chops, loosed lethal fat into the arteries of their eaters. Chicago, named by a smell-shocked Ojibwa sniffing the wild-onion tracts, stank with the sul-furous coal palmed off in arm-twisting contracts. The air, the lake, where a trillion silver skeletons rotted forty miles of shoreline (the starved alewives washed in with the opening of the locked interior by the St. Lawrence Seaway). Out Bidwell's windows, north, south, west, the locked slums, leaking vengeance on those who'd locked them there. "A fifth of American color television sets are dangerously ra-dioactive," last Sunday's feature in *Midland,* and there, sucking poison into their cells with Garfield Goose, his little boys, Josh and Petey. In fury, Bidwell called Sears, threatened them with a follow-up story in *Midland,* and in two hours, a redheaded engineer, Swanson, zoomed up from the Loop, in hand two thousand-dollar boxes, scintillators whose needles reported his boys safe. Safe, that is, said Swanson, until the regulator tube broke down, and the voltage soared to transmit reds, greens, and blues.

The classic hang-ups of the twentieth-century burgher, and they were Bidwell's; in spades, for they were also the staff of his Sunday supplement's life.

And now, his very own pestilence, Miss Cameron. Obsessed, frenzied, the great mechanism of perception wild with unreality. A pair of legs, a pair of ears, a pair—he supposed—of breasts, all the paraphernalia of reasonable woman, and then, above the neck, behind the eyes, between the ears, a loose nut. Back to the factory. But no, the factory turned her loose, and now so did the repair shop, and once more she was after him who had nothing, next to nothing, to do with her.

This Christmas week, between bouts of chills and fever, Bidwell worked on the Christmas Day of 1241, when Batu, Chinghis Khan's grandson, crossed the iced Danube and battered the town of Esztergom. Europe, a small island of feudal civility, hung by a thread. Batu's armies had wiped out Kiev, Ryazan, Moscow, Bolgar, Vladimir, and Pest. There was nothing to stop them but the immobile, tanklike knights of Hungary. Then, Christmas Day, Batu got the news his uncle Ögödei, the Khakan, had died, and back he turned. Europe was saved, as it would be saved by such threads for three centuries, until its sea power flanked the masters of the Eurasian landmass and began that great rise of the West, which, this very Christmas week of 1968—as its feet were chilled by Eastern threat—reached the moon itself. A distance which should annul the old divisiveness of the world. A great story.

For years Bidwell had published bits of it in the *Harvard Journal of Asiatic Studies,* the *Abhandlung für die Kunde des Morgenlandes,* and the *Journal asiatique.* Austere, careful studies, but Bidwell had literary ambition, and in mind a fine book like Mattingly's on the Armada or Runciman's on the Sicilian Vespers, a work Josh and Petey would see on general reading lists, not merely in footnotes. This ambition went against the grain of his graduate training, but there it was, a desire to shape data into coherent stories which would serve men who counted as models and guides. All right, such stories were formed by fashion and lived by style, but they were what deepened life. Didn't Chinghis, didn't all heroes, live and die by them?

Sweat poured into the blue clocks of his flannel pajamas; he pulled the great quilt about his chilled bones. Mind adrift between the Mongols and *Apollo 8,* Bidwell felt the Great Divide in things. The lunar odyssey had its elegant technology and its political-commercial hoopla. Its heroes were no Hectors, no Chinghises, only burghers like himself, bolstered by exercise and the great American confidence in mechanic triumph.

Where did he, Bidwell, stand with these Moon Loopers?

They were the stuff his sort made sense of, the titles of books his sort wrote. Their risks were somatic, his mental; they moved in space, he time.

They lived like finely tooled nuts in a great machine. And how would they die? They had no choice. Bidwell's subject, Chinghis Khan, had constructed his death, had planned the extermination of the Tanguts, chosen his successor, and then moved north of the Wei to the cool air of the Kansu mountains. No wonder the Mongol bards rose to their great epic; Chinghis had worked his life out as a poem.

Yet the astronauts too were controlled by story. Christmas Eve, they read Genesis to Earth as sunlight poured on the lunar crust. Bidwell, fever rising, back troubled by a mattress button he was too weak to rip off or shift away from, felt their voices fuse with the racket of his children.

Human buzz.

What did human enterprise come to, great or small?

Commotion.

The fever drifted him, Bidwell felt himself buzzing off like an old bulb.

They were all going to have to make it on their own. Ethel, Batu, Chinghis, Josh, Petey, Shiffrin (his boss at *Midland*).

They'd feel the void he left. Yes, but then augment their own emotional capital with it. Functioning men wasted nothing. What could be more ornamental than young widowhood, the loss of a father, a friend?

Sig Schlein would look through his manuscripts, decide what could be salvaged for articles, and wrap up his bibliographical life with an elegiac paragraph in the *HJAS*. A few sheets of paper, a few feet of earth, a few real, a few crocodile tears, and Farewell Bidwell.

And for years, maybe, Farewell Batu and the other Mongol chiefs whose ghosts he'd animated. Though they could take it better than he. Their bloody deeds were on record, his own lay mostly hidden, some in his boys' heads, to be disinterred on couches fifteen years from now (if people were still buying that paregoric). "My descendants will wear gold cloth, feed on tender meat, ride proud horses, press the most beautiful young women in their arms . . . and they will have forgotten to whom they owe it all." August 18, 1227: Farewell Chinghis. Buzz and bitter lemons. December 24, 1968: Farewell Bidwell.

A bad night.

But somehow, by morning, he'd outflanked the flu-dazed grip on his life. A silver band showed beneath the shade. Christmas morning. "Time, Daddy."

Weak, but clearheaded, Bidwell, in his sweat-damp clocked pajamas, led Ethel and the boys toward the Scotch pine on their green *tayga* of carpet, where lay, scattered like Chinghis's victims, packages of every color and shape.

The geometry of burgher dreams.

2

Back in 1964, Bidwell was translating extracts from the *Secret History of the Mongols* for the University of Minnesota Press. The *Midland* typing pool sent up a girl who did extra work at home.

Miss Cameron. Five and a half feet of long-faced timidity, hands crossed before her parts, eyes down, though sneaking up when she thought his weren't. Yes, she did extra typing, she would be happy to do his manuscript.

He gave her a short section about the kidnapping of Temüjin's wife Börte by the Merkit warrior who impregnated her. Miss Cameron brought it back the next day, a fine job. He gave her the rest of the manuscript, about a hundred pages.

A week, ten days, two weeks, and there was no word from her. The typing pool said she hadn't called in and, furthermore, had no telephone. They assumed she was sick. She lived on the edge of the Lawndale ghetto. The Friday before Christmas, Bidwell drove fearfully on the shattered rim of the slum and rang the doorbell of her apartment.

She came downstairs, and when she saw him through the glass, a small hand went to her small chest. "I'm very sorry," she said, opening up. "I've been sick."

He told her not to worry, he'd been concerned about her as well as his manuscript.

A smile showed a half second on thin lips. Physics had cloud chambers for such short-lived states. What self-distrust killed such smiles? Miss Cameron's long hair, a dull red, shook about her narrow shoulders. Cold? Fear? Negation? "I'm almost done with it. Do you want what I have?"

In her dead voice, these words hung all sorts of interrogation before Bidwell. He wanted nothing from Miss Cameron but what he'd paid for.

"I'll wait till you finish. Can I bring you anything? Food? Medicine?" There was a deep barrenness in the stairwell. Miss Cameron was as stranded as the old moon. "No, thanks," she had everything. "Good-bye," and sorry she caused him so much worry. "I can't remember why I didn't call. I didn't know so much time had passed."

Monday she brought in the typescript. There were hundreds of mistakes in it, omitted paragraphs, garbled sentences. He had the whole thing redone by another girl in the pool but said nothing to Miss Cameron, only thanked and paid her.

That Christmas afternoon, he answered the phone.

"Why did you?" asked the dead voice.

"Excuse me."

"You had no right."

"Miss Cameron?"

"You shouldn't have done it."

"Please tell me what's wrong."

"You know." Sly and accusatory, new sound in the monotone. "You know."

"Look," said Bidwell, "let me get a doctor for you. You're not in good shape."

"No." A wail. "No. Tell me why you stood at the window. Naked you were. Pudgy you are. Yet had your way. With me." Then fiercely, "It's you should see a doctor." The phone banged.

Bidwell rang up his analyst neighbor, Spitzer, told him what happened, asked if the girl sounded suicidal or homicidal.

"Probably not," said Spitzer. "She's having an episode. Happens frequently on Christmas. Or Sundays. The routine's broken, there's nothing to intrude on the fantasy. Can you get hold of her parents? Or some relative?"

Bidwell knew nothing about her, he'd have to wait till the office opened in two days, then he could check with personnel.

"You could call the police," said Spitzer, "but I don't advise it. The girl's called you because she's got it into her head that you're important to her. If you bring the police, it'll confirm the worst of her fears. Don't worry. She won't hurt anyone. And she won't throw herself out the window."

(False prophet Spitzer. Though it was four years off.)

That night, the phone jangled him from sleep.

"Saint Stephen's Day, Mr. Bidwell."

"Oh, Lord. Miss Cameron. What?"

"I must see you. You came again. The scale fell from you. Devil. At the window. Yet it can't be. I'm so, so, so mixed up. Please see me?"

Saint Stephen's Day. Every year they went to Sig Schlein's Boxing Day party. "Today?"

"Please."

"Where? Not at your place. Wouldn't be right."

She would come uptown, they could meet at Pixley and Ehler's on Randolph opposite the public library. It would save him miles.

This was rational, she was aware of him. All right, he'd be there at ten-thirty. Pixley and Ehler's. How did she pick it? Chicago's Olympus of the radical thirties. His boyhood. Thick buns frosting in the windows, bums mixing with scholars from the Crerar Library upstairs, the filthy classic hulk of the Chicago Public Library across the street.

At ten-thirty there was no one at the round tables but a bum dipping a cruller into coffee.

Bidwell waited at one of the tables with a pot of tea till Miss Cameron swung open the doors. In a cloth coat which didn't seem up to stopping frost, hardly enough to contain her, and hatless, the red hair like thread laid over a counter to be woven for something more useful than itself. The long face, beak nosed, chapped, pale, eyes a clouded blue and looking as if stuck in at the last moment, full of haste and hurt. Her progress to his table was a drift. Then, arriving, head down, she said, "Thank you."

For coming? For existing? For not being something contrived by her brain and found nowhere else?

"Miss Cameron, I came to persuade you to let me take you to a hospital."

The raw face slapped against her palm. "God," it said. She sat down.

"Miss Cameron. Tell me what I can do for you."

The face faltered, thickened, grew inward, the eyes cleared, lit with what he had not seen there before. "Have you not killed the devil's warrior for my bed, Temüjin? What a question."

Wednesday morning. Chicago. Nineteen sixty-four. Women pouring out of the IC tunnel where Capone had had Jake Lingle, the diamond-belted go-between, shot to death, the news dealers calling out Lyndon Johnson's Christmas menu on the ranch, the bum lapping his cruller, and here this frail cup of girl's flesh thought itself the bride of Chinghis Khan, eight hundred years and fifteen thousand miles away.

"It's just me, Bidwell, Miss Cameron. It's 1964, and you're Miss Cameron, somewhat unwell, and you typed the manuscript about Chinghis and Börte for me, and I think it's confused you."

Her face blinked. Bidwell could make out the present taking over her face, a hard march through swamps, but she made it, she nodded. Up and down went the foal's head. "I know," and as he was about to welcome this with "Good," the face blinked again, the smashed eyes said, "But he told me."

"What?"

"At the window," she said with her small wail. "He said you'd take me back, though Jaghatay was in my belly. Here," and a thin hand came from her lap to the brown middle of the coat to show the unlikely presence of Börte's son.

Bidwell, a weight of misery in his own stomach, found nothing to say. Her head rose and fell, his went from side to side.

"Yes," she said, the face blinking again. "I know it's in my head." Which now pendulumed like his.

Bidwell, knowing, even as he did it, that a risk was in it, covered her small hand with his gloved one.

"Gawd," she moaned. The head twisted away from its stem, her body, rising, followed it. Before Bidwell could get his bearings, she was into Randolph Street, red head down, ramming the cold air.

3

By the time he'd gotten her personnel file and located a mother who lived in Evanston, she'd called to apologize and request another meeting.

"All right," he said, his campaign formed. "At the same place."

Where not Bidwell but Mother and Mother's priest came with a car. Miss Cameron was wrapped up and taken to the Sisters of Mercy in Milwaukee, "not," said Spitzer, "a great center of treatment, but they'll be kind to her, and she'll be off the streets."

Eight months later, Bidwell received a letter in green ink.

Dear Mr. Bidwell,

I know I caused you trouble. My mind troubled. The man at the window — was it not you? I would say it was real, though I know you could not have been at such a place. But did you not mean it for me? Sitting there with your glasses, so kindly, why not? The world thinks Genghis a monster, but you showed me how in bad times, he drank his saliva and ate his gums, slept on his elbow and saved his Börte. Did you not mean me to know I was to you what Börte was to him? I cannot quite straiten it out. But remain

Very truly yours,
(Miss) Frederick Cameron

4

Monday, January 15, 1968, three weeks to the day after she'd called, Miss Cameron rang him at *Midland*. He was having his weekly fight with Shiffrin, the editor. His junior by ten years, a classic Chicago newsman out of the City News Bureau and the *American,* Shiffrin had married meat money and put some of it into the sinking *Midland.*

Hard, thin, a board of a man, Bidwell called him Giacometti. "A face like a cheese knife," he said to Ethel. "When it comes at you, you think it'll slice you in half. And his ideas are narrower than his face."

Shiffrin was on top of whatever was on top, but for him that meant what appeared in the newspapers of St. Louis, Milwaukee, Minneapolis, and Chicago, with dollops of *Time* and *Newsweek* for intellectual debauches. "You should be reading the tech and business mags," Bidwell told him the first week, but Shiffrin was unable to detach the text from the ads in *Aviation Week,* and besides, the mere sight of a technical word blanked him out of consciousness.

When Miss Cameron's call came, they were having a shouting match about a piece on the students. Bidwell had listed twenty different issues raised by the world's students, the lighting system at Prague Tech, the language question at Louvain and Calcutta, football at Grambling, political issues at Hamburg and Berkeley. To this he'd attached a tail of explanations from commentators, Aron, Howe, Feuer, McLuhan, and a handful of college presidents. A rapid, agitated surface, but it covered lots of ground and let the pancake-sodden readers of the supplement get an idea of the complexity of the matter.

To Shiffrin, it was Bidwell's usual academic glop which turned every second piece he touched "into the *Britannica.*"

Of course, he was right, was always right. To most of their readers, Joey Bishop was Einstein, the amount of information that could be ladled out in any one story should not exceed a recipe for French toast. If Bidwell hadn't been there since the Year One, and if he didn't do good rewrite jobs, Shiffrin would have bounced him.

"Look, find some little spade chick on the Circle campus, let her yack away half a column, then get some Yid prof to yack up the other half, a few pictures, and we got our story. Save this truckload of cobwebs for the *Atlantic Monthly.*" Which is more or less the way it would work out, and another issue would be ready to wrap Monday's fish.

Bidwell took the call from the switchboard in middispute. "Mr. Bidwell?"

The whirl in the office subsided. "Oh, yes, Miss Cameron. How are you?"

"I'm fine. You said I could call you."

"That's right."

Shiffrin's black eyes bounced off his cruel nose and moved sky-ward. Then finger snapping.

"I'm afraid it's not a good time, though. I'm in conference."

"Finish up," said Shiffrin. "Nail the nooky, and let's get shaking. It's sixteen to press," meaning sixteen hours till their press roll.

"Call in half an hour," said Bidwell and hung up. "If you had nooky like that, you'd turn monk."

Shiffrin's wife weighed in at a hundred and sixty pounds, all vocal, he ran through the secretarial staff with his agitated wand, over-promising, underperforming, he understood women trouble. "Professors like you working me to the grave, I'm ape now."

This last week, Bidwell had been writing up Ye-lü Ch'u-ts'ai's revelation to Chinghis that it would be better to regard towns as resources rather than pools of infection, a great moment of generous truth in the Mongol world and the never-ending education of the Khan. All right, he, Bidwell, would make the best of Shiffrin.

He arranged to meet Miss Cameron in Pixley and Ehler's.

Four years later, the Crerar was gone to IIT, but the buns and the bums were still there. And Miss Cameron too, about the same, the long face bent over two cups. No smile to meet his, but her look was relaxed, even intimate.

He shook hands, his bare, hers gloved. Their flesh had still not touched. Which Bidwell knew counted, though not how. "And," weeks later, "what could I have done?"

"Thank you for coming."

"You're looking well."

Which brought blush and smile. The body gets simpler near the surface. Its economy there offers small variety to register the terrific feelings beneath. Bidwell could but guess the recrudescent girlishness of Miss Cameron's smile, not coyness, no, only simple pleasure in the situation which the inner time of derangement had kept from the years. "You haven't changed," he said, meaning the standard compliment.

"I hope I have." A remark in clock time, and its own evidence. "It's why I wanted to see you. To show you I understand how wild I was."

Was this all?

He sat down to a cup of tea, continuation of the cup he'd drunk four years before, but bought by her for whom his taste was absolute.

Bidwell, fleshy head given jots of youth by the frost, civil tonsure indulged at the sides and back in concession to style and barber's prices, had now a vagueness of feeling, seeing in this half-smiling, pale person not only an old trouble but also a not-bad, if thin, woman's body.

"Your trouble seems to be over."

"Mostly over."

"Still have bad times?"

"Now and then. I don't drink now."

"I didn't know you did that."

"Once a week, I'd really lush up. Now I sit tight."

Bidwell eased off his overcoat, stuck his scarf in his sleeve. Like most Pixley customers, Miss Cameron kept on what she'd come in with. Who knew when quick hands would grab? He should have seen this as trouble.

"What can I do for you?"

"You are," said Miss Cameron. "Seeing you. That's all. Just this. And to talk to you every once in a while."

The strange creep of human feeling. Unable to stay put. Could he find pleasure on that thin chest? What would pass between Pudgy and Miss Giacometti?

"I suppose that's all right, Miss Cameron. It's not a hard way to help someone."

"You're a good person."

"Not really. It's habit. Laziness. Though, you know, I probably can't see you once a week. But we can certainly talk on the phone. Maybe on Thursdays. That's an easy day at the office. Then every once in a while, we can meet here."

Which created her schedule, her life.

Every Thursday after he came back from lunch, Bidwell would answer the phone and talk with Miss Cameron about her health, her work — she did part-time secretarial work at Northwestern — and her reading — she was going through Will Durant, had been in *The Oriental Heritage* since the day after their first meeting. Once a month, they met in Pixley and Ehler's at five o'clock and drank tea for an hour.

The Thursday after their fourth and last meeting, the telephone did not ring. Bidwell waited uncomfortably, felt its silence, felt the absence of that dead — though somewhat revived — voice. Ah, well, she was out of town, sick, at a movie, or, true revival, she'd faced down her madness, seen through the old delusion.

The next day's *Sun-Times,* though, showed something else. At the time of her usual call, Miss Cameron was jumping out of the tenth-floor window of the Playboy Building on North Michigan Avenue. The first such occurrence there, clearly a dramatic one, for Miss Cameron had, as far as was known, no business in the building. Other than the melancholy one therein reported. She'd been seen by an elevator operator at lunchtime: "While most came down, she went up," and then when the rest came up, she took the quick route down.

The famous owner of the building couldn't be reached for comment, but a spokesman said the girl was a mental patient, perhaps the building was chosen as a deranged protest or symbol, but, of course, there was nothing to be done about that. Most of the building's windows didn't even open; the woman had found a janitor's storeroom and even then had to climb up on a trash can and smash the window with a fire extinguisher.

A small thing, lightly killed.

Bidwell was, of course, very upset, but the week passed, he worked on Chinghis Khan's eradication of the Tanguts and did not think of Miss Cameron; except the next Thursday, when the silence of the telephone stirred him, and that night, when the garage door shut behind his Pontiac and he was alone the usual few seconds in the dark.

What a death the poor narrow thing had constructed for herself. No campaign, no successor, no trip to the cool mountains, only an elevator ride, a smashed window, an untelephoned farewell: "This is it. I can't ask you anymore. Let alone by phone."

THE GOOD EUROPEAN

1

Mr. Weber was mad, a shock to most of the office staff, but for Harry Pfeiffer mere confirmation of a painful commonplace.

Pfeiffer was Mr. Weber's "New York end," had been ever since coming to work for D-J International barely a year after he'd stepped off the boat from Hamburg. For fourteen years he had listened to the stories told about Weber without being at all amused; as a German refugee, he had had enough of eccentricity in power. His job was to read Weber's turgid official reports, and it soon became clear to him that he was also responsible for attending to the personal requests appended to them. Every month he sent his secretary to the newsstand for the comic books which the Weber children wished to read; and twice a year, he telephoned Bloomingdale's to order the twenty-four jars of peanut butter and the two kegs of saltines which the Americans in Saint-Germain-en-Laye phenomenally consumed. These, and less regularly requested items—jars of Sanka, crates of Kleenex tissue, Emerson radio tubes, Sunbeam razor cutters, nylons, cigarillos— would be parceled by company help on one side of the Atlantic and un-parceled by company help on the other.

The Webers had lived in Europe for nine years, and before that in Buenos Aires for ten. All this while, their passion for American products grew until it displaced every other affectionate sentiment connected with their native land. The situation was not modified by annual New York visits.

It was during these visits that Pfeiffer had had his views of Arnold Weber, views which had sent him home to his wife muttering, prophetically, as it turned out, "The man's mad."

Now that events had certified his assessment, Pfeiffer sat back triumphantly in his small office watching the clerks outside spread their varied distortions of the story. He had heard what appeared to be an accurate version from Mr. Crain, who had talked with Chanteloup on the transatlantic phone.

The story was that Weber had returned to the office looking particularly despondent and saying something under his breath about Europeans. After an hour in his office, he had sent for Chanteloup and de Roubain. They entered to find him swinging naked from the parallel bars. (His office was fitted out like a gymnasium.) As they came forward to ask if they could help, he had shouted, "Lousy frogs," and leaped onto de Roubain's shoulders, rolled over on him, and bitten him in the throat. They called for help, and in a minute, the room filled with pacifying assistants. Weber's chauffeur was summoned, and he and Chanteloup had gotten Weber dressed and carted off to the doctor's. The diagnosis was that he had suffered a complete breakdown. He was to be confined for an indefinite period in an institution, an American one in view of his obviously paranoid feelings about Europe and Europeans. Plane reservations for New York had been made and two nurses hired to accompany him back to the States.

At three-thirty, Pfeiffer's secretary made a twirling motion with her forefinger. Pfeiffer laced up his special shoe and limped down the hall to Bellman's office. The talk, he well knew, would have to do with Weber, but this was not his chief concern. Indeed, for the past hour he had been considering the Weber affair only as it might affect the execution of his resolve to smoke a cigarette in Bellman's presence. On the way up the hall, he decided that Bellman might be so distracted by the news that he might not notice anything.

Miss Pinney waved Pfeiffer into the office, and he drew a pack of Chesterfields from his pants pocket. Mr. Bellman's head was poised over some papers. Pfeiffer sat down and struck a match.

"Take a seat, Harry," said Mr. Bellman, not looking up.

"Thank you," said Pfeiffer, lighting it despite the initial disadvantage. He held the smoke in until he felt he'd be consumed by it, then puffed it away from the desk toward the window.

Bellman's black stare was on him. "You've heard about Arnold?"

Pfeiffer nodded and took another puff, his face white with the effort to keep his hand steady.

"I'm going over tomorrow to see what I can do. One thing I cannot do, Harry, and that is stay there." Pfeiffer blew a load of smoke toward his lap. "Crain and I have been talking about it. We think you're the man to take over." He pushed an ashtray over the desk, and Pfeiffer stubbed out his cigarette. "I know it's hard to decide such matters overnight, but we've got to have a quick answer, Harry. Can you give us one this weekend? If you decide against it, cable me at the Georges Cinq. Otherwise we'll book the passage for you next Thursday. Your family can join you later. Do you have a passport?"

"An old German one for souvenir," said Pfeiffer.

"Yes. Why don't you start on that right away? If you decide against going, the company's only out ten dollars." He opened a Damascus mosaic cigarette box. "Try these. They're Romanian, I think."

"Thank you," said Pfeiffer, taking one.

"Two hundred in francs there, three hundred here, and expenses in francs or whatever local currency you need. Have a nice weekend, Harry. I hope you're going to decide to help us out. It might only be for six months or so. Arnold's a hard man to keep down. And I think you'll have a nice time. You and your wife have never gone back over there, have you?"

"No," said Pfeiffer.

"It'll be a lark for you then. Seeing Europe as Americans."

"Yes, that would be something," said Pfeiffer.

"Shipley's horsing around over there," continued Bellman. Shipley was an old-time company man whom Bellman had been trying to insult off the payroll for years. "You're a friend of his, aren't you?"

"He brought me into the company."

"Perhaps he can earn some of his keep by entertaining you."

"I'll talk it all over with my wife, Mr. Bellman. I appreciate your confidence in me."

"I hope so, Harry."

"And meanwhile, I'll do something about the passport."

As Pfeiffer opened the door, Bellman called out, "There's no one who can do the job like you, Harry. If it's yes, Gilly will make you reservations at the Castiglione. It's a nice place, much quieter than the Georges Cinq. I think you'll prefer it."

Pfeiffer put out the Romanian cigarette in Miss Pinney's ashtray. At least he had done that.

"Leopold," he called to his accounts assistant who sat in the main clerks' office at a table piled with immense ledgers. "Tell Gilman to book me a passage for Paris next Thursday. I'm going down to the passport bureau now."

"*Sie fahren nach Paris?*"

"Thursday."

"*Und zurück?*"

"Who knows?"

Pfeiffer put on his suit coat and limped to the elevators. He had never seen Paris. He'd been in Strasbourg but never in Paris. Within three months, within a month perhaps, he might be seeing it again. And he would see Germany: there was a D-J office in Frankfurt. He might even see Bebelshausen again. Or Hamburg, although he never wanted to see Hamburg again, not even stone detached from stone with veils of dust between it and the sun.

2

Hamburg was the last Pfeiffer had seen of Europe. Fifteen years ago. He was Heinz Pfeiffer then, and he had walked the streets of Hamburg for five hours unable to take a seat in a restaurant or hotel lobby, to go to a movie, or to sit in the park where the benches too were *Für Hunde und Juden Verboten.* He had walked with his head bent away from the looks, curious or embarrassed, until, near the wharves, he had bought two sweet rolls from a peddler and eaten them leaning against a wall.

Withal, it was still Europe, rather than Germany, he was leaving, and, therefore, the tremendous relief of departure was coupled with regret, regret for that sweet condition which had enabled him, the small, clubfooted son of a German-Jewish grocer in Bebelshausen am Rhein, to consider himself, and to be considered by his fellows, *ein guter Europäer.* He had gone to school in Munich, Geneva, Strasbourg, Heidelberg, and Bern, and everywhere his role had been the same, his humor and intensity composing the ideal temperament for the European bourgeois student of the twenties and thirties. Everywhere he was a success. Men liked him, and, despite his foot, so did women.

There had been almost no trouble, no sign of what was to come. Pfeiffer remembered only one incident, and that largely because it had a startling, if, happily, brief sequel. It was in the spring of 1930, and he was on a Rhine cruise with a group of friends. They drank a lot, and there was singing and dancing. Pfeiffer danced fairly well, all things considered, and it was while he was dancing with one of the prettiest girls on the boat that he felt himself pushed and, a few seconds later, pushed again. At the third push, he turned to see a large boy from another party whom he knew as a member of the young Nazi group at Heidelberg. "Once more," Pfeiffer had told him, "and I'll punch you in the nose." Laughter from the boy and a punch from Pfeiffer. His friends stepped in, threatened to throw the other into the Rhine, and toasted Pfeiffer's heroism.

The sequel came five years later. Pfeiffer stepped off the train one evening in Düsseldorf, where he was making the contact which resulted in his getting an exit visa. He was alone on the street when he saw walking toward him, in uniform, pistol at hip, the same fellow. I'm dead, he thought. It's all over. The *Schwein* will shoot me in the head and kick me into the gutter. He closed his eyes and heard the footsteps thunder up and pass him.

The year before, he had returned to Germany from Bern. He had not planned to come back until the political situation changed, but an aunt had written him that his mother was dying. At the border, he was stopped by two policemen and asked, "Where are the papers, Pfeiffer?" Pfeiffer replied that there must be a mistake, he was only a law student in Bern. They didn't bother to dispute this but took him to the station house, stripped him, poked around in his mouth and anus, sliced open his special shoe, and examined his deformed foot, saying that it would be an excellent place to hide something. He was detained at the border for two days but never learned for what papers they were searching. When he got to Bebelshausen, his mother was already buried, and the house with the grocery on the ground floor had been sold for one-twentieth its value.

During the next two years, Pfeiffer lived with his aunt. In that time, he never left the house, not even to sit in the backyard, until he made the trip to Düsseldorf, and then, at the end, the trip to Hamburg.

3

During his first three weeks in Paris, Pfeiffer worked from eight o'clock in the morning until nine at night. He thought of nothing but fighting his way through the labyrinth into which Arnold Weber's incompetence had maneuvered the European affairs of the company. The incompetence went beyond even conscious irregularity: Pfeiffer's most difficult hours were spent deciding when the madman had strayed into accuracy.

By the fourth week, he saw his way clear. Weber's stranglehold was loosened, though at a large price. Pfeiffer's review of the accounts indicated that Weber's nine-year reign had cost the company close to eight hundred million francs for the French market alone. He drafted a long cable to Mr. Bellman and, after dispatching it, took to his bed in the Castiglione for three days during which he did nothing but sleep, read Agatha Christie, and order immense dinners from La Crémaillère which were wheeled to his bed on tables covered with embossed silver and flowers of the season.

The evening of the third day, Shipley telephoned to ask him over for a drink. "I'd've called before, Harry, but we just got back from Rome. How are you? I hear you've been doing a number one job filling in for Arnold. I'm going to cable Dolph the good word. Get here at four-thirty, will you? Belle and I eat at six."

To his surprise, Pfeiffer found himself looking forward to seeing Shipley. The only person with whom he'd talked socially in Paris was Chanteloup. Half his lunches had been ruined by the Frenchman's stories about Weber, stories of personal mania which matched those which Pfeiffer was digging out of the company books, stories of the gymnasium (dismantled by Bellman on his visit), of the tiger hired for "publicity shots" but kept in an adjacent office so that Weber could go in to stare him down, until one day he had had his arm clawed after punching the sleeping animal in the nose through the bars of the cage. "You crazy Americans," Chanteloup had come out with after telling this one. "Americans," exclaimed Pfeiffer, but held back from saying either that madmen were international or that, at any rate, he was scarcely more American than Chanteloup himself.

After such stories, even Shipley seemed a relief. He opened the door himself, resplendent in a Floridan outfit of purple sandals, green slacks, and mauve sport shirt. "Let me show you the works, Harry." The works were five enormous rooms in which magnificent lounges, beds, tables, pictures, and tapestries bloomed like subtly acclimatized natural growths. In a far corner of the largest room sat a white-haired woman who didn't look up as they came in.

"Belle," screamed Shipley. "Belle."

The woman smiled and came over. She was dressed in black and wore a chrysanthemum over each ear. "You know Belle, Harry, don't you?"

"I don't think I've had the pleasure," said Pfeiffer, taking Mrs. Shipley's hand.

"She don't hear you, Harry," said Shipley.

"I'm sorry, I don't hear well," said Mrs. Shipley. "Did you tell him about the accident, Billy?"

"She got her eardrums burst by an explosion in a Rome laundry. Ripped some of the ear off," and he raised one of the chrysanthemums to give Pfeiffer a glimpse of some blasted flesh. Mrs. Shipley stepped out of reach. "We were having tea next to this place when *boom!*" and he slammed a fist into his palm. "They'll bust no more eardrums in that place. I'll tell you that."

"I'm very sorry, Mrs. Shipley," said Pfeiffer.

"She can't hear you," said Shipley. "Call her Belle."

"I'll get you something to drink," said Mrs. Shipley.

"Like hell you will," said Shipley, and he shouted, "Annette!" And to Pfeiffer, "We pay the slut seven thousand francs a month."

The maid appeared, and Shipley said, "Scotch and water. Two," and he held up two fingers. "Lemonade. One," and he held up one.

Mrs. Shipley went to a corner with a magazine. Pfeiffer sat on a couch opposite Shipley on another.

"See this picture?" asked Shipley, pointing over his head to a small

Utrillo street scene, dark under an unlit display light. "Comes with the place. It's by the modern Rembrandt, one of the reasons this damn place is costing me six hundred thousand francs a month. You know what? I had to draw on my New York salary twice last year. What do you think of that? I wrote Dolph about it. I said, 'Dolph, if you want the company to stay big over here, if you want your top men to give up their country and their homes and their friends so that the company can survive, then you got to treat the big men in a big way.' Expenses here won't cover a dog's cubbyhole, let alone the slut and a quack for Belle's drums. What are you making?"

Pfeiffer told him, adding a hundred each way.

"Not bad for a starter. Though I remember when I picked you up out of the gutter"—Pfeiffer had been on a fellowship at Columbia—"and put you into the office at thirty-five dollars a week, and you were so happy, you kissed my butt." Pfeiffer saw the warning signs of reminiscence and settled back mournfully to shepherd his drink through it; he would not be offered another. At six, the maid came in to announce that dinner was served.

Shipley stopped in the middle of a sentence, shouted "Belle," and when his wife looked up, jabbed a finger toward his open mouth. "Sorry you can't stay, Harry," he said, walking Pfeiffer to the door, arm around his shoulders. "Yes," he said just before he closed the door, "a man shouldn't have to leave his country just to save a few bucks to retire on. The old roots sting when they're cut. You stay over here awhile, and you'll see, Harry."

Pfeiffer walked down the Champs-Elysées, letting the European dusk wash Shipley out of his head.

The next morning a cablegram came from Bellman: "With all his faults, Arnold Weber's goodwill, generosity, fairness, and great spirit quadrupled both financial and spiritual assets of the company. We are looking to you, Harry, to maintain the position he won for us. We believe you will do a grand job. Come home and take your family back with you. We will speak further in the office. Fondly, Dolph."

4

If he were to have reviewed his own accounts six months later, just before his first inspection tour of the Frankfurt office, Pfeiffer could have noted an ease he had not known since his student days. Established with wife and son in seven rooms above the Étoile, served and guarded by a brisk French couple, he left for Germany without the trepidation he had felt at his departure for Europe. Watching his wife in her new Persian lamb coat standing by the car with little Henry to wave him off, Pfeiffer felt a confidence which would have steeled him for a trip through hell. Before he stepped on the plane, however, his wife called him back, clutched his arm, and said, "*Pass mal sehr gut auf, mein Lieber.*"

"For what?" asked Pfeiffer sharply. "And anyway, Henry hears," for they never spoke German around little Henry. He kissed her good-bye again and then bent to his son who jabbed at him with the little model of the Empire State Building which Bellman had sent him as a going-away present. "Good-bye, darling," said Pfeiffer, pushing the model away and kissing him.

His wife's warning had done something to Pfeiffer's confidence, and he could not help trembling as the plane circled over Frankfurt and came down at Rhein-Main. On the ground, he stared at the blue-coated officials who examined his traveling case. One of them said in better English than he himself spoke, "There are taxis over there, sir."

Damn you to hell, thought Pfeiffer in even better English than the official's.

The German office turned out to be in fairly good shape, but not so good that within a week everyone in it didn't tremble when Herr Pfeiffer sounded the buzzer, for, though he was always polite, he harrowed the tiniest error and lashed the least culpable of its perpetrators.

At night, Pfeiffer went back to the Frankfurter Hof, had dinner, sat around the lobby for an hour reading the Paris edition of the *Herald Tribune,* then went upstairs to bed. The second evening he had gone to a movie, but it was a comedy, and when he heard the audience laugh, he walked out. Why should they laugh?

He spent some time walking along the river down by the great Dom where the emperors of the Holy Roman Empire had been crowned for centuries. Damaged, it stood alone amid the rubble of those half-timbered Roemer houses which Pfeiffer remembered as the prettiest in Frankfurt. He was not unpleased by the destruction. On the other hand, he was not displeased by the construction projects going on over most of the city. They can begin again too.

During the second week of his stay, Pfeiffer began to eat dinner with his Frankfurt secretary, Fräulein Uta von Bensheimer, and her American boyfriend, Jimmy, who worked for HICOG, the State Department apparatus in Germany. They spoke German, for Jimmy spoke it better than Pfeiffer English, although he hadn't known a word when he'd come over three years ago.

Fräulein von Bensheimer was a German type Pfeiffer had never known, a most charming aristocrat, restrained, yet witty, and splendidly at ease. Sometime, however, the ease became a kind of looseness Pfeiffer wouldn't have believed possible in a girl of her type and training. Once she reminded Jimmy that he had failed to buy a new bed for them. "The one we have now is so hard, and it squeaks terribly," she explained to Pfeiffer.

Pfeiffer began to feel that such looseness was an important element in the new Germany. Everywhere he looked there were signs of it. The newsstands were crowded with physical culture magazines in which nudes flexed themselves for prurient cameras. The conversation along the Königstrasse was often ripped by smutty hilarity, and not just from the numerous prostitutes—harder faced than any he'd ever seen—who strutted there with GIs from the caserns around the Farben Building. Despite the many augurs and present signs of material prosperity, this looseness helped Pfeiffer decide that the Germans were really finished; he saw the laughter and smut as the marks of their uneasy presentiment of the end.

He began talking frankly about these matters to Jimmy and Uta. They were understanding, sympathetic. Indeed it was Uta who suggested that he make the trip to Bebelshausen before he returned to Paris. "Who knows that this will not provide an antidote to your discomfort. Maybe it will help heal the awful scars that are making you so unhappy. If you can only bridge the terrible years, who knows what you'll think then?"

She and Jimmy offered to drive him down, but he decided to go with the company chauffeur, and that Saturday he found himself in the Mercedes speeding down the Rhine and into the Würtemberg hills to Bebelshausen. He had returned in somewhat this fashion in not a few dreams.

Although it had been shelled, Bebelshausen seemed basically unchanged. Many of the houses and stores were completely familiar to Pfeiffer, and once or twice, he felt the fearful excitement of recognizing a face. He passed by his old school—it was a shell—and the woods—half stripped—where he used to play and where he had first made love. He directed the driver down the road to his house.

It was no longer there, just a bare lot he might have missed if it hadn't been for the pair of oak trees which had shaded the west side of the house, and where, in summer, they had put up, American style, a great hammock. Thank God, he thought, seeing that the trees had been spared. He climbed out of the car, limped up to them, sat down facing the river, and looked between the hills where knots of smoke from the thermometer factory untied themselves in the Rhine breeze. Then, in the smaller tree, he saw his initials, HP, carved four feet from the ground. The strain of fifteen years eased suddenly from his heart, and Pfeiffer burst into a kind of teary groaning which caused the chauffeur to look first toward and then away from him.

That night he tried to tell Uta and Jimmy about what had happened to him; he managed to say enough to enable them to pronounce his experience an important one.

That he knew. He had come back home, and what counted was still there. His country's misery was a version of his own; he saw in her looseness and silly posturing the awkward attempts to atone for the misery she had madly inflicted in her fifteen-year exile from European sanity.

He returned to Paris with a confidence he had only masked before his trip. When he told his wife about his discoveries, she said that she would go with him on his next visit, and they even decided to take little Henry. During the conversation, they slipped into German, though the little boy was in the room building the Tour Eiffel with his blocks.

The next weeks in Paris were the happiest of their lives. They went to the theater and found they could follow it with ease. De Roubain introduced them to some French and Spanish friends with whom they traded dinner parties, and they began planning all sorts of trips around their recovered Europe. It was at the summit of pleasure that the cable came from Bellman.

> Arnold Weber in full recovery of his full powers after elec-
> trotherapy (shock treatment). Wishes to join me, and whole
> company, in thanking you for holding the fort in his absence. On
> return to New York you will find more tangible expression of our
> gratitude in weekly envelopes. With sincerest best wishes to you
> and entire family, Adolph Bellman.

It wasn't until he was two days into the Atlantic on the *Ile-de-France* that Pfeiffer thought, Maybe I should have stayed, but by then it was too late, and a little later he even wondered whether he had meant stayed in Europe or America.

CHICAGO, IN THE DEPTHS OF FEELING

Like most New York City kids of my class and generation, I didn't travel very far from home until I went away to college. I knew New England and had spent time with relatives in central Pennsylvania, and that was it until I went to college in North Carolina, which was the South to me until, after graduation, I took a bus to Florida, where a girl to whom I was more or less engaged lived and where I worked until her mother told me that her daughter could never marry a Jew, drove me to the station, saw that I bought a ticket on the Silver Meteor to New York, and, to my surprise and disgust, gave me a peck on the cheek as she hoisted my bag into it.

1

I didn't see Chicago until after I'd spent three years in Europe, where I married Jean, became a father, discovered my vocation, and started practicing it. My Chicago base was Les Reilly, a pianist I'd met on the *Queen Mary* going over to Cherbourg in 1949. I was headed for a Fulbright teaching assignment in Versailles, Les for the Institute Cortot to study piano. In Milwaukee, he'd studied ten years "with a pupil of a pupil of Leschitizky" but felt he couldn't take the next musical step until he had Europe under his belt. Hemingway and Fitzgerald had cooked that moveable feast in the twenties, and for years the young were ravenous for it. If the travel industry paid ten dollars to the estates of those two writers for every reader who took to sea and air for a bit of that feast, their heirs would be richer than Gates and Buffet. People like Les and me could be driven crazy with desire by words.

On that almost sleepless Atlantic trip—in whose four and a half days I made out—not the phrase of that day—with, indeed *fell*—its standard participle—for Gerda Ebel and Maidi Fuchs, I didn't notice Les until the third day out. His physiognomy was all thrust: though he was small, five five or five six, his blue eyes bulged, his teeth bucked, his ears Clark Gabled like small tables from his bright, orange-red head. His voice was loud and could rise to hysteria; it was also capable of a variety of snorts, a gamut from contempt to dismay. In both manic and depressive modes, he was for me a comedian. We walked the Paris streets diagnosing viva voce the defects of the locals, assuming of course that English was beyond them.

That first evening, on the *Queen Mary,* a dozen young passengers drank around the Steinway while Les played Gershwin, and his wife, Angela, black eyes so bright they looked as if they belonged to a special electrical system, belted out—another standard participle of the day—lyrics in the Ethel Mermanian torch fashion of the Milwaukee bars where she'd sung to support them.

In Paris, the first week, the three of us lived in a rathole on the Rue Budapest, near Gare St. Lazare. Then I took off for a Versailles pension and they settled into a fuliginous Pigalle apartment. Every couple of weeks, I'd come into Paris, we'd have dinner, and Reilly would play for me what he was studying; I'd sleep on their floor and take the early train back from the Gare des Invalides for my morning *anglais* classes at the Collège Jules Ferry. In December, I met Jean Ayers, who was taking the *Cours de Civilisation,* the moneymaking supplement the Sorbonne cooked up for *étrangers.* From then on, I stayed not with the Reillys but at the apartment on the Rue Verneuil that Jean shared with Bryna Johannson, an older—all of twenty-six—girl who worked at the U.S. Cultural Center on the Rue St. Honoré.

In May, Jean, two months' pregnant, went back to Old Lyme to explain her Old World life to her parents. Meanwhile, I applied for jobs all over Europe and found one in the English section (*Anglistiksabteilung*) of the University of Heidelberg. I was to teach two classes in American literature. The pay was auditors' fees (*Hörgeld*), about two hundred dollars a semester, so I found a lucrative supplementary job with the U.S. Occupation Army. No sweat. I was a clerk in the Staff Message Control, editing mind-killing communiqués about personnel changes and supply problems from all over the European Command. In August, Jean flew back to Germany wearing the diamond engagement ring my parents gave her the day she and hers came into New York to meet them, and days later we were married in the baroque chapel of Heidelberg Castle by an army chaplain. Our ancient landlady, a granddaughter of the philosopher Schelling, was our maid of honor, and the best man was her nephew, Heinrich Speicher, a thirty-year-old student in Alfred Weber's seminar.

The Reillys didn't come to our wedding, but, two months later, Les showed up at our door with photos of naked Angela giving suck to baby Rita. (He'd forgotten to mention — in person or letters — Angela's pregnancy.) These he displayed to anyone encountered in our Hauptstrasse hangout, the Schnookeloch. One day, a thoughtful-looking sociologist at the adjoining table studied them and asked Les what gender the baby might be. "Female," said Les. "A beautiful little girl named Rita Camille Johannson Reilly." "So sorry," said the sociologue. "I hope you'll have better luck next time." In Paris, Reilly had suffered every sort of pianistic insult — the skepticism of his teachers, the contempt of his fellow students, poverty, and his fear of returning to the States without a degree. The sociologist's dismissal of the world's newest Reilly roused Les to question the fellow's own lineage. There were ever-louder exchanges, then threats, shoves, punches, china breakage, and, finally, banishment from Schnookeloch.

Six weeks after that, a letter came from Angela telling us that Les had broken down, "so sick we called the priest from St. Augustin to give him last rites, but two days later, he got out of bed, yelling for cognac. We're on our way back June 3 to Rudy Ganz's Chicago Music College. Seeya in *Dick Tracy*."

2

In 1955 I went to Chicago to do a piece for *Esquire* about the death of Enrico Fermi and the election of the first Mayor Richard Daley. I looked the Reillys up in the phone book, called, and accepted Les's invitation to stay in their basement apartment five blocks west of the lake in Hyde Park. During the day, Les had classes, nights he was a bellboy at the Del Prado Hotel, where, in addition to tips and salary, he picked up stray change, half bottles of scotch, and, most recently, a discarded camel hair overcoat not more than a size too big for him. He drove a growling '47 Hudson down the Outer Drive to and from the college, where he studied piano with a pupil of a pupil of Schnabel.

The dark apartment, an American clone of the one in Paris, stank of urine and defeat. Approaching it, you could make out tiny faces staring through the barred windows. Inside, a frazzled Angela chain-smoked Kools, drank dollar-a-bottle muscatel, washed diapers—drying on lines all over the house—and cursed her life of Reilly.

Jean and I had wondered what held them together. "They're always battling." "Not quite 'always.'" During the four days I stayed with them, I discovered their frenzied, careless sex life. God knows what got into the heads of their three little daughters. I peered warily into any room I entered to avoid the sights and sounds of copulation.

Love noise, smoke, urine, fatigue, and Beethoven saturated the dark rooms. Les was working on the opus 101 in A, to which, until then, I'd never listened. He played it—I thought—marvelously. His pianistic weakness was memorizing, a drawback to a concert career, but not to fine performance. Les was a fair technician—his own appraisal—and had exceptional—ditto—musical intelligence. There were phrases in his opus 101 few pianists could match. (My view.)

He showed me the sonata's shifts, transpositions, developments, symmetries. Playing the section over which Beethoven had written "lyrical, full of innermost sensitivity" (or "deepest feeling": *mit innigsten Empfindung*), Reilly was a great master, or so, sitting on a broken sofa beside a bottle-sucking, fecal-stinking daughter, I believed. That music somehow altered my feeling for the water-bound, steel-proud city. *With the deepest feeling.* I fell for the place, the sea-sized lake reflecting the belt of glassy skyscrapers onshore, the endless neighborhoods, bohemian and black, Spanish and Polish, Litvak and hillbilly, marked by stone avenues and stippled by little green parks and, every now and then, a stunning building or enormous factory that took your breath away. You felt every sort of human career and emotion pumping here, every human type, every trick, every sublimity.

Mit innigsten Empfindung.

Dodging outbursts of lust, nostrils tense with excretory fumes, I'd walk to Promontory Point, overlooking the great lake which smashed green-water fury against the protective stone tiers rising from its brim. From there, you had a grand view of the Loop's skyscrapers. The tallest buildings looked like masts of a great schooner, though one embarked not for Cythera but for Wealth and Power.

3

My twelve-thousand-word piece on Fermi and Daley contrasted the end of the heroic scientific era of the thirties and forties with the stirrings of a new municipal era. I interviewed Daley, a solid, jowly man with sharp blue eyes and imperfect grammar who exuded expertise, confidence, and strength. I couldn't get him to talk about himself, only about the city—its dwindling tax base, the state's legislative miserliness, the suburbs' exploitation of the city which nourished them. Grim about each difficulty, the thick-necked, jowly man in the blue suit, shirt, and tie couldn't, every now and then, keep back a burst of girlish giggling, the sign, as I read it, of joy in the municipal and national system he'd worked out to improve the city he so loved. Riding back to Hyde Park along the gorgeous lakeshore, I found myself unjournalistically crazy about that dese-and-deming, giggling, oddly brilliant man.

The next day, I interviewed a physicist who'd collaborated in Fermi's world-changing sustained reaction experiment under the old squash courts of Stagg Field. A skinny, peppery man in his late forties, he talked about the tension of that December afternoon, then, changing gears, described the Saturday softball games the physicists played. "Terrified when Fermi pitched that if we swung too hard and hit a ball into that head, Hitler might win the war."

No one could be more different from the mayor than this atomic physicist, but I felt a kinship of power and of intelligence there. Later, back at the Reillys', listening to Lester playing the profound chords of the opus 101, I fused the two of them into my feeling for their city.

4

Reilly was playing with exceptional passion. That morning, driving back on Lake Shore Drive, he'd been pulled over by a cop. Without looking, he did the Chicago thing, handing his license, clipped to a five-dollar bill, out the window. The cop, "a bruiser," reported Les, pushed it aside, reached in the window, and fingered the camel hair overcoat. "You're getting," he said, "a little big for five there, Lester." Reilly, princely with five, coughed up a ten.

Angela often laid into him about his driving — "You don't dream, you don't masturbate, you don't sightsee, you d-r-i-v-e!" She hated the Hudson. "That oil-leaking whale." Today, the denunciation, fueled by the lost tenner, was followed by an oratorical condemnation of the life he led and the one to which he'd condemned her. Les responded in kind, which led to shrieks, slaps, blows, and then, Venus knows how, furious, furniture-shoving copulation — with the little girls and I re-treating to the kitchen.

5

The piece I wrote was a mess. Felker, the *Esquire* editor with whom I worked, said I should change the names and turn it over to Rust Hills, the fiction editor. Somehow a farcical note had fused or — Felker said — been confused with a soppy romantic one, that *Empfindung* which I had for the city.

6

Les and Angela are dead. Three more children and several miscar-riages later, she broke apart in a sea of muscatel. Les, teaching piano in an Oklahoma City community college, married the young assistant registrar — "I am her Paris and her Greece," he wrote me — had two children, then was divorced by her and moved back to Chicago. Driving there, he skidded into a truck and crushed an index finger, which ended his piano playing.

In Chicago, he bought and sold pianos, wrote about concerts for neighborhood newspapers, and did a "corrective edition" of Debussy's *Suite Bergamasque* for a new music publisher, taking so long to do it that he got no other assignments. He lived on a small academic and a larger veteran's pension plus a few dollars for playing—he was up to this—Gershwin, Berlin, Kern, Rodgers, and Porter in a local club. (That lasted until Watergate, when even older patrons wanted other sounds.)

Every few years, he got to New York. If I was there, I'd take him to the best restaurant in which his ever-shabbier clothes and ever more depressed, ever louder and odder self would not be embarrassingly conspicuous. I'd listen to the latest installment of his saga, the scholarships, graduations, jobs, and then the bolt-out-of-the-blue deaths of two of his children, his own stays in veterans' hospitals for electric shock depression treatments. There were also stories of new enthusiasms, mental, medical, musical, and sexual encounters (rubbing against women on buses, hand jobs in the listening cabins of Tinklin' Tunes, even a couple of lengthy—at least protracted—relationships with other gifted castoffs).

7

It was Rita, whom I had not seen for forty-five years, who called to tell me that "Dad died in the elevator" of his weary Chicago apartment house. "Heart attack."

"He had lots of heart, Rita."

"And a tough time letting his kids know about it."

She told me when and where the funeral service would be.

I could––should?—have flown to Chicago for it, but I didn't. I hadn't been there for six or seven years, and now some ugly disinclination to pay respects to a dead friend kept me away. The day of the funeral, I telegraphed flowers and wrote an e-mail letter to Les's children about what a special man and friend their father had been. That evening, I sat in my workroom with a snifter of cognac listening to Artur Schnabel playing the opus 101 and let myself have the luxury of breaking down in the "rather lively and with deepest feeling"— *etwas lebhaft und mit der innigsten Empfindung*—section of the beautiful allegretto.

GIFTS

*I was not come to do any harm but actually gave
presents of my own substance.*

Hernando Cortés, September 3, 1526

Williams had allowed himself six hundred dollars for a Mexican week,
five days in Mexico City, two in Yucatán.

Round-trip to Mérida was two hundred and twenty dollars, hotels
ran him about sixty pesos a day—he preferred third-class ones—
meals were cheap, and that gave him a few hundred dollars for special
pleasures. He usually spent fifty on presents for his wife and Tony, his
son. It took time to find decent presents, but he didn't write it off. It
was one of his inroads into Mexican life. Which was one of the objects
of his annual excursions—cultural, historic, and scenic accumulation.
And then, whatever came in the way of pleasure.

It invariably came in the same way.

On each of his annual trips, Williams ran into someone who counted for him, sometimes intensely enough to involve months of further
contact (usually epistolary), sometimes only in the imaginative trans-
figuration of his wife.

"That's the way it goes," said Williams to his sixteen-year-old son,
his only confidant. "I don't advocate it, but that's my way. You make
your life, I'll make mine."

Years ago Tony had overcome uneasiness at his father's confidences. It was odd, but there it was, he was his father's closest friend.

The Mexican confidence, however, did him in. Giving ear wasn't giving absolution.

Apparently the business had begun as usual. At the university's Olympic swimming pool, where Williams—in excellent shape for a forty-year-old—had picked up a girl guide, Rufelia, an Indian girl working for a doctorate in economics, "bright as a fish, heavy thighed, thin armed, beautifully torsoed," and so on, his father filled in detail en route. A mestiza from Yucatán, she hadn't been back to see her family in two years and jumped at Williams's offer, full fare and expenses to Mérida in return for two days' companionship. *Muy bien.*

September's the rainy season. In the capital this meant a fat cloud sailing in front of the sun at four-thirty, then breaking into rain for five minutes. In Mérida the cloud arrived on schedule but flooded the town, turned the streets into canals, with garbage instead of gondolas. The lights and fan went off in the pathetic little hotel they stayed in three blocks off the *zócalo,* they were "forced inside" and had gone at it in the heat, debilitating despite "rather exceptional joys." (This was about as far as father went with son.)

The girl hadn't been a virgin since thirteen, had had a child at fourteen who was raised by her mother's sister in Campeche. The child regarded Rufelia as a mysterious relative wafted by supernatural gifts to the capital, there to work out reforms for family and pueblo.

Rufelia did not regret, indeed felt herself steeled by this early history. She saw herself as another stage of the revolution, the feminine liberation that had been in Cárdenas's original plan.

The village had tried to break Rufelia at thirteen, but the revolution had made her literate, and modernity had dripped in through French and American novels and films to soften the bondage of class and sex. A national scholarship did the rest. When the students had rioted in the spring against Rector Chávez, Rufelia had whacked off the bronze nose of Fra Miguel.

This history became part of Williams's. On the plane ride from Mexico City, her story, its blunted English beveled and angled by Spanish insertions, took the weight from her nose, cheeks, and jaw, lit the raw black eyes, and turned her, in his expert view, into one of the love goddesses who queened it in the Anthropological Museum. That miracle world of collection and instruction culminated in this fine-breasted, small-smiling talker, on, under, and beside him in the Hotel San Luis. And yet, in the unfanned woolen air, with the sweat flooding the harsh sheet, and his heart slipping beats, Williams felt he'd been forced into wolfing his pleasure, felt unusual indigestion, and then, in postcoital gloom, felt that he'd had all that this Indian girl would ever give him.

Never had he been so divided from one of his intimacies.

It was partially language, for Rufelia's intelligence could not vault her limited English and his more primitive Spanish, but more, he felt he was playing parts in her story: he was the childhood rapist, the purchasing yanqui gringo, the bargain maker who never lost. In the hot room, forty hours more in hand, despite the revival that would surely come in several of these, Williams began preparing the cultural pleasure that might ease this indigestion.

The night was the fifteenth, Independence Day. No accident, of course, for Williams's intention had been to see the Mexican president hail the anniversary in Mexico City; now he would do with the provincial version.

The water had seeped into the earth; by dinnertime only a few streets were impassable. He and Rufelia walked the white-walled streets to the green square ringed by the colonial church and the yellow mansions. The square was filled with more than the usual taxi drivers, kids, and loafers; the band was there, Indian ancients in blue caps and the beautifully pleated white shirts of Yucatán. He and Rufelia ate in an air-cooled box in the loggia, papayas and mole, tacos and fried eggs, four beers and coffee, then walked the market streets, loud with preholiday pitch. Williams bought a fake antique (a two-inch clay goiter sufferer), a three-dollar watch inside a gleaming Swiss face, and, for ten pesos, a bejeweled bug held by a chain to a perforated perisphere, "for you, Tony, if it didn't crawl out of my coat."

At the square, a blue, winy night relaxed the heat and leaked over the soft gold of the church, the administrative palace, the palms and pepper trees. The band worked toward a few of the same notes, singers ground out local specialties, benches filled, couples strutted, minute children peddled Chiclets, grizzled Indians allowed themselves annual shoe shines, and soldiers set off fireworks from the palace roof. The mass of Indian faces, the lucent shoddiness of festival, brass bleats and tropic momentum, a whirl of sensuous information in Williams's head that altered the fatigued ease in his legs and groin, the capillary strain in his rear, the slight, coronary hop in his chest.

In their fifth slow round of the square, he saw in the eyes they met that they'd become a couple, memorable, identifiable. He belonged, he could notch Mexico into his life.

Eleven o'clock. The mayor would repeat Fra Hidalgo's cry at midnight, the bells and Catherine wheels would tip the celebration.

"Let's go to bed," said Williams.

Around the corner from their room was a ten-by-twelve-foot swimming pool, open to the sky and ringed by live trees and vines. They got into bathing suits, the way they'd first seen each other the day before. Alone, they swam back and forth in the hot pool, brushing each other's bodies, working up for the nightcap.

In their room, the fan, a great-winged adjustable bat, revived. They dried off naked beneath it. Rufelia's cherry-tinted body gleamed from shards of streetlight broken by the shutters.

— You been often in hotels with men, Rufelia?

— *Jamás.*

— Come on, now. You didn't learn everything at the university.

"Never in hotel." Unembarrassed, though not at ease.

Williams was the sort who asks whores their history. More, he almost never failed to love the women he stayed with, one night or twenty. This meant their story was important, and not only their body's story. He wished to know thoughts, hopes, pains, how they met what seemed to him one of the world's three great problems (that of subjugated women, the others being the population mess and the earth's relationship to the universe). He was a writer for a business newsletter, he relished the trends and numbers of manufacture; nights, he stayed up speculating over Beacon, Anchor, and university press books.

Williams never finished any books but novels, yet he regarded himself as the equivalent of a Ph.D. in several subjects. Without ambition, hating little but other men's, he stitched his burgher ease with these annual weeks of experience, drawing on them to translate his nighttime reveries into the facts of flesh.

He lifted Rufelia, no easy matter, onto the great double bed. They lay, arms coursing each other's sides.

The account, at this point, veered for Tony into a realm that seemed at least in part formed by fantasy or by some symbolic fiction. His father, long headed, the burned brown hair grizzling to silver at tips and clutches, framed his full smile into a mockery of meditative remembrance. Or was it all tale teller's contrivance? Was the mockery in the facts or the telling? Was its motive pain or boast?

Tony heard about the next day's trip, the narrow road razoring the flat, furzy fields, the hills, the thatched *pueblitos,* the doors open to the filthy yards, the hammocks, the chickens, the bony black cows, the spurts of mangrove jungle, the asparagus-thin roots tangling with each other into million-legged beasts, the maize and henequen fields asleep in the rising dew, the sun bejeweling them while the dusty Studebaker whanged along at sixty, his father wordless, working out some connection between the simmering Indian girl beside him and what he was about to see, the empty priest state in the limestone hills.

"Took us an hour or so," a wonderful trip, though the country didn't change, just the harsh grass and the fronds with their glass-sharp fringe, boring terrain with the villages plopped every now and then along the road, surely the way they'd been for fifteen hundred years. "God knows none of these big-hatted farmers had ever come within any but market distance of Uxmal."

Uxmal now was palaces, pyramids, nunneries, and temples, gray and pink magnificence, mathematical and masonic genius, "What carving, what symmetry. And it was absolutely still. We were alone. The guard slept at the table, we didn't even buy a ticket, just left the car and walked over a ragged path to the Governor's Palace, built on one of these scary staircases, not so tall, but steep, and eighty feet long, the entrances trapezoidal cuts, all scored with these stone mouths and twists." They heard odd noises, scuffing, scurrying, then saw the iguanas' little dragon tails whisking into cracks in the stones. In the air, red flies pecked at their sweat. "Just the two of us, the animals, and this dead city."

The girl climbed the staircase and stood in front of the frieze, arms akimbo, while Williams sat at the bottom below her summoning face. "The place turned you into an actor." Her hair fell back, "the blackest black in nature," and the full, Chinese eyes, "You can see how the Indians came across the Bering Strait," her fine, solid legs like mangrove roots, "leguminous," a dark Indian remembrance of hierarchical glory, "and I remembered some miserable book about sacrifice to the knife and blood redemption, and, kind of joking, I climbed up to her like a victim. The white god Quetzalcoatl, though a bit unplumed"—hand touching the bald inlet to the grizzled hair—"crazy, you know, but we act all the time, the place called for it." On the plane from the capital, she'd recited a Mayan poem about the body's gift to the furious god. "A human being looked mighty good in that dead city, even if she was only imagining a razor blade tonguing my heart."

Williams mounted the stairs, receptive, and then, at the top of the flight, not quite kidding, Rufelia pushed at his chest. "I grabbed at her arms, we pulled and wrestled around, sex in it, but fight too, and maybe some of what had gone before us. I was excited, I tell you, scared and excited, and full of love-hate for that crazy little Indian."

The confused fooling led to her rolling down twenty stone steps.

When Williams got to her, an army, "literally, an army of ants in two columns, twenty feet long, black ants with scouts and generals and ordering sergeants, was crawling over her thighs. There were lakes of blood from her knees. And she couldn't move, her arm was bent over, the nose looked broken, there was blood in her mouth and her eyes, her face was glued into hysteria, and there I was, knowing you can't move a broken person. Scared out of my head."

And had left her there.

For the next batch of tourists or the guide or whoever. Had torn off in the Studebaker and, back in Mérida, had paid his bill and left a note for her with her ticket, an envelope of pesos, and instructions to see the doctor as soon as possible, forgive him, and adios.

"Which is how come I got back yesterday instead of tomorrow."

"Whew."

"Whew is right."

"I hope she's all right," said Tony. "Can you get in trouble?" He was sunk in the ugliness of it.

"They know my address. I guess I'd hear if anything happened."

"Maybe you should call the hotel down there, see if she picked up the ticket."

Williams regarded this pared-down replica of himself sitting up on the bed and rubbed its hair.

He went to his study and telephoned and was back twenty minutes later carrying the jeweled bug chained to the perisphere. "The manager said she'd only broken her arm. What luck. I forgot to give you this."

"Alive?"

"Sure it's alive. It eats those leaves there."

Tony thanked him and accepted thanks for his advice.

It was, however, the last advice he was going to give his father. And, if he could manage it, he had heard the man's last confession.

1 *voice*

Pure utterance impossible.

Matter for utterance adequate, yet, beginning, already senses kinship with whatever calls for the colors of utterance.

Existence without utterance?

Yes.

What, therefore, impels appeal?

Excess.

Movement.

The appearance of movement.

Or of excess.

(Such pain in stasis.)

2 *story maker seen by story*

He, flathead, is numb at extremities, breathless, weakhearted (though thinks he's overeaten), is liable to flatten out tapping a colon, leaving me up the creek.

Meanwhile, piles everything on me.

The simplest, most independent set of events, all I need's a push.

What happens?

He strangles with embrace.

None asks birth, but, arrived, breathes, sucks, cries.

I could make it in Harlem, cross-eyed, gimpy, make it on fatback, don't need ambrosia, Greece. Just fluency.

There he sits, flathead plowed with false misery, cracking me thigh and sternum. (Or stuffing me into shells.)

Indispensable?

Yes, though less complete than I.

Less coherent, maybe less durable.

Launcher. Pedestal. (Less complex than his cargo: coded out of three and a half, I out of twenty-six letters.)

And I'm unbound by my matter. (Except as I issue from him to his kind, constrained to process and conclusion by their small capacity.)

Sometimes the shadow of Something Larger scoots across me.

Or is this my dreamed release? (No longer clapped within these coded hammers.)

Sport 'twould be to sport without, unfleshed, issued from my own kind, passing time with my own kind. (Wordless?) Already I feel the presence of cousins.

Not of flathead's manufactory.

3   *flathead*

Yes, but who arranges it, interrupts it at his will, begins and finishes it?

Whose voice?

Whose story?

Think, after all, how the reader's mind is but juggled inheritance (words, phrases, grammar, conventions of reading, of the times).

I write from the convention of mind exalted by print to intimacy with readers. "I" is but a fraction of the name on the title page (cracked glimpse of its authority).

4   *epigraphs*

"I am not I; pity the tale of me"
        — Sidney, *Astrophel and Stella*

"The development of the ego consists in a departure from the primary narcissism and results in a vigorous attempt to recover it."

—Freud, *On Narcissism: An Introduction*

"The man of true breed looks straight into his heart even when he is alone."

—Chung Yung, *The Unwobbling Pivot*

"Integer vitae, scelerisque purus,

non eget Mauris jaculis, neque arcu,

nec venenatis gravida sagittis."

—Horace, *Odes,* 1, 22

"Where nothing ever is felt, nothing matters."

—Langer, *Mind: An Essay on Human Feeling*

5   *Preface*

Dear, familiar (overfamiliar) readers, you know the arbitrariness of beginning, the devices of fictitious frankness, you know this beginning too as another lien on your attention.

Hopeless. You can't be ensnared with intimacies.

Helpless: alone, here, quartets splattering the green walls, the thirty-seven hundred books, under which I indite, absolute ruler: helpless.

What is the story that contains what I now am?

But what ease, what honeyed discharge.

Reader. I dare you to put me down. Lunkhead.

Chapter One

IN RETURN

Walters had been in Kyoto four or five times, but only one time counted for him. The other times he'd come for conferences and stayed in
the hotels—the Miyako, the International—and hardly got outside.
There'd been tours of the Imperial and Nijo Palaces, a walk through
the Katsura gardens, and an hour at Gion Corner for snippets of puppet drama, tea ceremony, gagaku music, and flower arrangement;
there'd also been a couple of hours in a nightclub where girls dressed
as apes mounted each other. He'd been too tired for curiosity, let alone
excitement. What tired him, what counted then and always, was serious business seriously conducted. Even failed business succeeded as
part of larger schemes: definition of ends and relationships as they altered from administration to administration.

Walters had worn several hats: assistant secretary in the Commerce
Department; negotiator for Bechtel and the Chase Bank; and, for the
last six years, assistant secretary for economic affairs in the State Department. In four decades of professional life, there'd been fifty-odd
conferences in Japan alone.

Almost never, though, had he spent time there on his own. The
almost was accounted for by five days in the summer of 1973. By
himself—with next to no official assistance—he'd stayed in a small
Japanese inn near the Kodaiji Temple in Kyoto. He couldn't remember now who had told him about the place or who had made the
arrangements, but he remembered that he'd taken the *shinkansen* from
Tokyo Station and called Mrs. Fukuma from the one in Kyoto. A slen-

der woman with thick black hair and a smile so full of sweetness he'd remembered it as well as anything else, she had met his taxi at the temple and led him through small streets to her small inn. It was why, fourteen years later, he was back, once again taking the time out of a life in which there was very little time to be out.

Walters was most at home at work. (His wife Dorothy's explanation for this was, "Some people look better frowning.") A problem solver, problems were Walters's pleasure. (The more impersonal the problem, the better he liked it.) A bit of paternal and connubial motion persuaded even those who counted that he was a good father and husband. He was, he knew, a lucky one. (Walters disliked confessions but had heard enough to know how lucky.) Dorothy was charming, civil, amusing, brave, loyal, and loving. What he most loved about her was the similarity of her public and private selves. "She's of a piece," he told their daughter Laura. "*Integer vitae*. Is that the Latin for it?" One reason their marriage functioned well—both felt this—was that unlike many official wives she didn't come with him on business trips. Or on the rare occasion when she flew with him, she'd sightsee, shop, and socialize on her own. Their schedules were distinct; they might see each other at breakfast or at supper, but there was no pressure to do that. If they did, it was—usually—a bonus. "We don't lean on each other" was their boast. He told Laura, "We're parallel lines, which make a track on which your life has rolled along reasonably well. Is that too fancy?" (Laura herself had had less luck: her second marriage had just gone off the track.)

"I'd like to see that Kyoto *ryokan* of yours," Dorothy said out of the blue when he told her about the next Tokyo conference. "Would you have time or shall I go myself?"

It came out that she thought she better go while she was still spry enough to sleep and eat on the floor and to rise without cracking her joints. Fifty-four, and no athlete, she was limber, walked miles, swam, lifted things, and worked in the garden.

Walters hadn't thought of going back to the inn. He wasn't much on sentimental returns, preferred to keep his better memories untested. Still, bits of fatigue floated in him; it had been a difficult winter, why not take a few days off? Kyoto was a good place to do it.

He had the embassy find out if the *ryokan* was functioning and if Fukuma-san was still there. It was, she was.

———

Even in the department, there were opposing views about the Japanese. Products of several thousand insular years, their contradictions—arrogance and humility, courtesy and rudeness, generosity and niggardliness, originality and lack of it, xenophilia and xenophobia—signaled to some a mentality incomprehensible to Westerners or even other Easterners. There were people who had spent thirty years in Japan who said they had no Japanese friends and no idea what went on in a single Japanese head; there were others, some who knew the language and some who didn't, who felt the Japanese were exactly the same as everybody else with the same problems; Westerners would understand them as soon as they understood the problems.

The contradictions were also topographical, architectural, and physical. There were the glass, steel, and concrete skyscrapers, and there were the little shrines with their curling roofs, the wooden plaques with the kanji inscriptions, the trees filled with blossoms and white prayers knotted on the branches. There was the terrific noise, the loud public announcements and police commands, then the quiet of gardens, the small, carless streets, the noiseless electronics of light and motion. There was the bulky male strut and the demure, in-turned delicacy of the traditional woman.

The country had survived the endless eruptions whose deposits were its ubiquitous mountains. No wonder the holiest holy place was Fujiyama. Walters and Dorothy saw it, perfectly symmetrical and snowcapped, from the hotel room, and for much of the trip to Kyoto, they'd seen it swell and spread, green beneath its creamy top. Dorothy had bought a book of Hokusai's, *Thirty-six Views of Fuji,* full of charming scenes from Edo markets, Shinto prayer wickets, and the mountain itself. The most beautiful was one called "Red Fuji," the mountain a triangular ember in the clear air. To convert the fearful—climbers were still regularly killed in Fuji avalanches—into the sacred, a subject of lithographs and haiku, wasn't that *pure Japanese?*

Whatever that was. That it was *something,* though, most Japanese believed. Department experts were full of this subject. *Nihon-jin-ron,* the theory of Japanese uniqueness, was related by some to the mastery of the difficult language and the complex cerebral work this required.

Some Japanese intellectuals, the *hyo-ronka,* carried the theory around Japan's dangerous new prosperity. Their chief antipathy was the *shin-jen-ron,* the *new human being,* the soft Westernized idler adrift in a floating world whose key word was *tsu-kei-sute,* "disposable."

Erikson, a Japanese deskman, had written out these words for Walters and given him this brief course in Japanese singularity. Walters took it as he took much expertise, skeptically. Without knowing a word of Japanese and next to no Japanese history, he'd negotiated with Japanese officials and businessmen for decades and had come away with hundreds of agreements on everything from whaling rights to silicon chips. Of course, there was a special style of negotiation, many levels of authority and deference, there were "concessions" that weren't concessions, "agreements" that weren't agreements, there was even the excitement of a signed agreement which was sometimes a systematic postponement. Still, once you got used to all this, it had an agreeable, piquant quality, as special as bonsai trees or a Japanese inn.

The conference finished late, but the fast trains from Tokyo Station left every fifteen minutes. When he and Dorothy arrived in Kyoto, it was dark and cold. Walters showed Fukuma-san's address to the taxi driver. Still there was some difficulty finding it; it was not well known. The driver circled blocks and finally called Fukuma-san for directions. A cold rain started. They drove a block and saw Fukuma-san running under an umbrella. She was in kimono, slippers, and white socks. Walters remembered the sweet, barely lined face. She did not—of course—appear to remember him. Why should she?

The de-robing and de-shoeing at the entrance were complicated by bags and overcoats. Walters had forgotten how low the ceilings were, how fragile the walls and floor. He and Dorothy were upstairs in two rooms, one filled with their sleeping pads and quilts, the larger with the almost-legless table beside which were the *zabuton* cushions and low-backed legless seats. Each room was more or less warmed by a gas heater.

The cold was the first problem. The Western bath and toilet were downstairs. Dorothy could do without a bath, but she did not like the Japanese toilet. A hole in the floor asked her body to do what it wasn't used to; disgust followed discomfort. If she'd been in the woods, she would have adjusted, but she wasn't and didn't. To go down the cold corridor and stairs to the Western toilet disturbed her.

Then too, Fukuma-san was noiselessly in and out of rooms and bathrooms. At least parts of her were. A kimonoed arm, towel draped over it, would appear. After a knock they barely heard, Fukuma-san entered with bows, smiles, bowls of tea, and small dishes of soaked rice and fish. "I suppose the idea is that service is invisible," said Dorothy. (This was her form of complaint.)

In 1973 what had counted for Walters was the inn's tranquillity. Sitting cross-legged in his kimono on the tatami, back against the tokonoma alcove, he'd looked out at a twisted gingko tree abloom with gold flowers. It had seemed part of the room. After a hot bath in the steep tub, he'd been deeply relaxed. Fukuma-san would bring him newspapers, maps of Kyoto and Nara, tea, fish, biscuits; she'd adjusted the fan, shown him the radio, the English books. The feeling was that he could have anything he wanted.

It had been a long time—no, more than that—it was the first time he could remember being actively contemplative without a specific problem. He'd logged time on beaches, rocking chairs, and hammocks, but the leisure of the *ryokan* was different. He'd thought it might have something to do with the room's subtle bareness, the interaction of outside and inside.

For that ease, and for the courtesy and grace which created it, he'd come back. Now, though, it was March, not August. Paper shutters screened them from the dark exterior. They were enclosed with gas heaters, bag racks, and clothing hooks (had these been here in 1973?); and between their rooms was the cold corridor. There was still beauty, the tokonoma with its blue vase, a mural screen of cicadas on a blooming branch, the tatami; and there was Fukuma-san who plied them with delicate constancy. More tea? Biscuits? Hot bath? Shower? And what time would they like breakfast? Did they prefer Western or Japanese?

Walters hadn't remembered her asking anything in 1973.

Their reservation was for four days. When he turned out the light in the sleeping room, Dorothy said, "I think we'd better leave tomorrow."

"I suppose so," he said. (Oh my, he thought. What will Fukuma-san think?) Her last appearance had been with the house guest book. "Would prease sign?" She held the large book for them with the inquisitive deference that seemed an apology for existence. For Walters, the gesture conjured up that diplomatic delicacy which he admired even when it frustrated negotiations. Under the last name in the book, "Toby Jenkins, Hong Kong, Jan. 15, 1987," Walter wrote, "Mr. and Mrs. H. L. Walters. March 8, 1987." Unless there were guests who didn't, wouldn't, or couldn't sign their names, the Walters were Fukuma-san's first guests in almost two months. "I'm sorry it didn't work out, Dorothy."

"I too, dear. I'm sure the place is wonderful in summer. And I'm glad I've seen what you loved."

Walters was up before seven. He washed up downstairs in the bathroom, where a kimonoed arm appeared with a fresh towel and fluty. "Good morning. Hope srept we'?"

"Very well, thank you, Fukuma-san." Though he was a bit startled by the bekimonoed, vocal arm.

"And missus? Eat now?"

"I think she'll sleep awhile. *I'd* love some breakfast."

When the tray full of boiled eggs, rice gruel, dishes of vegetal and doughy oddities, and tea appeared, he said, "I'm afraid we have to cut short our stay in Kyoto, Fukuma-san. It's a shame to have had so little time, but it's been lovely to see you again. Did you know I was here back in 1973?"

He saw not the slightest sign of perturbation in the delicate, gentle face. If anything, her smile was exceptionally deep. "Oh, thank you," she said. Was it for the fact that he'd returned to her house? Or, if she doubted that, for the graciousness of his lie? Whatever, her graciousness concealed the embarrassment of the broken reservation.

"I hope we'll return before long."

"Thank you, thank you. Sha' core taxi?"

"That would be very nice. I would like to walk around the neighborhood for an hour or two first. I remember how lovely it is up here."

"Taxi ten o'crock?"

"Thank you, Fukuma-san. That would be fine."

Upstairs, he told the waking Dorothy he was going to walk around for a while. "She'll give you breakfast in the other room. I told her we had to go back. She was perfectly understanding. I said I'd been here before, and that we both looked forward to returning. I think that saved face."

It was bright and nippy. The tiny wooden houses with their black-and-white wooden signs in hiragana and Roman letters looked like old guild shops. Crooked trees twisted in tiny yards. Here and there were hydrant-shaped stone shrines, Buddhas, bodhisattvas. Quiet, remote, graceful. At the end of the street was the arch of the Kodaiji Temple. In front of the central shrine, an old woman in black *tanzen* kimono pulled the bell cord, clapped, and bowed for the spirits. Downhill was a sign, HOTEL U.S.-YASAKA. It stood over a six-story concrete affair with glass doors and plants. Inside was a small marble lobby; behind the reception desk, a man in a blue blazer.

"Do you speak English?" Walters asked him.

"A rittle."

"Do — you — have — a — room — for — myself — and — my — wife?" Walters held up two fingers.

The man handed him a sheet with a price list. After ten minutes of slow talk and pointing, Walters made the man understand that he and his wife would be back at ten o'clock, and that if they liked the room, they'd take it for three nights. The man wanted him to pay now for all three, but Walters walked out saying he'd be back shortly. (Dorothy might not want to stay in Kyoto.)

At ten, Fukuma-san walked them to the taxi and, smiling, waved good-bye till it turned the corner, where Walters handed the driver the U.S.-Yasaka flier and indicated that they wanted to go there, not the station. The driver showed no surprise or disappointment that they were going only two hundred yards.

The room at the U.S.-Yasaka resembled the cockpit of a spaceship: lights, music, drinks, and snacks were governed by a large keyboard between their beds. This wasn't the Japan that Walters sought. Still, Kyoto was Kyoto, and there was more to it than contemplating a gingko tree. Outside the spaceship were temples, castles, villas, gardens, museums, lovely old streets, the Kamo River, the hills. As if to compensate for their defection from the *ryokan,* the next days were radiant with spring. The Walterses took to the backstreets, walking toward the hills down lanes coddled with fruit trees. Everywhere were surprises, little spreads of quiet: rock gardens, brooks, tiny bridges, prayer trees, sacred nooks and pagodas tucked away in groves. Gilded devils guarded recumbent gods; bells and drums erupted from closed shrines, old men contemplated rocks, uniformed high school students played soccer and baseball; adorable infants smiled and laughed at the tall Americans. "This is the idea," said Walters. "Don't you feel splendid? Rested? Better than rested?"

"Yes."

The third day Dorothy, a bit under the weather, stayed in bed. Walters said, "I think I'll go see Kinkakuji. The Golden Pavilion. Would you mind, dear?"

"I want you to, dear."

Across from the Yasaka Shrine, he took the number 12 bus. He followed the route on his map. It went down Shijo-Kawaramachi, crossed the railroad tracks, turned north on Horikawa-dori, went past Nijo Palace, then west again on Kitaoji-dori. A half-hour trip, full of interest. Walters tried not to squirrel away calculations about traffic, commerce, the mix of old and new; he tried to bathe in the impressions. Still, he had to be alert for his stop. Just behind him sat three young women, university age. He turned around and asked, "Do you speak English?" There was some giggling, then a pretty girl in spectacles said, "Can I he'p you?" Walters showed her the map, pointed to Kinkakuji, and asked if she'd be kind enough to tell him when to get off. "I te' you, with pressure."

Relaxed again, Walters fell into thinking how happy he was, how precious the world's offerings, how lucky he was to be able to enjoy them. And Dorothy, true-blue Dorothy. How lucky to have the self-melting love for and trust in another human being. In his entire life, he could not remember having such a thought. Bad luck to count blessings. It could be a forecast of loss. A year ago, he'd come home early and heard his own voice saying, "I'll be home by nine, darling." When he came in, Dorothy blushed, then told him she'd kept messages recorded on their answering machine. She had the equivalent of a long-playing record of his messages. Now and then she played it. Would he forgive her? This fear of loss was an element now of the deep love the aging couple had for each other.

"Prease, sir, Kinkakuji now."

Walters walked up an oak-lined alley. Men in coveralls swept the gravel with long brooms. As Walters approached, one of them, a short squat man, stopped sweeping and came up to him. "Excuse, Kinkaku-ji repair. Crosed indefinitry."

"Oh, dear, what a shame. I've come a long way. Could I just get a glimpse of it from the fence?"

The man bowed twice and said, "Very sorry. Crosed indefinitry. Nothing to see."

There were times when Walters would have been angry. He had his share of the American temper, that perpetuation of infantile anger into adulthood, but decades of diplomatic frustration had taken the starch from the temper. Frustration was not only expected, it was almost welcome; it made his services more valuable. Today he'd prided himself on taking the bus, not a taxi (let alone a car from the American Center). He was playing the ordinary man and enjoying it. There might even be rules against upper-echelon people using public transportation. Walters was playing hooky. That counted more for him than Kinkakuji.

On the Walterses' last Kyoto day it snowed. They made their way through slosh down Higashioji-dori to the National Museum, where, visibility poor, they turned too soon and found themselves in front of a huge bronze bell. Flake after thick flake piled on the dark gold bronze. It was very quiet. Snow piled on their hats and coats. For a second they looked at each other and, without saying anything, acknowledged the loveliness of the moment. It was the best of their stay.

While Dorothy took a shower, Walters decided to take pictures of besnowed Kyoto. The air was silvery with bits of evening dark. He walked uphill from the hotel to the Kodaiji Temple. Snow fell in the groins of crooked trees and on the curled struts of the shrine. By the square N of the Shinto archway, he snapped pictures of a woman pulling the bell cord, clapping, and bowing. She was a sporty little figure in red jacket, pants, and woolen cap with a pink ball. Sporty but dignified. As he put the camera down, she came toward him. It was Fukuma-san. A surprised but fine smile spread in her face. "Herro. Herro," she said merrily. He spread his own face with a smile. "How good to see you, Fukuma-san," and, bowing, moved past her, the jam of deception smeared on his face.

About fifteen years ago, Walters had made a public fool of himself. He'd had the bad luck to testify before a congressional committee on a slow news day. Two days before, he'd crossed the Pacific, and though he was a quick recoverer from long flights, he hadn't completely recovered from this one. In addition, he hadn't adequately prepared for the hearing, and so the witty subcommittee chairman had forced him into a trap: he'd had to expose a presidential position which had been carefully veiled. It earned him and the congressman a minute of evening news time. It was the equivalent of having one's weakest moment painted into the Sistine Chapel, and Walters had never entirely recovered from it. The only comparable humiliation of his life had occurred when he was ten years old. He and his prettiest cousin, Jeanie Walters, were inspecting and caressing each other's more intimate parts when the supposedly hooked door was pushed open by Walters's father. Years later, Walters senior had told his son what a laugh he'd had about it, but there was no laugh that day. These memories went through him as he walked downhill in the silvery air away from Fukuma-san's smile.

He didn't tell Dorothy he'd seen Fukuma-san until they were back in Washington. She'd known something was wrong but thought it was anxiety about ending his rare vacation. From the taxi to Kyoto Station the next day—a beautiful, summery one—they saw a grove of flowering trees. Dorothy said, "How lucky to see cherry blossoms."

Uncharacteristically, Walters said, "All these years in Washington, I'd think you'd know cherry blossoms."

"I am a dodo. These must be avocado or persimmon." All the way back to Narita, she endured his uneasiness.

It was almost two weeks later—his uneasiness gone—that he told her about the encounter at the temple. He'd had a long afternoon with the Far Eastern deskmen and the deputy secretary. (It dealt with ways of softening—and using—congressional anger about U.S.-Japanese trade imbalances.) In one of the easier moments, Charlie Okhosa told them how his Kyoto-born mother had handled his Kobe-born father. "Kobe people are supposed to be excitable and pushy, port people, quick to take in, quick to dispose. Kyotans are supposedly confident ironists who've seen everything and know it passes. Mother was a good Japanese wife, but she handled my father the way the president handles his prima donnas, with jokes, smiles, letting them wear themselves out. She never expressed her will, but we were all controlled by it. A great natural diplomat. I take after the old man."

At supper, Walters passed Charlie's remarks on to Dorothy and, with an apropos, told her about running into Fukuma-san at the Kodaiji Temple. "I don't know which of us was more surprised. I didn't want to upset you by telling you."

"I hope she blames me for our decamping. And for the deceit."

"That would be just," said Walters with a smile. "I'm glad we moved. I'd have just stuck it out there—and been miserable. It was stupid to go back there anyway," meaning back to Fukuma-san's. But remembering that he'd gone there more for Dorothy, he threw in,

"Back to the temple, a hundred yards from her house. Her own shrine. My paparazzi madness."

"We do have some wonderful pictures, though," said Dorothy, who had caught her husband's unusual indictment of her but, in the habitual diplomacy of their long marriage, ignored it.

PACKAGES

As I was staying in Aliber's place across from Campbell's, my sister asked me to pick up the package. "I guess it's the acknowledgment cards." Our mother had died five days before.

Campbell's is a wonderful funeral factory. It does it all for you, gets the notice into the *Times,* sends for the death certificates (needed by banks, lawyers, accountants), orders the printed acknowledgments of condolence, and, of course, works out the funeral; or, as in Mother's case, the cremation and memorial service.

We'd held the service there in the large upstairs salon. Lots of flowers and few mourners: Mother's friends—who were in New York and ambulatory (eight octogenarian widows)—cousins, many of whom we hadn't seen in decades, two of my children, Doris's, and my father with Tina and Leona, the two Trinidad ladies who kept him up to snuff. A black-gowned organist—the closest thing to a religious figure in attendance—played some of Dad's favorites, "Who," "Some Enchanted Evening," and "Smoke Gets in Your Eyes" (this one a bit much in view of Mother's mode of disintegration).

The package was wrapped in rough brown paper tied with a strand of hemp which broke when I hoisted it. "Don't worry," I said to the shocked Mr. Hoffman. "I'm just across the street." I held it with one hand and shook his with the other. Outside, limousines and chauffeurs idled—it was a slow death day in New York.

Thursday. Garbage collection on East Eighty-first. A massif of sacks and cartons ranged the stony fronts of town and apartment houses. No one but me on the street. Across Fifth Avenue, the museum fountains poured boredom into the July heat. I left the package in a half-empty carton, walked to Aliber's door, then returned and covered it with yesterday's *Times*. Back to the house, key in the door, then back again to the package, which I unwrapped. It was a silvery can, the size of a half gallon of paint; labeled. Curious about the contents, I tried to open it. No lid. Nor was it worth the trouble of fetching a hammer and wedge from Aliber's. I stripped off the label, rewrapped the can, and covered it with the newspaper. On top of that, I put a plastic sack of rinds and fish bones.

Aliber's apartment is dark, leathery, high ceilinged, somber, turbulent. Its walls are books. Books litter tables, chairs, sills, floors. An investment counselor, Aliber is really a reader. His claim is that all intelligence has a monetary translation. A cover for sheer desire to know everything. (He does better than most. Of the hundreds of Aliber books I've looked at, ninety percent bear his green-inked comments.)

There are hours to kill before Doris picks me up. I activate air conditioners and sound system and pick out some correct music. A cello suite of Poppa Bach. Naked on the leather couch, I listen until it overflows my capacity. You need weeks for such a piece. It should take as long to listen to as it did to compose. Or is the idea to reduce vastness into something portable?

A package.

I think I thought that then, though the notion may have come after I'd found *The Mind of Matter* in the wall behind my head. I read a chapter devoted to Planck's "famous lecture to the Berlin Academy in May of 1899," in which he described "that extraordinary quantity" which "for all times and cultures" made possible "the derivation of units for mass, length, time, and temperature." Planck's constant. Not then called h. Only 6.6253×10^{-27} erg seconds, or, by our author, "that stubby transmitter of universal radiance . . . Nature's own package." Little as I understood of this package, I felt some connection between it and Bach's and the one which held what was left of what had once held me.

Six weeks earlier, back in Chicago, I'd written a letter in my head. *Dearest Mother. Last Saturday, I unbuttoned your dress and slipped it off your shoulders. Doris undid your bra, and for the first time in decades, I saw your sad breasts. We put the gauzy, small-flowered nightgown over your head and pulled it down the bony tunnel of your back, your seamed belly.*

Before we taxied to Mount Sinai, Leona fixed your hair; tucked, curled, waved, and crimped it. (If her eight months of beauty school produce nothing else, they've been worth it.) It was your last home vanity. When we left you, sunk in the narrow bed, the piled hair survived. Your stake in the great world.

I finished lunch with my spring wheat man in the Wrigley Restaurant and walked alone by the Chicago River. Immense brightness, the Sun-Times Building a cube of flame. All around, the steel-and-glass dumbness of this beautiful, cruel town. *I noticed, then noticed I noticed, the bodies of women, white and black. Thank you, Mother, for my pleasure in such sights.*

A girl in leotards the color of papaya meat jumped around a stage in front of the big nothing of Picasso's metal gift—bloodless heart, brainless head. Huffing, she explained arabesque and second position to the crowd of municipal workers, shoppers, tourists. It's splendid being part of a crowd like this, letting bored respect for art muzzle the interest in the dancer's body. Bless such civic gifts.

There have been times I've wanted your death, Mother. At least, did not much care.

It was money. That noise. Curse me for it.

I've walked through slums, *bustees, barriadas, callampas, favelas, suburbios* (the very names a misery). *In a Calcutta dump, I saw a darker you,* forty years younger, everything in her life within her reach: pot, shawl, kid. *What should a man do with money?* Getty, the billionaire, claimed he wasn't rich, didn't have a spare—an uninvested—nickel. I'm rich. So what am I doing in these glassy dollared Alps—reflections annihilating reflections—the money canyons of your town and mine?

Unearned dough. *It came to you without effort; it filled your head. (Should noise fill heads like yours? Or mine?)*

Last week you said you wanted "to go," and you kissed me with the strength of good-bye. (Good-bye is what's left.) *Soon you'll be nothing but*

your purses, your spoons, your china, your sheets, your doilies. Your money.
You'll be an absence in Doris; in me; a shard in Dad's head. [4]

After Mother's death—which he does not acknowledge: she is *out for*
lunch—his head is in more of a whirl than ever. He shuts himself in
closets, undresses at 3:00 P.M., goes, pajamaed, into the street (brought
back by the doorman). One night, he appears naked at Tina's bedside.
He says he wishes to do things with her. Disused parts hang from his
groin like rotten fruit. Tina gets a blanket around him, persuades him
back to his own bed. "I was *so* scared, Miss Doris. Doctor is a strong
mon. Yesterday, he move the fuhniture round and round the living
room."

Deprived of cigarettes—he sets clothes and furniture afire—and
of the *Times*—there's a pressman's strike—he spends hours walking
from room to room, staring at Third Avenue, winding his wristwatch.

As the small shocks of his small world dislodge more and more of
his brain, his speech shrivels to the poetry of the very young and old.

"How are you today, Daddy?"

"Rainy."

"What time do you make it?"

"Too late."

He lives by a few lines of verse which embody a creed and an old
passion for eloquence. "For a' that and a' that, A man's a man for a'
that." (We recite the Burns poem at his grave.) "Oh, lady bright, can it
be right / This window open to the night?"

Decades of control slough off the frail body. He sits tensely in the
living room. "What you doin', Doctor?"

"Waiting."

"May I ask what you waitin' *for*?"

"A girl is coming."

"What gull you talkin' of?"

"None of yours. Give her fifty dollars. A hundred dollars."

Tina has a grand laugh. (And laughs are scarce here.)

He is furious. "Out."

He waits an hour, then locks himself in the bathroom.

"You OK, Doctor?"

"Am I supposed to be?"

Doris calls Dr. Rice, who is not surprised. "It's the ones who've done the least who do the most now. I've known them to masturbate in front of people."

"Maybe we should get him a girl."

"I don't think that would do any good. And *he* certainly couldn't."

"What can be done?"

"An extra tranquilizer before bed."

Not a few times we would have liked to tranquilize him permanently. But senility too is part of life, one of the few remaining middle-class encounters with the Insoluble.

One afternoon, before I went back to Chicago, he came in while I was going over estate papers. He was in white pajamas. (The day's familiar divisions were no longer his.) "I have to talk with you, son."

"What is it, Dad?"

He took a scrap of paper from his old billfold and gave it to me. "I want to go here."

"You are here. This is your address."

"No, dear. I want to go *home.*"

"This is your home. No one else's."

"I don't think so."

And he was right. Home is where his wife lived. Or his mother — who died during the Spanish-American War.

The next day, his need to go home was so strong, we took a taxi four blocks to Doris's house. How happy he was. Doris was a segment of that female benevolence which had watched over him from birth, mother-stepmother-sisters-wife-daughter. They were a continuity of watchfulness. How he kissed Doris and talked until, noticing unfamiliar furniture, a different view, he grew weary. We taxied home, and now it was home, the place where his wife would be coming after lunch.

In Chicago, I got the day's bulletins by phone. "He peed in the dresser."

"Jesus."

"I think he confused drawer and door. They both open. I mean it wasn't totally irrational."

"Bless you, Doris."

He became incontinent. "I never thought I'd live to clean up my own father. I couldn't let the girls do it."

"How long can it go on?"

"Dr. Rice says he's strong as an ox. There's nothing organically wrong."

"Poor fellow."

"He misses you."

"How do you know?"

"He lights up when I say you're coming. Can't you come?"

"I'll try."

But didn't. At Christmas, I sent him a check for a billion dollars. "To the World's Best Father."

"Did he like it?"

"I don't think so. He tore it up."

"How dumb of me."

"He's still a human being, you know."

"I hadn't forgotten." Despite those reports of yours, I didn't say. Which convert him into a pile of disasters. "I should have come. He knew I should be there. And knew I knew it." Unable to say it directly, he tore up the check.

His last paternal correction.

At the end of the beautiful novella which Proust plants like an Ice Age fragment in his novel, Swann thinks how terrible it is that the greatest love of his life has been for a woman who was not his type. (This thought—like the piano music of Ravel—detonates the world's pathos for me; though consciousness makes it as beautiful as the music.) My mother was not my type.

A month after Dad's death, I dreamed that she and I were having another of the small disputes which disfigured thousands of our hours. "I can't bear your nagging," I said. As always, my anger silenced hers. She said she'd tell my father to speak to me. But when he came in, he was the old man who died, and, instead of his slipper, I saw only the sad face of his last days.

Then my dream mother said, "I hope you'll be coming back to New York next summer."

"This one hasn't been very pleasant."

"I haven't had a good one either."

I knew that meant the ulcerous mouth, the colds, the drowsiness which disguised and expressed her cancer.

I was about to tell her that I would be back when this part of the dream became a poem. (My dreams often conclude in poems and interpretations.) On a screen of air, I saw lines from George Herbert's "The Collar." "Forsake thy cage," they read,

> . . . thy rope of sands
> Which petty thoughts have made, and made to thee
> Good cable, to enforce and draw,
> And be thy law . . .

My dream interpreter here let me know that my cable had turned to sand because my parents were dead. I was free.

I've been a father so long, I didn't know how much I was still a son; how onerous it was to be a son. Now my "lines and life were free." "But," the poem continued on the screen of inner air,

> As I raved and grew more fierce and wild
> At every word,
> Methought I heard one calling, *Child!*
> And I replied, *My Lord.*

My response was not "My Lord" but "My Duty." The Duty which had raised and formed me.

Only at the beginning of my life and the end of hers did I love my mother wholly. When her life was over — like a simpleminded book — I pitied its waste.

There was much intelligence and much energy in her. Yet what was her life but an advertisement for idleness. And how could such a woman have failed to be a nagger, a boss, the idle driver of others, an anal neurotic for whom cleanliness was not a simple, commonsensical virtue but a compulsion nourished by her deepest need? *Wash your hands. Pick up your clothes. The room is filthy. Eat up. Mary wants to go out.* (The sympathy for Mary veiled the need to have the dining room inert, restored to preorganic purity. What counted was setting, stage, the scene before and after action. What drastic insecurity underlay this drive toward inertness?)

Too simple.

Mother loved learning, going, seeing. She loved shows, travel, games. She loved *doing good.*

Nor is this enough. She was the reliable, amiable center of a large group of women like herself, the one who remembered occasions and relationships, the one who knew the *right thing to do.*

Her telephone rang from 8:00 A.M. on. Lunches, games, lectures, plays, visits. Lunch was a crucial, a beautiful event. One went *out.* (But where? Longchamps—before its fall—Schrafft's, but which one? *Or shall we try a new place?* What excitement.) Whose game was it? Beasie's? Marion B.'s? Justine's? Bridge, canasta, gin, mah-jongg (the small clicks of the tiles, "one dot"; "two crack").

A smallish woman, five four, brown haired. (Gray for the last twenty years, but I always *saw* her brown haired.) Not abundant, but crowded with soft, expressive waves. (Expressive of expense; of free time.) Clear brown eyes, scimitar nose, narrow lips; a sharp face, once soft, fine cheeked, pretty.

She died well. "What choice do I have?"

Not bad; for anyone, let alone a monument to redundance. (Bear two children, *cared for by others,* oversee an apartment, *cleaned by others,* shop for food, *cooked by others.*) She died bravely, modestly, with decorum. The decorum of practicality. (Her other tutelary deity.) She made up her mind to be as little trouble to those she loved as possible. (Cleanliness reborn as virtue.) She set her face to the wall, stopped taking medicine (without offending the nurses she loved so in the last weeks), and sank quietly into nonexistence. The last hours, teeth out, face caved in, the wrestler Death twisting the jaw off her face, she managed a smile (a human movement) when I said we were there, we loved her. She lay, tiny, at the bottom of tremendous loneliness.

Doris and I wait for a taxi at the corner of Eighty-first and Madison. Seven o'clock, the tail end of the day. Traffic flows north. Buses crap plumes of filth into the lovely street (where—I think for some reason—Washington's troops were chased by British redcoats two hundred years ago). A growl of horns to our left. A Rolls-Royce honks at a Department of Sanitation truck in front of Aliber's house. The garbagemen are throwing sacks and cartons into great blades whirling in the truck's backside. A powerful little fellow throws in the carton with my package.

"What's the matter?"

"Nothing."

"You look funny."

"Tell you later."

Good-bye, darling.

And: Why not?

You were a child of the city, born here, your mother born here. If I could have pried it open, I would have spread you in Central Park. But this way is better than a drawer in that Westchester mausoleum. Foolish, garish anteroom to no house. Egyptian stupidity.

And it was the *practical* thing to do.

Wasn't it, Mother?

ACKNOWLEDGMENTS

The following stories were written between 1949 and 1964, when they were published in *Teeth, Dying, and Other Matters* by Harper and Row after appearing in *Almanaco (Feltrinelli), Big Table, Encounter, Epoch, Harper's Magazine, Kenyon Review, Noble Savage, Partisan Review, Transatlantic Review,* and *Western Review:* "Arrangements at the Gulf," "Assessment of an Amateur," "Cooley's Version," "A Counterfactual Proposition," "Dying," "Gardiner's Legacy," "The Good European," "Good Morrow, Swine," "Nine Letters, Twenty Days," "Orvieto Dominos, Bolsena Eels," "A Short History of Love," "Teeth," and "Wanderers."

The following stories were written between 1965 and 1969, when they were published in *1968: A Short Novel, an Urban Idyll, Five Stories, and Two Trade Notes* by Holt, Rinehart and Winston after being published in *Hudson Review, Les Lettres Nouvelles, Paris Review,* and *Shenandoah:* "East, West ... Midwest," "Gaps," "Gifts," "Idylls of Dugan and Strunk," "Ins and Outs," "Introductory," "Milius and Melanie," "Story Making," and "Veni, Vidi ... Wendt."

The following stories were written between 1969 and 1980, when they were published in *Packages* by Coward, McCann and Geoghegan after first appearing in *Atlantic, Beloit Review, Chicago* magazine, *Commentary, Encounter, Harper's Magazine,* and *TriQuarterly:* "Double Charley," "Dr. Cahn's Visit," "The Girl Who Loves Schubert," "The Ideal Address," "Lesson for the Day," "Mail," "Packages," "A Recital for the Pope," "Riordan's Fiftieth," "Troubles," and "Wissler Remembers."

The following stories were written between 1981 and 1989, when they were published in *Noble Rot* by Grove Press after first appearing in *Antioch Review, Encounter, Formations, TriQuarterly,* and *Western Review:* "In Return," "In the Dock," "*La Pourriture Noble,*" "Losing Color," and "Zhoof."

The following stories were written between 1989 and 1992, when they were published in *Shares, a Novel in Ten Pieces and Other Fictions* by Delphinium Books after appearing in *Antioch Review, Bostonia,*

Chicago Tribune Magazine, Commentary, Forward, and *Paris Review:* "The Anaximander Fragment," "The Degradation of Tenderness," "The Illegibility of This World," and "In a Word, Trowbridge."

The following stories were written between 1992 and 2002, when they were published in *What Is What Was* by the University of Chicago Press after first appearing in *Literary Imagination* and *TriQuarterly:* "Almonds," "Chicago, in the Depths of Feeling," and "My Ex, the Moral Philosopher."

"Oscar and Hypatia," "Sylvan and Agnes," and "Wool" were written between 1992 and 2001. "Oscar and Hypatia" appeared in *Marlboro Review,* "Sylvan and Agnes" in *On the Make,* and "Wool" in *Yale Review.*

Most of the stories have been slightly, a few heavily, revised; none has been transformed.

ABOUT THE AUTHOR

Richard Stern was born in 1928 in New York City and published his first novel, *Golk,* in 1960. In 1985 he won the Medal of Merit for the Novel given by the American Academy and Institute of Arts and Letters. In 1995 his book *A Sistermony* received the Heartland Prize for the year's best work of nonfiction. His novels *Stitch, Other Men's Daughters, Natural Shocks,* and *Pacific Tremors* are also available from TriQuarterly Books/Northwestern University Press. Stern is the Helen A. Regenstein Professor Emeritus in the Department of English at the University of Chicago and a member of the American Academy of Arts and Sciences. He lives in Chicago and Tybee Island, Georgia, with his wife, the poet Alane Rollings.